For Ruth and Floss

SWAN'S KNIGHT

DEBORAH HARVEY

Best wishes
Deborah Harvey

Llumina
Press

This is a work of fiction. Names, characters, places, and incidents either are the products of the author's imagination or are used fictitiously and any resemblance to actual persons, living or dead, business establishments, events, products, services, or locales is entirely coincidental.

ISBN: 978-1-60594-687-0 (PB)
978-1-60594-688-7 (EB)

Printed in the United States of America by Llumina Press

Library of Congress Control Number: 2011900664

Acknowledgments

Although many authors consider writing a solitary occupation, I am not one of them. *Swan's Knight* would never have been completed, much less published, without the tireless encouragement of my sister, Melissa Taggart, and a devoted group of readers who slogged their way through the original 260,000-word manuscript. These wonderful women, Laura Grover, Susan Hagood, Heidi Hansen, Karen Kramer, Cyn Maleski, and Mary Ruth Peele, were unfailingly generous with their praise and moderate in their criticism. I owe them a great debt of thanks.

Thanks go, too, to Kathryn Caskie, Donald McCaig, Richard McDonough, Jess Brallier, and Deborah Greenspan for their helpful advice and to editor John David Kudrick (www.johndavidkudrick.com) for his review of United States Marines protocol and procedures.

CONTENTS

Part 1

Part 2

PART 1

CHAPTER 1

There is nothing like the walking ring at upstate New York's Saratoga Race Course, under the trees. However, many oldtimers think it has never been the same since the New York State Racing Association, understandably concerned about liability, fenced the previously open ring to limit human access to the equine royalty circling a small knot of owners before every race during the thirty-five day summer racing season.

On this particular hot Thursday afternoon in early August, as the guest of the Thoroughbred's elderly owner, Swan Bolington stood watching her big chestnut homebred with the blaze face as he was being walked by his groom before the seventh race. She was in a champagne silk Chanel sheath, Chanel silk bi-color pumps, hose, and pearls, in homage to another Virginia horse breeder, Penny Chenery Tweedy, the owner in the 1970s of Secretariat and mistress of Meadow Stud. The grandfatherly owner of Perspicacious, Dr. Philip Deveroux of Philadelphia, stood next to Swan in a summer weight suit and a heap of anxiety. His trainer, Herman Detweiler, eyeballed the colt from under furrowed brows, but Swan thought he—the colt, not the trainer—looked up to the challenge: a mile on the turf, Grade III. On the other side of Swan was Dr. Deveroux's much younger lady friend, who was in a too snug low-cut summer dress, a broad-brimmed flowered hat, long white gloves, big sunglasses, and high heeled sandals. The lady could not have more accurately identified herself as a member of the *nouveau riche* if she had hung a sign around her neck, just as Swan's simple couture identified her as Virginia landed—albeit minor—gentry. Everyone had a role to play at the Spa in August. The *nouveau riche* funded the horse business. Without them, people like Swan would have been no more than struggling farmers with big property tax bills.

"He'll do," Swan said reassuringly to Dr. Deveroux, "Mr. Detweiler has brought him here in fine form, he loves a fast track, and he has fifteen generations of grass milers behind him to give him a boot in the . . . south side . . . if he needs it."

The paddock steward called riders up, and Detweiler's jock, Israel Diago, a regular at the Eastern racetracks, stood impassively for a few last-minute comments from the trainer, made primarily for the benefit of the owner, who heard "Get to the front at the jump if you can," and made neither head nor tail of much after that.

Swan was completely calm. She bred 'em, she didn't train 'em or ride 'em. She knew the colt was in a good spot for him. She looked out over the enormous crowd and recalled her mother's account of Saratoga in the early 1980s, seeing Mrs. Ringquist, as Penny Chenery was then known, with the two beautiful Carrington girls of the famous Queen Ranch, Heloise and Decca, all so cool, coifed, elegant, poised, as they watched their homebreds walk around the Saratoga ring just as Swan was doing now.

The horses filed out of the walking ring, followed along, like the guests behind ten brides and grooms, by the "connections," the owners, trainers, and families and guests of both, down the path, past the food vendors and park benches, under the stands. They then parted company with the horses, who stepped on to the main track. Swan and her party made their way into the wooden clubhouse, to white table cloths, bottles of Veuve Clicquot, and white-coated wait staff.

"Tip the waiter for luck," Swan murmured to Dr. Deveroux, with an impish smile, when they were settled at their table. "I'd suggest that you wheel the exacta, with our colt and the five horse."

"Phil is a win-only bettor," the flowered lady said. "One thousand to win, right, honey?"

Swan gave Dr. Deveroux a big smile: he deserved it, since he had never shown the slightest interest in her, the twenty-six-year-old breeder of his first and only racehorse. She smoothed her long tail of dark, heavy hair, a burden in the heat, and wished she'd tied it up.

"If you don't mind, I'll place my own bet, then," she said, since he was unaware that a gentleman, out of courtesy, should place a lady's bet on her behalf. No mind: Swan was the breeder, not the companion.

Although not a serious handicapper, Swan hedged. She placed a three-hundred-dollar bet on Spec and the five horse—to win and finish second, in either order. She collected at six to one when Spec, after a bobble out of the starting gate, rallied to finish driving, a scant neck behind the five horse. The trainer was well satisfied.

"Another head bob and we might have had the winner," he consoled Dr. Deveroux, a bit too optimistically. "The next start, we will be good to go, if he comes out of this one okay."

"Staying for the feature, Miss Bolington?" asked Detweiler, looking hopeful.

"No, with the yearling sale starting tomorrow, I want to stop by the barns and wish a couple of folks well," Swan said. "I'm heading home tomorrow, early; I'm on the eight-fifty out of Albany, spending a few hours in Manhattan, then it's on to LaGuardia and into Dulles. Horses need looking after." She turned to her owner and smiled again. "I have to make sure Dr. Deveroux's next campaigner from Belle Everley, whoever he may be, is getting his TLC."

She made a quick *de rigueur* stop at the venerable trackside watering hole, the Chrysanthemum, and another at the Oklahoma training track across the street from the main track, to see a few of the old-timers. Two rheumy hot walkers; Spec's elderly groom, called "Pops"; and a bent-over trainer or two still remembered Belle Everley racing stock from the glory days; they jumped up from where they sat on hay bales and uncovered their heads out of respect when she shook their hands warmly.

Then Swan turned her eyes toward Virginia. Taliaferro County. Belle Everley. Home to seven generations of Bolingtons.

Belle Everley was a classic Quaker farmhouse built of local materials and added to over time as family sizes and fortunes increased. The earliest section was a small log house, a two over two (two rooms above, two below); the largest, center section was limestone over frame; and another, slightly smaller adjacent section was made of fieldstone, with walls eighteen inches thick. The house boasted large windows in all but the log-house portion, with a fair view of the very lowest foothills of the Blue Ridge Mountains of northern Virginia from two vantages. Walk-in fireplaces were in several rooms on the main floor and three dependencies—a frame washhouse, tin-roofed summer kitchen, and log-and-horsehair-plaster smokehouse—remained within stone's throw of the main house. The barns were early twentieth-century structures, since every barn in the county had been burned late in the Civil War by Union troops fed up with the local bounty supporting Confederate raiders and militia from the Valley of Virginia eastward to the Potomac.

A few small but well-maintained historic gardens of native boxwood, azalea, dogwood, and fruit trees provided color from the first of March to Thanksgiving every year. A flagstone walkway brought visitors to the front steps from a graveled circular driveway that then snaked down to the three working barns below the house filled with horses. More than three hundred acres of prime Virginia farmland, under cultivation for more than two hundred years as pasture and cropland, swung around the house in all directions. Belle Everley had another priceless attribute: a pristine 360-degree nineteenth-century viewshed: no power lines, modern structures, or other evidence of post-Civil War life was visible from any vantage point.

Inside, the house's furnishings were simple family pieces, mostly made of walnut, poplar, and other indigenous natural woods, varnished to a high gleam (oldtimers could remember when a professional varnisher came to county houses annually to apply a new coat of the preservative). More humble pieces, made primarily for kitchen use out of pine and fruit woods, had been painted mustard, soldier blue, Spanish red, or hunter green over the years, with a rare salmon, robin's egg blue, or deep bittersweet dry sink, jelly cupboard, huntboard, or work table tucked into corners throughout the house.

Only Belle Everley's living room was done up in formal mahogany furniture, mostly early nineteenth-century tea tables, sideboards, windsor chairs, and settees. These were surrounded by paintings of hounds and race horses at rest, Aubusson carpets, and portraits of long-dead Bolingtons, Hexells, Swans, and their relatives in lemon gold frames. Heirlooms of the Confederacy—officers' swords, tintypes, cavalry stirrups, other militaria and framed ephemera—sterling silver racing trophies, and the occasional minor George Stubbs oil, acquired when Stubbs and his subject matter were very much out of fashion and affordable, caught the eye of connoisseurs shocked to see such treasures jumbled together next to humble family photos.

◆

Two days after her return from Saratoga, Swan buckled the chinstrap of her black Charles Owen helmet and walked to the round pen to watch as Eduardo slowly tacked up Oscar Mike. The colt was a strapping 16.2 hands as a rising three-year-old, black as pitch, with a restless, intelligent, vigorous eye that challenged all comers. He was named for Swan's first fiancé, Michael Delahunt Lee, an expeditionary force marine who had been killed in Iraq during his second tour of duty nine months before the colt was born. It seemed like the right name. Although not so dignified as those given The Fortress's other offspring, the name did carry through their military theme, since Oscar Mike was Marine Corps phonetic-alphabet speak for "On the move."

Swan had been determined to memorialize Hunt Lee in every possible way.

By the time Oscar Mike arrived, Swan's initial shock over Hunt Lee's death had morphed into a kind of grief that was eminently satisfying to her and frightening to her family. She had been besotted with it, letting it claim her every attention, nurturing it as if it were a child, just as she had devoted herself to Hunt Lee while he was alive. Their eighteen-month-long courtship and engagement had been the happiest time of her life, even though they had been separated for much of it: first, while she had finished her senior year at the College of William and Mary, then when he was redeployed and gone. Strangely, she had never worried about Hunt Lee once he was in Iraq. He had a reputation of being extraordinarily lucky, intuitive, and cunning in avoiding danger; athletic and accomplished, he seemed indestructible. Swan had so absorbed his own belief in that indestructibility that it seemed to her nothing short of treason to accept his death. It was not going to happen. This had driven the new man in her life, Army Special Forces Captain Carter Delaney Roland of Fluvanna County, close to crazy for the year they had dated. By the time they became engaged, however, he had rationalized Swan's feelings for Hunt Lee as the first-love hysteria of an extremely vulnerable and emotional girl, something the two of them would work through and resolve during their life together.

Of course, then Carter Roland got himself killed in Kabul. Swan did not name The Fortress's next foal after Carter Roland. It was a filly, out of Carnivorous. She called her Dress the Line.

After Roland's death, her next beau, Hastings Fitzhugh, went to Fallujah as a security advisor employed by Warburton and lost a lower arm to a roadside bomb. He and Swan had dated only briefly, thank God, before this disaster, and he was now back in Taliaferro County (which native Virginians, for reasons lost to time, pronounced "Tolliver"), almost completely recovered due to the care he received at the rehab center in Richmond. Nevertheless, Swan counted him among her unintended victims, and, anyone would have to admit, she had a strong case. The Fortress had another filly that spring, out of Dynamiter. Swan named her Enfilade.

Oscar Mike snorted several times, then half-reared, lifting Eduardo a foot off the ground as he held the colt's bridle, dropping his feet back to earth, only to go airborne once again, bouncing the small man rhythmically in a tense, sideways dance along the fence line.

"Uh-uh-uh-uh," Swan warned the colt sharply with her voice, and it was a credit to the colt's training that he did flick his ears her way and return all four feet to the ground, though not without some impressive head-whipping and snorting in the process.

Not for the first time, Swan revisited her own version of the *Black Stallion* fantasy:

The scene: the open plains of the American West. A wild stallion gallops around a wooden corral, neighing a challenge to all. A young girl watches the magnificent animal, so powerful and untamed, as a kindly ranch hand restrains her:

"No, señorita! You must not attempt to ride El Diablo—he is too much horse for any woman! He has already killed many riders before you! It is suicide!"

"Don't worry, Ramon. All he needs is gentle patience and loving firmness. He can be ridden, without breaking his spirit, and he will *be ridden—by me. Just wait and see!"*

It was Swan's view that this Walter Farley-inspired scenario basically embodied all young women's fantasies about men. The great truth, of course, was that, in real life, the El Diablos of the world always succeeded sooner or later in throwing off their gentle, patient would-be mistresses like the untamed broncs they were, causing grievous bodily injury in the process. Hunt Lee had done so by getting himself killed. So had Carter Roland. That they had chosen the identical means was quite secondary to the immutable fact that they had upended Swan's best intentions for her life. They had left her "stove up," as the old hardboots used to say, emotionally disabled in every important way. Although Hastings Fitzhugh had looked at her with no discernible distrust when she visited him that first time in Richmond, she didn't visit again and now scrupulously avoided him. What was the point?

Despite an endless reservoir of gentle patience and loving firmness, she had been thrown off too many El Diablos, too many times. She would stick with Thoroughbreds from now on.

"*Digame,* Eduardo," Swan asked, "do you want me to get on him or can Edgar do it?"

The small man shrugged. "Miguel loves his momma," he sighed. "He is a baby still, though *muy grande*."

"*Muy malo tambien*," Swan said, as Eduardo brought the colt to her perch on the fence.

"Leg up?"

"No, I'll mount from here," she said, and lightly dropped from the top fence board into Oscar Mike's saddle. "*Vámonos!* On to the rocket express."

In the next moment she was shot from a gun. The colt's first leap was a twenty-two-foot stride forward, then he took a a shorter, vertical one, then another forward stride: Swan had just enough time to motion to Eduardo to open the gate. Four more strides and they were out, at a rolling boil up the lane between the two mare fields, each stride more exhilarating, more frightening. Swan took a relaxing breath and settled in for a pipe-opener, a good fast gallop to give the colt the reassurance that he was going to get his own way at least part of the time. Her shoulders felt as though hot pokers had been jammed in their joints, her braced, crossed reins held up the colt's front end as he accelerated down the yielding ground of the grass lane. Swan caught a quick glimpse of The Fortress briefly matching her son stride for stride in the next field before they blew by, and then she was in their rearview mirror.

Oscar Mike leveled off, so Swan wrapped him up a bit. She turned south, toward the main road, and spied a white BMW convertible at the end of the hard-surface road adjoining the farm's driveway. This had to be her maternal aunt, Spaulding Swan Hexell, on her way to D.C. from Richmond. Mike ate up the distance to the intersection in a minute or two, and slowed when Swan asked him to, nicely, in front of the convertible.

"My God, Swan, what are you doing on that colt? Isn't that what you have Edgar for? He bounces better than you do," said Spaulding as Swan halted. She was in her late fifties, but looked ten years younger thanks to a great streak job by her hairdresser in Richmond, slim and slight, like Swan.

"I bred him, I ride him," Swan shrugged. "Hold him a sec—he is fine now, just feeling his—"

"Balls?" Spaulding supplied. She didn't reach for the colt's bridle, however, since he was snorting and blowing like a freight train.

"Not helpful," Swan said. She dismounted on her own and began to hand walk Oscar Mike in a small circle around the car. He champed his bit, clinking the metal impatiently, throwing mouth froth in a 360-degree circle as he tossed his head.

"I wanted to let you know that you may be receiving a phone call," Spaulding said, sweetly, stepping out of the range of the foam. Swan went on the alert. "Hunt Lee's former company commander is at Quantico these days, and he met General Clayton, who happened to say he knew me—although how that came up, I don't know—and the topic of your whereabouts somehow got into the conversation, and General Clayton agreed to ask me to ask you—"

"No, no, no, no, no. And I mean no," said Swan. "I know exactly how 'somehow it got into the conversation'! They all used to talk endlessly about the women they knew, or used to know, or wanted to know, when they were over there, until they got into each other's wet dreams about each other's girlfriends and fell in love with all of them, because they were all so screwed up."

"Swan, really. I don't think that is fair at all," Spaulding murmured.

"I know all about that guy, the officer," Swan continued, getting herself furious, "Captain God's Gift to Women, with a mountain range, for Christ's sake, tattooed across his shoulders because they are supposedly so freaking hot . . . divorced from a stag mag centerfold. From Texas by way of Kentucky. A moron."

"Well, he is a major now, apparently," Spaulding continued mildly. "And how big a moron can he be if he is posted at Quantico? Don't answer that," she said. "I did hear he is a . . . hunk," she struggled over the term, "but since when is that a crime? I thought Hunt liked him."

"Look, Spaulding, either he is an *Apocalypse Now* stalker who wants to meet a woman who has killed two men in two theatres of war or some other Armageddon-I'm-all-for-it freak. What difference does it make? I don't want anything to do with him—or any of them—anymore. I'd rather date Eduardo."

"Perhaps he would like to pay a courtesy call, out of respect to Hunt," Spaulding said, disapproval of Swan's attitude in her voice. "You know, there *are* such gentlemen still in the military. Hunt was one of them. One or two may even be from Texas by way of Kentucky."

"What good will it do, after all this time? I know you want me to start to see people again, but, in the name of God, what good will it do? Really? Let him make his courtesy calls to the Lees; I'm sure they'd appreciate them."

"At least he would be someone who isn't going back into a combat zone," said Spaulding. "At this point, I don't think anyone at Quantico is going to rotate back anywhere that will see any action; it's still seven months overseas followed by six months at home, rinse and repeat, for the Marines. He's safe from you," she smiled weakly. "And who says he's going to fall in love with you? Let's face it, if a centerfold is his ideal wife, what danger is he in?"

"With my luck, he'll suddenly yearn for a size six, thirty-four-C racehorse-breeding spinster, descendent of a FFV, who is hanging on to the last bit of the family farm, only to have his humvee hit a pothole on Snickers Gap Road, overturn, and crush him," Swan said bleakly.

"Now, don't get your hopes all up, honey," said Spaulding, turning back to the convertible. "Men—even good-looking Texas men—are perfectly capable of making their own fatal mistakes without your help. That's what we love about them. It has absolutely nothing to do with you . . . . That horse looks good and cooled out for now."

"Give me a leg up before you go on down the road," Swan said, and Spaulding did.

◆

The next day, Swan was sitting down to breakfast (hot black tea, fresh fruit, thinly sliced country bacon, and half a piece of toast) when the Bolingtons' longtime Québécois housekeeper, Mathilde, called from the hall.

"Phone for you, Miss Swan." Swan's throat closed a bit. Call it a premonition.

"Take a message, please, Mathilde." Let him call back if he was so interested.

"Major Septimus Moore," said Mathilde. "From the Quantico Marine Base."

Septimus, Septimus, Septimus Smith, thought Swan, quoting *Mrs. Dalloway,* but not in a mocking way. On the contrary, the name pleased her. It sounded martial, noble—but unfamiliar. Was this caller the moron major with the tattooed shoulders, or not?

She went upstairs to the study. An eighteenth-century walnut and mahogany desk in one corner held the complete and unexpurgated war correspondence of the late Sergeant Michael Delahunt Lee to Miss Susannah Swan Everett Bolington of Belle Everley.

Swan hesitated. She had worked very hard not to read the forty-nine letters more than once every few months and had succeeded for almost a year. She was not permitted to read the letters for another forty-three days under her current regimen. If she opened any letters now, she would have to reset that clock, even if she only read the twenty-four letters she recollected mentioned—or might have mentioned—Captain Moore.

It wasn't worth it.

Better to wait and see if he called again.

◆

Three days later, she was eating a crab salad lunch in the dining room.

"Major Septimus Moore, Miss Swan," called Mathilde from the hall phone, "from the Quantico Marine Base."

"Not at home," said Swan. She pulled on the custom-made brown Vogel boots, brown gloves, and her brown Charles Owen, and headed down to the mare barn.

Kezia Hardaway, D.V.M., was examining The Fortress's oldest daughter, Serve the Guns, who was 180 days in foal to Carnivorous. Eduardo held the mare's February foal by the same sire close to his dam. He was due to be weaned "by the sign" (an old horseman's methodology based on the phases of the moon) in the next few days, then go on to his new owner in Kentucky.

By way of Texas.

No.

Hunt once said there were only two kinds of men: those who slept with other women and, because they loved you, told you about it, and those who slept with other women and, because they loved you, didn't tell you about it.

Swan believed in this axiom as scripture.

It was now clear to her that she was afraid of everything to do with Major Septimus Moore, whether he was from Quantico, or Kentucky, or Texas. She was disappointed in herself.

◆

On Saturday Swan pulled into the Artisan Saddlery parking lot in downtown Waverly mid-afternoon. Josiah Yoder stood impassively in a leather apron in the cramped office that fronted the work room. Above the counter was a large, hand-lettered sign: "Poor planning on your part does not an emergency make on our part," a dictum the customer in front of Swan was attempting to counter. "These billets," the teenager moaned, holding her expensive French saddle as though it was an accident victim, "these billets . . . ."

Josiah turned briefly to Swan, who looked down sadly at her black Vogels. "The lining again?" he asked.

"Just needs a tack-down, I think," Swan said, flashing a winning smile. "I tore it on the gate latch going into Stone Chimneys."

"Go up to the Crossroads. Have lunch," Josiah said mirthlessly. "We'll bring them up."

Swan used the boot jack on the counter to pry off the Vogels, leaving her in her stocking feet. She beamed at the Amishman. There was some benefit to being a regular customer, she was the first to admit. She hobbled back to the dually. An old pair of muck mocs was behind the driver's seat, and she slipped into them to walk the two blocks to the local Main Street watering hole for the Waverly citizenry.

The Crossroads consisted of a small bar, ten formica-topped tables, and eight leather banquettes that were in as much demand as those at Manhattan's Four Seasons Hotel. Locals snapped them up greedily at lunchtime and stayed in them forever. The tables were for the rest of the huddled masses—tourists mostly, but also an overflow of grooms, horse trainers, and tradesmen who wanted more than a quick sub sandwich from the 7-Eleven. This late in the afternoon, however, the restaurant was almost empty.

Swan slid into the banquette closest to the door. She slipped out of the mocs and propped her stocking feet on the bench seat, pointing her red painted toes and stretching her calves, enjoying the freedom from the tall boots and taking the opportunity to discreetly admire her small feet and slim ankles.

When she looked up, she saw a man doing the same from the facing table. He was tall, huge, really, very broad-shouldered, early thirties. Blue eyes, steady, unapologetic gaze, blond hair in a buzz cut around his ears, a little longer on top. A sports jacket over an old sweatshirt and jeans; battered cowboy boots with a roper heel. *Much too big to be a rider*, she thought, perhaps he was a broodmare owner from out of town?

All-righty, then, Swan thought, but she didn't put her feet back on the floor. She did turn to the server, an earnest local high school girl working the weekend shift, as she approached with a menu.

"Egg-white omelette, please, Kitty—with mushrooms and asparagus? And an iced tea," Swan said, knowing she was still being watched and not caring. When she looked back, the man was studying one of the local freebie papers touting the county's upcoming steeplechase and winery seasons. *Tourist, then.* From the plates still in front of him, it looked as though he had done some justice to a large burger and fries and a Dos Equis or two.

"Coffee, please," the man said, when the server came to clear his table. He looked again at Swan, taking her in from top to bottom, in a way that triggered in her a little spasm of pleasure. This was followed by a panic attack so unexpected that, if Swan hadn't been barefoot, waiting for the Vogels, she would have paid her bill and fled the restaurant. Instead, she swung her feet back on the floor and turned toward the banquette table. This faced her away from the man and gave her some time to breathe.

At that moment, her cell phone rang, and Swan was able to spend ten minutes describing to Edgar in Spanglish the exact location of the new German-made elevator bit, how to fit it, and why it had to be used on the five-year-old lay-up they were boarding for a neighbor.

By the time she was done, Swan's omelette had arrived. The tall man nursed his coffee as she ate. He didn't stare in an offensive way—there was nothing she could set herself against to let her anger build—but he never completely re-immersed himself in the newspaper either. This annoyed her. The minutes continued to crawl by. Swan ordered coffee, extra light, fixed an expression of a complete lack of interest on her face, and chanced another look.

The man was amused, now, having figured out what was going on, but he gave her a break and broke his gaze first. He had a handsome face—fair brow, strong, clean-shaven jaw, classic profile—the whole nine yards. Bad, bad news all around.

Thankfully, by the time Swan finished her second cup of coffee, the stone-faced apprentice from the Artisan was walking through the front door, holding the Vogels and a pair of boot hooks as if they were gold, frankincense, and myrrh.

The man watched riveted as Swan stood up and put her hand on the apprentice's shoulder for balance. The boy hooked the boot hooks into the boot tabs, then she wriggled, with as much dignity as she could summon in four-way-stretch breeches, into one extremely snug tall boot, then the other. It was something she had done a thousand times at the in-gate of a horse show or on a shedrow at a racetrack, but in the restaurant, in front of a small but appreciative audience, it felt like getting dressed from the underwear out. She twisted around to check the fit of the Vogels from the back, then nodded at the impassive apprentice.

"Good to go," she said, and he disappeared out the front door before she could pull together a tip.

Swan paid her check at the counter, glad to see that in the meantime, the man had left. She strode out the door and turned west into the lowering sun, down the brick sidewalk, heading back toward where she had parked the dually.

She almost ran into the man, who was standing next to a truck of his own, parked two doors down from the Crossroads entrance. Swan had to step abruptly sideways, away from the open passenger-side door, to get by him. The afternoon sun was hot, and he had just shucked off his sports coat to lay it on the front seat. The sleeves of his sweatshirt were cut out; he had enormous arms, with prominent veins running up his biceps. Visible under the sweatshirt were the outside margins of elaborate cobalt-blue tattoos snaking across his shoulders, which were huge.

Christ—this had to be Major Mountain Range himself, Swan realized, as she brushed past him. It all fit. She felt him turn to look once more, his eyes following her to the corner, where she went south and out of sight.

◆

Swan drove slowly all the way back to the house. She came to the conclusion that meeting Septimus Moore—formally—was now unavoidable. It was going to happen, perhaps as soon as today (why else would he be in Waverly?). Her objective under the circumstances had to be to formulate a strategy that would allow her to emerge from that meeting as the unqualified victor. Victory was defined as making clear to him her absolute unavailability, while at the same time extending to him every possible courtesy of Taliaferro County hospitality. This, at the most basic level, is simply what a lady did, day in and day out. Sometimes it was a more difficult task than others.

Her specific strategy was (1) to minimize in her own mind any evidence of Septimus Moore's attraction to her (2) to ridicule, undercut, and discount all evidence of her intense attraction to him, and (3) to shore up her previously held view of him as a West Texas womanizing lout.

Simple, effective, and elegant, really.

◆

Once home, she went upstairs to the study. She looked at the desk again, envisioning herself opening the letters from Hunt Lee, separating those that mentioned Septimus Moore from those that described other members of the rifle company, the platoon L.T., the food, the mission, the civilians, the dead, the ordnance, the humvees, the missile strikes, his hopes for their life together, the despair, the camaraderie, the fuck-ups. She stood there in the doorway for a long time.

So it really was no surprise to her to hear an eight-cylinder truck engine cut off in the circular driveway twenty minutes later. Damn. She had hoped to have a shower first. Mathilde answered the door at the second knock. Swan had placed herself in the comfortable, sunny little parlor, filled with overstuffed furniture, built-in bookshelves, and racing memorabilia.

"Major Septimus Moore," Mathilde announced, a bit breathlessly, rolling her eyes to give Swan a pantomimed *Wowie wow wow* she was hoping would be invisible to the tall man in the sports coat behind her.

Swan stood up.

"Miss Bolington," he said, his face a grim mask, then without waiting for acknowledgment, "I won't trouble you. It was inexcusable of me not to introduce myself in the restaurant once I realized who you were. I recognized you from Sergeant Lee's photograph, and your cap confirmed it. I do apologize, most sincerely. I would never have presumed to present myself in this way now, at your home and uninvited, if General Clayton had not been kind enough to inform your aunt of my wish to make your acquaintance.

"Please don't take my discourtesy as an indication of any lack of regard for Sergeant Lee, who was a valued member of my company and a true patriot."

He nodded a bow. "My compliments to you," he said and turned to leave.

Swan remained standing, speechless and amazed at her good fortune. Her visitor by his own reckoning had accomplished singlehandedly his own complete social immolation; she had to do absolutely nothing to finish him off. The one nagging bit of business was what Spaulding's opinion would be of her conduct in the next, oh, thirty seconds.

"Major Moore," she said sweetly, "don't go. Your apology is accepted. This is not the Court of St. James. All you did was look at a girl sitting in her stocking feet in the Crossroads."

"You are very kind," he said, and Swan saw in his handsome face a moment of uncertainty, his desire to stay in conflict with the more rational and prudent option to withdraw. He had flirted in a way that made it impossible to go back to being a courtly stranger now. To her astonishment, she began to suspect that somehow this Septimus Moore had fallen in love with her and had been in love for some time. Swan knew she had that effect on a certain kind of man. It had happened, unbelievably, before.

Well.

There went option (l): "to minimize in her own mind any evidence of Septimus Moore's attraction to her."

Moving on.

She sank back into one slipcovered chair.

"So you are at Quantico, Major Moore," Swan said brightly, as he sat opposite her.

"Yes, since late last month," he said.

"I know better than to ask anything," Swan said. "My stepfather is at D.O.D., working in the office of the Secretary of Defense."

He smiled, but faintly.

"I have heard that you breed racehorses, Miss Bolington, and you certainly have a beautiful farm here," he said, with no trace of a Texas accent. They continued chatting until Moore suddenly said, "I heard, too, that you named a great prospect after Sergeant Lee. I'd love to see him, if that would be possible. We don't have many Thoroughbreds in Buena Vista, Texas, but I've learned to appreciate them since I've been East. I attended Officer Candidate School and The Basic at Quantico eleven years ago."

Swan hesitated. She was suddenly reluctant to show Oscar Mike to Septimus Moore. She didn't trust herself even to say the colt's name out loud to someone who knew Hunt Lee as well as Moore did; who might think it not a good thing to have done.

But what else could she do?

They started toward the barn in the late afternoon sun. The colt was in his small paddock adjacent to the barn for the night, and he nickered as he heard Swan walk towards him. He mock-charged the fence line, tossed his head and blew loud, stallion-like blasts of air through his nostrils in their direction, just to show off.

It was Moore's turn to say "Wow."

"Oscar Mike," Swan said simply.

"Perfect," said Moore, still looking at the colt.

Swan burst into tears.

Moore stood in front her, at a complete loss, while she wept into her hands for several minutes. Finally she raised her head and wiped the tears from her face, without apology.

Moore said, "Any chance of seeing what that guy can do under tack?" which was, under the circumstances, the best possible response.

Swan called out for Edgar, and in a couple of minutes both the exercise rider and Eduardo emerged from the office in the training barn. They had the schooling saddle, racing bridle, and Troxell schooling helmet with them. Swan introduced Moore to them, "This is a friend of *Señor* Hunt's."

The colt took to the tack with more equanimity now—no hijinks. He'd been out for a school earlier in the day, and two weeks of Swan and Eduardo's low-pressure training had improved his manners considerably.

Swan briefly considered putting Edgar in the irons, but she couldn't resist showing off. Impulsively she took a leg up from Eduardo instead. The colt was all business today, letting her jog him nicely down the farm lane for three quarters of a mile, then wheeling at the turn onto the little schooling oval, and opening up a bit on the way back.

Swan dismounted next to the three men and handed the reins to Eduardo.

"My beautiful, beautiful boy," she murmured to the colt, smoothing his forelock under the bridle's crown piece. Eduardo and Edgar ran the irons up the stirrup leathers, loosened the colt's girth, and walked him, still on his toes, toward the barn's wash stall.

Swan turned back to Septimus Moore.

"Pretty spectacular," he said, in a way that made her think he wasn't talking just about the colt.

"Yeah, we are going slowly with him since he is so growthy," Swan replied, ignoring any *double entendre*. "He spent a couple of months at the Waverly Training Center earlier in the year, but he is home for now. I'm not sure he is a graded-stakes horse, but the breeding is there, definitely, so we will see. He has the mind of a raw—"

"Recruit?" offered Moore.

"Yeah, he hasn't finished basic training—not yet. But eventually he will get with the program."

"May I ask you—your staff seems pretty protective of you," Moore began cautiously. "Your manager doesn't seem to be a big fan of mine."

"Uh-oh," said Swan.

"Well, they felt pretty free to . . . speculate . . . *en español* about who I might be in terms of your social life and who they don't want me to be . . . . Neither of them knew I spoke Spanish, of course, *hasta que me puse a la derecha.*"

"'Until you set them right'?" said Swan. "They mean well," she sighed, "but it was very rude of them, nonetheless."

"Their opinion seems to be that you should stick with Miguel for . . . ah . . . romance and tell 'the rest of us' to get the hell out. I thought you might want to know, since I could have been . . . anyone," Moore said, his voice trailing off.

"'Miguel' is Oscar Mike," said Swan, and turned to walk back to the house.

Moore made a formal departure from the driveway; he did not come back indoors because Swan didn't invite him in. She knew she should have asked him to stay for dinner, but then it would have been impossible to avoid talking about Hunt and Iraq. He had probably seen enough of the wreckage not to want to go there. No doubt he knew the general outline of the disaster. He would have gotten the lowdown from Hunt's buddies, or the Lees, or General Clayton even, about her "she's lost her mind to grief" phase; her "let's get us another warrior" phase; and her "she almost killed a third guy" phase.

Now she was apparently in the "she's dating her horse" phase. Not appealing.

His early departure did allow her time to speculate on how Moore had come to be in love with her and why he had finally decided to see for himself what it meant. She didn't need to refer to Hunt Lee's letters to recall his amused description of the relentlessly sex-saturated obsessions of the expeditionary force marines of his battalion. That he felt he could not quote to her a single anecdote—his own or anyone else's—word for word left little to the imagination, and she was probably as familiar with the contents of *AfterDark*, *Knockers*, or *Beaver Extra* as the average twenty-first-century woman.

She had concluded from Hunt's letters that combat soldiers were the most devoted sexual fantasizers on the planet. They poured over every explicit photo that came their way as though it was part of the Dead Sea Scrolls, comparing notes, divining hidden meanings, then discussing it all endlessly on long, dusty "grocery runs" protecting supply convoys, in stinking holes in the sand, calling down air support on hostile villages. In Swan's opinion, the same testosterone that fueled marines, in particular, to think *Hey, let's the six of us go into this town filled with mujahadeen and get acquainted with the rocket launchers they have trained on the rest of our unit* made them the *DaVinci Code* scholars of porn.

Swan had not appeared in any of the publications held in high esteem by the Armed Forces of the United States. She had, however, given Hunt Lee a photo that was later found among his possessions and eventually returned to his family from Iraq.

It had been taken at the Upperville Horse and Colt Show the June before his last deployment. Swan was standing near the in-gate, holding a bay gelding catch ride. She was in a salmon-colored sleeveless shirt tucked into brown four-way-stretch Pikuers, the black Vogels, and her black Charles Owen. About to be twisted up and confined in a net, her hair was a thick dark tail down her back. She was facing the show ring, her brown Pikuer jacket folded at her feet, her thighs and butt model-worthy. Although she had been reviewing the course in her mind when the photo was taken, the morning light made her look pensive, even sweet, in the way Hunt Lee had loved. She had kidded him about it: to him she looked romantic, entitled—a belle—but she had been all business: the 20 percent commission she was due on the sale of the catch ride came through the next day.

The outer edge of the photo carried a faint Spanish red-brown stain, and Swan assumed that was why the Lees had returned the photo to her, many months later, without comment. The stain probably was not blood, but the possibility made it impossible for them to keep it.

Perhaps, *Terminator*-style ("Sarah Connor, I came back through time for you"), Moore had seen this photo and wanted to know the woman in it. What other explanation could there be? Hunt Lee had not been the type to pour his heart out either to his men or to the officers above him. He wasn't like any of them, really. He'd gone to the Hill School, then Harvard, and was on his way to U. Va. Law School before joining the Marines. He'd rejected O.C.S. for the expeditionary force, only to find himself among Orange County surfers, hill country backwoods boys, and midwestern Methodists for G.W. Bush.

◆

On Sunday afternoon, Swan called Spaulding, who was spending the weekend on the Eastern Shore at a old Swan family homestead in Onancock, to give her the 411.

"So he came by the farm," Swan said by way of an introduction, having decided to omit the whole Crossroads episode, "your major."

"Reeeally? And he was—"

"Cordial," said Swan, then was silent.

"How nice for you both." Spaulding was trying to help things along.

"No, it was fine," Swan said, but guardedly. "You are right. He just wanted to—" What had he wanted, other than to apologize for flirting in the restaurant? "Make my acquaintance." Yeah, he had said that.

"No full frontal assault? No moronic declaration of love? No flouting of decorum and decency in the face of Virginia womanhood?" Spaulding was on a roll.

"No—as you will be disappointed to hear, I'm sure," Swan said stiffly. Then she was silent.

"Well, this is . . . painful," said Spaulding, frustrated. "Was he hot, at least?"

"Oh, yeah," said Swan. "He was the Number One Texas freight train of smoking hotness."

"Now we are finally getting somewhere," her aunt beamed through the phone line.

The following Thursday, Mathilde's day off, Swan answered the phone on the first ring.

"I'm sorry to be calling so late in the week." It was Septimus Moore. "But I was wondering if you were free for dinner on Sunday night? I've got to be in Warrenton during the afternoon, and I thought we might go to the Reynard Inn in Waverly."

Swan had been prepared for this eventuality: him asking her out. In Warrenton for the afternoon? From Quantico? Hardly likely.

"That sounds lovely, Major," she said, following the script according to Spaulding.

"Seven-thirty?" he asked. "By then I hope you will have given some thought to calling me Sam."

"Oh," she said.

"My initials—S.A.M.," he said, "Septimus Anderson Moore. It is that or 'Moron,' as in 'Moore-on.' Which is the very affectionate nickname given to me as a L.T. by my rifle platoon," he explained. "Such subtle humor, but so appropriate for a young combat officer, I suppose."

Swan laughed. "I'm thinking I'm going to go with Sam. But with a nickname like Moron, it is amazing that you have gone on to have a successful military career—even getting yourself to Quantico."

"There are so many punchlines for that set up, it is hardly worth it," Moore sighed.

"His officers called R.E. Lee 'Granny' when he first assumed command of the Army of Northern Virginia," said Swan quietly, "before he became a living god to the South."

"I don't think I'm in any danger of becoming a god to the South or to anyplace else, since I think my days of standing before the enemy may be over."

"Are they?" said Swan, a bit too sharply. "Truly?"

◆

On Friday Eduardo weaned the Serve the Guns colt from his dam by the astrological "sign," since on that date the sign was in the feet (the optimum predictor of future soundness—as opposed to the breast or leg or elsewhere in the body), and Swan went to the lumber yard in Hume to inspect the hundred locust posts she was purchasing for fence repair in the mare fields.

◆

On Saturday Serve the Guns slipped her foal, for no apparent reason, since the fetus looked well-formed when Eduardo found it in the field. Swan was keenly disappointed. Not only did the loss mean a potential $150,000 out the door but it also threatened to undercut her faith in the "sign" as an infallible predictor of an uneventful weaning (which technically it had been, at least from the live foal's perspective). She would get a free rebreeding of the mare in February, so it was the loss of a year in the mare's reproductive life that was the hardest to take.

Under these circumstances, Swan had little time to focus on her big date much before six P.M. Sunday. She was going with the black tube minidress, garnet-red jewel box purse, and the black Miu Miu open-toed pumps with red silk four-inch heels. Moore was tall, very tall. She could get away with murder, height-wise, with him so long as she could get into his vehicle without the minidress causing a riot. She ran a quick dress rehearsal in the dually to make sure, barely returning to the house before Moore turned into the driveway. She needn't have worried. He was in a little Mercedes roadster, not the truck after all.

When she opened the front door, he took one look and said, "Holy shit."

"I'm taking that as a compliment," Swan said.

"Meant as one."

There wasn't much conversation back into Waverly. Moore seemed pretty much speechless (although he did find a way to let her know the Mercedes was borrowed; his truck was in the shop) and almost everything Swan thought to say by way of small talk was dwarfed by her strong desire just to look at him, to take him in. He was dressed in a vanilla linen shirt, a natural-shouldered blue jacket, and khakis. He wore clothes well, since he was not barrel chested, with a slim waist: someone somewhere had taught him how to dress himself.

That said, it was Swan's long, bare legs and world-class caboose (thank God for Spanx) that brought conversation in the restaurant to a standstill as the two of them followed the host to their table.

"If eighty percent of the guys in here weren't . . . conflicted relative to their sexual orientation, I'd have some concerns," Moore said balefully, eyeing several same-sex couples at nearby tables. "In a D.C. sports bar, five guys would have had their hands up your dress by the time we'd gotten this far."

"I'm taking that as a compliment," Swan said.

"Meant as one."

Over the local-produce entrée, Swan got Moore to talk about Buena Vista, a tiny, flat, flyblown spec of dirt outside San Antonio, home to cattle, Mexicano cowhands, and not much else. His father, originally from Kentucky, had tried wild catting in the oil fields, raising cattle on leased land, and apparently, liquor, as his final career move before dying when Moore was fifteen. Moore's mother was a retired teacher also from Kentucky; like Swan's, she had remarried and was living in Corpus Christi. Moore had gotten a football scholarship to Texas Tech. By coffee, they were getting to his path to the Marines when Spaulding suddenly appeared in the Reynard's doorway, in evening wear.

"My aunt, Miss Hexell," Swan said as Moore rose from his chair. "Spaulding, Major Septimus Moore."

"How *do* you do," said Spaulding, turning on the charm. "I was just coming from the Kennedy Center to see *La Bohème*—which was fabulous—and I recalled that you said you might be in town, Swan." Spaulding gave them both a blinding smile.

"I don't want to interrupt your evening, but I'm hoping you and Major Moore might come to my little reception next Sunday, for Hospice, at the Willow's Edge. Very informal, just a few folks at my cottage, but it is possible that General Clayton will be able to get away to attend. And Swan's stepfather, too, and the secretary of defense if *he* can get away. And of course Senator and Mrs. Avery, since they are our neighbors and the honorary chairpeople of the committee," Spaulding beamed at them both, as she sat down.

Swan, having been bushwhacked, was mortified, but Moore seemed cautiously enthusiastic.

"I'd be delighted," he said.

"And of course please feel free to bring a guest, both of you," said Spaulding breezily, as if that had even remotely been her expectation. She got up from the table, and Moore rose again. "So nice to meet you, Major Moore. Good-night, darling." Then she flitted out into the night.

"You don't have to come," Swan said immediately. "I can't imagine that you'd want to haul yourself out here two weekends in a row—well, three really—and certainly not for my aunt's Hospice fund-raiser."

"Can't you?" he asked.

"No, not unless you have some idea to—"

"Oh, I have some idea," Moore said. "Some very specific idea. And I've had it from the first minute I saw you in the Crossroads, as you well know."

"Before that," she said, so quietly that he wasn't sure he had heard her, "before the Crossroads."

"Yes." He motioned for the check.

The ride back to the farm was as quiet as the earlier ride. Swan didn't want to say anything to move her suitor any farther in any direction—forward or backward—since she wasn't prepared with a countermove for either eventuality. One thing she had learned training horses: the best way to get the best of a young horse was to precipitate a bout of bad behavior once you had your disciplinary strategy in mind, so you could act decisively rather than wait for dangerous hijinks to catch you by surprise. Any military mind would know this as well: preparation is everything; fight on ground of your own choosing.

Things were quiet, uneventful but busy around the farm, until ten A.M. Thursday. Swan impulsively had undertaken some half-hearted weeding of the flower bed at the side of the house, pulling up the spent day lilies, cutting back leggy roses, removing the last signs of the Japanese beetle infestation in July.

To Swan's surprise, strolling down the hard-topped service road that led to the mare barn was Hastings Fitzhugh. His surname was pronounced "Fitchy," in the peculiar way of old Virginia, although no one outside a fifty-mile radius of the Newport News/Norfolk area typically managed it on the first try.

"Fitch!" Swan called, from the side of the house. "Up here!" and he made an about-face.

His terrible injury had not affected his long, elegant stride, the general ease with which he carried himself, the legacy of a lifetime spent in the saddle, cross country and over fences. The rehab staff in Richmond had been impressed by his laconic fortitude, which quite successfully concealed a tightly locked down anger.

"Mathilde thought you were still at the barn," he said as he got closer. The left sleeve of his summer-weight jacket was pinned up below the elbow. "The three of them do nothing but try to keep tabs on you all day, and they still don't succeed."

"Darling, you look wonderful," Swan said, in the lightest of tones, as though it had been days, not months, since they had seen each other. He gave her a quick kiss on the cheek. "How are you feeling?"

"Put out," Fitch said, with a mock scowl. "I have to hear from Patty and Lorenzo that you were canoodling with some hulking blond and generally making a spectacle of yourself in the Reynard last week."

"I do my best," Swan said, with a modest smile. "Someone has to raise hell in downtown Waverly. None of the teenagers is holding up his end of things. They are all earning honest livings in the Crossroads or driving Meals on Wheels to shut-ins these days. Although, as restaurateurs, Patty and Lorenzo should mind their own business."

"That's my girl," Fitch said approvingly. "Waverly has been dead ever since David Edgeworth shot Connie Edgeworth on Main Street in broad daylight and got probation. So you are confirming this outrageous bit of misconduct? I *should* be ashamed of you."

"Well, no one had to turn the fire hoses on us, like dogs in the road. It was Hunt's captain, Septimus Moore, just in the neighborhood and making a courtesy call." That phrase was proving handy.

"Four years late, isn't he?" Fitch's tone was still lighter than air, but with an edge. "Wasn't he the one Hunt said was supposed to have married Miss November? She must be thrilled for you both."

"Fitch, really, that's enough." Swan avoided the bait. "How's the rehab—the . . . prosthesis?"

"*Forsan et haec olim meminisse iuvabit,*" Fitch replied, quoting Virgil. *Perhaps someday it will help to have remembered even these things.* "It's a pisser, all the way around. I'm happier without it." His face darkened.

"Let's get back to your *cinq à sept* with soldier boy." He rallied. "Seriously, Swan: are you dating this guy? Everyone in town is talking about it. You haven't had a real date since you waved your hankie at me at Dulles on my way to the show." Fitch meant Iraq. "I'm not counting those drop-outs you were tutoring for their GED exams while I was locked up. Be careful how you answer, because I bet Patty and Lorenzo one hundred bucks you'd sink your teeth in Josiah Yoder next. I've seen the kind of service you get at the Artisan."

"You are hopeless." Swan smiled in spite of herself. "I see we are not going to get anywhere. Come inside, let's discuss the hunt's work day to rebuild those coops in my fallow field."

Fitch followed her up the steps, into the house, to the cool parlor.

"You know, technically, I should be aggrieved." He wasn't joking any more. "We never formally broke up, as I recall."

"Fitch, please: we haven't been a couple since your return, a return I, for one, am deeply thankful for." Swan changed the subject, though none too smoothly. "Tell me what your plans are. Are you going back to work, when you feel up to it?"

"Oh, they say they want me back—too much invested in me, by them and, before that, at Langley and . . . elsewhere." Interpol and CIA careers predated Fitch's stint at Warburton. "But my first priority is seeing if good old James, bless his Thoroughbred heart, will hunt fairly with me holding the reins one handed. I don't trust the prosthesis to do the job, although it can probably hold the whip. After that, maybe some teaching position or some think tank, who knows?" He sounded restless, unhappy, defensive.

"Some folks are talking county politics."

"Fuck—with my mouth?" he snorted. "That's not likely. What about us?"

"You have had a lot to deal with, and, frankly, so have I, although in no way has it been comparable," Swan said cautiously.

"Listen, I don't give a damn about this bad-luck-doomed-love shit of yours. There is nothing to it, never was. Hunt felt the same way, so did Roland. But, of course, my . . . physical problems . . . are a lot for anyone else to deal with."

"You know that's not it. I'd finish the IED's job and kill you myself if I thought you really believed that was a factor," Swan said testily, "and there is no 'bad-luck-doomed-love shit' as far as I'm concerned."

"So we both just need to get on with our lives? You might take your own advice and start a fire in the fireplace with those letters of Hunt Lee's, or are you still reading them ten times a day? You should know them all by heart."

"I think it would be best I showed you out," Swan said gently.

"So nice to have had this little *élaircissement,*" he replied, "most enlightening. Soldier boy is going to find himself up in the shit, if he isn't there already."

"He's a marine, not a soldier."

"Well, look on the bright side: if he has gotten rid of Miss Buck Nekkid, chances are he has already gone through his skank phase. Or do you plan to share him with her? I hope, for your sake, that at least he's good in the sack," Fitch said, walking out the door.

"Thanks for stopping by," she sighed, forgiving him for everything.

The next day, calla lilies and yellow Abe Lincoln roses arrived in a large turn-of-the-century sterling equestrian trophy from the Waverly Florist.

"My darling," was on the card. There was no signature, but the handwriting was Fitch's.

Swan placed the trophy in the entranceway, on the round eighteenth-century mahogany pedestal table, next to two framed photos. The first was of Swan's grandfather in a trilby hat, proudly holding a Bolington homebred after the gelding won the St. George Cup on the grass at Doncaster in the 1970s. The trophy, not impressive by American standards but gleaming like a silver jewel, had pride of place in the center of the table.

The second photo had been taken by Spaulding at the engagement party of Swan and Hunt Lee at the Willow's Edge. Swan had put her hair up to show off the Cartier diamond studs Hunt had given her as a surprise engagement party present. They matched her diamond engagement ring perfectly. Swan was in an emerald Ralph Rucci *prêt à porter* cocktail dress, Hunt in his marine dress blues. They were looking at each other. There were days that Swan placed this photo face down on the table. On such days, Mathilde passed by the table many times, but she never righted the photo herself. Sooner or later, she had learned, the photo and frame would face the front door again, as if by magic.

◆

The next morning, Swan sent Eduardo with the dually to Waverly Motors for a tune up and tires. She was expecting her Mennonite neighbors, Katie and Hannah Yoder, with the tractor and manure wagon to pick up the manure pile behind the mare barn and training barns.

The Yoders really did this as a favor to Swan. It cost a fortune for a professional pick up service from the race track, and local rose and mushroom farmers could not keep up with the twenty-four/seven production department of twenty-five mares, foals, and boarders at the farm. Unlike other farm owners, Swan had an abhorrence of spreading even aged manure on fields that horses were going to graze on; it offended her parasite management protocols.

About eight A.M., Swan heard the girls arrive with the old International pulling an enormous open wagon. They headed down the service road. About nine o'clock, she heard them start up the tractor with a full load of manure. Swan remembered that the gooseneck horse trailer was on blocks near the manure pile, which rose like the Blue Ridge between the fence line and the end of the hard surface service road.

Swan pulled on a CIA ball cap and her Bean boots, tucking her jeans into the leather uppers, and hot-footed it down the road. Too late: Katie and Hannah had backed the wagon at a fatally awkward angle to the manure pile, against the gooseneck. Both were gazing unhappily at the tires of the wagon and the tractor, sunk into the soft shoulder off the service road.

"Son of a bitch," Swan muttered, while the Mennonites weren't yet within hearing range. Katie looked up apologetically, Hannah with exasperation, wiping her hand across her forehead and tucking a wisp of hair into her prayer cap.

"Good morning!" Swan said cheerily.

Katie looked at her in frustration. "I'm a baker, not a farmer."

"Eben offered to come, but they are so behind with the soybeans," Hannah began.

"*No problemo*," Swan said confidently, then, reconsidered. "Uh-oh. Eduardo has the dually. I can't hook up the gooseneck to move it out of our way."

"Well, we got the tractor in here, we should be able to get it out," said Katie. "Could Edgar help?"

"Day off," replied Swan, "and, frankly, horses are Edgar's specialty, not internal combustion engines.

"Fire her up," she directed, but without hope.

Hannah got the gleaming International to crank and turned the steering wheel, but it was clear that extricating the rig was beyond them. She cut the engine before she dug herself in any deeper.

"Son of a *bitch!*" Swan said again, and this time she didn't bother to shield the girls from her voice.

"I suppose we could unload the manure . . ." Katie began, "or call Brother or Dad."

"Oh, no!" said Swan. "We'd never hear the end of it; and I could never let you guys come all the way up here with a clear conscience again."

Then Hannah and Katie's heads shot up like white-tailed deer on the first morning of hunting season.

"This doesn't look good," observed someone from behind Swan.

She turned around. Septimus Moore was standing a little way up the service road. He was in his desert camouflage battle dress, in solidarity with the troops in the field.

"I don't suppose you have a trailer hitch in the bed of your truck," Swan said, trying to envision Moore's F-250, her mind still on the problem of moving the gooseneck.

"Sorry," said Moore, with genuine regret.

Only then did she realize she hadn't even said hello.

"Major, what a pleasant surprise," she backtracked. "Katie Yoder, Hannah Yoder, this is Major Moore, who served with Hunt, uh, overseas."

Both girls looked down shyly.

"Ladies," Moore said, removing his head cover. "I see I've dropped in at a bad time. Why don't we move the gooseneck with the dually I saw when I was here?"

"*We* would have done that already if the dually weren't in Waverly getting lubed with Eduardo," Swan said a bit sharply, only recognizing the awkward syntax afterward.

"Well, would you like any help or not?" asked Moore with almost no smile.

"No thank you, Sam," Swan said. It was the first time she had ever called him by name. "You are obviously going somewhere, or have been somewhere, and you will get filthy."

"May I at least offer a suggestion?"

"No, but much appreciated."

Katie and Hannah looked stricken.

"Oh, Christ," Sam muttered, Mennonites or no Mennonites, and in three or four long strides he was next to the tractor, lifting Hannah out of the driver's seat. She jumped down gratefully, holding her long polyester skirt a little above her running shoes and stockings. He cranked the tractor once again, turned the steering wheel sharply away from the gooseneck, and held it there.

Then he jumped down, helping Hannah clamber back into the seat. He put her hands where his had been on the steering wheel and went to the back of the wagon.

"Now go!" he ordered and gave the wagon a huge, two-man push upward and forward from under the tailgate to release the back tires. Hannah got the tractor to lurch forward, find solid ground under its wheels, and buck itself onto the hard surface road.

"We're Oscar Mike," he said, grinning under a generous spattering of manure, turf, and guck.

"Roger that," Swan said dryly. Hannah's face was awash with relief. Katie's social antennae, deadly accurate, caught an undertone in the exchange.

"Thank you so very much, we were well and truly stuck," Katie said to Sam. "We should be getting back." She was reluctant.

"Let's have some coffee up to the house," said Swan, "and, Sam, I think you need a towel, or—"

So they all trooped back up the drive. Swan pointed Sam to the bathroom tucked behind the center hall; there would be towels stacked in the corner.

"Mathilde, could we have four coffees, please," Swan called out, to be heard in the kitchen.

When Sam emerged, he looked at the roses and calla lilies in the trophy on the pedestal table. He saw the photos displayed there, including the one of Hunt and Swan, as he followed the women through the first floor. When they were settled in the parlor, Swan started fretting again.

"So annoying . . . . If only the dually had been here."

"Don't worry, Swan," said Sam, the first time he had used *her* first name. "I'm well aware that you three would have found a very good solution. We do have women in the Marines, you know." He'd picked up on what was bothering her. "We're just used to finding a way or making a way."

"Finding a way of giving yourself a hernia, you mean," Swan muttered, still fussing.

The banter shocked Katie, not its subject matter (Mennonites weren't prudish) but its familiarity—Swan knew Sam and liked him, and Katie hadn't known anything about him. This was unusual.

Sam didn't rise to the bait.

"Occasionally it is helpful to be six-four instead of—" His voice trailed off.

"A shrimp," Swan finished for him. "Believe me, I know. Although that is more useful in riding Thoroughbreds."

"Point taken," Sam said.

The conversation then turned to Hannah and Katie, but as was often the case, it was awkward going with the two women in the presence of *ein English* man. Sam saw this pretty quickly and, as the uninvited late arrival, prepared to leave them to themselves.

"I hope you can make yourself presentable before you go wherever you are going," said Swan, refusing to consider the possibility that Sam's visit was anything but a spur-of-the-moment detour on his part.

"Don't worry, I'm on my way back to Quantico." Sam replaced his head cover. "Always 'invigorating' to see you, Miss Swan," he said, "and to meet you two ladies, of course."

He was down the front steps, on the flagstone walkway and headed to his truck, which was head-out in front of the tractor in the drive.

"Six on Sunday?" he called back to Swan.

"Yes, six." The Hospice reception.

Katie and Hannah sat like two polyester-clad stones, right where Swan had left them.

"I know you need to be getting the tractor back," Swan prompted, hoping to dislodge them. No such luck.

"He's a friend of Spaulding's." Swan answered their unspoken question. "She asked him to the Hospice fund-raiser, and we are going to go together. That's all."

Katie remained silent.

"He just paid a courtesy call, a couple of weeks ago," Swan continued, trying to anticipate their next question.

"Is he the man you had dinner with in the Reynard?" Hannah asked matter-of-factly, "and before that, at the Crossroads? We've heard about it all."

"Can't anyone have dinner in a public place without the town turning upside down?" Swan was defensive, knowing the answer to that question as well as the girls did. "The Crossroads was just a coincidental . . . . It's nothing, nothing."

"Oh, *Schwan,*" Katie said, "he is *ein soldat.*" *A soldier*. She said it despairingly, as though she had said, "He has terminal cancer" or "He's married."

"Don't worry. It's nothing. Nothing," Swan repeated reassuringly, but she didn't like the way she felt when she did so.

"Will Mr. Fitzhugh be there? At your aunt's house?" Katie asked, her intentions clear.

This stopped Swan short.

"I don't know," she said. She realized she had better find out.

Chapter 2

For the second consecutive Sunday, Swan stood looking at herself in the mirror prior to an evening with Septimus Moore. The detour to Manhattan on her way back from Saratoga had been to pick up some new clothes. She had invested in a strapless pencil-skirted Christian Seriano cocktail dress in blue and black silk. Silk in the same fabric had been ruched into a saucy little ruffle that wrapped on the bias from hem to waist and was banded in silver silk. She added blue and black silk D&G pumps, a tiny silver purse and Hunt's diamond engagement-party studs. She had worn the earrings only rarely in the four years she had had them, mostly when she was seeing Carter Roland, but never after they had become engaged. She viewed them as talismen against any imprudent conduct on her part, a substitute for Hunt Lee's combat medals and marble tombstone at Arlington National Cemetery. If she could have, she would have worn the medals and the headstone around her neck on her evening with Sam. She hoped he would admire the earrings, so she would have an excuse to tell him their provenance. She wanted to see if it would hurt him, if evidence not only of Hunt's love but also of his means would have an impact, would begin to push him away.

She looked like a sapphire blue confection in the dress. She knew it.

Sam arrived on time and in his dress blues, complete with dress sword, white gloves, and ribbons on his enormous chest. The sight was spectacular.

"You look absolutely lovely," he said, as she picked up her blue silk purse from the hallway table.

"Likewise, I'm sure," she smiled. For the first time, Swan felt in Sam some anxiety. She was surprised, touched: he was a country boy from a Texas shit hole, after all. She sought to reassure him. “This isn’t the Emmitsburg Road, Major. Spaulding loves officers, particularly tall, good-looking ones. Don’t be surprised if she monopolizes you all evening. She’ll want to show you off and take credit for you, since she’s convinced you are her own personal discovery.”

“I’ll try to live up to her . . . expectations,” Sam said, “and yours.” Swan’s arcane reference to the nemesis of Pickett’s Charge had brought a hint of a smile to his face.

Swan’s coolness toward him vanished. She felt strangely jumpy, excited, in a way she hadn’t felt in a long time. As they walked down the flagstone walkway, Swan saw the Mercedes parked as usual.

“I’m growing attached to this,” she said, looking at the car. “The truck will be a shock when it comes back.” She stopped abruptly. She had made an assumption that she would be seeing Sam again. That was a mistake. He picked it up, and she saw him smile in the growing dark.

◆

They drove an hour south of Belle Everley to the Willow’s Edge. Swan held up her end of the conversation via a short history of the house, another remnant of the Hexell and Bolington families’ dwindling land holdings north of Richmond. Like Belle Everley, the farm house dated from the 1820s. Although Spaulding always referred to it as a cottage, it was another example of the quirky Quaker-inspired building style of northern Virginia. The original section was frame, with a large fieldstone addition of generously proportioned rooms on two floors. Early in the twentieth century, a solarium had been added on the south side of the house. Walk-in fireplaces were situated in both main sections, one in what had been the original kitchen.

A spring-fed pond at the front of the house provided the setting for the willows that had given the house its name, and a fieldstone springhouse had been restored to serve as a summer folly, furnished with a scrub top table, herb drying racks, and Adirondack chairs. A fieldstone step-down to the spring head provided a ledge on which generations of children had dangled their feet in cool water in the summertime.

◆

They arrived at the house at seven fifteen, but twenty cars were already parked helter skelter in the driveway that snaked around the back of the house. Sam helped Swan out of the car and, as they approached the massive front door, she took his arm protectively.

Spaulding's butler, Alfredo, led them into the crowded downstairs living room. A string quartet and a bar occupied a corner near the kitchen, but the rest of the floor space was wall to wall with people in black tie. Spaulding saw them almost immediately, since Sam's tall figure was impossible to miss. But before she got to them through the crowd of other guests, Swan was turned around from behind, embraced, and kissed—long, wet, and open-mouthed.

It was Hastings Fitzhugh, of course.

"My darling," he said, when he came up for air. He had been drinking.

Swan looked immediately from Fitch to Sam. The marine was white as a sheet, mystified, and to her surprise, furious, but was already working very hard to conceal it. Swan pushed gently but firmly away from Fitch and took a step back into Sam's body as both an acknowledgment of his claim on her and a warning against his overreaction.

"Hastings Fitzhugh, Septimus Moore," she said coolly.

"Major, my sincere apologies," said Fitch smoothly enough as they shook hands. "I hope you will excuse an old friend greeting an old . . . friend."

"Of course," said Sam, who was still angry but was beginning to see how the land lay. Then Spaulding Hexell descended upon the three of them in a flutter of greetings, defusing the tension in a moment. Spaulding had made an instantaneous decision to separate Fitch from Sam and Swan in the most expedient way possible.

"Swan," Spaulding said smoothly, "I know the major will want to pay his respects to General Clayton, and I want him to meet the Averys, of course, since they cannot stay long: there is an early vote tomorrow in the Senate, so I must take you both from Fitch—well, right away, I'm afraid."

As if by magic, she was holding by the hand the lovely teenage Townsend Brooke, niece of an aging movie star who had just relocated to Taliaferro County, as an offering to Fitch. Spaulding kept a laser eye on the young thing in Fitch's company even as she was herding Swan and Sam toward the Averys, who were deep in discussion with Swan's stepfather, the grey-headed and distinguished Bertrand Davis. Fitch, to his credit, was on his way back to being a perfect gentleman now that he had done the damage he had intended. Miss Brooke was laughing and flirting sweetly, by all appearances.

Small talk with the suave senator and his lady was smooth as silk, so Spaulding felt free to return to Fitch and Townsend within a few minutes. Swan carried Sam along with her in conversation with the Averys, who nonetheless were soon spirited away to discuss tax breaks for small business with two local entrepreneurs, leaving Swan and Sam to Davis.

"So, how are you enjoying being stateside, Major?" said Davis, guardedly. "I hope you agree that we are seeing positive developments politically in both theatres—"

Sam was politically adept enough to let Davis's observations go unchallenged. For Swan's part, she had a cordial, if mostly distant, attachment to her stepfather; he had been married to Swan's mother only a year, the three of them living together at Belle Everley, before Lucinda Bolington Davis had died.

"Bert, it would be lovely if we could at least get a drink—," she began, and Sam instantly took the cue to head to the bar for the three of them.

"I see Fitch wasted no time in acting the jackass," Bert said grimly, when Sam was out of earshot. "He thinks he can get away with murder these days. He must have a death wish, tweaking this guy's nose—a big combat marine who looks as though he has his own built-in body armor. What's Fitch's game, Swan? Does he have any reason for pulling this stunt tonight, other than too many shots of Johnnie Walker Black?"

"Oh, Bert," Swan sighed, "he is disappointed in love, I'm sorry to say."

"Well, disappointment isn't what it used to be, apparently," Bert said dryly. "If he had had two good arms, your major would have cleaned his clock for him—General Clayton or no General Clayton. Everybody could see that—," but he broke off as Sam rejoined them.

A few minutes later, Sam made his way to the side of the general himself, whom he had greeted on his way to the bar.

"Enjoying yourself, Major?" asked General Clayton coolly.

"Very much so, thank you, sir."

"Swan Bolington is a beautiful girl, the most beautiful girl in the South, many say," said General Clayton, watching Swan from across the room. "I've known the family for years. The Bolingtons, and the Hexells, too, have ties to some of our oldest families, the FFVs—the first families of Virginia—though no one these days knows who or what those are."

"I believe Swan mentioned that they are descendents of the signers of the Declaration of Independence."

"The Bolingtons are related to the Balls, Martha Washington's people, and the Hexells, although they have been in the Valley for generations, are related to the Tidewater Randolphs, and therefore the Jefferson grandchildren, via marriage."

Sam could think of nothing to say.

"She was going to make Delahunt Lee a simply marvelous wife," Clayton said, still looking at Swan, "and was prevented from doing so only through . . . unfortunate circumstances."

"Yes, sir," said Sam, beginning to see where things were going.

"Although she made a brief . . . foray . . . in a different direction . . ."

Clayton must mean Swan's doomed engagement to the Army's Carter Roland, Sam thought.

"Also most unfortunate, since Captain Roland was a fine young officer himself. The difficulty is that we Virginians are all so tied to the land, and through the land, to history. Sometimes, too much so for our own good. The same places, the same people, the same losses, the same victories. We're never really happy outside that world, and few people ever really join us from the outside. All that aside, I'd hate to see Miss Swan lost to the Marine Corps . . . permanently. Is there any chance of that happening, Major?" asked Clayton.

"I'm not sure I'm taking your point, sir. But if I understand you correctly, I'd say we are experiencing some . . . blue on blue fire." He thought of Eduardo and Edgar's efforts to undermine him, and he wasn't so sure about the Yoder girls, either. "But I think we can get that sorted out."

"Do we have the enemy's position well scouted?" Clayton continued. Sam struggled for a few seconds: *Hastings Fitzhugh? Must be. He had made this scene, tonight, that's true, but Swan never mentioned him.*

"Affirmative, sir," he said.

"Good. Good work," said Clayton. "Did you know, Major, that Delahunt Lee was a superb horseman? Gentleman Rider of the Year—an amateur, of course—in the annual point-to-point series of races over fences? He could have been a professional jump rider and would probably have ended up master of foxhounds of the Waverly Hunt. His family was not related to R.E. Lee, more's the pity, but his mother was a distant descendent of 'King' Carter, who received three hundred thousand acres via Lord Fairfax, courtesy of Charles the Second."

"Yes, sir," said Sam grimly.

"Mr. Fitzhugh, whom I believe you met this evening, is the current M.F.H. of Waverly," said Clayton, as he watched his wife join Swan and Bert near the fireplace. "Do you ride, Major? Being from Texas, I suspect you know your way around a horse."

"Just 4-H, quarter horses, sir. Nothing like . . . this," Sam replied, sweeping the air vaguely with his hand.

Clayton was silent.

"Weren't you a halfback at Texas Tech?" he asked suddenly, "in Coach Keach's spread offense?"

"Tight end, sir, briefly."

"Ah, so you did some blocking," said Clayton. "Shall we join the ladies?"

Two hours later, Swan and Sam were making their good-byes. They walked silently to the Mercedes in the cool evening. Swan got in the passenger side as Sam held the door. He slid into the driver's seat and reached to turn the key in the ignition. Swan impulsively leaned across the seat. He turned his head and she kissed him full and hard, on the mouth.

"Thank you, thank you, thank you," she murmured. His arms were around her; in a second he had not only caught up with her but had also taken over the lead; then, in another moment, he was way ahead of her. Only then did she pull back—all the way to the passenger door. He sank back in his seat and dropped his arms. He looked at her.

"What a funny girl you are," he said, giving his head half a shake. "You don't let me within a mile of you for weeks, then you jump me just because I didn't take a swing at a one-armed drunk."

Swan laughed.

He started the car and headed north, to Belle Everley. He was trying to figure everything out on his own, silently; either he didn't want to question her directly or he didn't trust any answers he might get. He left her at her front door willingly. He knew better than to try his luck in the romance department. Not only did he have the benefit, via Hunt Lee, of the *CliffsNotes* on Swan Bolington, who was first and foremost a lady, but like many exceedingly handsome men, he also was patient. Women always came to him, sooner or later. Let her think things over for now.

The next morning, Swan simply sat and waited for the call from Spaulding. It came at eight thirty-five A.M.

"Are you alone?"

"Yes, of course," said Swan.

"Well, did he spend the night?" Spaulding asked.

"No."

"Did he want to?"

"Did not ask."

"Did you invite him in?"

"Did not."

"Oh, Christ on a cracker!" said Spaulding in complete disgust. "What are you playing, Swan?"

"Wait, aren't the roles being reversed here? Just a little? Shouldn't you be counseling me to slow down, be cautious? I've seen this man a total of four times—ever," Swan said, aggrieved.

"Swan, don't think you can get away using your usual bag of tricks with him," Spaulding warned. "He isn't some lovesick college kid or indulgent fiancé. This is a man used to getting his own way with women. I mean, look at him. Do you think he is going to put up with your games for long?"

"My God," Swan said, suddenly enlightened. "*You* are in love with him! You are protecting *him* from *me*. Don't worry—I'll share: there is enough of him to go around."

"Oh, please," Spaulding said, pityingly. "Of course, I do have eyes in my head. I do still have a pulse. He is a handsome guy. That height, those looks, that uniform—"

"That body," Swan supplied, just to tweak her. "Your point?"

"I just would not play games," Spaulding said, keeping the light tone, but with the slightest bit of effort. "If you aren't interested, why don't you send him on down the road?"

Swan's heart sank.

"What do you know?" she asked.

"Nothing."

"Don't. Don't do this. Please."

"Nothing."

"Please. I don't deserve it."

Spaulding sighed.

"After you two left, General Clayton and Bert—"

"What?"

"You only have to read the newspaper."

"What?"

"Nothing. That's all I'm saying."

"I thought you said no one at Quantico would be rotated back."

"I did say that."

"Is it true?"

"There are marine majors doing their fifth tour, right now."

Swan was silent.

Then she said, "I've got to go." She hung up the phone. Then she stepped into the bathroom off the hallway and vomited into the toilet.

◆

The next morning, Swan was up and dressed early. She paired a vanilla linen shirt with her blue Vogels and a soldier blue split riding skirt for an old-fashioned, elegant change from the Pikeurs. She was expecting non-horsey company in the form of Mrs. Yoder and the girls, and a courtesy call from the Waverly Hooved Animal Rescue League later in the morning. She had been unable to formulate overnight a strategy to deal with Spaulding's cryptic warning, and that always made her jittery and anxious. Her plan was to stay preoccupied with the many details of life as she knew it, as she had always known it, apart from the personal tragedies in which she had played starring roles.

When she sat down to breakfast, Mathilde brought news with the fruit, local honey, and croissants: "Dr. Hardaway called while you were in the shower," she said cautiously. "She'll be by within the hour to drop off some . . . supplement she wants to talk to you about . . . for the . . . mare." Despite fifteen years with the Bolingtons, Mathilde was still not very horse savvy.

"Really?" Swan said. "She called here rather than down at the barn for Eduardo? Well, no big deal, I suppose." She changed her immediate plans from a quick ride on a sale horse to tackling paperwork in the study. Forty minutes later, she heard the unmistakable sound of hooves trotting up the drive at a high rate of speed and the crunch of one-hundred-year-old wheels on the gravel.

"Halloo, the house," sang out a familiar voice. Fitch.

She went to the front door. He was in khakis and cap behind his two strapping chestnut Oldenburgs, who were put to a lightweight two-seat, four-wheeled spider lux cart. Fitch was driving coachman style, only reversed: the reins were in his right hand and his whip, in the hated prosthesis, in his left. He had a huge smile on his face.

Swan grinned back.

"Well, don't you look smart."

"I phoned Mathilde and convinced her to tell a little fib about Kezia to make sure you'd be home this morning," Fitch said, pleased with himself. "So now you have to come for a ride as a reward for me wearing this fucking fake hand . . . and to let me make amends for my inexcusable behavior at Spaulding's."

"Oh, Fitch." Swan was ambivalent.

"Hurry up, for Christ's sake," he laughed. "The 'halt' on these two leaves something to be desired." This last comment was proved true by the snorting horses jigging in place as they champed their bits, and it was clear that Hurricane and Hollywood had every intention of taking Fitch, the spider lux, and all on another very fast circuit around the driveway. "I can't jump down to help you up, I'm afraid, it's catch as catch can. Hurry or I'll kidnap Mathilde. I need ballast!"

"How flattering," Swan said, but she couldn't resist: she was down the stairs and into the cart at the same moment Fitch let his pair take off down the service road.

The lightweight cart bucked them up and down, spewing gravel in their wake as Fitch made a show of being unable to control the horses at all. They nearly upended Eduardo and the wheelbarrow along the fence line of Oscar Mike's paddock, and Swan heard the colt bolting around in his stall at the commotion outside. She ducked her head guiltily at her manager's disapproving look, but she was having too much fun, really, to care. They hit a swale in the gravel that forced Swan to seize Fitch's arm in a death grip to keep from being bounced out and made the turn toward the training oval on one wheel, its metal hub creaking in protest.

"My God, Fitch, enough is enough! You are going to kill us both," she protested, still laughing.

"One circuit on the track, then we'll ease up," he promised and let the horses trot at the equine equivalent of warp speed, dirt clods exploding under their hooves in the good footing of the oval.

Only after two full circuits was Fitch satisfied to let the powerful siblings come back to his hand and, eventually to a flat-footed walk. Swan made an effort to untangle her long loose hair, but it was thoroughly knotted beyond the efforts of her hands alone. She gave up.

"Fitch, this spider was never intended to be sacrificed to these two monsters—it is criminal—it will be turned into kindling if you keep this up," she began, leaning toward him to lecture, but Fitch cut her off with a light, open-mouthed kiss on her surprised lips.

"Darling, please don't scold," he grinned. "We survived."

He was so cheerful, Swan let the kiss settle her hash. She began again on another tack entirely.

"The hand seems most . . . serviceable, at any rate," she said, cautiously. Fitch's prosthesis was state-of-the-art freaky and covered in "flesh." Its fingers could move separately, albeit slowly, by way of muscle signals that were picked up by electrodes on the "skin" surface, then telegraphed to electronics in the hand.

"Fuck the hand. Let's go to the village for the mail, and on the way I can tell you how sorry I am for being such an ass at Spaulding's."

Swan sighed. This was typical Fitch behavior: outrageous, followed by contrite, followed by outrageous, then contrite . . . over and over. Anything to keep things between them in flux, she suspected. She just didn't know why, all of a sudden, he was back causing trouble. Then she knew: of course—Septimus Moore.

They trucked along in silence for fifteen minutes or so, keeping out of the way of the occasional car or farm vehicle lumbering down the road behind the cart.

"Spaulding called me yesterday and read me the riot act, very justifiably, I might add. Bert weighed in all the way from D.O.D., so I'm in the shit big time, I guess," Fitch began, sounding forlorn. "How did Major Shoulder Porn take it? Did he cast you aside once he saw how fickle you are?"

"Well, he wasn't very happy, but between General Clayton's presence and your obvious inebriation, he felt that decking a one-armed man would be an overreaction." Swan was still aggravated; Fitch winced at "one-armed." "*I* can forgive you because I know you, but it was a dirty trick on Spaulding, who had to spend time smoothing everything over when she should have been sweet-talking her donors."

"Swan, I am truly sorry." Fitch looked her in the eyes as he turned the cart onto the hard surface road toward the village. "I know I can be a shithead, it's just—well, I don't have an excuse." He played at glum. "But I did truck these two to the hunt box yesterday and made Javier get up at three A.M. to bring down the spider and the harness so I could create a sensation for you today."

He brightened up. "Anyway, I don't think you have to worry about your major. Now that I've seen him, he doesn't look completely . . . heterosexual. Do they still have 'Don't ask, don't tell' in the Marines? All those body builder types look suspect to me. I'll bet good money he is a top, though, not a bottom."

"You are truly delusional," Swan sighed. "I pity you. Why Spaulding put you on the Hospice board is a mystery to me. You have the sensitivity of a toad."

"But you love me anyway," Fitch said smugly, "and we are about to make a splash at the Everley Post Office, where, if I'm not mistaken, my new pinque coat has arrived from Saville Row, London."

"And you think *Sam* is gay," Swan said dryly, holding the reins as Fitch dropped off the driver's side of the cart. He popped into the little brick building that housed a small convenience store/gas station on one side and the post office on the other. This, a small antiques store, and the Everley United Methodist Church made up the entirety of the village of Everley. When Fitch returned with the enormous coat box, he handed it up to Swan, since it was not going to be safe in the backseat. He took advantage of his proximity to plant another kiss on her lips, in full view of the elderly postmistress through the window.

"Damn it, Fitch, I *will* slap you the next time you do that, hand or no hand," Swan said angrily, as he wheeled the horses around, toward Belle Everley. "Enough is enough! You know what it is like around here. You want the rumor mill to process the fact that you are still in the 'game,' hoping word gets back to Sam that I'm the harlot of Waverly."

"My darling, you wound me," Fitch pouted. "Your reputation is above reproach. Mother Teresa is the harlot of Waverly compared to you—assuming there *is* a 'harlot of Waverly'—I simply want Shoulder Porn to have to earn whatever he gets, if and when he gets it."

"You are sick," Swan said.

"Swannie, I'm doing you a favor. Anyone can put over the Lochinvar shit weekend after weekend: let's see what he is really like. You don't think he is down on I Street getting his candle waxed A.C./D.C. during the week? Unless—unless I'm mistaken: are you already banging him?"

"When we get back to the house, don't plan on being invited in," Swan said coolly. "I mean it."

"That's what I love about you," Fitch said sweetly. "No, you don't."

Chapter 3

The phone rang Thursday afternoon.

"It's Mrs. Delaney!" called Mathilde to Swan. "They're back!"

"Hetty, where are you?" Swan demanded into the phone. Her sister, Henrietta Bolington Delaney, and her anesthesiologist husband, Boyd, had spent much of the summer in the south of France. Swan's sister had married a first cousin of Carter Delaney Roland right after her graduation from the University of Virginia five years earlier. Boyd worked at the Richmond Hospital, part of the medical center where Fitch had been rehabbed. Hetty stayed at home in a Richmond suburb raising Boyd Junior, aged eighteen months, and hoping to add another child to the family.

"Darling, we are still at Dulles. The baggage situation is indescribable. Could we crash at the farm tonight and head down to Richmond tomorrow? The baby is exhausted, and Boyd doesn't have to be back to work until Saturday," Hetty said. "We could be there in an hour and a half. I know it is short notice, but we were two hours late out of Orly and we are exhausted."

"Of course: just let me tell Mathilde—hold on." Swan turned her head toward the kitchen, "Mathilde!" she called, "Dr. and Mrs. Delaney are going to stay here tonight; could you please freshen up the front bedroom? Flowers, et cetera? They may want the baby in with them, but, if not, let's put him in the room across the hall. Could we have that jalapeño corn side dish Dr. Delaney likes at dinner? The steaks will be fine. And make sure we have enough raspberries, please." Swan turned back to the phone.

"How was the flight otherwise?"

"A horror show. And with a baby? Please. He was a saint for the first couple of hours, but then—well, we'll never see any of those people again, so what does it matter? So much for business class.

They made me take off the baby's little shoes at security, while I'm taking off my Bruno Magli's and still holding him—he was having a meltdown, a real screamathon, then they rooted like hogs through the diaper bag, and—," Hetty took a breath. "Anyway, we're here now. He's asleep, although by the time we get to you, he will be absolutely wild."

"Don't worry, we'll put him to bed as soon as you get here," Swan soothed. "He's probably jet lagged, still on Aixe time. Did you get to Chantilly? Oh, never mind: you can tell me when you get here."

"Can't wait—and, Swan, don't expect scintillating conversation from Boyd, he is in a funk. He's got to face that situation in the department when he gets back, so—"

"Don't worry. See you soon," said Swan. An evening with a stone-faced anesthesiologist and a cranky toddler seemed like a bleak prospect. Swan briefly considered scaring up another man for dinner to take the pressure off Boyd, who was neither horsey nor immersed in local Waverly intrigue, both sure to be topics of conversation once the obligatory vacation travelogue had been dispatched. Spaulding was back on the Eastern Shore, although she would have loved to have come over if there had been time. Who would be available—and amenable—so late in the afternoon?

On a whim, she punched Fitch's cell phone number into her phone.

"I won't torture you with Boyd for dinner, but please come by for dessert so Hetty and I can talk a bit afterwards. You can talk health care reform with Boyd much better than we can—or want to," pleaded Swan. "And I'll let you swing Boyd Junior around by his ankles til he spits up if you can do it without Hetty seeing you."

"Sure thing, sweetie. You caught me as I was about to leave the hunt box anyway. I'm meeting the council for a late afternoon wrap up on the zoning decision; I'll grab something to eat in Delafield with that new county planner—she's attractive, by the way—and head to you about eight o'clock."

"It will be an early night—they will still be on French time. You are a gem. Although you should do it just because you owe me."

"For which? The post office kissing scene? The Hospice party outrage? The insults directed at your intended's ambiguous orientation? There is so much to choose from. Are you guys dressing?"

"God, no. Come as you are," Swan said, "but, Fitch, have a care: remember, Carter was Boyd's cousin. It's only been twenty months. He will not be interested in your version of my so-called new romance."

Swan cancelled plans for clocking Oscar Mike around the training oval and instead helped Mathilde. The simple sterling, not the Grande Baroque; zinnias and late season greens for a trophy bowl table centerpiece; wine, plus all the old, out of fashion liqueurs she could rustle up at short notice on the hunt board. She and Hetty liked a *kir*; Boyd would stick with a microbrew. Fitch would be looking for Johnnie Walker Black Label—again.The family black and white Staffordshire transfer ware, with a few odd pieces in green, rose, and brown transfer to fill out the table settings, not the Chinese export porcelain. A typical Swan tablescape.

Swan had time for a quick shower and scan of the upstairs before the travelers' arrival. She jumped into ballet flats, black summer-weight slacks, and a soft cotton shirt in a dusty peach.

The Delaneys piled out of their rented SUV packed with luggage. Hetty could almost have been Swan's twin, except her hair was red rather than dark black-brown and cut very short, in a French *gamine* style. She was also an inch or two shorter. The sisters laughed as they reached out to each other on the front step: they were dressed identically, except Hetty's shirt was lilac, not peach, a better compliment to her coloring.

Boyd Junior was grumpy; Boyd Senior, a stoic thirty-something six-footer tending a bit toward the blocky, thick-waisted type in khakis and button-down Brooks Brothers style. They settled into the parlor with drinks, Swan dandling the solemn baby in her lap.

"Hetty, he is so big; has it been only six weeks?" Swan marveled, and they were on to the trip for the next hour. By the time they sat down to dinner, Boyd Junior was having a snooze upstairs and they were on to the subject of the Chantilly Racecourse.

"As I told you on the phone, we saw the Prix de Jockey Club in July and the Chantilly Chateau is fabulous," began Hetty. "It was just as Mom described it. Swan, the fields of lavender—" and another hour flew by.

They ate dinner in the dining room, and Swan brought them up to date on the horse-business side of things. To their credit, they listened attentively about Oscar Mike and Saratoga, primarily for her benefit. Swan had just shooed Mathilde out for the evening when she heard Fitch's Porsche roadster throttling down in the driveway.

"Oh, I forgot to tell you guys: I invited Fitch in for a quick drink," Swan said, about to tell another bald-faced lie. "When he heard you were going to spend the night, he asked if he could pop in and see you."

Hetty fixed a determined little smile on her face; Boyd was impassive. Fitch breezed in, trying to be on his best behavior.

"Hetty, how could you have spent six weeks in France and lost weight?" he asked, giving her cheek an air kiss. "If Swan had gone, she would have parked herself in front of *une pâtisserie* and eaten *une religieuse* at every meal."

"Oh, I had my share of cream puffs," Hetty said sweetly.

"As did Swan, only here at home. The non-caloric kind," Fitch replied archly. "Did Spaulding tell you about your sister's new beau? He is very charming, for a bisexual. We all thought so—even General Clayton—didn't we, Swan?"

It looked like they were going to be off to the races right there at home.

Fitch launched in on a comparatively tame version of the Hospice reception, then followed it up with a dramatic interpretation of the Reynard dinner, both of which were punctuated by Swan's *soto voce* corrections and emendations.

"Grandpa Fitzhugh always used to say a gentleman should be able to ride, shoot, kiss, drink, and dance," said Fitch, "although not necessarily in that order. We know our *belle fille*'s new beau can shoot. As for the other accomplishments, *tempus est optimus iudex*."

"Or perhaps 'Swan' is the best judge, not 'time.' She should have seen him do all of those things by now," Hetty said archly when Boyd was in the kitchen getting ice, "although I doubt there is a horse on the place she would trust him on. Even The Fortress is too much for a Texas cowpoke to handle, and she is what—twenty-five?"

"Twenty-two in February," Swan corrected, "and a draft horse breed cross would be best for Sam. At six foot four, he needs a lot of horse."

"And probably a lot of woman, too," Fitch said, sweetly, "or haven't we gotten to the 'kiss' part yet?

"My hope is that 'we' won't get to it at all," Swan said with finality. "I thought you all wanted to get some sleep."

"My recollection of Mr. Fitzhugh Senior was that 'kiss' is a substitute for another verb all together," growled Boyd, coming back into the parlor. He seemed fine with Swan's new romance, at least what he'd heard about it thus far. Everyone was on his second after-dinner cordial when the phone rang in the entranceway. Swan picked it up.

"Swan, it's Sam."

A bit of a surprise. He seldom called this late in the evening.

"I wanted to thank you again for last weekend. I really enjoyed myself," he said.

Swan moved so the phone was further from the commotion in the parlor.

"Well, I did, too," she said, resisting the impulse to say *we were just talking about you.*

"I was hoping we could get together this weekend, assuming you were free," Sam said, "but I'm afraid now that can't happen."

"Really?" Swan said very slowly. She felt something astir in his voice.

"I've been called out of town."

Swan breathed deeply. There was a burst of laughter from Fitch in the other room, followed by Hetty's remonstration.

"Really," Swan said again. "How far out of town?"

Sam hesitated.

"Did you have some particular place in mind?" he asked.

"Abu Ghraib, Baghdad, Habbaniya, Fallujah, Husaybah, Ramadi, Rhino, Leatherneck, or Kandahar would be of interest to me," she said evenly, rattling off the marine bases in Iraq and Afganistan in one breath, "anyplace else—San Antonio, Jacksonville, Oceanside—not so much."

Boyd and Fitch were talking base-rate health care plans in a way that caused Boyd to protest, loudly.

"Well," Sam said, "your more . . . local . . . thinking is probably more on target." San Antonio was the home base of the Fourth Marine Division; Jacksonville, North Carolina, the Second Marine Division; Oceanside, California, the Tenth. All had expeditionary units, task forces designed for quick reaction. Sam's outfit.

Swan was relieved.

"How long will you be gone?" she asked, not idly. The time for playing dating games on that subject was long since over for her.

"Only a week or so, it looks like," He was reassuring, "but I probably won't be able to call you til I get back."

Swan thought, *sounds like a a time zone thing—Camp Pendleton in Oceanside, then.* She perked up.

"I'll be here," she said brightly, and there was another burst of laughter from the dining room.

"Sounds as though I've interrupted your evening," Sam said regretfully.

"My sister and brother-in-law are back from France today, and—Fitch came by after dinner." She thought that sounded casual enough.

"Why does that not surprise me?" Sam was rueful.

"I hope you have a safe trip," she said, and she meant it.

"Swan! Come on! We're bushed and Fitch wants to go to bed!" Hetty called out from the dining room. Swan considered how that was going to sound at the other end of the phone line.

"Don't get engaged while I'm gone," was all Sam had to say.

"Don't worry. That option is pretty much off the table," Swan said glumly, "given how well it's worked in the past."

"Well, don't fall off the horse, either," Sam said, "or the tractor."

"Copy that, although you've got a lot of orders, Major, for someone who is going to be off the coms for an extended period of time," Swan said pertly. But she relented: "I'll miss you."

"That's my girl," Sam said tenderly. "Take care of your little self." Then he was gone.

"Who's calling so late, in the country?" Hetty asked when Swan returned.

"Just—," Swan floundered, reaching for a lie.

Fitch connected the dots immediately.

"*Est homo ipse!*" he exclaimed archly, modifying "It is the man himself"—*Est vir ipse*— in favor of the more modern usage of "homo."

"You wish." Swan batted back the slur. Then she shooed him out and sent her company up to bed.

◆

After she bid good-bye to the Delaneys the next morning, for the first time in a long time, Swan scanned major news websites for current information on the war against terrorism. She had checked obsessively when Hunt and Carter had been in theatre, much less often when Fitch had been overseas (how naïve that seemed to her now, in light of the events that transpired).

She was marginally aware that there were one hundred thousand U.S. troops in Afghanistan, where both Sam and Carter had been deployed. There were thirty to fifty U.S. combat deaths there a month; mostly from roadside bombs, but marines were all over the country, particularly in the southern Helmand province, fortifying their bases, patrolling villages, trying to give locals protection from the Taliban insurgency. The opium trade, smuggling, guns, fear of Taliban retribution, and mistrust of the U.S. presence complicated the marines' task; some units had to answer to NATO and Afghan leaders rather than the U.S. command, an awkward arrangement. And years after the glorious invasion, Operation Iraqi Freedom, there were still more than sixty thousand U.S. troops in Iraq, where Sam and Lee had served.

Swan didn't like the sound of any of this. Sam had to be among the youngest majors in the Marines; most of that rank were rotating in and out of both Iraq and Afghanistan, seven months overseas/six months at home. The expeditionary forces were pretty regularly utilized, although often on missions for which they had not been specifically trained but for which they'd been assigned by the senior military geniuses. Marines who felt their fighting days were behind them typically were attached to the Fourth Marine Division, reserves based in San Antonio, but the Fourth had seen plenty of action, particularly in Iraq in the early days of the war.

That was about as far as it went in terms of her current knowledge. Once Hunt had been killed in Iraq, she'd wanted nothing more to do with the Marines; then her focus had turned to the U.S. Army, to twenty-nine-year-old Carter Roland. When his unit deployed to Afganistan, she ramped up her knowledge of a new theatre, a new deployment strategy. Her short tutorial came to a violent close so quickly, with Roland's death, that she shucked off the Army and never looked back. She hadn't tried to read the entrails in the way of ancient augurs, playing "what if" and "if only" the way she had with Hunt. She had not tried to understand what had happened to Carter; she knew from experience that such an exercise brought no comfort or closure. Instead she had alternated between dumb grief and cheerful fortitude, both for the benefit of the heartbroken Rolands and to fend off the well wishers who wanted to see the freak show—the twice thwarted-by-death fiancée—first-hand.

Swan had sought refuge in the insular, petty, on occasion borderline criminal, and provincial little horse world. It—and Waverly—had saved her. She could sell, breed, and occasionally race the Belle Everley stock, offer a few empty stalls to starvation cases seized by the Waverly Hooved Animal Rescue League, schmooze railside with trainers at local horse shows, and reminisce with the oldtimers to her heart's content.

◆

The days after Sam's departure stayed busy, just as they had before his arrival in her life.

Swan happily took possession of her new four-horse van, a custom model she had just had repainted by Waverly Motors in the Belle Everley racing colors, light brown, vermillion, and cream. She had purchased the almost-new vehicle from her neighbor Virgilia Osmond, who was going through a financial rough patch.

"It's the van or the Osmond family silver," Virgilia chuckled morosely. "I should have paid a bit more attention during the stock market bloodbath, and of course the property taxes and management fees—"

"I'm grateful you thought of me—it will help me out tremendously," Swan said, telling another bald-faced lie. "I'd been about to look for one, and you have saved me all that trouble."

The great difference between Virgilia's distressing financial predicament and Swan's comfortable one could be expressed in two words: The Fortress. Swan's homebred future "blue hen" mare, the elite of the elite in breeding circles, had produced five graded-stakes winners, including Serve the Guns, from nine foals to get to the races. Most had been sold at the Saratoga yearling sales at the top of the market. The mare was continuing to foal top racehorses at the end of her breeding lifetime.

Oscar Mike was The Fortress's only foal by the fiery Storm Cloud, who was a grandson of Secretariat through his champion daughter, Terlingua. Mike was from one of Storm Cloud's last full seasons at stud and worth a king's ransom to every race-oriented owner in the country. Swan saw Mike as her best chance to syndicate a stallion for millions, assuming he gave a good account of himself at the races. The Fortress was carrying a full sibling to Mike, 180 days along. Swan planned to breed her to the turf specialist Carnivorous for her last foal, in the spring. Swan still had three of her youngsters in the barn—Mike, Enfilade, and Dress the Line—as well as the middle-aged Serve the Guns.

Mike was flourishing at home, putting on "stud" weight—beef and muscle—cleaning up his feed, enjoying life as only a young Thoroughbred stallion-to-be can. He had been radiographed top to bottom by the local equine lameness guru and given a clean bill of health. Swan now had to put Mike back in the hands of her local trainer, who oversaw flat racers at the Waverly Training Center as well as Swan's two steeplechase horses, former flat race horses who had come home to campaign as hurdlers and timber horses in Belle Everley colors. If Mike did well at Waverly, he would go to successful Maryland trainer Oliver Lentz to begin his career as a grass or dirt racer.

In the meantime, he would be ridden by Declan Flynn, the steeplechase jock and exercise rider Jerusha had brought over from Ireland two years earlier. Declan was a cheery fatalist with an uncanny way with grass horses, great balance, and soft hands. He was too heavy to be a flat jock in the United States, so he had moved his tack to Waverly and earned a good living as a result.

◆

The next morning, Swan drove the SUV to the training center, arriving just in time to hear Jerusha Dutton ream out a silent groom for wrapping a front tendon on a two-year-old too tightly for her satisfaction.

Jerusha Dutton was a tall, thin, no-nonsense, tweedy Englishwoman from the Midlands, right out of central casting. She stopped her tirade to jerk her head at Declan Flynn, who was lounging on a hay bale nearby: he jumped to his feet and doffed his tweed cap at the sight of his owner.

"So the boyo is ready to pick up his lunchpail and come back to work," Declan observed, guessing the reason for Swan's visit.

"He seems so to me," she replied mildly. "He's up two hundred pounds and another half-inch at the withers. Dr. Kenworth says the knees are closed."

"We'll take him and start walking. Then we'll get him in the gate and see when we can put him on the work tab," Jerusha said calmly.

"He's got to get off the teat sooner or later, missus," Declan said to Swan, trying to comfort her. Swan smiled wanly. Everyone knew how she felt about Mike.

"Well, you're here: let's look at Punch and Judy," Jerusha ordered briskly, using the barn names for Swan's timber horse, Route Step, and The Fortress's hurdler, Battle Streamer.

They were in immaculately bedded stalls down the shedrow, tucking into large hay nets filled with local alfalfa. Nine and twelve years old, respectively, Judy had proved barren after her flat racing career, and former limited-stakes winner Punch was a gelding, so of no use in Swan's breeding program. Both were enormous compared to the flat racing Thoroughbreds typical of U.S. bloodstock, sound as a dollar, and sported the banged tails of U.K. grass racers.

"They'll be ready for the fall," Jerusha promised, pulling the two out of their stalls in turn and walking them up the shedrow for Swan's inspection. They talked about spots in the fall steeplechase season as Declan listened respectfully. Punch and Judy would earn their keep, but the steeplechase season was primarily a local social event. Pari-mutuel betting was very limited, so purses were low. Swan kept the racers to support the game, as Belle Everley owners had for more than one hundred years.

"Let's see where we can enter," Swan said briskly. She suddenly thought of Sam, of taking him to the local races, the *haute cuisine* of the tailgating set, with silver julep cups, steamship roast beef and lamb; the flower arrangements, all spread out behind SUVs and Rolls Royces, surrounded by the gentry and the wannabes, discreetly drinking and gossiping throughout a day of racing. He might as well see it all, and they might as well see him. He'd make quite a splash, she decided, and smiled involuntarily.

Sam.

Her good mood disappeared. What if he was deployed?

She had put the thought successfully out of her mind all week. Now she ran the worst case scenario: he was going to be pulled back in. This trip was the beginning. She wouldn't know until the last minute if it was going to happen. He wouldn't—couldn't—tell her, no one else would have the heart, it would all happen again.

She pushed the panic away.

She had Belle Everley, Mike and The Fortress, the life her family had lived for two hundred years. That was all, really.

"So," Jerusha was saying, "when is he coming?"

"Friday," said Swan, "we'll bring Mike on Friday."

Chapter 4

Unlike his earlier stay at the Waverly Training Center, Friday's trip would be Mike's last before his racing career began in earnest. Theoretically, the colt could go from Waverly to the Lentz barn, then to racetracks throughout the mid-Atlantic and, if successful, on to stand in Kentucky as a syndicated stallion, never returning to Belle Everley again. If he did return, it would be as an injured or disappointing runner, to live out his life as the embodiement of the end of Swan's dream. Edgar knew how hard it was for Swan to let the big colt out of her sight. He had already fed Mike his breakfast, given him a warm bath, and dressed him in a Belle Everley stable sheet, leather halter, and leather head bumper before Swan came to the barn. She was in her horse transport attire—jeans, cowhide gloves, cotton shirt, and hard-toed paddock boots. Eduardo had taken to the new van like a duck to water, reveling in its handling ability and its fuel-injected automatic transmission, so he was unusually cheerful as he backed it up to the barn entrance. Swan pressed her lips together and gave Edgar a short wave as Eduardo pulled away.

"*Muy bonito*," Eduardo said admiringly, as the new van accelerated smoothly onto the hard surface road, but other than that, they rode in silence. Twenty-five minutes later, they were parked adjacent to Jerusha's stalls in the shedrow. Seated in a collapsible deck chair in front of Judy's stall, Jerusha was her usual, no-nonsense self.

"Back at last, are we?" she asked, and her keen eye watched every step Mike took off the van. Eduardo handed the lead shank to Judy's groom, the silent Hector, and just like that, Mike's fate was out of Swan's hands.

Swan and Jerusha reviewed Mike's feed, veterinary, and farriery schedule for the final time. Mike would sport custom-made racing plates that afternoon. Both Swan and Eduardo gave the colt a quick but heart-felt pat good-bye, but he was already exploring his full hay net and Judy's inquisitive gaze. Suddenly Mike gave a high-pitched, ringing whinny, and they all smiled. Then it was unceremoniously back into the van for the Belle Everley contingent.

Declan gave them a wave as the van slowly crept back to the center's entrance.

"*Tienes solamente uno hombre grande ahora, señorita,*" Eduardo said to Swan, venturing a little joke to lighten her mood for the ride home.

"Yes," Swan said, "I have only one big man now."

The one week of Sam's absence had turned the corner into the second, with no word from him.

Jerusha reported that Mike was settling in nicely, walking and jogging under Declan's calm hands. On Wednesday, she went over to watch the colt walk the shedrow and pick at some grass afterwards. There was not much more to look at until he began serious training. On Thursday, the phone rang. Mathilde trotted quickly into the dining room with a smile. "The major," she announced. Swan went to the hallway phone.

"Swan?"

"Well, hello, there," she said, unsuccessfully trying to keep the warm pleasure from her voice.

"Listen, I've got about thirty seconds—are you free Saturday night?" Sam asked, his voice rushed.

"I've promised to go to the fund-raiser for the local fire and rescue squad," Swan said, "but we could do something more . . . entertaining . . . afterward."

"Damn, I was hoping you could come to Quantico, but let's make it work out your way."

"They start serving at six P.M.," Swan said, "unless you want to pass on dinner and come out afterward."

"Six it is," he said and hung up.

She was cheered now, knowing she would be seeing him in forty-eight hours. She allowed the daily routine to absorb her: keeping a sharp eye on the mares entering the last halves of their eleven-month-long pregnancies, overseeing the endless amount of upkeep that went with a two- hundred-year-old house and one-hundred-year old barns.

◆

On Saturday afternoon, the weather was still summer warm. Swan chose a little feather-light saffron-colored silk skirt and silk shell, bare legs, and saffron silk open-toed ef-me pumps for her audience of one. She was surprised when Sam arrived, in a black leather jacket, t-shirt, and jeans, with the little Mercedes once again. She let him give her an appreciative once-over before she threw him a questioning look. "You said you were going to miss the Mercedes when I got the truck back," he said, "so it's here for good." Swan wondered how he had made that happen.

She asked nothing about his trip. Her view was that he dropped off the face of the earth when he wasn't in Waverly. But her mind was churning with enough facts on its own. She was very, very glad to see him, and she focused on concealing that from him as completely as possible. She volunteered farm updates when he asked, particularly about Oscar Mike's progress as a home-schooled race horse and his move to the training center, and filled him in on Hetty and Boyd's back story. She studiously avoided the subject of Hastings Fitzhugh.

She purposely looked out the window as they drove through Waverly, past the landfill and the animal shelter, to the rescue squad's utilitarian building on the far edge of town. The parking lot was already full at five after six: people eat early in the country.

Inside local folk, including some from Waverly's Amish and Mennonite communities, were swarming around long metal tables covered in paper tablecloths. Several Amish women in dark skirts and white prayer caps replenished huge yellowware bowls of cooked pasta, greens, homemade rolls, and cut up homegrown melons arrayed on the tables. Others watched over a four-burner hot plate holding metal pots of spaghetti sauce, simmering just below the boil. A long table held two enormous burbling coffee makers and a flotilla of fruit and nut pies—walnut, pecan, apple, strawberry rhubarb, peach, cherry. Iced tea rings the size of small automobile tires and filled with cinnamon and raisins provided non-pie options for dessert. Twenty long metal tables and folding chairs were already filled with diners. Dozens of small children, Mennonite and English alike, scampered from one table to another as their parents ate, chatted, and supervised.

"My treat," said Swan, smiling, as they passed a hand-lettered sign reading "Free will offering for Waverly Volunteer Fire and Rescue" at the entrance table. She dropped five fifty-dollar bills into the cardboard box marked "Donations."

"Looks like every chow line on earth," Sam observed wryly. "May I fix you a plate?"

"That would be lovely." Swan began to look for empty chairs. The closest were next to the teenaged Rachel Zook and the clean-shaven Elias Schrock, a courting Amish couple.

"May we join you?" Swan asked as Rachel looked up shyly. Elias nodded, half-rising.

Sam caught sight of her through the hubbub as he headed back with paper plates.

"Rachel, Elias, this is Sam Moore," Swan said. "Sam, Rachel and Elias are to be married next month."

"On the twenty-third—not that we're counting," said Rachel, catching Elias's eye. He blushed.

"And you will be living—," Swan began.

"Oh, in one of the doublewides on the Schrock farm," Rachel blurted out, then *she* blushed. She should have let Elias answer.

"Sounds wonderful," Sam said, with a genuine smile for them both. That was all the encouragement Rachel needed to launch in on her plans for the trailer—hooking up a gas-generator-powered washing machine, planting a little truck garden, storing her handmade quilts—a bombardment of domestic chatter. Sam made a second trip to the food tables and returned with coffee for Swan. By that time Rachel and Elias had gone on their way.

"That has to be the sweetest couple in the world," he mused. "What are they? Eighteen?"

"Just turned. Elias works one of the Schrocks' dairy farms, with three of his brothers and one of his sisters. They'll be fine."

"I've got combat marines only a little older than that," he said. After they had eaten, the hall began to empty out. It was still early. Swan had an idea.

"Do you like to dance? Not military cotillion/embassy row stuff, but low-down, roadhouse dancing."

"Hell, I'm from Texas, that all we've got down there," Sam said. "We're Oscar Mike."

Swan pointed him south, down the center of the state, through the darkening night. Sam had C.C. Adcock and the Lafayette Marquis, Lou Reed, and Waylon Jennings in the CD player.

"What are you thinking about?" Swan asked, after ten minutes of uncharacteristic silence.

"Those Amish kids. It's nice to see someone's fairy tale come true."

"You sound like you don't believe that can happen."

"It didn't for you. Didn't for me, either."

Swan could think of nothing to say to lighten his mood and that dampened her spirits, too. They rode on in silence.

◆

In another half hour, they pulled into the parking lot of a little two-story frame tavern on a lay-by off Route 29. The Scarab was a dive; it attracted truckers, bikers, horse trainers, and trailer trash, in just about equal measure. Swan had only been there once—with Fitch.

They walked in the door, into a wall of smoke. It was hot, almost pitch dark, stuffy, and crowded, even this early on a Saturday night—at the bar, on the little dance floor, and at the tables. Sam took a look around at the slimy clientele and, as if it were an afterthought, shrugged out of his jacket. When Swan saw his enormous shoulders and arms with their exotic blue mountain range under the racerback t-shirt, she was blindsided by a longing so intense she was surprised it wasn't visible to everyone in the bar. She followed Sam to a little table in a far corner being vacated by three bikers. He was subconsciously clenching and relaxing his fists, flexing his shoulders and arms in a way that parted the crowd like Moses at the Red Sea. A powerful contraction gripped her. She had never felt anything like it. At one moment, she wanted to lick the cephalic vein running up his bicep or brush her lips along the cords of muscle standing at attention on his neck; at the next she wanted to turn around and get out of Dodge, to give herself a chance to think through what was happening to her. She decided ultimately that she didn't want to move one inch further away from him. She had all she could do to keep from crawling into his lap as he sat down, sliding her hands under his shirt, and kissing him in front of everyone. She knew that as soon as he saw her face, he'd see it, feel it, for himself. The panic almost made her sick. She tried to convince herself again to turn and run. When he did look at her sitting across from him, he searched her face for a long time, willing her to look at him.

"Finally," he said. Then he stood up and deliberately walked to the bar. He came back with two Scotches, one ostensibly for her, and a beer for himself. He immediately downed the beer and the shot. After a few moments, he looked at her, then took her shot and drank it, too.

The juke box was playing a bluesy cajun ballad, swampy, smokey, and sad. Sam pulled Swan to the dance floor without a word. He put his arms around her as though he had done it a thousand times before. They danced, her arms around his neck, his hands on her hips, sliding lower until they rested on her bottom. He closed his eyes and bent down low to kiss her on the mouth, along her jaw, down her throat, nuzzling her ear through her hair, back to her mouth. He danced only as an excuse to kiss her, as she gently rocked her hips back and forth against him. He would have been perfectly content for them to be the only couple on the floor, oblivious to the fact that all eyes were watching them. Fitch's friends, townees from Waverly, the bartender—all of them watched goggle-eyed as he made love to her on the dance floor. Swan's mind was racing—they were only dancing, after all—trying to plot out her next move, but his mouth was too warm, his scent too strong, his body too overpowering, for her to stay ahead of him.

They danced for as long as people dropped quarters in the juke box. The bar finally began to empty out, and they moved toward their table to leave. Swan picked up her purse and folded his heavy leather jacket over her arm. They walked out to the Mercedes in the warm, buzzy night, still not talking, then he turned her against the passenger door of the big truck parked next to the roadster and began to kiss her in earnest, in that focused, I-mean-business way.

She began to tremble; she couldn't help it. She hardly knew this guy.

"You're not scared, are you?" he teased, his mouth still on hers, "because I'm the one who should be scared. Look at me: I'm terrified. You are very scary."

That made her laugh a little and relax into him, because he didn't act scared at all: his mouth and hands were busy exploring her pretty much at will. His hand slipped under her skirt, between her legs, but so gently, and she was letting it happen, hoping it would happen. The dim lights across the parking lot slowly winked out, one by one, as the bar closed for the night. They were in the dark now, and the lot was empty, though there still were voices far away. She tried to push him away just a little, with her palms against his collarbone, so she could slide toward the Mercedes. But she couldn't control the excitement, and when she felt him slip her lacy panties down her legs, she stepped out of them silently. He lifted her bare leg, hooking it around his hip, hiking up the silk skirt with his hand. He unbuttoned his jeans, holding her against the car with his upper body, not his arms; she felt him fumble in his pocket for a condom. She was offended, not reassured. She didn't want that, although she realized that she damn well should. Instead, she reached down to caress him, stop him, touching herself first, then lubricating his entire length with her slippery hand. She was shocked at how big he was, huge-girthed from base to head, two hard counterweights beneath his rock-hard erection, but it was too late to turn back. She wanted to feel what it was like. She wanted to give him what he wanted, and she couldn't wait, wouldn't wait. It was going to happen, it was about to happen, and then it did happen: he was inside her with a quick intake of breath. It felt like she was being choked from the inside out, like he had had gone into her all the way to the base of her throat, but then each thrust opened her wider, deeper. She felt the spreading heat, the delicious friction along the entire length of her tight, taut entranceway. She was moaning "Mmmn, mmmnn," now, a rhythmic, provocative sound faster, then slower, with each thrust, a little mantra of pleasure for him alone.

She turned her body, pushing against his chest with her hands until he had lifted her up off the ground, driving against her, but in a controlled, powerful motion. When she felt she couldn't last any longer, ashamed but defiant, too—decency be damned—she came for him. She arched her back, gently at first when she felt the strong contractions inside her, then she moved more purposefully to prolong the afterspasms as her muscles tightened like a fist around him. She felt hot, then cold, then hot again, as a last hard contraction shook her from top to bottom. She gasped, and then he came in a thick, hot flood. He collapsed into her, propping himself up against the truck with his hands, pulling the air into his lungs. She unwrapped her legs from around him and gently set both high heels back on the ground. She was soaked. For a second, it sounded as though a voice was coming closer, and he moved to shield her body with his, but then it faded and it was quiet again.

"Not scared any more?" he asked, when he was able to speak. She shook her head, once.

"Me neither," Sam said. "We'd probably better go." He kissed her on the mouth and started to pull away, but then came back again, kissing her hard. His breathing turned fast and deep, his erection swelling, bursting against her, demanding attention. Swan thought, *God, he's ready again.* Shock and excitement rolled over her, but the fear of discovery was too great. She pushed him away and he reluctantly stepped back from her.

"I need to find my . . . underwear," Swan said weakly. *Who said romance was dead?*

He sidled down to the Mercedes and opened the driver's side door so the overhead light could help. Swan smoothed down her skirt. She found her panties, just a scrap of wet lace, and quickly slipped them on. It was humiliating: she was glad for the dark. They drove back to the farm in silence, except for Lou Reed and 50 Cent. Swan stole looks at him the whole way, but he looked at her only occasionally. He seemed lost in his thoughts. In her driveway, he pulled her out of the Mercedes but then kept his arms around her.

"Shall I come in?" he said, "We should—"

"It's late," she said, turning away a little.

"No. Let me come upstairs. Now that we've had sex, I want to see what you look like with your clothes off. I want to make love in a real bed. If I leave now, you'll convince yourself what just happened never happened," he whispered.

She gave up the small amount of resistance she had had to the idea. He followed her inside, creeping up the stairs. Once in her bedroom, Sam pulled off his clothes in an instant; then hers, too. When they were naked, she hesitated for a moment, suddenly intimidated by his enormous size. Barefoot, she barely reached his nipples. But his body was wonderful, slim waisted, veiny, sculpted, and she wasn't afraid, not really, not there in her own room. He would probably be gone in the morning, gone for good, after his conquest. She might never have a chance like this again. She stepped close to him, his enormous, engorged cock pressed high on her body, and inspected the entire expanse of the famous tattoos for the first time.

"How? Why?" she asked, looking up at him.

"Nineteen. Stinking drunk, Laredo, Texas," he smiled thinly. "It seemed like a good idea at the time."

"I've never seen anything like them. They must have taken a lot of work."

"Well, I got them half done before passing out, then I had to get them finished," he said. "It took a lot of time, and a lot of cash, which I didn't have. I arm-wrestled drunks in a bar to pay them off.

"I know," he said, reading her expression, "what a jackass."

"No," she said, "they're beautiful." He lifted her off her feet as she reached up to kiss them.

About dawn, Swan roused herself. She dug out from under the quilts, Indian silk throws, antique textiles, and scarf pillow shams that dressed the old family bed and hobbled to the open window. She looked out over the mares and fields, the mist still hugging the grassy surfaces, turning them dewy. She turned back and looked at the huge naked man she'd left behind. He was on his belly, arms stretched out, bare to his round muscular butt, and deeply asleep stretched across her entire bed. She smiled: he deserved it after the night he'd put in. Every inch of her had been kissed, fondled, explored, and adored, without apology, without persuasion or sweet talk, almost without any words at all. She thought back. Five times. Six counting the Scarab. A high school hormone-storm calibre performance.

Swan looked down. Her skin was covered in day-old-beard burn, her nipples were swollen, her hair was tangled and knotted down her back. A plum-colored hickey was emerging above one breast, another was blossoming on her inner thigh. Sam's racerback t-shirt was on the floor next to the bed. She tiptoed to it, pulled it over her head. It was huge on her. The arm holes were loose, the neck so low that she was as much uncovered as covered. The shirt smelled good—sweaty, yes, but smokey, like the bar, and fragrant with Scotch, aftershave, her perfume. She crawled back into the bed, into the small space unoccupied by his big body, and gently eased herself next to him. He opened his eyes and rolled over.

"I'm wrecked," Sam groaned. He looked at her critically, his brow furrowed. "You look rested."

"You did all the work," she grinned, then winced. "I, however, feel like I had a telephone pole up my . . . skirt . . . all night."

"I should apologize, but it isn't all my fault. You are so, so tight, so . . . delicious. No wonder you were the platoon's wet dream." His voice was appreciative and regretful at the same time: the night was over.

"I'm not complaining," she teased. Septimus Moore had been a perfect ten in size, strength, and stamina. "That was unbelievable. But you know that." She paused. "I hope you know, what happened last night, in the parking lot—nothing like that—That is not my . . . typical behavior," she struggled. "I'm not the kind of person who . . . who—" It was galling to try to explain the indefensible.

"It was pretty much unprecedented from my perspective as well," Sam said carefully. "Not SOP, at all. Pretty . . . fantastic . . . from my perspective . . . as well." But he saw that reality was sinking in for her.

"Christ, if anyone from around here saw anything, *anything,* I'll have to sell out and start a new life under an assumed name," Swan said, and she was beginning to think she really meant it. "What went on in the Scarab was bad enough."

"I'm pretty sure that no one could have seen." Sam wasn't 100 percent certain he was right, and he was afraid that anything he said would only make things worse. The afterglow was definitely evaporating. He could see her mind beginning to work and work. He had hoped she would want to stay in bed and make love throughout the long lazy Sunday, but that time, if it had ever existed in her mind, was past.

"You do know I'm crazy about you, don't you?" he asked instead. "I couldn't keep my hands off you—and I can't now." He was rueful."But I can see you don't want me anymore."

"No—I wanted it all to happen. I would have jumped you if you hadn't thought of it first. I'm not sorry about anything other than the . . . venue." She laughed. "I wish we'd done what you suggested and met at Quantico, but everything will be okay. I'm just tired of being the center of everyone's morbid attention, that's all." She looked at him, stretched out next to her in the early daylight, vast male acreage to be admired and explored. When would she ever have the chance to enjoy a body this glorious again?

"And I *do* want you—"

She twisted his dog tags gently in her hand, then she leaned down to kiss his rock-hard belly, below his navel, slowly and deliberately trailing her tongue through the fine blond hair, down the thick, engorged shaft to his foreskin. His erection was like a weapon, hard as a tire iron or a baseball bat. It filled her mouth and she teased it and rewarded it with her tongue at the same time as it swelled and rose. Then she retraced her path, back up the deep groove delineating the muscles of his chest, to his collar bone, then to his mouth, slowly. Up, then down. Again. He lifted her hips so his first thrust into her was both cautious and hard, just so he could hear that little reflexive gasp that acknowledged his claim to all of her, inside and out. She wrapped her legs around him so he could lift her hips and legs off the bed with each thrust, and she heard herself saying, *Yes, yes, more, more*. He didn't hurry, though. He took his sweet time, moving her around under him, on top of him, beside him. He was happy to show her just about everything he could think of, which was about twenty times more than everything she could think of, just to see if she liked it. And she did, every bit of it—his moans, hoarse, whispered expletives, murmured endearments—she relished her power over him. She felt as though she was the Queen of Sheba or the whore of Babylon, or some other legendary temptress instead of a farm girl enjoying her first one-night stand. Each time she explored the juncture of their two bodies with her hand, his uneven, ragged, pumping breaths let her know when he was on the verge of his own release. Hot and cold, she felt the friction would cause her to catch fire, like flint against stone. He growled, thrust, and she came, too. She was wiped out afterward, lying on him face down, in a kind of shocked contentment. This final time, he looked at her with the sappy grin of a teenager after a night at the drive-in. His easy confidence began to dissipate, though, when he saw her begin to fret with what little energy she had left. He cobbled together some story about another commitment later in the day while he pulled on his clothes, just to let her off the hook.

"I'll call you this evening—okay?" he asked anxiously. She could make a case for a one-night-only so easily, he could almost see the wheels turning. Who knew what she would come up with if he let her think things through on her own for too long?

He was cheered by one thing, though. When he left just before noon, after a thirty-minute shower and an enormous breakfast she had cooked herself, Swan had asked Sam to leave the racerback shirt with her. He had given her one last long, warm kiss at the front steps in just his leather jacket and jeans. She had slid her hands under the open jacket to press herself, still in his t-shirt, against his bare chest, and for a moment he thought he might have a chance to go back to Plan A. But he'd let her run the show. He'd be happy with what he had, for now.

"Tonight, tonight. Remember," he said.

◆

After he left, Swan put on a silk kimono over his shirt and started another pot of tea in the kitchen. She wanted to think. By that time Mathilde had returned from Mass at Our Lady of Fatima and a late breakfast with other parishioners in Waverly. She took one look at Swan's *déshabillé,* and her expression could have won her an award for Best Housekeeper Minding Her Own Business. She had to have seen the Mercedes in the driveway when she had headed out; now it was gone. Mathilde retreated to her bed/sitting room suite behind the kitchen to read the Sunday papers, keeping her thoughts to herself.

Swan mulled over the fact that she knew nothing, really, about Septimus Moore, nothing that was going to have an impact on her, that is. She wanted to know how long he'd been married, how long he'd been divorced, if he had children. She wanted to hear about the wife—and all the others—the way all women want to hear about other women, to be convinced that they meant nothing. But first, she wanted to relive every minute of Saturday night. She wanted to replay it from the time he arrived for dinner, through the drive to the Scarab, to the moment he pulled off the jacket, almost as a warning to everyone in the bar, the first hard, spontaneous grapple in the dark, the long, ardent love play in bed, then—

The phone rang.

"Swan." It was Spaulding. "You know, darling, when your mother died, I vowed to myself never to start a sentence with, 'If your mother were still alive—'"

Swan felt the bottom drop out of her stomach.

"I got a call from Miranda Hastings right after church, who said Fitch heard from the bartender at the Scarab, of all God-forsaken places, that you or your twin were in there last night with what has to have been either one of the Hell's Angels or more likely, given his physical description, Septimus Moore. And that the two of you put on a performance that would have made the people of Sodom and Gomorrah very proud.

"Apparently the bartender could not wait to give this news to Fitch, who most of the Scarab's upscale clientele apparently believe is still dating you. This is obviously too ridiculous for words, and I will kill Fitch if this is another twisted joke from the cesspool of his utterly depraved psyche. Accusing you of the kind of behavior he pays for in whatever den of iniquity he wallows in is so beyond—" Spaulding finally ran out of verbal steam.

Swan waited a beat or two.

"Darling, please don't worry about it," she said calmly.

Spaulding absorbed this for several long moments.

"So, is there some tiny grain of truth to it, then?" she asked hesitantly, "because if there is, there is . . . more."

"Tell me."

"Well, Fitch apparently was not happy to have been awakened at the crack of dawn, and he told the bartender to go . . . do violence . . . to himself in no uncertain terms, and the bartender said Fitch might feel differently if he knew the whole story, that there had been a security camera in the parking lot since that drug arrest at the Scarab last year."

"Go on."

"The bartender said this couple's car was in the parking lot partially out of camera range but there was some 'activity' in the lot after closing that might be construed—"

As far as Swan was concerned, "partially out of camera range" was the pertinent information.

"Darling, don't blame Fitch," she said smoothly. "Sam and I did go to the Scarab after the rescue dinner. I . . . I thought it might be fun to dance. We did get pretty cosy, which tends to happen when you drink and dance for hours at a time. Last time I checked, that was not against the law in the Commonwealth of Virginia. Most of the Scarab's clientele, including the master of mixology behind the bar, were in the bag before we even got there, so I would count on a certain amount of exaggeration to be part of the narrative, wouldn't you?"

"So," Spaulding was processing this intel, "did he spend the night?"

"Yes, you will be happy to hear. Yes, he did.

"And now, I have to go. I've got horses to ride. Please don't worry about anything. I know what I'm doing, believe me. I do appreciate the call, though." She hung up the phone before her aunt could dispute the "know what I'm doing" business.

Then Swan sat mulling. Could her sterling reputation, the locals' pity, and Fitch's disbelief shut down the hot rumor that easily? She was beginning to think that they could, and she cheerfully helped Edgar refresh the yearlings' ground manners and provided logistical support to Eduardo as he hooked the bush hog to the tractor. She had just flopped down in a settee in the parlor about five o'clock when Mathilde appeared in the parlor doorway. "Mr. Fitch on the phone for you." Swan went to the hall with some hesitation, prepared for the worst.

"Fitch?"

"What in the name of God have you been up to, you degenerate whore of Satan?" he began and his tone wasn't jokey, but cold as ice.

"Hello to you, too," she replied calmly. "Having a nice afternoon?"

"I should be, but I'm not, thanks to Susannah Swan Everett Bolington," he groused. "I've spent most of it trying to kill off an unbelievable story out of the Scarab last night."

"Really?" Swan said.

"Don't tell me you haven't talked to Spaulding." Fitch's voice had turned from ice to steel. "I know Miranda must have called her thirty seconds after the benediction at Green Pines Methodist. I had a total of three hours' sleep before I heard from that cretinous bartender, Scar, at seven A.M. He was drunk as a skunk but unfortunately hadn't passed out before calling to report that my lady friend had been in the Scarab all night putting on a live sex show that continued in the parking lot and to ask if that concerned me at all?"

"Really?"

"Yes the fuck 'really'! Unless that was Hetty Delaney coked up in a black wig, I'd like to hear what happened so I don't look like the biggest jackass in Taliaferro County, if it's all the same to you. And if you say 'Really?' one more time, I'm going to—"

"Now, Fitch," Swan said, "whatever happened has nothing to do with you. I appreciate your gallantry in defending me, but gallantry is wasted on anyone in the Scarab, so consider yourself off the hook, thank you very much, and enjoy the rest of your day."

"Goddamn it, something did happen." Fitch was now truly shocked. "What?"

"Fitch, stay out of it, please," Swan said, trying again to head him off. "I'm sorry if your scheme to keep people thinking we are a couple has blown back on you, but that was going to happen sooner or later."

"Well, I sure as hell never thought it was going to happen in the Scarab. What were you doing in that dump, anyway? The one time I took you there I thought you were going to run yourself through the car wash when we left, you were so disgusted by it."

"We went there for fun, the same reason everyone goes there. It's no big deal," Swan said.

"Hillary Clinton working in a titty bar is no big deal—*this* is a big deal," Fitch growled, but he was beginning to sense it was a losing battle. She wasn't going to tell him anything. "Whatever you've decided to do with this guy, Swan, is your business, but to do it on pay-per-view in my fucking backyard is low. I don't see how I deserve it from you." He was really hurt.

"I'm sorry, truly. We won't do it again."

"Some comfort that is. But if it's all the same to you, I'm going to stick with plausible deniability, for my own benefit: it wasn't you, as far as I'm concerned."

"We were at the Waverly fire and rescue supper before the Scarab, if that is any help," Swan said gently.

"Oh, a big help—from the Amish social to sex in a bar parking lot," he sighed, but she could see he was beginning to make his peace with it. "If I'd known your predilections lay in that direction, I'd have done things differently when we *were* a couple. But I'm happy to play the fool if it helps you out."

"Thanks, kiddo. I guess you were right: I am the 'harlot of Waverly' after all."

They had dodged the bullet: Fitch was going to take it in the heart for her instead. When Sam called about nine P.M., she was almost giddy with relief.

"Fitch has found it more expedient to defend me than to dignify the tale making the rounds," she reported. "He is so sensitive to pity, he can't tolerate even a whiff of it."

"Probably just as well I didn't flatten him at your aunt's place, then," Sam said. "Everything okay . . . from your point of view?"

"I'm just sorry I chose the Scarab, not for anything else."

"Then I can be in Warrenton Wednesday night, say about eight: meet me somewhere." His voice was velvety, ardent.

"Anyplace without a parking lot."

Two days later Spaulding was on the phone once again.

"Did you hear? Fitch was in the Reynard last night, hot and heavy at a corner table with Townsend Brooke! She is barely eighteen! One handed or not, he is a terror—and almost twice her age! What have I done?" Spaulding wailed.

"You haven't done anything; it's what I've done," Swan reassured her. "He had to do something with someone to save face. She is from a Hollywood family, she can take care of herself. If she thinks she can ride El Diablo, more power to her."

"You are hard, Swan," Spaulding said. "It doesn't become you at all."

◆

On Wednesday Swan decided to take the silver BMW SUV; it was easier to navigate than the dually in Warrenton's small downtown. She was to meet Sam at the Trainyard, a too-quaintly restored landmark hard by the railroad tracks where they could get coffee or a sandwich without having to order from the dinner menu. Black jeans and a pumpkin colored linen shirt were all she needed for the bistro. The ballet flats and ponytail tied at the base of her neck were going to make her look like his daughter, she decided ruefully, but too late. When she pulled up, he was waiting next to his F-250 still in battle dress, a change from the racerback. Just the thought of it brought back Sunday morning and made her flush, so she was ready for his very public kiss as she got out of the SUV.

"I've missed you," he said softly, and she felt the swelling evidence as he kept her against him. "I think about your body all the time. Have you missed me? Tell me."

"I haven't had time," she teased, with a toss of her head. "I've been busy dodging a scarlet letter from the citizens of Waverly—and trying to run a horse business."

"No excuse—I've been hunting down evil-doers on two continents and I've had a hard-on since Sunday. Feel it. Use your hand," he said hoarsely.

"No!" she laughed. "Behave: I can't afford another PDA, even in a different town." She made as though she was pulling away from him, but he held her effortlessly in his embrace so the effect was lost.

"Let's get something to eat, then. Are you hungry? I was hoping you'd spend the night at my place at Quantico afterward."

"I didn't plan on doing any traveling," she said, a little uneasily.

"I've got anything you need there. I'll even lend you a t-shirt to sleep in."

"Sounds like you've done this before."

"Just following proper combat-readiness protocols." He still held her firmly, and she was conscious of the heat of his body warming her from top to bottom. She was wet against him, her heart pounding, her breathing already ragged. Her desire—and her curiosity—eroded her resolve like a sand castle at high tide.

"Okay, then." Eduardo could hold the fort in the morning.

Swan popped open her cell phone and left a message for Mathilde on the housekeeper's own phone to tell Eduardo when he arrived at five-thirty A.M. It felt strange; spontaneity was a rare commodity on a working farm.

Cheerful now, Sam ordered a Porterhouse; Swan settled for a bowl of soup, a glass of merlot, and the fresh fruit garnish from his plate. She felt like they were in high school, sharing private jokes in a booth far from the door, in a world of their own. But now that they knew they were spending the night together, it was all either of them could think about. Soon Sam paid the check and she followed his truck down Route 17 away from Warrenton and toward Quantico, thirty miles to the east.

Swan hadn't given any thought to how or where Sam lived. It was part of his nonexistence away from Belle Everley. She knew there was base housing at Quantico for military and civilian families that looked like housing developments in any community anywhere, but she had no idea what billeting was available for unmarried officers. Hunt had spent his career in Oceanside, in Iraq, or in the ground.

When Sam pulled into a sprawling apartment complex near the base, Swan followed. She parked in front of a two-story building and trailed him into a stairwell, up a flight, then into the prototypical bachelor's digs. Two or three pieces of high-end weight training equipment, a black leather couch, a huge plasma TV hooked up to a high-end I-Mac, a cable box, DVD, DVR/CD set up that looked as though it could monitor surface-to-air missile launches over Iraq—that was about it. An oversized funky chair made out of cattle horns and cowhide had to be some Texas thing. Swan's attention was drawn to framed photos on a chrome table in the long hallway. She was on the hunt for evidence of women, but all of the photos seemed to be from his deployments or on leave in what looked to be Hawaii and Australia. One faded photo was of a small boy, Sam himself, she assumed, with his grim-faced mother and father taken in what might be Kentucky, from the foliage. Swan was disappointed—she was curious about the ex—but relieved as well; unlike Swan, Sam seemed over his first love. Tucked into one of the photo frames was a restaurant receipt. Swan didn't need to examine it: she knew it was from the Crossroads.

He came up behind her and put his arms around her without a word. They picked up from where they had left off on Sunday morning. By the middle of the night, though, she was ready to talk. She laid back against him as he was propped up against the headboard, and she pulled his big arms around her like a coat. The time had come to talk about The Ex-Wife.

"Sam, you know everything about my romantic life. Everybody does. I was a virgin with Hunt Lee, and I only slept with Carter after we were engaged—which was six weeks before he went overseas. That's it."

Sam looked down at her.

"What about Fitzhugh?" he asked quietly. "The whole town thinks he's carrying a weapons-grade torch for you, that it's only a matter of him getting back on his feet before he sweet-talks you into getting serious."

"It isn't like that," Swan said, a bit testily. "We just dated briefly before his accident. We've been friends a long time, run in the same circles, since it is impossible not to in Waverly. I was in no shape to jump into bed before he left for Iraq. So now you *know* you know everything about me. I'm wondering what I should know about you."

"'Love'-wise?" Sam grimaced.

"You could put it that way."

"Starting when? Because I'll tell you right now that that kiss between Allorene Smith and me behind the mini-mart was just the kind of thing any fifth grader is going to think up when school lets out early—nothing more. And besides, she kissed me first."

Swan rolled her eyes.

"Let's jump past Allorene Smith, then, if we can," she said. "Unless she turns out to have ended up your ex-wife."

"Swan," said Sam patiently, "I was a High School All American tight end out of Buena Vista Regional; I was on the Texas Tech varsity, although I didn't get much playing time, for which I am grateful, since everyone who did is scheduling knee replacement surgery. Let's just say that the varsity cheerleading squads in both schools and I were on more than speaking terms."

"The entire varsity?"

"I might have missed one or two ladies," Sam said.

Swan mulled that over. "Moving on."

"My senior year at Tech I met a Lubbock townie, Lorraine Haver. We went to Las Vegas during spring break and got married, just for the hell of it, but we did try to make it work, for a year or two. Then I found out she had been seeing another guy, who sent pictures of her in to *AfterDark.* They decided to fly her to L.A. to do a photo test shoot, unbeknownst to me. This guy flew out, too, and by the time they decided they wanted her to be in the magazine, she and the guy wanted to be together, so we got divorced. I was in the Marines by then, anyway.

"So despite my reputation in the rifle company, I was never married to a centerfold, I was married to someone who *later* became a centerfold with some other guy. Which to my mind is completely different," said Sam. "Once I was in the Marines, there was a nice girl at Camp Pendleton, but the timing wasn't right. There were weekends on leave in Gibraltar, the bar scene—"

Swan interrupted: "Are we getting even close to the end of this?"

Sam was silent.

"She must have had a great body."

"Are we back on Lorraine again?" Sam sighed. "I've spent more time explaining her to other . . . people . . . than I did being married to her. And, anyway, you have nothing to worry about in that department. Lorraine had nothing on you."

"Oh, please!" Swan was disbelieving.

"Hey, I know what I'm talking about," Sam said, running his hand over her bare skin appreciatively. "When I saw your beautiful little feet in the Crossroads, your beautiful, beautiful bottom—I'll never forget it." He closed his eyes for a moment. "Never."

"You're a marine, anything looks good to you," she said dismissively.

"No way. I've lived with a centerfold, remember," Sam groused. "You could be Miss Any Month if you wanted to be. Although if I had to change anything, I wouldn't mind more of you in the height department. You are like a little cupcake—a few bites more would be . . . delicious." He cupped her breasts in his big hands, caressing her nipples, bending his head across her shoulder, and she could feel exactly how his mind was straying from the topic at hand. "More like two vanilla cupcakes, covered with icing . . . with cherries on top."

"Let's get back to you," Swan said, gently moving her breasts from his grasp. "You would have had more than one serious relationship in the last ten years if you were really over Lorraine. How many women *have* you slept with?"

"If you are worried about my . . . status, I've been tested very recently. Otherwise, I would have never had sex with you without protection, the way I—we—did, no matter what your 'preferences' were at the time. I'd like to think of myself as a gentleman in that regard."

"How many?"

"I thought we were talking about my love life, not my sex life."

"Hunt called you God's Gift to Women. I want to know why," Swan pursued, frustrated.

"I would have thought the reason was evident once my fly was open in the parking lot." Sam had had just about enough. "That's usually a conversation stopper."

"Oh. Oh," Swan said, finally seeing what an idiot she had been.

"And I *have* had another serious relationship in the last ten years. I've been in one for the last four years. It's just that the other party hasn't known about it up until now."

Swan let that sink in.

"A couple weeks before Hunt's death, he'd been talking about premonitions," said Sam finally. "How Civil War soldiers would go into battle just fatalistic in general—'It's God's will'— that kind of thing—then before some engagement they would have premonitions. They would give away all their belongings, write farewell letters, pin notes with their names and units to their clothes so their bodies could be identified. These guys always seemed to die in those battles—or at least the books always said they did. Hunt knew a lot about the war—all of you seem to, since it was fought here in your own fields, I guess.

"So one night my guys got tired of listing every movie star they wanted to bang—which didn't happen often—and Hunt told them the soldiers with premonitions knew it was going to happen, they sucked it up, and they accepted it. Fatalism was kind of a new idea to my guys, but they got it."

Swan said nothing. She had no idea where he was going.

"A few days later the company's digging their graves—bedding down for the night—on the road to Fallujah. Hunt's Alpha team leader, he and I are catching up, housekeeping shit. He says, 'Captain, when this is all over, you should look us up in Waverly. Sweetface and I, we'll be loving life: good horses, good Scotch, Smithfield ham—you'll like it.' I said, 'I don't think that's my scene,' and I laughed—he was the blue-blooded sergeant and I was the redneck captain. I'd been to Quantico: I knew the gentry, the old warrior class. Then out of the blue he says, 'If something happens, go see Sweetface. She'd like you, and you'd like her. Otherwise, she'll end up with some bin Laden-loving shithead Democrat, and that will seriously piss me off in hell.'

"He told me how you'd held the farm together for your dad when he had his stroke. Planning the matings of the mares, paying the bills, without anyone knowing your dad couldn't do it anymore, from when you were seventeen. Coming home every weekend instead of partying at college. No wonder you didn't date anybody but your cousin til your senior year, and even then it was a local guy."

"I sound perfect," Swan said softly. She hadn't heard Hunt's nickname for her in years; he'd named his M-16 after her. "I also spent too much money on clothes, sassed my mother til she wept; and got three speeding tickets that had to be 'fixed' so I wouldn't lose my license."

"Well, you *were* perfect—to him," Sam said, "and he made you perfect to me, too. Fast-forward to the twelfth, and the shit hits the fan outside Rashid. Mudj attack our rigs from two sides; Hunt is hit by an EFP before he can get a round off. The corpsman tries to get him stabilized on scene, but there was no part of his body that you couldn't feel the shrapnel . . . ." He looked down, then met her eyes again. "Then he gets cas-evac'd to Shock Trauma, ready to be airlifted out—but you know all of that.

"I saw him. He was conscious, mostly, although in a lot of . . . discomfort." He took a deep breath. "Hunt says, 'Captain, Sweetface is worth fifty of whatever you've been getting. You should give it a shot.'"

Now Swan was beginning to see. The panic was back. It was going to swallow her up.

"He says, 'She's yours.' And he gave me your picture. The one at the horse show. He says, 'Tell her it was all good, and I was Oscar Mike.' "

Swan was stunned.

"I take the picture, thinking I'll get it back to him, but then . . . he died. So I keep it; I look at it every fucking night. I think about the kind of life someone could have with a girl like you—someone beautiful, sure, but independent, kind of defiant, and loving, too." He gave a short laugh. "A pretty lethal combination. I don't rotate out for six months, and when I do get stateside, I hear through the grapevine that I'm already too late; there's someone else. So I figure, that's it. It's over. I send the picture to the Lees, telling them it had been misplaced in the transfer of Hunt's effects from base to hospital. They were his next of kin, not you. Then, I hear your new guy is deployed and then M.I.A. and then dead in Kabul, just when I'm going back to Iraq. What the fuck? All the while, I'm thinking about you, Swan. But it's been so long, you've been through the wringer, you won't want to be reminded of any of it: who would?

"I'm posted to Quantico, and I'm not going to wait any longer. If I hadn't found out General Clayton's connection with your family, I'd just shown up anyway. I hadn't figured out the rest of it but—"

Swan thought about Hunt's letters. There had been no hint that Hunt thought he was going to die, no hint that he'd thought of Sam for her. Like most enlisted guys, he had little use for officers; the more he saw the fewer he liked. Every once in a while he found one who he thought didn't have his head up his ass, but not often. He mocked officers and feared their ability to fuck everyone up. Hunt Lee *had* kidded that, if anything happened to him, he'd come back and haunt her. Belle Everley was haunted by Mosby's Rangers—the fox-hunting county boys who had made up the Confederate irregulars in the Civil War. Swan had teased him right back—that she wouldn't be able to tell him from all the other ghosts tramping up and down the staircase every night. Hunt had said, "I'll be the only one saying 'We're Oscar Mike' though."

When Sam had heard her say Mike's name that first day, he knew it was all going to play out just as Hunt Lee had orchestrated it. The pieces had fallen into place for Sam then: she would believe him when she knew everything. Swan slipped out of the bed and retrieved her purse from the hallway table. She opened it and withdrew the dog-earred photo from the horse show.

"Here," she said, holding it out to him, "is something of yours."

When she saw how he looked at it, she knew he was telling her the truth. He loved her. She just didn't know what she was to do about it.

"But, Sam," Swan said finally, "if there is any chance that you might be sent back there—anywhere—as an advisor or an observer or a trainer or a liaison, or whatever the Pentagon calls it—and I mean Iraq, Afghanistan, Pakistan, Osama bin Laden's supposed former cave, Karsai's back porch—anywhere—if there is any chance of that happening, you have to go. Now.

"You are all the same: you don't believe in the 'bad-luck-doomed-love shit' until it is too late and you are already dead. I have to make you see that you have only escaped up until now because you haven't actually known me. Because if you don't leave, and you are deployed after all, I will make you very sorry you stayed."

He listened calmly.

"There is no such thing as 'bad luck doomed love,'" he said. "I could be hit by lightning or run over by a supply truck on the base tomorrow. We've all told you that, but you won't let yourself believe it. Let me convince you I'm right."

The next morning, she watched him shower and shave. She toweled him off, marveling at the muscles rippling across his back and chest as he brushed his hair, applied deodorant, and grinned as he caught her staring in admiration. She rustled up a light breakfast from the slim pickings in the refrigerator. They kissed like a married couple, him in battle dress, about to go out the door, her in one of his t-shirts.

"I love having you in my bed," he said, as he was about to leave. "I wish you were going to be here when I get back tonight." He kissed her just as he had in the Scarab, the heat of his body warming her from without as his mouth warmed her within.

"Come out to the farm on Saturday," she said, impulsively. "I'll cook, just for the two of us." She should be pushing him away, not playing Martha Stewart, sleeping in his shirts . . . falling in love with him.

He sighed. "Three days—"

Now she was warmed by the longing in his voice. But he had to go.

“Another satisfied customer,” she smiled, and then she pushed him out the door.

On her way back to Belle Everley, she went over all of it in her mind. Sam had felt this longing-from-a-distance love for her. Now that he had slept with her, she wanted to know his plan, how he figured everything was going to go from here. She would have to make him understand that she was bad luck to him. But all of that wasn’t going to happen this week. For now, she decided, she was secretly going to be in love.

Chapter 5

They settled into a routine: Saturday nights into late Sunday mornings at Belle Everley, Swan sending Sam back to his apartment with fresh fruits, breads, and veggies; Wednesday nights in Warrenton or Fredericksburg for dinner and then to Quantico and his big bed. That it was a routine didn't mean it became routine. The sex stayed molten hot. If she hadn't fully appreciated the power of testosterone before she knew Septimus Moore, she was a believer now. She could feel how needy he was each time they were together and how satisfied he was when they parted. It reassured her, without them ever discussing it, that he was sleeping with no one else. She had never felt safer than she did in bed wrapped in Sam's huge arms. They were a phenomenon of nature, her private stronghold. They were hers by rights. She could move him away from her by the lightest of touches. She could pull him toward her with a look or gesture. It was thrilling.

◆

For those two nights, they were in their own little world. For the rest of the week they were still on planet Earth, although one milestone did come and go. For the first time, Swan let the date on which she would have permitted herself to read Hunt Lee's letters pass, and she did not read them on the days that followed.

Then Jerusha Dutton entered Punch in a two-mile-long timber race and Judy in a maiden hurdle at the Thornton Hill Hounds Point to Point Races in Sperryville, in late-September. The Sperryville races boasted a beautiful view of the Blue Ridge Mountains, a hospitality tent for corporate spenders, and an adequate supply of local bigwigs and gentry for ambience. Like virtually all of the seasonal hunt races, the event was held, not at a bricks and mortar racetrack, but on a course laid out in mowed fields, over undulating terrain, with a wooden announcers' booth permanently erected for a view of the course itself.

Swan invited Spaulding, the Delaneys (minus Boyd Junior), and Sam to come out to see the Belle Everley string on race day. She reserved two parking places close to the finish line and arranged for a catered spread from the Reynard to spare Mathilde until dinner, when she'd have everyone back for a late snack before the Richmond crowd headed south.

Although Jerusha proclaimed herself confident, Swan was not sanguine about her chances, particularly with Punch. He would be in top company, even this early in the season, and Swan had learned, primarily through a few veiled comments from Declan, that the gelding's heart didn't seem to be in his racing career any longer. There was no physical problem, Punch had apparently just "been there, done that" to his satisfaction. It happened. Swan said nothing to Jerusha, but if Punch didn't enjoy himself anymore, she intended to bring him home as her foxhunter with the Waverly Hunt. Jerusha could soldier on with Judy, since Mike would move to Oliver Lentz's barn in November or December.

The morning of the races, Hetty and Boyd arrived at Belle Everley first, with Spaulding in the convertible—it was still sunny and unseasonably warm— not far behind. The ladies were in linen dresses, lightweight linen jackets, straw hats, and flat heeled shoes. Boyd was in brick-red go-to-hell slacks, button-down shirt, and Orvis mocs.

Swan could read Hetty. She was intensely curious about Sam, due to Spaulding and Fitch's hyperbolic—and diametrically opposite—accounts of the mountain range major.

He arrived in the little Mercedes about noon as they were packing the Reynard picnic—cold chicken, Smithfield ham on homemade biscuits, champagne, German potato salad, crudités and dip, petit fours, huge oatmeal raisin cookies, a basket of trophy pears and apples, condiments, a giant thermos of black coffee and another of iced tea—into Swan's SUV.

He loomed over all of them, in pressed jeans, sports jacket, denim shirt with a collar, cowboy boots, and battered marine ballcap.

Spaulding greeted Sam with her ubiquitous air kiss, to both Swan's and Sam's surprise, telegraphing her approval of him, Swan thought. She turned to Boyd.

"Boyd Delaney, Septimus Moore," she said simply.

"My condolences on the loss of Captain Roland, Dr. Delaney," Sam said solemnly, as he shook Boyd's hand. Boyd was surprised and touched.

"Boyd," he said. He smiled.

That left Hetty, who looked up at her sister's beau with keen interest.

"Your reputation precedes you, Major," Hetty said in a rare show of Southern belle-ishness.

"I apologize in advance for all of my shortcomings," Sam replied solemnly, and Swan and Hetty recognized simultaneously the Clark-Gable-as-Rhett-Butler line from *Gone with the Wind.*

That turned Hetty pretty much to jelly.

◆

The short trip to Sperryville was occupied with a detailed primer on racing over fences for Sam's benefit and an assessment of the Belle Everley horses' chances in their respective races. Hetty hadn't spent a lifetime as a Bolington for nothing—she could contribute astute comments when called upon. But she was clearly more interested in winkling details of Sam's personal life out of him, and he was interested in providing satisfactory replies while revealing as little as possible. Sam and Hetty were well matched, and by the time they pulled into the host farm property, Swan judged their Q&A a draw.

Once they had parked head-first against the fence bordering the course itself, Spaulding took over hosting duties, assembling the meal in the back of the SUV, while Hetty and Boyd entertained Sam. Boyd was in hog heaven cross-examining Sam on his brief glory days as a Red Raider in Lubbock. Swan, sporting her owner's badge, headed to the adjacent mowed field where Jerusha's van was parked, Punch and Judy pulling contentedly at hay nets in their stalls an hour before their races.

"Grand day, missus," observed Declan, heading in the opposite direction from Swan. He had a mount in the second race, so was sporting another owner's silks over his white breeches and black boots. "We'll do our best, but I think we've left himself in the barn." Declan meant Oscar Mike. "He is not playing Jack the lad any longer; he's going to be the real deal." In an unusual gesture of intimacy, he gave Swan a big smile and a brief, awkward hug.

Swan felt a surge of excitement: the diffident jock was confirming her own growing suspicion, that Oscar Mike was the great triumph of one hundred years of Belle Everley breeding. First, however, they had a timber race and an open hurdle to contend with.

Jerusha and Swan had a quick conference. "I'm going to have Declan lay off the pace with Punch and then see if he can move up on the front runners when they start to back up; he really only has one big move in him," said Jerusha. "Judy won't be rated, she's going to want to get out there and go. I'm worried about that six horse and Jonathan's mare, but we'll see if she will be there at the end."

"See you in the paddock," said Swan, nodding in agreement.

As she headed back to the SUV, she saw Fitch in a tweed hacking jacket, with a chicken leg in his good hand and his disabled arm half way around Hetty. Swan picked up her pace, but from everyone's body language, all was calm in the Belle Everley party.

"Darling, great to see you," said Fitch, as Swan approached, but he was more respectful than he had been at the Willow's Edge or Belle Everley. He made no move to kiss her and had apparently been on his good behavior.

"I had to come out to support Thornton Hill's day, but, as Waverly's master, I hope I can count on you all for our races in the spring," he continued, his glance including not just the Bolington girls but Sam as well. "I wish you well with Punch and Judy, they look terrific."

"Knock wood," Swan responded ominously. "If Punch can't pull the trigger, you may see him a lot sooner than the spring."

"Always a place for our landowners in the first flight," said Fitch. Property owners who allowed the local hunt access to their land were welcome to join the field of members anytime the hunt went out. "And now, I'm afraid I have to go: I've given Townsend over to the company of a couple of VMI cadets who, although no doubt gentlemen, are most probably not to be left to their own devices for a long period of time.

"Have a lovely day," Fitch said, nodding to each of them in turn, and he was off, striding toward the Porsche parked in the V.I.P. section, close to the stewards' stand.

Spaulding raised her eyebrows purposefully in Swan's direction, making sure nothing in Fitch's comments were lost on her. Hetty made it crystal clear anyway.

"He's seeing Townsend Brooke?" she blurted out to Spaulding. "My God, is she even of legal age?"

Spaulding's shrug said everything and nothing, and they turned their attention to the food and the race card. Other Waverly and horsey folk drifted by during the afternoon, ostensibly to offer best wishes for Punch and Judy or to catch up with Hetty and Boyd, but Swan suspected their primary purpose was to get a gander at the whore of Satan and her new hunk of man, still the piping-hot talk of the county after eight weeks of an all-too-public courtship.

When the time came for Punch's race, Swan took Sam into the make-shift paddock, created out of decidedly unglamorous orange snow fencing, to watch Jerusha saddle her runner and give Declan a leg up. Sam was enjoying himself, but suddenly he seemed preoccupied; he had a melancholy look that he pushed out of his eyes when he saw her glance at him.

"Safe trip, Declan," was all Swan said as Jerusha led Punch out of the paddock at the call "Riders up!"

As she expected, Punch broke slowly from the start and never really got uncorked. He jumped the big, unforgiving fences carefully enough, but fell further and further behind the leaders. He eventually finished seventh out of nine starters, twenty lengths behind the winner. Jerusha could not conceal her disappointment. When it came time for Judy's hurdle race late in the afternoon, Swan repeated her visit to the paddock, this time with Hetty and Boyd. Hetty got teary when she saw Declan in the light brown, cream, and vermillion.

"Oh Swan, don't you think of Mom and Dad when you see our silks in the paddock, like the old days? And Grandpa Bolington?" she said, her voice quavering, and Boyd gave her a comforting squeeze. Swan pressed her lips together in a struggle to maintain her composure and managed to give Hetty a supportive little smile.

◆

In the hurdle race, Judy went to the lead almost immediately, her white-blazed face unmistakable. She jumped around in fine form, avoiding traffic in the ten-horse field, and held on for a strong second place, just half a length behind the winner. Jerusha was satisfied, Declan stoic, and the Belle Everley crowd hopeful as they packed up and started for the farm, inching their way down the narrow country roads choked with traffic. Swan would get an update from Jerusha on how Punch and Judy came out of their races, but her mind was pretty much made up: Punch was coming home.

They trooped into the house just as Mathilde was laying out a light supper—cold roast beef, the very last of the Pennsylvania peaches, fresh tomatoes, the jalopeño corn Boyd craved, homemade oatmeal bread, and English trifle. She then retreated to her suite behind the kitchen and the low drone of the television evening news.

"Beer, Sam?" Boyd called, but he didn't wait for an answer as he hunted around in the Sub Zero for what he wanted. "Dos Equis okay? Oh, I guess so: that's probably why it's here. And what about you girls?"

The others settled into the parlor. As Sam was about to sit down, Hetty turned to him.

"So when are we going to see these famous tattoos we've heard so much about?" she asked, vixenishly.

"Henrietta Hexell Bolington Delaney!" Spaulding exclaimed; Swan looked at her sister goggle-eyed.

"What?" Hetty was defensive. "I just asked."

Sam looked at Hetty for a moment and then grinned a huge grin. He shrugged out of his coat and began unceremoniously to unbutton his denim shirt.

"It's fine with me: she's a taxpayer, she should see what she's paying for," he said calmly.

He shrugged off the shirt. His jeans had shucked down his hips, and he slowly turned around, letting Hetty get a good look at the tectonic plates of muscle over his shoulder blades covered in cobalt blue mountains all the way to his heavy biceps. "I have no problem with nudity: anyone's—"

"Well, I have," Swan protested, interrupting, "with virtually everyone's." She shook her head: "Marines."

"Mother of God," said Boyd, coming in with beers in both hands. "How much time do you spend in the gym?"

"Not so much any more," Sam said. "Overseas you have down time you can devote to it—kind of like being in prison."

Spaulding looked like she was going to have a stroke. Hetty was still openly admiring.

"Wow, what a bod," she said, "look at those abs! No wonder you landed a centerfold." Swan rolled her eyes at her.

"Show's over," Swan grumped after another minute, handing Sam his shirt, "unless, Hetty, you'd like to show us your stretch marks from Boyd Junior. No? Let's eat, then, shall we?"

When they had finished their dinner, Sam helped Swan clear up the dishes and take them in the kitchen. The others could see him from the parlor as he looked down at her, laughing, searching her gaze for approval of some sally of his.

"He's got it bad," whispered Hetty to Spaulding and Boyd as they settled in with coffee.

"I know," Spaulding said glumly, "and I don't know what anyone can do about it. She's sure she has already started the Doomsday clock for him, just by knowing her."

"Does Bert think he's going to be sent back?" Hetty whispered again.

"Talking to Bert is like talking to the Sibyl: you get an answer that is open to fifty interpretations," Spaulding said, frustrated. "It boils down to 'If he is going to go, he is going to go—she has to be prepared for anything,' for all the good that does us. Even assuming Bert wants to help her, to do what's best for her, which of course he does, his hands are tied. 'National security' includes troop deployments."

"Look at these majors and colonels going back for their fifth and sixth tours," said Boyd quietly. "He's done three. Unless they plan to move him over to the Pentagon, his days are numbered—I mean, his stateside days."

"How many majors with no political connections or special expertise land at the Pentagon?" Spaulding asked bleakly. "Zero. Bert has made that clear in the past."

"Oh, God," said Hetty, "the poor kid."

After their company had departed, Sam and Swan undressed and climbed into her old bed. She reached across his body and just barely touched her fingertips to the big cephalic vein above his elbow. She traced the vein's course up the inside of his bicep, under the smooth sunburned skin, and back down again. It made them both shiver.

He wanted just to enjoy the sensation, the subtle provocation of it, but that was impossible. Instead he pulled her to him, pressing his open hand against her lower back until her pelvis was snugly tucked up against his, her breasts and their hard nipples against his rib cage. Then he pulled her up his body, turning her, kissing her mouth with enough force to push her shoulders back against the headboard, and that shifted the whole bed against the wall with a thud.

"Have some care for the family heirlooms, if you please, in your . . . romancing," she murmured. But he didn't laugh. Instead, he kissed her with no let up. He flexed his arms so she could feel the muscles roll and swell under her hands. Her breathing became faster, deeper. Then his hands crept under her little nightgown, and she felt his fingertips brush her nipples over and over, ranging across her skin at will.

Lubricant—warm, slippery, viscous—seemed to soak her, Brazilian wax and all.

"God, I love how wet you are," he said, moving his hand down her body, between her legs. "You are . . . syrupy. Maybe I should strip for your family more often."

It was her turn not to laugh.

"All your fault," she said, trying to catch her breath, "I've never been like this . . . until now. It's embarrassing but—"

"Your body is learning to know me—*me*."

"You mean, 'Here comes the boss's monster dick—we'd better get lubed, quick'?" she teased gently. "'Otherwise we'll never—' Oh!" she said, gasping as he entered her. She opened her hips, tipping her knees out a little so he could push deep inside her, and then she put her arms around him. She nuzzled the hair on his chest, letting her tongue explore his taut skin and hard nipples. "Oh, my beautiful boy," she said.

His breathing became deep, rhythmic, rough. He sounded just like the colt galloping, pulling the oxygen into his lungs, fueling his heart, pumping the blood to the muscles under his skin, and he felt just like the colt in her arms, big, powerful, barely under control. She felt the heat and cold, the girth of him in her. She would barely recover from one thrust before the next one was pushing into her, in a relentless rhythm that seemed to carry her along with it. He pulled out and turned her hips, entering her now from the side, pressing against her, letting her feel the new trajectory of his cock staking his claim in her, increasing the tempo until her breathing couldn't keep up with him and she felt the contractions cascade through her and dash themselves against him.

She came, hard; him, too.

They drowsed then for many minutes, enjoying the little after-contractions, the delicious sensation the smallest movement gave them both. So much of his body was tangled in her hair that she was trapped under him, trussed up, bound. Eventually she wriggled enough to begin to break free, but he pushed back, keeping her against him. The panic suddenly began to set in for her. He had wanted her, just like Hunt Lee, no matter what the consequences. He had her now, she'd never be able to get away.

"More," he said, "again," and he began to move on her. "Feel this."

"No." Swan felt trapped. This was all too soon—too, too soon. It was overwhelming, frightening. "You got what you wanted," she said, "now, go."

He rolled to his side, facing her, looking right at her, now that she had ruined everything.

"'Go? *Go*?' I can understand why you'd want to kill any feelings you have for me," he said bitterly. "What I can't understand is why you want to kill the feelings I have for you. I would have thought you'd enjoy seeing me suffer. You're so sure I'm a hound that fucks every woman he sees."

"That isn't it," she said, her voice like stone.

He sat up, looking right at her, angry but pleading, too.

"Christ, I know I've done everything wrong. I don't know what would have been right, from your point of view, but I guess I've fucked everything up, right from the start. I shouldn't have told you Hunt Lee wanted me to have you. I shouldn't have stared at you in the Crossroads or come to the house. I shouldn't have asked General Clayton to talk to Spaulding. I shouldn't have gotten married. I guess I should even have backed my parents up from the alter.

"But you have problems that have nothing to do with me. You've sucked in guy after guy, but you've never given up Hunt Lee, not really. Well, Swan, he's gone for good. So he is going to get pushed out of this bed, inch by fucking inch, once and for all, and I'm the one who's going to do it."

Swan suddenly knew why Sam had been so pensive at the races: Hunt Lee. Sam was living Lee's life, right down to the Smithfield ham. She wanted to try to explain the Doomsday clock, the "bad-luck-doomed-love shit," although she didn't see why he needed to have it explained to him again, but he kept on.

"I'm begging you. I'm begging you to care for me. To love me and *tell* me you love me. Because I don't think you've ever done that, for anyone, til after they all were dead. That is why you are so fucked up over them all."

Then he let his head drop gently into his hands.

"I'm begging you, and I've never begged anyone for anything in my life."

"Let me think," Swan said, in an almost-normal voice. "Please, go home for now. I can't do this anymore tonight."

He got up and dressed without a word. She got out of bed and put on the silk kimono, then led him downstairs and opened the front door. She looked up at him, way up, trying to read his mind.

"What do you really want?" she asked softly. "Tell me the truth."

"I want us to get married. Soon." Then he laughed. "Although I guess this isn't much of a proposal. It hasn't been much of a courtship either, I guess, by your standards. Short on the flowers, the steeplechase races, the hunt balls." He shrugged. "That is what I want. You asked. I answered."

"Come back to bed, then," she said simply, burying her head against him. "I don't want you to go."

He did go—the next morning, as usual.

Swan dreaded the post-mortem phone call from Spaulding, viewing the comfortable cheer in which they had all parted and the dark drama that had taken place over night as being separated by centuries. She was still processing the overnight part. The effort she was going to have to expend to maintain the cheeriness seemed beyond her energy level. She was surprised with the first call was from Hetty, not Spaulding.

"Well, well, *well*, well, well," Hetty said provocatively. "You certainly know how to pick them, Swan: your major was all that he was hyped to be, and more. Those blue eyes and shoulders like Mike's—big, broad, and built for endurance. Have you ever even seen arms like that? What a babe!" she began admiringly. "And he actually seems to be a normal guy for a career-warrior-slash-true-believer." When this opening was met with silence, Hetty's mood detector sounded the alarm. She changed tone immediately.

"What's up?" she said softly. "You aren't upset about the shirt thing, are you?"

"We had a . . . disagreement . . . after you all left," Swan sighed. "I think it ended up okay, but it was . . . difficult."

"Do you want to talk about it? I can listen as well as Spaulding can when I want to," Hetty offered.

"No, it's just, well, a baggage issue, I think." Swan had made a snap decision not to mention the whole "I want us to get married" part of the evening. But she was going to have to give Hetty something. "I think he wants to go faster than I'm comfortable with, not surprising given the fighting man's awareness of the illusory nature of time."

"Well, faster is better than slower, *I* always say; and don't *you* always say you can always slow down a racehorse but you can't always speed one up?" Hetty queried, her tone lighter.

Swan sighed.

"I do always say that, but I'm beginning to believe that not all racing truisms can be extrapolated into decision making in real life," she said. She was feeling better. After all, no real harm had been done overnight; Sam had staked out his position, she had staked out hers. The make-up sex had been phenomenal.

"What has it been, eight weeks? That is . . . accelerated . . . by any measure, for sure, but Boyd and I both liked him—alot. And you know Spaulding already thinks he's the second coming, although anybody with his looks who is not a paroled ax murderer would probably get the same reception. Spaulding talks a good game about common aspirations and the blending of two minds but, when it comes to men, the packaging is everything."

Hetty paused suddenly and backtracked. "What do you mean, 'he wants to go faster'? You two have already circled the proverbial bases dozens of times. What else can he want? Exclusivity? That should be no problem for you, since you've made it clear that Fitch is—oh!" Hetty was shocked into a brief silence. "Don't tell me he popped the question. No!"

"No, of course not, not in any formal way," Swan replied, seizing upon a tiny semantic peg to hang the lie. "It was just in a manner of him illustrating how we look at the future differently," she finished lamely, not knowing what she was talking about herself.

"Well, you obviously have been able to commit in the past, and you'd think he'd want to take it slowly, given his marital history. He's probably had loads of women," Hetty mused. "I'm amazed he's fallen for you—well, not amazed, but—you know . . . . Sorry."

"No, you're right. It's hard to figure," Swan agreed.

"He has to understand that, with what you've been through, you would be . . . ambivalent . . . about the prospect of marriage in the near future," Hetty reasoned, "and it is, by all objective measures, too, too soon."

"Except 'all objective measures' go out the window in wartime. Plus, I just hate the drama."

"Well, look on the bright side, kiddo. Whatever you had, you've still got," Hetty teased."You've landed Major Hunk in record time, even for you. Who would have thought?"

Any other topic was anti-climactic, but Swan listened with interest while Hetty recounted Boyd Junior's charming little doings in his parents' absence so the conversation could be brought to a comfortable close. She had time to fill a cup from the teapot under a cozy on the sideboard and pass through the entranceway before the phone rang again. Spaulding.

"We had a lovely time, darling."

Swan listened as Spaulding confirmed the Delaneys' satisfaction with Sam.

"We did have one question for you: who are his people? I think you said they were originally from Kentucky—Lexington, by any chance?" Spaulding was using code for the big horse farms for which the Bluegrass State was famous. "Sam seems to appreciate a good racehorse."

"No, dear, not from Lexington. Probably from Wingo, or Vicco, or Sadieville, or Salt Lick. I gather they were of extremely limited means, both before they moved to Texas and after."

"Oh." A pregnant pause from Spaulding. "Are his parents still alive, I wonder?"

"His father is dead. I'm not sure about his mother. She remarried," Swan was trying to retrieve bits of information she'd gotten, when? At the Reynard. It seemed eons ago. "She was a teacher."

"I gather he went to Texas Tech on a scholarship?" Spaulding probed. Swan decided to put her out of her misery.

"I think we can be assured that there was no family money, no land. He got through school on a football scholarship and student loans. He lives in a rental apartment outside Quantico. He makes one hundred thousand a year, which is pretty outstanding, it seems to me, but small potatoes for what he's asked to do. He drives an old truck and apparently has put himself in hock to buy the little Mercedes I was stupid enough to say I thought was cute when he borrowed it. His dad had a problem with alcohol before he died pretty much broke. I think that covers it," Swan said bluntly.

"Honey," Spaulding said softly, "you don't need to defend him to me."

"Sorry . . . sorry." Who had been on his side from the very beginning?

"Oh, Swannie, you love him. We kind of thought he had fallen for you, but you—"

"Gotta go, Spaulding. I'll talk to you later."

◆

That afternoon, for the first time in a long time, Swan thought about the wedding plans she had made with Hunt Lee. Her mother had wanted the ceremony at Belle Everley Methodist, but it was Mrs. Lee's wish that Hunt be married in the National Cathedral in Washington after his final deployment; Mr. Lee Senior had been a warden there, and it was more centrally located for many of the guests. Swan had decided on the Cathedral, with the reception at the farm.

Then disaster—and instead they were at Hunt Lee's funeral, which Swan barely remembered. She had begged Mrs. Lee to put her engagement ring in the casket with Hunt Lee's remains "so he isn't completely alone." She was reasonably sure Mrs. Lee, after a heartfelt attempt to dissuade Swan, had done what she'd asked; in any case, if the thirty-thousand dollar diamond was not resting in Arlington, Swan hoped she would never find out about it.

She suddenly wanted to talk to Mrs. Lee. She and Mr. Lee had rented out their Taliaferro County house and moved to Florida; they couldn't bear to be around the people and country Hunt had loved. They exchanged Christmas cards, and a single rose was delivered to Swan and to Mrs. Lee on the anniversary of Hunt's death every year, anonymously. Of course they were from Mr. Lee.

After lunch Swan rang them; Mrs. Lee answered.

"My dear girl," she said on hearing Swan's voice, and they caught up a bit on the local news for each of them before Swan got to the point.

"Mother, did you know much about Hunt's captain over there the last time—Captain Moore?" Swan asked. "Did Hunt tell you about him?"

"Moore . . . the tall man with the strange tattoos? Was that him?" Mrs. Lee fumbled through her recollections. "He was in the company picture, the one Hunt sent us when they first got there, wasn't he? He sent us a lovely letter after the official one, with your photo, which we very much appreciated. I think Hunt said he had been in Afghanistan before . . . before Iraq. He had had some unhappy marriage or something . . . the men made fun of it? Or am I thinking of someone else?"

Swan began to cry.

"Mother, he's here. He's here. And he wants—" Swan was sobbing.

Mrs. Lee was at a loss. "Who's there, dear? Who's there?"

Swan realized she thought Swan meant Hunt Lee . . . or his ghost, anyway. If only that were the problem.

"Mother, did Hunt . . . blame Captain Moore for anything? Did he think he was a good officer? Hunt was such a survivor. He had such great instincts . . . . Did he think Captain Moore was . . . unlucky?"

Mrs. Lee was trying to make sense of it all.

"My dear girl," she began, again, but helplessly, "it just happened. It all just . . . happened."

Swan saw it was hopeless. She gave up.

◆

On Tuesday, Spaulding called.

"Daniel is back," she announced to Swan cautiously.

"Our Daniel? Daniel Spaulding?" Swan was surprised. Her maternal cousin by marriage had done two stints in rehab since graduation from William and Mary, with a degree in finance, two years before Swan. He had been Swan's first boyfriend during her sophmore year at W&M. He had gone on to get his MBA at Harvard before his life fell apart.

"He was interviewing at one of the banks in town," Spaulding explained; she meant Washington, D.C. "Do you have any interest in seeing him? I know he'd like to see you, very much."

"We've been out of touch for so long," Swan began, but she heard something akin to pleading in Spaulding's voice. Much of the family had written Daniel off long ago, but he had been a favorite of both Spaulding and Swan's mother, Lucinda.

"I can't take a day off to go into town—," Swan continued.

"I think he'd meet you in Waverly. I know Wednesday is Sam's, but how about later? He'll be heading back to Strasburg to wait out the interview process."

That is how Swan found herself at the Reynard on Thursday. She let the genial Patty show her to a table, but no sooner had she been seated than Daniel, in a Gucci suit, headed toward her. He was on the slight side but he had a steely elegance and smoldering eyes that made him attractive to women who liked a tortured rake to wreak havoc in their lives. Fortunately, Swan had not been one of them; her attraction to him as a college girl had been based on family attachment, not physical chemistry.

"How's my favorite cousin?" Daniel began, with a kiss on her cheek.

"Well, thanks. And it is great to see you looking well," Swan said, trying to put some genuine affection into her voice.

"How long has it been? Two years at least."

"Three, I think."

"Yes, of course. Hunt had passed away and I was trying to get back on my feet at New Beginnings. I've always regretted not being in any condition to be of more help to you, Swannie, during all of . . . that."

"Your note about Carter was very sweet. I did appreciate it," Swan said, and she was struck anew by how completely her life had been bifurcated into the time before Her Troubles and the time afterward. "There really wasn't much anyone could do, when it comes right down to it."

They ordered Lorenzo's seafood special, and Swan, after a moment's hesitation, ordered a glass of the house merlot; Daniel stuck with sparkling water.

"The good news is that with an aunt like Spaulding, we have no catching up to do, since she's told each of us about the other in mind-numbing detail," Daniel said, in an attempt at humor. "So you probably know that this assistant V.P. job at Tidewater Commercial's D.C. office is most likely my best shot at getting off the family dole." Daniel's habits had made a significant dent in his comfortable trust fund; Swan knew he was trying to replenish his coffers.

"You'd move from Strasburg to D.C., then?" Swan thought out loud, "closer to the rest of us nosy relatives?"

"A mixed blessing . . . ." Daniel took her meaning, "but I've got to grow up eventually, just like Oscar Mike."

That opening let Swan brag about the colt for a few minutes. They ate their way through Hetty and Boyd, Bert, the state of the varous family manses—almost everything but Daniel's recent history. As their plates were being cleared away, she let Daniel change the subject.

"I hear you and Fitch aren't together anymore," he said.

"If you know that, you must know that I'm getting kind of involved with Hunt's former company commander."

"How's that working for you?" Daniel smiled.

"You tell me: I'm sure you've heard everyone's take on it."

"The jury is out on the timing, but everyone seems to have drunk the Kool-Aid on the guy himself. I wish you luck, kid. You and I are the family casualties, you know," he mused. "You, because of things beyond your control, and me because I'm—me, I guess. The Hettys and the Spauldings and the Berts seem to breeze uneventfully through life."

"That sounds as though it would be nice."

"Yeah. At least it's something we have in common," Daniel said quietly. "But I'd better get on my horse: I'm bunking at the Willow's Edge, and Spaulding will be peering out the window in her nightcap if I don't get there at a reasonable hour."

"It was lovely to see you, Daniel." Swan was wistful.

"Then let me give you a piece of advice." He had risen from the table, after leaving cash to cover the check, and turned toward her. "Stay out of the Scarab. You can cross the paths of some unsavory customers there." He smiled, and then he was gone.

◆

On Saturday, before Sam's arrival, Swan sent Eduardo to retrieve Punch from Jerusha's barn. The trainer had been philosophical: The Fortress's "long" yearling filly, Dress the Line, would be coming to her in early spring, after Edgar had backed her at Belle Everley, to begin her racing education.

Swan was comforted to see Punch's beloved face in his old stall in the main barn. It made her miss Mike a bit less. Punch had hunted two seasons with Swan before going to Jerusha as a timber horse, and Swan looked forward to having him for her own pleasure once again. The Waverly Hunt was about to start its fall season. Within a few weeks, Punch would be let down in fitness enough to roll along with Waverly, which had a reputation as a social hunt, with many diplomats and other professional, weekend-only riders among its membership. (The Tuscarora, which hunted the adjacent country, was a hard-riding, hard-drinking crowd, the Hell's Angels of the region's recognized hunts.) Punch had plenty of speed to keep up with Tuscarora, but Swan would have had to pay a capping fee as a guest there. With Waverly she hunted for free.

As Waverly's master, Fitch had cubbed—the informal "pre-season" of hunting in August and early September—successfully with jerry-rigged reins and prosthesis, on his saint of a staff horse, James. A M.F.H. led with his knowledge of local terrain and political skills (in keeping landowners and members alike happy and generous), which Fitch had in abundance, not with brute strength and athleticism. The whippers-in and professional huntsman knew their hounds, their foxes, and their coverts and were intensely loyal to Fitch. Everyone wanted him to succeed, including Swan. In the back of her mind Swan had thought that, if James could not adjust to Fitch's new riding style, she'd offer him Punch. Now it seemed that would not be necessary.

So, when Sam arrived, Swan was cheerful. They had called a truce the previous Wednesday at Quantico. They were going to let the difficult subjects of Saturday night lie for the time being and just live life through the fall. That, they both agreed, is what a couple in their situation would have been doing if Swan's history hadn't hung over them. Despite her terrible fear, Swan had picked up no evidence of Sam's imminent deployment, no sign that he was going to extricate himself from her life—not yet. When he came into the parlor in a racer-t and jeans and sat down next to her on the settee, to his delight she climbed into his lap immediately. He ran his big hand up her calf and thigh, all the way under her terrycloth shorts and tickled her feet until she wriggled in protest.

"I'm going to hate autumn," he said, "if it means six months until it's bare legs' season again."

"Speaking of summer activities," Swan turned cautiously serious, "Harry Edwards told me that you sold him your Harley, the Fat Boy, so you could buy the Mercedes. I got the impression from him that the motorcycle was your pride and joy: why would you do that, if that is true?"

"And how did Captain Edwards think to bring this up?"

"Once, when I left the apartment, he had parked the 'hog' in the space you vacated when you took the SLK to the base," she explained, "and when I came out, he was there. He assumed, I guess, that I knew you had sold the Harley to 'make room' for the Mercedes."

"I decided that the truck and the Mercedes were more practical than the truck and the hog," Sam said evenly, "but Edwards was right: I did set quite a store by the Harley."

"I hope it wasn't anything I said that made you—"

Edwards had told her Sam had bought the roadster for her, going into debt to do so.

"Swan, a motorcycle isn't like Oscar Mike, if that's what you're thinking," Sam said gently. "It isn't going to feel betrayed by me selling it."

Then he grinned.

"You do realize that you whisper the same sweet nothings to me when we make love that you do to Mike, don't you? The very same words. Don't you think that's strange?"

Swan was taken aback.

"Well, I do." Sam answered his own question. "Not that I mind sharing you with a horse, but, by my calculations, Mike is the equivalent in age to a nine-year-old boy. That is disturbing. I don't see the similarities, myself."

Swan rallied.

"I can think of one," she said, slipping her hand down the front of his jeans.

Chapter 6

Swan made sure she had nothing scheduled for the Tuesday of the second week of October. It was the anniversary of Hunt Lee's death, and Swan, as she had for the previous four years, planned to go to Arlington National Cemetery, to Section 60, where the Operation Iraqi Freedom and Operation Enduring Freedom combat fatalities were buried. She had not mentioned the date or her planned visit to Sam.

She always went alone. Even when she had dated Carter Roland, it had been understood that she would give Hunt her undivided attention on that day. She preferred it to Memorial Day, Veteran's Day, or Christmas. For her, the wretched, keening grief of the other families was more bearable on the anniversary than on the holidays.

Mathilde, who knew the date's ritual well, made breakfast without her typical chatter, and she did not turn on the flat screen for the U.K. morning racing feed. She gave Swan's shoulder a sympathetic squeeze as she sat down in the dining room and left Swan to her thoughts.

◆

Mid-morning, Swan made sure the two arrangements of greens and chrysthanemums from the Waverly Florist were carefully tucked into the back of the SUV, added a lightweight jacket to her black sweater and slacks, and headed east. In an hour and a half, the grand skeleton of Arlington House, Mrs. Robert E. Lee's ancestral home, loomed above the Potomac River.

Swan parked in visitor parking and made her way to Section 60, clearly identifiable by the enormous number of brightly decorated graves compared to those of fallen heroes from wars past. Children, some barely out of strollers, stood with their young mothers, placing handwritten notes, toys, balloons, and keepsakes on one headstone or another. Older folks in garrison caps or fatigue jackets sat in lawn chairs, covered by quilts, weeping quietly or staring at the headstones of their darlings. A classroom of solemn children on a field trip clustered under a spreading oak nearby. An ancient veteran in a VFW cap and wheelchair was being slowly trundled back to the hard-surface road, by a young soldier in uniform.

The white marble headstones were placed ten feet apart. Swan went directly to Hunt's grave, identified by a four-digit number. Now that the Lees were in Florida, she was the only regular visitor, so she was surprised to see a fresh wreath: the card read *Rest well. Maj. Septimus A. Moore, USMC.*

She gently repositioned Sam's wreath to make room for her two. One bore a card reading *From Mother and Dad, Always* and the other, a card with the Emily Dickinson quote *Because I could not stop for Death/He kindly stopped for me.* It was signed *Swan.*

"You're safe here, my darling. They can't hurt you anymore," Swan said, as she always did, looking at the marker. She was so happy it was true. She saw Hunt, his long legs crossed in front of the fireplace at Belle Everley as he slipped the huge diamond on her finger; swaggering toward the plane, looking over his shoulder, winking at her as she waved, her arms wrapped in Mother Lee's . . . .

He'd come home in pieces. Everyone said the team at Dover did a fantastic job on the bodies, but they all knew the truth.

Tiny stones rested on the polished edge of Hunt's marker, left by the nameless visitors who had wanted to show their witness of the sacrifice and the grief. But Swan felt like something had changed. She felt a distance, not only from Hunt but also from the other heartbroken mourners surrounding her. It didn't alarm her, it wasn't painful, it was like riding a racehorse in a dream, pulling away from the field; a slow, steady, quiet acceleration, without the fear, the concussion, the sound of pounding hooves. She let the sensation wash over her.

She turned at the sound of horses' metal-shod hooves on a hard surface. A flag-draped caisson was rounding the bend above Section 60 with full military escort from the Army's Old Guard; the gray horses pulling the limber seemed like personal friends. Swan felt a cameraderie with them, a closeness. These horses had brought Hunt here, to Section 60. They understood her as she understood them.

She took the caisson's approach as her sign to leave, and she charted a path back to the visitors' parking that arc-ed well clear of the melancholy procession heading to a cluster of chairs around a freshly dug grave. She was glad the Rolands had decided to bury Carter in the Confederate cemetery in Fluvanna County, closer to them, rather than at Arlington. Two such anniversaries would have been unendurable.

When she came home, a long stemmed white rose was in a tall sterling bud vase on the round table in the entranceway. Swan gently placed the engagement picture on its face and went upstairs. She went in to her bedroom and loaded Mozart's *Requiem* into the CD player. Then she closed the door.

Swan had decided over the previous weekend to try Punch with the Waverly Hunt the following morning, Wednesday, suspecting she could use the pick-me-up of a fast ride in good company before meeting Sam for their regular date night. Eduardo had Punch's mane and tail braided impeccably and the gleaming gelding tacked up in Lucinda Bolington's side saddle when she emerged from the house. With a nod he loaded Punch into the new van as Swan climbed into the passenger seat. It was a luxury to have a groom's assistance at the fixture, and Swan was able to concentrate on the finishing touches to her wardrobe and hair on the short jaunt to the great house at Arcadia, the hunt's departure point.

She was wearing a black melton hunt coat, canary waistcoat and breeches, stock tie and pin, tan gloves, and black side saddle apron—meticulously correct guest attire, although as a landowner she could have shown up in a thong and horned Viking helmet and been given a warm welcome. She had paper-thin-sliced ham on white in her sandwich case, brandy in her sterling silver flask, and her black Vogels polished to a jewel-like finish. Her hair was braided tightly then confined in a hairnet, elegant under a black silk top hat and veil. She carried her grandmother Hexell's one-hundred-year-old silver-handled, leather-covered stick, mandatory for a lady riding aside.

The field was already gathered when Eduardo pulled the van into the historic farm. Fourteen couple of crossbred foxhounds milled around the huntsman, the professional Ezra Wilky, and the whippers-in, two local women. With Eduardo's help, Swan swung up on Punch, adjusted her inside leg on the saddle's second pommel, and walked directly to Fitch. He was in his glory in his pinque hunt coat, black velvet hunt cap, and brown-leather-topped boots aboard the elegant dark bay James. Punch needed no reintroduction to hunt decorum, and he tolerated the milling hounds with equanimity. Only his erect head carriage and bright eyes telegraphed his anticipation of a long, pipe-opening gallop. Swan's voice correction kept the old steeplechaser at a flat-footed halt as she greeted Fitch.

"Fine morning for scent, Master. The pack looks marvelous—is that Manic and Mayhem?" Swan asked, indicating two crossbred hound littermates she had puppy walked the preceding year.

"The very same," Fitch said, with a welcoming grin. He was in great good humor. "It's grand to see you 'aside,' Miss Swan. You look a picture: we'll try to give you a good run for your money, girlie."

Following protocol, Swan greeted the hunt secretary, then the hunt members, including Kezia Hardaway, all of whom were identifiable by their coat buttons and collar facings in the Waverly colors of saffron and navy. Edwardo would take the van home and return after the hunt breakfast at Arcadia House. She made a special effort to greet the pale blonde Townsend Brooke, who was astride one of Fitch's very serviceable hunt horses and in correct, off-the-rack guest attire. She looked uncomfortable on a horse nonetheless, and Swan had a moment's concern about the teenager's ability to negotiate the trappy country surrounding Arcadia. She hoped Townsend would stay in the second flight, those riders who opted to take gate and road options rather than jump fences to keep up with the pack. The Arcadia butler, acting as a hunt servant, brought around bone china stirrup cups shaped like fox heads in a sterling tray, raising it to stirrup height for the riders' libation in a gesture right out of a George Stubbs painting. Then the field set off promptly, the staff roading hounds to likely coverts.

Punch was happy as a clam in first flight, his long strides and deep snorting breaths showed his enthusiasm for his old pastime. To Swan's relief, Townsend remained with the slower riders as hounds were cast for the first time. Before long, they found the scent of one of the many red foxes populating the region. The field was off, first at a strong trot then at a ground-covering canter, negotiating coops and rail fences through cattle fields, down dirt and gravel roads, through plowed fields now fallow, with their crops of soybeans and corn already harvested. At several checks, or halts, where the hounds lost the scent, most of the field went to their flasks, since the morning was cold and more than one rider used the brandy for courage over fences that dropped off alarmingly on the off side, or hugged the cut banks of the streams running through the vast Arcadia acreage.

◆

About a hour and half into the day, Swan was aware of activity behind them and she felt a ping of alarm. She eased Punch and looked back over the coop they had negotiated as they brought up the rear of the first flight. Townsend was on the ground some distance behind her, with a dismounted lady rider offering assistance. Swan made a quick mental note of their location: they were on a loop heading back toward Arcadia House. She held up as first flight disappeared ahead of her and turned Punch to jump the coop backwards, child's play for the old campaigner.

"Townsend, are you all right?" Swan called out. The teenager looked white as a sheet but was being helped to her feet. Another rider had caught up Townsend's horse, and the rest of the second flight was slowly moving off, having determined that no life or limb was in danger.

"If you can get mounted, I'll lead you back to the house," Swan offered.

The mortified girl looked grateful, as did the two members who were watching the rest of the second flight disappear. One gave Townsend a careful leg up back into the saddle, and Swan made sure Punch understood that their day was coming to an end. The other riders moved off briskly to catch up, and the two girls stayed halted until they were alone. Then Swan gave a lead toward a dirt road that would take them back to their starting place.

"I think my wrist is sprained," Townsend said bleakly, as she rode one-handed.

"No worries," Swan comforted her. "Someone will take you to the Urgent Care Center in Waverly to have it x-rayed; we'll be back at the house in twenty-five minutes. Do you think you can make it?"

Townsend nodded, and the color seemed to be coming back into her face. "I'm sorry to ruin your morning, with you looking so beautiful, like a Victorian picture, in your skirt and veil."

"No worries," Swan said again. "You are doing me a favor; Punch is probably not up to the whole day's sport anyway." A small fib.

"Didn't he race at Sperryville?" Townsend asked, perking up, and they recalled that day at the races. Then Swan revealed the mysteries of side-saddle riding; soon the plaster-covered mansion came into sight, to the great relief of the teenager.

"Fitch is going to be furious."

"No, no, not at all," Swan said reassuringly. "We've all come off many times, Fitch included—he'll just be glad you are all right. Don't worry, really."

"He loves you, Swan," Townsend said sadly.

"No, no, not at all," Swan repeated. "We're just good friends."

"Really?" Townsend brightened.

"Really."

"Has he had many . . . girlfriends?" Townsend's infatuation was almost painful to see.

"I'd say he has had his share." Swan thought honesty the best policy. She was struck by the irony: Townsend sounded like Swan did when she was thinking about Sam. Women.

Kezia Hardaway's husband, William, was waiting at the great house with a car for the patient, and Eduardo was just turning into the driveway with the van. Someone had alerted them by cell phone to the girls' early return. Two or three people hurried to help Townsend dismount and put her horse on Fitch's van. Eduardo swung Swan out of the saddle in a graceful dismount, then loaded Punch for the trip home.

"I'll stay for breakfast, Eduardo," Swan decided, "in case Miss Brooke returns. I'll catch a ride later."

The butler brought her a large mug of hot tea as she awaited the field's return in the library of Acadia, which was much more the archetypical plantation house than was Belle Everley. The owner, Mrs. Jeptha Braddock, was in the field, so Swan was on her own. Within the hour, she heard the riders making the turn down the long lane. She met them at the door.

"How is she?" Fitch asked Swan as he dismounted, Eugenia Braddock right behind him.

"It may be a sprained wrist, but she is a trouper," Swan reported. "They took her to Urgent Care just to be cautious."

"You were a darling to bring her back," he said gratefully.

"No worries. Anyone else would have had to cut their day short or lose their capping fee. I'm a freeloader, I knew the shortcut home, so it made perfect sense."

Fitch sighed, and Swan sensed he was comparing in his mind the girl he had with the girl he wished he had.

"She is a sweetie and very brave," she said to him. "Now what's for breakfast? I'm starving."

"Darling Swan, try the grits and the sausage," urged Eugenia. "I'll make sure Townsend gets back from Urgent Care."

"Let me fix you a plate," Fitch offered in a voice like honey on a fresh biscuit, "and extend a formal invitation to the Waverly Hunt Ball, which we have decided to hold two weekends before Christmas."

Swan was surprised. Hunt balls typically were held in the spring, after the hunting season had ended.

"Yes." Fitch could have been reading her mind. "You may recall that they cancelled in the spring because of my recovery. Very nice of them, although they certainly should have gone on with it, in my opinion. Now that I'm back they've decided to hold it after all, at the Reynard, in the private ballroom upstairs."

"That should be beautiful," Swan said carefully, because she suddenly had an alarming thought: was Fitch about to invite her as his date? "I'm sure Sam and I would love to come."

Fitch's expression revealed nothing.

"We'll be happy to see you both, so long as you save me at least one dance," he said mischievously. "They've decided to do the traditional black, white, or gold." This was the arcane custom of a limited palette of colors for the ladies' formal dress.

"The military uniform is always most appropriate, as you know," he added. "But I will enjoy the opportunity to christen the scarlet tailcoat we picked up at the post office. I had the sleeves tailored for my new . . . physique."

Swan imagined Sam in the spectacular marine evening dress uniform; she was willing to bet it would trump Fitch's scarlet tailcoat. No matter what she came up with, she decided, she'd place a distant third to her two peacocks. That night she described the day's events to Sam over dinner at the Wayside Tavern in Fredericksburg.

"I have to hand it to Fitch," he said grudgingly, "for a guy you aren't dating, he sees a lot more of you than I do. Fox-hunting, family dinners, carriage rides . . . . He's even come up with a white tie event at which he'll be the host and you'll be at his beck and call."

Later, in bed at Quantico he was pensive as he held her.

"Sometimes I still can't believe I'm here with you," he said. "It all seems unreal, as though it couldn't have happened—after all this time wanting it to happen, I mean."

She raised her head from his chest, and her heavy hair fell around both of them.

"Is that why you sent the wreath to the gravesite yesterday? To convince yourself that it had happened? Hunt's death, I mean? That *it* had to happen for *us* to happen?"

"No," he said. "I sent it because I was pretty sure you were going to be there, and I wanted to be there with you, somehow."

She was silent.

"I love you very much," he said.

"Spaulding thinks that if Carter had returned from Afghanistan, I would have broken our engagement," Swan said softly. "She thinks that as soon as I am engaged, I began to regret it. She will probably say the same thing to you if you persist in thinking we should be together."

"Your past does not intimidate me. I'll either win you for myself or not. It will not depend on what your family says or what the Marine Corps does with me."

"I don't deserve happiness, I've lost my chance. I don't want to lose you yours."

"I wish I could make you see things the way I see them, but the only way we'll ever prove who's right is to look back after everything has played itself out. We'll either be sitting surrounded by our children and grandchildren or—"

Or you'll be in Section 60, Swan thought.

◆

On Saturday they went to bed about midnight. The phone rang forty-five minutes later, and instinctively Sam rolled over and picked it up.

"Hello?" he growled.

"Ah, is Mrs. Smith there?" A woman's voice.

"Wrong number," Sam growled again, but Swan clambered over his broad back as though he were a piece of furniture to pull the phone out of his hands.

"Mrs. Smith?" she asked.

"Yes. Mrs. Smith?" It was Patty Lombardini from the Reynard.

"Yes."

"I wasn't expecting you to have company or I would never have called," Patty said cautiously.

"No. It is quite alright. What's up?" said Swan, holding Sam's quizzical gaze across the pillows.

"I'm afraid we are in need of a night's lodging for two . . . parties," Patty said, cautious still. "Our coverage for this situation has developed food poisoning or flu or . . . well, is unavailable and—"

"Say no more," Swan said. "You were right to call. What can you tell me?"

"A restraining order has been in place for several weeks and our clients have been at the safe house on and off during that time, but that location has been discovered by the 'restrained' party," said Patty. "Mrs. Smith and her son had to leave home suddenly again tonight and another location would be optimal, if that could be arranged."

"Of course, that sounds absolutely right," said Swan. "How soon might I expect my guests?"

"Half an hour?"

"We'll be ready. Turn your headlights off as you come up to the house," said Swan.

"Thanks, Mrs. Smith," said Patty.

Swan placed the phone back in its cradle.

"Okay," she said to Sam, "here's the deal. We are going to have two overnight guests in thirty minutes. I'll fill you in on the rest after I've gone downstairs to wake Mathilde. But first . . . ."

Swan opened the drawer of the nightstand on her side of the bed and removed a leather holster holding Grandpa Bolington's World War II German Walther .32 semi-automatic pistol. Under the pistol was a full ammunition clip, which she slipped into the pistol's handle with a click. She engaged the safety and placed the pistol on the nightstand, muzzle facing the wall.

"Damn, you could cover a sector in one of my platoons any day," Sam said, admiringly.

"It would be a great help if you could put this on top of the dresser where you could retrieve it if needed but where it would be out of reach of someone any shorter than you are, even using a chair," Swan said, pulling on her silk kimono.

Sam obediently jumped up to place the pistol on top of the seven-foot-tall eighteenth-century wardrobe in the corner of the bedroom.

"Please check that the shotgun is locked in the gun case in the closet," Swan said as she slipped downstairs. "You don't have your sidearm, do you? One of our guests is going to be a child."

"Aye, aye, ma'am, and, no, no sidearm here. Locked up at Quantico."

She tapped on Mathilde's door.

"Mathilde? It's Mrs. Smith," Swan said. The housekeeper was at the door in a few seconds.

"We are having guests, Mrs. Smith and her son, in half an hour. Please do your best with the front bedroom, will you—towels, et cetera?"

"What about Major Moore?" Mathilde asked in a whisper.

"I think it best if he stays in my room til our guests are settled in."

She turned on the light on the front steps and flew back upstairs.

Sam was sitting on the bed, partially dressed.

"Okay," she began. "I'm on the board of directors of the House of Mary Magdalene, which is the county's abused women's shelter. Most of us don't broadcast this fact for reasons such as the circumstance we face now. We have a small house, secure, the actual address of which is held pretty much on a need-to-know basis, where our clients can stay until they get their situations settled. Since most of our clients know the county pretty well, occasionally someone discovers the address and makes trouble for . . . someone. So we find it prudent to move certain clients out of the shelter til we can get the restraining order . . . straightened out.

"So we are about to have two clients, Mrs. Smith and her son, to stay the night," Swan finished.

"Sounds like a lot of Smiths."

"Yes, well, as you might imagine, sometimes families are reunited and children may be 'asked' by their fathers where Mom has been staying, who has been helping her, et cetera, and it is better if—"

"Understood."

"So, for the same reason, I'm afraid you will have to stay here while I get our guests settled," Swan explained.

Sam was perplexed. "You mean, because I'm a man? Too intimidating?"

Swan smiled for the first time since the phone rang.

"No, sweetie, because you are so damn tall," she said. "If this child describes a young dark-haired woman, a farm house, and a tall man with tattoos and a military haircut, Dad won't have to do much detective work if he wants to pay us a visit now or . . . later, will he?"

"Bring him on," Sam said, in a way that made the hair on the back of Swan's neck rise. For the first time, she had heard the voice of the combat-tested killer.

"Hey, this is somebody's father," she said quietly. "But, thanks, anyway."

"Consider me confined," Sam said, resignedly.

Swan gave the front bedroom and bath a once over, with Mathilde at her heels. She pulled out a box of toys, games, and DVDs from the closet.

"Not much for a boy to choose from," she muttered. "We'll have to do better next time, Mrs. Smith."

Within a few minutes, a compact car pulled in front of Belle Everley with its headlights off. Swan was at the door by the time the three passengers were about to knock. Patty Lombardini was leading a thirtyish woman wearing an old car coat over a nightgown and a nine-year-old boy in pajamas and robe. She had a canvas duffle bag in one hand and a folder of paperwork in the other.

"Mrs. Smith," Swan said warmly to Patty, then turned to the woman and child.

"Welcome, Mrs. Smith," Swan said, "and you are—"

"Peter," said the boy shyly.

"Come on in, it's cold out here. This is another Mrs. Smith, Peter," Swan said wryly, introducing Mathilde, in robe and curlers.

"Are you hungry?" Mathilde asked them. "How about a cup of tea?"

"No, thanks," the woman said wearily, "it's already been kind of a long night."

"Mrs. Smith will take you both upstairs, then," Swan said briskly, but kindly. "You can have a bath or drop right into bed. And, please, don't worry about anything tonight. We are very happy to have you. This Mrs. Smith and I will just go over a few things downstairs first." Swan looked at Patty.

Mathilde picked up the duffle bag and led the two strangers up the stairs. Swan turned off the downstairs lights and pulled Patty into the dark parlor.

"Thanks, again," Patty began. "Can you feed them in the morning? We have an emergency hearing before the magistrate with Social Services at ten A.M. If we need a warrant, we'll go to the sheriff's office right away. They are adding patrols past the safe house tonight. We think it will be okay; he's threatened to pull this kind of thing in the past and he's always been just talk, you know, but—"

"No, no—better safe than sorry," Swan reassured her. A similar situation had not turned out well three years previously.

"I'm concerned about Major Moore," Patty said. "Is it going to be awkward?"

"Absolutely not. I'm keeping him under wraps til our guests leave. Don't worry. He is a senior serving intel officer, he knows how to keep a secret."

"I hope to be back here by eleven thirty A.M. We need to get them into the thrift shop; they have nothing but the clothes they ran out of their house in and a few things we were able to scrounge. Normally, I'd have taken them there tonight and let them choose some things, but under the circumstances we thought it would be best to get them settled securely first. By tomorrow we'll have the bench warrant and then he'll be the sheriff's problem."

"That will be fine." Swan showed Patty to the door, signed the housing paperwork for the county, and gave her a quick embrace. "Go right home, Mrs. Smith."

"Don't worry, Mrs. Smith," Patty replied, pushing blonde curly hair out of her eyes. "Lorenzo is waiting up for me."

Swan returned to bed, snuggling close to Sam in his skivvies.

"Everything okay?" he murmured into her hair. "I'd better get some respectable nightwear to keep here if this is going to be a regular occurrence."

"Not a regular one," Swan said, "But I do miss my old German Shepherd, Nell. She would make sure that, if anyone got in, he'd never get out in one piece."

"I'll try to take Nell's place, at least for tonight." Sam wrapped his arms around her. She felt absolutely safe, absolutely secure. It felt wonderful.

Swan's unhappy guests did their best to do justice to Mathilde's full breakfast the next morning. Peter half-heartedly amused himself with the old DVDs and games Swan had been able to round up until Swan found an old copy of *Treasure Island*. He pounced on it, bringing a small smile to his mother's drawn and despairing face. But amusement was the last thing they needed; so Swan left them to themselves.

◆

Patty came back at eleven-thirty with promising news on the legal front, and mother and son were outfitted with cast-off clothes that would do until they made a friendly raid on the shelter's thrift shop on the edge of Waverly. Then they were off, with *Treasure Island,* as quickly as they had arrived.

"Sorry our weekend got screwed up," Swan apologized over a late lunch. "Saturday nights are always bad in this business." She looked pensive. "And you thought all the misery in the world was in Kandahar and Baghdad. We generate plenty of it right here in Taliaferro County."

"Maybe we could generate a little love this afternoon," proposed Sam. Swan thought of the vast difference between men and women. A man has to have sex to feel close to someone; a woman must feel close to have sex.

"That might be arranged. Can you stay overnight and go back to Quantico early in the morning?" she asked.

And just like that, Sam began spending the whole of every weekend at Belle Everley. He watched Judy contest two more hurdle races in November; the mare finished first once and third once and seemed to relish both outings. He watched Oscar Mike learn how to navigate the training center's loading gate, always a perilous lesson for a colt as big as Mike, and to launch himself as soon as the electrical current holding the stall doors closed was interrupted by the starter. He held Mike as Declan Flynn was boosted into the saddle on the training track to whet Mike's appetite for competition and build his confidence in the company of a less talented rival.

Swan hunted three more Wednesdays through the fall, since Sam was still at Quantico during the week, but without the company of Townsend Brooke, who had suffered a hairline fracture, not a sprain, that kept her out of the saddle for the rest of the season.

Bertrand Davis and Spaulding invited Swan and Sam to a performance of *Our American Cousin* at Ford's Theatre in the District, followed by dinner at a Capitol Hill eatery one Saturday night. It was during this dinner that Sam learned how Swan's mother had died: an accidental drowning during a boating party on the Potomac River three years previously. Lucinda Bolington Davis had been almost forty when she had Hetty, and Swan had followed eighteen months later. A slim and youthful sixty-three, she had still considered herself a bride after thirteen months of marriage to Bert, a politically connected long-time Defense Department/defense industry insider. Her death came soon after Hunt Lee's and was a terrible shock. Bert had moved to a townhouse on Capitol Hill almost immediately thereafter. Swan received the farm outright in acknowledgment of her years running the family horse business; Hetty, a pre-arranged lump sum since her life was in Richmond with Boyd.

When Swan starting dating Septimus Moore, Bert was put in an awkward position. He was reluctant to discuss Sam's future with a sister-in-law who showed no ability to keep a secret. He had developed oblique answers and hypotheses that could be parsed a number of ways so that no useful information of any value got into Spaulding's hands, to her great frustration. It seemed to Spaulding that concrete answers to Swan's questions were within sight but always out of reach, so far as Bert was concerned, and the relationship between the two began to cool over the fall.

"If she has the information, she doesn't need 'emotional support,'" Spaulding had burst out during one of these tense conversations. She read Bert's reticence as evidence of his divided loyalty, between D.O.D. and the Bolingtons. She felt he had chosen D.O.D. and was watching as Swan headed toward potential disaster.

This uneasy truce continued into Thanksgiving, with Swan oblivious to much of the tension. The Delaneys, Swan, Sam, and Bert had celebrated at the Willow's Edge, giving Swan's workers several days with their families, thanks to two local college girls' willingness to undertake the basic horse care at Belle Everley in everyone's absence.

Bert and Sam had taken advantage of some unusually fine late-November weather to sit by the pond in front of the historic house alone for a couple of hours before dinner while Boyd had been wrapped up in TV football. The women had looked out the window frequently; Sam had been talking and Bert listening for much of the time. Their topic could be nothing but the wars. If nothing else, at least Swan had given Sam the opportunity to speak off the record with one of the men potentially responsible for his life or death.

The second weekend of December was the Waverly Hunt Ball.

◆

The night of the ball was cool, almost cold. If left to her own choice, Swan would have worn something in scarlet or sapphire to compliment Sam's uniform, but her options were limited by the hunt's black/white/gold edict. She had chosen a heavy silk *prêt à porter* dress, in a hand-blocked black-and-white Japanese print reminscent of an Edo-period geisha's understated kimono. It had a high neck and was backless to below the waist. A scarlet silk lining was visible along its border. A black shirred silk shrug warded off the cool night air, and black silk peep-toed platform pumps with sky-high heels would help close a few inches of the twelve-inch height difference between Swan and Sam when they danced. Her hair was pulled back from her face in a bun at the base of her neck from which a tendril or two escaped.

Sam arrived in the Mercedes. No matter how often she had seen the marine evening dress uniform, with its short blue coat, scarlet cummerbund, striped trousers, and battle decorations, she still found herself short of breath at the sight of him.

They drove toward Waverly in silence. Sam looked at Swan furtively as they traveled the dark dirt roads. She was so beautiful to him: she reminded him of a dragonfly that had briefly alighted on some dark flowerhead in the moonlight. *Unattainable . . . unattainable . . . unattainable.* He thought of the girls he had known in Texas, their nasal accents and ignorant, brayed vulgarities, their blowsy ValUmart knock-offs of what passed for fashion among teenage TV sitcom stars. He thought of the sad promiscuity of the girls who frequented the bars in Oceanside, desperate to land a serviceman. Swan wasn't just a different kind of girl; she was a completely different species, to him anyway. He parked in the small lot behind the restaurant, which twinkled with white Christmas lights. Sam deliberately pulled a tiny box from the pocket of his dress coat and half turned toward her. Swan had seen such a box before, more than once. Time seemed suspended, then stopped permanently.

"Susannah Swan Bolington," Sam began quietly, "I love you and want to spend the rest of my life with you." He gently placed the box in Swan's limp hand, unsnapping the lid as though she lacked the strength to do it herself. All she had to do was raise the lid to see the box's contents. "Will you marry me?"

Swan cupped the box in her hands as though she were lifting water from a stream to her lips. She opened the lid. A ring with a Victorian platinum setting held a perfect round diamond flanked by a smaller round Kashmir sapphire and a matching Burma ruby. The multicolored stones picked up the reflection of the Christmas lights surrounding the car.

"Yes." She looked at him.

Relief washed over Sam's face. He reached across her lap and took the ring from the box. He placed the ring on her left hand, then lifted her hand to his lips and kissed the back of her fingers.

She sat as if in a trance.

"This ring has been in my family for five generations," he said. "It used to have two sapphires flanking the diamond, but one was lost from the setting one hundred years ago. I had a jeweler in Washington look for a matching sapphire of the same age, but he found a Victorian ruby instead. Red, white, and blue. Unusual for an engagement ring, I know," he added hurriedly, "and if you'd rather, the jeweler said he'd replace the ruby with a sapphire since that's more traditional."

"It's perfect," she said. She looked at her hand as though it belonged to someone else. It didn't look like the hand that had held the huge diamond of Hunt Lee or the modern hand-hammered band of Carter Roland. For this she was very grateful.

"Shall we go in?" Sam asked quietly, and the spell was broken.

Swan walked with him toward the Reynard's entrance, and they joined a knot of couples laughing and pretending to huddle together in the chill. Amidst the ill-fitting, low-cut satin ballgowns of the hunt ladies, she looked like an exotic black orchid edged in white.

She glanced at Sam, his eyes ablaze with triumph, as they climbed upstairs to the low-ceilinged second story ballroom. English and native boxwood, long branches of holly and magnolia, fresh persimmons, lemons, and pomegranates decorated the hallway and the mantels in the ballroom; beeswax tapers provided colonial-era lighting and fragrance.

The Lester Lanin quintet, imported from New York City, was already playing dance music for a crowd of folks aged eighty to twenty. Only Townsend Brooke, on Fitch's arm, looked fashionably different from the bustier'd hunt ladies, in a white satin micro-mini dress with a tulip-shaped skirt and white platform heels. Fitch was resplendent in his new tailcoat, with its navy blue and saffron facings, and black tuxedo pants. The coat draped beautifully over the prosthesis, and only a careful examination would reveal the subtle alterations that made that possible. He reached a white-gloved hand to Swan in greeting, then pulled back as if he had touched a live wire. He had caught sight of the ring and didn't take his eyes from it for a long moment. Then he lifted his eyes to Swan's.

"I see felicitations are in order," he said quietly, as if they were the only two people in the room. He gave her a melancholy smile and a tender kiss on the cheek.

"Congratulations, Major," Fitch said, turning to Sam with a handshake. "You've won our great belle. I hope you both will be very happy."

"Thank you, Mr. Fitzhugh. I'm the luckiest man in the South," Sam said, somewhat formally. Their eyes met briefly, then Sam turned to Townsend.

"You look lovely, Miss Brooke," he said gallantly, "I hope you'll save a dance for me, since I know Fitch has claimed my fiancée for the . . . gavotte, Fitch?" Sam joked—no one had danced a gavotte since the reign of Elizabeth I.

"The carioca." Fitch countered with the show dance Fred and Ginger made all the rage in *Flying Down to Rio*.

"You two had better dance together, then," said Swan, rolling her eyes, "since I don't know either of those. Foxtrot, hustle, tango, waltz: take your pick, gents."

"Oh, Swan, are you really engaged?" Townsend interrupted, unable to contain her excitement. "When? Where? Just tonight? May I see your ring? Oh, it is fabulous, so unusual—Patty, come here, look! Swan and Major Moore are engaged, did you know?"

Suddenly, Swan and Sam were surrounded by the couples who were not dancing. After silent communiqué with Swan, Fitch made his way to the quintet and its microphone.

"May I have your attention, everyone?" Fitch smiled at the crowd, signaling for silence. "With great pleasure, in the absence of Bertrand Davis, allow me to share with you the happy news that Miss Susannah Bolington has accepted the proposal of marriage of Major Septimus Moore, of Texas and the Quantico Marine Base. Swan and Sam, on behalf of the Waverly Hunt Club, I offer our warmest best wishes. Sam, welcome to our celebration, to our town, and to our hearts."

"Thank you, Fitch," said Sam, and as if on cue, the quintet struck up "The Most Beautiful Girl in the World." Sam took Swan's hand, and they began to waltz alone. A flurry of applause followed, then Fitch and Townsend and Patty and Lorenzo joined them. A few steps later and the whole room was filled with dancing couples. *Is there anyone happier than I am,* Swan wondered, *here in this little tavern two weeks before Christmas?*

◆

The rest of the evening seemed to float by. Swan danced not only with Fitch but also with Daniel Spaulding, who had materialized out of nowhere as the escort of Waverly member and former prep school flame Wickie Gardener, Lorenzo Lombardini, William Hardaway, even Declan Flynn, who was technically Virgilia Osmond's guest but spent most of his evening drinking and manning the stag line, such as it was.

Sam was left to partner all of the ladies in turn; Swan admired him most from across the floor when paired with the tall, trophy-worthy Townsend.

"So, you've chosen the big man after all, girlie," Fitch was saying as he turned her in gentle foxtrot half circles to "The Way You Look Tonight."

"I hope you meant it when you said you were happy for me," Swan replied, looking him in the eye once again.

"Of course I did. No one on earth deserves it more than you do. If he's the one for you, then he's the one for me. Do you have a wedding date?"

"Until an hour ago, I didn't have a fiancé. So, no, we don't have a date."

"This hasn't come about due to an impending deployment, has it—or any other impending . . . event?"

The smile faded from Swan's face.

"No."

"Good," he hastened. "I'm glad to hear that. So, does Spaulding know? Bert Davis? Hetty?"

Swan shook her head. "I think this was news to everyone tonight."

◆

At midnight, Patty and Lorenzo led everyone downstairs to the now-closed restaurant for a buffet of steamship roast beef, local duckling, horseradish dressing, popovers, Beluga caviar, steamed fruit compote, fire-roasted squash, baby peas, plum pudding, and the best Virginia red wines from local vineyards. A jeroboam of Mumms provided champagne toasts.

◆

By two-thirty, Swan and Sam were unlocking the door at Belle Everley once again. Sam shed his accoutrements and climbed silently to the bedroom. He stirred up the moribund fire in the fireplace until he found a live ember or two, which he patiently nurtured while Swan showered. He was sitting in the wing chair in front of the fireplace, watching the flames flicker to life when she emerged from the bathroom in a little satin full slip. Swan slowly came over to the fire, letting him watch her as she sat on his lap, facing him, her knees straddling his hips.

"This is different," Sam murmured delightedly when he realized she had on nothing beneath the slip. He slid the silk even further up her thighs with appreciative hands. "Are you invading my perimeter, Sergeant? You never come to me for sex. I always have to chase after you."

She slowly unzipped his dress trousers and placed her hand inside them, without taking her eyes from his face.

"How can I ever come to you? Your engine is always running, all I have to do is put you in gear. I never have to step on the gas, much less turn the key in the ignition—" She gently explored him further, til she reached what she wanted.

"That's not the reason. Sometimes I forget how inexperienced you really are—" He stopped abruptly. "Chiclet, did you used to ask and not get?"

Swan pulled back slightly, but he held her hand in place.

"Because that isn't going to happen with me," he continued quietly. "I can guarantee you are going to get whatever you want, whenever you want, from now on."

Swan relaxed.

"You seem to be . . . out of uniform, Major."

She had undone his cummerbund and trouser waistband; now she nuzzled his neck under his open collar.

"Do you know what is nice about your cock?" she continued, giving him a little smile while looking him in the eye. "It's very big and hard, which is very . . . useful, but it's also . . . flexible," she gently raised herself above him, "kind of like Gumby. You can deploy it for optimal directional capability." She demonstrated, lowering herself onto him, guiding him with her hand. He exhaled a long, low sigh. She began to move so slowly and deliberately that she knew he wouldn't be able to wait her out.

"Well, Gumby is plenty interested in you right at the moment." He began to take over. "God, I've never raw-dogged it with anyone the way I have with you. It's fantastic," he sighed.

A minute later, she said, "Good-bye, Gumby; hellooo, Pokey—" Later still, when she was writhing beneath him as his powerful body continued its relentless, rhythmic thrusting, she gasped, "We're naming the next foal Battering Ram."

"You know, there are things we can do in bed that you might like to try after we're married," Sam said quietly the next morning, as she snuggled in against him, not yet ready to leave their cocoon of private pleasure.

"Things you . . . like?"

"Alternatives, sure, but I'm easy to please. You'll see."

"I've only had what you would call conventional sex, despite having known three men of the world," Swan said shyly. "Of course, I know about . . . things. I surf the Internet, talk to my friends. I'm not some repressed, narrow-minded—at least, I don't think I am, but given what every teenager seems to know and do—" Her voice trailed off.

"A man can find a fifteen-year-old on any street corner in any city in the world willing to do anything he wants," Sam said quietly. "Some men like some things held back for marriage, particularly southern men."

"You sound like someone out of the eighteen sixties—'held back for marriage.' Who thinks that way anymore?"

"It isn't when a man is born, it was when his father was born, or when *his* father was born and taught *him* how things should be. You of all people should understand that." Sam wrapped his arms around Swan with a satisfied little groan.

"What I do understand is that in the next two hours we will have an onslaught of phone calls and visits from my well-intentioned loved ones asking questions that we won't have the answers to, unless you have thought of them," Swan said quietly.

"Such as?" He had turned serious.

"When we will be married and where; where will we live; will you be staying in the Marines and, if you won't be, what you have in your mind to do, to start with," Swan said.

"Let's keep them in suspense."

"Maybe we shouldn't have said anything about our engagement until we had thought things through a little more," Swan said, sounding hesitant.

"Not reconsidering, I hope." Sam successfully kept his anxiety out of his voice.

"No! Not at all."

"Well, then, let's not worry. Anyway, if there is one thing I've learned about Waverly, it's that no one can keep a secret for long."

As Swan had predicted, the phone began to ring off the hook before breakfast. Spaulding offered the Willow's Edge for the reception, Hetty wanted the go-ahead to plan an engagement party for New Year's Eve; Bertrand Davis was fatherly toward Swan and genuinely delighted for them both. The surprise call was from General Clayton, late in the afternoon.

"Major, I hesitate to say this, but, 'Mission accomplished,'" said the general after offering the traditional congratulations.

"Thank you, sir."

"Do you have a date in mind?"

"Not as yet. This was all a bit of a surprise to my fiancée," Sam replied evenly.

"Well, sometimes that is for the best," General Clayton said. "It will make a nice story for your children and grandchildren. However," he continued, "I wouldn't wait too long."

By dinner time, Swan was feeling the effects of too much food, too much champagne, too much talk.

"Do you want to call your mother?" she asked Sam tentatively as they sat by the parlor fire in front of soup and sandwiches. "Isn't she in Corpus?"

"Probably a good idea."

"Will she be surprised?" Swan had never heard Sam mention speaking with his mother.

"Probably, but pleased."

"Of course, she's been down this road before," Swan said, thinking of Lorraine.

"She's going to love you." Sam didn't move. "It's too nice here by the fire; I'll call her tomorrow."

"I thought Fitch and Townsend made a lovely couple, didn't you?" Swan said cozily, turning to a bit of gossip.

"Lovely, yes, for one in completely over her head."

"You mean head over heels?"

"No, I mean there isn't an eighteen-year-old in the country who could hold Hastings Fitzhugh for long," Sam said, "particularly in his condition. But she might as well learn that the hard way."

Swan was suddenly certain the condition Sam was referring to was not Fitch's prosthesis.

"Why should she waste time on someone who's so obviously in love with someone else's girl?" he continued. "If I were Fitch, I'd wait this engagement out. Who knows whether he might still get his chance? Fitch isn't the only one: your cousin Daniel watched you all night—did you notice? That Flynn thinks you're pretty special. It's disconcerting to see so many rivals circling not only you but also each other, all at the same time. God knows how many more there are, tucked away on these old ruined farms."

"Now you do sound like Fitch," Swan said, a bit testily, "and you are quite wrong about Daniel. He's family."

"You forget: I got the scoop from your many friends during tonight's festivities; everyone I danced with seemed to think it an appropriate occasion to fill me in on the romances you had prior to the ones I was already aware of."

"Like me going to the Texas Tech cheerleader reunion?" Swan said, seeing her opening.

Sam ceded the point. "Time for lights out."

◆

The next day Sam was on the road back to Quantico as usual. Spaulding wasted no time in calling Swan before she knew her niece would be busy at the barn.

"Well, no one can talk about anything else, so what do you expect?" Spaulding said defensively when tweaked about the early hour. "I should leave this to Bert, but you might want to give a thought to a pre-nuptial agreement. You have extensive holdings, Swan, despite your claims of poverty, and once you're married, all of your income, even from assets held separately prior to your marriage, will become community property."

"This isn't a topic I expected from you, that's for sure," Swan said coolly. "I thought you'd be all about 'Are you getting a dress from Dora Tang's atelier or Dominique Lalique's, or are you going vintage?' You've never been concerned about a prenup before."

"If he is leaving the Marine Corps, unless he goes to Warburton or Black Rock for risks and analytic support, or the CIA, he may have a period of time without income. He won't qualify for a military pension without twenty years."

"Who said he is leaving the Corps?" Swan said, feeling the old panic. "Have you been talking to General Clayton? He spoke with Sam yesterday, but I am not going to ask him to give up his career, and I don't want anyone in the family to ask him to. I would fight it if he decided to do so on my account. That would doom us. Doom us! You must see that."

"I can think of worse things that could happen," Spaulding said carefully. "I assumed you would have made that a condition of accepting him."

"If you mean that I would go certifiably crazy if Sam was deployed and injured—or worse—you are absolutely correct," Swan said calmly. "Unfortunately, you would have to stand by and watch that happen. But Sam—and Hunt and Carter—have devoted their lives to the military war against terrorism. Two of them are in the ground because of it. Yes, the war is failing, by any measure other than that there has not been another Nine-Eleven. Everyone can see it except the D.O.D. holdouts from the Bush era. One hundred thousand troops in southern Afghanistan, fifty thousand in Baghdad for the next decade— the country simply won't stand for it. The only reason it's tolerated it for this long is that everyone being killed is either a volunteer or a mercenary.

"But, don't you see? If I ask him to turn his back on it now because I think the wars have been failures—mistakes—my sacrifice will have been for nothing, too. I'll be admitting that it wasn't worth it all—losing Carter and Hunt and ending up as screwed up as I am—so screwed up that, whether Sam is deployed or not, I have at least a fifty-fifty chance of driving him away. If I let him go back and he's captured and beheaded, or held for ransom, or blown up by a homemade bomb on some mountain donkey path, it will be my fault. And if I force him out of the Corps, *that* will be my fault.

"If he goes and comes back fine—not just the next time, but the next, and the next after that—and we live happily ever after, maybe I'll be able to be a normal girl again. So I'm giving myself a one-out-of-three chance of making it through the next ten years."

"I wish to God I had never asked you to meet him," Spaulding said quietly.

"Don't worry. I've got to go—horses to ride."

"I love you, my darling," Spaulding said, "but this is all too sad," and she hung up the phone.

◆

Later that day, Swan went online and reviewed the profiles of all the dead military personnel in Iraq and Afghanistan to that point, by rank. Sergeants in particular seemed to have targets painted on them, something she knew from bitter experience. More marines had been killed in Afghanistan than soldiers, unusual because the Army was much larger than was the Marine Corps. Members of the marine expeditionary forces, the Army's Tenth Mountain Division, and the 101st Airborne Division had suffered disproportionately.

She looked at all fatalities above the rank of captain the most carefully. There were dozens of them. Clearly, even being attached to the Pentagon or the Medical Corps or the P.R. Department couldn't inoculate you against disaster.

Chapter 7

When she saw Sam on Wednesday at the Wayside in Fredericksburg, she had good news: Mike was set to go to Oliver Lentz's barn at the Furnace Mountain Training Center in Maryland; The Fortress was entering the last sixty days of her pregnancy; and Dress the Line had worn tack for the first time in her stall, under Edgar's gentle hands.

"You are so efficient, you might want to begin to think about a wedding date," Sam said matter-of-factly.

"I thought we could discuss that after the holidays."

"Don't you need a lot of lead time to reserve churches and halls and . . . things?"

"You didn't."

"Well, I'm smart enough to know that Vegas is not an option, not for this family." He was smiling but he could sense her mood. He let the subject drop.

"Are you planning to go to Corpus for Christmas?" Swan asked.

He looked perplexed.

"Why would I do that?"

Swan waited a beat.

"Oh. Ah, no. Christmas with my mother is Chik-fil-A on TV trays in front of *It's a Wonderful Life*. Nothing I can't miss."

"Well, I can't leave the farm," Swan began, "but if you'd like to invite her and your stepfather here, they would be most welcome." Then she had a thought. "You have told them about us?"

"I tried them on Monday: no answer."

"I think that is the first outright lie you've told me," she said quietly. "I'm not accusing you; I've told plenty when I've felt that was going to work for me. If talking about your folks forces you to lie, then let's not talk about them."

He looked at her.

"Boy, did I luck out in landing you," he said.

◆

On Thursday morning, after she had returned from Quantico, Swan helped Edgar with Dress the Line. The spunky filly let them put the saddle and simple racing bridle on her in her stall with no complaint. Then Swan boosted Edgar across the filly's back, his belly on the saddle but his feet free to jump back to earth if she objected to his 125 pounds. Swan walked the two of them around Linny's twelve-by-twelve stall, making sure to keep Edgar's feet away from the walls. Then, trusting a lifetime's worth of instinct, she pushed Edgar into the irons and led Linny out of the wide stall door for a little jaunt down the shedrow. The filly walked tentatively, struggling to balance Edgar's unfamiliar live weight; Swan smiled at the widely held misconception that Thoroughbreds buck like broncos when first backed. Linny was no Mike, no El Diablo. She was a sensible little horse. Edgar's ride was only ten minutes long; the filly was looking a bit stressed but pleased with herself, so they called it a day. Swan was in an ebullient mood when she walked into the house for lunch at noon. Mathilde was holding the phone out to her.

"I thought I might catch you," said Sam casually.

"Just walked in the door from backing Linny. First step on her way to the winner's circle—Saratoga, here we come. What's up?"

"I'm going to be in your neighborhood later; are you going to be home? Maybe around six?" Something in his voice shot Swan's threat-level alert system to Code Red level.

"Of course. This is unusual. Anything going on?" Swan kept her voice even.

"I'll tell you tonight."

"Tell me now."

"Chiclet, that's only six hours from now."

"Tell me now."

"No. Wait til I see you."

"Tell me or I'm driving back to the base with ten sticks of dynamite and a detonator strapped to my ribcage."

"Goddamn it, Swan—not funny. Tonight. I mean it."

"I'm hanging up now. See you shortly: you can tell the sentries I'll be the girl in the blue dually and the bulky coat."

"Son of a motherfucking bitch! I'll be there in fifty-five minutes." Sam hung up.

"Mathilde," Swan said, walking toward the kitchen, trying to keep her voice matter of fact. "Major Moore is coming by unexpectedly for lunch. Isn't that nice? What can we give him? Turkey clubs and crab soup? And any of that apple crisp that is left. Oh, are you making brownies?"

Mathilde stopped beating eggs into the homemade brownie dough. Her eyes met Swan's for a long moment.

"What is it, Miss Swan? Deployment?" Mathilde whispered the word as an obscenity.

"What else could it be?" Swan said, her voice suddenly breaking. "It has to be. Oh, God. Oh, God."

"Maybe it's someplace safe, like . . . England? Or, where is NATO headquarters? Belgium? It could be someplace like that, couldn't it?"

"If it were someplace okay, he would have told me on the phone, like 'Guess what, it's Germany in March' or something like that. I'm not an idiot. It's seven months overseas; six months at home. Everybody knows that; it's just the Quantico and the 'three tours already' thing that made me think it wouldn't follow the normal schedule. Oh, God," Swan felt the tears welling up, spilling over. "It's going to be fucking Kandahar again; I just know it. Goddamned Helmand Province. This fucking, fucking surge! I hope George W. Bush burns in hell!"

"Monsieur Bush hasn't been president for years. Go upstairs," Mathilde said briskly, "while I get lunch started. Cry yourself out in the shower, then put an ice-cold cloth on your face. You'll have it out of your system by the time he gets here. We'll show the Marines we can man up, *ma chèr*."

When Sam pulled in the circular driveway, Swan was in the parlor, just like the first time he came to the house. She had put Great-grandpa Bolington's black Mason's frock coat over her jeans and white linen shirt and had poked the fire to a lively blaze, but she was still freezing. Sam stormed in the door, but his anger drained out of him as soon as he saw her face.

"Do you want a drink?" she asked him dully, barely responding when he put his arms around her.

"Can't, honey." He took her left hand and kissed her engagement ring. That's when she knew it was a done deal. She resisted the urge to say, "Just kill me now."

"Okay," he said as they sat down, "here's the deal."

"It's Kandahar in March," she said, staring into the fire, "Helmand Province, which has never been held by us permanently in ten years."

"Yes."

"March first or March thirtieth?"

"March first."

Seventy-five days.

"Tell me," she said, and her voice sounded as though she was already on a tranquilizer.

"The Tenth Marine Expeditionary Force had been skedded to go back even before the troop buildup was requested there; I know you've been sniffing around news sites for weeks so I won't go over the details you already know," Sam said calmly.

"The Tenth Marine Expeditionary isn't your unit," Swan said.

"The major attached to that unit just suffered an accident," Sam said. "Since I've had relatively recent experience in Helmand, know many of the tribal leaders still in place there, and most importantly, know some of the company command structure, ISAF commanders, and new C.O. from my tour in Iraq, they asked me to step in."

"That means you are going to Oceanside if it's the Tenth," Swan said lifelessly. "It couldn't be Camp LeJeune, commuting distance."

"Afraid not."

"How long have you known?" she asked. "It that why you went out there in August?"

"No, unrelated—but I did stop in and see personnel I had known on previous tours. Maybe that's why I popped up on their radar when this happened. It was only finalized this morning."

"When do you have to be there?"

"Right after New Year's. There's a lot to do."

"What happened to the major?"

"Non-combat related."

She was silent. The minutes began to tick by, but she had proved she could wait him out.

"Self-inflicted gunshot wound," he said finally, "fifth tour coming up."

Could it get any worse? she asked herself.

"Well, at least his family won't have to wonder what is going to happen to him over there. It already happened here." She thought a minute. "Doesn't someone already in the unit get promoted when there is an . . . opening . . . like that?"

"No, sometimes just the opposite. In this case, the captains are all relatively inexperienced due to . . . turnover . . . they've already encountered. Majors are often reassigned. Unit cohesion isn't always possible."

Mathilde materialized in the doorway. "Lunch is ready, Miss Swan."

"Thanks, Mathilde. Let's eat."

After Mathilde had served them, Sam tried again.

"I'm thinking we have a couple of options," he began patiently. "First of all, the deployment is only going to be seven months. They only send part of the unit each tour. We can go ahead and plan the wedding for right after I return at the end of September. That's probably when you were thinking of anyway—summers here are so humid, you said. Or we could go to Las Vegas on my way to Oceanside—I've done it before." He tried making a joke.

"And look how well that turned out," she said. "No. We're not going to hit the Elvis Chapel followed by the five P.M. all-you-can-eat buffet at the Lucky Strike, with slot machines as bridesmaids. End of discussion," she said, her face like stone. "With the holidays, anything we tried to gin up around here before New Year's would be some thrown-together thing . . . too pathetic and depressing."

"The end of September it is, then," he said. "Agreed?"

"Agreed."

"Swannie, I'm sorry," he said. "Sorry about the whole damn thing."

"Oh, you don't know what sorry is, not yet," she said, bitterly. "At least we had a few good months."

"Say whatever you want, if it makes you feel better. I know I started that Doomsday clock in your head, and I wish to God I hadn't, but it's done." He finished his lunch and pushed back from the table, making ready to leave. She saw how truly miserable he was. She jumped up and put her arms around him, willing him to embrace her.

"I love you, Sam! You asked me to tell you that once. So I'm telling you now," she said brokenly.

"As I love you, soon-to-be Mrs. Moore. I'm still the happiest guy on the planet—go figure. Maybe it's because I get to kill bad guys again while you're stuck here worrying." He lifted her straight up, off her feet, by her elbows, as though she were a little paper parasol, and kissed her, then headed for the front door.

"If you told them at Quantico that I had some kind of breakdown or seizure or something, could you stay another hour?" Swan asked. "I hate pet names for body parts, but I could do with a visit from Major Gumby."

Sam turned back. "He'd like to visit you, too."

That night Swan had a dream. She was a bride coming down the aisle—at the Cathedral? The stairs at Belle Everley? And as she got to the alter, Delahunt Lee, Carter Roland, and Septimus Moore, in uniform, were waiting for her. She was getting married to all three of them, in Heaven. It would have been ludicrous if it hadn't been so pathetic.

◆

After that, she woke every day planning how soon she could get to Quantico or how soon Sam could get to her. She knew from experience that, after he was gone, she would intensely regret every minute they had spent apart prior to his departure for Oceanside. Once he was gone she would have to rely on her ability to relive every moment they had been in physical contact. Phone calls, e-mails, text messages, video hook-ups would be problematic and unreliable in Afghanistan. No technology would replace the chemical attraction at the cellular level, the pure physical pleasure of being next to him in bed or in his arms. She began to sleep in his t-shirts again, the ones he'd already worn that carried his scent, so that she woke with it on her own body. The sex became more intense and all-consuming than in even the early days of their relationship. She had never felt it before with anyone. If she brushed her lips over him, anywhere—his collarbone, his hip, his ear, the small of his back—it would rouse him, even from a sound sleep, arouse him as though Pavlov had rung his bell. Then she would do anything for him—did do anything for him— night after night. She held nothing back, not now.

Hetty had the unenviable task of revisiting her earlier offer of an engagement party on New Year's Eve.

"God, how wake-like would it be," Swan said bleakly. "Everyone standing around toasting the New Year while the Fiancée of Doom clutches her next victim."

"Well, we could go to Plan B; just have local folks on Christmas Eve there at the farm for a buffet open house. No dancing or toasting or anything engagement-y," Hetty countered. "Mathilde, Eduardo, Edgar, but none of the other folks, the Averies, or Claytons, or the Waverly Hunt crowd.

"And just for the record, Swan, we've talked: we all believe Septimus Moore can take care of himself, big time. One: he is a major, not a combat team leader on foot patrol seven days a week; two: he will probably be pushing paper at NATO/ISAF or division headquarters, up the rear ends of generals when he isn't in the field with the guys. Generals work hard at not being anywhere near any real danger and succeed very well. Three: he knows the territory—the bad guys, the good guys, and the screw-ups—and won't have to spend time sorting everybody out all over again. Four: the Taliban aren't winning any popularity contests, and current policy is to pull back from the vulnerable outposts where trouble has been, try to tame Helmand, and get the water and electricity running in Kabul and women in school." Hetty grinned through the phone line. "And, five, he is a Mars-the-God-of-War-like specimen of superhero proportions, who is probably as close to being indestructible as the fevered brains of warfare could have dreamed up. He could go *mano a mano* with the entire Taliban high command, donkey cavalry and all, and come out way ahead."

"Sounds like somebody has been talking to Bert," Swan said, impressed. "All but for that last Mars the God of War bit, which probably came from Spaulding's 'fevered brain.'"

After a discussion with Sam, Swan agreed with Hetty's Christmas Eve buffet plan in lieu of an engagement party. Patty and Lorenzo outdid themselves: a bisque so thick with lobster that it could be cut with a knife; crown roast of pork; coquilles Saint Jacques; Yorkshire pudding; parsnips and herbs; a whole Gruyère cheese filled with fresh raspberries and broiled til creamy; an alter made of glacéed fruit; a Lady Baltimore cake, frosted in white buttercream and filled with candied orange peel and raisins; a chocolate iced roll cake festooned with handmade spearmint gumdrops; and six-foot-tall arrangements of gladiolas and calla lilies for the entranceway, the living room, and the parlor. The rest of the downstairs was decorated for Christmas—eight-foot-tall evergreens cut from Belle Everley's own fields; one decorated all in Victorian spun cotton fruit ornaments; one in white lights and Victorian wood and tin toys; and one in German blown glass kugels shaped like fruits, pine cones, and Santas.

Swan had decided that the party would be low-key, except for her outfit. She had a mid-thigh Chinese inspired vermillion silk cocktail dress, part of her post-Saratoga horde, and matching silk pumps. Might as well pull out all the stops. Hetty thought it was the loveliest she'd ever seen her sister, and she couldn't wait for Swan to see Sam's engagement gift to her: ruby studs, which Hetty had helped him choose, from a European antiquarian jeweler on Fifth Avenue.

Hetty, in long-sleeved green velvet, directed the Reynard team, with Mathilde as her deputy— laying fires, lighting candles, dressing the tables, setting up the bar, positioning the string trio under the stairs in the entranceway, lit by huge pillar candles in floor candelabra—before she shooed Mathilde out to dress as a guest herself. Hetty jiggled Boyd Junior but, like all babies, he generated a low gurgling sound, punctuated occasionally by little yips that could disrupt any somber mood. Bert Davis stood in front of the mantelpiece and raised his glass cup, for a single toast.

"Sam, please know you are in our hearts tonight and will be every night you are away from us. Swan, darling, you and Hetty are as dear to me as my own daughters, and if you and Sam are half as happy as your mother and I were before she was taken from us, you will be very happy indeed. Please raise your glasses—to Swan and Sam," he said. Everyone drank cheerfully.

Spaulding made Swan and Sam sit in the loveseat in front of the mantel for a photo, then squeezed the family together in a fruitless attempt to fit them into her little digital camera's viewfinder. At Hetty's urging, Sam produced the earrings, to Swan's stunned surprise. Since Sam had never asked about the diamond studs, that night many centuries before at the Hospice fund-raiser, he could not know that he had replicated Hunt's gift to Swan, although Hetty, of course, did. She helped Swan place them in her ears and kissed her lovingly.

Then the knocks began at the door in earnest, the string trio lifted its instruments, the waiters began their rounds, and time started up again. Sam and Swan held up damn well, all things considered. Finally it was all over. Spaulding and the three Delaneys were tucked into guest bedrooms. Swan escorted Bert to his car in the dark, starry night; he had plans for Christmas Day in D.C., but he turned to her first.

"Listen to me. You've got to pull yourself together. Don't make it any harder for him. He shouldn't have to apologize to you for what he has to do. This was going to happen sooner or later unless we came up with some instant-victory strategy at the Pentagon, and you *know* the chances of that. Couples with much less going for them than you do are doing it without the drama, with no family support or with too many kids and not enough money. Do you want him to feel as guilty about leaving as you do about being 'bad luck'? No, I know you don't," he said to her bowed head. "So show him you are everything he thinks you are. And Merry Christmas."

Swan cried a little on his shoulder, then stepped back. "I can do that."

◆

Later Swan and Sam were in the old walnut bed under the quilts and silks in front of the fire once again. She snuggled against his big arm. She might as well give it a try right then.

"I've been such a crybaby about all of this," she began, tentatively. "I haven't even asked you how you feel about it. Are you . . . happy . . . to be going back or are you disappointed it wasn't Boblingen or Khe Sanh or Diego Garcia?"

"Well, I couldn't see putting in for another desk rotation at Quantico, even if it meant I could court you fulltime, not with my guys up the line," Sam said, contemplatively. "The taxpayer has sunk a lot of dough into me over the years, and it wasn't to make nice at NATO headquarters or play touch football at some Japanese marine base. When there are two wars going on, to be someplace else is to be Second Assistant Spear Carrier when the star is playing Hamlet center stage."

Swan looked at him in amazement: how differently they viewed things!

"If I weren't being such an idiot, you'd be happy to be going back?" she said.

"I suppose you could put it that way. Like with any job, when the boss says go, you go."

"You don't view it as bad luck?"

"Swan, bad luck is being hit by lightning," he said. "I'm a marine, a human weapon. I belong where my trade is . . . practiced."

"It's going to be your fourth tour. Aren't you worried about—" Swan stopped.

"Cracking up?" he supplied. "Like the major I'm replacing? No. It would have happened by now. That's no reflection on the guys who do, but many of them had personal problems before they enlisted, or have a history of substance abuse, or were so damned young . . . . Of course, it was hard to lose Hunt in Rashad—damn hard. I had about six months of dreams afterward, and I was there for most of that time. But I was a captain by then and had top L.T.s, and the best sergeants in the outfit watching my ass.

"Anyway, most injuries are to extremities, disfiguring but nonfatal; twenty-six percent are to the head and neck—they make up sixty-four percent of all deaths. These are the parts of the body not protected by body armor, obviously. If an IED is going to get you, it's going to get you. It isn't like dodging a bullet—" he grinned sardonically, "which requires some skill."

"You find that comforting."

"It's reality. Marines make up only six percent of all deaths. Pretty good odds, I think."

"For anyone not dating me," she said. She couldn't help it.

"Swan," he said, "I wouldn't trade these five months with you for any five years of my life up until now. You talk about all of my escapades, but at least you've known real love—Hunt, Carter . . .

me, I hope. A quickie marriage and one-night stands followed by months in desert shit holes don't equal happiness. After ten years, I'm the poster boy for combat fatigue with women, the wonked-out Vietnam veteran of love. Without Hunt and the Marines, I could never have won a second look from you, do you realize that? Be honest: why did you take me to the Scarab?"

"Why?" Swan was brought up short. "Well, I'd taken you to such stuffy, snobby little events: the Hospice thing, the rescue dinner. I figured I owed you something more . . . lively."

"That's not why," Sam said. "You knew it was my kind of place, what I'd be comfortable with—like a thousand bars in a hundred towns all over the world, Tulsa, Oceanside, Bankok, Melbourne. But you would never have been there with anyone in your crowd, certainly not with Hunt or Carter Roland."

"That's not true—Daniel goes; so does Fitch."

"Cousin Daniel is a drug addict," Sam said evenly, "and Fitch has his own thing going on. He's probably on a first-name basis with every coke distributor and unlicensed gun dealer within forty miles.

"But I'm not talking about them. Tell the truth: if you *had* been in the Scarab with a girlfriend and you'd seen me arrive on the Harley, long-haired, tattooed, muscle shirt, standing at the bar— would you have let me buy you a drink?"

He looked at her face.

"No," he said softly, "I didn't think so. I wouldn't have had a chance, not in a million years. It took ten years of social polishing by the Marines—and a dress uniform and a sharp haircut. Even then I needed somebody to die and hand you to me. If I don't meet you, I have nothing. I'm in the Scarab, hitting on skanks," he said. "The End."

She didn't move. He tried to get her interested in his body, but she was too wound up. So he changed things up.

"Listen," he said, seriously, "I think I'm beginning to get you, a little anyway. We've never talked about having a family or anything. After the condom fiasco, I've kept off this subject, but I'm assuming you've been using something, which is fine with me. But if you decide for your own reasons to stop, in the hopes that I'll leave you with a baby before I go, and you don't want to tell me, I'm okay with it. And if you want to talk about a family after we are married, I'm okay with that, too. I'm not going to melt down over things you do without telling me until you are ready."

She looked at him, amazed.

"You are beginning to get me a little," she said.

CHAPTER 8

The next morning, Boyd Junior made sure everyone was up with the sun. Mathilde had laid in breakfast and a superb roasted goose dinner (with leftovers from the night before in case anyone got hungry in between), then headed off to Mass and a well-deserved day off with her cousins and sister-in-law in Richmond. Edgar and Eduardo were with the Salvadoran community in nearby Sterling, with the college girl back-ups happy to handle horse duties for pay on Christmas Day.

Gifts were mostly fun, thoughtful, or unexpected, typical for families who basically could buy themselves whatever they wanted throughout the year. The Bolingtons had paid special attention to Sam: a bespoke sports jacket from The Custom Gentleman in D.C., and a raft of custom-made shirts, the first-made-to-order civilian clothes—clothes that actually fit—he'd ever had in his life. A handful of silk ties, and a wool topcoat rounded things out. There was nothing for him from Swan under the tree, but he said nothing about it. There was nothing for her from him, either.

A treasure trove of toys and goodies from Santa provided the family with the pleasure of a delighted Boyd Junior ripping open boxes, pounding a red drum, pretending to pedal a toy car suitable for a little boy twice his age. After breakfast around the fire, Hetty smiled at everyone.

"Well, you might as well know—a little stranger's on the way in June: either Bolington Hexell Delaney or Lucinda Swan Delaney. Boyd Junior is getting a sibling."

That news made Christmas gifts anti-climactic, but after lunch, Sam said, "Sorry, everyone: I'm afraid I've got a delivery that can't be put off. Orders straight from Santa. I'll be back in a couple of hours."

Swan stood up: "Funny—same guy has sent me on an errand. I'll be back a little sooner, though."

Everyone oohed and aah-ed as Swan and Sam exchanged raised-eyebrow looks and jumped into their vehicles.

Swan drove the dually to Virgilia Osmond's Stone Chimneys; she backed it up to the door of the tractor shed and gently maneuvered the hitch under a small vehicle trailer. A cinch. She was pulling into the Belle Everley driveway in under an hour. Spaulding came out first, followed by Boyd and Hetty.

"This is it? His pride and joy?" Spaulding said, at a bit of a loss.

Swan looked at the motorcycle with satisfaction.

"This is it. I paid Captain Edwards enough for him to find a newer model and laid on the old Bolington charm until he caved. I've hidden it at Virgilia's all week."

"Swan, do you think he'll be mad you spent so much?" Hetty asked the question they all had in their minds.

"Don't know; don't care," she said. "We've agreed he's going to leave all of his things here when he goes to Oceanside and give up the Quantico apartment; the Marines can pay to move the Fat Boy cross country so he can ride it for two months in the good weather and enjoy himself before he's deployed. Plus, I can ride with him when I visit out there."

Boyd was impressed.

"He is going to be blown away, absolutely," he said, admiringly.

"That's what I was going for," Swan said.

An hour later, Sam's pick-up was back. They heard the driver's door slam as he got out.

He gave Swan a long look as she came to the steps.

"Merry Christmas, Major," she beamed. He looked at the Harley in disbelief.

"Son of a fucking bitch," he gasped. He looked like he was going to run over to the trailer and kiss the motorcycle right in front of them.

"Now, that's not very Christmasy-language, is it?" She came down the steps and hugged him.

"Thank you, thank you, thank you," he said. An enormous bark boomed from the F-250 passenger side. It was Swan's turn to look stunned.

Sam grinned and turned back to the truck. He opened the passenger door and grabbed the leash of a ninety-pound black German Shepherd.

"Meet Flagg, military working dog, retired: he's yours."

Swan didn't move.

"He's a four-year-old explosives detection dog who has been mustered out," Sam said. "Seems that his female handler in Iraq got a medical discharge and Flagg, here, didn't cotton to working with a handler of the male persuasion, despite months of retraining. He would work, but not up to the standard required. So Flagg was categorized as expendable military property, meaning he could be adopted by the handler, or by someone else in the military. She couldn't take him, so a few months ago, I put in for him. I went to Dulles to pick him up from Lackland Airforce Base, where he's been since his return from Iraq.

"He's yours—technically mine, but I used this address for the paperwork and, since we'll be married in a few months, it's all above board. 'Course, these guys only know the German Schutzhund commands."

Swan looked at the dog. She could see his wonderful character in his face, calm, standing his ground but not challenging anyone in his new environment. He had eyes only for her.

"*Sprechen ze Deutsch, mein hund*?" she asked the dog quietly, reaching out her hand.

Sam grinned knowingly. "Merry Christmas, Chiclet."

That night, after the Delaneys and Spaulding had left, Swan and Moore tucked themselves into bed, with Flagg at its foot.

"*Platz*—lie down," Swan said to him quietly, translating for Sam's benefit, and the Shepherd obediently settled down onto the thick carpet with a big sigh. "*Bleib*—stay," she said. "*Guden hund.*"

"They've been kenneled all their lives, but I hear they adjust really quickly. When you said you missed Nell, it got me thinking. He can keep an eye on you when I'm not here."

"He is the best present in the world," she said. "I can't believe you engineered it without me knowing."

"Well, I did check it out with Eduardo; I wanted to make sure you guys had a secure kennel in case it was needed, and you'll find the mare barn has about two hundred pounds of dog food, dog beds, everything you'll need til the stores open and you get a chance to get whatever else you want, all on me."

"Eduardo must have told you I knew the Schutzhund commands: I used them with Nell. You and Eduardo seem to have a thing going," Swan observed slyly. "You two are in cahoots too much for my liking these days."

"I think I'd like to get in your cahoots instead. Let me see if I can find them." Sam pulled her to him. "*Platz*."

◆

The week after Christmas they spent packing up Sam's stereo, flat screen, exercise equipment, Mercedes, and truck for storage at Belle Everley and readying the few things he was taking to Oceanside for the military movers. The weather was mild enough to ride the hog around Waverly's hard-surface roads. By unspoken agreement, they kept their conversations light, the heavy going they'd put off until he left Oceanside in March.

Flagg proved remarkably mellow about his new life outside the Green Zone. He bonded with Swan seemingly overnight, and after he spent a few tentative days on a long leather leash tethered to her belt, she began to let him loose. Staying close to Swan always seemed better than straying from her, in Flagg's mind, an attitude that amused Sam.

"Christ, he has it as bad as I do," he grumbled, stumbling over Flagg's body velcroed to Swan's legs in front of the big screen TV. "I don't have to worry about another guy; you couldn't fit a piece of paper between the two of you."

"Hey, we're in love, aren't we, buddy?" Swan crooned to the dog. "He deserves spoiling—he put in his time chasing bad guys, just like you. Now he gets his retirement." Flagg thumped his egg-beater-like tail at her voice.

"Speaking of which," Sam cleared his throat, " I don't want you to freak out in advance."

Swan stopped tickling Flagg's taut belly and looked up.

"I'm going to change my medical power of attorney from my mother to you when I get to Oceanside," he said calmly, "and I'm making you my executor and beneficiary in my will."

He stopped her from interrupting with a look.

"It makes sense since they could take Flagg back; he's nontransferable otherwise. So don't freak out. We're going to be married in a few months anyway, and you will become my next of kin. This just tidies things up before I ship out."

She sighed.

"Well, let's decide where you are going to be buried, then. Arlington would be convenient, since I like all my fiancés in one place if possible. Too bad you are due back before Hunt's death date; I could decorate both graves in one trip."

"I'm thinking this means that you're okay with this plan," he said cautiously.

She shrugged. "Sure, no problem, I already have the black outfit."

"You're taking this better than I thought you would; I'm impressed."

"Hey, I'm back in the Marines, now, baby," she said.

They spent a quiet New Year's Eve at Belle Everley, by choice. Sam was leaving less than forty-eight hours later. Swan had three trips to Oceanside planned for the sixty days Sam would be there. January and February were her busiest time of year, foaling out all of the high-priced Thoroughbred mares Swan owned or boarded. She typically never left the farm then: with The Fortress an elderly matron carrying a foal potentially worth five hundred thousand dollars, there was no higher priority for her than that safe delivery, they agreed. Swan typically hired foal watchers and extra stall muckers for these weeks to spell her, Kezia, and Eduardo and to deal with the extra work that stalling ten mares and new foals around the clock would entail.

Sam occupied Swan's time with discussions of the wedding details he supposed, naïvely, absorbed her thoughts. She had to conceal her utter lack of interest in the ludicrous exercise of planning a third wedding when neither of the previous two had come to pass.

"Well, at least you will finally meet the mother at the wedding," Spaulding said sensibly,"unless—"

"Oh, I have no intention of waiting til then," Swan said. "One of these return trips from Oceanside is going to have a stop in Corpus. The poor woman deserves to see her daughter-in-law in time to voice her opinion before it is too late. If I heard my only son was going to marry someone on her third fiancé, I'd sure want to see her before the wedding day, wouldn't you?"

"Don't you want Sam to decide when you meet her?" Spaulding asked, but she saw Swan's mind was made up.

◆

The morning of January third, Swan drove Sam, in uniform, to Dulles for the general aviation flight to Oceanside. She wore one of Moore's favorite dresses, short, cheerful, in raspberry wool, and the ruby earrings. She left her hair loose; he liked it that way best. She took Flagg with them, in his old K-9 service jacket, for moral support, and he passed into the terminal without challenge.

"I'll call you when I get there," Sam said calmly as they called his flight at the gate. "God knows what the apartment is going to be like, but it will do for sixty days."

"Sounds like a plan," Swan said, determined not to get herself worked up.

"Chiclet, try to see it from my perspective: it's just like Bert catching the six-thirty Metro into the Pentagon; or Boyd getting on the two ninety-five bypass going to the medical center. Really." His eyes drilled into hers for signs he was convincing her.

"I know," she said, but she felt the back of her throat begin to close. "Let's not talk about it any more."

"Swan, it's going to be fine," Sam tried again.

"Please. I mean it. Not helpful." She was thinking of other Virginia women who had said good-bye to men on their way to Valley Forge, Manassas, Gettysburg, the Marne, Normandy, Bastogne, Khe Sahn, Saigon, Kuwait City, Baghdad, Herat. Only the lies would have been different: "It's just like catching the stagecoach to Trenton—" or "It's just like catching the train to Catlett's Station—"

He wrapped her in his arms, lifting her far off the ground so he could whisper to her.

"I wish we could turn around and get back into your nice old bed," he murmured. "I should have collapsed the damn thing last night, once and for all, to give you something to remember me by."

She managed a sickly imitation of a smile. "Your performance was the stuff of legends, no need to bust up the furniture."

"Keep your cell phone on. I don't want to rely on Mathilde and that damned phone in the entranceway. Although the hall does have one asset: I saw the picture Spaulding took of us last week is now on the table."

"Yep, it's there for the duration," she said, but immediately regretted the ambiguity of the last word. "Please take care of yourself, on the hog especially."

"That would be perfect: to take myself out on the Five before I even get to Kandahar." He turned to Flagg, ruffling his ears, "I'm leaving you in charge, Private."

Last call: Swan just held him tighter, reprising the embrace of two hundred thousand loved ones of two hundred thousand service members before her.

"I'll call you," he said. "Everything is going to be fine. Stay away from Fitch, will you, please?" and then he was gone.

Swan started back toward the parking area. Flagg pressed himself against her, but the force field of the big black military dog cleared a wide path in front of them like a canine mine sweeper.

"I should be getting better at saying good-bye: I've had so much damn practice," she muttered. The dog looked up.

"Flagg, *Aus*," she said and they were on their way home.

◆

The next day, the first call was from Fitch.

"Okay, I see it as my patriotic duty to amuse you now that you are on your own."

"No need. I've got mares to—"

"Yeah, yeah, blah blah blah, too bad," he interrupted. "Let's drive Hurricane and Hollywood all the way into Waverly unescorted, like Willowby and Mary Anne Dashwood in *Sense and Sensibility*. Or we could see the *Twilight* movie marathon at the Waverly Cinema and neck in the balcony."

"Sounds too much like my stunt at the Scarab, but I've got a better idea if you really are fixated on this."

"Ouch. I am. Lay it on me."

"I want to go to Furnace Mountain and see Mike. I want to talk to Oliver in person now that the colt's been there for a few days. Decca may be there, and you adore her."

"The beautiful Mrs. Lentz? Fifty looking thirty, a goddess among women. When shall we go?"

"Kezia promises me The Fortress is still three weeks away from delivery, and she's our first one due. The weather is supposed to be clear for the next few days. Frankly, I could use a pick me up: let's go tomorrow. But with one understanding," Swan warned.

"No groping?"

Swan sighed. "That's a given. No—that you let Townsend know this is just a pity date," she said, patiently but firmly, "or we could bring her along."

"I'll call the kid and fill her in. She gets her wrist looked at for the last time tomorrow anyway, I think. She goes back to school at the end of the week."

"I'll drive," Swan said, "and I'm bringing Flagg."

"Christ, between the engagement ring and *der Reichstaghund*, I'm not going to stand much of a chance, am I?" Fitch said, disgusted. "I suppose the chastity belt is locked and loaded as well."

"This from a man dating an eighteen-year-old," Swan sighed. "You are like Bluebeard. At least she's out of prep school now."

◆

The next morning, Fitch arrived in the roadster at six for the two-hour trip to Furnace Mountain, in the northeast corner of Maryland. Fitch seemed determined to be on his best behavior. He was tweedy in a custom-made hacking jacket—and gallant.

"I've brought you a late Christmas gift," he said tentatively, as he got into the dually. He gave Flagg, in the back of the extended cab, a baleful look: "God, the hound from hell. He's not going to bite my head off from the back seat, is he?"

He handed her a wrapped box.

"I have nothing for you," Swan protested.

"What a surprise. Open it," he said.

A pair of hunter green leather gauntlets, butter soft and beautifully stitched and fringed.

"They match your green Vogels," Fitch explained. "I had them made up in New York two months ago by blind French nuns, but that was before—"

Before her engagement.

"You are a darling," she breathed. She put them on immediately; with the melton Mason's frock coat, hunter green wool pants, and black paddock boots, she looked like an exotic bird.

"About time you were beginning to notice."

Furnace Mountain was ten times the size of the Waverly Training Center and attracted big name trainers, who sent runners to New York, Delaware, Virginia, and Pennsylvania tracks. On 350 acres of prime Maryland farmland, it included twenty privately owned barns, of frame, metal, adobe, each with a distinctive style, as well as tracks, gallops, and a veterinary center. The weather was mild and appealing 90 percent of the year, with just a few potentially snowy weeks in January and early February.

They drove along the winding main road, past barns with romantic names: Pebblewood, Featherbed, the Grove. They stopped in front of Green Forest I and II, stuccoed, long, low structures with lovely landscaping and welcoming office/reception rooms at their entrances.

Oliver Lentz owned the two barns outright. They were filled with top race horses, including three full brothers to Kentucky Derby winner Cartouche, owned by Thurgood and Grace Templeton of Pennsylvania. Lentz was a legendary horseman and married to one of the fabled racing Carrington sisters. He had trained Serve the Guns during her racing career—Punch and Judy, too—and the Fortress gelding Broadsword for another owner.

"Swan, dear," Oliver Lentz, a handsome, athletic man of fifty-five, approached the dually with outstretched arms, "soon-to-be Mrs. Moore—I couldn't be happier for you. And, Master, always a pleasure to see you," Oliver smiled at Fitch. "You are looking splendid."

"Oliver, it's been a long time," Fitch offered Lentz his right hand. "I hope the lovely Decca is here today."

"Sorry, she's back at our farm—foaling season," Oliver said.

"Where I should be," Swan added, "but I had to see Mike. What do you think, Oliver?"

"Oh, too soon to tell, particularly with these big ones," Oliver said smoothly, repeating the conventional wisdom. "But I like his attitude, kind of like this nice guy here." Oliver looked at Flagg standing at Swan's side."Of course, the turf is a natural for him, given his late start in the year and his breeding, but we'll get him on the work tab and see him on the all-weather surface."

They walked down the center aisle of the immaculate barn, surrounded by the sound of horses busy at their feed tubs and hay nets. Suddenly, there was a familiar nicker.

"My beautiful boy," Swan said delightedly. Mike's huge black head popped up, his eyes bright with recognition, from a stall in the center of the barn.

"Christ, just like Black Beauty," Fitch teased. "He does look grand, Oliver."

The trainer pulled the colt out of his stall and stood him up in the aisle way. "He's eating good, drinking good, walking good. No complaints. We have all his films sent up by Jerusha. I've got a new girl to start riding him in the morning; she's got a sweet touch. A lot like you, Swan, so he should take to her." A sturdy girl in chaps, helmet, paddock boots and protective vest, toting a saddle, appeared in the aisle as if on command.

"Hope Fluellen, this is Miss Bolington," Oliver said. Hope was five-foot six and one hundred and thirty-five pounds of riding power; she had an open, friendly face, with lots of blonde curly hair tamed by braids.

"With me, Mike likes to think he's running the show a little," Swan said modestly, "probably my fault, but he will rate kindly if he senses you two are on the same side. His mom was the same way—a little light-mouthed," she finished up apologetically. Swan ran her hand over Mike's blooming coat approvingly.

A young Englishman popped his head out of an adjoining stall.

"Swan, this is Philip St. John Cross," Oliver said, using the British pronunciation "Sinjon," "my assistant trainer. He'll oversee the string here while I'm campaigning the Templetons' colt."

"A pleasure, Miss," Sinjon said, doffing his cap. "He's a grand colt."

"You can't beat The Fortress on the bottom—and of course, Storm Cloud," Oliver continued, turning back to Mike. The dam line was on the bottom half of a pedigree chart. "I just wish I'd had a chance at her twenty years ago myself. She was something else at up to a mile and a half. Now, let's look at my plan for Mike and see if we can win some races to cheer you up while Major Moore is away."

They admired the three siblings—aged two, three and four— of Cartouche: Roisterous had made a late start due to injury; the three-year-old Calypso was pointed to the Kentucky Derby; Devotee had just joined the Lentz string the week before. In the office Oliver described a couple of allowance races at Delaware and Maryland tracks in late February and early March for Swan's consideration. Swan's cellphone rang. She looked at the number. California.

"I've got to take this," she said and stepped outside for better reception.

"Hi." Sam's voice filled her.

"Hi," she said softly. "You made it."

"Yeah. Three hours late into Oceanside, then another two hours into the apartment. I fell into bed, then on to the base for an all-day meeting yesterday, although being on East Coast time still helps. It's oh-dawn-thirty out here."

Two horses being led behind Swan whinnied at each other.

"Where are you? Down at the mare barn?" Sam asked. "Aren't you at the house eating breakfast?"

"I'm in Maryland," Swan said, "at Furnace Mountain. I decided I needed to visit my other boyfriend, Oscar Mike."

"How's the Mike-man liking Maryland?"

"Swan, honey, we are going to get coffee. Extra light, no sugar for you, right?" Fitch called from the aisle way.

"Well, that didn't take long." Sam's voice was like ice.

"He came along for the ride," Swan said to appease him. "I asked him to come."

"You have to give him credit. I told you he'd wait me out," Sam sighed.

"Don't. Look, I've got to go, Oliver is a busy guy and he's waiting on me to wind things up here. I'll call you tonight? What is a good time?"

"Anytime is a good time for you, Chiclet," he said gently. "But try to shake loose of Fitch. Please."

"You're my guy," she said, "my human guy, anyway. I've got Mike and Flagg, too."

"I wouldn't mind if Flagg had been attack trained about now," he said glumly.

"How about me? You are surrounded by eighteen-year-olds in thong bikinis and I'm dressed like the Michelin man."

"More layers to take off; more fun," he growled, but she had put him in a better mood, she could tell. "Love you."

"Love you more."

Swan clicked the phone closed.

"How's Major Shoulder Porn?" Fitch said, coming up behind her with a giant paper coffee cup from the track kitchen.

"Fine—missing me," she said lightly. "Let's meet Mike's new groom before we head home."

The ride back was companionable. "I hear Hetty is expecting the next young lord of the Bolington empire," Fitch said when they were heading south, out of the Furnace Mountain driveway. "I'm sure Boyd is happy."

"Yes, we all are."

"She'll have her figure back then in time for the wedding. I'm available as a bridesmaid. I look good in fall colors—just a hint. I'm not going to hold my breath for an invitation to be a groomsman."

"Thanks for the offer," Swan said sweetly. "We're looking at the first week of October. At the house. Small."

"Small can be good. I'm not going to pester you, but I do want to make sure your spirits stay up in the meantime. An attack dog isn't going to be enough companionship, despite your major's best intentions. I don't want to hear that you are sitting home watching *Pandora's Box* over and over again, and I'm as big a Louise Brooks fan as the next guy.

"So let's make a standing date: once a week—something fun. We'll work it around foaling season," he said. "Don't think I'm carrying a torch—I've got a perfectly good little cream puff of my own in Townsend. I'll keep the gossips satisfied that I'm not trying to steal you away from one of our fighting men."

"Fitch, I know you mean well—"

"Good—it's settled."

When Swan got home in the afternoon, she checked on The Fortress: all was well. The house was empty. Swan was giving

Mathilde more time off after the hectic autumn. She wanted only a light dinner on a tray most nights, and Mathilde spent them with the Catholic Ladies Relief Society or with her Richmond relatives.

Swan waited until ten P.M. to call Sam.

"Did you have a good day?" he began but didn't wait for an answer. "So is he gone? Fitch?"

"No, he's here in bed. I try to betray all my fiancés with other men before I kill them, preferably within forty-eight hours of their departure," Swan said calmly.

"God, I deserve that," he groaned. "I'm never going to make it the three weeks til I see you at this rate."

"Not at this rate."

"This is the longest we've been apart—physically—in months." He sounded low. "I need something before you come out here—a new photo."

"I thought this was 'just a day at the office,'" Swan said softly, worried.

"I want to take the horse show photo with me, but it has a lot of miles on it; a new one would be nice, too," he said, sounding more like himself. "Nothing too raunchy—"

"Yeah, I have a lot of those," she said sarcastically, "but I'll see what I can come up with."

"How's The Fortress?" Sam said, but he meant *when will she foal so you can come out here.*

"She's doing fine, but not close enough to put on foal watch. I've got two boarders who look as far along as she does—" Swan launched into a short update on the horse side of things, then how Hetty was feeling and newsy notes, but soon she got to the point.

"What do they want you to do on this deployment? Kill bad guys and pacify the locals? Pacify the bad guys and kill the locals? Or what?"

"Sounds like you've been sitting in on our strategy meetings," Sam said wearily. "I don't know enough yet to tell you, but the staff officers I've met seem to have their heads on straight."

◆

That night, Swan had the Marriage in Heaven dream for the second time—Carter, Hunt, and Sam in their dress uniforms and her coming down the aisle to all three of them. The next morning she pondered whether she could sound blasé enough to tell someone about it—Spaulding or Hetty—so they could laugh about it and neutralize her fears. The dream would have been more reassuring if Carter and Hunt had been onlookers or trying to prevent her marriage, but to have all three of them shoulder to shoulder—any Psych 101 student could figure that out.

So she said nothing. She continued the new routine: horse business during the day, visits from Kezia, phone calls to mare owners and from Oliver Lentz with updates; weekly lunches with Spaulding at the Willow's Edge, chats with Hetty; nightly calls to Sam; and jaunts with Fitch that were frequent enough and public enough to begin a low buzz of talk around Waverly. Her defenders were vocal: Patty and Lorenzo; Kezia Hardaway; Mathilde and Eduardo, of course, who through the network of farm employees around town made it clear that Fitch never spent the night at Belle Everley and the mistress never spent the night away from it. Flagg was her constant companion, and Swan's staff doubted the dog would let Fitch, or any other man, make any moves in any case.

Swan remained ignorant of the talk, primarily since no one, not even Spaulding, dared to bring it up to her. She slowly narrowed her focus to The Fortress, as the mare grew low-bellied, irascible, and uncooperative, sure signs of impending motherhood. The old matron was now being watched by a foal cam mounted in the stall and hooked up to monitors in the house and the barn office, where Eduardo and the hired foal watchers began sleeping in shifts. Night after night, The Fortress's episodic tail rubbing, yawning, rolling, backing up against the wooden stall walls, looking at her belly, groaning, lying down and getting back up again, were observed and charted, without any signs of a foal. Kezia Hardaway stopped by every few days, as befitting a patient virtually made of solid gold.

Chapter 9

At the end of the third week of January, the old mare had had enough. One midnight, she laid down and gave birth to a full brother to Oscar Mike. The foal was big and healthy; the mare her usual ferociously maternal self. Swan and her team had little time to congratulate each other, however, since two of the boarder mares foaled out in the following forty-eight hours.

It was four days later before Swan could schedule her first trip to Oceanside. She felt guilty about leaving Eduardo, even for four days, but she was wild to see Sam. She'd had the Marriage in Heaven dream at least twice a week since he'd been gone, and she hoped that lying next to him would eradicate it from her subconscious. She found a direct flight for late the next morning and bought her ticket.

"I'll be there tomorrow afternoon," she promised Sam.

Swan tried to be happy. As eager as she was to see Sam, she knew that it meant only that his departure was that much closer. She put Flagg in his kennel next to the house; Eduardo would care for him while she was gone. It was so painful, so familiar a feeling that, when she saw him waiting at the gate, she threw herself at him. Feeling his arms around her, feeling him lift her up the way he had when he had left Dulles, feeling the urgency of his kiss—it was as though they had been apart for months, not weeks.

"Do you want something to eat, or do you want to go straight to the apartment?" he asked when they were able to catch a breath.

"The apartment," she said without hesitation. She felt the way she had in the parking lot of the Scarab, attracted and aroused in a way she had never felt with another man. Sam had borrowed a car, since the Harley had no room for her bag, and they drove toward Camp Pendleton smiling at each other like schoolkids.

"If this were my car, I'd pull over right now and throw you on your back here in broad daylight," Sam said. "As it is, we've got a twenty-five minute drive to think about it, which may be almost as much fun." He looked at her admiringly. "At least you dressed for the weather here: thank God bare legs' season is back. It makes the move out here worth it." He reached over and ran his hand up her calf and thigh in his old way, his caress tickling and arousing her as it always did.

"Careful: let's not have an accident on the Five," she warned, but she almost imperceptibly opened her legs to his hand. "Oh, God," he said, and for the next few minutes he silently explored her, slipping his hand into her silken underthings as he drove, then under them, until she shuddered with pleasure.

Then it was her hand doing the exploring: "Don't look down," she teased him, breathlessly, "eyes on the road at all times." She lubricated her hand between her legs and began to move it on the already engorged length inside his trousers. He was so hungry for her it was easy to satisfy him long before they got to the base.

"Christ, what a drive," he moaned, as they set their clothing to rights to clear the sentries into the beachfront base. "The sad thing is, I'm already hard for you again."

Swan laughed; she reached for him. "Too bad we have bucket seats and the shift console between us." They stopped at the sentry post on their way into the compound.

"No, we can't, damn it—surveillance," he said. "One hand job in fifteen minutes is enough. I'm getting into a real fucking bed with you, Chiclet." They pulled up to an apartment complex that was the twin of the one at Quantico. "Won't you please come in and then take your clothes off?"

Once the door to the second floor apartment was closed behind them, however, he wanted to take everything off himself. He took his time, under the circumstances, lingering over the lemon silk camisole, bra, and panties while she unbuttoned his shirt, unbuckled his belt, whimpering as she struggled with everything that made the uniform a challenge to speedy disrobing.

Then they were in bed and his mouth was kissing her, between her breasts, down her belly, and between her legs, his tongue probing and caressing in its own sweet way. She looked down at him, pressing her hands against the plates of muscle on his shoulders beneath her, then down his spine, and grabbing hold of him when his tongue found what he'd been seeking. She shuddered again. When she pulled him back up to her, in one thrust he began the long and deep rhythm they had perfected between them. They murmured their own little endearments for each other, nothing profound or witty, just heartfelt, tender.

Eventually Sam rolled off her and looked down at her mass of hair spread across his chest.

"There has never been anyone like you, Swannie, not for me—ever," he said, tangling his fingers into her thick mane.

"You think that now," she said, snuggling into the great cavern of his arms.

"I know you feel the same way about me—I can feel it. Why don't you think it can be the same for me?" Sam asked.

"Is it?" she asked, just to hear him say it again. "There have been so many before—"

"There has never been anyone like you, not for me." He kissed her neck under her heavy, loose hair, inhaling its scent. "What do you want to do while you're out here?" he asked.

"Oh, please," she said.

"Other than this." He kissed her throat and shoulder.

She lifted her ribcage so her breasts pressed against the fine blond hair on his chest. She gently rubbed them up, then down; up, then down. His mouth followed them, found her nipples, and he began to move on her again.

"You can't be serious . . . not yet—" Her voice was teasing, but she wriggled back in response, just to make sure.

"Turn around," he said hoarsely, "Turn around, wife."

It was dark when they untangled themselves.

"Do you want to go out so I can show you off, or should I call for take out?" he said.

"If we go out, we have to shower," she said dreamily, "and if we shower, we'll just start this up all over again. We'll never get anywhere."

"Take out then."

While they waited for their food, he started in on updates from Waverly.

"So you're happy with this new foal? Everything is okay?" he asked. "You're not really going to name him Battering Ram, after me, are you?"

"All okay." She sensed he was really interested in somebody else. "Fitch is his usual annoying self, but he is being a perfect gentleman. And, no, I'm not naming the colt Battering Ram." She laughed. "I'm going to ask The Jockey Club for Trebuchet, with Holdfast as the alternate."

"Have you made any progress on the wedding stuff?"

"Enough that, if you show up at Belle Everley on October 2, you should expect to leave a married man." His smile was so genuine, it touched her.

"Fitch asked to be bridesmaid. I said okay."

"Yeah, I bet he'd take the groom slot, too, if that happens to open up," Sam groused, as the Chinese food arrived. But he let it go. "You're sure you don't want to see anything while you're here?"

"Why would I want to tour the countryside when we could be together like this?" she asked. "When you are gone, do you think I'll want to remember the early architecture of Oceanside? If, God forbid, something happens—"

"Don't."

"I won't want to reproach myself that I wasted our time together. We've had a few months, not years, like other couples. I just want to be with you," she cried. "What if I'm snowed in, or orders change and you go over early, and this is our only visit before you deploy?" She began to tear up.

He put his arms around her, his mood not playful anymore.

"God, I'm sorry to put you through this," he said.

"I'm okay, just—" She pulled herself back together. "I'd like to talk to you about something now, so you can think about it before I go back. I'd like to stop in Corpus and meet your parents, just a quick howdy, so it isn't weird at the wedding . . . for that to be the first time."

Sam sighed.

"Every family isn't like yours, Swan," he said carefully. "When my father was drinking, my mother chose him over me, time after time. I don't hold it against her. It was her choice. When he died, she remarried within nine months and left Buena Vista, warehousing me with a neighbor to finish high school. The school counselor helped me fill out my app to Texas Tech; I packed up and left on my own, with a bus ticket to Lubbock paid for by my high school football coach. When I graduated, when I got married to Lorraine, not a word from her. When I joined the Marines, graduated from O.C.S., I was the only member of the class who didn't have one person in the audience to see me do it.

"I'm her only kid, and I just don't make her list of priorities. So I don't have a lot of interest in reestablishing some family relationship," Sam said in a dead voice. "I don't want you to go there thinking you are going to be welcomed with open arms as the daughter she never had, or something. And she is not going to be at Belle Everley when we get married."

Swan's heart went out to him: going to war time after time with no one to care whether he came back or not. No wonder he had fallen in love with a picture.

"My beautiful boy," she crooned, pulling him to her. "I'm going to make it all up to you."

They laid in each other's arms for a long time. Then Swan said, "I've got lots of well-meaning, nosy, bossy relatives, so I'll give you some of mine. They'll call you every day if you have a head cold; inquire if you are overdrawn at the bank; advise you on your love life; and basically make damned nuisances of themselves. That will be my wedding gift to you."

Swan slipped out of bed and walked barefoot to the hall.

"But, for now, I've brought the picture you wanted."

She pulled an envelope of reinforced cardboard out of her purse. In it was a photo taken by Fitch just before Mike's move to Furnace Mountain on an unusually mild day. She was sitting on the colt bareback and barefoot, her little saffron silk skirt hiked above her knees. The colt's eyes were wide, his neck arched, looking as though he was about to launch himself into the air. Her hair fell loose around her, almost to her waist. It seemed to tangle in his mane. Swan was looking down into the camera lens, with an expression both humorous and triumphant. She looked like a model on one of those romance novel covers, but only a model who had gone to rodeo college could have sat on Mike.

Sam shook his head gently when he saw it.

"You and I are going to have sex a thousand times when we get to the desert," he said solemnly, addressing the photo directly. "Or, at least my hand and I are going to have sex, and you are going to watch us."

"I take it you like it," Swan chuckled gently. She burrowed deep against him, resting her cheek on his massive bicep as though it was a piece of furniture. "These pillows are terrible; let me sleep on your muscle."

◆

For the rest of her visit, they stayed in the sparsely furnished apartment eating take-out, soaking in the bathtub, watching movies, taking the Harley for spins after dark through the warm seacoast town, everything that was impossible at Belle Everley with its relentless, exhausting, absorbing demands. Swan didn't ask how Sam got the four days off; he went out for meetings each day but returned within hours. Sleeping in his arms kept the Marriage in Heaven away. When she got on the plane to Dulles, she made a reservation for a return trip in two weeks.

At the farm, The Fortress and her new son were in the pink, Flagg was happy to see her, and all else was right in her world. All, except that the Marriage in Heaven became virtually a nightly occurrence. She still wasn't ready to discuss it with anyone, but she did talk to Hetty in an oblique way when she told her sister about her trip.

"If all soldiers were women," Swan said, "there wouldn't be any ground wars like Afghanistan and Iraq. If women had been ordered to storm the beaches at Normandy, to charge into a hailstorm of fire, not one woman would have gotten off the landing crafts in the Atlantic. We'd all have said, 'Hey, this isn't going to work for us. We need a Plan B, like a volunteer to sleep with Hitler and poison him.' That is something a woman would do."

"Men will never refuse an order to go forward and risk looking like a coward to their buddies," Hetty agreed, "they'd always rather die. They would stand in line to die on Normandy to prove they aren't cowards."

"Self defense—a woman could do that."

"When you're in it, maybe everything seems like self defense," Hetty said sensibly.

◆

Fitch took Swan to the Reynard for dinner the Thursday after she returned. When he came to pick her up in the Porsche, a manila envelope was on the passenger seat.

"*Pour toi*," he said, "but, fair warning: it has to do with your good major and his previous life. If you don't want to know, don't open it; throw it out the window and we'll go to dinner."

"What woman alive would do that?" Swan asked, reaching for the envelope. His hand stopped her.

"Ayn Rand said, 'Tell me what a man finds sexually attractive and I will tell you his entire philosophy of life,'" he said.

Swan's blood went cold. She reached for the envelope. It held a magazine. *It least it isn't surveillance photos,* she thought. She tore open the envelope: *AfterDark,* an eleven-year-old issue. Swan was so worked up she still hadn't connected the dots. She looked at Fitch.

"Centerfold," he said. Swan briefly considered throwing the magazine out the window. Fitch read her perfectly; he reached to take the issue from her. She let it fall open at the center stitching instead.

Miss November. Lorrie Haver, age 21. Hennaed red hair, curly, piled on her head, early Brigitte Bardot style. *Green eyes; 125 lbs., 5'9". Hometown: Lubbock, Texas, vital statistics: 38DD-23-36.* Slim legs a mile long, teeth like pearls, saucy, but with a demure downward-cast to her eyes. A spectacular vixen.

Swan starred at the double-page spread, fixating on the pneumatic bosom while she arranged her face into an expression she hoped was unreadable. Fitch watched, impressed.

"There are other photos," he said.

"Are her breasts smaller in any of them?"

"You wish. All natural, too. Her favorite band is the Grateful Dead: who would have pegged her for a Deadhead? Movie: *Top Gun*. Ugh. No wonder he divorced her."

"She divorced him," Swan corrected him mechanically. "What else?"

"Goal: to be famous. Quote, I love a man who knows what he wants and how to get it, unquote." Fitch seemed to be reciting from memory.

"Five nine," Swan repeated. "That would be six feet in heels."

"They must have looked great together," Fitch murmured, still watching her.

Swan sighed.

"At least her goal wasn't 'Getting my ex back,'" she said.

"It's a gift," Fitch said, referring to the magazine. "Take it or toss it."

She took it.

When she told Hetty the next day, her sister was speechless for a long minute.

"Damn," she finally said. "Five nine?"

"My thought exactly," Swan said.

"Well, she must be . . . thirty-two. Her boobs are probably almost to her knees by now. At least you have six years on her. But she is definitely out of the picture, correct?"

"Yes. But when you see this layout, you will see how very much of her is *in* the picture. I don't have anything she doesn't have bigger and better of."

◆

The next Thursday Fitch took her to the Reynard again, this time with Townsend Brooke, who was home for the weekend, at Swan's insistence. The teenager was so smitten it was painful to witness. She said virtually nothing for the whole meal. She had worn a dress that looked like something Swan might have chosen if she shopped in a Rodeo Drive boutique. Townsend even seemed to be growing her hair out, although, it would never be as thick or long as Swan's.

Just before she left for Camp Pendleton, Swan got a call from Sinjon Cross with an update on Mike.

"He's beginning to gallop with authority," Cross said happily. "We'll breeze in the next couple of weeks, probably three furlongs—twenty-five-and-twelve kind of thing. See if he wants to be a racehorse."

This cheered Swan immensely. Then it was back to Oceanside. Swan had mulled over the Marriage in Heaven and the centerfold situation on the flight out, and when she and Sam were in bed the first night, she took the plunge.

"I've been having a dream," she began tentatively.

"What kind of dream, Chiclet? Winning the Derby?" he teased.

"No."

Sam took the warning. He gathered her up tightly.

"Tell me."

"I'm coming down the aisle at my wedding. I'm not sure exactly where, but I'm in a big white dress. When I get to the alter, all three of you are there: Hunt Lee, Carter, and you, in uniform, smiling and waiting for me. And I'm totally okay with that, until I realize that all of us are in Heaven. Then I wake up. It's not a nightmare exactly, but it is not good, either." She stopped. "It is . . . scary."

"Do you think that because of the dream I'm going to die," Sam asked quietly, "or that because of the dream *you're* going to die? At least it sounds like we all had a nice wedding together." He was joking, but one look at her face and he gave it up.

"Honey, for my first three months in Afghanistan as an L.T., I dreamed about cutting off bin Laden's head and eating it with a knife and fork. Every night. And it was a *good* dream," he said grimly. "Eventually it went away. Anxiety. That's what it was."

"How many people have you killed, do you think?"

"Directly? Probably fifteen, if you don't include the villages where I called down fire as a company commander. Almost all in Iraq—we all got us some. RPG nests. How do you think I got promoted so quickly? I rocked and rolled. My C.O. wrote me up for the Bronze Star. Anyone can get any commendation if it's written up the right way." He shrugged.

Swan still looked pensive.

"What else?" he asked.

"Nothing, really. Let's go to sleep."

"What else, Chiclet? We're running out of time to talk about . . . things."

"Well. How tall was Lorraine? Your wife?" Swan asked abruptly.

He was cautious.

"Tall."

"And beautiful? She must have been."

"I thought we'd been all over this."

"Not *all* over it."

"Okay," he said, trying to see where she was going. "Yes, she was lovely—I'll say that for her. And, you know, they airbrushed those magazine photos long before Photoshop was invented."

"I saw the issue of *AfterDark* she was . . . in."

His face darkened considerably.

"Let me guess: someone else 'found' it for you."

Swan was silent.

"I'll say this much for him: he is a tenacious bastard, although why anyone who loves you would purposely hurt you when it's so easy to do, is beyond me. There's no challenge to it. You're defenseless, really." He sighed. "Okey-doke. What do you want to know?"

"Was she a virgin when you married her?"

"She was a virgin when I met her—not by the time we got married."

"Was that important to you? That you were her first?" Swan asked.

"I suppose so. But she was probably my twentieth, so it all evened out."

She thought about that for a minute. "The sex must have been great."

"That's not a question."

"Was the sex great?"

"Yes, eventually. But, like I told you: there's never been anyone like you. Not for me."

"Did you try to get her back from that other guy? The one she went to California with?" Swan asked.

"Define 'get her back.'"

"Did you call her? Follow her to California? See her?"

"I was at Quantico, finishing my ten weeks at O.C.S. and on my way to The Basic School by then."

"Did you see her? Did you try to get back together?"

"I saw her. I tried to get her back."

"And?"

"And she was pregnant and ready to marry the other guy."

Swan thought about that.

"Are you sorry I wasn't a virgin when we met?"

"Chiclet, I'm not sorry about anything about you. I *am* sorry I'm not worth twenty-five million dollars, like Fitch," he said.

Swan pulled out of his arms to look at him.

"You are kidding, right? Fitch isn't worth that much."

"Everyone in Waverly must know that other than you. And that excludes the five hundred acres and manor house in Delafield, the hunt box outside Waverly, and the jewelry he will inherit when his mother passes away. FYI: I'm worth closer to twenty-five thousand, by way of comparison.

"I've only been a major for a year and paid off a shitload of student loans before then. No house in Delafield, Delaware, or Dela-anywhere. You've got the only jewelry I own other than my Tech college ring, which I bought on installments. Tomorrow I'll give you my bank account number and pass code and you can review my complete financial history, Fitch, too. That should give him a good laugh. Anything else?"

"Are you sorry I'm not taller?" Swan asked in a small voice. "If we have kids, I'll probably have sons the size of dwarves."

He exploded with laughter.

"Yes, I'm very sorry you aren't taller, that's a big disappointment for me. So you know I must love you very much—otherwise it would be a deal-breaker, big time." He kissed her. "If you're right, we'll find them jobs in the circus."

◆

The next day, she watched him towel off after his shower.

"God, you look like you're getting bigger—is that even possible?" she said.

"I've been hitting the gym hard since I've been here. I want to keep everything nice and tight for you," he grinned. "Plus, I've got to keep up with the new crop of twenty-year-olds coming in for every deployment."

She looked at him, bare chested, unshaven, his uniform trousers shucked down his hips, a modern Pagliacci bronze of an idealized male, with the crest of muscle running along his waist, the deep channel of his spine defined in a way seemingly impossible in the human male.

"I want a picture of you like this before you go," she said.

"To jack off to while I'm gone?" he teased, "I thought that's what our engagement photo was for."

"Just get one taken before I come back. Find some gay photographer in Oceanside—he'll know what I want."

He snorted: "As if I'd let some horny perv pull my pants down. But I get your drift." He went to his closet and rummaged around, coming back with a digital camera.

"Here. Take one yourself right now." He grinned. "Take your clothes off while you do it."

She laughed.

"You know how I feel about nudity," she said, but she did stay in her underwear and was rewarded with his smokey, molten expression. She clicked off a half dozen frames; downloaded them to Sam's PC laptop; and hit *send* as an e-mail attachment to his I-Mac hooked up at Belle Everley.

Three nights later, her last in Oceanside, they joined two couples for dinner off the base. Major Browning and his wife were from Grand Prairie; Colonel Aaronson and his wife from the Mississippi Delta.

"When Sam said his fiancée was a Virginia farm girl, we figured you would look like . . . well, a checkered apron, braids maybe, big hands and feet—" said Browning.

"Sounds like a milkmaid," Swan responded, perplexed.

"Gilbert!" his wife interrupted, "we did not! Really!"

But her husband blundered on.

"Well, not like a movie star, which is what you do look like," Browning continued, admiringly, checking out her black, cinch-waisted Ralph Rucci dress with cut out panels across the shoulders.

"Thank you." Swan knew a compliment when she heard it.

"How are you going to like being a marine wife?" Aaronson asked. "Hard to bring horses onto a base in the Philippines."

"We haven't gotten that far, I guess," Swan said tentatively. "I'm hoping for Quantico or the Pentagon when you all return stateside."

"God," snorted Browning, disgusted. "We'd rather be dodging Mehsud rocket attacks on the Wiziristan border."

"Swan's stepfather is at D.O.D.," Sam said quietly.

"Oh. My apologies," said Browning. "Politics is not my forte, as you can see."

"Well, I'm not a military lawyer or an expert on scientific warfare. I'm just your garden-variety, killing-machine kind of major," Sam said cheerfully. "I don't think the Pentagon is in my future."

Swan was silent. Mrs. Aaronson read her mood perfectly.

"My, what a lovely engagement ring, Miss Bolington," she said, smoothly changing course. "So patriotic, and the colors of the Texas flag, too." Then their food arrived.

Swan's mood was somber when she walked through the Dulles terminal the next day. In two weeks, he'd be gone. She could not remember how she had felt when Hunt had left; when Carter had left. They had both been surrounded by living, loving parents, other relatives, as well as her, the fiancée, at their departure. She hadn't felt that the entire farewell ritual rested on her shoulders the way she did now. She'd been arm candy waving a hanky, just as Fitch had described her.

Fitch. Sam was right. For someone who had never slept with her, never been engaged to her, never married to her, he was manipulating, controlling, everything. Lorraine was nothing compared to Fitch.

Swan sighed. For two weeks she had to act as though her focus was on Belle Everley. She was going to send Linny to Jerusha for her early race training. She had agreed to open the house for the Waverly Garden Club's tour of historic houses in April. During Historic Garden Week, busloads of garden enthusiasts came from all over the east coast to tour historic houses in the Tidewater, Colonial Williamsburg, Richmond, the Shenandoah Valley, and on the Eastern Shore, over a nine-day period. It was like the biblical attack of the locusts, but without the desperately needed funds they provided for garden renovation, magnificent American landmarks and historic houses would be in jeopardy. The old house had last been on the tour seven years previously, and Swan had agreed to open it that year before she had met Sam. Now she would have to prepare the house, barns, and gardens for ten thousand visitors over a two-day period. It could easily take twenty thousand dollars to do so.

The first phone call once she came in the door was from Sinjon Cross.

"How's Mike?" she asked eagerly.

"Doing well: real well. We got that three at twenty five and twelve on Friday, while you were out of town. Like it was nothing. Hope says he was just cruising along when she just thought about letting him out and, boom. Like a shot out of a gun. Came back good, ate good, loving life. He's a monster. Next work will be a black line work—guaranteed." That was the quickest work of the day, as measured by clockers; it indicated race readiness. And monster was about as good as it got in the racing business.

"He's not the Big Horse yet, though . . . " she teased—the top earner in any racing string.

"Not yet," Cross chuckled, "but Oliver is thinking about a March fifteenth allowance race at Delaware Park. Six furlongs on the dirt. Just to get his feet wet. Then we've got a couple who are probably going to Belmont in April. There are good spots there—and Big Sandy has always agreed with the Belle Everley horses."

"Sounds like a plan," Swan said.

She went to Sam's I-Mac in a guest bedroom and pulled up her e-mail account. She downloaded the photos she'd sent from the apartment. Sam was half-turned toward her, looking like a lusty, grinning god. In each photo, he came closer and closer to her, even though she was backing up to keep him in the frame, until he had lunged at her, the last a blurred image of his chest while she was in his embrace. In a final image, he had held the camera at his long arm's length, his other arm around her as she nestled in front of him, facing the lens. They were smiling, snuggling, looking like they didn't have a care in the world. Swan clicked out of the photos. She'd get them printed up professionally, she decided.

She walked out of the bedroom and passed the door to the upstairs office. She looked at the old desk. Without hesitation, she opened the drawer. She pulled out the Hunt Lee letters, lovingly stacked in chronological order, and tied together with an antique silk ribbon, their envelopes smoothed right to their very corners. With great care she placed the whole stack in the fireplace. Then she lit a match.

Edgar continued to work with Linny at home, up and down the shedrow, walking the farm road between the barns. Mares continued to foal out under their watchful eyes. Swan knew Fitch was wild with curiosity to learn Sam's reaction to the *AfterDark* revelations but Swan never mentioned it. She reported on the officers' dinner, the attractions of Oceanside, and watched him fume with considerable satisfaction.

Townsend Brooke stopped by the next weekend, home from William and Mary. Swan was finishing a cup of coffee in the parlor when Townsend appeared at the door, looking collegiate in a wool hacking jacket and jeans. The teenager offered some half-hearted chitchat about Swan's alma mater.

"I really enjoyed having dinner with you at the Reynard," Townsend said then. "Fitch knows so much—you, too, Swan. I'm taking Latin and Art History but, honestly, I feel like I wasted years growing up in Hollywood. No one talks about *The Lady's Not for Burning* or Myna Plensk-whatever's 'Dying Swan' there. That's what you two talk about all the time." She was despairing.

"Maya Plisetskaya. Don't worry about it," Swan said, patting Flagg by the fire. "You have other qualities he admires. You are so lovely and sweet, for one thing. Fitch appreciates that."

"He never takes me anywhere I might learn something," Townsend fretted. "It's always dinner and . . . bed," she sighed heavily. "Maybe if I had a reading list or if I could learn to ride better—"

"When Sam is deployed in a couple of weeks, I'll have more time," Swan said. "We could go to the National Gallery of Art during Spring Break and look at the Vermeers. People come from all over the country to see them. I could give you more riding lessons, then, too, but until you can ride every day, it is hard to really improve."

"Oh, Swan," Townsend wailed, "it doesn't matter; he'll always love you best. It's hopeless."

"I know what we can do," Swan said. "Fitch loves scones and they are easy to make. Currants, sugar, flour, butter, milk. I'll show you how while Mathilde is out of the kitchen, and you can surprise him."

Swan sent Townsend back to Delafield with a yellowware bowl full of scones and the recipe, but deep down, they both knew it was a lost cause. Sam had been right. No eighteen-year-old could hold Hastings Fitzhugh. The next day, Swan had a surly phone message.

"Fuck," Fitch snarled, "no need to send her to me with food. And no Vermeers: she's not your fucking project."

Townsend called from her college dorm that evening, in a state.

"He was furious. He knew I must have said something that let you know we aren't happy. He says the fact that a monster stud like Sam is marrying you, when he could have anyone, means you must be unbelievable in bed, and yet you gave Fitch the run around. I can't repeat his actual words . . . . He said it's all about Eugene Ickes—whoever he is—or that Sam is after your money. He's drinking more than he was before Christmas."

Swan listened impassively.

"Townsend, I'm very sorry. It is very wrong of him to say these kinds of things. He is angry over his injury and bitter that someone he cared for has . . . moved on," Swan said. "I suspect he didn't say 'Eugene Ickes,' but 'eugenics,' which is mating people based on their physical perfection to 'improve' the human bloodline. From the Nazi era and a pretty low thing to say."

But there was nothing else she could do. She did nothing to break the silence with Fitch.

◆

The days ticked down to her last trip to Camp Pendleton. She had assembled a wardrobe for the occasion: a deep amethyst silk sheath, with cut-out sleeves and matching elbow-length, fingerless gloves; an acid green kimono jacket; a black silk petal miniskirt; wide-legged chocolate silk trousers and a cream silk peplum jacket, ruched and lined with the chocolate silk; a champagne-colored silk shirtwaist dress with chocolate silk-covered buttons; platform peep-toed shoes and tiny purses to match them all. They had set her back a year's salary for a marine captain, a fact that bothered her not a bit. They had been worth every penny. Their four days together flew by.

The last morning, he showered and dressed, cheerful and resolute, but he turned to her.

"Don't shower this morning—don't wash me off you," he pleaded. "Stay just the way I've left you, with me still in you." Swan did as he asked, and then they were standing with the other families and service personnel at the Air Force base, awaiting the convoluted processing that would be the first leg of the trip to Kandahar Airfield, Afghanistan.

It is really happening, Swan thought over and over again. *It is finally happening.*

"You know my GPO address, and I'll send you everything else when I know it," Sam said. "Check your e-mail til you see that I've gotten through. The Skype connection is set on the I-Mac video cam through the high-speed satellite connection. I'm having my pay direct deposited; I added your name to my account at the Waverly Bank. Just fill out a signature card and you have access to my funds."

Swan choked up. His pitiful savings.

"Why would you do that?" she whispered.

"Good practice for October," he said cheerfully. That started the waterworks.

"Don't . . . don't . . . don't," he pleaded, but she buried her head in his jacket, sniffling, her eyes wet. She swallowed, liquidy, thick swallows.

He tried a different tack.

"I've never told you how great it is to be engaged to you. I've never been engaged before. Lorraine and I went to Vegas, remember? I'm an engagement virgin." He was trying to get a smile from her. "You've never been married and I've never been engaged. A perfect match." It wasn't working. "Hey, a major's girl should be able to handle this, you know," he said softly.

She wiped her eyes on his field jacket as though it was a towel, then she pressed her cheek against his chest. His heart was pounding, the muscles in his arms were quivering, giving the lie to his calm.

"You missed your other farewells; I'm giving you 'farewell to the second lieutenant,' 'farewell to the captain,' *and* 'farewell to the major,'" she said, sniffling loudly. "I might as well say good-bye to all of you at once."

That made him laugh.

"You've got to be the funniest girl in the world," he said, lifting her off the ground one last time, his huge duffle bag over his shoulder. He kissed her, and then he was gone, tall above the crowd, the line moving toward Customs, the snaking pathway ending in a fly-blown desert filled with warring tribes, whirring drones, cave-dwelling fanatics. He turned back to catch her gaze:

"My beautiful boy!" she cried out, "be careful! Be careful! I love you!"

"I love you," he mouthed back.

Swan turned away when he was out of sight. *I've got to get out of here,* she thought. She headed toward the rental car and Belle Everley. Home.

Swan opened her front door with great relief. She had called Mathilde from Dulles, so she had a dinner plate in the warming drawer of the kitchen's big English Aga cooker ready for her. The housekeeper bustled around preparing a tray, with a pot of English Breakfast tea from the mahogany tea chest, a hot turkey sandwich, cranberry relish, bread pudding—comfort food, in front of the parlor fire. Then she sat down unceremoniously next to Swan.

"So, tell me how it went, *ma chèr,*" she said in a no-nonsense voice.

Swan looked at her dear, concerned face, framed by grey hair pulled into an untidy bun.

"I held it together, pretty much," she started, tentatively. "I was able to joke up to the end, I think."

"On a scale of one to ten—"

"I'm giving myself an eight: there were tears, but I was able to smile through them. I did wipe my nose on his jacket: half a point down for that, now that I think of it," she said. "Ten would have been dry eyes, cheerful, patriotic demeanor, bravely comforting others. However, nobody had to call the paramedics—that would have been a one."

Mathilde gave her a smile as she topped off Swan's teacup.

"I'm very proud of you: your dear parents would be, too," she said. "Do you want to hear who called?"

"Miss Spaulding and Miss Hetty, I assume. Mr. Bertrand?"

"And Mr. Fitzhugh, full of apologies, as— "

"Usual?" Swan finished.

"He said he would 'stand in the driveway and let you flog him with his master's lash,' for being such a complete—well, he's not going to get me to use his language, no matter how charming he is,"

Mathilde said disapprovingly. "He said if I could get you to forgive him, he would come to Mass, convert to the Faith, then marry me in front of the whole parish. I know he's disappointed in love, but, really! The major has to put up with a great deal from that man."

"You like the major, don't you, Mathilde?" Swan teased her gently. "You are just like Miss Spaulding—you always fall for a handsome face, particularly if there is a uniform collar under it. Me, too, I guess." She was pensive.

"As for Mr. Fitch, I have to put up with him but you shouldn't have to. I'll call them all back, later. They are just concerned about me."

"Why don't you finish eating, then have yourself a little nap first, right here by the fire? This has been hanging over you for weeks. These trips. You are worn out. Was the major happy to have you there to say good-bye? You said he'd always had to go alone before."

"Yes, yes, he was," Swan took a few more bites, then half-heartedly put the plate aside. She let Flagg lick her fingers, absent-absentmindedly. "I *am* tired."

Mathilde jumped up to take the plate, tucked a homespun coverlet draped across the loveseat around Swan's legs, and lifted them onto the cushion. She wiped Swan's fingers with a wet-wipe as though she were a little girl again.

Then she let Swan fall deeply asleep. When Swan woke up more than an hour later, it was to the sound of the phone. "I'm awake," she called to prevent Mathilde from taking a message.

"Mr. Fitzhugh."

Swan groaned.

"Fitch," she said when she got to the phone.

"How'd it go?"

"Fine. He's on his way," she said. "Thanks for checking, but you needn't worry."

"I'm worried that you are going to get fed up with me once and for all. No one would blame you," he said. "I thought you were going to make Mathilde take a message and blow me off. Did she tell you about the whipping option I offered? I thought that might appeal to you."

"What would be the point?" Swan asked absent-absentmindedly; he could hear that she was not interested in the conversation at all.

"Okay, I'll make this short and sweet—you are exhausted," he said. "I apologize. I've only been dating Townsend all season to make you jealous, which anyone with eyes has seen from the beginning. When you tried to patch things up between us, it hurt my feelings because it proved just how little you cared about my love life."

"So are you and Townsend on or off?" Swan tried to summon some modicum of interest for his sake.

"Off. I did her a favor and sent her on her way, to the relief of one hundred frat boys at William and Mary and, no doubt, a host of beard-seeking Young Hollywood pretty boys."

"The game-playing is getting old," she acknowledged, "and that sex stuff with her, about me: unacceptable."

"Understood. So I have a peace offering— to take you to a tea dance at the British Embassy on the twenty-fifth, where a lot of hot and cold running NATO and U.K./ISAF types not beholden to the Pentagon are due to show up. You might be able to pick up some intel that Bert can't or won't divulge to you, particularly if your dress is tight enough," Fitch proposed.

"That would be great, I think. Why can't you be like this all the time? Everyone would love you."

"Everyone but one," he said brightly.

"I'll think about the Embassy. I'm just too tired to do any ideas any justice tonight."

"I'm forgiven, then?"

"Forgiven, without the whipping business. But I reserve the right to reinstate the punishment if you act like this big of a jackass again."

◆

Forty-eight hours later, an e-mail popped up on the I-Mac.

Here. All okay. Phones intermittent. Hot and dusty as I remembered. Flies, snakes, rodents all happy to see me back. Internet connection slow and in heavy demand. Food is fast but won't win awards. Miss you lots. Keep the bed warm. LU, Sam.

There was a photo attachment. Sam was in his desert camo, grinning, at some pancake-flat, un-I.D.ed location, but Swan bet it was the Kandahar Airfield.

Twenty thousand people—military, media, medical personnel, contractors—were based there. The smell of the "poop pond" (an open sewage treatment facility) seemed a topic of everyone's conversation. Institutional laundry and food service, a big gym, duty-free stores, but long lines everywhere to get anything. Tents for sleeping. Monotonous but relatively safe. Sam wouldn't be there long, she suspected.

She hit *reply*: *Home. All okay. Cold and wintry as I remembered. Horses, dog, family all happy to see me back. Internet connection waiting on e-mails from the boss. Love the photo. Sounds like the bed's already warm there. Miss you lots. LU, S.* She hit *send.*

Swan was cheered to have anything from him, anything at all. She was sleeping in his t-shirts, sometimes two at a time against the cold, over her nightgown, to keep his scent close. But the Marriage in Heaven was still taking place every night.

She was of two minds about Fitch. She could handle him with one hand tied behind her back, but she didn't like Townsend and others suffering the resulting collateral damage. She'd let things cool for a while. She put him off on the tea dance, concentrating on Mike's continued progress toward his race mid-month.

Hetty's pregnancy also began to occupy her thoughts. The Sam drama had absorbed the family throughout the fall: Hetty and Boyd deserved the spotlight now. The baby was a boy— Bolington Delaney would arrive in mid-June. Every couple of days, Swan checked in with Hetty and resumed her routine established when Sam was in Oceanside. She got two more short e-mails throughout the rest of the week, but then the phone rang a week to the day after he left.

"Swan?" he sounded like he was at the bottom of a very dry well, far away.

"Sam?"

"Hiya, Chiclet."

"Hi, hi, hi," she said, trying to get a handle on her surprise. "Where are you?"

"Oh, I'm at the QuikMart in Waverly: didn't I tell you? I've been reassigned."

"Sorry, sorry," she said, rushed, afraid they were going to be cut off. "I shouldn't ask, I know."

"That's okay," his voice was warm, loving. "Boy, it's great to hear you."

"I'm so glad you caught me: I was about to do a barn check on a mare."

"Everything okay?"

"Yep, seven mares down, three to go, all in the next week or so."

"How's my boy, Flagg? And everyone?"

"Great, everything's great . . . ." Her mind searched for something more meaningful to say, while it was ticking: time, time, time. "The Fat Boy was delivered today, safe and sound."

"Great. No riding while I'm gone, though, hear? Remember the tractor incident?"

She laughed, relieved. Everything sounded normal. He sounded normal.

"And The Fortress and Major are going to Kentucky for her to be bred to Carnivorous, and Gunny is ready to come back from being bred to him, this week," she said chattily.

"That Carnie must be one lucky guy . . . . Wait—Major?"

She laughed guiltily.

"Didn't I tell you? When I decided not to name the new colt Battering Ram, we'd already started calling him after you."

"I don't know if I should be flattered or insulted. I think I'll go with flattered."

"Do you need anything sent? Or anything?" she suddenly asked, worried that they were running out of phone time.

"Just my fiancée, preferably in that black silky nightie," he said. "Could you box yourself up and get Fed-Ex-ed here?"

She laughed. "Do you think I'd clear security?"

"Without the nightie: guaranteed."

"Everything going okay at your end of things?"

"Oh, you know, as well as can be expected." He was guarded, and she remembered there was typically a line, even for officers, within hearing distance waiting to use the phone cubicles at a base.

"Does anyone know what you are going to be asked to do? Or anything?"

"I think they are trying to sort that out."

"You sound like Bert."

That got a laugh.

"Yeah, there's a lot of that going around. How's Hetty?"

Back in safe territory.

"She feels fine, happy it's another boy," Swan said. "But in another month, she's going to see how hard it is to run after Boyd Junior and tote that belly around at the same time. Her face will look like The Fortress's."

"Don't tease her—you never know, you may find yourself in the same boat some day," he said.

"You never know," Swan agreed, trying to toss off the line. "But by then, she will have used up all the good family names."

"You mean like Bolington Swan Hexell Spaulding Bolington?"

"Hey—" she protested.

"Sorry. Oh. Listen, honey, gotta go. Line's going around out the door. I'll try again next week, if not sooner, about this time. Love you."

"Love you. Love you!" she called out, and the phone disconnected.

Chapter 10

For the next week, it was mares and foals, mares and foals, twenty-four-seven. One older mare had a difficult delivery. Kezia despaired of saving the foal and the mare both, then the foal got repositioned on the third try, and suddenly, there she was—small, wet, stunned, but alive—and within fifteen minutes up and looking for breakfast. Swan was in sweatpants, hunting boots, flannel shirt, down vest, pretty much around the clock on days like that; so was Eduardo. Only Kezia looked like she had showered and changed between visits, as her big dually rocked oldies in the driveways of one barn after another in Waverly.

The Gold Chip van arrived one midnight to load The Fortress and Major for the return trip to the Bluegrass, the mare's last in a long, illustrious career. Swan was sending Eduardo with the farm's most precious cargo. He bedded down in the empty stall next to the mare on a collapsible cot; he would catch a commuter plane back to Dulles in a day or so, once he was sure the mare had settled in. Edgar would pull double duty with Swan, handling the farm work. It was the price of keeping mares at home—every popular stallion was in Kentucky. Mares trekked there from all over the East, foals in tow, to be bred, and confirmed in foal by the Kentucky reproduction specialists. Many, like Swan's, returned to their home farms for the rest of their eleven-month gestation for more TLC than was available at the big broodmare "factories" of the Bluegrass.

Then Sinjon Cross called Swan: Mike was going into a race on the fifteenth at Delaware Park. Swan planned to go north, hope for a safe trip as a first time out for her colt, and return the same day—long on mileage, but she was reluctant to be away from home for an entire night. Only her visits with Sam had been completely anxiety-free, she realized. She had been so absorbed in him that it seemed as though the farm had been on some other planet. Eduardo had carried the burden during those weeks. She would give him a paid week off as soon as the weather changed and the mares and foals were in their pastures around the clock.

Sam's e-mails were a cryptic combination of objective reporting and endearments; his next call was another one short on details and emotions. They both were trying hard, but everything seemed rushed, abbreviated, superficial, compared to how she had communicated with both Hunt Lee and Carter. There had been less frequency when communication had been primarily via letters but more intimacy. She fretted. Were they going to have seven months of "Everything okay?" backing and forthing?

Then a real letter arrived. She was shocked to feel it in her hand. It reminded her of the Hunt Lee letter exchange, the fruits of which were ash residue in the office fireplace upstairs.

Sunday

My sweetest girl,

I've gotten tired of shouting at you from the phone bank and keystroking five-sentence e-mails. The shitty Internet availability is fucking everything up.

They can't even cure the stink of the outdoor sewer around here so we shouldn't be surprised, but I miss you a lot tonight and thought you might get a kick out of a letter from me.

I feel great about one thing: we aren't counting down to when I leave anymore but to when I get back. It's just hit me that I'll step off the plane at Dulles October 1 and twenty-four hours later will be standing in the living room at Belle Everley watching you come down the stairs at our wedding without knowing one thing about who's going to be there, what we are going to eat, what you will be wearing, other than what you shout at me or tell me in a letter or ask my opinion about. I'll basically be Second Assistant Spear Carrier at my own wedding, but I guess almost every groom is. It may be kind of fun to do it that way so long as we end up hitched. I still can't believe—that night you asked me what I wanted and I said for us to be married—that it's actually going to happen. When I said it, I thought you would throw me out and never see me again. So already I'm way ahead of where I ever thought I'd be.

I wish I could tell you what's shaking over here, but that's pretty much impossible. The NATO folks and the U.S. military folks work well together in many cases, but for some of our units, it's a new experience to be reporting to NATO rather than the U.S. command structure. That much is being reported in the papers back home so it's no secret. It's also a challenge to ask grunts who have been trained to kill insurgents to instead get the trust of the people away from the Taliban. In some ways, your Aunt Spaulding is better suited to the task we've got than are leathernecks armed and equipped to look like invaders from outer space. You can imagine how much you'd enjoy even the nicest military presence on the front lawn of Belle Everley after eight years. Correction: you don't need to imagine. Your ancestors experienced four years of it in the 1860s. My time in Virginia has given me a better idea of how an occupying force can wear out whatever welcome it's had sooner or later. Some of the kids who welcomed me as an L.T. seven years ago are probably fighting against us in the hills south and east of here. That is sad.

Anyway, I am thinking of you just about all of the time. Someone will say some crazy thing out of the blue, and I'll think, that's something Swan would say. *Or I'll hear some song blaring, one that was on the jukebox that night in the Scarab, and I'll think of us dancing for the first time. How it felt.*

Another thing I've learned. Although it's my fourth tour, it's my first tour actually missing somebody. I used to envy the guys mooning over their sweethearts at night. Now that I'm in their shoes I see it's not always all that great. You are still lonely, but lonely in a different way. It's so much better to have someone than not to that it's so worth it.

You have been the most wonderful thing that's ever happened to me. I think you know that by now, but, in case you don't, I want you to have it here in black and white in my handwriting and not printed out on the laser printer upstairs.

I wish I could just hold your sweet little body or feel you climb into my arms like you do every night, like I'm a jungle gym or a tree or something. That always cracks me up. Anyway. We are going to have a great life together to make up for all the shit that has happened up until now. I really believe that.

Love from your battered old marine,

Sam

Swan sat down right where she was, on the floor in the hallway. Flagg took advantage of her being at his level to lick her face, but when she didn't respond, he flopped down contentedly. She read the letter again, word by word, several times. It filled her with longing but with peace of mind, too. It was comforting to hold the paper, to know he had held it only a week before, that he had made the strokes of the ballpoint that were impressed on the sheets. His saliva was on the gummed envelope, his DNA. It was a piece of him.

She thought it the most wonderful letter she'd ever received. She couldn't imagine how she could answer it, or equal it. She didn't have to, not right then. She refolded it carefully, and put it back in the envelope.

She sent him an e-mail when she went upstairs to bed: *Loved your letter; love you.*

She was still thinking about it as she got in the SUV heading to Delaware Park. She had considered taking Eduardo with her, but he had just returned from Kentucky, and he and Edgar would have their hands full for the day she was gone. They'd be able to see the race live on the flat screen with Mathilde at least.

◆

She arrived mid-afternoon, an hour before the race itself. She would meet Sinjon in the paddock; no point in making a nuisance of herself any earlier. Her credentials got her into the clubhouse, which was a far cry from the storied ambience and scorching sun of Saratoga. The crowd was sparse on the weekday, and definitely packed with senior citizens, who remembered racing from its long-past glory years.

The race before Mike's went off; and that was her signal to make her way downstairs to the paddock, a green but unglamorous spot under the clubhouse itself. The little winner's circle was adjacent. It always looked so festive in "win" photos, but the connections always seemed to ruin them, dressed as though they were heading to a wienie roast; in leisure suits from the seventies; in halter tops, like they had taken a detour from Coney Island and hadn't expected their horse to win at all.

Swan was in a silk shirtwaist dress, pumps, and an unstructured matching jacket that acknowledged Delaware's still cool March weather. She reached out her hand to Sinjon, who was standing with the "second call" jockey for the Lentz barn, Allerio D'amboise. Tomás Iglesias, the top jock for the barn, was riding the Templetons' Calypso in Florida. The Cajun Allerio was a regular at Delaware, and a good choice, but not the best fit for Mike. Swan felt a little twinge of concern, then forced herself to let it go. This was what she had Sinjon for. Her throat caught a little as she looked at Allerio standing next to her in the Bolington silks, going out in a flat race on a major racetrack. *Mom and Dad,* Swan thought, *I hope you can see this.* She shook Allerio's hand and he gave her the "owner's nod," deferential, smiling, but businesslike. Until Mike proved himself, he was just another horse on the jock's dance card.

Mike entered the paddock "on the muscle," typical of a first-time starter: inattentive, barging ahead of his groom in the paddock, dancing sideways at the small crowd around him. Swan resisted clucking to him. It was his first day on the job: let Sinjon run the show. Mike had had two more strong breezes since his first, one at five furlongs and another at six—not a lot of work but enough to give him a shot at the company contesting the seventh race. Sinjon exchanged a few words with Allerio, then came and stood next to Swan.

"Like old times for you?" he asked with a smile, never taking his eyes from Mike. "Let's see what we're going to see." At "Riders up!" he gave Allerio a boost into the saddle, then the eight horses who made up the field were gone. Sinjon and Swan headed to their seats in the clubhouse.

"The five horse is going to be the rabbit," Sinjon said, thinking out loud. "We've got the rail."

The inside post was not ideal for a big, first time starter like Mike, who was going to be in danger of getting squeezed early on. There would be some bumping for position at the first turn. Swan hoped Mike would take it if it came his way, settle in, figure things out, not get rattled. Hang in and try. Winning was a much lower priority.

The field was on its way to the gate. Six furlongs—three-quarters of a mile—was the standard sprint distance on American tracks. Not a lot of time for a young horse to recover from a slow start or a misstep. Swan just hoped for the best.

Mike loaded smoothly but not happily, she noticed through her binoculars. The assistant starter held his head straight as the other seven horses loaded after Mike. She saw his head bump up and down a couple of times in the tiny stall and her heart sank. Then the gate flew open. There was a quick scramble as the front-running horses went to the lead, choking Mike back, off the rail, but Allerio wisely kept Mike out of trouble. He tried to settle the colt into a rhythm, laying fourth around the first turn. Swan didn't even check the time: she cared about the "trip"—the way the race was run—not how fast they ran. He'd get the winner's share so long as he was the first across the finish line, whether they flew or crawled.

The field began to stretch out in the middle of the race. Allerio was "sitting chilly," letting the colt cruise, not fighting him, and Swan relaxed a bit. No matter how Mike finished, she was going to be happy. He was tougher than she gave him credit for. He didn't have two great racehorses as parents for nothing.

◆

Turning for home, Sinjon started to pound his rolled up program against the palm of his hand: "Here we go, here we go," he said, as

Allerio asked Mike to make his move. The colt exploded forward, but awkwardly. He lugged out for a stride or two, and another colt got ahead of him in the final strides toward the finish line. The other horses started tiring, "going backward," while Mike seemed like he was just getting the message, *Hey, we're in a horse race.* He finished a strong second. Sinjon looked at Swan and they gave each other that *Good effort, we're satisfied* nod. The winner's connections were doing the classic jump-up-and-down-and-hug nearby. You would think they had won the Triple Crown. Swan smiled. She knew how they felt.

"We've got a miler here, maybe more," Sinjon said, sounding quietly confident. Belmont Park, they were on their way.

Swan walked out of the clubhouse with Sinjon and followed Mike and his groom to the backside stabling area. Mike was blowing hard but happy; still looking around, trying to figure out what had happened, processing the whole thing. She now speeded up to catch him, giving him a reassuring pat, but the colt's mind was on his surroundings, not his mommy.

They'd see how Mike came out of the race—no physical injury, not underlying illness—see how he cleaned up his dinner, how he slept, how his less than two minutes of effort had affected him. Swan knew the colt would be exhausted, as much from the mental stimulation as from the physical effort, and sleep like the dead, snoring flat on his side, that night.

"Let Allerio know: great job," she said to Sinjon. "Call me tomorrow. Good effort today." Then she turned to her colt.

"Good boy, buddy," she crooned to Mike, who was being hand-walked to cool out before his warm bath. The colt whinnied; although she knew it was just another indication of excitement and greenness, she took it as a personnel farewell.

Once again, Swan headed for the road.

She was glad to get back, as always. She hugged Eduardo and Edgar, who were waiting in the parlor for a brief celebration, after her phone call had alerted them she was on her way home. Mathilde brought in the Mumms, and they all had a glass before the phone started ringing.

"We saw it on TV!" Hetty shouted excitedly when she called. "It was fantastic! Swan, you've done a wonderful job with him! If only

Mom and Dad could have seen him! I thought Boyd was going to have a coronary while I called the race to him at the hospital!"

Fitch was next; Spaulding not far behind. Swan thought she'd hear from Bert after he got home and returned her text message on his Blackberry.

She e-mailed Sam: *Mike second in strong effort today at Delaware Park. See attached smile.* She had attached a photo taken by Sinjon as she stood grinning in front of Mike's stall after the race. She has started and stopped several letters to him since receiving his, but none sounded right. She was content for the time being with e-mail and hoped talking to him by phone would let him hear how much it had meant to her.

She had decided to go to the tea dance with Fitch but not to tell Sam until afterwards. The Ambassador's House at the British Embassy was a sought-after invitation. If someone proved charming, witty, and attractive enough, he might be invited back during the rare but highly visible visits from members of the Royal Family, even relatively minor ones. Fitch had been admitted into this circle; Swan recalled he had been at a brief garden reception for the brother of the heir to the realm several years previously.

She was delighted to get a call from Sam the next night.

"So are we rolling in dough from Mike's big finish?" he teased.

"Not by finishing second, we aren't, but his training fees are paid up for the next few months, at least. He'll go to Belmont at the end of next month. I wish you could have been there to see him," she said wistfully. "Judy won over hurdles last week at Glen Meade, in Rappahannock County. I couldn't get there because of foaling, but Jerusha said she ran like a tiger, though there were only five in the field."

"I wish I could have seen it. Why don't you write me all about it," he said.

"I'm intimidated; I can't match your wonderful letter to me," she said truthfully. "I am putting together some packages for anymarine.com—socks, beanie babies, foot powder, dried fruit, beef jerky, batteries—for some of the forward units. Mathilde and Patti Lombardini are helping me."

"Oh, that's great—some of our guys get no mail at all," Sam said. He'd been one of them. "The rest of you have real lives to live. We're either bored out of our minds, lonely as hell, or scared shitless. That's the Marines."

"And I'm going to a dance in Washington in the next week or two." She had suddenly changed her mind about telling him. "It's with Fitch, but we think there may be some military NATO types who might know what's going on over there." She hesitated. "I won't go if you think it isn't a good idea."

"Why would I think that?" he asked.

"Because of Fitch."

"I'm twelve thousand miles away," he said, calmly. "Chiclet, you're going to do what you're going to do."

"I won't go if you don't want me to."

"It's not a big deal, not to me." She suddenly felt a pang.

"I miss you. I don't want to do anything that you don't want me to," she said, a little desperation creeping into her voice.

"I'm going to be here seven months, Swan," he said. "You can't anguish over every decision. I trust you—completely. Shouldn't I?"

"Yes, yes. You should. As I trust you," she said, her pleasure evaporating. "At least you are still at the airfield. That is safe, isn't it?"

He hesitated a beat.

"Who said I was at the airfield?"

"You talked in your letter about . . . a bad sanitation system, and there are blogs on the Internet that talk about a 'poop pit' at the Kandahar Airfield, so I put two and two together, I guess."

He laughed.

"You are wasted in Waverly: you should be at D.I.A.," he said, but her heart was warmed by his voice now. "Just write me a letter, baby."

"Is my picture doing its job?"

"Big time, and thanks for sending the one of us at Oceanside." Swan had had the one from the apartment printed up for him. Her copy was framed but in her bedside table, next to the Walther, for her eyes only.

"Love you. Love you. Love you."

So she decided to go to the Embassy reception with Fitch with a clear conscience.

She wore the black Rucci dress from the dinner with Sam's officers in Oceanside. She'd had her hair professionally braided and pinned up in an intricate, unusual way, much more like New York than anything Washington typically saw, and her diamond earrings. Black gloves. A bit of beaded black silk and veil on a band, a "fascinator," technically served as a hat in deference to protocol.

Fitch looked handsome as ever in a custom suit with detachable collar that fit him like a glove, Italian shoes, and a silk tie. The weather was unseasonably warm and hazy. Fitch folded Swan into the Porsche with great care, glancing appreciatively at her legs as she swung them into the well of the passenger side, and sighed.

"If I hadn't been blown up in Baghdad, we'd be married by now," he said. "That would have made it much harder for the gallant major to have gotten up your skirt."

"Hard to know 'what ifs,'" she said mildly, "but obviously if we'd been married, he never would have tried."

"If I had to lose you, I have to admit, I've lost you to a class act. He seems like the real deal."

"I'm pretty partial to him."

"Do you think he'll re-up again?"

"We haven't talked about anything much beyond this deployment, quite frankly. If he stays, he stays. I don't seem him going to Black Rock or U.S.A.I.D. I'm hoping for Quantico for his return."

"Well, I'd like to keep an eye out for a nice big draft cross hunter for him over the summer. A good safe guy he can learn to hunt on and come back alive. Consider it my wedding present to you both," Fitch said, keeping his eyes on the road. "As master of Belle Everley, he'll have hunting privileges with Waverly, of course. Order him some military breeches and boots; he can hunt in his uniform coat."

They rode in silence into D.C., to the British Ambassador's Residence, where the reception was to take place. The 1920s red brick and stone building was a graceful next door neighbor to the brick and glass embassy on Massachusetts Avenue.

Swan and Fitch made their way through the receiving line, then found their way to the dance floor, where a British military band played sprightly fox trots suitable for the staid crowd. Yellow gladiolas, like great lemon spears, stood by the dozens in silver vases, sentinels matching the yellow scagliola strategically placed around the ballroom. Fitch danced beautifully, leading her as expertly as a captain at a cavalry charge. Swan couldn't help but remember the last time they had danced together—at the hunt ball, celebrating her engagement. There was no Major Septimus Moore with his arms around her, but here still was the charming Hastings Fitzhugh, who was so much more suited to her in background, education, predilection, even height.

"This feels more like it," Fitch murmured as they turned, then turned, then turned, "more like it used to be. More like it should have been. More like it should be now."

Swan was silent. What was the harm in letting him say what he was thinking? He was going to think it, whether she allowed him to say it or not.

No. She should not let him.

"Perhaps we could have something to eat?" she said evenly, as though he had said nothing at all.

Tiny, perfectly constructed cucumber, watercress, and smoked salmon sandwiches, lemon curd, China tea, fluted tartlettes, chocolate bon bons shaped like flowers, candied fruits and spun sugar-dipped berries, and sauvignon blanc were offered by a wait staff circulating throughout the ballroom.

It was a lovely afternoon, but it became clear that the NATO military bigwigs Fitch had been promised were conspicuously absent. Swan was philosophical. If Sam's C.O. had been passing pickled ham sandwiches to her himself, she doubted what intel he could have handed her; and what she could have done with the information if she'd had it. Her days as a military operative were over, she decided. Devoted fiancée at home was her role. They drove companionably on the way back to Waverly.

"I'm sorry this turned out to be a bust as far as intel is concerned," Fitch said.

Swan sighed.

"Fitch, do you believe in this war? Do you believe we can win it? Is it winnable—by anyone?"

He turned to look at her, surprised.

"Strange. You and I have never discussed this subject. Hunt, Carter, Warburton, Iraq, Afghanistan—we've never discussed any of it, not in substantive terms."

She stared out the window of the roadster.

"*Senatus Populusque Romanus,*" Fitch said. "The Senate and the People of Rome. They so decree and they are never wrong. A small number of us make the ultimate sacrifice, or something less, that is still . . . painful . . . while the rest amuse themselves with bread and circuses. The world goes on." He looked pensive.

"*Roma victa,*" Swan quoted the traditional cry of the Roman legions.

"Yes, of course. Rome conquers all," Fitch replied. "Eventually. With the help of Warburton and Black Rock, of course."

They both were silent, then, and melancholy; he mourning his loss, she her own, possibly still untotaled. It was unbearable.

"Mike will be going to Belmont soon," she said.

He followed her lead willingly. Discussion of Mike's campaign, her anymarine.com package project, Hetty's pregnancy, and the Waverly steeplechase races, to be held at Waverly Park the second week of April, occupied most of the rest of their trip.

"I gather you have given the Scarab a wide berth," Fitch said, as they passed through Waverly, abruptly changing the subject. "I just wish Mr. Spaulding would do the same."

"Daniel?" She felt an icy undercurrent of warning.

"He'd better get his shit together," Fitch said ominously. "Or else he's going to get felony drug possession. That will send Tidewater Commercial running for the hills. Tell Spaulding that if she has any influence, she should boot his behind back to Strasberg. And I mean that in the nicest possible way."

"Well . . . ." She mulled that over.

"I'm serious," he said, looking at the driveway as he turned into Belle Everley.

"I know you are. Warning delivered." She gave him a quick kiss on the cheek and slipped out of the roadster before he could come around to open her door. "And appreciated."

He looked up at her as she started up the steps, the couture dress; the ludicrous little hat, the thick hair braided and twisted. She looked like a pre-Raphaelite painting of Guinevere, the medieval exemplar of female beauty.

"God, why did I ever let you go?" he asked quietly. "You are perfection."

She looked back at him.

"If things don't work out with Sam for whatever reason, would I ever have another chance with you, do you think?" He had to ask.

"You mean, if Sam didn't come back? If Sam doesn't come back, why would I be interested in anyone ever again?" She opened the old front door.

"May I come in? For old times' sake?"

"That would not be a good idea," she said pityingly.

"Not today?" He was hopeful.

"Not today," she replied, "not anymore, Fitch." She turned back to the door.

Fitch shifted the roadster and drove down the driveway—and away.

◆

For the next three weeks, Fitch prepared for the Waverly Hunt Races and Swan prepped Belle Everley for its garden week visitors. Weeding, sodding, pruning, painting, grouting, masonry repair, mowing, floor refinishing, window cleaning, fence staining, and one hundred other tasks were necessary to make a two-hundred-year-old house, outbuilding, and barn complex ready for its visitors. Some tasks were maintenance deferred over the year for this very event, some were beautification that could have been postponed but provided the cosmetic finishing touches to the bones of the property. Swan had drastically underestimated the cost of this work, but it had to be done. Easter weekend had come and gone, with a small dinner with Spaulding, Bert, and the Delaneys at the Willow's Edge. The mares and foals were now turned out into their pastures, lush with spring grass, around the clock, allowing a thorough cleaning and disinfecting of the barns, an annual ritual. Every week Swan and Mathilde were sending ten boxes of food stuffs and dry goods to front-line military outposts with contacts on anymarine.com. One unit needed a microwave; another a small electric washing machine to replace hand-washing of clothes for fifteen marines. Patrol units asked for beanie babies to tuck in their body armor for children terrified of the U.S. fighters prowling their villages in night-vision goggles, with automatic weapons. All of the units seemed to need socks, beef jerky, dried fruits, and the Oakley boots that trumped the standard-issue footwear. Swan wanted to ask Bert why these simple necessities weren't provided, given the billions of tax dollars hemorrhaging the national economy, but she was reluctant to do so. She suspected the answer would be that those millions were needed for drones, not tube socks.

Fitch was running a paramilitary operation of his own—his hunt committee volunteers for his day of racing at Waverly Park. Snow fencing had to be installed to mark out the course, parking, and paddock areas; veterinary, farriery and E.M.T. services retained; volunteer parking attendants, outriders, stewards, fence judges, concession operators, hospitality tent coordinators were hired. Tractors were put in place for vehicles that might become stuck in the fields used for parking if April rains soaked them. Then there were the entry secretaries, paddock judges, tent rentals, even sheriff's deputies to handle traffic coming in off the state hard-surface road at Waverly Park.

The two days Belle Everley was on view were the two days of the Waverly Hunt weekend, so she and Fitch would be unable to assist at each other's grand event. She was going to vacate the house at Belle Everley during the tours, but they all were staying on site to provide security to the barns and horses in the fields. They'd use the mare barn office as their base of operations; it had sofas, telephone and TV, refrigerator, and restroom facilities enough to keep them comfortable. After the last tour finished up at five P.M., they'd be released from their self-imposed exile; the property would belong to them again.

◆

Two days before the garden tour, a dozen garden club volunteers in woolen slacks and sweater sets descended upon Belle Everley to lay down plastic protective sheeting over the carpets on the first floor, direct the installation of portable toilets and signage around the driveway, and familiarize themselves, as docents, with the rooms they would protect and describe to the visitors, twelve at a time, as they toured the house. Another half dozen ladies brought enormous tubs of fresh cut flowers to dress all of the downstairs rooms. They prepared arrangements of calla lilies, irises, anthurium, orchids, gladiolas, daffodils, freesia, fancy tulips, roses and branches of magnolia, dogwood, and forsythia. These dressed the entranceway table, the kitchen, the living room, parlor, even the downstairs bathroom.

The docents had asked about the property's history, the provenance of the furnishings, the origins of the gardens, and the success of the racing stable, to share with their visitors.

◆

The Saturday of the Waverly races and the Belle Everley tour was unusually hot after several cold rainy days earlier in the week. Swan performed an early inspection, with Thérèse Malloy, president of the Waverly Garden Club, in tow. The old farm, one of six on the tour, looked spectacular. The pastures and lawns were in their early green finery, the spring bulbs peaking at their full glory—the late varieties of daffodils, the early ruffled tulips and the just budding irises filling the flowerbeds. The dogwoods and forsythias were still showy and the trees were in hazy-red buds. The outbuildings had been power washed and swept within an inch of their figurative lives; pots of azaleas and boxwood had been placed in their doorways. Swan suddenly teared up: her mother and father had been alive for the last garden club tour. Hetty had been seeing a young pre-med student—Boyd Delaney. Daniel had been squiring Swan—Hunt Lee was still two years in her future.

Edwardo and Edgar fed the horses, cleaned and filled the water troughs in the mare and foal fields, brought up the yearlings to keep them out of trouble from the hoards of visitors, filled the barn fridge with bottled water and sodas, and settled into the office. Swan had positioned lawn chairs and traffic cone barricades at the entrance to the barn driveways to make sure no vehicles or visitors strayed beyond their boundaries. Mathilde took the first watch, with a panama hat, sunglasses, and a romance novel to keep her company. Swan flopped down on a sofa with Flagg and her manager and groom. The Shepherd panted anxiously, not happy with all of the hubbub.

Edgar, the twenty-two-year-old rider, stall cleaner, groom, and all-around man of the farm, grinned a gold-toothed grin.

"We should charge the *gringos, señorita,*" he teased, "if not for the tour, for a soda or for *cinco minutos* on the sofa to rest their feet."

"Or for pony rides?" Swan said. "We could sell rides on Punch."

"Or on Miguel—let's bring him back from *Señor* Lentz," suggested Eduardo with a fiendish grin. "A ride they would never forget. *Muy rapido, muy stupendo.*"

"No, he would throw them off so quickly, they'd all have concussions—they'd have rides they would never remember, not rides they would never forget," Swan chuckled.

Edgar looked perplexed.

"*Como se dice* 'concussion,' Eduardo?" Swan asked.

"*La conmoción cerebral,*" Eduardo translated helpfully.

The vision of the garden clubbers being catapulted through the air on the rocket express struck all three of them as funny at the same time. Swan took a swig of soda.

"We should sit around like this all day every day," she joked.

She felt good, happy even, for one of the few times since Sam had been gone. Mike's first race had been another one, of course; the tea dance . . . yes, sort of, before the drive home. She was looking forward to Mike's trip to Belmont Park, to Hetty's new baby, to Linny beginning her career as a racehorse . . . the wedding, of course.

Her cell phone rang. Spaulding's number came up on the screen.

"Something's happened to Fitch," Spaulding said breathlessly. "He's at Waverly Hospital. They suspect septicemia," she said ominously. "The stump."

"The stump? What about the stump?" Swan sat bolt upright on the sofa, and the two men went silent. "*Señor* Fitch—*muy malo,*" she mouthed in their direction. "What happened?"

"He woke on Wednesday, apparently, with chills and fever," Spaulding said. "He suspected flu, but he had to go on one of the zoning board's wild goose chases, walking the Hazelton place, I believe, out in the cold rain all day. The next day he was worse, Miranda says, but he said he'd had enough of hospitals—he had to go to Waverly Park and watch the course being laid out for the races. Yesterday he was willing to stay in bed but his blood pressure dropped; Miranda convinced him to go to the emergency room, and he became so ill they admitted him to intensive care last night. They are pumping him with antibiotics. He is extremely ill."

"But the stump is healed!" Swan exclaimed. "It has been for months! He's wearing the prosthesis all the time. There is a sleeve under it."

"They think some some small area of skin was rubbed, some small wound that he ignored, and as much as he is around horses and the barn, some bacteria found its way in under the sleeve. There is inflammation at the site, that is what points to the stump as the problem."

"Can he have visitors?"

"Only family for now. They've called his mother. I don't see how Persis can get up here tonight; I believe Olivia is thinking of driving her up tomorrow," Spaulding fretted.

Boston-bred Persis Hastings Fitzhugh had moved from Waverly to Myrtle Beach when Fitch had joined the CIA. She kept in regular touch with her only child and her sister Miranda, who had moved to Virginia to be near her and had stayed after Persis had relocated. Persis had suffered a riding accident when Fitch was a child and got around primarily using crutches. She lived with her other sister, Olivia, in relative seclusion.

"Do they need anything? Can we do anything? Shall I call Persis? Miranda?" Swan asked helplessly. "Oh, God, the races today!"

Spaulding sighed.

"I think the hunt members are scrambling to fill the gaps. The hospitality people are going to be the most disappointed, but, you'll never guess: Townsend heard all of this and she called Dexter Gaylord to come schmooze the corporate types in Fitch's place. Most folks still remember his TV show," Spaulding reported. "It helps to have famous relatives, I guess."

Swan sat down and gave Eduardo and Edgar the news. She wanted to Google *septicemia*, but she couldn't get back into the house until the afternoon to get to the I-Mac. Her laptop was inside, her Blackberry kaput after a riding-related unplanned dismount. Until then, she'd have to let her memory and imagination work overtime. She knew septicemia was a blood infection. She knew that if it was diagnosed in time, it could be treated with antibiotics. Healthy people almost always recovered, but people who were immune suppressed often died, very often.

HIV.

She had never considered the possibility. Would they not have disclosed it when he had lost his hand, if it were true? She thought over what she knew of Fitch's sexual history: other than Townsend, who was little more than a child, and herself, who had never slept with him, who had he dated seriously? Florenza Burkholdt, a jet setter from Antibes, daughter of some minor Black Forest duchess. Gala Pierce, State Department—sweet but certainly not a "player." Candace Franks, Harvard instructor, separated from her husband; Vicki Waters: she had come and gone so quickly she hardly counted. All were well and thriving, so far as she knew. One-night stands—probably in the scores, but Fitch was no fool. He would have used protection whether on the streets of D.C. or in the brothels of the Middle East.

Swan ducked into the little bathroom next to the barn office. She vomited: nerves. Swan sighed as she came out and caught Eduardo's gaze. What difference did it make now? She and Spaulding would never know the truth anyway.

CHAPTER 11

The afternoon was a long nightmare, particularly when contrasted with the festive mood of the visitors pouring out of cars and minibuses to tour Belle Everley House. Hetty had been brought up to speed by Spaulding and called Swan from Richmond; the Lombardinis called Swan to make sure she had already heard, everyone was waiting on updates from the hospital, which would only talk to Persis, still in Myrtle Beach. Finally Swan got a condition report through the hospital reception desk: "intensive care" equaled "critical." Miranda decided to stay at the Waverly Hospital to talk to the doctors.

◆

In mid-afternoon, Spaulding reported Olivia and Persis were on their way. Normally Swan would have offered to put them up at Belle Everley, but the garden tour horror show made that impossible. They didn't feel comfortable at High View, Fitch's estate near Delafield; they were going to stay in one of the Reynard guest rooms, close to the hospital.

◆

At five o'clock sharp Swan raced back into her house, almost running down the hot, tired docents. She asked Mathilde to oversee their departure—typically they were given refreshments before they left—and wasted no time getting on the Internet to see what septicemia was. Just as she thought: it was bad news for a small percentage of patients who were well; very bad news for anyone with HIV. She considered going to the Waverly Hospital and thought better of it. The prospect of another day guarding the barns from the garden folks was unendurable.

Swan e-mailed Sam: *Fitch very ill: septicemia. Intensive care.*

Within eight hours, her cell phone rang as she sat in the parlor, exhausted.

"What's up?" Sam said.

"The stump," Swan said, "they think. Some barn bacteria. Bad, very bad."

"What is being done?" Swan heard the military officer beginning to assess and gather data.

"I think he's getting the best care possible, though they are talking about a consultation at Walter Reed in case it's something linked to his stint in Iraq. His mother's pretty much a basket case, and it's hard to get much out of her. No one else can do anything without her. She's next of kin."

"You sound worried."

"I'm scared shitless, actually."

"Not 'bad luck doomed love' again?"

"I've started seeing him again—as a friend. He's fine the nine months he and I aren't speaking. He's fine while you and I are dating. He's fine until you go to Kandahar and I start taking him to Furnace Mountain and going to dinner and dances. Now he's suddenly sick enough to die," Swan burst out.

"What did he say? What has he said?" Sam asked. So he had read between the lines.

"He asked, if anything happened to you, would he and I have any chance of a future together."

"What else?"

"What else did he need to say? I might just as well have put a gun to his head."

"Did you say yes?"

"Yes? Yes to what?"

"When he asked if you two could have a future if I died, did you say yes?" Sam asked patiently.

"I don't remember. I don't think so. He was blathering on and on, the way he does when we are alone together and he gets on the what-ifs. I don't pay any attention to him. We'd been talking about finding you a horse to hunt once we are married."

"Hmm. He wants to keep you, even if that means toting me along in the hunt field. I'm going to ride back in the kiddie section while he makes love to you at the front of the field. He must think I'm a complete idiot."

"He didn't mean it that way. He meant it as a peace offering, a wedding present."

Sam snorted. "Some present."

"Well, it doesn't matter now. There's no use arguing about it."

"Septicemia responds well to drug therapy, unless—"

"Yes—'unless.' I don't know . . . I don't know anything."

Sam considered this.

"Swan—" he began cautiously.

"I told you: I never slept with him! I *haven't* slept with him! I'm not going to sleep with him!" she burst out. "You do know I *hate* the fact that you've slept with a hundred women? You do know that, don't you? I don't want you to be in any doubt about that."

"Yes, I know you hate it." Sam had the good sense to say that, at least, and not reproach her about *her* impulsiveness, *her* risk-taking behavior. "Although I could make a good case it wasn't a hundred."

"Because how would you feel if I had slept with hundreds of men all over the world? *That* I would like to know," she stormed on; she was letting it all out. "You seem so judgmental of me sometimes, when I've done nothing wrong!"

"But I've done wrong? By sleeping with women before I knew you—" He was trying to follow the logic.

"Yes. No! Not just 'women'! A *hundred* women! Because you should have known that whoever you married, whether it was me or . . . or . . . some 'skank'—you should have known how hurtful it would be to her—whoever—to me. You should have known! Why didn't you?"

She heard him sigh from twelve thousand miles away.

"I didn't set out to sleep with 'a hundred' women. If I'd met you when I was fourteen, you would have been the only one, or pretty damned close to being the only one. But I didn't meet you until I was thirty-two and divorced. I hope even you don't hold it against me that I slept with my own wife," Sam said mildly.

"Don't be idiotic! You should be apologizing to me instead of making me feel like I've done something wrong, when I haven't." Swan was one breath away from beginning to sob; she could feel it.

"I apologize. I apologize for making you feel like you've done something wrong. I have no trouble with Fitch—or any of them—

when I'm there: bring 'em on, all at once or one at a time. I just feel them working on you when I'm not there. It gets to me. But I shouldn't be taking potshots at you when you're so upset."

Well, that did it: she burst into tears.

"I thought all I'd have to promise is to be faithful from now on. I didn't realize I'd have to promise to regret everything I've done up til now," he said gently, "but if that's part of the deal, count me in. Don't cry, honey. I know how worked up you are. I called to make you feel better, not worse."

She tried to stop crying. "I guess I can't blame you. You are so good-looking, women have probably thrown themselves at you from the time you hit puberty. On a scale of one to ten, you are a twenty. Even homely men think they deserve anything they're offered."

"You are a little kid in so many ways," he said. His voice was soft. "I've got to go, and you must be wiped out. Only one more day on this stupid garden tour, right?"

"Yes—over tomorrow afternoon."

"Let me know if anything happens. Honey, I'm so sorry you have to go through this. I assume you'll go to see him if they let you. You and Townsend, too. Has she come up from school?"

"I don't know. No one's mentioned her. They broke up last month."

She listened to his silence.

"I told you that." She heard his mind connecting the dots.

"Not the time to go into it now," he said smoothly. "Gotta go, Chiclet. Love you."

"Love you. Love you."

Swan was miserable when they had hung up. What the hell had happened? His jealousy over Fitch had morphed into her jealousy over the unnamed hundred in his past, obviously, and she had bitten his head off. But hadn't he deserved it?

There was only so much she could fret about at one time. Fitch.

She fell into an exhausted sleep, with Flagg at the foot of the bed, dreading six A.M. and the repeat of the garden tour circus. Thérèse Malloy arrived first, horrified and apologetic for putting Swan through the tour again.

"I'm sure you would rather be at the hospital or helping out at Waverly Park," she said frankly. "If we weren't here, you'd feel comfortable leaving Belle Everley, I know. But you can't, not with all of this going on. I'm so very sorry. Have you heard how Fitch is doing today?"

"No, I'm waiting on a call from Spaulding about Persis Fitzhugh—if she has arrived from Myrtle Beach," Swan said carefully. "Of course we are all concerned about Fitch," she said. "Major Moore particularly asked me to be sure Fitch lacks for nothing when I spoke with him last night."

"Of course, of course!" Thérèse realized her gaff; she tried to recover. "All of Fitch's friends are wild to help in whatever way we can. Major Moore is quite right."

Swan's cell phone rang. Spaulding.

"You'll have to excuse me, Thérèse. Good luck with today's turnout. Looks like good weather at least."

"Persis went over this morning. They let her in for a few minutes, with Miranda." Spaulding sounded breathless. "Swan, it's very bad. They say we all need to prepare ourselves for the worst."

"Why? How? Aren't the antibiotics working?"

"Persis broke down completely. To have reconciled herself to his disability and then to have everything go bad like this, out of the blue, it's too cruel. I don't know if she's going to be able to stand it. Miranda doesn't either."

"Did he know them when they saw him?"

"He had so many tubes, ventilator, fever, so much in so little time. Organ failure, dehydration. He seems to, but they were told not to let him talk. He probably won't remember they were there anyway."

"What is the plan if what they are doing isn't working?"

"Continue the current regimen until they see him turn it around."

"It's only been thirty-six hours. Even I.V. antibiotics, even Mithrozax, need time to work, to begin to turn things around." Swan heard call waiting beep."Spaulding, I'll call you back."

It was Persis Fitzhugh.

"He wants to see you, Swan. Can you come?"

"How is he?" Swan asked.

"Not good. Not good at all. They don't know why."

"I'll be there in half an hour, Mrs. F. Please don't worry. We're all praying for him."

Swan tore upstairs for the fastest shower on record. She threw on the first things she reached for— linen shirt, slacks—pulled her hair into a tail, and called Eduardo at the barn to tell him she was heading to the hospital. She'd be back before the ten A.M. Sunday tour opening. She left a note for Mathilde and jumped in the SUV.

She thought over her demeanor, her deportment. Honest concern or cheerful optimism? Stoic acceptance or indomitable *We'll fight this thing to a standstill*? She still didn't know when she ran up the steps at Waverly Hospital. One look at Persis's stricken face, though, took cheery optimism off the table. Persis looked like Fitch's grandmother, not his mother, sitting in the waiting room, her crutches propped next to her.

"What does the doctor say?" Swan asked, "Where is he? What are they doing for him?"

"They can't get ahead of the infection. They talked last night about going in again and re-amputating the arm to try to stem the—but it's systemic now," said Persis numbly.

"Oh, God," Swan moaned; she couldn't help it.

"Go in, please."

Swan took a deep breath and went into Intensive Care. Eight beds were arranged around a central nurse's station. Swan caught a young nurse's eye as she strode to Fitch's bedside. "Five minutes," she warned, but then she smiled as she caught sight of Swan's engagement ring. *Okay. We can play it that way,* Swan decided. *The Pity Strategy.*

"Hiya, kiddo," she said quietly, looking at Fitch.

He opened his eyes, but it was like someone on a slab in the morgue regaining consciousness.

"You look good in yellow," he rasped, eyeing her linen shirt.

"Thanks, but I'm not rocking my best look today." Swan's voice was shaky. He looked frighteningly bad. "Need anything? Anything hurt?"

"Thirsty as hell." The fever.

Swan looked around helplessly. The ventilator was off but standing at the ready, next to the bed.

"I don't know how long before they put me back on that thing," Fitch said, his eyes moving to the ventilator. "Then I can't talk."

"I know, honey," Swan said, filled with compassion for him. "I'll see if I can get something for you to drink, or ice cubes, at least."

"Don't. Not yet."

She looked at him expectantly.

"If this doesn't work out . . . okay," he said painfully. "I want you to know . . . to know—"

"I know, darling. I know. I wish things could have been different, for your sake."

"We would have been great together. We could have had little whippers-in, instead of little whipper . . . snappers," He smiled, trying to make the joke. "*Je t'aime pour toujours et jamais.*"

"*Ti amo,*" she said quietly, "*caro mio.*" She gently squeezed his good shoulder. They looked at each other. She just sat quietly with him, letting the silence soothe them both.

"Time," whispered the nurse from the central station.

"He's thirsty, nurse," Swan protested. "Can't he have something? Ice? He's burning up."

"We'll take care of it," she said reassuringly, but as Swan was leaving, she stopped her. "I think they will be taking him to Walter Reed tonight. Don't say anything to Mrs. Fitzhugh. They haven't decided yet."

Walter Reed National Medical Center. So it was true: they suspected Iraq somehow, not HIV, Swan thought, but she was alarmed nonetheless. To move an intensive care patient to a military hospital: it must be a last resort.

To tell Persis or not? Swan composed her features as she stepped out of the ICU.

"He's dying," Persis said to her lifelessly.

Swan said again, "I'm so very sorry." She put her arms around Persis, crutches and all. She thought about staying, to beg for another few minutes in another hour or so. But he had his aunts and Persis, his family, all wanting to be with him. If he was better the next day, she'd come back, or go to Walter Reed if necessary. Swan saw Townsend Brooke striding toward her, looking stricken. She embraced the teenager, then gently took Townsend's arms from around her and placed them around Persis. She turned and escaped down the hallway, her mind roiling with fear.

◆

She drove slowly back to Belle Everley. The driveway was crowded with docents and volunteers. Swan went directly to the barn office once again, grabbing a cup of tea off the hot plate. One look at her face kept Eduardo, Edgar, and Mathilde from saying a word. Swan gave them the grim prognosis. Then all sat with heads bent; Mathilde and the men made the sign of the cross and began reciting the Lord's Prayer. Swan joined them.

Swan talked to Spaulding, Bert, Hetty, and Boyd by phone about her visit with Fitch. Spaulding was going to drive up from the Willow's Edge to spend the night at Belle Everley. Mathilde volunteered to work all night, if need be, to whip the house back into shape so Persis and Miranda could move there from the Reynard the following day. Swan wondered if Townsend needed a place to stay as well or if she planned to get back to William and Mary. Her relationship with Fitch was so ambiguous, everyone was reluctant to make assumptions either way. It was awkward.

Swan e-mailed Sam: *Saw Fitch. Talked to him a little. He was feverish but off the ventilator. He's going to have to turn things around himself. Spaulding, his mother, and aunt here starting tomorrow. Sorry for being such a bitch yesterday: how I could think things are worse for me than they are for you is beyond me. LU very much.*

Spaulding arrived just after dark. She had a tray for dinner, then talked to Miranda at the Reynard by phone. Fitch had not improved during the day; he was back on the ventilator. No one was talking about Walter Reed anymore. Swan didn't know if that was better or worse. A different concoction of antibiotics was going to be layered on over the first. It sounded like a prescription for We've Got to Try Anything, How about the Kitchen Sink.

It was a great relief to have the garden tour over, at least. The plastic sheeting had preserved the carpets, but every bibelot had been moved, every table jostled out of place, every window smudged, every picture tipped off center on the walls, every drapery crumpled somehow. The front yard looked like it had been trampled by a herd of friendly but bumbling cattle. The portable toilets wouldn't be picked up until the next day. It would take Mathilde weeks to get things back to normal. And to have to cook and tidy up for a houseful of company at the same time—Swan sighed. At least the spectacular flower arrangements had been left for her company to enjoy.

"Mathilde," she said, once Spaulding had gone to her room. "If you want to get one of the town girls in to help us with the housework this week, let's do it. I'm going to have to ferry everyone to the hospital and be what help I can be to Mrs. Fitzhugh. I'll see if the hunt needs anything done— trailering or anything—in Mr. Fitch's absence. I may have to ask Edgar to go to Waverly Park to help them after the races, and if I do, I'll have to get on the horses tomorrow."

"Miss Swan, I can handle it," Mathilde said confidently. "I don't want any more strangers in the house with things as they are, after this weekend, do you?"

"No, no, I don't," Swan said, relieved. She gave Mathilde a hug. "No wonder I love you."

But by morning, all of Swan's plans had been rendered obsolete. Fitch had gone into a coma overnight. He died without regaining consciousness at three in the afternoon, his mother and both aunts weeping at his bedside. He was thirty-four.

When Swan heard the news from Spaulding, who had heard it from Miranda while she was still at the hospital, she said, "Thank God they didn't re-amputate the arm; he was spared that, at least."

Instead of coming to Belle Everley, the three bereaved women drove to High View. They had not wanted to go there while Fitch was alive, but now that he was gone, they wanted to be alone, together, to find solace and to make their arrangements.

Spaulding stayed with Swan. They made themselves a fire in the parlor fireplace and sat there all afternoon, talking, not talking, drinking pot after pot of tea delivered by a silent Mathilde. Everything seemed to have fallen apart so quickly.

"I can't believe Persis has lost him," Spaulding said. "First Francis, then Fitch. He always was such a character, such a scoundrel, but so, so charming, when he wanted to be. We all thought he'd be a comfort to her when Francis died . . . marry well, have children with some understanding wife."

Swan sat silently.

"He loved you very much," Spaulding said. "Everyone knows it."

"I wish he hadn't," Swan said, and she meant it. "It would have saved him a lot of heartache."

"If this was going to happen, I'm glad you refused him." Spaulding was suddenly fierce. "If you two had been about to get married . . . then this—"

"Yes. I'd have been certifiable. I'm not that far away as it is."

"Persis doesn't want an autopsy; she said he's been through enough. We'll never know if there was some underlying condition . . . ."

Swan couldn't take any more.

"Good night, darling," she said, kissing Spaulding on the cheek. She called to Flagg and went up the stairs to the I-Mac in the study. She typed in Sam's e-mail address: *Fitch died today 3 P.M. EDT.* When the phone rang in the middle of the night, she wasn't surprised.

"How are you holding up?" Sam asked anxiously.

"I can't believe it's all over, so . . . over," she said mournfully. "Yesterday it was, 'We must do this, do that, we have to get this,' and today, it was . . . over."

"His mother?"

"She is still in the 'wake me from this nightmare' stage."

"She's a widow, right? It's good she has her sisters and all of . . . you."

"I guess. Although when you are going through it, no one is much real help. Choosing between mahogany or brazilian cherry for the casket? Funeral home or church for the funeral? What difference does it make?" she murmured.

He was silent.

"I've thought about what you said yesterday," he said then, "about our pasts. About why I slept with so many women."

Now she was silent.

"I think I was looking for you, all along," he said. "I just didn't know how to find you. I thought I'd sleep with someone and it would hit me, like, *this is the one*. I assumed that whoever 'you' turned out to be would be doing the same thing. Sleeping with men to find the right man, I mean."

Swan sighed heavily.

"Women date to find the right one, they don't sleep around to do it, Sam. If you'd passed twenty men in Waverly, knowing I'd slept with half of them, you'd have had no problem saying, 'Hi, how're doing?' to them? Oh, please!" she scoffed. "You are the one who's naïve!"

"Given how I earn my living, it seemed like an operational strategy at the time."

Swan considered that.

"Well, it's a moot point. Everyone I've ever slept with is dead. And now, everyone who has ever truly loved me is dead, too."

"Except for me, you mean," he corrected her gently.

"Yes," she said, "except for you."

When she fell asleep this time, the Marriage in Heaven had no trouble starting itself back up again for another go 'round. Fitch was now the lucky groom, with Sam, Hunt Lee, and Carter Roland a kind of Greek chorus next to him, everyone smiling beatifically at her as she came down the aisle. It *was* a lovely wedding.

◆

On Friday, they all drove to Green Pines United Methodist, a tiny clapboard and brick church dating from the early nineteenth century. It was Miranda's church, outside Delafield, even though she now lived forty-five minutes to its south. Bertrand Davis could not get away, but he had sent a huge flower arrangement, as had Fitch's former colleagues at the CIA, Hetty and Boyd, the Waverly Hunt, the Artisan, the Piedmont Preservation Trust, the Crossroads, the Oliver Lentz Stable, and the Tuscarora Hunt, among many others.

Swan was surprised and touched to see how many people attended. Daniel Spaulding had come out to support Spaulding, and Swan, too, when it came down to it; Virgilia Osmond; Fitch's devoted farm manager, Javier, and his three grooms and farm workers; Eduardo, Edgar, and Mathilde. The Lombardinis had closed the Reynard for the afternoon. A number of Warburton executives sat behind Persis, Miranda, and Olivia—Swan didn't recognize any of them. She smiled wanly at Horatio Gonzalez, Fitch's retired farm manager, and his wife, and at Fitch's ex Gala Pierce. She embraced Townsend and Dexter Gaylord. Townsend looked absolutely shattered, as bad as Persis. Members of the Waverly Zoning Board, Taliaferro County

Planning Committee, several members of Spaulding's Hospice board who had served with Fitch, Thérèse Malloy from the Garden Club . . . there were more, as well.

After the hymns, the prayers, and the short eulogy delivered by Ezekiel Harrington from the PPT, the pastor asked Swan to come to the front of the little church. Daniel, who was sitting next to her, gave her an encouraging hug as she stood up. Once before the congregation, Swan opened a small volume of poetry she had brought with her.

"This is a poem by Jane Kenyon," Swan said in a clear, calm voice, "another gifted individual who died much too young. It's called, 'Let Evening Come.'"

Let the light of late afternoon
shine through chinks in the barn, moving
up the bales as the sun moves down.

Let the cricket take up chafing
as a woman takes up her needles
and her yarn. Let evening come.

Let dew collect on the hoe abandoned
in long grass. Let the stars appear
and the moon disclose her silver horn.

Let the fox go back to its sandy den.
Let the wind die down. Let the shed
go black inside. Let evening come.

To the bottle in the ditch, to the scoop
in the oats, to air in the lung
let evening come.

Let it come, as it will, and don't
be afraid. God does not leave us
comfortless, so let evening come.

She made it through the last verse, her voice still strong. She was proud of that. She squeezed Persis's hand as she passed the first pew and returned to her seat. Then she pulled out a wad of tissues and placed the whole thing firmly against her eyes, mascara be damned, to staunch the flow of tears.

The final hymn was "Shall We Gather at the River," from the alter-call, tent-revival days of the old South. The cremation urn was carried out and placed in the hearse, then the vehicle drove off. The congregation filed out and scattered to their cars. There was one more stop to make. Swan drove alone, slowly, from the little church through Delafield, and on to High View. The sunny day was turning overcast, with big, scudding clouds obscuring the sun. The wind picked up. Swan made the turn down the service road. Fifteen or twenty cars were behind her, Daniel's the first, following her lead. She drove carefully as the hard surface road turned to gravel, then to nothing more than a sunken lane, compacted after two hundred years of cart and farm wagon use. The wind had done its job; the flat ground was dry enough for a four-wheel-drive vehicle to navigate. Then even the farm lane seemed to disappear. Swan continued more slowly now, heading into an open field not yet plowed for the spring planting. The hillocky ground bumped the SUV up and down, and the cars behind Swan slowed to a crawl. She was facing west, toward the foothills of the Blue Ridge. At a small marker she parked the SUV, and the cars behind her lined up to park in a row next to her, obediently, as though they were lining up for the start on a racetrack.

"Take my arm, Swannie," murmured Daniel solicitously, as they disembarked.

Ahead of her, Swan saw the funeral home's black Lincoln Town Car driving to an unmarked spot, out of view, toward a low ridge. She and Daniel began to walk toward it, and as they did so, a knot of mounted horsemen in a stand of trees to the east caught her eye. Swan recognized them after a moment. At the fence line, she stopped. A four-foot tall natural log drop had been built into the sagging wire fencing bordering the field twenty years earlier. Grapevine, locust saplings, poison ivy, wild raspberry bushes, and thistle had overgrown the fence itself. In April it was alive with goldfinches, Eastern bluebirds, mockingbirds, thrushes, and wrens.

Fitch had led the Waverly Hunt over this daunting fence hundreds of times, from the time he turned fourteen and his father master before him. On the other side of the fence was the hearse, its back doors opening onto a small trench. Persis, Miranda, and Olivia were seated, none too steadily, in folding chairs, next to the pastor, at the graveside. The other mourners caught up to the site, and when all had gathered, the pastor stood.

"*I am the resurrection and the life*," he intoned. At the end of the reading, he motioned to William Hardaway, who began reciting Robert Louis Stevenson's "Requiem" from memory.

Under the wide and starry sky
Dig the grave and let me lie
Glad did I live and gladly die
And I laid me down with a will.
This be the verse you 'grave for me
'Here he lies where he long'd to be
Home is the sailor, home from the sea
And the hunter, home from the hill.'

The distant riders were moving toward them. The Waverly foxhounds swirled around the horses like autumn leaves caught in a gust of wind. Kezia Hardaway, the acting M.F.H., led the staff, wearing black armbands, with black cloth covering the buttons and facings of their hunt coats. The whippers-in and huntsman Ezra Wilky fanned out behind Kezia as they approached the other mourners. Forty riders galloped slowly, in a half seat, taking the stone wall on the far side of the field in perfect order, as though they were a Stubbs painting come to life. Even at that distance, Swan recognized Declan Flynn, Jerusha Dutton, in the hunt field for the first time in ten years, and the masters of Tuscarora, Cheswick, and the Grange hunts, as well as the Alamand Hunt from Maryland. She felt a hand grip hers: Townsend Brooke had crept to her and leaned against her for support.

Kezia brought the riders and hounds among the mourners, to their astonishment, and halted at the graveside. She nodded, once. The gentlemen members as one doffed their velvet hunt caps and helmets, the lady members dropping their heads in formal salute to their fallen master.

"*Ashes to ashes, dust to dust,*" intoned the pastor, then all joined in the Lord's Prayer. After a moment of silence, Wilky blew the long, drawn out blast of "Gone Away" on his horn. The loss of the quarry. End of the day. Kezia nodded once again. The gentlemen replaced their hunt caps and gathered up their reins. Wilky lifted the cheerful, open-mouthed hounds as the field turned back to the east, away from the grave. Kezia swung them all at a slow gallop in a large circle around the mourners, then turned the pack toward home. A flock of sparrows flew up in protest at the hubbub and briefly darkened the sky over the grave.

Toot-toot toot-toot tooooot, toot-toot toot-toot tooooooot.

The huntsman's horn, unmistakable, noble, melancholy, rang out. The field galloped slowly, a controlled retreat from them, a thrilling sight. Soon, soon, they were far away and then, gone.

Swan looked at Spaulding, who was embracing Persis in her chair through a soaking cascade of tears. Persis looked blankly at those approaching her, kissing her cheek, patting her shoulder, in a futile effort to comfort her. Fitch's mother looked only moments away from collapse. One of the funeral home staff gently helped her to her feet, then toward the car. The other mourners straggled back to their cars, weary, silent, dispirited. Swan kept her arm around Townsend but could offer her no comfort. She could think of nothing to say. She followed the others.

Squirrels and nesting birds chattered obliviously in the fencerows, busy with the tiny, urgent details of life. Swan took one last look around High View, now without its master, without an heir. She wondered if she'd ever have the heart to walk, much less ride, these fields again. Perhaps she'd come back to see the grave when it had settled, the grass grown over it, the copper marker affixed to a large field stone adjacent to the gravesite itself. The sun burst out from behind the scudding clouds.

Daniel kissed Swan briefly and got in his car. She stood beside her SUV, then threw herself into the driver's seat. Swan wanted Belle Everley. She wanted Sam. She wanted life.

Thinking of you today, began Sam's e-mail when she checked on the I-Mac at home. *I hope his family is bearing up. I may not be able to call for a day or two. Give your dog a hug for me. LU always, Sam.*

Spaulding went home the next day. She was going to stop at High View to see Persis and Olivia, who were returning to Myrtle Beach to see to Fitch's affairs from there. There was already some discreet interest in the fate of High View: no one thought Persis would move back into the manor house. Its steep, narrow nineteenth-century staircases and non-wheelchair friendly bathrooms made it a difficult house for someone not completely ambulatory, and the huge acreage was daunting to manage. The community feared that the great estate would be prime for purchase by developers, but Persis had just put her only son in the ground there and Fitch had been an implacable foe of development. More likely was that Persis would find a tenant who would want the farm as it was, at least for the time being.

That left the fate of the employees up in the air, and Swan knew Eduardo and Edgar in particular were anxious for Javier, a fellow countryman. When Kezia called her the next day, Swan assumed it was to discuss employment opportunities for Fitch's loyal workers.

"Swan, this may come as a surprise to you, but when Fitch was in the hospital, he told Mrs. Fitzhugh that he wanted you to have James if he did not recover. He thought James might suit Major Moore, and Fitch said he had promised you a hunt horse as a wedding present," the veterinarian said. "Mrs. Fitzhugh agreed that it would make sense to send James over immediately rather than wait for probate. I said I would help place the other horses as time permits, and I believe the cattle are going to be sold at public auction."

"James . . . for me?"

"Yes, as soon as you are ready for him. Shall I send the van?"

Swan felt a sudden pang: dear James, who had carried Fitch and kept him safe all year long, despite his terrible injury, and for years before that, now without his master.

"No, I'll send Eduardo to pick him up this afternoon. I want him here as soon as possible. If Fitch wanted me to have him, I don't want him to be alone."

Eduardo felt the same way about James. He had the big gelding off the van and bedded in the stall next to Punch right after lunch, with a full hay net to munch on. James looked cheerful and calm when Swan went to the barn to give him a welcoming pat.

"What do you think, Eduardo? Will he do for the major when he returns in the fall?" she asked, her spirits lifting for the first time since Fitch was taken ill.

"If you give *el mayor* riding lessons, Jaime will take care of him the way he took care of *Señor* Fitch," said Eduardo soulfully.

"Eduardo, we are going to have to take very good care of the major when he comes home," Swan said, suddenly very serious. "We can't let anything happen to him."

◆

Two days later, another surprise.

"Daniel is going to rent High View from Persis," Spaulding announced breathlessly, when she called, "at least month to month. He hates the District, says there are too many 'distractions,' and he has always liked Delafield."

"My God, how can he afford it?"

"I think Persis just wants someone in there she knows, whose rent will pay the taxes and insurance and who will oversee things while Fitch's will goes through probate," Spaulding said. "It's better than letting the house sit empty and letting the staff go, particularly with Persis out of state. There will have to be a property assessment, and as executor, Persis is responsible for securing the assets, so it is just good fiduciary responsibility. And to have a banker as a tenant . . . ."

A tenant who is also a cocaine user, Swan thought grimly, but she said nothing. She had plenty to tell Sam, though, when he finally got through by phone late that night.

"Daniel at Fitch's? Well, you all certainly know how to keep it in the family," he said in amazement. "But I can see how it would make sense. A banker will be helpful in making things happen for Fitch's mother, disabled as she is. I assume she is his heir."

"Well, it isn't me, if that is what you are thinking," Swan said, a little defensively, "though he did bequeath us something."

"Us?"

"Yes, his M.F.H.'s horse, James—for you, really. To ride. Just like he said," Swan explained, feeling Fitch had been vindicated. "He is a wonderful horse, very reliable and beautifully trained for a gentleman rider. I've already got him here in the barn."

"Waiting for me?" Sam said, in wonderment.

"Yes, for you, sweetie."

"But doesn't the master's horse travel at the front? Will he be happy packing a novice back in the peanut gallery?"

"James is very adaptable. Once he understands his new job, he'll get you around fine. And no horse knows Waverly country better than James—every fence, every ford, every ditch. If there is such a thing as a point and shoot horse, James is your guy."

"Well, I've got to give Fitch credit: he was a man about the whole thing, after all." Sam was grudgingly appreciative. "Listen, I'm up for trying the Skype again, tomorrow night, if possible. How about you?" Their three previous attempts had been foiled by a thunderstorm in Waverly, slow feeds out of Afghanistan, and one Internet blackout. It wasn't acknowledged, but these blackouts took place when there were casualties the brass didn't want communicated to families prior to the official notices going out.

"Yes, I want to see you, not just talk to you." There was yearning in her voice.

By the next morning there was other news. Oliver Lentz had entered Mike in a maiden special weight at Belmont on April 28. Oliver was back from Florida and overseeing his string at Furnace Mountain personally.

"You won't guess what else is going on that evening," Spaulding remarked, when she heard the news. "*Tristan und Isolde* is at the Met, at Lincoln Center. You can make the seventh race and still get there. You should go."

Swan considered this. The temptation was strong.

"*Tristan* was Fitch's favorite; I don't know if I'm up to it," she said.

"I think it would be good for you. You love Wagner. Let me get two tickets, and you can decide later if you want to go; you can always sell them if you change your mind."

Swan was still undecided.

"Let me talk to Sam tonight and think about it in the meantime."

She made sure she was dressed, made up, and smiling when they tried the video Skype feed that night. They lucked out. After a short delay, Swan suddenly saw Sam on the big I-Mac in the study. His face broke into a huge smile, so she knew he saw her, too.

"Hey, baby," he said delightedly. He was sunburned, in his camouflage utility uniform, with a black and white Keffiyeh scarf around his neck and his hair newly shorn under headphones. She could see he was in a huge, USO-style tent with Internet cubicles made out of canvas and plastic chairs visible behind him. Each chair was filled by a service person of one branch of the military or another, judging by the uniforms.

"God, it's great to finally see you," he said, but she could see the anxiety in his face nonetheless. She tried to smile more naturally in response.

"Sam," was all she could say, before she suddenly started to tear up.

"I know, I know," he said sympathetically. "But we don't have much time."

Swan wiped her eyes on her sleeve.

"You look great," he said encouragingly.

"You, too. New haircut?" She tried to match his cheerfulness.

"Yeah, cooler," he grinned, and her heart warmed in her throat. More tears trickled down her face. "If you are going to do that the whole time, we aren't going to get very far, honey," he said, still trying to help her.

"I know, I know." She wiped her face furiously. "I'm not really this bad, I'm usually okay."

"Yes, you are one tough little cupcake," he teased. "So how's my new horse? And my dog?"

"They're both fine. Flagg is right here," she sniffled. "Flagg, say 'hi' to Dad: *Gib laut!*" She turned to the Shepherd's big dark eyes and, with a little encouragement, the dog gave a ferocious bark.

Sam laughed. "I hope James is in the barn and not there in the house, too, waiting to say 'hi.'"

"Affirmative." She was recovering now, finally and could give him a genuine smile. "He's eating us out of house and home, though, Sam. He's a big guy."

"As big as Mike? Cut us big guys some slack—we need our chow." Then his voice softened again. "How's my girl doing tonight?"

"Hanging in there," Swan said. "We are all still in complete shock. But what about you? Are you seeing any . . . activity? Are you staying . . . put?"

"Negative and negative," he answered carefully.

"MREs any better this tour?" She moved into safer territory. She knew he was in a dining hall facility somewhere, but it was all she could think of to ask.

"Tasteless, goopy, and processed," he reported cheerfully. "I could go for some of Mathilde's cooking about now. I had a dream about Boyd's jalepeño corn last night, so you know how bad it must be," he joked. "I should be dreaming about my honey, not fresh vegetables."

Swan thought about the Marriage in Heaven dream, now starring Fitch. "Me, too."

"Looks like your hair is getting longer," Sam said softly, "Turn around and show me." She turned her head. "Not just your head, honey, stand up and let me see all of you."

"Too long?" she asked, twisting around so she could look at the monitor.

"Can't be too long for me," he said. "Don't cut it til I get back, at least." He sighed appreciatively. "Man, what a caboose. That's what we're over here fighting for—that beautiful backside I first saw in the Crossroads."

That did make her laugh. "You are a hopeless sex maniac."

"Lucky for you."

"I forgot to ask—did you get the things I sent for Easter?" Swan had mailed a chocolate Easter basket wrapped in cold packs, as well as batteries, foot powder, auto magazines, baby wipes, just before the weekend of disaster.

His face lit up.

"Oh yeah, even the chocolate was okay. The dry ice packs worked great and you just got in under the wire—no chocolate over here from mid-April to October, because of the heat. We sat around and ate little chocolate bunnies like real warriors."

She laughed again. "No wonder I miss you."

"I'm still waiting on my letter, baby." His voice was persuasive. "But I'm not complaining, it's great to have someone to wait on."

"I wish you were here—home!" Swan burst out suddenly, anguished. "I'm still having that Marriage in Heaven dream, for one thing, and this nightmare with Fitch . . . . I'm worried about Daniel being at High View, and I've got to go see Mike in New York by myself when I really just want to stay home. Hetty's beginning to feel miserable. This stuff doesn't happen when you're here!"

"Yes it does, but you handle it better when you're getting some TLC from the old man," he chuckled gently. "I feel the same way about you." His voice became low, rough, intense. "The only time I'm really happy is when I'm in your body."

"Don't. Don't say things like that. It makes it harder," she moaned, "but better, too, I guess. I'm acting like an idiot." Swan swallowed, sniffed hard, then hiccuped unceremoniously. "You know, you are really a great guy," she said weakly.

"That's what the Taliban tell me," he said, relieved to hear her rally. "But, honey, I've gotta go, you should see the line here. Love ya."

"I miss you, I miss you . . . . Call me when you can!" she cried. The monitor lost the feed. She put her head down on her arms and wept, very gently.

◆

The next day she called Hetty for an update on baby Bolington. Still eight weeks from delivery, Hetty was tired, grouchy, and experiencing a little uptick in her blood pressure. Swan knew Hetty didn't want to complain under the circumstances, but she needed sisterly commiseration. She let her ventilate a little, and she could hear Hetty was grateful for the attention and the sympathy.

Then Spaulding called.

"I have the opera tickets and a good idea. Why don't you take Daniel with you to New York? He can go to the races and escort you to Lincoln Center, then you can catch a midnight flight back to Dulles, or you can get up first thing the next morning, catch the shuttle, and be home in time for Mathilde to put breakfast on the table. You know how much you want to see Mike run at the big track, and we'd all feel better if you were in New York with an escort."

Spaulding was right. Who know what might happen—this could be Mike's last race. Daniel was congenial, urbane, gallant. Whatever else he was or did, he was still family.

"I'll think it over."

The next day she impulsively called Daniel at Tidewater Commercial.

"Sure, Swan, I'd enjoy going to Lincoln Center and seeing Oscar Mike, too. I haven't been to Belmont since your parents and Spaulding took us all—God, it must have been seven or eight years ago. Didn't we see Punch run in a handicap race? No, it was before Punch's time. But it was a great day," Daniel said amiably.

Swan e-mailed Sam and the next day had a reply: *Glad you are going to New York; looks like we're moving out somewhere. I'll try to call later in the week.*

She tried to parse this particular message but was unable to trigger that well-honed alarm system in her head, the one that after long and bitter experience could cut through the "don't worry" bullshit she'd been feed so many times, the condescension, the unintended arrogance of these men who thought they were bulletproof, all evidence to the contrary. What was the use? Unless she flew to Kandahar and ran interference in front of his humvee with her SUV down the old Silk Road, what could she do but accept the "don't worry" story once again?

Accept did not mean believe.

The only remedy was to immerse herself in the life she knew and could control. She stopped in to see Jerusha and Declan school the poised two-year-old Dress the Line at the training center and oversaw the first veterinary exams of the new foals, still happily learning about life in the fields in front of the old house. A Gold Chip van arrived one evening to unload Serve the Guns, safely in foal, and Swan was happy to return her to her herd. Gunny was the deputy while The Fortress was in Kentucky, and she calmed asserted her authority in the mare and foal field.

Swan took a picture of herself standing on tiptoe in front of James in the barn aisle, her head easily fitting under his towering head, and sent it to Sam as an e-mail attachment: *Your new horse,* she captioned it and hoped he would get a laugh at how tiny she looked. She had thought of sending a more provocative one via mail, perhaps in a t-shirt *sans* bra, but her natural modesty won out; there was no such thing as privacy, even in officers' quarters. There were strict rules on what visual images could be sent into the religiously conservative Afghanistan, anyway.

What would they do if he was assigned to Oceanside for his next stateside rotation? She really had no plan other than a renewal of the shuttling she'd done in the winter. But to see him so little, only to have him rotate back overseas, was unendurable. In the back of her mind Swan had the idea of asking Bert Davis to pull strings for him—well, for her, really—and have him posted back at Quantico. It was inexcusable in wartime to even think about it, but that didn't prevent her from keeping it as an option in her mind. She got comfort from it. Perhaps by the time he was eligible for another rotation overseas, the wars would have settled into a garrison type situation, with marine units not exposed in the villages but acting as urban police forces tamping down tribal violence. Or she could rent the house at Belle Everley, leave Eduardo in charge of the barns and the horses, put her carpetbag on her back, and follow him to—wherever.

Chapter 12

The night before Mike's race at Belmont Park, Swan was taking stock of her wardrobe. She planned to wear the blue Seriano to Lincoln Center; it was not opening night at the Met, so she needn't be any more formal than that. Daniel had made dinner reservations at the Evergreen Inn in midtown, owned by a famously well connected magazine publisher, and they were going to stay at the nearby Algonquin Hotel before catching a seven A.M. shuttle back to Dulles.

Oliver Lentz had vanned Mike to Belmont Park the weekend before and had given the colt several days' work over the enormous track's dirt surface, with encouraging results. His breezes from Furnace Mountain, his second place finish at Delaware and his impeccable bloodlines might have earned him a bit more attention from handicappers and track media, except it was just before Kentucky Derby week, when all eyes turned to Churchill Downs, not Belmont Park.

Swan planned to call Bert Davis upon her return. She had spent time on the Internet, in chat rooms and on blogs, to try to piece together the activities of Sam's unit. There had been several spectacularly bad weeks of casualties—U.N. observers, D.E.A. agents, a fixed-wing aircraft crash involving senior military personnel—then a week of relative calm. Swan wanted a better take on the real story. Why she wanted this was clear in her own mind, although she refused to acknowledge it otherwise: she thought if she had enough information, her "impending doom" radar would either kick in or stay silent.

◆

The next morning, she met Daniel, in a Gucci suit and an elegant haircut, at the gate at Dulles. She was wearing the champagne silk shirtwaist dress with chocolate silk-covered buttons she'd worn in Oceanside—for luck, she felt. They'd be the best-looking owners in the winner's circle. A quick call to Oliver confirmed that Mike was good to go for the afternoon. Their forty-five-minute flight was consumed with chat: Daniel's impending move to High View, Hetty's progress, Persis's recovery, Belle Everley and Waverly doings.

Swan detoured Daniel to Clarissa of Boston for a wedding dress. Swan's first dress, for her marriage to Hunt Lee, had been from Dara Tang. When she had cancelled the order, Tang had not charged her anything for the alterations or the dress, out of respect. Her second dress, for Carter Roland, had been ordered but not fitted at Renfields of New York City. They had cancelled it without penalty, shocked by her second loss.

Once the Clarissa bridal consultant figured out that Daniel wasn't the bridegroom, it was relatively simple to choose a strapless ball gown with a fitted bodice and buttons down the back in a white silk satin that would compliment Hetty's vermillion silk satin matron of honor's gown. Swan had the tiny buttons covered in vermillion satin and—with Daniel's approval—long gloves in the same material. She wanted something different this time. Swan had already decided to have the service for 125 guests at Waverly Methodist, which was larger than tiny Everley Methodist, and the reception at Belle Everley: all the work done for Historic Garden Week had left the old house picture perfect. She had asked Patty and Lorenzo to handle the catering and Waverly Florist to provide the flowers, with the help of a floral designer from the garden club. Lester Lanin would provide the dance music; a string quartet at the church, a D.J. for late night partying. It helped immensely that she had researched two previous such soirées.

"If I plan any more of these things," Swan said to Daniel, as she made her down payment at Clarissa's, "I might as well go into it as a career."

They cabbed it to Long Island, to the Belmont Park clubhouse, for the seventh race. Swan and Daniel would see Mike in the paddock with Oliver and, for the first time, Tomás Iglesias. The jock was scheduled to ride not the Templetons' homebred but the Derby favorite, Izquierdo, the following week on Kentucky Derby day.

Soon it was time to gather in the paddock with the other connections around the impressive bronze sculpture of Secretariat in full gallop. Swan had eyes only for her magnificent Mike when the groom brought him in to be saddled. The colt seemed six inches taller than when she had seen him at Delaware the month before, coal black now, but still with that restless, competitive eye that Swan had seen in Belle Everley horses ever since The Fortress had been foaled almost a quarter of a century earlier.

Oliver Lentz was calm in front of a slim crowd of ten thousand weekday racing fans. He reached out to Swan, looking more like a prosperous realtor rather than a member of horse racing's Hall of Fame.

"My dear Swan, and Mr. Spaulding—good to see you, too," Oliver said, grasping her hand in his. He looked deeply into her eyes. "So very, very sorry about Fitch, we were all heartbroken."

"Yes, he would have liked to have had a wager on Oscar Mike today," Swan said, forcing a bright smile.

"We've covered his numbers nicely," added Daniel, holding up several win and triple tickets.

"Well, let's see if we can boot one home for the master of Waverly Hunt this afternoon," Oliver said calmly, turning to Tomás. "You remember Miss Bolington of Belle Everley, Tomás?"

The top rider of the just-completed Aqueduct meet caught the name of the Virginia farm before he registered Swan's identity, but he smiled cordially. His eyes, however, were on Mike, his non-winning mount from Delaware Park. This was not the first handsome homebred with stellar connections that he'd thrown his leg over—it was just another day at the office for Tomás. If this colt didn't have the goods, he'd be on one who did the next time.

They walked behind the horses, under the grandstand, up to the cavernous clubhouse. On Belmont Day, six weeks away, forty thousand people would fill the seats, while another fifty thousand wedged their way in to see the greatest race of the Triple Crown. Compared to other racetracks, Belmont was enormous. The ring was a mile and a half in circumference, and the horses looked like they were running to Long Island's furthest reaches when they made for the first turn.

Today the field was only seven runners, including Mike.

Swan had two thousand dollars worth of win tickets on her colt, who was at odds of seven-to-two based solely on his connections: Tomás and Oliver were reason enough to grab the attention of those who couldn't see a reason to bet another horse in the field.

Tomás was a rail specialist who loved the inside post position, not the best spot for a horse slow to take off like Mike, but he had a clock in his head, a great feel for the horses around him, and nerves of steel. If Mike was going to get anywhere, Tomás was going to get him there.

◆

After years of preparation, they were at Belmont Park. Swan's horse was walking in the footsteps of Secretariat, Affirmed, Seattle Slew, Spectacular Bid. Then suddenly, the post parade—with Mike in the Belle Everley silks, prancing past them—was over. The horses were loaded in the starting gate in ninety seconds. The gate flew open: Mike's huge leap forward gave him a good start. Tomás let the field settle into position, like a chess grandmaster: the speedsters shooting to the front, Tomás sliding from post position four into the rail behind the leaders, letting Mike roll along as the dirt from Big Sandy flew into his face off the heels of the horse in front.

"Okay, okay, okay," murmured Oliver, as the horses cruised on the far turn, then suddenly Mike's black head was creeping between the two frontrunners, through a small hole that opened like a merge lane on the expressway, Tomás moving Mike into the next gear, smooth as silk.

"Here we go, here we go," Oliver was pounding his race program rhythmically, just like Sinjon had at Delaware Park, his voice increasing in tempo.

"Yes! Yes! Yes!"

Mike was making the famous turn for home, and for the first time Swan was screaming for her colt as he made the lead.

"Here comes Oscar Mike," announced the race caller, "with Go with the Flow hanging on gamely . . . ."

The colt was flying now. Tomás had released his hold and was urging him on for more speed.

"Yes! Yes! Yes! Yes! Yes! Yes! Yes! Yes! YESSSSSSSS!" Swan was screaming like a banshee, jumping up and down, grabbing Daniel, like all of the half-crazed owners of all the runners who ever crossed the finish line first.

"It's going to be Oscar Mike, by a length, over Go with the Flow, and Raison d'Etre for third," came the call. Oliver had a serene smile, Daniel a fistful of winning tickets, Swan a huge lump in her throat.

"For Fitch," Daniel said to her, and her eyes welled up with tears. But she still jumped up and down.

Daniel took her arm as they all headed to the winner's circle. A few horseplayers patted Oliver's shoulder, shouting congratulations, as they worked their way down to the main level of the track; Lentz had become recognizable by the national audience during Cartouche's campaign. Everyone else immediately turned their heads back to the *Daily Racing Form*, to the next race, due to begin in twenty minutes.

"Here's where we belong," said Oliver, grinning to Tomás as the grooms brought Mike, blowing but triumphant, from the racetrack through the opening in the rail, into the winner's circle. Swan confidently took her colt's bridle, and Mike neighed when he felt her touch, a boyish, ringing whinny that made the rail birds laugh and clap. Oliver gallantly stood just to her side, letting his owner feel that thrill of victory on her own. Then the winner's circle photo was taken and Tomás jumped off to weigh out, return to the jockey's room, and don the silks of the owner of his mount in the next race. But first, he turned to Swan.

"*Miguel es muy rapido, señorita,*" he grinned, and the man who had ridden three Kentucky Derby winners gave her a thumbs up.

It was like being hugged by the president of the United States. Oliver took Mike as they left the winner's circle, expertly layering his halter over the bridle, Swan's moment in the sun over. They all walked joyfully to the backside, the stabling area where Daniel and Swan watched the hot walker and Hope Fuellen hand walk Mike around the stable area before giving him his bath.

"We've got to go," said Swan to Oliver. "Many, many thanks. For everything."

"Let's make this a habit, shall we?" Oliver said with a smile. "I'll call you tomorrow, but he looks like he came out of it okay."

Daniel and Swan checked into the Algonquin with just enough time to change and dash to the Evergreen Inn for an early dinner. Daniel had brought his tuxedo but wore it sans tie, in the European mode. Swan called Edwardo, Spaulding, and Hetty with the good news from the cab; she left a message for Jerusha Dutton on her voice-mail. Eduardo had seen the race on TV and was so excited his Spanish was too fast for Swan to comprehend. She just laughed whenever he took a breath. Once in the clubby Evergreen, they ordered dim sum, white chocolate mousse, and champagne. While they waited to be served, their talk finally turned to Septimus Moore.

"Well, Swan, give me all the news about Sam," Daniel said sardonically."I suppose he is happy as a clam to be back banging heads with the same warlords he was chasing six years ago."

"Daniel, the reason the war is going so badly in Afghanistan is because the opium trade is fueling the Taliban's ability to mount a vigorous defense. The guys buying dope on U Street —or in the Scarab—are directly funding the guys shooting at Sam right now! Anyone doing heroin might as well declare themselves enemy combatants as far as I'm concerned," Swan said angrily, "or they should get hooked on crystal meth. At least that's a homegrown product."

"Of course—you have every reason to feel that way," Daniel said sympathetically. "He seems like a really patriotic guy. We need more like him—willing to lay themselves on the line for politicians who blow one way one day and another the next. That takes guts," he continued, placating her. "On your part, too, sweetie. It is damned unfair for a relative few and their loved ones to shoulder the whole burden while the rest of us . . . ." He left his sentiment unfinished, and Swan moved them into safer territory: the Wagnerian love story they were about to see.

They immersed themselves in the opera once they were at Lincoln Center—those singers who could do justice to the Wagnerian repertoire were few and far between. Swan wept during the love duet; Daniel handed her his monogramed handkerchief. Then they had a nightcap at the Algonquin's storied piano bar, twelve-stepping or no for Daniel. He had been charming and courtly all day, and Swan teased him on how he'd attracted the attention of several women, both during the performance and at the hotel before they called it a night. The next morning, Swan and Daniel returned triumphantly to Dulles. They parted, Daniel to D.C. and Swan to the farm, with the promise that they'd catch up with each other once he had moved in to High View.

Swan dragged her overnight bag into the entranceway with relief. Mathilde had taken messages for her, leaving the pink slips on the hall table: Oliver Lentz, with an okay on Mike's post-race recovery; Townsend Brooke; Sam. Oh: she had missed him last night. Had he forgotten that she was going to be in New York? Eduardo, Edgar, and Mathilde converged upon her, and she happily gave them a second by second account of the race before trudging upstairs to change from the chocolate silk pants into green Pikuers and the green Vogels. She sent Sam an e-mail: *Sorry to have missed you; Mike won convincingly at Belmont, at 7-2. Spent the night in NYC. Great fun but I'd given it all to have had you there instead. LU, Swan.*

Then Swan went downstairs to write a check to the Waverly Hooved Animal Rescue League for two thousand dollars, Fitch's winnings on Mike at Belmont Park, in memory of Hastings Fitzhugh.

She wanted to call Townsend before she did anything else. She hadn't talked to her since Fitch's funeral, primarily because catching her between classes or in the dorm at night was a challenge. No sooner did she reach the phone than it rang on its own.

"I was just going to call you," Swan said when she heard the teenager on the line. "How are things going, sweetie?"Swan settled into the hall chair, Flagg happily on her feet.

Townsend sighed.

"I just feel so low, Swan. Sometimes I feel we might have gotten back together, and other times I know Fitch always carried a torch for you. That's what everyone thinks: Uncle Dex, your Aunt Spaulding—everyone."

Swan hesitated, mulling over a lie.

"Well, everyone is wrong. The last time we were together, Fitch and I agreed that the past was past. We were over. What would have happened if things had turned out differently, no one will ever know."

"I just wish our relationship hadn't seemed to have been mostly about . . . sex," Townsend said sadly.

"Honey, for men, most of any relationship is about sex. They are taught to suppress every emotion—no crying, no fear—their whole lives, then they are expected to go hog wild during sex. It's the only time they are allowed to let go, be real, be emotional. No wonder it's all they think about, really," Swan said. "It is amazing they can hold jobs or function at all, when you think about it."

"I guess, when you put it that way . . . ." Townsend sounded like she was buying it.

"I know he liked you very much. He gave you some great memories, and you were such fun to be around for him. Try to think of things that way. And you should begin to think about dating again. You are finishing up your freshman year. You should be meeting people. What are your plans for the summer: back to L.A.?"

"I'm not sure yet. I'd like to stick around here—Virginia, I mean. My parents are on location in Budapest for the summer. Uncle Dex says I can stay at his place. He'll be gone for a few weeks promoting that indie film he shot last year, but otherwise around. I just don't know."

"Well, you know you have friends here. My cousin Daniel is moving out to High View. He was at the hunt ball in December, do you remember? He's a little closer to you in age: well, he is twenty-eight and a banker, but still . . . and my offer of riding lessons stands. I've got Fitch's James here now, too, for Sam to ride when he comes home."

"We could have lunch and . . . stuff?"

"Absolutely. My Oscar Mike won a race at Belmont Park just yesterday. We could go to one of his races. Have you ever been to a real racetrack, not a steeplechase course, I mean?" Swan felt suddenly protective of Townsend, she was so forlorn. "And my sister, Hetty, will be having a baby in June. She's in Richmond, but I'm sure she will be up here for a visit. And of course, I'll be planning my wedding. I've just ordered my gown, with vermillion, cream and saffron as my accent colors. Food, flowers, music—we'll be choosing them over the summer."

"Sounds like fun." Townsend was warming to the whole idea.

They rang off. Swan felt good about her lie. What was the harm? Townsend was miserable, Fitch was in the ground, and fronting the lie in a good cause might hold "bad luck doomed love" at bay. Swan went upstairs and checked her e-mail. Nothing from Sam. She left a message for Bert Davis at D.O.D. and was pleasantly surprised to hear from him before she left the house for the barn.

"Do you know what is up with Sam, mission-wise? With all we've been through with Fitch, it would help if I knew he was, well, safe, or as safe as he can be over there. No details, just reassurance." Swan heard Bert's voice go cautious immediately.

"What has Sam said?"

"Absolutely nothing. That is why I'm asking you." She tried to laugh naturally, but it came out shaky and forced.

"Well, you know how fluid things are. We've got our hands full. We've put our senior guys in a difficult position politically, but they have said all along that they are up to it. The have to be. They've been given thc funds, so they are expected to deliver, even if the mission is . . . transformed."

"You mean acting like an urban police force instead of fighting armies?"

"That could be part of it. The thing is, Swan, and this is the salient point, Sam needs to watch his step while he's there. The players have changed, the terrain has changed. The rules have changed. The Administration is open to all points of view, but serving officers at his level need to be prudent."

Swan felt a chill.

"It's volatile, Swan. Not all of our allies are Boy Scouts, not all officials there, as here, are above reproach. Sam needs to remember that."

Swan could tell Bert had said all he was planning to say. Even that much was more than he'd say to anyone who wasn't family. Sam must have said something, done something . . . or something.

"Thank you, Bert. I mean it. Thank you."

"Honey, I like Sam. He could have a brilliant military career. But he needs to keep his ear to the ground."

"And his mouth shut?"

"Don't be alarmed," Bert sounded fatherly again. "He's not in harm's way . . . not directly anyway. We are all working toward a solution. Now I've got to run. The Secretary is calling."

"Can I say anything to Sam?" she asked cautiously. "Should I?"

"Use your judgment, honey, just use your own judgment."

Well, it could have been worse, Swan thought. No political cesspools were as dangerous as an AK-47 pointed at unprotected areas of the anatomy. She felt an alarming little surge of relief at the thought: what if Sam did not have a brilliant military career in his future? She envisioned them at Belle Everley: community leaders, parents perhaps, charity board members, racehorse owners . . . but Sam would hate it all if it wasn't his decision, if he was forced out.

The Marines were his life, his family. Didn't he all but tell her so when he told her about his mother? The Marines had given him the polish, the recognition, the purpose—everything Fitch didn't have at the end. Everything that not having had made Fitch bitter and angry. Did she want to see Sam turn into Fitch?

Swan went to the barn. She wanted to clear her head, to become totally absorbed in the horse's way of seeing, of thinking, of reacting. Edgar was getting off James as she walked in. The old campaigner needed just a stretch of his legs to keep fit. Swan pulled a sugar lump from her pocket. She wanted James to begin to bond with her and trust his new surroundings. Even the most unflappable horse was flummoxed by drastic changes in housing, handlers, routine. Swan couldn't help Fitch anymore, but she could help James.

"I'd like to ride him," she said to Edgar, "just around the property." She got a leg up and felt James's smooth, powerful Rolls Royce of an engine move her off in huge, ground-covering strides. Within moments she was slowly but surely being run away with, as James moved forward, oblivious to her riding aids. Typical man's horse, Swan thought, bemused.

"Hey, James," she said, her voice a warning. "This little peanut up here is in charge." She gave him a sharp reminder with the reins and banged her butt in the saddle a couple of times to get his attention. James seemed to realize she was on board, but he picked up speed anyway, reaching out with his stride farther and farther. Swan let him roll on as she slowly exerted her authority, using her balance, voice, and timing to compensate for not being the five-foot-eleven, one-hundred-eighty-five-pound rider James was used to. She laughed—she was fearless, really, on horseback—and began to enjoy herself. How ludicrous it was: she who had broken the rocket express, Oscar Mike, was now barreling down her own driveway virtually without any control at all. It felt as though the wheel had come off the steering column in her hands while speeding down Route 95. James, who thought they were on the same page, just kept on agoin' as they reached the intersection with the hard surface road. Swan's brake pedals were disconnected from the wheels. James made the turn toward High View.

A familiar Volvo appeared, coming toward them: Daniel. His quizzical expression turned to alarm as he saw the speed at which Swan was approaching. He suddenly turned the Volvo across both lanes of the road, put the car into park, and jumped out, leaving the driver's side door open to create an even larger barrier. In another second he was walking toward Swan, arms outstretched. This caught James's attention and he slowed. Swan got the big gelding under control and brought him to a halt in front of the car.

"Holy mother of God," Daniel said.

"Thanks," said Swan, out of breath. "We would have stopped eventually."

"You think?" Daniel was disbelieving. "When? Meeting a semi coming from Waverly?"

"Upper body strength," Swan gasped. "I don't have enough of it for James. He'll be fine for Sam—he has no problem in that department."

"Did Fitch want you to join him in the Beyond?" asked Daniel dubiously. "Is that why he gave you this monster?"

Swan laughed. "Just a matter of riding styles. James is saying, 'Let me drive. I know what I'm doing. Relax and enjoy the ride, little girl.' Typical man's horse. Typically man, when it comes down to it."

Daniel grimaced.

"I was on my way to High View for a quick look-see, but now I think I should escort you home. Why don't you get in and we'll lash James to the bumper?"

"We're fine," said Swan confidently. "You go on." She wheeled James and pointed him up the driveway. He was willing to do her bidding now. Brakes and steering had been restored to normal function.

"See you!" she called over her shoulder. "See you!"

Her little flirtation with disaster had gotten her adrenaline pumping. Swan vaulted off James at the barn and handed him off to Edgar. He must have seen the speed at which she had taken the intersection.

"What?" Swan mock-challenged him.

"*De nada, nada,*" Edgar said. "You're the boss—but just stay alive," Swan heard him mutter under his breath behind her.

Swan decided not to tell anyone about her conversation with Bert. She had never known an officer as senior as Sam in her personal life; she was reluctant to meddle. She hoped Sam would bring up the topic of politics himself, but he didn't. He was lonely, loving, and loyal, as always. She was his future wife, not his boss. She should keep it that way. Over the next few weeks, life began to return to normal. Swan and Spaulding still talked almost every day, only now it was about Hetty or Persis, not Sam. Swan talked to Hetty, too, planning a quick dash to Richmond before Memorial Day made Route 95 traffic a living hell. A long shot, Painted Silk, won the Kentucky Derby, and Izquierdo won the Preakness, so there would be no Triple Crown winner that year. Calypso was now one of the favorites for the Belmont Stakes, so Oliver was already at Belmont Park. Tomás would be on the Templeton colt, after all, at Big Sandy.

The Fortress and Major returned from the court of Carnivorous, the old mare in foal for the last time, the colt broncky and full of himself. Kezia Hardaway arranged to sell Hurricane and Hollywood to a Charlottesville horse dealer who promised to keep the two raucous siblings together when he sold them on, out of unrequited affection for Fitch, Swan suspected. Kezia was named the new M.F.H. of Waverly Hunt, becoming the first lady master in 120 years.

Then the roof fell in.

"Swan." It was Bert on the phone one morning. "Sam is in some trouble."

Swan sat down on the floor of the hallway, phone in hand, the velcro Flagg flopping down on her legs as usual.

"Have you seen today's *Washington Sun*?" Bert asked. "Look on the front page. A serving officer has had some devastating quotes associated with him. He obviously said things 'on background' to some embedded journalist that he thought would be 'off the record.' The shit's hitting the fan." Swan had never heard Bert use a vulgarity before.

"Tell me," she said calmly.

"He basically says we are not just in bed with the criminal drug traffickers in Helmand Province but we are 'so far up their asses' is the phrase used, funding the entire heroin trade, not just the farmers, which is an open secret—or subject of discussion, I should say—but the whole pipeline, right up through ISAF and D.O.D."

"How do you know it was Sam? I thought 'on background' meant no names were attached."

"I know it is Sam because, number one, we've heard he has acknowledged it and, two, because—," Bert inhaled deeply, "some of what he said came word for word from me."

Swan thought back to Thanksgiving and Christmas Eve; Sam and Bert together for hours.

"Can it be traced back to you?" she asked grimly.

"Already has been," Bert said calmly. "He's about to become my stepson-in-law. Doesn't take much detective work to connect those dots."

"Oh, Bert," Swan said, "I'm so sorry. What does it all mean?"

"Don't know yet. We're doing damage control now. The *Sun* is just the beginning. CNN, the other cable news networks, they all want ISAF to produce the officer. The Bronze Star winning, multi-tour combat major from Texas, who has hung the command over there out to dry."

Sam was done for.

"Have you talked to him?" D.O.D. could get through to anywhere whenever it wanted via the Pentagon. "Can I talk to him?"

"Let me handle it for now, honey," Bert said. "Command will control access to him pretty tightly under the circumstances. I've been asked to confirm some points that obviously came from someone at

D.O.D. We're looking for a friendly reporter to throw me a couple of softballs to help with the packaging of the counter information. I've talked to General Clayton. He thinks we can weather this."

"What do you think?"

"I'm not so sure. This is the kind of thing that gets under the Secretary's skin. He's pretty worked up."

"Is ISAF going to throw Sam overboard?" Swan asked.

"I don't see how it can be avoided, frankly," Bert said. "He's pretty much overboarded himself."

"Okay," said Swan quietly. "Thanks, Bert. I know this must be terrible for you. Let me know if you talk to Sam, will you? Can I e-mail him or anything?"

"If you do, just make an oblique reference to the situation. You know. You can let him know *you* know and are okay. That kind of thing."

Swan hung up the phone and walked into the kitchen. Mathilde still read the *Sun* in the paper version; Swan read it online upstairs.

She found the story, below the fold, a very small presence on the front page, with a larger section after the jump to page nine. Several officers were quoted, but the "most passionate" was clearly the Texas marine. What could have caused him to make such a mistake? Swan looked at the byline: Allorene Archer. Unusual name, Allorene . . . Allorene—Smith? The fifth grade kissing expert from Buena Vista? Swan sank to the floor again. Flagg threw himself on her legs with a sigh.

A Texas girl at the *Sun*? Was that even possible? If she was newly assigned to cover the war, she'd have come across his unusual name (how many Septimus Moores were there?); he would have trusted her, Swan had no doubt. Allorene would have scored a coup. His gallantry, his guard down with a woman. He was so naïve that way.

Swan went upstairs and did an Internet search. Allorene Smith. Graduated from Holyrood College, in San Antonio, Columbiana Journalism School. Three years at *Texas Weekly*. Two years at the *Fort Worth Telegraph*. Two years at *The Alabaman*. Just hired by the *Sun*. It was her, alright: his fifth grade crush had overboarded him, her wonderful Sam.

She e-mailed him: *Honey, things sounding hot over there. Everything okay here. LU and MU, Swan.* She thought that was benign enough.

For three days there was silence. Bert received the white-glove treatment from the *Sun's* conservative rival, the *Tribune*, which let Bert qualify, put in context, add perspective, and blah blah blah himself to the point of neutralizing the impact of the naïve observations of an idealistic but out-of-touch lower level officer. Several marine and army generals handled by P.R. pros took condescending issue with the *Sun* story, pointing out the lack of experience of the female reporter who obviously was relying on a few disgruntled officers for her facts. It was enough to make Swan ill, but if it was too late to help Sam and could possibly help Bert, she decided it had to be done.

Bert called with an update.

"This Allorene Archer is newly married to Ned Archer of EyeintheSky.com, the political muckraking blog. Interestingly, she looks a little like you: same coloring, height," Bert remarked.

"Sam knew her. A childhood friend." *Looks like me,* Swan thought. *He's lonely . . . deprived. He suddenly runs into his little sweetheart in the most unlikely place in the world.* She probably took one look at Mars the God of War, all six-foot-four of him, and said, *Thank you, Jesus.*

He slept with her.

That's how she got the dirt out of him. She slept with him.

"How'd the Secretary take it, Bert?" Swan asked.

"He's still on a slow boil. Some senators are rumbling about an internal investigation, maybe even a hearing."

"If there is a congressional hearing, Sam might as well go over to the Taliban. Otherwise he'll be directing donkey traffic in a Herat bazaar."

"I may be applying to be his deputy," said Bert, grimly. "It may look like a good career move for me, too."

Swan hung up. She analyzed the likelihood that Sam had slept with Allorene Smith from several angles. First: opportunity. A liaison at Kandahar Airfield would have been difficult but not impossible. Second: motive. Allorene's would have been obvious. His—a chance to resume his fifteen-year career as God's Gift to Women. Because how strong could his attachment to Swan be after only five months of real courtship? Third: risk versus benefit. Sam would never have had to mention seeing Allorene at all if the interview hadn't caused such a brouhaha. There wouldn't be any career consequences for Sam, even if a liaison had been suspected, other than a warning not to fraternize. Fourth: vulnerability. She could assess Sam's but what about Allorene's? She was a new bride, shouldn't she be happy then, if ever? But stranger things had happened.

The thought didn't alarm her. She had experienced so much worse: Disasters from Which You Don't Recover. She had been expecting him to be unfaithful, dreading it but expecting it. You don't sleep with one hundred women and suddenly become monogamous overnight, even if you want to be. If she could sleep with him, she would know the truth. She was sure of that. She knew how he was when he'd had sex, real sex, not, as he said, sex between him and . . . himself. But sleeping with him wasn't possible from twelve thousand miles away. She thought of his arms, his breathing when he was on her but not yet in her. His mouth, hungry, exploring her, the weight of him as he moved onto her. His solicitude fighting against his need. He was careful with her because she was small.

"Oh, God." The thought of him being that careful with someone else was suddenly unbearable, like being fully conscious while under the knife. If he'd slept with that woman, she would kill herself. Then him. The illogic of that brought her around. Non-sequential suicide/murder would have to wait. He had promised. He wanted to be married, didn't he? If he had thought she would find out, he would never have done it. But she never would have found out. Ever.

The phone rang: Spaulding.

"Honey, I'm so sorry. Bert told me Sam's gotten himself into some kind of a fix. I read the story in the *Sun* and it didn't sound that bad to me. Just more of what the commentators say all the time on the cable news channels. What does Sam say about it?"

"I haven't heard from him, so I don't know. I was about to check my e-mail," Swan was a little irritated, unreasonably.

Spaulding backed off, apologetic. "I just wanted you to know I'm concerned, Honey. Bert seemed so . . . stressed."

"I know."

"And I'm wondering why you were riding a runaway down Everley Road," Spaulding continued. "Which I just heard about from Daniel. Is that wise, given everything going on? Isn't that what you have Edgar for?"

"Gotta go, darling."

She was about to head upstairs when the phone rang again.

"Hiya, hon." From that dry well in the desert somewhere.

"Hey," she said softly, settling into the hallway chair. "What's up?"

"Nothing good." He sighed. "What have you heard?"

"Bert filled me in a little. Who knew Allorene Smith would go from fifth grade Jezebel to *Washington Sun* war reporter in twenty short years?" Swan's humor was forced.

"Swan. I didn't sleep with her. I swear to God."

"I hear she looks like me."

"She doesn't. We didn't. I wouldn't."

"I suppose I should be grateful that Lorraine didn't take a journalism course."

"I knew that's what you'd think."

"Tell me then, if that isn't it."

He sighed. "I can't—they made that clear. They only let me call you because I knew what you'd be thinking when you heard who it was. I practically begged them. I hoped that, if you heard me say it didn't happen, you'd believe it."

"What will they do to you?"

"Don't know yet." He sounded as tense as she had ever heard him. "I just need to know . . . it would be easier if I knew . . . you believed me."

She was silent.

"It's one thing to lose the fucking career. I've done that to myself. But not you, too. Over nothing that happened." He struggled. "I mean, over nothing that didn't happen. Nothing *happened*."

Swan was silent.

"Swan. Please. Please."

Hearing him plead was horrible but she had to make him do it.

"Tell me again," she said.

"I didn't sleep with her."

He wasn't apologetic—he was indignant. She thought about it.

"I believe you."

He exhaled.

"Sometime I'll tell you the whole story. It wasn't as bad as—but I gotta go. I said I'd only need a few minutes, that if I could talk to you, hear you—"

"If they send you home, call me. I'll be at Dulles, or Andrews, or Oceanside, wherever," Swan said.

"I'd love that," he said, his voice hoarse, needy, the way she wanted it to be in order to believe him. "I wish . . . ."

"Yeah," she said softly. "Me, too." She cleared her throat."Call me when you can. Let me know if we can do anything here. I love you."

"Love you, too."

Suddenly she didn't want to let the conversation end like that. So tense. So intense.

"Would you like to hear about our wedding?" she asked him.

He brightened.

"Fill me in."

"Have you thought of who you would like as a best man? Hetty is standing up for me, of course."

"Well, I'd thought of Bert, but I guess he's going to be busy being father of the bride. Harry Edwards will probably be deployed by then, although he hasn't heard for sure yet. How about General Clayton? He is the one who got us together, after all."

Swan snorted at the thought of a major general next to her major.

"Oh, great. Then I'll be the third prettiest person at the alter," she groused. "We could add the Commander in Chief and make the sideshow complete."

"What about Boyd? Never hurts to have a doctor in the wedding party."

"I'm sure he'd be honored," Swan said warmly. "I'm letting Spaulding fuss over the menu with Patty and Lorenzo: peanut soup and steamed clams, steamship roast beef with baby local vegetables and green tomato chutney; a vegetarian option we're still discussing; field greens with pecans and raspberry vinaigrette, mango gelato in cantaloupe cups, white chocolate mousse wedding cake. And champagne and—well, that's how far we've gotten. Tents, tables, and linens. I doubt you are interested in the flowers, other than hearing we are going to have some."

"Wow," he whispered. "Wow."

"Too much? Not enough?" she asked anxiously.

"Sounds like a State Dinner. Are you sure I'm worth it?"

"I'm sure." She wanted to say more but she didn't dare. She'd be crying in twenty seconds, max. "Your dog says 'hi.'" she looked at Flagg, who was watching her face intently, as always.

"*Gib laut!*" The big dog barked. But the line had gone dead.

Then it rang again. She snatched the phone, hoping it was Sam.

"Swan?" It was Hetty.

"Oh." Swan sounded so disappointed to herself that she scrambled to make amends. "Sorry. I thought it might be Sam. Anything wrong, Hetts?"

"I should be asking you that. Spaulding said—"

"Yes, well, I don't know much other than what's in the *Sun*. Sam said . . . not to worry." *No, he didn't*, but that's what she was going with.

"You sound okay about the whole thing." Hetty was admiring but skeptical.

"Anything not involving short-range projectiles coming into contact with soft tissue is 'okay' by me. How's the big tummy?"

Hetty groaned. "Mad. Has a child ever kicked his way out, I wonder?"

"Only in horror movies," Swan said dryly. "How's the sibling?"

"Also mad, I'm afraid. He still wants to be picked up, and I'm trying not to do that. Boyd's mother wants to come and 'help' when Bolington is born but—"

Swan's call waiting beeped.

"Can I call you back? It may be Bert," she apologized. "Bert? I just got off the phone with Sam," she said.

Bert waited.

"No denial on his part, Bert. He said he couldn't talk about it, but he did say . . . she didn't sleep with him to get him to talk."

Bert was surprised, and not in a good way.

"Why would that possibility even come up, Swan?"

"Because Sam knows me."

"You mean, he knows that's what you'd suspect?"

Swan was silent.

"Oh, Swan." Bert's pity was almost palpable. "Are you sure you know what you're doing?"

"It's not his fault. It's me. You know I'm a lunatic about this subject and . . . everything," she finished weakly.

"Is he that much of a womanizer, then?" Bert's voice was ice cold. "Obviously, he's a good-looking man, but still—"

Swan felt his goodwill towards Sam drain away.

"He was, I guess, in the past. Before . . . me, but I was suspicious because he is so lonely, so vulnerable. He knows her from childhood and—"

"So he's had a relationship with her? In the past?"

"No! No! That's not what I mean." Swan was desperate. "There was nothing. It's me and my crazy suspicions about . . . everything."

"Because, if they've had a relationship and it all comes out," Bert continued. "Well, they both will be so compromised that whatever she has reported will be overshadowed by their—I'm sorry. Just thinking aloud. Inexcusable," he said.

"No. I'm sorry I said anything."

"You haven't known him all that long. It's not too late. No one would blame you."

"It's me, not him," Swan repeated miserably. "I'm a basket case. Everyone knows that." She felt everything that could go wrong in the conversation had gone wrong, and she had a terrible feeling that she had lost Bert as an ally for Sam.

"It's me. He's done nothing. Really."

They said good-bye. Swan hung up the phone. She should call Hetty back. Poor Hetty—she'd hardly had a shred of Swan's genuine attention for months.

She'd call Hetty.

But first she'd just go into the hall bathroom and throw up.

Flagg waited patiently until she came out.

◆

For the next week, behind the scenes mechanizations having nothing to do with Sam took place at D.O.D. and at ISAF in Kabul.

Journalists sympathetic to the current administration's position were given access to officers with different viewpoints on the Afghan drug trade, and they got their stories good positions in influential papers. The Marines were able to keep Sam away from any other media and, although a few columnists ranted and raved about muzzling honest disagreement within the ranks of the fighting forces, events spiraled away from the first day's fireworks. Another thirty soldiers, U.N. observers, and marines were killed in roadside bomb attacks and an unfortunate case of friendly fire, and the news cycle moved on.

With the exception of a couple of e-mails, Swan heard nothing from Sam. He attached a photo to one e-mail, standing outside a headquarters tent, his face looking drawn, she thought. Understandable, under the circumstances.

Chapter 13

Swan rose early on Memorial Day to place potted azaleas on the graves of her parents in the Everley Methodist cemetery. She grouped the pots carefully against the headstones. They looked cheerful for the other visitors to the cemetery over the long weekend. She wished her mother had known Sam. Her father, ten years her mother's senior, had been in his fifties when the girls were very young; in his sixties when they were growing up as teenagers. He would have been beside himself over the previous four years, trying to protect her from fate.

Swan made a detour to High View on her way back to Belle Everley. She had filled a silver julep cup with peonies, their stems cut short, that she planned to leave on Fitch's grave. The flowers would only last a few days, and leaving the valuable little silver cup was the height of idiocy, but it was something of a county tradition for its horsemen. Swan parked the SUV and hiked to the log jump. The day was warm. Monarch butterflies were already busy in the spiky budding thistles and Joe Pye Weed in the field. A disgruntled groundhog had climbed a bent trunk of a fruit tree twisted around the fence, his long claws scratching the bark as he went higher in response to Swan's interruption. "*Ti amo*," she said, looking at the tablet. *Hastings Eliot Fitzhugh. Beloved son, neighbor, friend, master of foxhounds.* She turned on her heel and walked back to her car.

◆

The next morning, she was leaving the house as usual when the phone rang. Mathilde picked it up on the first ring and motioned Swan back inside with an anxious look.

"Miss Susannah Bolington?" The voice was far away. "This is Captain April Gallagher at Three Multinational Hospital in

Kandahar, Afghanistan. You are the next of kin of Major Septimus Moore, USMC?"

"I'm his fiancée and hold his medical power of attorney," Swan replied in a measured voice. *Here it is. Here it is.*

"Please don't be alarmed," said the voice. "Major Moore has been admitted to our facility for symptoms that forty-eight hours ago we diagnosed as the flu. We have some concerns, however."

"What concerns?"

"He's got a high fever, one hundred and four degrees, and vomiting. We are testing him for a couple of possibilities. Leishmania is one. It's common among front-line personnel in the desert; not always easy to diagnose. We are treating the major with fluid therapy until all the blood tests come back, but we'd like to see a better response, particularly given his robust physical condition. He has, of course, given us permission to treat him here, but I wanted to let you know his status."

"Does he have a phone? Can I talk to him?" Swan asked, anxiously.

"Not at present. He's on a ward and pretty uncomfortable."

"Captain—Gallagher, is it? Are you a doctor, Captain?" Swan asked.

"Yes, ma'am. Someone will be in touch with you again in twenty-four hours with a status update."

"Thank you. Thank you very much. Please tell Major Moore that I love him and hope he feels better."

"I will," said the doctor, and she hung up.

Swan's thoughts were roiling through her brain. *Here it is. Here it is.* The blade of the guillotine sliding down toward her outstretched neck.

She went up on the Internet and typed in "leash," "lesh," and Google helpfully prompted her: leishmaniasis. A parasitic disease in two forms, one more serious than the other. Symptoms of the visceral form were fever, vomiting, and malaise. Sand flies were the carriers, and it was endemic in Iraq, Afghanistan, and parts of South America. Untreated or undiagnosed cases of the visceral form could cause organ failure. It was hard to diagnose. Patients usually had low red blood cell counts, white blood cell counts, and platelet counts. People with visceral leishmaniasis usually became sick within months, but sometimes not until years later. The cutaneous form caused skin sores, unsightly but less serious.

Swan called Bert, tamping down her panic.

"Something's wrong with Sam. He's been admitted to the military hospital at Kandahar. They think it may be leishman . . . iasis . . . sis." Swan stumbled over the name. "Have you heard of it?"

"Oh, yes, we're seeing hundreds of cases each year now, in both theaters," Bert said. "Some of our personnel are bitten hundreds of times by the damned sand flies."

"Is it dangerous?" Swan asked anxiously.

"Has he been diagnosed yet?" asked Bert.

"No, they are testing him now, but he has a temperature and vomiting," Swan said.

"Let's wait til they work him up then, before we get too far ahead of ourselves," Bert said. "He's a big strong guy in the prime of life."

"If it is leishmananai—" Swan tried again.

"Let's not borrow trouble, honey," Bert said. "When you get something more definitive, call me A-SAP."

Swan fretted. She tried to think of who she could call, who she could pump for information. Oh: Boyd, of course. She left a message at the hospital.

"I know your message said it wasn't urgent," said her brother-in-law when he returned her call two hours later, "but—"

Swan filled him in.

"Well, if it *is* leischmaniasis, it is certainly treatable, although the visceral form, as you discovered, can be serious if not treated. It is extremely rare. The symptoms are unpleasant. We use liposomal amphotericin here, but sodium stibogluconate is used on both forms in the military. It has its own side effects—debilitating fevers and headaches, overwhelming fatigue—and sometimes worse—during treatment," Boyd said. "The symptoms are reversible after the drugs are withdrawn. I think they are administered through military facilities, since sodium stibogluconate is not approved by the FDA. It's available under an investigational protocol due to the great influx of recent cases in U.S. service personnel. Is the diagnosis confirmed? I'm quoting from memory here."

"Not yet," Swan said. "I suppose it could be food poisoning or something like that, but if it were, they wouldn't have called me, would they?"

"Swan, you know the military," Boyd said calmly. "They do things their own way, in their own time. Call me when you hear anything more and try not to worry."

"Thanks, Boyd, thanks so much. I know you've got a lot on your mind," Swan said. "Not long to wait now."

"Probably another couple of weeks," Boyd agreed. "Hetty is so ready for it to be over, I think she would cartwheel up the stairs to the maternity ward today if they let her."

"That would be a sight I'd like to see," Swan said dryly, but she was preoccupied with Sam. She rang off before he could hear how half-hearted was her concern for Hetty in comparison. She puttered around the barn for the rest of the morning and received some sympathetic looks from Mathilde when she came back to the house for lunch.

"We seem always to be on the brink of disaster," Swan said weakly, when she'd explained the captain's call.

"At least it wasn't—"

"Yes, at least it wasn't a bomb," Swan finished. "If he's in the hospital, he isn't on the damn roads."

Despite Captain Gallagher's promise, no one did call from Kandahar twenty-four hours later; it was more like forty-eight hours.

"We've tentatively confirmed visceral leishmaniasas, Miss Bolington," said a male voice, another doctor. "We'll begin some aggressive drug therapy here. Then—"

"Then what, typically?"

"There are several options, depending on his reaction to the drugs and what subsequent tests indicate."

"Did anyone tell him you talked to me? That I'm concerned? When can I talk to him?"

"I don't see anything here. I'll make a note though."

"Please do. I don't want him to think I'm not concerned."

"No, of course not," the doctor said.

"Do you have a contact phone number? Or someone I can call?" Swan asked. "What is the actual facility?"

"The Role Three Multinational Hospital in Kandahar. There is a family/dependents' phone line. It isn't the most reliable, this is still somewhat of a bare-bones operation, but it's something," the voice said. He gave her the phone number.

"Thank you," Swan said, her mind racing.

She called Bert.

"Bert, I don't want to jump ahead in the line, but how can I be sure Sam's getting the care he needs, that he doesn't need anything, when I can't talk to him?"

"The Role Three is a decent operation; it was set up and staffed by the Canadians for several years but has been under the management of U.S. personnel for some time. The level of care is pretty high, though lacking the amenities—it caters to trauma patients," Bert explained. "They'll keep Sam there through his course of treatment, most probably, but if there is more organ involvement, or anything like that, he will probably be flown back here."

"Back here?" Swan hadn't thought of that possibility. "Back to Bethesda? The naval hospital here?" It hit her like a thunderbolt. That would be too good to be true: Sam home in weeks.

"No, to the Brooke Army Medical Center at Fort Sam Houston, San Antonio," Bert said, "or Walter Reed Medical Center, not Bethesda. They are the only facilities in the country that deal with leishmaniasis patients."

"Texas," Swan's heart sank. "No! Bert, we have to get him here! There's no one in San Antonio for him. This is his home now. Here!"

"Swan, he's coming in from the west—Afghanistan. That probably means Texas."

"No, no! We've got to get him here, Bert, please."

"Swan, one thing at a time."

"Bert. If his career is . . . finished . . . the only thing we can do for him is to get him here. Home. Please. If there is only one string to pull, please pull it now, for this," she said. "Should we call General Clayton?"

Bert sighed.

"Let me look into what that would entail. Sam is not a general officer," Bert said, deliberately, "perhaps some kind of hardship dispensation."

"I'd pay any extra airfare," Swan said vehemently, "the taxpayer would not have to pay a penny beyond San Antonio."

"It's not the airfare. His records will naturally be processed through San Antonio, not Walter Reed. Iraq patients, from the east, come to Walter Reed, depending on their illness or injury. The red tape will probably be a nightmare."

"Bert—"

"One thing at a time."

Swan had to be satisfied with that.

"So he might be coming home?" Spaulding said, surprised, when she heard from Swan. "Because of this leash . . . mysos . . . is?"

"Yes, to recover, perhaps indefinitely, once he is out of the hospital, if Bert can get him here."

"And if not?"

"I'll have to go to San Antonio until *I* can get him here."

"Then we'll have to get Bert to get him here somehow."

"Yes. Yes. Spaulding— "

"Yes, darling?"

"Some of these patients have serious difficulties . . . like organ failure," Swan said carefully. "He may have had this as long ago as Iraq and not been correctly diagnosed. The blood tests aren't always accurate. If he's been concealing symptoms, he may have not gotten it during this tour in Afghanistan. That would mean he's been untreated longer, and that would be . . . worse."

"Well, he is a great strapping specimen, he'll shake off this flea bite."

"Fly bite, Spaulding," Swan corrected gently. "A sand fly bit him. Maybe more than one."

"Too bad one didn't bite the Taliban bad guys," Spaulding said grimly.

"Yes," Swan had to smile at that. "Yes, it is."

She went upstairs and finally wrote Sam the letter he'd been asking for.

◆

Darling,

I'm so frustrated that I can't talk to you. The doctors tell me you are miserable, vomiting, headaches, fever, sick as a dog. Sicker, maybe. I wish I could be the one taking care of you, but Bert says the medical team there is top notch. We are all becoming experts on leishmaniasis, Boyd included, so by the time you return stateside, we will be the world's foremost experts on caring for a patient who has been bitten by a sand fly.

I hope you don't mind: I've got Bert working on getting you returned to Walter Reed rather than San Antonio if you are flown home. It will be much easier to care for you, get you back and forth to the doctors, et cetera, if you are here where Mathilde and I can fuss over you. This isn't going to change our plans to get married in October, I want you to know that. You will just be here sooner to help us choose the napkins for the reception and things. Something for you to look forward to.

I love you and . . .

Here Swan stopped. She knew this would be read to him, more than likely, so she was reluctant to say everything she wanted to say for some stranger's eyes.

. . . miss you, my darling. I'm hoping they will let you call me or let me call you before long. In the meantime, I'll try to find out what you might want or need and send it to you. Hetty is less than two weeks away from her big event, we think. Perhaps you'll be here in time to be godfather to Bolington in July.

Love, love from your own

Swan

Swan folded up the letter and addressed the envelope carefully. She placed it on her nightstand, took Flagg outside for his evening constitutional, and went to bed.

The phone rang at two A.M. Swan had been having the Marriage in Heaven dream, she recalled, when she woke up.

"Miss Susannah Bolington?" Another strange male voice.

"Yes? Yes?" She was trying to shake off sleep.

"This is Captain Ellis at Role Three, Kandahar," the voice said. "We wanted to let you know—"

Here it is. Here it is. Swan's heart was pounding.

"Major Septimus Moore is being evac'd to the Brooke Army Medical Center and will arrive in the next twelve hours."

"What? What? What?" Swan was in a fog.

The voice repeated the message, word for word.

"Why? What is wrong?" Swan asked, her voice raised.

"Nothing, ma'am. This is standard protocol. His infection is stabilized and his treatment will be continued at Brooke."

"I thought he would stay in Kandahar?"

"Protocol is that treatment continue stateside. We need the beds here for trauma and more acute cases. The major does not qualify under those guidelines."

"He needs to come to Walter Reed, then, not Brooke!" Swan was shouting now. "Not San Antonio!"

"I'm sorry, ma'am. That is the information I've been given," said the voice calmly, as though it gave bad news to families every hour on the hour. Which it probably did.

Swan banged the phone down. She dreaded what she was about to do: call Bert's emergency cell phone, to be used primarily in the event of a nuclear missile launch, she had always thought.

"Yes, Swan?" Bert answered calmly, under the circumstances. With two wars ongoing, Bert was used to being awakened.

She told him the message.

"I'll get on the horn to the Pentagon," Bert said. "I'll see if we can get Sam rerouted to Walter Reed. May be tricky on this short notice, but they must be filling up in Kandahar. More troops, more trauma. I should have called General Clayton yesterday, when we talked, but I had other things on my plate."

"Of course. I'm sorry to lay this on you, with all you have to do."

"That's okay, hon. That's what dads are for," Bert said gently.

Swan ran downstairs, turning lights on throughout the house, Flagg bounding at her heels.

First she booked a nonrefundable ticket on a flight to San Antonio for the next afternoon.

That woke Mathilde, in curlers. Swan gave her the news, pacing around the dining room until Mathilde was dizzy.

"If I have to go to San Antonio, I'll go to San Antonio," she told Mathilde calmly. "I want him to see me when he arrives, wherever it is. Then I'll worry about getting him here."

She looked at Mathilde's dear face.

"I'm going to see him in the next twenty-four hours, one way or the other," she said, trying to absorb it.

"My nerves can't take it," Mathilde said weakly. "We *have* to get out of the Marines."

Swan laughed.

"I'll tell the major that when I see him."

Three hours and two pots of tea later, Swan was packed for San Antonio. The sun was beginning to make its early summer appearance.

The phone rang.

"Miss Susannah Bolington? General Clayton on the line for you," said a military aide, and in a moment, the general was indeed there.

"Good morning, Miss Swan," he said genially, as though it were a garden party at noon.

"Good morning, General," Swan said hopefully. "Sorry to bother you so early."

"Early? Oh-five-hundred?" the general snorted, "SOP. SOP." Standard Operating Procedure. "Sounds like you want a certain major here at Walter Reed."

"More than anything. Please. Please."

"How does twenty-three hundred hours sound to you?"

Swan sat down with a thump, on the big old bed: eleven P.M.

"Tonight? Tonight?"

"Affirmative. Touch down at Andrews. Then he'll be taken to Walter Reed for an 'eval.' You should be able to see him tomorrow."

"I can't believe it! I can't believe it."

"What good is being a general if you can't make a thing or two happen if you want it to?" Clayton asked gruffly.

Swan started to cry, the tension flowing out of her.

"Thank you so much. I can't thank you enough," she sobbed. "For Sam, too."

"Come on now. You're going to be a marine wife. You know what you need to do," Clayton said.

"Suck it up," Swan said, still choking.

"Affirmative."

"Sucking, sir," Swan sniffled, "ooh-rah." The marine battle cry sounded odd through her tears.

"Ooh-rah," said Clayton cheerfully. "Give Major Moore my best wishes, and let me know if he isn't being treated to your satisfaction at Walter Reed. We've had problems there in the past, but my understanding is there's been much improvement."

"I'll be eternally grateful, General," Swan said. "We'll never be able to thank you."

"Just get him on his feet for that wedding," Clayton said, and suddenly he was gone.

Swan knew Mathilde had been outside her closed bedroom door because as soon as she hung up the phone, there was a tap.

"He's coming home tonight," Swan said, in a daze. "He'll be in D.C. tonight." Thirty miles from Belle Everley. Mathilde came to her in a rush, and they hugged on the bed for a long time.

When she had unpacked her bags and had breakfast, she was still trying to process how everything had changed. She was going to have a very sick guy to care for, but he was going to be in virtually a local hospital. She'd be able to see him every day, come home to Belle Everley every night, nurse him when he was discharged. Get him well. It would be completely different from Fitch.

Fitch. Bad luck doomed love. It stabbed at her, through her happiness and relief. Fitch came home, too. Fitch had recovered until she returned to his life. Fitch . . . .

No one was safe. Not from her.

Swan forced herself back to the present. She was all he had. She would make him get well. Then they would see.

◆

Swan spent the rest of the morning checking in with Boyd, Bert, Hetty, and Spaulding, counting on them to spread the news that Sam was coming home. She confirmed that she would not be permitted to meet the flight at Andrews Air Force Base in Maryland; that nursing staff would accompany all of those coming in to Walter Reed, and that getting Sam settled there and stabilized would probably take the whole night. The next morning she would head to D.C. She still found something to fret about: would Sam know what was happening, would he know that she knew where he was, or would he still be so ill that he'd be pretty much out of the whole thing? His sudden redirection might mean a paperwork snafu, and the extra time in the air might not have been in his best interest. All of this caused her continued anxiety until she was able to see him for herself.

She fretted the whole day and into the evening. She slept very badly—infuriating because she wanted to look well and rested for Sam. She forced herself not to call Walter Reed until the visitor phone line opened the next morning at nine A.M.

"Yes, Major S.A. Moore, USMC. We have him admitted as of oh-two-hundred hours today," said the receptionist checking the patient list. He was there. That at least was a relief.

Swan showered and changed into an apricot-silk shirt, summer weight brown slacks, flat shoes. Hospitals could be hot or cold; hallways long; parking lots full. She wouldn't need couture to see someone as ill as Sam must be. She tied her hair back, checked that she had all the paperwork she might need, and jumped into the SUV.

◆

She drove up Georgia Avenue an hour later. Walter Reed was a sprawling complex of up-to-date wards, kept spic and span for visitors, including the Commander in Chief, and older, almost decrepit buildings that had been the subject of exposés over filth and mismanagement by the major Washington newspapers for years.

Security was tight, but Swan made it through, parked, and found her way to Ward 63, the Leishmaniasis Treatment Center, Infectious Disease Service. She was passed through another thorough security check. She was not gowned and gloved; leishmaniasis was transmitted from person to person rarely, by blood transfusion or sexual contact, not through the air.

She was shown into a ward and her eyes began to search for Sam immediately. She was directed to a bed with the curtains drawn. When she saw him, she was shocked. He was at least twenty-five pounds lighter than he'd been on the first of March, his skin pale green, hooked up to I.V.'s, semi-conscious. She rushed to him, oblivious to the other patients, most of whom had lesions indicative of the cutaneous form of the disease.

She took his huge hand. "Sam, Sam," she called to him quietly. "Honey."

"He needs his sleep, he had a long trip," a nurse murmured. "The disease presents with extreme exhaustion as well as fever. But he is responding to the drugs. He is strong as a bull."

Swan nodded, torn. She wanted him to know she was there, but she didn't want to rouse him unnecessarily. It was enough to see him, to know he was home.

"When can I talk to a doctor?" Swan asked anxiously.

"Are you staying in town?"

"No, I live in northern Virginia—Taliaferro County."

"Oh, well, that is convenient," the nurse said sympathetically. "They're on rounds now, and it would be better if they could observe him for twenty-four to forty-eight hours before giving you their assessment, but his chart shows that he is responding as well as can be expected. He's only been on the drug therapy for four days. The protocol is seventeen to twenty-one days."

"Yes, yes, I know." Swan kept her eyes on him, drinking him in. She wanted to embrace him but didn't dare. "Do you know, has he been awake at all? Does he know where he is? What's happened?"

"I've only been here since oh-six hundred," the nurse replied. "Looks as though he's been conscious, but not since I've been on, I'm afraid," the nurse said. "You'd be better off talking to the doctor."

"If he wakes, please tell him I was here; that I'll be back, that I'm taking care of everything," Swan said authoritatively.

"We will," the nurse said. "We understand you and the major are special friends of General Clayton and Undersecretary Davis at the Department of Defense."

Swan heard the slight undercurrent of "attitude." She didn't remotely care. String pulling was an art form at Walter Reed and in Washington, in general.

"Yes, yes, we are," Swan said coolly, "and of Senator Avery, of Virginia, too." Pushing to the front of the line, if need be, didn't distress her at all. Whatever it took for Sam. "Shall I stay? Will he wake up this morning?"

"Probably not til this afternoon. He needs all the rest he can get. He may sleep a full twenty-four hours."

"I'd written him a letter, just before I learned he was coming home," Swan said tentatively, pulling the envelope out of her pocket. "If he wakes up and you have a moment, could you read it to him?"

"Of course," the nurse said. "Sometimes Red Cross personnel come through the wards; they will do things like this, too."

"Thank you," Swan said sincerely, "I'll be back tomorrow."

Swan sat next to Sam for some time, watching him breathe, watching his poor gaunt face, trying to will him to awaken just for a minute to register her presence. She wanted to rest her head on his shoulder, place his hand on her cheek, even if he was deeply asleep, but she did not.

Then she left Walter Reed and headed for home.

◆

The rest of the day Swan spent catching everyone up on Sam's arrival, explaining what she still didn't completely understand herself on the course of events. The best explanation was simply Boyd's "You know the military." Swan knew that Sam would be worried about the men he had left behind, the political mess he'd stuck himself into, everything—but it was useless for her to try to help with that. She was still shocked as how close they had come to San Antonio instead of D.C. She was also humbled by Bert's willingness to intercede, probably at great professional cost, on behalf of the man who had most likely dealt his career a serious injury, if not a death blow.

Daniel Spaulding offered to stop by Walter Reed late in the afternoon, just as visiting hours were winding down, but Sam still had not awakened, he said, when he talked to Swan that evening.

"I'll stop over in the late afternoons, if it will make you feel better, so you know he'll have at least two sets of family eyeballs on him every day. I must say, the poor guy looks like hell. This damn disease can be fatal if it's not treated, you know, Swan. It's a good thing he's back here."

"Yes, yes, I know," Swan said. "Bert said he would stop by as well. I really appreciate you going over."

"Anything for you, honeykins," Daniel said.

◆

The next day, Swan was thrilled to see Sam's eyes open at last. His expression when he caught sight of her was something Swan would never forget. Ever.

"Well, here's someone to see you," the nurse said, stating the obvious, as she changed out one of his I.V.s."Only a few minutes, please, ma'am, he's got a blood work up in ten minutes."

"Hey," Swan said softly, "hey, kiddo." She wanted to say something more tender but she didn't want to make a scene. She just walked to him, gratitude and worry in equal measure in her face.

His eyes were full.

"Thank God you're home. Was it a horrible trip? Did they tell you that I hijacked you from Fort Sam Houston? Do you need anything? What do the doctors say? What happened?"

The nurse chuckled gently.

"He doesn't have time to answer even half of all that," she said.

Just then, Sam leaned over and vomited heavily into a plastic hospital container. Swan reached to hold it for him, and he pushed at her gently to keep her back. He groaned.

"Honey, I'm so sorry," she said helplessly, as he fell back in bed.

"He had a rough night." The nurse smoothed his sheets. "He's still pretty wiped out from the trip."

"Hi," he said to Swan. He looked feverish. "It's great to see you."

"What are you doing for him?" Swan asked, never taking her eyes from his.

"He's getting an experimental drug that should clear up the parasitic infection—" The nurse stopped short. "The doctor can explain it all. We are trying to make him comfortable in the meantime."

"Yes, I'll want to talk to the doctor after Major Moore goes for his tests, if that's possible," Swan said. She looked at him closely.

"You are so skinny," she said, taking his hand. "I've got Bert and Boyd—and everyone—working on this whole thing. We'll make sure the doctors are doing everything, and I'll be here every day. Please don't worry about anything. You've got about two weeks more of these drugs, and the side effects are as bad as the original symptoms, I'm afraid, did they tell you? But you should recover completely and be discharged. Then I'll take you to Belle Everley and you can take all the time you need to get completely well and get your strength back," she smiled encouragingly.

He smiled wanly.

"You look so skinny," she repeated, disbelieving. "Cousin Daniel will stop by in the afternoons in case you need anything or the doctors have anything to talk to us about. I've added him and Bert to the family visitors' list at the reception desk. I hope that's okay."

Swan put her hand on his forehead, brushing his buzz-cut hair above his ears.

"We're keeping him hydrated," the nurse said. "I'm afraid we've got to get him to the lab."

Swan realized Sam had barely said two words to her, but she was satisfied. She tried to find a doctor but none was on the ward; they had made their rounds, she knew, before visiting hours, purposely. When Sam returned he was wiped out and Swan stayed only a few minutes before leaving him to rest. She brushed her lips to her fingertips and placed her hand on his forehead, but then she couldn't resist: she gave him a half hug around his shoulders. He smiled but didn't lift his head.

Swan tried all day to reach the Walter Reed doctors by phone, with no luck, and in frustration she called Boyd in Richmond.

"I know doctors are happier to talk to other doctors than to family: could you call up there and find out what is going on?" she asked. "It's a lot to ask, but I think they view him as government property and are just treating him without any discussion with me at all."

"Sure, Swan," Boyd said, hearing the stress in her voice. "How did he look?"

"Absolutely terrible. Could he have lost so much weight in two months? It looks like thirty pounds, at least. Skin looks sallow and feverish," she reported dismally. "He vomited his guts out while I was there and looked so weak—"

"Yes, that all sounds pretty much like what you'd expect. I'll see what I can do. Do you have the name of any of the attending physicians or ward doctor?" Boyd asked. Swan gave him what she had gleaned and tried not to be frustrated by the medical bureaucracy of the military.

◆

The next day, Swan wore watermelon silk and Louboutin pumps. She wanted Sam to see a treat.

He looked appreciably better, although still far from well, and she was finally able to talk to him.

"Wow," he said, taking in her short dress and bare legs.

"How are you, Major?" Swan said, grinning. "You finally look like you're actually going to live."

"Feels like it," he said.

"What do the doctors say?" she asked, and she bent over to kiss him. He was barely able to lift his head in response, so she settled for sitting chummily next to him. She rested her cheek against his arm like the old days: it felt wonderful.

"Couple more weeks and I should be out of here, that's the important thing," he said, and just then a doctor in a long coat stopped at the foot of the bed. Swan introduced herself.

"Major Arthur," he said. "I'm an infectious disease specialist. We are monitoring his organ function, but the drugs are beginning to take hold and beat back this parasitic assault."

"That's what we want to hear," Sam said with the ghost of a smile.

"He doesn't complain, but when can he get some relief from the vomiting and diarrhea?" Swan had been filled in by Boyd before driving to D.C.

"If we are lucky, in the next few days, but some of the symptoms may linger, unfortunately, throughout the treatment," the tall, forty-ish doctor replied. "Typically, a visceral leishmaniasis patient is a Third World street person; it helps that Major Moore is physically a beast," he smiled wanly.

"Thank you, Doctor," Swan said, and Arthur was on his way down the row of beds. "I think he is hot for you," she whispered to Sam, with a baleful look.

"They all are," he said conspiratorially. "It's the vomiting that gets them." For the first time he began to sound like himself. "Why don't you tell me what the hell has been going on?"

Swan started with the phone call from Kandahar and took him right through the whole story.

Then he gave her his version.

"I'd been feeling like shit, but I'd been so preoccupied with mission C-two and the news story bullshit that I hadn't focused on it until I woke up with a temp of one-oh-four." He stopped, swallowed, then went on. "That was—hell, I don't know what day it was. Next thing I know, I'm at Role Three, and next thing I know after that I'm on my way stateside. Then I hear my wife has called the Pentagon or the chairman of the Joint Chiefs to get me to Walter Reed. I was so out of it, I wasn't sure who my 'wife' was supposed to be. I thought, what's Lorraine got to do with it? Then I figured they'd confused me with somebody else and I was going to get my leg amputated in error or something. Just shows what a fever can do . . . and I remember checking my tag to be sure I was still I.D.'d as me.

"I think I was here . . . two days before I figured out that my wife was you," he smiled. "Did you come to see me? I thought you did, but I thought I had dreamed it."

"I came to see you," she said softly. "I called General Clayton, Bert, Boyd—and I would have called the chairman of the Joint Chiefs if I thought it would have helped. I didn't want you to go to Brooke, which is where they were sending you."

"How'd you divert me here?"

"I'm not sure. General Clayton was in charge of that bit of business. I just knew it would be a long commute from Belle Everley to San Antonio," Swan said dryly. "But I don't want to tire you out. You aren't out of the woods yet." She stood up to go. "Get some rest." She put her hand to her lips and then to his forehead as a substitute kiss. "Don't make a pass at anyone while I'm gone."

Swan returned to the farm with a heart lighter than it had been in days. She was almost euphoric. She had intervened and it seemed to have worked. Sam was on the mend. The phone was ringing when she came in: Spaulding. Swan gave her the upbeat update.

"Well, I'm very glad to hear he's improving," Spaulding said sincerely. "I hope Sam realizes how generous it was of Bert to cash in so many chits to get him here when Sam's misjudgment has cost Bert so much."

Swan was cautious.

"We haven't discussed the whole *Sun* flap, Spaulding," she said. "We've been busy saving Sam's life for the last few days." That was a bit of an exaggeration, but she wanted to make the point. "And I believe it was General Clayton who made the flight happen, but, of course, we are grateful nonetheless."

"I'm glad to hear it," Spaulding said, and her tone was kind. "I just meant that we tried to warn him, I know Bert tried to warn you that Sam was in deep water over there, politically. It took both General Clayton and Bert to pull him out. I hope he doesn't make a habit of it."

"Until I hear Sam's side of the story, I plan to give him the benefit of the doubt," Swan said stoutly. "His body was the one in bullet-stopping mode, not Bert's or the general's. And I mean that with all the respect and affection in the world."

"I'm sure you do, honeykins. When the time is right, I'm sure you'll hear the whole thing. Particularly this . . . girl . . . and how she got to him." Allorene Archer.

"It's ancient history," Swan replied, "and I suspect that Sam was already ill and trying to slog on when he talked to the woman anyway. I wouldn't be surprised if his judgment was compromised. If you saw how sick he's been—"

"I'm sure you're right."

◆

The next day, Sam looked better yet.

"Bert stopped by last evening, did he tell you?" Sam said.

She shook her head.

"I was glad to have a chance to thank him in person and to apologize for my screw up over there. I guess I really caused a stink that we still haven't gotten aired out."

"Don't worry about that now. I'm just glad you two had a chance to talk."

"Where's my gear? I asked Daniel when he dropped by last night, but no one seemed to know."

"Your duffle and your suitcases, you mean? I hope they made their way here and didn't go to San Antonio without you," Swan said anxiously. "I'll get on it."

"When you find it, there's a little present in there for you."

"What? What did you bring me?" she asked excitedly.

"Nothing fancy, just something authentic . . . from Afghanistan."

"Is it a burka?" she teased.

"Wait and see," he said. "And you can tell Daniel thanks, but he needn't trek over here every evening."

"We want to keep a second set of family eyes on you."

"You're all I need," he said softly, "I got to read your letter. Better late than ever." He smiled. "God, I can't wait to actually hold you. Do you know how long it's been?"

"Three months, seven days, and assorted hours," she replied. "Which brings me to Hetty's due date. It's tomorrow. Doesn't mean anything, but second babies are usually on time, not late. She'll want me to buzz down there and see Bud when he's born, just for the day, so I may not be able to get up here. I'll try to call the nurse's station when it happens."

"Bud?"

"Bolington Upshaw Delaney—'B.U.D.'" Swan grimaced. "Don't blame me, I didn't choose any of it."

"What are we going to call ours?"

"Ours?"

"Our Bolington. Bolington Moore," Sam said patiently.

She gave him a phantom kiss as her answer, then she left him.

Hetty went into labor the next night and delivered a seven-pound baby boy the following morning before dawn. Swan threw together an overnight bag, drove to Richmond Hospital, and picked up a dozen roses at the hospital florist for the new mother. One hospital to another, she thought with a sigh. She had made sure to wear nothing that had been to Walter Reed, pack nothing that had even touched anything that had been to Walter Reed, just to be on the safe side for the new mother and baby.

"Have you seen him?" Hetty asked proudly from her hospital bed, her red hair pulled back in a headband and a matching bed jacket over her hospital gown. "Isn't he a monster?"

"A certifiable monster," Swan said approvingly, kissing Hetty on the top of her head. "We've already heard from the Redskins; they are interested, but want to keep their option money for now. How are you, Mom?"

"Oh, glad it's over, as usual," Hetty said with a martyred sigh. "There has got to be a better way of getting children into the world." She looked at Swan with affection. "I'm so glad to see you. I know it is a hassle, with all you've been through with Sam, to charge down here."

"I wouldn't miss it," Swan said. "Who knows whether I'll ever see the inside of a maternity ward again?"

"Speak for yourself," Hetty said, "although I suspect your fiancé has different ideas. He looks like he'd be good for fertilizing an egg or two."

"Not right now, he doesn't," Swan said grimly.

"How's he doing?" Boyd suddenly appeared in the doorway in his role as happy father.

"He seems 'on the improve,'" Swan said. "But who knows with a disease like this? Some of the statistics are frightening, if you look them up on the Internet."

"Better you don't do that," Boyd said, "but he'll have to be monitored closely for the foreseeable future. Sometimes there are long-term issues that have to be addressed."

"At least we have him here if there are," Swan said. "Boyd, Sam and I are so very grateful. I know you put a boot up the rear end of the doctors up there. No sooner did I arrive at Walter Reed after I talked to you than a Dr. Arthur appeared to give me a cheery update."

"They are run off their feet," Boyd said sympathetically. "I wouldn't be practicing VA medicine for all the tea in China. Oh. That doesn't sound very reassuring," he stumbled. "I mean, they are doing the best they can with many more cases than they typically want to handle.

"At least he isn't a PTSD patient. Those poor buggers are really up shit's creek: they are so short of military psychiatrists, they can't help half the patients they should be seeing. It's a national disgrace as far as I'm concerned." It was rare to see Boyd this worked up. "But an infectious disease is an infectious disease. He'll be in good hands. As soon as his course of drugs is completed, they will want to punt him out of there to free up a bed and get him into your hands as an outpatient. He may have crippling fatigue far beyond the hospitalization; you should be prepared to have him in bed twenty hours a day once he comes home. It's going to be a full-time job, for you and Mathilde," Boyd said seriously. "No tooting off to Belmont Park to see Mike, no flouncing off to the Met with Daniel."

"I understand," Swan said soberly.

"Here's someone for Mommy," sang out a nurse in the doorway, bringing the new member of the family to Hetty's arms, "and for Papa, too, of course, Dr. Delaney."

"Hiya, Bud," Swan said, grinning at the nickname. The solemn baby looked at her suspiciously as he tried to focus on all his new relatives.

"Give you any ideas, Swannie?" Hetty teased, tucking her newborn expertly against her.

Swan and Hetty talked babies and weddings until visiting hours in the maternity ward wound to a close. Spaulding, who was helping Boyd with Boyd Junior at the condo, promised to come the next day to see her new grand-nephew. Mrs. Delaney, Boyd's mother, was coming up from Charleston the following day to spell Spaulding. Hetty would have her hands full "recovering."

Swan thought through everything Boyd said on the drive back to Belle Everley the next morning. She had been so focused on Sam's immediate needs that she hadn't considered a long recuperation and rehabilitation. In some ways, she welcomed it. Their five months together had been a whirlwind courtship. They had had only a few days as an engaged couple before his deployment had thrown everything up in the air. If he was going to be home in bed, they'd have a chance to plot out a future beyond October second under the tents at Belle Everley.

◆

In two-and-a-half weeks, the team at Walter Reed was ready to move Sam out of the leishmaniasis ward to outpatient status. Swan had reconfigured the big bedroom that had been hers and Sam's into a bed sitting room for him. Two more comfortable chairs had been moved in front of the fireplace and rented hospital equipment had pushed out Swan's wardrobe to occupy the closets. A mini fridge had been installed next to the bed and a new flat-screen TV with satellite connection was on the opposite wall. Swan moved herself, and Flagg's dog bed, into the guest bedroom next to Sam's.

She had buzzed up to Furnace Mountain two or three times to see Mike before Sam's release. He was blooming. Swan and Oliver decided to send Mike to Belmont for a second race the first week of June. Swan was torn. She wanted to see the colt run again at the big track, but she was reluctant to leave the Washington area—too superstitious. She decided to let Oliver take the colt and run him. She would see his next race.

Mike boomed around Belmont like a big cannon, with Tomás directing the fire. Swan screamed at the flat screen in Sam's bedroom, with Eduardo, Edgar, and Mathilde, as they watched Mike demolish a group of second-tier three-year-olds at a mile and an eighth. Oliver calmly stood in the winner's circle, looking like it was just another day at the races, and the Belle Everley crowd continued to scream and jump up and down.

When he called later in the afternoon, he said, "Why don't we think of the Virginia Derby next month? It's against older horses and on the turf, but he's been training well at Furnace Mountain on the synthetic surface, let's let him roll." The Virginia Derby was the only top-rated race in Mike's home state, held at the only race track in the state. So much for the vaunted history of flat racing in the home of Secretariat.

Swan was beside herself with excitement.

"A Grade One? Is he ready?"

"Why not? He's got the blood to do it," Oliver said calmly. That is what Swan liked about Oliver: he, like her, believed in the enormous power of Thoroughbred genetics.

◆

The day of Sam's release from Walter Reed, the physician's transport service delivered him via ambulance, and two burly off-duty EMTs hoisted him up the steep Belle Everley main stairway and got him safely in bed. His long-missing duffle bag and cases had found their way from Kandahar to San Antonio to Walter Reed, and had finally met up with their owner as he was heading to Waverly.

"Open it," Sam said to Swan as he was settled in bed upstairs. A small parcel wrapped in paper now sat in her lap. Out came a black and white tribal scarf, identical to the one Sam had worn in the Skype feed, a gift from a Northern chieftain. Inside that was a thin silver chain with a pieces of blue stone affixed like charms to its links.

"Lapis," Sam said, "from the local lapis lazuli mines along the Silk Road. In production for hundreds, maybe thousands of years. These bits and shards I found on the side of the road. Some had been dipped in silver centuries ago as bits of jewelry and ended up as flotsam and jetsam, blown up by the drones, I suppose.

"Perfectly legal to pick up and bring home," he continued in a rush. "None of the bits were attached to any site, or big enough really to have any value beyond their great age."

Swan picked up the necklace, it felt ancient in her hand.

"The chain I had made by a local silversmith before I came back; I didn't have enough time to get you a proper present, being evac'd and all," Sam finished, in an attempt at humor.

"I love it. I love them both. No one has ever brought me anything from over there," she said delightedly. *Because you're the first one to return alive*. She immediately put on the scarf and the necklace over it, for his approval.

"You could wear anything and look terrific," he pronounced, his eyes appreciative.

"You need your rest," Swan said solicitously. "I've had strict orders; no visitors right away, no exertion. Mathilde wonders what you'd like to eat. She's prepared to whip up anything."

"Nothing right now." Sam was green around the gills.

"Maybe later. Everybody wants to know if you need anything—Townsend, the Lombardinis, Spaulding—"

"That's very nice of them, but your family has its hands full with the new baby."

"Maybe later," she repeated softly. "Get some rest now, you're home." She looked at him, her eyes full. She blinked back the tears. "You're home."

◆

That night, Swan took Flagg into the spare guest room. She left the door ajar in case Sam needed her in the night. She slept deeply, the windows open to let the late June breeze waft through the room.

"At your three o'clock! Hunt! Goddamn it! Your three o'clock! Now!"

Swan woke bolt upright. Flagg growled— a deep, menacing sound—and jumped to his feet. It took her a moment to determine whether she had dreamt it or heard it. Flagg's response confirmed it: a raised voice, a man's.

"Corpsman! Fuck!"

She rushed into Sam's room, her heart bursting through her throat. He was soaked in sweat, despite the breeze, and sound asleep.

"Sam! Sam!" she whispered loudly; she sat on the side of the bed.

He half jumped up, arms flexed, and his eyes opened.

"What?"

"You were having a bad dream," she said gently. She pulled him to her and he folded down, his head buried in her lap.

"It's okay now," she said. She suddenly thought of his mother—the mothering he'd been denied by the wife of an alcoholic. Swan wanted to mother him now. He murmured unintelligibly and wrapped his arms around her waist. Then he was completely asleep again. She held him like that until she heard Mathilde begin to stir in the kitchen. She waited until he had showered and gotten down a bit of breakfast before she stole into the downstairs entranceway and picked up the phone to call Boyd.

"He's having nightmares," she whispered to her brother-in-law when she reached him at the hospital. "About . . . about Hunt. He said he'd had them after Hunt died, but that was almost five years ago. Then they went away. Hunt was the only guy Sam lost in combat. Why would the dreams start up again now? He's been deployed twice since Iraq. The leishmaniasis drugs?"

"Are you sure the dreams ever stopped?" Boyd asked logically.

"Well, he didn't have them last year."

"You weren't spending every night together were you, not all the time, before he went to Oceanside," Boyd reminded her. "Maybe he's always had them sporadically."

Swan wasn't convinced.

"They've come back," she said. "They've come back because this was his first deployment since he met me. Since we've been engaged. I'm bringing it all back for him."

"Now don't get yourself worked up over nothing," Boyd said calmly. "Nightmares are typical, and if you're right, he worked himself out of them before. Watch and see."

"Watch what?"

"His liquor consumption, for one thing. He doesn't have a sidearm in bed with him, does he? Under the pillow? Check and see. Does he flinch at loud noises? Hear voices? Think people are following him? Watching him? Is he hearing small-arms fire? Bombs exploding?"

"Oh, God." Swan was despairing. "Boyd, what am I going to do?"

"You would have two choices. Take him to a Walter Reed psychiatrist, if he will go, and if you can get an appointment with one. They are so shorthanded. They will either give him a clean bill of health or patch him up and certify him as combat fit. They need majors. Or you can take him to a private doctor and pay out of your own pocket. They have less experience with PTSD but more time to devote to each patient. Some drugs help some PTSDs, assuming he is willing to acknowledge PTSD is a possibility. But you are getting way ahead of yourself. It's just a nightmare."

"What would you do?" Swan asked.

"Employ watchful waiting. He's still recovering from the leishmaniasis, for crying out loud. And lock up all weapons in the gun cabinet."

"Oh, God," she moaned again. Then she was silent. "Don't tell Hetty, or Bert, or Spaulding, please."

"I won't," Boyd said, kindly. "I wouldn't."

◆

Two nights later, Swan was awakened again.

"I'll kill you if you do that again. I swear it. I'll fucking kill you."

Swan rushed into his room. He was asleep but he looked straight at her.

◆

The next morning, Swan sat with him as he tried to get down tea and toast.

"I want to start sleeping in here again," she said, matter-of-factly. "Just to make sure you're okay."

He looked at her closely.

"Why wouldn't I be okay?"

"You've been having dreams," she said cautiously.

He waited.

"Dreams about Hunt being killed."

"I've had those before. I told you about it. Dreams don't bother me."

Swan looked down.

"Do they bother you?" he asked.

She was silent.

"Do you think I'm fucked up?"

"If you are, it makes two of us," Swan said grimly.

"Where's the Walther?" he asked suddenly. "It's not in the top drawer, here." He gestured at the nightstand.

"I've locked it in the gun case with the shotgun. You're home, and I've got Flagg. I don't need any more protection than that. Boyd Junior's two and a half now: when he's here, he's into everything." But she couldn't look at him.

"You think I'm fucked," Sam said sadly. "What have I done? Tell me."

"You haven't done anything, sweetie."

"If you've had to start lying to me, we're fucked."

She looked at him carefully.

"Okay. You said you'd kill me if I did 'that' again," Swan said.

"It was a dream. It wasn't about you. I never dream about you," Sam said. "Not in that way."

"Maybe if you had the getting married in Heaven dream, we'd be there together," Swan joked half-heartedly.

"I'd never hurt you in a million years. And, yes, I'd love it if you came back in here to sleep."

"Do you think I'm the reason the dreams have come back? Do you feel guilty? Guilty about Hunt's death?" She had to ask.

"I don't know, baby. We believe we're the best of the best—best weaponry, best technology, best reason to fight, best country, of course, to be fighting for. But I just don't know. Didn't some writer say, 'The past isn't dead. It's not even past'?"

"William Faulkner." Swan paused.

"Would you want to go to a psychiatrist?" she asked, looking out the window at the summer pasture.

"Do you want me to?"

"When you're ready." She felt better.

"They say it's a sure sign you're fucked if you say you're *not* fucked," he said, resigned. "So if I gotta go, I gotta go."

"When you're ready."

"I'd never hurt you—not in a million years," he repeated.

"You'd tell me if you were having . . . symptoms, wouldn't you?" she asked, trying not to sound anxious. "You don't have your sidearm under your pillow, or anything?"

He lifted the pillows obediently.

"You aren't hearing voices? Or gunfire? Thinking we are watching you? Having . . . intrusive thoughts?"

Sam looked at her so disbelievingly, so hurt.

"No. Do I act like I do those things? Am I . . . fucked?"

"No, sweetie. You're fine, like I said." She wrapped her arms around him, like the old days. She felt him stir for the first time since his return home.

"Then can we, you know . . ." He started to nuzzle her, tentatively.

"What?" she teased, pretending she didn't understand him. But she giggled, giving herself away. "The bedroom door isn't completely closed. Mathilde."

"She can watch," he murmured agreeably, "or join in, if she wants."

"You are sick—you are still sick, I mean," Swan said, but she felt herself slowly being lowered into the pillows behind her.

"I know. I need—" he slipped his hand under her shirt, behind her back, "special treatment." His hands fumbled with her waistband. "A great deal of special treatment." He was kissing her breasts. "You smell so good."

"Miss Swan?" Mathilde's voice wafted up the stairs. "Miss Lucy and Miss Hannah Yoder. They've brung some baked goods for the major."

Sam groaned. "No. Go away."

Swan laughed and began to straighten her clothes.

"They're concerned about you."

"Tell them we're busy," he tried one more time. "Physical therapy."

"I can't. They're Mennonites."

He groaned in defeat.

"So close. Hard. Buttons almost all undone."

"They probably have brought apple dumplings."

She kissed him chastely on the forehead. Then she went downstairs.

CHAPTER 14

By the time the Yoder girls had left, Sam had become feverish again and he had fallen asleep. Swan got him to eat chicken broth with vegetables and some of Mathilde's custard flan, with fresh strawberries, but he was listless. He dozed restlessly for the remainder of the evening, while she mulled over their dilemma. Dilemmas, really. Getting him well, keeping him safe, getting them married, keeping him home.

She looked at him asleep in her old bed. She forced herself to think of being without him, not just being without him but also setting him free for another woman to love. She forced herself to think of another woman in his arms, seeking shelter there, the way she had, and finding it. She thought of how he joked to make himself less intimidating. The little trick he had learned—where?—and perfected with her.

"*You are very scary,*" he had said.

Oh, this was painful.

But she had to do it. What would the woman be like? Small, again?

No: he'd look for someone who didn't remind him of her. Someone better matched to him physically, someone cheerful, optimistic, unscarred.

Swan summoned Her.

Tall, lush figure: that was really his type. A teacher would be a good choice for him. Someone who loved children, perhaps from a military family, who understood what he did and why he did it better than she did. Someone who was hopeful.

God. It was agony.

All right: look at the alternative.

Sam dead.

Back to the Her, then.

She had a warm, nonjudgmental family, thrilled and proud of him. The two of them would have a nice house in a Houston suburb, or Oceanside. They would ride the Harley through the warm Oceanside nights. Her arms around his waist, her cheek against his broad back, her eyes closed as the warm breeze blew over them. Him kissing her mouth, running his hand up her bare leg. Her hands sliding up his arms, over the tattoos, down his belly.

Her beautiful boy.

Swan suddenly thought of riding James, racing down the hard surface road, rolling toward disaster and—oblivion. She yearned for it—to be the one dead for a change, to be out from under them all. Then she would not have to endure the nights knowing the Her had him, knowing he was in her, knowing what every second felt like.

She looked at him lying there, still hers for now. She took off her nightgown and robe and slipped into the bed next to him, into the small wedge of space not occupied by his body, and crawled into his arms. She kissed his too prominent collarbone, ran her lips over his chest, and she felt him rouse even though he was still asleep, snoring quietly. She ran her hand gently down his belly, below his navel, hesitated, then placed her hand on him, grasping him as he swelled to his huge, husband-sized arousal. She wriggled closer, opening her legs and raising herself enough, using her hand to guide him. She began to move on him, doing all the work for both of them. He moaned restlessly but he didn't wake up: the drugs. She didn't care. Sick, asleep, unresponsive—it didn't matter. Her time was running out. She pushed him into her, felt her pelvic muscles pull his response out of him. It made her breathe heavily, so heavily that she was afraid Mathilde might hear her from downstairs. She was moving hard, straddling him, not solicitous, pulling her orgasm out of him, then using her hand on the tight, swollen spheres and shaft until he exploded, pumping—warm, thick, sticky—into her and between her fingers.

She collapsed on him in a heap, feeling his feverish skin warm her whole body. Her legs were quivering with the effort. She ran her hands over him—his muscles, veins, sinews, bones. She never tired of it. She stayed in the old bed, dozing, but his restlessness kept her from a satisfying sleep. She rose at dawn and put on her robe, chirping quietly to Flagg, and crept downstairs to let him out. When he scuttled back in the door, she padded to the kitchen to make tea. She took the steeping pot and a bone china mug back upstairs to the sick room, the dog cheerfully underfoot as always.

In a few minutes, Sam opened his eyes.

"Hi," he said weakly.

"Hi, yourself," Swan smiled. He looked sweaty. She reached for a fresh, cool washcloth in the bowl next to the bed and began to sponge him off.

"I had a weird dream," he said drowsily.

"Really?" she said softly. "Were we getting married in Heaven?"

"No. You and I were making love. Here."

"And how was that?" she murmured, lifting him away from the pillows.

"Strange. I seemed to be watching, not . . . participating. But I feel as though I've had sex, real sex—not just a wet dream."

"Oh, you participated. Major Gumby just wasn't running the whole show like he usually does," she teased softly.

Sam looked at her, brow furrowed.

"It wasn't a dream?"

Swan smiled, sphinx-like.

"You fucked me while I was asleep?" He was skeptical for a moment. Then he grinned his old grin. "Hot damn. I missed the whole thing."

"Lie back down," she fussed over him, plumping the pillows. "Would you like a cup of tea? It's still very early."

"In a minute. I want to hear more about this sex thing."

"Well, when a man and a woman love each other—," she began in a parent-having-the-talk voice.

"You know what I mean."

She shrugged, trying to keep it light. "Consider it an experiment."

"Was it as good for me as it was for you?" he teased and pulled her to him. But he looked tired and gaunt, so she kissed his forehead to placate him.

"It was interesting, more like making love to an average man," she said quietly, "not so Mars the God of War."

"Who?"

"Inside joke."

"So that is . . . good?"

"Different," she said. "You're still sick, buddy. Your nurse should not be taking advantage of you."

"Just wake me up the next time." He nuzzled her.

"Drink this." She handed him the teacup. He took a few long swallows.

"You take good care of me," he said, eyes filled with gratitude. "No one has ever done that before."

"You've never needed it before," she said, matter-of-factly. "Any woman would do the same." She turned him over and began to massage cocoa butter from the nightstand into his skin.

"You are so dehydrated, your skin will be like an elephant's if we don't keep it greased up." She used her palms. "This is how I used to massage Punch and Mike. Same principle—," she rubbed him methodically, "different species."

"Mmmmmm. Don't stop."

She started over again, along the muscles in his back and shoulders. She heard his breathing deepen as he fell back asleep, and she rubbed until her arms were tired, until she heard a tap at the door.

"Come have your breakfast," whispered Mathilde from the hallway. "I'll bring up a tray for the major."

"He's asleep. He's all right for now," Swan said.

Sam woke enough to be left for a few hours. Swan had promised Daniel she'd meet him for a quick lunch at the Crossroads, now that he had moved to Delafield.

"How's your patient?" Daniel asked.

"Better." Swan wasn't as enthusiastic as he expected.

"You don't sound relieved."

"I am relieved. He still has a way to go, but I *am* relieved," Swan said. Daniel looked at her sharply, narrowing his eyes just a little.

"You are scared shitless. I've never seen it in you more than now, not even when Hunt was shooting his way through Fallujah. Who can blame you?" he asked warmly. "You've gotten worse and worse. When they patch Sam up and send him back in the line, you aren't going to make it, honeykins."

"Who says they are going to patch him up?"

"Leishmaniasis is completely curable, I thought. Is there something more?" Daniel was suddenly suspicious.

"Say there is."

"Then you either are going to be nurse-maiding an invalid at the farm or looking at Haldol from the nuthouse meds trolley when he goes back. Simple as that."

"Because if he goes back—"

"One way or another, you will do him in."

"You are the only one who understands," she murmured.

"You should give some serious thought to breaking it off then, honeykins," Daniel said gently.

"I love him. He loves me."

"I know. It's like watching the Titanic when you are on a nice cruise ship out of harm's way."

She tried to joke. "That sounds bleak."

"Maybe I'll pick up some survivors when the ship goes down," Daniel quipped, but neither of them laughed.

Swan thought about Daniel as Sam continued his recuperation at Belle Everley. She took his advice more seriously than the advice of Hetty or Spaulding. She must have thought men were more realistic about love, she decided. There are only two kinds of men, Hunt had said. A woman would never want to acknowledge that to herself, much less offer it as advice to another woman. But how often had it turned out to be true?

Swan brought up Allorene Archer only once.

"There was no sex, no drinking," Sam had said. "I had been in country a relatively short time, and I was sick at how much worse things were than before. Karsai is a gangster as far as I'm concerned, just a gangster with a genial exterior. He's made peace with the slimiest warlords, crooks, torturers, drug traffickers—brought them into his government to make it work—and their hands are out at every turn. Folks there have to pay for everything, their lights on, their legal cases heard, their daughters protected, with money they don't have, day after day. The drug trade makes Mexico look like the Waverly Methodist bake sale. This is the third poorest country in the world. The Afghan police are illiterate, drug-addled, demoralized, frightened. Our guys are basically dying so the Crips and Bloods can do business as usual every day of the fucking week.

"The people are terrified to cooperate with us, since the Taliban tell them they will be killed if they do, and the Taliban always come back. They are terrified *not* to cooperate, since we can draw down fire and engage the Taliban wherever we decide to. They all know we will leave eventually, and the Taliban will never leave. Any woman who applies for a driver's license will be dead the day we go.

"So much for nation building on our dime and our blood. ISEF and C-two see it, know it, the Pentagon, we're shoring up a regime we'd kick to the curb in a second if it set up shop here. Maybe if I hadn't been there before, seen our hopes, seen the way the people welcomed us the first time . . . .

"Anyway, when Allorene shows up at one of the press briefings, she asks for some observations on background, and I guess I vented. I knew when I was doing it that I was walking myself off the plank, but I guess I counted on her separating the ventilation from the observation. She did try. I said a lot worse to her—worse that she didn't print. But she was new to the *Sun*. It was a big step up for her, and she wanted to prove she could deliver some content that would make some waves back home. She talked to other guys, too, other sources. Maybe her new husband encouraged her to let it all hang out—he's a big blogger, which I didn't know at the time.

"I am sorry I threw in a couple of things Bert and I had talked about. It had been kind of blue-skying last year when we talked about it, but then it turned out to have come true so completely. It was more like, they knew this was happening, it wasn't a calculated risk, it was a done deal. That was my biggest regret. I owed Bert better than that."

When Swan asked if he thought he had been sick when he talked to Allorene, he shook his head.

"No, I fucked myself when I *was* myself—no excuses."

Swan was satisfied. She never asked again.

They did talk about everything else. Furnace Mountain. The embassy tea dance. Fitch's death, minute by minute. The fox hunt funeral. Mike's first win at Belmont. The birth of Bud Delaney. She sat and entertained him in a way nothing on the flat screen did, until he fell asleep. She felt like Scheherazade, spinning her stories day after day. She brought him up to speed on the wedding progress. He seemed inordinately interested in every detail, perplexed at the minutiae. She omitted the trip to Clarissa of Boston so the dress would remain a mystery. She had Eduardo bring James up to the house, walking him around the circular driveway, so Sam could see his horse. She omitted the story of her run-away ride.

"He looks fantastic," said Sam, looking down from the bedroom window. "I wonder how he's going to like being ridden by a novice cowboy."

"James is interested in two thing: three square meals a day," Swan reassured him, "and keeping up with any foxhound in a twenty-mile radius. He will be so happy to have a gentleman pilot. You two are made for each other."

◆

Week by week, Sam grew stronger. He came downstairs for the Fourth of July, dressed for the first time since he came back to Belle Everley. Swan had managed sleeping in the old bed with him for at least part of most nights, before his dreams or his restlessness forced her back into the guest room until the morning. Sam's nightmares continued, but they were less graphic than they had been. There was one exception: he had flailed so vigorously one night—shouting at Hunt to get down, get back—that he had clouted her on the forehead with his open hand, knocking her out of bed like a duckpin. She'd been scared witless for a minute but was able to dust herself off and watch him toss and turn before falling asleep again. The next morning she explained the knot on her head as the result of an altercation with a sale horse the day before. They had resumed their physical relationship, although it was not yet the night-long, world-rocking experience they had enjoyed before his departure. The nights they made love, he seemed to sleep more peacefully.

They decided to make the Virginia Derby a family outing, since the track was so close to Richmond, and let Hetty and Boyd show off Bud to Sam for the first time. The Delaneys would come later in the afternoon, since the big race was scheduled for six P.M. Swan was going to bring her staff: they could be back in time to feed and bed the horses in the evening, and it was seldom they could all get away at once. Even Jerusha decided to come to see her protege.

Daniel drove Swan's SUV, with Mathilde, Eduardo, and Edgar in tow, and Swan the dually, with Sam riding shotgun for the hour and half trip to Colonial Downs. Swan got them all situated in box seats at the finish line three races before Mike's. Spaulding arrived at the same time they did, and she kept up a constant chatter, filling Sam in on the arcane betting strategies of the Bolington clan.

Colonial Downs was a far cry from Saratoga and Belmont, charming and sunny, but with country-fair style food and casually dressed patrons. An hour before race time, the Delaneys arrived, jamming themselves into the snug box seats in the clubhouse. Sam and Bud gave each other a good eyeballing, then Hetty unceremoniously handed over the squirming, whining Boyd Junior in a way that looked permanent.

"Hi, Sam. You look on the mend. Here," she said, exasperated, as Boyd Senior struggled with the stroller, the diaper bag, and a satchel filled with Boyd Junior's toys. "You lead men—this one is just a little younger than the ones you're used to." Swan watched, bemused, but Sam was unflustered.

"Private Delaney," said Sam, stowing Junior under his arm like a football, "we're going to get along fine; let's get everybody a funnel cake." He strolled with the two-year-old in tow to a nearby food cart. Boyd Junior was speechless . . . and tamed.

"Thank God." Hetty, hot and flustered, handed off her newborn to the delighted Mathilde for a short cuddle. She flopped down in the box. "Happy birthday, Swannie." She gave her sister a quick smooch and a small gift, wrapped in flocked paper. "Don't let our sweaty carnival act put you off the joys of family life." She began to fan herself with her racing program. "I'm going to have to nurse Buddy; I just can't decide whether to do it in the restroom before the race or risk a milk explosion in the winner's circle. I don't want to miss going to the paddock."

Swan laughed. "I'd recommend option one. Oh, and you look great—looks like the baby weight is just about all gone."

"All but about ten pounds around the middle," Hetty said proudly, patting her linen-sheathed belly. "Pilates. What do you think, Mathilde?" she asked, "how do you like Mr. Buddy?"

"He looks just like the old master," Mathilde said disbelievingly. "Look at those eyes, that jaw."

That broke everyone up; the bald newborn and the white-haired Everett Bolington were hard to envision as twins. Hetty and Spaulding took Bud to the ladies room for a snack, just as Sam returned with powdered-sugar-covered platters of fried dough that were neither funnels nor cakes.

"Private Delaney needs a trip to the men's room," Sam announced, "or a fresh diaper."

Boyd Senior groaned. "That's me. I've got the bag; you've got the kid."

"I'm out of my league," confessed Daniel from the next box. "I work in a bank."

Swan took pity on all of them.

"Much as I'd like to see you guys handle this mission, I'm going to give you all a break."

She motioned to Sam and they headed to the ladies room, not far behind Hetty and Spaulding, with the diaper bag. Boyd Junior was still under Sam's considerable spell, and Swan was able to get him into the ladies room, onto the changing table, and out again, with no difficulty.

"The key to this is to have two to three times as many adults as children under the age of four," she said to Sam as she emerged. The toddler immediately started to wail. Sam produced a piece of sugared dough from his jacket pocket, and the crying stopped as if by magic.

"The key to this is funnel cake," he corrected Swan. "Napoleon said, 'The army moves on its stomach.'"

No sooner was everyone back at their seats than it was time to head to the paddock. Oliver greeted the whole crowd, including the children, with aplomb. Tomás Iglesias appeared from the jockeys' room with the Belle Everley silks once again on display.

"So this is the famous major," Oliver shook Sam's hand, "a pleasure, at long last."

"You've certainly given Swan some great days this spring," Sam said. "I'm very grateful."

"No, it's we who are grateful to you, Major, for your service and sacrifice," Oliver said. "We'll try to give you a great day today, by way of thanks."

Then came the call to the paddock—and then came Oscar Mike. Eduardo and Edgar were speechless with pride as the colt rocketed into the paddock looking like an equine Rolls Royce, powerful, elegant, huge. Tomás had come down from Belmont Park just to ride Mike in the big race and had already won on another mount on the under card. He was a rock star among the track patrons; many had never seen him or Oliver before in person. The rail birds pointed and waved. He spoke to Edgar and Eduardo briefly in Spanish, greeted Boyd and Hetty with deference, and gave Swan a confident grin.

Oh my God, Swan thought, *Tomás thinks we're going to win this thing.* The thought had never entered her mind. Most of the other ten horses were one to two years older than Mike—it was the equivalent of sending a Pop Warner quarterback against the college varsity defensive line. She had placed some serious bets on Mike, but she was now in a panic. Was it too late to get to the window and cover some more tickets? Maybe Daniel could sprint to a window upstairs.

"Riders up!" came the call.

"Swan, isn't this exciting?" Hetty said, clutching Buddy in one arm and Boyd Senior in the other. "Can you believe we're actually here? Boyd, can you believe it?"

Swan took Sam's arm as they followed the horses out of the paddock.

"Enjoying yourself?" she whispered, as they walked past the applauding crowd of rail birds.

"Wouldn't miss it," Sam grinned. "Is this how the other half lives?"

Swan suddenly pulled him with her: "Here's a window—watch and learn."

She put down two thousand dollars at the big-denomination betting window adjacent to the clubhouse entrance, wheeling the exacta with Mike and her second choice, an older turf specialist, and with Mike to win alone.

"That ain't the rent money, is it, Ma?" Sam asked, faking alarm.

"Yep, but who's counting?" They settled into their seats in time to watch the end of the post parade. Mike was four-to-one based on his two wins at Belmont and his Oliver-Tomás connections; his youth kept him from being the favorite. That was the turf specialist Swan had used in her betting strategy.

"If Mike wins, I'm going to pass out," Hetty announced excitedly, cradling Bud on her lap. Boyd Senior had Junior on his.

"If Mike comes even close, *I'm* going to pass out," countered Spaulding.

"You'll both miss being in the photo in the winner's circle," Daniel observed. "You'll be sorry if that happens."

"Okay, folks," said Oliver, smoothly. "Let's see if we are going to be in a horse race."

It never got old or predictable. The loading process was the overture or preamble, the assistant starters efficiently pressing each horse into the tiny stalls like packing oranges in a crate with divided sections, then swarmed around the predictably reluctant loader, draping a protective blanket, locking arms behind the animal's rump and pushing forward, in order to get a fair start for all the horses in the field. Then the gate clanged open, the race caller announced some variant of "They're off," and the two-minute drama unfolded with a front runner, a pace stalker, a come-from-behind-er, a winner.

"Yes . . ." Swan started her murmuring early, craning her neck as Mike found his stride behind the front runners on the green grass footing of the turf course. She grabbed Sam's huge arm, using it to raise herself on tiptoe on the far turn.

"Yes . . . yes . . . okay . . . okay . . . yes . . . yes. . . . ." Her mantra became faster and faster.

Oliver began pounding his program in his hand at the turn for home. Mike was beginning to fire, letting the Rolls Royce engine under his ribs fuel his great stride, dwarfing some of the horses he was beginning to pass, taking aim at the favorite until it was just the two of them battling to the finish.

"Yes! Yes! Yes!" Swan was screaming and she suddenly was lifted off her feet. Sam plunked her down on her seat so she was standing on it, obscuring the view of the patrons behind her, her hands on his rock-hard shoulders, with a glorious view of the finish line.

Edgar and Eduardo were shouting detailed instructions to Tomás over the din. The two horses battled right to the finish, neck and neck. The country crowd was on its feet; the race caller giving the call first to Mike, then to the turf horse, until they hit the finish line at almost the same time. Swan was sure Mike's huge neck had given him the head bob—the distance between him and the challenger at the finish line.

"Yes! *Yes! Yes !Yes!*" she screamed, jumping triumphantly into Sam's arms, never taking her eyes from the tote board, willing Mike's number three to blink on the top.

"Miguel! Miguel!" screamed Eduardo and Edgar. Then they were all screaming: "Three, four, six"—the order of finish.

"Oh my God! Oh my God!" Hetty was beside herself; Boyd Junior began to cry in fright until Hetty calmed down enough to reassure him. "It's okay, honey, we won the race! Mommy's happy!"

Hetty kissed Oliver not once but twice, Boyd pounded Eduardo on the back, Mathilde grabbed Bud to protect him from the general mayhem, Daniel raised his hands in triumph, and then they all followed Oliver, natty and serene, to the winner's circle. Jerusha Dutton grabbed them, her eyes full, as they went down the stairs and nodded vigorously, over and over.

"Great day," she said. "He looked like a champ. He'll do. He'll do fine!"

It was a repeat of the victory trek they'd taken at Belmont Park, the back pounding, the exhortations in Spanish for Tomás, particularly among the barn workers watching from the rail. A reporter from the horse-racing channel button-holed Oliver and, to her shock, Swan, on the way to the winner's circle.

"Yes, he's a great youngster, he really stepped it up today," said Oliver, courteous and self-deprecating. "I want to thank Miss Susannah Bolington for the opportunity to campaign him for her wonderful stable. No, we don't know where we will be pointing him next. We'll want to see how he comes out of this one first."

"We're very happy," Swan said in answer to the reporter's obvious question. "It's always gratifying to succeed with a homebred, here on Virginia soil."

Then they were next to Mike, who was blowing, not prancing and boyish now, he'd had to work hard that day. Swan took his bridle and put her hand on his glistening neck; he trumpeted his now-trademark whinny, tossing his head, pleasing the crowd and drawing a small smile from Oliver. He dragged Swan off her feet, and Sam instinctively pulled her back to him in a comic moment that was caught by the track photographer and the TV cameras as well.

"*Gracias, Tomás,*" Swan said as she caught her breath.

"*No—muchas gracias, Señorita Bolington.*" Tomás looked her in the eye triumphantly. Then he jumped off to be interviewed. Swan heard him describe his trip, but his English was so heavily accented that with the din she couldn't make out much of anything he said. He thanked her for the opportunity to ride a great horse, though. That she did hear.

The Belle Everley contingent continued to whoop, holler, kiss, and grab each other on the way back to their cars. They had originally thought to have dinner in Richmond to celebrate, but the children needed to get home and Swan was worried about getting Sam back as well. She was probably being overprotective, but they all agreed that they'd have time to relive everything later. They split up, got in their cars, and headed home.

"Happy birthday, darling Swannie," said Spaulding. "It looks like you got quite the birthday present."

As they were driving back toward home in the late twilight, Sam moved uncomfortably.

"I've got to use the head," he announced.

"Don't you want just to pull over . . . into the woods?" Swan asked helpfully.

"Not an option."

"The Scarab is just up the road," Swan reminded him.

"Problem solved."

They pulled into the packed parking lot. The joint was jumping—what a surprise. The only vacancies were two stools in the middle of the bar. Swan sat at one and put her purse on the other while Sam hit the men's room. "Order us a beer," he said, as he headed down the narrow hallway. She was conscious of her short skirt hiking itself up as she perched awkwardly on the high stool.

Within a few minutes, she became the focus of attention of a couple of bikers at the table immediately behind her. She thought she heard a rude expletive directed her way, followed by coarse laughter, but she decided ignoring it was her best option.

Then the men rose unsteadily. The larger of the two, a porcine redhead with a long braid, lunged toward her, leaning heavily on the bar with his back to the door, breathing directly into her face.

"I know you," he bleated conspiratorially. "You were in here last year." He looked back at his buddy, standing behind them. "You were fuck-dancing some tall dude all night."

Swan looked straight ahead. Where was Sam?

"I told you it was her," he said, talking to the smaller man over his shoulder.

"To keep a big body like that satisfied, you must be some cun—"

Mr. Pigtail suddenly seemed to levitate. He was being lifted six inches off the ground by the collar, then turned with his back to the bar. Sam's right fist landed on the bridge of his nose, effectively putting out all his cognitive lights, but Sam continued to bounce him against the bar, toward the door, landing a right with every third thunk or so, his left hand holding him upright by his t-shirt.

The barflies seems to evaporate as this was going on, each taking a few defensive steps backward but staying close enough to have front-row seats for the event itself. Swan bailed off the barstool and scooted toward Sam, standing next to a table evacuated by its occupants.

Pigtail's buddy now decided to be helpful. He lunged toward Sam's blind side, the blade of a hunting knife glinting in one hand. Swan picked up an overturned wooden chair nearby and hurled it the six or seven feet into his mid-section.

"Sam!" she shouted at the same time, and Sam dropped Unconscious Pigtail Man. He turned and landed an uppercut on Second Guy's jaw as he was collapsing into the chair. Second Guy went down like a log rolling off a truck. Smooth.

Swan and Sam looked at each other.

"*Vámonos!*" she shouted and lunged toward the door, pulling him after her by the hand. They hit the parking lot just as a sheriff's deputy was climbing out of his unit, light bar flashing. Swan pulled Sam to the dually, hoping they looked respectably innocent, avoiding eye contact with the deputy as he strode calmly toward the now open door of the Scarab.

"I'll drive," Swan said, and they slide into the front seat. Sam's eyes were still ablaze. He had a cut over his eye, but Swan didn't know how he got it. Neither guy had landed a blow. He shook his right hand, flexing it.

Swan turned over the engine. There was a tap on the window. She warned Sam with her eyes.

"Hi, Officer," she said sweetly. Tall, solemn Kenny Hardy of Waverly stood next to her.

"Miss Bolington?" he said tentatively. "Is that you?"

"Good evening, Kenny. Deputy Hardy, I mean," Swan smiled. Sam let his hand relax in his lap.

"I'm surprised to see you here," Kenny said calmly. "This is your . . . houseguest?"

"My fiancé, Major Moore," Swan replied, using her tea-party-at-the-Reynard voice.

"Good evening, sir. I heard you are just back from Afghanistan."

Swan relaxed.

"Yes, he is," she chirped.

"You seem . . . injured . . . Major," Kenny said, eyeing the cut. "Do you need an ambulance?"

"No, thanks," Swan said, as though Sam were a ventriloquist's dummy.

"That's a nasty cut," Kenny continued. "How did you get it?"

"We fell down," Swan said, giving him a big smile.

"That must have been painful." Swan realized Kenny was trying to determine whether they had been drinking. Thank God she hadn't had time to order those beers. She breathed right in his face.

"Yes, it's dark out here," she said idiotically. She jabbed Sam in the short ribs across the small front seat.

"Good night then," he said obediently.

"Miss Swan," Kenny began, his eyes narrowing, "I hope I'm not making a mistake in letting you head out of here. We got a call—"

"Oh, really?" Swan said brightly. "We just stopped in to use the restroom. Major Moore has been . . . ill."

"Yes, I heard about that," Kenny said. He'd made up his mind. "I hope you feel better real soon, Major, and thank you for your service. Now have a nice night."

Swan double-checked her rearview mirror and clicked on her blinker as she eased out of the parking lot, the most careful driver in Virginia on her way home. They looked at each other.

"What the hell did you do in there?" Sam asked disbelievingly. "Throw a fucking chair?"

"He had a knife. He was going to stab you in the—"

"But he didn't, did he?" Sam said calmly. "He didn't, because my little girl threw a chair in a bar fight with one hundred percent on-target accuracy."

"Just like bucking a hay bale," Swan replied modestly.

"Damn." He looked at her. "You could commit murder in Taliaferro County, you know that? That little smile, those eyes . . . ." He shook his head admiringly. "You walk on water around here."

They sat in silence the rest of the way back to the farm. As they got out, closing the car doors quietly so as not to rouse man or beast, Swan placed her hand on his arm.

"Sam, why did you take those guys out so fast?" she whispered. "I mean, they were disgusting, but they didn't actually touch me, not like Fitch, when he kissed me. It was almost like you were looking forward to decking them, relieved to be able to do it."

"They had it coming, honey. They knew it. I guarantee that it wasn't the first time they'd been punched out for being drunken assholes."

He patted her bottom, pushing her up the steps ahead of him, toward the front door.

"But, yes, I did enjoy it. And happy birthday."

He kissed her, lifting her off her feet. He handed her a little box. It was the ruby bracelet that matched the Christmas earrings from the Fifth Avenue jeweler. "They found it after they had already sold me the earrings and called me."

"It's beautiful," Swan said, fastening it on her wrist. And it was.

◆

The next morning, Swan was awake before Sam. She gently lifted his muscle-heavy arm from around her and thought back over the night. A bit more of the Major Gumby of old, less nightmaring. Moving in the right direction there. But the bar fight: had he detonated too quickly? Before he was deployed, would he have pounded those two with such relish or would he have extricated her and walked away? Big men didn't have to fight often; they were so intimidating that oafs like last night's steered clear unless they were on something. Swan believed the Scarab two thought she was alone at the bar; they hadn't seen her come in with Sam at all. It was a serious screw up on their part.

Another problem: without Fitch the Fixer, would Scar play ball or turn them in to Kenny Hardy? Scar had to have recognized her from the last Scarab episode, even though it was almost ten months previously and she was only in there for five minutes. How many girls in little skirts and nine-hundred-dollar shoes threw chairs in the Scarab, anyway?

Swan heard Mathilde stirring downstairs. She showered, changed into boots and breeches, and was sitting down to breakfast when the phone rang: Spaulding.

"Good morning," Swan said cheerily.

"Swan."

"What's wrong?" Swan was on high alert.

"I can't believe I'm having this conversation."

"What is the matter?" Swan had a sinking feeling.

"Were you and Sam in some sort of fight last night at the Scarab?" Spaulding said.

"Oh. That." She laughed. "We just missed some fuss, apparently. Sam had to use the men's room and there was some row at the bar, as there is every weekend, and—We were already leaving when it broke out, I think. We were in there for all of five minutes," she said, as usual mixing some truth into the lie stew she concocted. "What a rat hole that is. If we hadn't been desperate, we'd have used the bushes, they would have been more sanitary. Have you ever been in that rest—"

"Swan," Spaulding cut her off.

"Yes," she said quietly.

"That could have cost him his commission or time in the brig. Does he know that?" Spaulding's voice was icy. "Thank God he wasn't in battle dress. It would have been a disgrace to our fighting troops. One man has two broken cheekbones and a broken nose. The other's jaw is broken in two places."

"That sounds pretty serious."

"The only reason Kenny Hardy isn't at your door right now is because no one was willing to press charges or give any kind of statement. Virtually no one could have passed a sobriety test, drugs were found in the ladies room, and there was some kind of . . . sex act party . . . going on in the card room behind the bar. The only thing everybody did see was a knife in the hand of one of the victims, and everyone knew Sam's been so sick that no one thought he could knock two men out in two minutes."

"Oh."

"I cannot believe Sam put you in danger like that, Swan," Spaulding said. "While he was punching these guys, another . . . gang member . . . could have been raping you or knifing you while you stood there unprotected. There could have been a firearm. It wouldn't have been the first time."

"It wasn't like that."

"After all General Clayton and Bert have done to get him home . . . to get him to the front of the line at Walter Reed," Spaulding continued. "To repay them like this. They couldn't have bailed him out this time. He should have his head examined. And I don't mind telling him so to his face."

"Sam has been under a lot of stress," Swan said coldly. "He's not the same as he was before he left. He has things to work through."

"What things?" Spaulding asked carefully.

"That is his private business. Please try not to be so judgmental. Anything else?"

"No. I guess not," Spaulding said. "You know I've always liked him. And I only want you to be happy. But this—"

"I know," Swan said quietly. She heard him stirring upstairs. "He's getting up. You'd be doing me a big favor if you don't light into him. You saw how wonderful he was yesterday with Boyd Junior. Don't ruin everything. Who knows how long I'll even have him home?"

Spaulding was silent.

"All right. But, Swan, be careful. You read in the newspapers about veterans, active military, doing a lot of frightening things."

"Yes, yes, I know. But that would never be Sam. Ever."

Sam had been stirring but he didn't get up. The fight had wiped him out. He stayed in bed the whole day and the next one as well. But it marked a turning point. He began to get well, really well. He began to eat four meals a day. Mathilde could barely keep up. Steak, eggs, home fried potatoes, local berries by the quart; early corn from the Carolinas, early tomatoes, beans, sweet peas, more corn. Roasted local chickens. Loaves of homemade oat and wheat bread. Pork chops and rice. When Swan took him to his weekly check in at Walter Reed, Dr. Arthur was admiring but cautious.

"I'm still seeing some organ involvement, but the fact that the appetite is back is a very good sign. Don't try to get all thirty pounds back at once," he said with a smile, "but if you are hungry, eat."

Swan was busy weaning Major and the other eight foals in her fields by the sign during the third week of July, but she watched Sam with satisfaction. She was able to talk enthusiastically with Oliver about Oscar Mike's possible appearance at Saratoga in August. They were thinking about a Grade II stakes, the Merry Widower, at the end of the meet. She buzzed over to Jerusha's at the training center to see Dress the Line work at the training track; Jerusha felt the filly would be ready to go to Oliver by November. Linny was all business, smaller but more mature than Mike at that age. Judy was cooking along, too, not too far from a start over hurdles in the early autumn.

The first of August was Sam's birthday. They celebrated with lobsters and champagne. Swan had given him his first set of gentlemen's hunting boots from Vogel and military breeches from Fitch's Saville Row tailor. She had Fitch's magnificent Hermès saddle, which would do for Sam to get started in; he had five inches on Fitch and would need more flap to fit his long legs.

◆

That morning Swan found Sam setting up his weight equipment in the bedroom. He started slowly but seriously, building up to serious lifting. Swan watched him at first, then stopped. To her mortification, she found it too interesting for her comfort. It took him a week to catch on.

"I know you can't spot me, but I don't know why you don't at least sit and talk to me," he complained one day as he was finishing up on the weight bench. "It's not like I'm working out for hours at a time. You can ride or check those foals half an hour later."

"I've got a lot to do," she said, turning to leave, "not like you—you do your reps, shower, and take a nap. Then you eat lunch." She was lacing up the green Vogel field boots, adjusting the collar on her shirt, tucking the green gauntlets in her pocket.

"I suppose I smell like a locker room," he mused, "but still."

"I'm out of here." She turned to go.

"Wait a minute." He slid off the flat weight bench, letting the weight bar fall with a clang. "Come back." He grinned. "I'll let you towel me off."

"No. Edgar is waiting."

"Come back," he teased. "I need you."

"No." But her voice was no longer determined.

He caught her around the waist before she got to the door. She tried to squirm out of his arms.

"We can't. Mathilde is right downstairs."

"So what? She's never heard people laugh in a bedroom before?" He nuzzled her hopefully and pushed the door closed with his foot. He kissed her hard, and, although she twisted away, she also slid her hands up his bare arms, standing on tiptoe.

"You're hot," he said delightedly. "You're so turned on." He pushed her gently against the wall and started kissing her in earnest. "What's brought this on?" He started tickling her gently until she squirmed, her hips twisting against his daunting, insistent erection. "Don't tell me you're a gym groupie. How come I didn't know this before now?"

"Stop . . . that. Mathilde—she's just at the bottom of the stairs," warned Swan again, still trying to extricate herself, but her hands lingered on him even as she pushed him away.

"You are! You're a freak! You want it on the weight bench," he grinned, and he picked her up off her feet. "Your tongue's hanging out, you want me so much."

"Eww. No, I don't. It's sweaty and disgusting." She was beginning to giggle.

"Come on: I'll bench press you. You know you want to."

"I just got all dressed," she protested, trying to sound determined.

"You can just get all undressed," he proposed, pushing her down on the bench. "I'll help you."

He began unlacing the Vogels, trying to take the Pikuers with them at the same time.

"Stop," she pretended to protest, "these are three hundred bucks a pair!"

"Well, get them off yourself then; they won't survive what's about to happen to them otherwise."

Twenty minutes later, he rolled off her, pulling her close so that her heart pressed against his, her ripe breast pressed against his unyielding pec, their nipples locked in a kiss of their own.

"Your heart is pounding so hard, it feel like it's going to rocket out of your chest," Swan gasped.

"All for you, baby; always for you," Sam said, his voice hoarse. "You could bring me back from the fucking dead. As a matter of fact, you have." He swallowed hard and tried to lighten the mood. "We're doing this on the weight bench from now on."

Swan kissed his armpit, the closest part of his body to her, and sat up, retrieving her sports bra, her cotton jersey shirt, the elastic band that had held her hair, her belt.

"Have you seen my other earring?" she asked. "My gloves?" She looked under the weight bench: her panties, the Pikeurs, one boot.

"You are all about getting everything off, not so much on getting it all back from . . . wherever," she observed. His lovemaking—so powerful, assured, joyful—had been much more like the old, pre-leishmaniasis days, but she was unsettled. She didn't know why.

"Don't go, not yet," Sam said. He was looking moonily about, sitting next to her, not bothering with clothes since he was about to shower. He corralled both of her bare feet, with their pink polished toes, in one big hand.

"What's wrong?" he said, finally focusing on her furrowed brow. "You seemed . . . into it."

"Oh, I was into it," she said quietly. "I was so into it. I just hope you didn't . . . overdo." That was not the reason, but he bought it. She rubbed him, up and down his arms, eyeing him as though he were a horse.

"How much have you gained back? Twenty?"

"Twenty-five," he said. "It's all this healthy activity." He tentatively began nuzzling her again. "But I need more quality time."

"Oh, no you don't, fella," Swan said. "I've just gotten all my clothes back on, and Edgar is going to think I've drowned in the water trough." For the first time since he'd come home, Sam was up—literally—for a doubleheader. Major Gumby was back.

She kissed him quickly and swung her boots over the weight bench.

"Enjoy your nap," she smiled, "then after lunch, if you're up to it, maybe we'll reinstall your big old hard drive."

Walking to the barn, she mulled. He was on his way to being well. She should be rejoicing. The Hunt dreams were still a problem, but they hadn't gotten worse. She still didn't know what triggered the bar fight. If he continued to improve, he'd be cleared to go back on the line, even though his deployment with the Tenth was to end September 30. She didn't know whether he'd get another seven months home and rotate back with the unit or if his redeployment would be triggered as soon as he was cleared. Daniel was right, though. The Marines weren't going to let him sit home all winter and learn how to foxhunt and be a husband. They would have something very different in mind.

The wedding was fewer than sixty days away. Clarissa had express-mailed Swan's gown to a Waverly dressmaker for a final fitting, and the dress was back at Clarissa's for the last details to be completed. Boyd had agreed to be Sam's best man. He owned his own cutaway. Hetty's dress, sent to Richmond for fitting, would be taken in last to give her more time to get her figure back to her pre-Buddy days. The idea of Boyd Junior as a ring bearer had been discarded after his Colonial Downs hijinks. Spaulding had a lovely saffron-colored day dress. Everything was resolved.

Everything except Swan's choking fears, which were so overwhelming at times that she couldn't speak. She felt she was being crushed in a vice: if Sam recovered completely, it would only let "bad luck doomed love" have another chance at him; if he stayed sick, mentally or physically, it simply proved "bad luck doomed love" had triumphed once again.

She considered the slim possibility that Sam might leave the Marines. It was unspoken between them, and confirmed gently by Bert, that Sam's career had been irreparably damaged by the *Sun* episode. However, she knew her man: with his units on battlefields in two countries, he'd do whatever the Marines asked—oversee a toilet paper depot or pull the leader of the Taliban out of the Korengal barehanded. He had said once he would leave for her, but she didn't believe him. After her ride, while Sam was napping, she called Bert.

"I'm glad to hear he's improving," Bert said, and it sounded genuine. "Naturally, I'm still concerned about the Scarab thing. A repeat of that would be—"

"Remote as a possibility," Swan said. "I think that was an isolated episode. But what do you think of me asking him to make an appointment with a military psychiatrist, just as an information-gathering exercise?"

Bert was silent.

"What are you afraid of, Swan?" he asked.

"Nothing, nothing." She was afraid of herself.

"He is a big, powerful guy," Bert said. "If you have any concerns about your safety, don't be foolish."

"No, he's wonderful. I'm concerned about him, not me," she said, but Bert seemed not to have heard her.

"Because Spaulding and I have been talking," he continued. "We're wondering if perhaps, after all that has happened, you two may be moving too fast."

"Too fast?" Swan's heart sank. "We've been engaged for eight months."

"But not your typical eight months," Bert said, evenly. "Fitch's illness and death; the brouhaha with the *Sun*, Sam's illness, his recovery, redeployment . . . . It's a lot to get through."

"What's wrong?" Swan said.

"We didn't want to worry you."

"Worry me now."

"There was apparently an incident in Afghanistan," Bert said, "between Sam and another officer. There was some talk about PTSD then."

"Tell me," Swan said, her voice barely audible.

"The details are not important. No action was taken. It is a closed book, but I thought you should know. Spaulding disagreed. But we do agree that you should rethink things, given what has gone on."

"You don't think we should get married?" Swan said.

"In a word, honey: no," Bert said. Swan thought her heart would explode; or maybe her head; maybe both. "Neither of us . . ."

"And . . .?"

"And neither does Boyd or Hetty."

Swan sat down heavily, the phone still in her hand. At that moment, the bright little life she had constructed for her and Sam dimmed.

"Swan?" Bert asked. "Are you there, dear? Listen, I have to go. I didn't want to upset you. Spaulding felt we should discuss this with you face to face, not over the phone, but I'm not sure the timing is going to let that happen."

"No, it's better that I know now," Swan said faintly. "Thanks, Bert. Thanks for everything you have done for us both. I mean that."

"We love you very much, honey. We all do."

Swan hung up and sat there, looking at the engagement photo Spaulding had taken at Christmas in front of the fireplace in the parlor. It was on the entranceway table, as it had been since before Sam went to Oceanside. She realized that, while she had been focused on getting Sam well, everyone she loved had been focused on something else. The carefree day at Colonial Downs must have been a glorified family counseling session, with all of them assessing, dissecting, and evaluating her and Sam—how he looked, what he said, what he did. She went over everything that had happened: nothing had happened. But they were all against him now.

Or, at least against him for her. Perhaps that was the salient point.

Really, what were they thinking that was so different from what she was thinking? She had the right to think it, because she was . . . well, nuts. They had no right to be thinking it, no right to be agreeing with her. Swan didn't know what to do with it. She didn't want to confront them, act hurt or betrayed. She didn't have it in her. Sam had mouthed off to an old girlfriend, gotten sick, punched two drunks. That was all. He would have every right to be furious, and he wouldn't have the slightest idea how to counterattack or even mount a defense. He had no experience in navigating family waters. Unlike Fitch, who had skirted trouble all his life, Sam didn't have the ability to tell half truths, charm and dissemble, backtrack, reinvent, lie, double back, until no one could remember what the truth was anymore. Swan didn't care about the incident with the other officer. Whether it had happened or not, who was to blame—it would mean nothing to her. She called Daniel from the barn.

"Are you free for lunch at the Crossroads?" she asked him. It was Sunday.

"What's up, honeykins?" Daniel asked calmly.

"I'd just like to talk to you," Swan said. "Maybe you know what it is about."

"Maybe I do, now that you mention it," Daniel said. "I'll see you there in forty-five minutes."

Swan punched in the Belle Everley main number.

"Mathilde, please tell Major Moore when he wakes up that I've gone into Waverly for a couple of hours. Make sure he eats a good lunch, won't you?"

She went into the Crossroads and flopped down on the banquette nearest the door. Daniel was there within five minutes. He was looking the country gentleman in a lightweight hacking jacket and chinos, paddock boots, oxford cloth button-down shirt. No Gucci today. His hair was shorter, his skin tanner. Country life seemed to agree with him. Kitty gave him a tentative little smile when she brought them their food. He gave her a scoundrelly look. She dropped a side dish of slaw.

"Are you aware of the family's feeling that Sam and I are moving a little too . . . fast?" Swan asked, framing a euphemism for *everyone wants us to break up.*

"Yeah," Daniel said softly. "I've gotten that impression recently."

"Do you still . . . agree?"

"Yeah, but they think he is the problem; I think you are the problem," he said coolly.

"What have they said?"

"Well, there was something in Kandahar, apparently, that was hushed up. It was at the same time the manure hit the propeller on the *Sun* story," Daniel confirmed.

"Sam has never mentioned it, and I'm not going to ask him. It's beside the point, since the whole Scarab thing seems to be much more of an issue, at least to Spaulding."

"Yes, that was a pretty impressive performance. Remind me not to get on his bad side."

"That's unfair." Swan was defensive and fired up. "Sam was defending me, in his mind. There's no doubt about that. They instigated the whole thing. It was two against one, and they had a knife. You know what it's like—a pit," she said contemptuously. "We wouldn't have been caught dead there if we hadn't had to use the restroom."

"I'm well aware of its . . . limitations."

"How did Spaulding learned of our scrape so early the following morning?" Swan asked. "Someone must have brought her an eyewitness account. Was it you?"

"I have the advantage over Sam," Daniel said. "Put me in mufti, I can pretty well blend in anywhere."

"What would you do if you were me?"

"I told you. I'd break it off now before I caused him and myself any more pain."

"I don't know if he would even agree . . . to break up, I mean. He is pretty determined. He thinks he knows what he wants." Swan stared down at her sandwich.

"He wants to make you happy. If breaking it off will make you happy, he'll accept it." Daniel ate methodically.

"It will make me want to die."

"Have you ever thought of getting to know someone who isn't hell bent on marrying you right out of the blocks before he sets off for the desert? Letting things evolve at a leisurely pace? Not be constantly jacked around by the Pentagon? Men see you, set their minds on you, win your consent, then—"

"Yes: 'then.'"

Now Daniel stared down at his lunch.

"If Fitch hadn't died . . . ." Swan thought out loud.

"Yes." Daniel looked up. "I have another advantage over Sam. I've never considered myself invulnerable. I have a healthy respect for human weakness."

"Do you have any idea what would make them all like him again?"

"I suppose getting out of the Marines; seeking psychiatric help; taking some high-paying, no-risk consultancy; getting a completely clean bill of health from Walter Reed . . . ."

Swan sighed. "Thanks for coming over."

"Anything for you, honeykins," he said. "You have done one thing for me. You've make me very, very glad I've never really been in love." He kissed her quickly on the cheek.

Swan paid the check and headed for Belle Everley. She was in an airless, windowless cell, a box. A box of despair. How happy could she make Sam? She couldn't turn him out while he was ill, with no place to go, no one to care for him. When she was convinced he was well, she would have to tell him.

In the meantime, she followed the progress of Mike toward his date with destiny at Saratoga and of Linny and Judy with Jerusha Dutton; the developing pregnancies of The Fortress, Serve the Guns, and the other mares; the growth spurts of Major and Lady and the other yearlings. She sold a yearling for a good price in advance of the Saratoga sales mid-month.

And she watched Sam eat, lift weights, become restless, impatient with his recovery, and get well. At night, they began to make love as they had when they first met. He viewed it as getting back to normal; she as the glorious finale of their life together. She was more in love with him than ever, and she often watched him as he slept, trying to imagine the bed empty, without him, with only Flagg at its foot. She looked around the bedroom in the dark, at the weight equipment, his uniforms carefully hung and pressed in the closet, his jeans and racer back t-shirts folded in the big clothes press, his shaving kit in the bathroom. Imagining all of it gone, with her tall boots in their boot bags in place of his dress shoes, all sign of him erased, was agony.

◆

By the end of the month, she felt like those poor research animals shocked randomly over and over again until they lay motionless, catatonic: learned helplessness, scientists called it. Three days before her departure for Saratoga, they made love late at night. For the first time ever, she felt as though she was just going through the motions.

"What's wrong? Why are you being like this?" he asked sharply.

"Like what?"

"Like this. Proficient, distant, mechanical."

"That's not very flattering. What am I usually?" she asked, avoiding his gaze.

"Sweet. Ticklish. Responsive. Warm."

"I don't know what you are talking about. I thought we just had great sex."

"Christ," he said contemptuously, "add 'mendacious' to the first list."

"I'm sorry you weren't satisfied. Head to the Complaint Department for a refund."

"What have I done? What happened?" His brow furrowed.

"Nothing," she said. She smiled and moved herself further down the bed. He realized what she was up to; he pulled her back up to his eye level.

"Don't. Do you think that will make everything fine?"

"Apparently, I can't do anything right," Swan said stiffly. "I'm going to get up and take a shower then."

"You're turning away from me. Why?" he asked, worriedly. "What's happened? You're the way you were that night you told me to go. I'd 'gotten what I wanted.' Do you think I want sex like this? From you? I can go to any bar and get sex like this."

"Perhaps we should give it a rest and talk in the morning. I've got to get some sleep," she huffed.

He narrowed his eyes.

"Are you trying to pick a fight?"

"You're the one trying to fight! Listen to yourself: 'We've had sex and I want to know why.' Ridiculous," she said.

"You always make it about sex when you want to fight with me. Why not try a different subject? The Marines? Why not haul out the one hundred women again?"

"You seem to be arguing with yourself, Sam. Supplying both sides of the argument, yours and mine." Swan rolled over in bed, away from him.

"Just do us both a favor and tell me where this is going. It will waste less time," he said bitterly.

"Well, I'm obviously getting on your nerves somehow, getting the third degree like this. Perhaps we should take a break for a few days. Cool things off." Swan stayed facing away from him so she did not have to meet his eyes.

He was thunderstruck.

"So that's it. 'Take a break for a few days.' We already took a 'break'—all the way to fucking Afghanistan! You are giving me the boot. I didn't see that coming." He was stunned. "Now I suppose I'll have to use the Magic Eight-Ball to figure out why. Whenever you get these lunatic ideas, you know you can't make a logical case for them." He fumed. "Not lunatic *ideas*; always the same idea, over and over again. 'Bad luck, doomed love.'"

"I've got to get up early and meet Patty at the florist."

"Oh, no you don't, not if we are taking a fucking 'break.' What got 'bad luck doomed love' going in your brain this time?"

"Do you think it's constructive to begin every discussion by insulting me? How has that worked for you so far?" Swan kept her back to him but she did prop herself on one elbow.

He sighed and she knew he was making the effort.

"Okay. Something has set you off. Something somebody has said. Something somebody has done."

"I'm going to do an errand in the morning. I'm not giving you the boot."

"The hell you aren't! If I've got to use the Magic Eight-Ball, you're going to stay right here and watch me do it. 'Take a break.' *Give* me a fucking break!"

"We've been over everything a million times."

"Yeah, and I don't budge and you don't budge."

"You were fine til you met me."

"Number One: I was not fine. I was lonely as hell. Number Two: I *was* sick but I'm recovering, so I'm *now* fine." He tried to turn her to look at him.

"Fitch was fine when I started going out with him. Then he lost his arm. We broke up and he recovered. We got back together—as friends, I mean—and he died. He *died*. Within weeks. I don't want that to happen to you."

"It won't happen to me. Look at me." He rolled her over to put her hand on his chest. "I'm a beast. Doctor said so."

"You were fine," Swan insisted. "You had a great career and then you meet my stepfather, through *me*, and your career goes down the tubes. Then you come down with this rare disease. It's only because you *are* a beast that you are recovering as well as you are. Dr. Arthur said you might lose a kidney or your spleen or . . . something worse."

"I can live without a spleen and I can live fine with one kidney. It's only the liver—" His voice trailed off.

"I can't take that chance. What about pancreatitis? Or PTSD? The only way I can be sure you are okay is to—"

"Break up with me so your bad luck won't kill me? It's *my* liver, isn't it? Let me decide if it's worth the risk." He sounded certain.

"If something happens to you, I'll go crazy. I mean it."

"Something *has* happened to me! *You've* happened to me! You are driving *me* crazy. Check me into the psych ward. You'll be doing me a favor." He was boiling over.

"That's why we need to take a break," said Swan, trying to make him see. "Hunt told me that when the Marines were first in Iraq, you refused to eat the candy in the MREs—not only refused to eat it but wouldn't even let it in the humvees. You thought it was bad luck because somebody's humvee was blown up while the team was eating—?"

"Charms," Sam said woodenly. "Pure superstition."

"Yes, but you threw all the candy out anyway, didn't you?" she said. "If you saw three humvees trip IEDs and blow up, one after another, before your eyes, would you still go right on behind them or would you stop, chart another course? That's how it looks to me."

"Swan, when I send a platoon forward or call down fire on a village, I'm taking a risk that something will go wrong. If I don't make a decision, if I can't absorb the consequences of risk, I'll be paralyzed. Do you understand that?"

"You've chosen to put yourself in that position. You can live with it, apparently."

"What are you going to do? Join a nunnery? Date men you dislike so that when you kill them you won't feel bad?"

"Mockery is so helpful."

"What else can I do? Take 'bad luck doomed love' seriously?"

"You could agree that we need to take a break without making a federal case out of it."

"If taking a break will help, we'll take a break, but I'm telling you right now: you're breaking it off. You don't have the guts to admit it, that's all. And it's all for nothing."

"I'm screwed up," Swan said miserably. She looked down.

"Heads, you win: tails, I lose," he said. He looked one hundred years old. "If I didn't love you so much, this would be laughable. Three and a half tours in hell, a rare deadly disease, a political shitstorm, I'm here safe and sound, and you're breaking us up anyway. "

"I want us to take a break," she repeated mechanically.

"Then that's what we'll do."

"I wish you could understand," she whispered. "If you could do something to keep me safe, wouldn't you do it? You would. This is something I can do. I have to do."

He pulled her to him and he was all over her, in her, not careful any more, showing her his anger and his need. She wanted him, and as he drove into her, there were tears in his eyes. It went on all night, without let up. He would say, "Don't do this to us," and "You're killing me," trying to break her down, but it was hopeless. By daybreak, she felt like he had pounded her into the ground. He got up and silently showered. She laid in bed with her eyes closed. She heard him dress and throw his uniforms and all of his other clothes into his suitcases, stepping over Flagg as he went back and forth from the closets to the dresser to the clothes press.

Finally he turned to her, knowing she was awake.

"I'll be staying with Harry Edwards at Quantico," he announced. "If this 'break' is a 'break up,' I'll send for my stuff." Then he lifted the duffle bag, the three suitcases, looked around the bedroom one last time, and was gone.

Swan staggered toward the shower an hour later. She looked in the driveway. The truck was gone; the Harley and the Mercedes were where he had left them. She went back into the bathroom and vomited. Then she went downstairs. Mathilde looked at her, shocked, alarmed, and silent. Swan went into the entranceway and picked up the phone. When Spaulding answered, she said, "You'll all be relieved to know that I've sent Sam away" and hung up.

To their credit, the whole family left her alone. She flew to Albany, rented a car to drive to Saratoga, and watched Mike run in the Merry Widower as if in a dream. When he won in his usual driving fashion, she walked to the winner's circle with Oliver, smiled holding the trophy, talked to the horse racing channel's on-camera reporter, patted Mike and heard him whinny, and turned around and drove back to Albany.

When she came home, the Mercedes, the Harley, the flat screen, and the weight equipment were all gone. She became hysterical, and Mathilde for the first time in her life called Boyd Senior at home in a panic. He called Dr. Cavendish in Waverly, who called in a prescription that Mathilde picked up that night.

◆

Daniel Spaulding came to Belle Everley and moved into the spare guest room. Over the next week, Daniel called Clarissa of Boston, the Waverly florist, the tent company, Patty Lombardini, the Lester Lanin orchestra, the D.J., and the pastor at Waverly Methodist. He told them all, "Send us a bill."

He spoke with Hetty or Spaulding every day. He called Tidewater Commercial and told them he had a family emergency. At night he would talk briefly to Swan about Eduardo's tasks for the next day, about instructions for Oliver and Jerusha. He talked to the owners boarding horses at Belle Everley and to Kezia Hardaway. He told them Swan had the flu and had lost her voice. Some of them believed him. He opened the mail and brought her check book to Swan to pay her bills. He would sit with her in front of the fireplace in her bedroom and watch her stare at her untouched dinner, night after night. Some nights she vomited or had the dry heaves. Some nights she wept silently, the tears trickling down her face until Daniel had to wipe them off with a handkerchief.

Then another bombshell was dropped by Persis Fitzhugh. A new will had been discovered: Fitch had left High View and four million dollars to Susannah Swan Everett Bolington. It was dated the day after the embassy tea dance and had been witnessed and executed the same day. Everyone was speechless. Persis would get twenty-one million and the hunt box; Swan the five-hundred-acre farm and enough money to pay the taxes and upkeep on it in perpetuity. She didn't know how to feel. She was now a woman with two historic houses and no husband. No one knew what to say except Daniel, who said, "I guess I should start making my rent checks out to you now."

At the end of September, the family talked about what to do on October 2. They thought of instituting an informal suicide watch, which Daniel rejected contemptuously.

"She's tougher than she looks; otherwise she could never have sent him away. She'll be okay."

And she was.

Daniel started going back to work for half days. On one of them, he was contacted by Septimus Moore. They agreed to meet at a coffee shop near Walter Reed when Sam was in town for his check up. They saw each other in the parking lot. Sam was in his desert camo battle dress, looking fit and bulked up. He strode up to Daniel and shook his hand grimly.

"How is she?" he asked.

"She's fine," said Daniel smoothly. This was not strictly true.

"I hope you're all happy," Sam said, bitterly, and for the first time Daniel was acutely conscious of the great physical disparity between them. He didn't feel threatened, but he stepped back a step or two, just the same.

"Do you think you were doing her any favors by constantly dismissing her fears? Didn't you see how desperate that made her? Didn't you want to help her at all?" Daniel asked.

"I appreciate your insight," Sam said, sarcastically. "But I think I know her as well as you do."

"Do you? You might have tried to show it."

"How? By burying a chicken in the back yard for good juju? By sending her to a shrink? What would he diagnose? PTSD? Clinical depression? Thanks, but when I need advice from a—"

"Cokehead?" Daniel said it for him. "You *are* clueless, aren't you? I can see why you screwed yourself in Kandahar. She's not making it up, you know, they all *have* died. It's not like she's seeing UFOs. A psychiatrist might have something to offer. It is possible. Otherwise, she was all alone, trying not to lose it completely—and trying to protect you."

"Protect me? From what? I'm home now and recovering," Sam said dismissively.

"From her, you stupid, blind shit."

"And *you* know this how?" Sam was getting angrier.

"Did you ever see *The Lion in Winter*? Richard the Lionheart says to Philip of France, 'I've wandered every street in hell.' And Philip replies, 'Funny, I've never seen you there.'"

"Yeah, you've made no secret of the fact that you and Swan share this mystical bond." Sam was contemptuous. "What a nice angle that is to hook up with her yourself. Landing Swan would make you scion of the Bolingtons, wouldn't it? Swan can work fourteen hours a day on the farm while you do—what? Play at banking and snort your salary up your nose?"

Daniel looked him in the eye. "Marrying Swan would make *you* part of the landed gentry, wouldn't it? You and your dirt-poor offspring. You're hopeless. You've gotten what you deserve."

He turned back to his car and got in. In his rear-view mirror he saw Sam, standing motionless next to his truck in the lot behind him. He didn't tell Swan about this meeting.

Swan looked like hell. Everyone said so. She was pale and wan. She sleepwalked through her days, mechanically directing Eduardo and Edgar's activities as though she were underwater. Hetty and Spaulding were desperate, but Daniel counseled patience. Swan would talk to them on the phone but would not see them, which hurt Hetty, in particular, terribly. Spaulding tried to come up with something to say, something that would interest her. Townsend Brooke had not returned to the College of William and Mary, Spaulding said, and had transferred to UCLA, majoring in film. She had begun dating a star of a teen drama on the KW network, Bernardo Holtzman, and was happy again.

◆

By mid-October, Daniel was spending some nights at High View, but never more than two or three consecutively away from Swan. He was never seen in the Scarab. On the anniversary of Hunt's death, Swan went to Section 60 by herself and sat in front of Hunt's grave with her two wreaths for hours. Then she turned around and came home. She did not look at the card on the third wreath.

Mathilde shopped, cooked food, and cleaned the house for a ghost. Flagg watched Swan anxiously from morning til night. He never let Daniel touch him.

◆

One day Daniel drove Swan to Furnace Mountain, since everyone thought it would be good for her to see Mike. It did seem to cheer her up, and she talked to Oliver and Sinjon like the old days. The Templetons' colts were beginning to win big, like Mike, and the Templetons themselves stopped in just as she and Daniel were leaving. She seemed to enjoy that.

She began to eat again. Three good meals a day. She gained back the weight she had lost, most of it anyway. In November, Mike won another Grade I race, at Belmont Park, but Swan didn't go up to see it. She did, however, insist on driving herself to Furnace Mountain to see Dress the Line transferred from Jerusha's barn to Oliver's and seemed pleased to see the sister stabled next to her brother Mike, both of them next to the Templetons' three colts.

She rode Punch once with the Waverly Hunt. Kezia was glad to see her looking relatively well and riding wonderfully aside, as always. No one asked about James. On an impulse, Swan trailered Punch to High View. She walked into the enormous manor house, the main part brick, with a front portico, and two flanking additions in a pale yellow plaster. It still felt like Fitch's house, but walking on the two-hundred-year-old chestnut floors, running her hands along the carved mantel pieces, gave her solace. She rode Punch through the fields closest to the house, marveling at the rich earth, clean streams, undulating terrain, now that it was all hers. She met with the Piedmont Preservation Trust to discuss placing a historic easement on High View and agreed to let the Garden Club tour her new house during the spring Historic Garden Week.

Swan overheard Mathilde on the phone in her suite behind the kitchen telling her Richmond sister-in-law that there had been a terrible scene at the Willow's Edge. Sam had asked to talk to all of them there—Bert, Boyd and Hetty, Spaulding, Daniel. He had become increasingly agitated until he had melted down completely, shouting that they had tried to sabotage him from the beginning, that they had wanted Daniel for Swan all along. They all had been truly shaken, and when he stormed out and jumped on the Harley, they had called Mathilde at Belle Everley to warn her that Sam might be on his way there in a rage.

"As if he would ever harm a hair on her head," Mathilde was saying on the phone. "I saw that man every day for months. Major Moore would give his life for her and that—" Mathilde had stopped, suddenly aware that Swan was in the kitchen.

"Dog, that Flagg," she finished. Swan could hear her sniffling.

Swan refused to join the family for Thanksgiving but insisted everyone else go to their families for the holidays, including Daniel. She and the college girls managed the Belle Everley barns for the four-day weekend.

◆

The Saturday after Thanksgiving, she drove to the Willow's Edge. Daniel had dictated guidelines to Spaulding, who hadn't seen Swan in months: no talk about Sam; no questions about the future; no apologies. They drank tea and talked about Boyd Junior and Bud, Mike, Swan's plans for High View. Kezia had asked her to be joint master of foxhounds, Swan said. They sank into silence. Swan looked out the window at the little pond and the willows in the dusk. Then she said she had to go. After she drove away, Spaulding put her head in her hands and cried.

On her way back to Belle Everley, Swan passed the Scarab. She had been so preoccupied that she hadn't realized she was there until she saw the neon sign in front of the frame building. The parking lot was full. She almost drove past, but at the last minute she saw an empty spot and sharply turned the dually into it. She didn't know why. Old times' sake probably—Fitch . . . Sam.

It was unseasonably cold. She wasn't dressed for slumming: black leather pants setting off her slim legs and perfect derrière, a black faux fur cossack's hat, the long tail of dark hair almost to her waist, the Mason's frock coat and Afghan scarf; black leather gauntlets, boots—more like a costume. It would have looked ridiculous on anyone else, but on Swan it was distinctive, eye-catching. Her pale, creamy skin was visible only on her beautiful face.

Every leering eye followed her as she snaked her way past the dancing couples toward a table, though without Septimus Moore she felt little, vulnerable, lost. She saw no one she knew; just as well. The bartender, the reptilian Scar, took it on himself to bring her a beer, with a wink, open to any suggestion. She was reluctant to catch anyone's eye, almost impossible anyway due to the smoke, darkness, the glare of a strobe light and glow from the jukebox. What a mistake this had been. She had no sooner taken off her gloves than she had decided to pay her tab and leave. The glimpse of a tall man's broad back at the bar stopped her as she rose. She would need to get out at that very moment if she was to avoid what was about to happen.

Too late. Scar had made sure of that.

She was still standing as Sam slowly turned around. He got himself a good look, then picked up his beer and made his way to Swan's table, cutting off her exit route. She sank into the chair, never taking her eyes off him.

"I've been coming here every Saturday for three months hoping you'd remember what we talked about on Christmas Eve," he said. He was in jeans, t-shirt, camo jacket; his face was stubbly. "I told the bartender it was five hundred bucks if he let me know whether you ever came in. You never did." He looked well, as big as ever physically, sunburned, but still pale under his eyes.

"Christmas Eve? The looking-for-skanks thing? I was on my way home from Spaulding's and stopped in for . . . for I don't know why. I was about to leave," Swan said.

"So I see." He eyed her untouched draft, her bare hands. "You've lost the ring."

Swan was silent. Then she said, "I'll give it back."

He snorted, disgusted. "If you do, I'll—" but he stopped himself with a sigh. He started over.

"So, it's you and Daniel, now. Who'd have thought?" But he was sarcastic. "I suppose you still have your shared mystical bond."

"We aren't sleeping together, if that's what you're thinking. We are cousins. Anyway, I assumed you'd . . . moved on," she murmured, and he leaned over the little table to hear her.

"Moved on? Moved on?" He was contemptuous. "This is how far I can move away from you," he pulled her outstretched arm to him, resting her palm on his chest. "The thought of anyone else makes me want to puke my guts out." His touch sent a charge up her arm, hot and electric.

"You could always have come to the house," Swan said, pulling her hand back gently.

"And watch you think of ways of keeping me out or getting me out? Somehow, standing on the front steps with the door closing in my face wasn't that appealing," he said grimly. "And, now that I've seen you, I won't be coming in here again either. So you needn't worry." He shucked off his jacket. He was wearing the black racer-back-t even though it was the first of December.

He turned slightly. Even in the smokey dark she could see a swan, its neck arched, beak to its breast, wings raised, tattooed on his huge bicep just below where the great mountain range ended. He saw her look, and he turned so she could see its twin on his other arm.

He stared her down, daring her to say something, but she looked away.

"Do you think you will deploy again?" Swan asked, still not looking at him. "Kandahar? Boblingen? You look . . . completely recovered."

He shrugged. "Depends on Walter Reed. If they clear me, they can send me wherever they want. It doesn't matter to me."

The jukebox was blaring C.C. Adcock: *I've been through hell/I know it well/ I'm ready for my final date with the devil.*

His tone changed. He looked at her pleadingly.

"Listen," he said, raising his voice so she could hear. "I told you I'd leave the Corps if that's what you want. I don't think you even *know* what you want."

"If you left and we were still unhappy, you would have left for nothing—or worse, for me."

"We haven't been unhappy; *you've* been unhappy! Just tell me what you want to do and I'll do it, but I won't hang around like a dog begging for kitchen scraps. I don't see the percentage in it. You don't love me. Just say it and put us both out of our misery."

"I do love you," Swan said, "but I warned you. I told you that if you deployed again, I'd make you sorry you'd ever met me."

"Okay. For the last time: I didn't fuck up my career because of you. I didn't get sick because of you. Fitch didn't die because of you," he said, "neither did Carter Roland or Hunt Lee. Your goddamn family went off me because my career is in the toilet, I'm probably going to have health problems down the road—PTSD or worse. I'm a nobody—no money, no land, no family, no political connections. They are all afraid you'll end up nursemaiding me, supporting me, while you are trying to run the farm—two farms, now, I hear—and you'll run yourself into the ground. You have your whole life in front of you. They think you can do much better.

"And you've bought into their whole thing. They say it's dark, it's dark; they say it's light, it's light. Underneath all that tally-hoing and opera-going and charity shit, they are worse than the fucking Taliban. Talk about mind control: Sheik Omar could learn a lot from the Bolingtons," he said.

"If they are trying to 'save' me from 'man trouble,' then why are they handing me to Daniel on a silver platter?" Swan asked calmly. "They have always been there for me, through Hunt, Carter, Fitch, and now—I can't turn my back on them. How could I? If something else—*anything* else—happened, without them, I'd go crazy."

"Oh, Daniel is only the family's little caretaker. They know he'll self destruct. He is just supposed to serve his purpose now—til I give up and get out," Sam said bitterly, draining his beer. "Before I deployed, did you ever go off the pill? Maybe if we'd had a baby . . . ." He stared at her, then seemed to force himself to look away, but he turned back to study her face. He swallowed hard.

"You look fantastic," he said, his voice suddenly soft, choked, "as ever. Better even." He swallowed again. He looked away. Then he got up from the table and threw down a twenty.

You are better off without me, she thought.

He jammed his arms into the sleeves of his jacket and made his way toward the front door, without looking back. She counted the seconds. Soon she heard the Harley roar to life. She felt tears wet her face in the dark.

She looked down at her belly. Still so flat. She'd pulled that off, at least. Her appointment at the women's health center in Delaware was three days away. She hadn't wanted to go anyplace locally. She had gone up after she had seen Linny and Mike at Furnace

Mountain. She was coming to the end of her first trimester, they had said. Absolutely no more waiting. If she delayed any longer, she'd have to go to Canada.

She would stop by to see Mike and Linny again on the way, she decided. That's where her future lay anyway. She gently rested her hand on the waistband of her leather pants. The gesture quieted her nerves. She hadn't had the Marriage in Heaven dream since she'd taken the home test. Funny. She'd carefully hidden the kit, kept it out of the bathroom wastebaskets, but Swan suspected Mathilde had put two and two together.

She still had a few days to think about it. That was the important thing.

Swan stood up and pulled on the gauntlets. She walked slowly out of the Scarab, thinking, thinking. Mostly, she was thinking about The Her. Maybe she wasn't in Oceanside at all, but in the Scarab right now, the five-foot-nine happy-go-lucky gal without Swan's array of psychoses to torment him. This imaginary Her was still Swan's best friend. The two of them would go arm in arm through her brain until Sam deployed again or gave up and left for good. Maybe if Swan came back in a few weeks, she'd see the woman holding on to his arm, looking up at him, glommed on to that prime male real estate. Because, be realistic: how long was a man like Sam going to pine away?

She wound her way through the dark lot, her head down. Well, isn't that what she had connived for, denied herself for? The Her? Swan had done it to herself. After all she had put them—and the whole family—through, the second circle of hell's worth of misery, how could she backslide now?

She stood in front of the driver's-side door of the SUV.

"Sam," she said in anguish. She pressed her head against the door frame, her eyes wet in the dark.

She felt a sudden wave of longing, not just from her own heart, from her own self, but from somebody else, whoever was in her, for the same thing. It was overpowering.

"I'm right here, baby."

Swan looked up in disbelief.

Sitting propped against the seat of the Harley, arms folded, jacket collar turned up against the cold—there he was. Under the trees shading the parking lot, almost invisible. Sam.

"I heard you go," she said.

"Yeah, I moved the Harley over here next to your car so I wouldn't miss you. Did you really think I'd leave you in there alone, after what happened the last time?" he said softly. "Not likely."

"Sam, I have to tell you—"

"I don't want to hear it. I've heard enough," he said, still quiet but firm. "You talk and talk yourself into such a fucking state of panic. We aren't going to do it anymore. Not tonight. Tonight you are just the little cupcake I'm taking home."

She looked at him cautiously.

"Sex doesn't solve everything. Even great sex." She should know.

"I should know," Sam said with a grimace. "We have problems. Big problems."

"A skank from the Scarab," she murmured, still looking at him. "A one-nighter. It doesn't change anything."

"My kind of girl—absolutely."

"What about the car?" she asked, as she walked toward him.

"It'll be here in the morning," he said.

Part 2

Chapter 15

Three days later, Swan was on Route 95, between the Furnace Mountain Training Center and the Delaware border. She had never truly examined her feelings about motherhood. To have it now looming, through no conscious decision of her own, and short-circuit it permanently was frightening and disheartening. She imagined her return trip down the interstate in a few hours, no longer pregnant, no longer troubled by this glitch in an already complicated life. The thought left her uncertain, worried, alone.

"I think of you every day. Every night. The way you used to cry out for me. I can't think of anything else. Can you? If you say you can, you're lying," Sam had said to her after they had left the Scarab. Despite their night together, all their problems remained, problems that would be magnified a hundredfold if she had this baby.

Swan took the next off-ramp, where a QuikMart and a bevy of gas stations clustered around a fast-food outlet in the grim, rainy December gloom. If she kept going, she would be over it all. If she turned around, she was changing her destiny, and her family's, forever.

Swan had never craved motherhood the way Hetty had. Most of her friends and neighbors rode straight through their pregnancies, to the eighth month if there weren't any complications. Waverly obstetricians were used to such patients. So long as you had been a regular rider before you became pregnant, it was okay to continue. Falling off . . . well, that carried the same risks whether you were pregnant or not.

Some folks were working with their horses within a few weeks of delivery and riding astride a few weeks after that. Edwardo and

Edgar could handle the riding chores until she was back on her feet. Mathilde could help with the house and Spaulding and Hetty would pitch in when she needed them. She didn't need logistical support. She needed reassurance that she would be a good single mother.

But she couldn't confide in anyone to get it.

She had postponed, wavered, equivocated, until her time had run out. She was going to have a baby or an abortion. Swan thought about everything one more time, spooling through the reel of memory just to be sure that she had not overlooked anything.

By everything, she meant everything she'd been to everyone she had cared about.

Her father's dutiful partner; her mother's loving challenge. Hunt Lee's vivacious college sweetheart; Carter's grieving, hopeful fiancée; Fitch's unrequited love; the one constant in the lives of three men engaged in the great battle of the day, or at least what they thought was the great battle. Of course, the great battle had really been waged by Swan, the great internal battle to survive when everyone else had been wrenched away, sacrificed on the alter of his country, because of her.

She had survived to walk around among the living as if she were still alive herself, in the sense that she was impervious to fate, and to love a man who refused to believe the truth, that she had killed them all. Now she was going to have this man's baby or kill this man's baby. There was nothing to stop her, no moral qualms, no overwhelming desire for motherhood, no family opprobrium to hold her hostage. It was an absolutely value-neutral question before her. Anyone who didn't see that hadn't lived her life.

She knew it was a boy as well as she had ever known anything.

Thinking this through had taken time. She had sat in the dually so long that it was too late to get to her appointment. She picked up her cell phone and called the women's health center. She cancelled. It did not give her any any relief, any satisfaction, or joy at all.

She took the on-ramp south, toward home.

By the time Swan turned into the circular drive, the sun was setting on the short December day. Mathilde had lit the lamps, and the front steps were festooned with holiday greens, large branches of local holly, thick with berries, and long swags of magnolia. An enormous volley of barking greeted the sound of the SUV's purring engine: Flagg made sure Mathilde knew that Swan was back long before she skipped up the front steps. Mathilde came to the door, anxiously twisting her brown to grey hair behind her ear, reluctant to acknowledge the purpose of the trip north.

"How are you feeling, Miss Swan?" she said softly. "Do you want to go straight to bed?"

Swan smiled wanly.

"Why would I want to do that? What's for dinner? *Jawvohl, mein hund,*" she said to Flagg, who was bouncing up and down in place, trying to catch her attention. Mathilde looked at her carefully, the long black tail of hair down her back, the slim figure, and creamy skin, and then burst into tears.

"Oh, thank you, Jesus, Mary, and Joseph!" Mathilde blubbered into her apron. "I've prayed the whole day. The blessed Virgin heard me. Thank you, thank you, thank you." She dabbed at her eyes. "Now, you mustn't worry about a thing, *ma chèr*, we'll handle everything. I'm from a family of ten, you know. Nothing is too hard for the Lord to manage."

"My old darling, what are you talking about?" Swan teased her gently. "I went to see Oscar Mike and Linny, like always. You really are being so silly." She hugged her though and gave her a smooch on her cheek.

"I've got a nice chicken pie in the oven for your dinner," Mathilde fussed, "cranberry and orange relish; peas from the root cellar; a fresh custard tart *a la francaise* for your dessert, and a big pot of tea, already steeping, since you called from town."

"Sounds wonderful," Swan said, and she made herself comfortable at the long mahogany table in the dining room. "I could eat a horse." Then she considered the portent of that statement. "Any calls?"

"Mr. Daniel Spaulding, Mrs. Delaney, and—"

"And?"

"No one else."

"Mathilde: who?"

"No one, *mademoiselle*." Mathilde bustled around preparing a plate for Swan, who patted the place setting beside her. Mathilde quickly made up another plate of food and plopped down next to

Swan, pouring them both large bone china mugs of tea from the pot under a tea cozy on the sideboard.

"He hung up, I mean."

"Who hung up?" Swan said.

"Whoever hung up . . . hung up." Mathilde struggled. "That's who I mean."

"You know how to use caller I.D., Mathilde," Swan said calmly. "Was it the major?"

"He hung up." Mathilde had her story and she was sticking to it.

"Mathilde, whatever happens is none of the major's business, you must understand that," Swan said carefully. "Whatever happens concerns me alone."

"Yes, Miss Swan, only . . . ."

"It is the only way I'll be able to get through things, do you see? It has to be my way, *my* way," Swan said, gently but firmly. "I did see the major in the Scarab on Saturday, quite unexpectedly, but he needs to move on with his life. He needs to find someone else, start a family, and live far away from here."

"How can he once he finds out . . . this?" Mathilde asked sensibly.

Swan sighed.

"I don't know. But we must keep the major out of . . . things . . . here. I will need your help," she smiled. "He knows how much you like him. He likes you, too. I wouldn't be surprised if you two decided to try to get me to change my mind about how things have to be, but you must promise me you won't interfere." Swan drank from her mug. "Interference, well-meant interference, got us into this predicament to begin with," she said softly, "so promise me."

Mathilde nodded.

"But how can you keep it from him? You're going to start to show." So Mathilde knew the whole story after all.

"Big shirts, to begin with," Swan said. "No more tucked in, fitted riding shirts. You saw how small Miss Hetty was with Boyd Junior and Bud. Maybe I'll stay small, too, although—" she reconsidered, "Major Moore is . . . big. And gussets in the waistbands of my breeches," she mused. She envisioned a giant Moore baby growing . . . growing . . .growing.

"I'll get you a big glass of milk," Mathilde said, jumping up from the table. "No backtalk. At least two glasses a day; three would be better. And yogurt." She looked at Swan critically. "Knowing the major, any child of his will be not just big . . . but hungry."

"I've already gone up one bra size—do you think anyone has noticed?" Swan asked innocently.

Mathilde rolled her eyes. "You haven't been paying much attention, have you?"

"What do you mean? Has there been speculation? Talk?"

"Miss Swan, there has been nothing but talk, nonstop, since you sent the major on his way in September. Nothing." Mathilde shook her head. "Some people are taking bets on when he'll get you back from—"

"From?"

"It is nothing but tabloid gossip; I won't repeat it," Mathilde said primly.

"From? Or I won't drink a swallow of this," Swan bargained, holding the milk hostage.

"Mr. Spaulding."

"Mr. Daniel is my *cousin*—and my tenant. That is all. Anyone with a brain has to know that. Anything else is ridiculous."

"The major believes otherwise. Mr. Spaulding is your cousin *by marriage*. Your cousin Mary's stepson; not related to you by blood at all," argued Mathilde.

"That makes no difference." Swan downed the glass of milk and made a face. "I need time to think. And to tell everyone in my own way. I want to tell Miss Spaulding and Miss Hetty first, and Mr. Bert and Mr. Daniel. Yes, I'll have a tummy in a few weeks but, other than the Scarab—" Swan did not want to tell Mathilde about Sam's bounty offer. "No one who suspects anything knows how to get in touch with the major. He is staying with Captain Edwards. Anyone nosy—and mean spirited—enough to tell him will have to do some serious digging to find him and want to cause trouble between me and a very big man, who may not take kindly to interference."

Mathilde listened soberly.

"The major may be medically cleared and deployed before he even finds out the state of things. So I'm going along as we are now, for as long as possible. I'm going to see Dr. Cavendish for a routine check up this week, no big deal."

◆

Swan was able to avoid saying anything to her family because she didn't see any of them for three weeks. By the time they all met for Christmas week, however, anyone would see immediately that her traffic-stopping figure had undergone a change that was impossible to explain via anything but the truth. Spaulding was the first to arrive, resplendent in forest green Chanel wool pants, pearl earrings, short, highlighted haircut, and a red cashmere sweater set. Once she had placed a small mountain of gifts under the tree in the Belle Everley parlor, she sat down abruptly in front of the fire. She had caught sight of Swan's silhouette as she sat with her feet tucked in next to Flagg.

"Oh," Spaulding breathed. "Oh, oh, oh. Oh."

"What's done is done," Swan shrugged, defensively. She was in an oversized wool shirt, long sweater vest, and stretch corduroy leggings; layering was her friend. But still . . . .

"Oh, Swannie . . . . Oh."

"Yes. I know."

"Does Sam know?" asked Spaulding.

"No, but now it looks as though he's not deploying soon enough for me to keep it from him. I plan to tell him after Christmas. He is out of town, with Harry Edwards's family near Camp LeJeune, for a few days," Swan said. "This is according to Mathilde, who apparently has some pipeline into a pipeline that eventually leads to Quantico's officers' mess." Swan was not going to acknowledge to anyone but Mathilde her meeting with Sam at the Scarab.

"How far gone are you?"

"Almost four months; it must have been the day we separated, believe it or not, or not much before. I was using protection but nothing is perfect," Swan said, trying to sound matter of fact, ready for anything.

"What are your plans?"

"My plans are to raise the baby as a single parent, like a million women have before me."

"What do you think Sam's plans will be?"

"Well, I'm hoping he will understand that this doesn't trigger a revisiting of why I broke it off to begin with in the fall," Swan said, "and I hope that he sees that this does not have any real impact on his life. He is still a guy who could marry any of a million women if he just crooked his little finger; and I hope that he will not want to complicate my already complicated life by trying to intrude into it."

"That is a lot of hoping," Spaulding stated the obvious. "What do you *think* he'll do?"

Swan sighed.

"I suspect some version of a nuclear-warhead detonation. I've got to come up with a way to put this in some context for him, to lead him to my way of thinking. I've had some time to absorb this; none of the rest of you, including Sam, have. I understand that."

"He blames us for everything," Spaulding said sadly. "Our active working against his . . . suit, our refusal to confront you about your attitude toward 'bad luck doomed love,' our designs on your . . . romantic future. He thinks we have ruined not just his life but yours, too. That we are 'toxic' and an impediment to your happiness.

"Swannie, do you think this is true?" Spaulding asked. "I am heartsick. I've tried my best to give you the kind of advice I thought our Lucinda would have given you. But to see you this way, so broken . . . the way you were when you visited me in the fall, so ill—"

"Yes, well, it has been difficult," said Swan in a whisper. "The fall was . . . very hard. But much of it must have been first-trimester blues and hormone storms. And Sam was ill, too, remember. He's so big and strong on the outside—the 'Mars the God of War' thing you and Hetty hung on him. People assume he is indestructible, but he wasn't recovered completely from the leishmaniasis. His state of mind."

"You always defend him," Spaulding observed gently. "You defend us, too, but you blame him for nothing. You can't. You must love him very much."

"That's why I had to give him up. It had nothing to do with your opposition or acceptance of him or us," Swan replied, and she was suddenly very tired. This statement was not entirely true.

"How can we help you, my darling?" asked Spaulding, reaching out to hold her hand.

"Well, you could fill in Hetty, Daniel, Bert, and Boyd before they arrive," she said. "I don't know if I could go through this whole discussion three more times."

To their credit, they all rallied once they got over the shock. Hetty was pleased for Swan—she was a huge proponent of motherhood, but she simply couldn't envision Swan's road as a single mother. Boyd was the typical doctor, asking questions about Swan's eating and sleeping habits, as though Dr. Cavendish wasn't doing the same thing; Daniel kept his head on straight and kept his mouth shut. Bert Davis was flummoxed. He didn't know whether to be happy or anxious, but Swan's demeanor finally tipped him toward happy. Boyd Junior and Bud were the perfect antidotes to worry, chortling carols, chasing the ever patient Flagg, trying to climb the Christmas trees, and generally wreaking holiday mayhem before everyone split up for their homes. Mathilde, Eduardo, and Edgar had dispersed to family get-togethers, and Swan was making do with the college girls. A few days before New Year's, the Belle Everley crew was reunited, and Swan felt comfortable enough to make the phone call she dreaded, to Septimus Moore.

"Sam, I need to talk to you. Could you meet me somewhere convenient?"

He was surprised—big time—to hear from her, she could tell.

"Shall I come to the farm?" he asked cautiously.

"No, that's a long drive." *It was a long drive for someone who wasn't going to be spending the night,* she meant. She wanted it to be someplace public, to decrease the possibility of a scene.

"Crossroads?"

"No." If he was angry enough, he might follow her back to the house to harangue her. "What about the Wayside? Or the Trainyard?" she suggested.

"Wherever you like. When?"

Better sooner than later.

"How is tonight? I know it is odd timing, between Christmas and New Year's, but—"

"It's all the same to me," he said cheerfully.

"Sam, I just want you to know. This has nothing to do with us getting back together or anything like that," she said by way of a warning.

"Are you okay? Is everything okay?" he asked, clearly disappointed.

"Absolutely. How about seven thirty at the Trainyard?"

"I'll be there."

Swan assessed her closet. None of her outfits from New York was designed with a baby bump in mind. She went with an oversized shirt, elastic waistband leggings, long wool sweater, ballet flats. At the last minute, she added an oversized quilted corduroy vest. She pulled her hair into a low ponytail and got in the dually.

When she pulled into the Trainyard parking lot, Sam was leaning against his F-250 in the dark. His typical off-duty uniform of jeans, sweatshirt with the sleeves cut out, low-heeled cowboy boots and a combat jacket were enough for the relatively mild January early evening. He looked at her intently, trying to read her demeanor, looking for any sign of warmth, of desire, of need, and found none. He reached for her arm, but Swan scooted into the restaurant ahead of him, out of the cold and out of the glare of the parking lot lights. The hostess gave Sam a five-thousand-megawatt smile and showed them to a booth. Swan looked at the tight squeeze her camouflaged belly was about to endure and turned to Sam:

"Do you think we could have a table instead?"

The hostess led them to a window table. The holiday lights inside the restaurant made everyone look red and green. Swan ordered: crab cake, tea, and custard tart. Her first trimester nausea was gone; her appetite was firing on all eight cylinders.

"Okay," she said to him when the waitress had left them. "First, please promise not to get upset by what I'm going to say."

"No fucking way," Sam shot back. "If this is what I think it is, I'm not going to promise anything. You're going to make the biggest mistake of your life." He was clenching and unclenching his hands—that was disconcerting.

Swan hadn't expected this. How did he know?

"If you won't promise, would you at least try to not get upset?" She forced a smile.

"You're getting married," he said lifelessly. He shucked out of his camo jacket and as usual, his tattooed arms generated admiring looks from every woman in the restaurant not on life-support equipment. He ignored them all. Swan had to look away. *Married?*

"Married?" Swan had to keep from laughing in his face. "Who would I be marrying? Cousin Daniel? We're not in some Tennessee holler, you know."

"Then what's the deal?" he said, but she saw the relief on his face, and his tone was much softer. Obviously, that was what he had been dreading since her call. Good: he suspected nothing. Swan went for a cheery, cable newswoman's smile for the delivery of bad news. She took a deep breath.

"Sam, when you went overseas, I stopped taking my birth control pills, and although I started back up when we began sleeping together again last summer, I didn't do so in time to prevent something I'm sure we both now wish hadn't happened." She said this all in one breath, so he took a moment to process it.

Sam looked at her, and she saw disbelief, disbelief, disbelief, uncertainty, cautious half-certainty, growing certainty, then certainty march across his face.

"You said you'd try not to get upset," she said. He hadn't, but she was going with wishing making it so.

"How far along?" he managed to ask.

"Just shy of four months."

"May I . . . see?"

Swan surreptitiously opened her long sweater and gathered the loose folds of the oxford cloth shirt around the profile of her bump, conscious of the fact that she was virtually a window display.

"Four months. That would make it—"

"June first," she interjected helpfully. "Forty weeks. But I want you to know that you needn't worry about anything. I won't be naming you on the birth certificate, or seeking child support, or going to the military for medical benefits, or anything like that."

He looked at her as though she had said, "I won't be running buck naked down Main Street."

"None of that is what I would be worrying about," he said, matching her demeanor. "I assume you knew this at the Scarab."

"Yes."

"And you didn't tell me then—"

"Well, I was surprised to see you, of course, and the conversation went south kind of fast," she said. "Then, when we went to Quantico, you said you didn't want to talk about all the things between us, just be . . . together . . . ." She trailed off.

"What did you think I'd do?" he asked.

"I'm not sure, now. You've been so worked up, and for me to spring this on you in bed, when we agreed it was a one-night thing—"

Was he buying any of this? Would she, if she'd heard herself?

"Yeah. I guess. I would have liked to know if we were doing any harm to . . . it, though."

"We didn't. We couldn't."

"We were pretty . . . wild," he said. "It had been so long since we'd been . . . together . . . and I wasn't as careful as I could have been. We both know I'm way too big for you—I could have ruptured you." They'd made love all night—nonstop—in many ways.

"No—not a problem. People do it up to the day of delivery if they want to. Some doctors think it's good for you," Swan said. "Well, not for *you*, but, I mean, good for the mother."

"So I guess you didn't care," he said.

"More coffee?" The waitress was back and bright as a new penny, looking at Sam's heavy biceps swell and roll as he clenched and unclenched his hands.

"Do you have any herbal tea?" Swan asked, and the waitress bustled right off to bring her a cup.

"Didn't care?" she tried to pick up the thread of his conversation.

"You didn't care if you told me or not, and you didn't care if we hurt . . . things."

"Are you listening at all? I just ordered caffeine-free tea and, I told you, we couldn't hurt a fetus as small as this one was then." Her patience was beginning to ebb. "I don't intend to hurt anything."

"But *then* you didn't care. I assumed you were back on the pill so you weren't worried about us getting pregnant. I'm so fucking stupid. It never dawned on me you already were." He looked at her "What a liar you are. You should work for D.I.A."

"I'm not getting it, Sam," she said coolly, "I'm telling you now. What does it matter what I did then? We are only talking a few weeks."

"You didn't tell me and you didn't care because you didn't think you'd have to care for long." His voice was cold, as cold as she'd ever heard it. “I assume you’re telling me now because concealing it at this point—” he dropped his eyes to her waist, “is no longer an option. You figured I’d find out and—what? Go ballistic? Accuse Daniel? Demand we get married?”

“All of the above,” she said. Sam looked at her until she began to be uncomfortable.

“Well,” he said calmly.“I want to thank you.” He looked away.

“I want to thank you for not killing my little kid.”

Swan sat stunned. He knew what had been in her mind—why she had gone for weeks without telling him anything; why she didn’t care if they’d hurt the pregnancy. She had been going to terminate it anyway.

His words cut, shocked, hurt her. They were true. She was offended nonetheless.

“It wasn’t like that. You aren’t a woman. You can’t understand the emotions you experience. If I had done it, it would have been for the best. My decision, mine, on my own—like you said before you were deployed.” She was suddenly trembling all over.

“What made up your mind?” he asked.

“I decided I would never marry, that this would be my only chance at having a family. It had nothing to do with you—nothing whatsoever. You happen to be the biological father, but this will be my child.”

“I appreciate your point of view,” he said with equanimity, “fortunately, though, the Commonwealth of Virginia will have a different take on things.”

“Sam, be reasonable: you will be deployed overseas once you are cleared by Walter Reed, probably within weeks. You will be permanently posted at Oceanside or Camp LeJeune or San Antonio, all of them far away from here,” Swan said. “You will not have the opportunity to form any real bond.”

“That doesn’t change the fact that this is my child, Swan. Nothing changes that. Nothing.”

She considered this.

“I don’t understand why you don’t just cut yourself off from me! I’ve done nothing but make you unhappy. You are a wonderful, great-looking guy. A million women would get down on their knees every night and thank God to be married to you and give you all the children you could ever want."

"Well, that would certainly let you off the hook," he said sarcastically. "You seem to forget I tried that 'million women' approach and it didn't work out so well." He took a deep breath and tried again. "Look, I've accepted that I have a crazy girl on my hands, one made crazier by her family. But let me be sure I understand your current thinking: I'm getting well, and that is because you and I have broken up. Even though we are now going to have a child, it is more important that we stay apart so I can stay safe from 'bad luck doomed love.'"

"You don't have to mock me. I know it is illogical," she said miserably.

"I give you credit: you've sat here and let me say my piece instead of high-tailing it like you usually do when the conversation starts not going your way," Sam said, but he was still scowling.

She was silent. Miserable, but silent.

"Okay, where do we go from here? Do you know if it is a boy or a girl?" he asked.

"Too soon. Not til the end of January/middle of February. Ultrasound will show it."

"And you feel okay?"

"I do now. I was pretty sick much of the fall."

"Yeah." His voice broke a little before he inhaled sharply. "Fall sucked all the way around." He recovered. "The family is okay with all this?"

"Yes. They support me."

"Yeah, I'll bet they do. They get a kid and jettison the sperm donor, just like they've wanted."

Swan was stung.

"With all the women you've known, you probably have children out there already! If you're so eager for fatherhood, why don't you track them down?" she hit back. Something in his eyes made Swan immediately sorry she had done so, however.

"I'm going to let you get away with that crack because I know how truly, truly clueless you are," Sam said, his anger tightly under wraps. "Condoms have been my friend many times, little girl, as a matter of fact, right up until my famous meeting with Swan the Fucking Bolington. I've had no interest in being roped into fatherhood by a skank looking for a government support check." He searched her face. "Have you understood anything I've ever said about us? Christ, you think men are dense! You make me look like the Einstein of relationships!"

Swan decided not to rise to the bait a second time. Wise. She watched him clench his jaw, then his hands, for a long moment. He searched her face and sighed heavily.

"How could you not tell me?" Sam asked softly, and he was not bitter now but vulnerable. "We laid there that whole night, and I told you I was so happy to have your sweet little body back in my arms. Didn't that make you want to tell me, to say, 'Sam, our baby is in me, right now,' even once? You were going to get rid of it—what, the next day? You must be made of stone."

"Don't." She was defensive. "We agreed: it was going to be one night only, no questions, no arguments. And I'm telling you now. I didn't want you to be blindsided."

"Oh, yeah. Thank goodness that's not what happened tonight." He paused. "Let's, for argument's sake, consider getting married before this kid makes his appearance—just hear me out," he said as he saw her begin to bridle and pull back.

"One: he gets to be legitimate."

Swan shrugged and began to interrupt.

"Please! Two: you qualify for all military benefits: medical, insurance, the whole nine yards. Three: if the Taliban gets me, you get a quarter of a million for the kiddo. Four: 'bad luck doomed love' will be neutralized—you won't be marrying me voluntarily, it will be at the muzzle of the proverbial shotgun. If your family is worried that I'm some gigolo, now that you're a huge landowner, I'll sign a pre-nup; I'll take nothing if we split up down the road, whether it's in six months or sixty years."

"Sam, I told you: this has nothing to do with you. If you had left Quantico three weeks ago, I'd never even have told you. You would have moved on, and it would have been a non-issue. I think that's the way it should be now." Swan set her chin, determined.

"You think we should pretend I have nothing to do with this kid, and I think we should get married to have this kid. You thought you'd keep this a secret from me?" He shook his head. "Maybe your luck will change, and I'll be deployed to Timbuktu. Because otherwise, you've guaranteed that I'll be in your life for the next eighteen years.

"Look at me, baby." He held his arms out in front of her, flexing them, inspecting the results with satisfaction. "Eighteen inch biceps." Then he grinned down at her. "I'm the jealous, muscled up ex-fiancé, the stood-up PTSD'd marine, and the baby daddy, all rolled into one. Your next guy's worst nightmare."

She smiled back: "You are going to be twelve thousand miles away for fifty percent of the year, no matter what lawyer you get. You will get tired of me running the show. I know you: you'll eventually get pissed off enough to find a woman who doesn't have my history, my issues, my attitude about everything. Ninety-eight percent of all divorced and single fathers are out of their children's lives by age eighteen. Look it up."

They eyeballed each other.

"I should probably get going," she said.

"I'll get the check." She could see how reluctant he was. But he walked with her to the dually and stood while she hunted for her keys in her purse.

"Okay if I put my hand on—it?" he asked, not meeting her eyes.

Swan shrugged; she turned her head away as he gently spread his fingers over her belly, under the oversized shirt.

"A baby," he said. "This isn't the end of this. Not by a long shot." Then he bent down and kissed her very, very lightly on the forehead.

Swan got in the dually and rolled down the window. "Good-bye, Sam."

CHAPTER 16

Dressed in her mid-pregnancy uniform of oxford cloth man's shirt, skinny corduroy leggings, down vest, ballet flats and long, dark ponytail, Swan met Daniel in the Crossroads the following Saturday. Swan had told him about the meeting at the Trainyard, and he'd been able to see the irony of it all, to his credit.

"Well, this certainly wasn't in the plan, was it, honeykins?" Daniel said, greeting her. He looked at her bump, but discreetly. "You still look lovely, of course, nothing could ever change that."

"Oh, you!" She fended off the compliment.

"How doth the happy father?" he asked, as they settled into the banquette closest to the door.

"About as you'd expect," Swan said, soberly. "He wants us to get married so the baby is legitimate, try to work things out. Failing that, he seems pretty determined to be part of the baby's life in a way I didn't . . . plan on."

"And your plan is—"

"Like I've told everyone: have the baby and raise it as a single parent."

Daniel looked at her, skeptically.

"Well Sam's going to be gone half of every year. As in 'gone' gone—in one armpit of the world or another. The other half either in Oceanside or at LeJeune, not Quantico, so other than e-mail, he isn't going to have much opportunity for input, is he?" Swan said.

"Precisely," Daniel agreed, "although I suspect you can't cut him out completely. The courts seem to have strayed from that line of thinking."

"Yes," Swan acknowledged, "though it doesn't matter, really. I don't ever plan to marry, so it won't be the complication it might be otherwise. He'll see that and give up. We just have to outlast him."

They ordered peanut soup, crab cakes broiled on crispy rolls, cole slaw, and iced teas with lemon. Then an unmistakeable figure stepped in the door out of the pale sunlight of Main Street.

Sam was in his Christmas tweed sports jacket, USMC sweatshirt, jeans, ropers. As always, he set off a little tremblar of interest among the diners, who discreetly raised their heads mid-mouthful as he began to stride to an empty stool at the far end of the bar. Daniel cleared his throat to draw his attention.

"Major, won't you join Swan and me? We've just ordered," Daniel said serenely, rising from the banquette.

"Thanks, happy to." Sam looked unsurprised to see them. And, just like that, they were all cozy as you please, Sam on one side of Swan, Daniel on the other.

"You look a treat, Swannie," Sam said calmly, but he made no move to kiss her hello. Swan was the most rattled of the three of them, hands down.

"This is an unexpected pleasure. Aren't you a bit far afield?" asked Daniel, as Sam studied the menu.

"I had some business out here. I met with a realtor about a property," Sam said, not looking up.

"A property?" Swan widened her eyes to Daniel.

"Yes. Persis Fitzhugh's hunt box."

Swan and Daniel looked as though they had been hit between the eyes with some large flat object.

"Fitch's hunt box?" Swan repeated, stunned. "What made you interested in that place?" The unique combination residence/barn built on High View's far boundary, closest to Belle Everley, made for convenient overnight lodging when the hunt was meeting a distance from the main house.

"It is affordable and close by. It wouldn't suit everyone: a tack room with half bath, a feed room, and two stalls downstairs; two smallish bedrooms, one that can be a nursery, living room, dining room, newly redone kitchen, full bath with spa tub, deck, upstairs, built into a hillside," Sam said genially. "No doubt you know it well, Swan. Five fenced acres. A one-hundred-year-old fieldstone exterior. Mrs. Fitzhugh wants it sold, and the real estate market has dropped so much that a rent-with-option-to-buy agreement makes sense to her."

"A nursery?" Swan was trying to take this in.

"Yes, for my days."

"Your . . . days?" She was mystified.

"Sure. I'll want him—or her— some days, and nights, too," he said.

"You can't be serious," she said.

"Very serious. Swan, this little kid is going to have a father. That father happens to be me," Sam said genially but with an undertone of rock-hard certainty. "I'm not going to be some zoo exhibit he—or she—sees for an hour on Saturday while you are at the Artisan or the track. He's going to have a father, a dog, a swing set, and his own little bed in his father's house. When his father is deployed, he will live with his mother full-time. You are free to go your own way, but our little kid is going to have a normal two-parent life." He looked directly at her. "Do you understand me?"

He continued, not waiting for her response.

"I'm going to want to come to the doctor's appointments."

"No," she said.

"Then I'll schedule my own appointment separately with the pediatrician."

"You aren't going to be here when he is born. You aren't going to be here most of the time," she argued.

"I'll want the bills for your doctors' visits."

"No."

"And I'll be paying child support."

"No."

"Then when I come back, I'll buy things for him myself. His clothes, his diapers, his little shoes, everything."

"No." None of this had been part of her plan. Sam and the baby tooling around Waverly in an SUV, showing up at library story time? She didn't think so.

"Don't you get tired of saying that over and over? You should have chosen a different guy. I'll want to look at my little kid in a car seat that I bought for him, in overalls that I bought for him, eating formula I bought for him. I'll look the doctors in the eye knowing I paid the co-payment, I bought the antibiotics or whatever he needs. I'm going to be living in this town. People are going to say, 'That's

Sam Moore's kid' as often as they say, 'That's Swan Bolington's kid.'" Sam looked at the little waitress with a smile. "Hamburger special, please, Kitty, and a Dos Equis."

"Well, well," was all Daniel could muster. He suspected that most of Sam's speech had been for the Bolingtons, by way of him.

Just then, two local construction workers in wife beaters and jeans strolled in the front door and made their way to the bar. Sam took that as the go-ahead to shuck off his jacket. Swan knew his Alpha male game well; Sam wanted Daniel to see the swan tattoos he'd added in the fall. *He might as well piss a circle on the ground around me,* she thought. *I already have his kid in me, what else does he want?*

Well, he put his bare arm around her now, that's one thing he wanted.

Men.

"Mr. Spaulding: if we are going to eat together, I'd like to apologize for the dust up at your aunt's place last fall. I was upset. I'm sure I said things that were . . . imprudent. Seeing as how we are now going to be related through this baby, I want you to know I am genuinely sorry," said Sam.

Daniel nodded curtly. Daniel and Swan's food arrived. Swan barely had the appetite for it.

"Sam, talk sense: how are you going to manage to live here when you are going to be based elsewhere?" she asked, determined to soldier on to the more pertinent issue.

"Well there is no guarantee that I can't get back to Quantico and pull desk duty, although I do have a short mission overseas coming up," he said, genially. "ISEF is hosting an international conference on Afghanistan in the U.K. to formulate plans for transferring power to the local authorities. Someone involved thought I'd be useful. So I will miss the birth, as we expected."

"So you've been cleared medically?" Swan asked robotically. She still hadn't grasped the hunt box part yet, and, although she had been prepared for his redeployment in theory, she realized she wasn't ready for it in actuality.

"Not completely, but enough for paper pushing—which is what this is." Sam turned to Daniel. "And the hunt box is a good investment, regardless. Who knows where I'll be? Or any of us, really? For example, are you enjoying High View, Mr. Spaulding?"

"Yes, yes, of course," Daniel said. He floundered. "This is a lot to take in."

"Mrs. Fitzhugh's realtor indicated that there might be changes afoot," Sam said chattily.

"Who?"

"The realtor associated with Lige Davenport—Tabb Fletcher," Sam said.

"Lige Davenport?" asked Daniel, "the resort/golf course/ business park guy?"

"That's him," said Sam, "Mrs. Fletcher said that he had been sniffing around Virgilia Osmond's place. Virgilia was gauging interest in her farm, I gather, reading between the lines."

"What would Lige Davenport want with a farm?" Swan said stupidly. "It isn't zoned commercial and the land can't perk."

"What was it the old farmers used to say, Swan—?" Daniel murmured.

"'Any land will perk if enough money changes hands,'" Swan recalled. "I know the recession has hit Virgilia hard, but to sell Stone Chimneys, two hundred years in the family." She frowned.

"Has she said anything to you?" Daniel asked, ignoring Sam, who was digging into his burger.

"Not a word . . . not a word." Swan was processing the possibilities; none was good. "Maybe Persis would buy it? She has the resources."

"She's divesting herself of property, not buying it, not here anyway," replied Daniel, logically. "Swan, you could buy it: put High View up as collateral; then sell Stone Chimneys when the market improves." He wasn't a banker for nothing. "You could be sure to sell it for farm use then."

"Three farms?" she mused. "I'd own three farms?"

"But Swan's eventual buyer could turn around and sell it to Davenport," Sam said, looking up from his food.

"Not if Swan put an easement on it—scenic, agricultural, or historic," Daniel explained, "although that would cut its commercial value to nothing and its value to another kind of buyer in half."

"Couldn't Davenport bid up the price on Swan with Virgilia now, til he broke her?" Sam said.

Daniel grimaced.

"That's certainly possible. Virginia is a Dillon's Rule state: individual counties have limited ability to carve out restrictions on land use, and Davenport knows that better than anyone. Swan would have to rely on Virgilia's preference for keeping Waverly the way it is."

"I can't believe this," Swan murmured, thinking, thinking, thinking her way through the problem. "Maybe Virgilia *would* consider a private sale to me. Selling out to development is one step above selling yourself on the streets of Waverly. If only Fitch were alive! He'd have eaten Elijah Davenport for breakfast. He had the county planning board in his back pocket.

"Daniel," she said, turning to him in anguish, "if Virgilia sells to Lige, life won't be worth living at Belle Everley—or High View."

"I know, honeykins," he said. "With all you've got to deal with already, it's a damned shame this has popped up. But . . . " he smiled, "I'll be right here every step of the way. We'll talk to Virgilia, suss things out, to the PPT, Davenport himself if we have to. And of course, I'll put you in touch with the right people at Tidewater Commercial. I couldn't handle any loan myself—conflict of interest—but there are very capable financial officers there who could help you out."

"Me, too, Swannie," Sam said sweetly.

"With all respect, Major, this is a family matter," Daniel observed genially, but with an edge.

"Yep, I agree." Sam was cheerful. "Our baby will be Swan's heir and, although I don't have an interest in her business dealings on my own behalf, it would be prudent for me to know what she is doing with the assets in relation to our minor child."

Daniel was dumbfounded.

"I can't see how that would be necessary," Daniel tried again, "although I'm sure Swan appreciates—"

"Mr. Spaulding," said Sam, his eyes narrowing, his voice lowered to barely a whisper, "you are a two-time-losing little cokehead. You are in no position to help Swan, particularly if you need to buzz off to Get Clean Acres at short notice—again."

Daniel stood up.

"Fuck you, you Hadji-murdering, butt-banging freak," he said.

Sam launched himself out of the banquette with both fists ready to go. Swan reached out and touched his bare arm, freezing him in place.

"Sam," she said quietly.

He stared at Daniel, towering over him like an ultimate fighter/body guard/club bouncer. He wasn't happy about it, but he did relax his hands. Swan and Daniel could see the effort it took. The instantaneous, palpable alarm of the lunch patrons dissipated.

"Swan, I'll pay the check at the register and meet you at the car," Daniel spat. He turned on his heel and left.

"I think we all understand each other," Sam said, a little unsteadily, but he slowly dropped back to his seat. "Isn't family life fun?"

"Marines," Swan said, but it wasn't a judgment. "You know, I won't always be around to cool things off whenever you two bang antlers."

"I'm not going to let them push me around," he fumed. "He counted on you stopping me. If I weren't so batshit crazy about you, I would have torn his fucking head off. They've screwed in my life enough." He looked at Swan almost pleadingly. "Do you really mind that I'm buying the hunt box? Not that it would change anything."

"I don't know how I feel. I've got a baby on the way and a huge financial decision to make and two farms to run. If I end up having to buy the Osmond place, I'll have to generate enough cash to support the baby and me and pay the loan as well. I won't have The Fortress popping out top-dollar foals anymore, and campaigning Mike, Linny–and now Enfilade—costs a lot of money unless they continually win big," Swan said. "I don't know how I feel."

"I'll support you," Sam said. He was calmer now. "I can do it. I want to do it." Swan smiled a little; Sam made a decent living but he had almost no savings and now would have a mortgage himself.

"Thanks, I appreciate that," she said. "Anyone who thought you wanted to marry me for my money would be having a good laugh about now." She stood up. All eyes were still on them.

Sam caught her around the hips as she turned to leave; his torso was so long that she was not that far above him while he was seated. He pulled her onto his lap for a warm, full-on-the-mouth kiss that sent the hormones of every woman—and most of the men—in the restaurant into combat readiness. Swan didn't push him away; she rewarded him for his restraint with Daniel, letting him go on until he came up for air, sliding her hands appreciatively up the huge muscles of his arms. Then she smiled and patted him on the cheek like a bad little boy.

"Daniel will be waiting," she said, and she was up, out the door, and gone.

She and Daniel rode toward Belle Everley in silence, Daniel roiling along at a full boil.

"Who the fuck does he think he is, Swan?" he said as soon as they were out of Waverly. "He's a PTSD nut job—everybody knows it! You should get a restraining order against him, he could kill you with one blow. It was the Scarab all over again."

"You provoked him," she said mildly. "You know he can have a short fuse. He's like a silverback gorilla—pretty tough on everybody until they acknowledge his . . . authority."

"He called me some coked up shithead or something, didn't he? Christ, he's a human M-sixteen—no wonder he loves going to Iraq over and over again."

"Don't say that!" she said sharply. "Never say that!"

"Well, I've got to hand it to you, he obeys you like some goddamn dog. You stopped him cold. Impressive."

She decided silence was her best option: no reason to mention the guy-on-girl action he missed in the Crossroads while he was fuming in the car.

"Where does he get off thinking—" Daniel looked at her so intensely that she was worried they'd drive into the ditch. "Swan, when you saw him in the Trainyard—you didn't go home with him, did you?"

"No, of course not. Please keep your eyes on the road, won't you?" Swan fussed.

"He didn't ask you to? He didn't try?"

"He didn't ask me. We didn't go back to Quantico. I was tired," she said. No, she hadn't slept with Sam after the Trainyard meeting; she'd gone home with him after the Scarab. Just as bad.

"Swan, you are like Bill Clinton. You avoid outright lies but you don't volunteer the truth either," Daniel said. "But I do trust your good sense. Getting back with him, after all you've been through—after all you've put all of us through—would be a fucking disaster.

"Septimus Moore isn't going to run our family, no matter how big a gorilla he is. He's just a red-dirt Marine with a bad attitude and a rundown little property on the edge of town. He's not going to be lord of the manor, now that you've sent him on his way for good."

Swan watched as the winter countryside rolled passed; the horses in the fields, dressed in their green waterproof all-weather blankets, the cattle stoically recumbent, with their legs drawn up against the cold light rain in the air.

"Daniel, you have to accept the possibility that Sam and I are bonded for life," she said quietly. "Once I cut him out of me, there will never be anyone else. And, sad to say, there may never be anyone else for him either."

Swan did call on Virgilia Osmond. Stone Chimneys was three hundred and fifty acres, small by development standards, but it was bordered by hard-surface roads on three sides, rare in a county where 75 percent of all roads were unpaved. The main house was a 1799 beauty, with walls more than a foot thick and magnificent views from three of four sides. Only the north was marred by a power-line right-of-way on a distant hill. A deep stream bifurcated the property, providing water to all of the fenced and cross-fenced fields, which were filled with cattle and sheep. Three big old barns nestled in small swales near the house, and a frame washhouse and a log and tin-roofed smokehouse were tucked against a rise between the barns and the house. Old box elders and newer red maples shaded the house itself, and a long driveway from the hard surface road was lined with cedars.

When Swan drove up to the house—in a long sweater and linen duster over leggings and flat-heeled boots—Virgilia was at the door, wringing her hands in distress over her Talbot's sweater set.

"I should have called you," the middle-aged widow said to Swan immediately, "but I was too embarrassed, really." They went in to the parlor and sat by the crackling January fire. A sterling teapot and a salver of scones sat on a side table.

"I've had to let Laurencia go, I just have a cleaning lady once a week now," Virgilia said, her woes pouring out of her. "If George were still alive, none of this would have happened."

"What *has* happened, Virgilia?" Swan asked calmly, buttering her scone.

"Well, the taxes are one thing, and, of course, the farm does not pay for itself without support from my investment portfolio. I'm not throwing off income enough to maintain this house, and the upkeep—the fencing, the mowing, the barn maintenance—I cannot afford a full time crew and I can't afford to have the work done piecemeal. I'm really sick of the whole thing. It's overwhelming at my time of life."

"I understand, darling, I do. What can I do to help?"

"Nothing, really. I met with Tabb Fletcher. She has been asked by Elijah Davenport to identify a few properties that might be suitable for mixed-use development near Waverly."

"But Virgilia, I don't believe your property is suitable for any use other than farming. It's all hard pan. The soil can't pass a perk test for septic systems for residential or business use." Swan had learned that much from Fitch before he died.

"I don't think houses are Davenport's specialty; it would be a mixed-use complex, with a special-exemption permit process via the county planners . . . something like that. Golf-course-slash-executive-retreat. He would itemize proffers and the county would partner with him on some sanitation system or well set up, the way it's been done in Myopia and Jeffersonville. You know how much I would hate to do it, but it is postponing the inevitable. I can't have the farm bankrupt me. I have my later years to think about."

"Virgilia, you know those 'golf course-retreats' always turn into strip malls or office parks once the commercial use exemption is granted. Would you consider selling a piece for some ready cash, say, enough to perhaps provide you with some security?" asked Swan carefully.

"The farm isn't big enough to slice up that way, and I'd still have the maintenance headaches, here on my own," said Virgilia sadly. "Maximum value will come from selling in one piece. I am most sorry for you, Swan, since your farms would be most affected by a change in zoning, traffic, et cetera. If I had children, it would be different. My cousins are in their fifties and their children live in Seattle. Stone Chimneys is just a few faded photographs to them."

"Would you be willing to sit down with Tabb and me, and perhaps Mr. Davenport, to see if some accommodation might be possible? I know the Piedmont Preservation Trust has expressed concern about something like this happening. That kind of . . . resistance . . . can tie things up for years, which I suspect you would not want." Virgilia would be a pariah if she had to live in Waverly as her neighbors fought her via the PPT.

"Well, I suppose I owe you that, but I'd hate to see you drawn in, given the year you've had. Losing Fitch, seeing Major Moore deployed to a war zone then coming home so ill—and now. . . ." Her voice trailed off awkwardly.

Swan looked at her.

"Yes," Swan said softly. "'And now.' Things can happen that change your future overnight. If we meet with Tabb, I'd like to bring Daniel in on things. He may have some option you haven't thought of. I'd hate to lose you as a neighbor."

Virgilia nodded. "I'm sorry."

"I know you will do what is best," Swan said gently. "One sometimes suddenly thinks about the future in a different way, I'm living proof of that. Let me see what I can set up with Tabb, first, then, perhaps with Mr. Davenport."

Chapter 17

Tabb Fletcher did not wish to meet with Swan. She referred her to Lige Davenport directly. Swan suspected Tabb had been raked over the coals in previous interactions with Waverly's farmers when the "development" word had been broached. Swan decided not to bring Daniel along, opting instead for a nice, friendly get together around the Stone Chimneys fireplace— Red Riding Hood, Grandma, and the Big Bad Wolf.

Dressed as a country gentlewoman, in a long russet sweater, green A-line wool skirt, green Vogels and gloves, Swan skipped up the steps at Stone Chimneys on a cold, overcast afternoon, and, with a knock, let herself in. Virgilia was in the parlor off the front hallway, standing in front of the crackling fire, with a robust, barrel-chested man, a six-footer in his mid-thirties with wavy brown hair, and melancholy eyes, deep and brown. He was in an immaculate classic suit—bespoke, Swan guessed, since it fit his physique perfectly, with an old-fashioned gold collar pin under a club tie in a Windsor knot.

"I'm Elijah Davenport, Miss Bolington. I'm very pleased to make your acquaintance," he said calmly, but Swan could see he was sizing her up as he shook her hand. "I hear Mrs. Osmond relies on your judgment and friendship; very neighborly country you have here."

"We'd like to keep it that way," Swan replied. Why beat around the bush? She helped herself to a cup of tea from the sideboard; Virgilia seemed paralyzed in the company of the daunting Mr. Davenport.

"No doubt," Davenport said. He was admiring; it still took a careful second look to see the signs of Swan's pregnancy.

"We think Stone Chimneys is a priceless asset to the county just as it is," Swan said, getting to the point. "At least it has been for two hundred years."

"Yes, of course," agreed Lige, smoothly. "We all feel the same way about these historic counties—Prince Arthur, Loudoun, Fauquier—all are feeling development pressure. We need to manage it."

"Hastings Fitzhugh didn't think so. He believed we needed to fight it, tooth and nail."

"Yes," said Lige. "I recollect that was his viewpoint."

"I have to wonder whether your sudden interest in Stone Chimneys may have to do with your conclusion that, with Mr. Fitzhugh gone, organized opposition to any land-use changes in Taliaferro County would be minimal." Swan was smiling as she said this.

"I only met Mr. Fitzhugh on a few occasions; I'm sure his loss is sadly felt by his family and devoted friends such as yourself," Lige Davenport smiled right back. He seemed to examine the scones on the sideboard, one by one. "You inherited his farm, did you not? Quite a surprise, that must have been, particularly to his aged mother."

"Fitch made sure she was very well provided for, as any gentleman would under the circumstances," Swan swatted back. "High View would never be suitable for her . . . limitations, and she lives elsewhere, in any case. He knew how challenging running a historic farm can be," Swan finished, "which brings us back to Stone Chimneys."

"Yes," said Lige. "As you know, Mrs. Osmond has expressed an interest in exploring the sale of her farm to me."

"For farming, I presume?" asked Swan.

"For evaluation for a number of purposes, farming being one of them," said Lige.

"Lige, I've told Swan that you might be interested in Stone Chimneys as a resort/retreat kind of place," Virginia said helpfully.

"Yes, some kind of mixed use would have to be considered, to maximize the potential of the property, including this beautiful old house." Lige was smiling at Virgilia.

You had to hand it to him. He could sling the bullshit with the best of them.

"As you might imagine, as an almost abutting landowner, I'm very concerned about any exemption to the agriculture zoning currently protecting the property," Swan said. "Please rest assured that Fitch left an active group of neighbors here who share his views, as will the PPT."

"Your concern is most commendable," Lige said, "given the many other demands on your time." He bent his head almost imperceptibly toward her mid-section. So he had finally caught on.

"Well," said Swan, standing up, "I don't want to monopolize your discussions with Virgilia; she is, of course, free to do with her property as she sees fit. I simply wished to meet you and be of any help to her that I can." She'd seen enough.

"Oh, Swan, don't go," cried Virgilia, looking desperate.

"Darling, I think Mr. Davenport would be more comfortable outlining his vision in privacy." Swan turned to the developer. "Nice to have met you, at last," she said, her old-Virginia manners not forgotten.

"I'd like to discuss my vision for the whole area with you, Miss Bolington," he replied smoothly. "You retain so much good will in the community, I'd want you to be fully informed. We have absolutely nothing to hide." Something in his voice sounded the "man interested" alert throughout Swan's nervous system. "Perhaps we could have dinner some evening, at the Reynard Inn?"

"One of my favorites," Swan answered with a smile. Pregnant or not, she wanted to see if there was an advantage to be had in doing a little number on Lige Davenport. As Hetty said, Swan still had "it."

"May I give you a call when my schedule is firmer?" Davenport grasped her hand and released it with a small additional squeeze. He moved quickly despite his stockiness.

"Please do," said Swan, "and now, Virgilia, I must go. We'll talk soon. It is a big decision and you'll want to look at every possible angle, I'm sure. I'll let myself out."

Swan half-skipped down the stairs of the old manse, her mind churning.

She saw one immediate impediment: Septimus Moore. She could not dine with Lige Davenport in the Reynard, or in any other place within one hundred miles, without him finding out and weighing in, all two hundred and fifty pounds of him. He was going to be a challenge to manage.

She popped open her cell phone on her way to the farm.

"Sam," she said sweetly. "Are you free for dinner at the farm tonight? I'd like to talk."

"You're not getting married, are you?"

"Oh, please," she said. "Sevenish?"

He sighed.

"I wish you called me when you just wanted to see me instead of when you wanted— something," he said, but he wasn't having any luck sounding martyred. He'd come for anything, and they both knew it.

Swan made sure Mathilde had time to make some of Sam's favorite dishes, and she dressed for him especially, a grenadine red silk shirt, elastic waist silk skirt, his ruby earrings, little red flats, her hair loose. He arrived in the truck, slamming the door in a way that made Swan's heart twist: so like the old days. Flagg's barkathon brought her back to the present, and after the dog had flung himself against Sam's body in greeting, it took them all a few moments to get settled in the parlor.

"You look wonderful," Sam said, kissing her warmly on the cheek, nuzzling her just enough, then stopping before she could protest. He was in an oxford cloth shirt open at the neck and USMC sweater over jeans, rocking a hint of beard stubble that gave him a sullen look. "How are you feeling?"

"Fine, fine," she said, giving her belly a reassuring little pat. Mathilde arrived with a beer in an icy pilsner glass and stirred the fire a bit.

"Welcome, Major," she said softly, hiding her pleasure at seeing him.

"Long time, no see," Sam grinned. It was awkward for both of them. Mathilde backed out discreetly, closing the door behind her.

He dropped the cheeriness.

"Let me have it," he said. He had noticed their engagement picture was no longer on the round table in the entranceway.

"Why don't we eat first?" Swan tried to sound upbeat. She sat next to him on the little sofa in front of the fire, but not too close. Proximity was not her friend.

"No. I want to know what's up so I can do justice to Mathilde's food after we've had our argument," he said logically.

"We aren't going to have an argument, or at least I hope we aren't," Swan said, still optimistic. "I do have some news: I've been to the doctor. Monday was ultrasound day. I thought you'd like to know—it's a boy."

Sam stared at her.

"A son. We're going to have a son." He looked down suddenly and Swan realized Mars the God of War's eyes were teary. She looked away, out the window. Oh, this was too painful. She heard him swallow, compose himself, swallow hard again.

"Well, that's fantastic as long as you are okay," he said, in a voice very nearly normal.

"Yes, everything is fine," she reassured him, brightly.

"Are you happy about it? Did you want a girl?" he asked tentatively.

"No, either one was going to be fine with me. I'm resigned."

"Resigned."

"I mean, I'm prepared." But the damage was done. She must have discovered a thousand ways to hurt him.

"Well, I've got some news, too. Looks like I'm going to the U.K. on Monday, probably for five months."

She did a quick calculation.

"That would put you back here July fifteenth."

"Yes."

"I'll miss you," she said, and her voice broke a little. "But I want you to do something for me that you aren't going to like or agree with one bit."

"That sounds promising," he smirked.

"I met Lige Davenport at Virgilia's today." She ignored the sarcasm. "I'm going to try to suss out his game plan for her farm, and I'm going to have to do it in a social setting. Over dinner, for instance—maybe a concert or a movie."

Sam's face turned to stone.

"I'm telling you this because people are going to notice us together and whoever you have keeping tabs on me is going to tell you all about it. I don't want you to be . . . alarmed . . . or get worked up, although, now that you are going overseas, it's probably a moot point. It will be strictly business on my part."

"And on his part?"

"Well, I did get a little vibe—"

Sam snorted in contempt. "What a shock."

"Please—"

"So, what do you want? My blessing for you to cock tease this guy around Waverly?" he growled, standing up suddenly enough to cause Flagg to jump, too.

"It isn't like that."

"So everyone is supposed to think you've thrown me over for good, even though you're going to have my baby in a few months?"

"Sam, I *have* thrown you over for good."

"The fuck you have! I could prove it right here on the goddamn sofa." He was walking around the smallish, book-filled room as though it were a cage.

"Be reasonable. Everyone is scared shitless of you. No one will come within a mile of me if they think you're going to have a meltdown over a dinner in a public place once you return stateside," Swan argued gently; she reached out to touch his sleeve as he stalked by. He sat back down next to her.

"Why don't you just fuck him in the Scarab parking lot and be done with it?" he growled bitterly.

"Well, if I did, at least I wouldn't have to worry about getting pregnant." Swan was conciliatory. She thought things were going well, all things considered. "If you're going to act possessive, I'll never get anywhere with this guy."

"I *am* possessive! Fucking possessive."

"I know you are," she said, softly, "but I want you to act like we've moved on, or moved on as much as two people who are expecting a baby in fifteen weeks *can* move on."

"No."

"Sam, keeping Belle Everley and High View safe is my first priority—" she smiled weakly, "after Mr. Baby. These farms are his inheritance. I don't want him to inherit a satellite parking lot for a business retreat-slash-spa-slash-rec center, and you don't either. I want him to inherit his family's historic farm, just like I did." She knew that would get him, the *coup de grâs*.

"All I'm going to do is have a meal or go to a show or something, report back to Daniel, and to you by e-mail, if you want. If you can think of a better plan, please tell me."

"Dinner," announced Mathilde.

They sat down to the typical big spread, oysters on the half shell, country ham, pickled beets, jalapeño corn, fruit salad, buttermilk biscuits, chess pie. Sam ate it all, his reward for listening to her scheme without blowing his stack, he said.

"Swan, it feels like pimping you out to this guy. I hate it," he growled, when he had finished.

She got up to get him some coffee, Mathilde having retired to her apartment behind the kitchen for the evening.

"It isn't like that," Swan said. "Please understand." She stood behind his chair and poured the coffee into the Staffordshire mug. He leaned back against her, and when she straightened up, she spontaneously put her arms around his neck, hugging him. He caught her arms in his hands.

"Show me," he said hoarsely. "Show me it isn't. Now that I know it won't hurt Mr. Baby."

He took the coffee pot from her hands and pulled her around him, onto his lap. He kissed her the way that always made her putty in his hands, made her yearn for him in every possible way. His hands slipped under the silk shirt to explore her burgeoning breasts and stroke the curve of her belly, and she fell deeper and deeper under the spell of his mouth.

There was a knock on the door: Virgilia Osmond, beside herself still.

Swan slid off Sam's lap with a jolt, her heels thumping onto the floor, tucking and buttoning her shirt, pulling her hair into a long tail and smoothing it down her back. She looked at him and he shrugged.

"You owe me," he said, arching his eyebrows. "You owe me some sexing, baby." But he followed them into the parlor and listened patiently to Swan soothe Virgilia, who was apologetic, confused, embarrassed, just looking for a way out.

"Davenport says he can give me three point two million, with an escape clause that says if he can't get a special exemption in sixteen months, he can back out with a two hundred thousand dollar penalty fee to be paid to me," Virgilia said. "In today's market, that's pretty much top dollar."

Swan swallowed hard.

"He must be pretty sure he can work the deal with the county," she said, "but, you know, Virgilia, delaying tactics by those opposed to the zoning change can easily eat up that sixteen months and more; traffic and noise studies, neighbors' objections, challenges to the zoning decision if the planning board rolls over for him. You'd be left with the two hundred thousand but no sale, and you would have mobilized the opposition to any subsequent zoning applicant. You'd have had another eighteen months of maintenance and headaches for nothing."

"What else can I do?" Virgilia asked, plaintively. "No one is going to be able to get financing for a farm other than a commercial developer, not with the way credit has been tightened at every bank in the country."

"Well, let me think about it a bit. It turns out that Major Moore is going overseas for a few months. I'll meet with Mr. Davenport to see if we can't come up with a compromise." Swan turned to the older woman and took her hand. "Tell me truthfully, if there was a non-contingent buyer interested in Stone Chimneys as a farm, how much would you want for it?"

Virgilia hesitated. "Let me talk to Tabb. She's representing Lige, yes, but I'd like her take on the price. I know it may be skewed in Lige's favor, but she has a duty to deal fairly with me, too."

"Fine," Swan said, calmly.

"Major, I'm glad you are feeling well enough to resume your service," said Virgilia, turning to Sam. "We will miss you here in the county. We've all become quite fond of you."

"Thank you, Mrs. Osmond," Sam said. Virgilia got up to leave.

"I'm so sorry, Swan," she said again. Swan wanted to comfort her.

"That's alright, really," Swan said, "and we've had good news: our baby is a boy."

"Oh, how wonderful! If George and I . . . ."

"Yes," Swan said, sympathetically, "yes, I know, dear."

After Virgilia left, Swan and Sam sat in the parlor watching the fire.

"If Lige offered her three point two million, he must be willing to go higher," Swan despaired. "God, what am I going to do?"

"I'm no help to you. Land in Texas is, like, one hundred and fifty dollars an acre. It's hard to believe it's so much more here, no matter how beautiful it is." Sam was quiet. "I don't know if I can get back out before Monday, assuming I would be invited. The next time I see you, it will be summer."

"At least it isn't Baghdad or Kandahar."

"Yes, at least that."

"I'd like to come to Andrews and see you off, I think," she said, tentatively.

"You would? Why?" He was genuinely surprised.

"Because you need someone there to say good-bye."

"Swan, you know I love you. While I'm gone, you are going to have our son. I want you to please think of what's best for him. Not just to inherit a beautiful farm but to have two parents taking care of him." He looked at her so intently she thought he was going to kiss her again, then and there.

"Nothing has changed. You are well, your career is back on track. Don't you see? Being apart from me is good for you. But I have decided one thing."

He looked at her expectantly.

"I'm going to see a psychiatrist. I want to hear what someone has to say about my . . . problem."

"What made you decide? The baby?"

"Yes, partially." She sighed. "He deserves a mother who has her head on straight, or straighter, at least, one who doesn't want to believe she could be a danger to her own little boy just by loving him, or his father, either. And partially . . . it was you. You were willing to go last summer if I said you needed to go. You can't fix my crazy head by yourself, plan or no plan—if it *can* be fixed."

"Who is this guy?"

"Woman. In Delafield. India. Fisher. She's a middle-aged person."

"Not a swami or anything?" Sam teased gently.

"No. The real deal; board certified."

"Wow. Well, I'm glad. Just don't let her talk you into sex therapy or anything—at least not without me."

He laughed suddenly.

"Did you hear Virgilia say everyone was going to miss me? Not likely, not the folks who want me committed as a PTSD'd maniac, like Cousin Daniel Spaulding. He's going to wet himself with glee once I'm gone. And Elijah Big Bucks is going to be able to get up your skirt without worrying about me at all, and there's nothing I can do about it."

"Well, if he tries, he's going to find it's crowded under there. Mr. Baby is well established in the neighborhood."

Sam put his arms around her.

"You owe me," he said softly, teasing. "You owe me some sexing. Consider it a farewell party for Major Gumby."

Swan felt herself warming as he talked. She turned her head away from his kiss but not enough to avoid it completely. He knew her little game well and nuzzled her with more enthusiasm.

"Let's go upstairs," he whispered. "Unless you want to hit the Scarab parking lot. I always seem to have good luck there."

"Upstairs," she said, "you silly beast."

That's how they ended up in the old bed. They made love like two healthy, fertile animals, comfortable in their winter's den, their task of procreation successfully accomplished. Afterward, he studied her changing body as though it were some ancient text to be deciphered by touch alone. She was secretly relieved: she sensed, as she always did, that he had had no one else since she had sent him away.

◆

By daylight they had torn all the bedding apart with their exertions; Swan snuck into the shower while he was asleep, but he soon joined her, helpfully holding her hair out of the shower's soaking blast as she soaped them both. He entered her one last time, pressing her against the shower wall, wrapping her legs around his waist, so she could be in no doubt of how much he still desired her. Then he ate breakfast with her and watched as Mathilde and Swan tried not to send each other telling glances around the dining room table.

"Surprised to see me here this morning, Mathilde?" he asked cheerfully, as he slathered homemade jam on two enormous pieces of oatmeal bread toast.

"No, sir," Mathilde started awkwardly. "I mean . . . yes, of course. Oh. Uh—sausage, Major?"

They all laughed, but Sam's deployment loomed large. Swan dreaded it and welcomed it. When Sam was near her she had to expend enormous amounts of energy fending him off, but when he was away, she was frantic with worry. Impossible.

Swan walked him to the front door and kissed him a long, lingering, good-bye in a way she would not have permitted herself if he hadn't been leaving in just a few days.

◆

The next day was Swan's first appointment with India Fisher. Sam was the only person she had told about her decision to see the psychiatrist. She wasn't ashamed, just cautious of raising her family's expectations. They had been thrilled with the news that the baby was a boy; let them enjoy that for now. Swan didn't know anyone who had been to a psychiatrist; she had just seen the same nutty television shows and movies that made fun of therapy everyone else had. But she saw no harm in giving it a try after all. If Sam was willing to do it, she should be, too.

Dr. Fisher's office was in her Delafield fieldstone house. It looked like a well appointed den or sitting room in any comfortable home in any prosperous suburb. It was filled with tropical plants, well-framed prints of still lifes, leather-bound books on psychiatry.

Dr. Fisher was a silent, still woman in her late forties, with untidy blonde-brown hair pulled back in a bun. She wore an unfashionable long skirt in a heather tweed, an oxford cloth blouse, and a heather cardigan that reached below her hipbones. She looked the prototypical old-style college professor, with shapeless clothes but an astute, compassionate face. She gestured for Swan to sit in one of two overstuffed chairs near the window.

"So, Miss Bolington, why are you here today? I assume you know I'm not an obstetrician," Dr. Fisher said, with an almost imperceptible nod toward Swan's mid-section.

Swan smiled weakly.

"Do you know who I am, Dr. Fisher?" she asked.

"Well, I know that you are in your family horse-breeding and racing business in Waverly, if that's what you mean," said the psychiatrist, settling into the other chair. The coffee table between the two chairs held several magazines. Swan looked at them with no interest.

"Do you know who I am?" she asked again.

"Tell me," said Dr. Fisher. She folded her hands.

"I'm the woman who kills every man who loves her."

"Then, yes, I do know who you are."

Swan seemed to examine the magazines. They both were silent.

"Miss Bolington, do you know what *cum hoc ergo propter hoc* means?"

"With this, therefore because of this," Swan translated softly.

"Do you know its context?"

"I believe it has to do with flawed cause and effect reasoning."

"Yes," Dr. Fisher said. "It's a term that describes the relationship between an event and a consequence. For example, you clap your hands in a thunderstorm and a bolt of lightning strikes at the same time. Clapping your hands does not trigger the lightning bolt, does it—no matter how closely together the two events take place?"

Swan was silent.

"Correlation does not imply causation," continued Dr. Fisher.

"No."

"Then why don't you tell me why you are here?"

"What if you clap your hands and lightning strikes, over and over again?"

"Is that what you think has happened?" Dr. Fisher looked directly at Swan.

Swan focused on the magazine covers: on one was a picture of a farm house, on another was a kitten.

"And what if . . . what if . . . you don't clap your hands and the lightning . . . doesn't strike?"

"Go on," encouraged the psychiatrist.

"And what if it isn't like clapping your hands? It isn't a . . . voluntary physical act like that . . . but an involuntary . . . emotion that . . . does it, that triggers . . . ." Swan looked up from the magazines and looked out the window.

"The lightning strike?"

Swan nodded. "What if that emotion returns, and in order to keep the . . . object of that emotion from . . . ." Swan was quiet for a few long, silent moments.

"From?"

"From being struck by lightning . . . you have to do something . . . some things . . . that might be . . . painful in the short term but . . . beneficial . . . in the long term. Not just beneficial but . . . necessary."

"Could you define 'necessary,' in your current frame of mind, Miss Bolington?" Dr. Fisher asked so very calmly, but Swan felt intense interest on the doctor's part in her answer.

"Unavoidable," said Swan sadly.

"How long have you had these feelings about things being . . . necessary?"

"For quite some time." The birds outside the office window were busy in the branches of a locust, a volunteer "trash" tree, not a variety anyone ever planted on purpose, but one well suited to a village landscape.

"Do you think anyone is telling your mind what is 'necessary' or 'unavoidable' in these difficult circumstances?" asked the psychiatrist, very softly.

"No one alive."

They sat there very companionably, for several minutes. Swan felt relaxed, at peace, really.

"Would you excuse me for a moment, Miss Bolington?" asked Dr. Fisher. She rose from her chair and left the office. When she returned, she looked at Swan.

"I've talked to Dr. Cavendish," she said. "Pregnancy often exacerbates feelings of anxiety, as it does so many physical functions. I think you might benefit from an anti-anxiety medication, something very mild that has no effects on the unborn child at all. I'd like to continue to see you, and Dr. Cavendish would like to see you, too. My nurse is scheduling an appointment now. How does that sound?"

"Fine," said Swan. "But I want to clarify something. When I said, 'No one alive,' I meant I often feel the presence of people whom I've lost influencing my thinking . . . not that I'm hearing voices of the devil or seeing visions or anything like that. Does that make sense?"

"Perfect sense. It is normal to feel the presence of our recently lost loved ones, to think they are voicing thoughts or ideas that really are our own."

"What do you think is wrong with me?" Swan looked directly at the doctor.

"Do you think there is something wrong with you?"

Swan sighed. "I'm not sure I know anymore. But if there is, I don't want it to affect my relationship with my baby. I want it . . . fixed."

"Well, I hesitate to make a diagnosis," said Dr. Fisher, but she was reassuring. "I will make some general observations. The human mind is constantly processing, evaluating, digesting data, some of it major, some of it very minor. If it receives repeated 'blows' in terms of traumatic events, it may try to come up with ways of dealing with those events, some of which are useful and some of which are less useful. These less useful ones may hinder a person's ability to function and form and keep relationships. They can involve abuse of substances, acting-out behaviors, risk-taking, even violence."

"That sounds kind of like PTSD."

"Yes, doesn't it? It may be a generalized anxiety disorder, like obsessive-compulsive disorder, hoarding, that kind of thing," said Dr. Fisher. "We have some medications that have proved helpful to patients experiencing the kinds of feelings you are describing. I suspect we will find one for you. I do want to ask you one thing: do you think you might harm yourself or your baby in your current state of mind? Have you had any thoughts along those lines, bidden or unbidden?"

"No, no," Swan said, then reconsidered. "I did consider terminating the pregnancy at one point." She paused to gauge the doctor's reaction; there was none.

"In a legal way, at a clinic," Swan continued. "It was an option that I felt needed to be explored. I am unmarried, and the father of the child is no longer part of my life. But I decided I could cope with the challenges of being a single mother and I'm looking forward to it now."

"Well, that sounds like a positive outlook," said Dr. Fisher. "You are due—"

"June first." Swan stood up.

The doctor bent to write a prescription.

"This is very mild, a very low dosage. Let's try this and talk again no later than early next week.

She shook Swan's hand.

"You have been through a very trying ordeal. No one could just bounce back from that," she said, "and the pregnancy on top of it."

"You don't think so?" Swan said, in a sad-yet-hopeful little voice.

"No. I've enjoyed meeting you," said Dr. Fisher, with a smile. "I'll see you next week."

Swan felt heartened. She had her prescription filled, and she carried the medication around with her for several days. She didn't want to start taking it until Sam had gone to England; she didn't want to get his hopes up and she didn't want to seem different in any way—medicated—when she said good-bye to him.

◆

On Monday she drove to Andrews, telling herself it was different from his previous deployment; no one would be shooting at him, for one thing, or planting roadside bombs to tear into his flesh and send his beautiful arms in fragments into the desert air. But in one way it would be the same; political booby traps would be as prevalent as scones and marmite and PG Tips.

She was bundled up against the cold; amethyst cashmere sweater over a lilac silk shirt and elastic-waisted black wool skirt. She had added the Mason's frock coat and her Afghan striped tribal scarf against the cold. When she saw him at the hanger in uniform, she looked at him and tried not to look at him at the same time. He grabbed her without hesitation, and she felt him rouse as she pushed her belly against him. It seemed to have grown even in the days since Sam spent the night at Belle Everley. She gave him another push and another, for him to feel and remember.

"I want e-mails, and I'll call, too," Sam said. "Look: I've replaced your picture with this." He held up the sonogram she'd given him. She didn't believe him; her photo was in his uniform next to his heart.

"Take care of yourself," he asked, his voice so very soft.

"You, too." Sam was still having nightmares about his combat tours. Swan knew this because he had dreams the night he spent at Belle Everley, although she didn't tell him so. He was always shouting to Hunt Lee to get back; to cover his sector; to get down before the IED's shrapnel Swiss-cheesed his body. Swan knew he wasn't well enough to go back into combat, Pentagon surge or no surge, and for that she was grateful.

"If this works out, do you think you will be . . . recognized . . . for being a help to it?" she asked, pushing him gently away. He moved only a fraction of an inch.

He shrugged. "Don't know. Don't really care. They will jerk me from one place to another, one time or another, that's the Marines."

"You would rather be back on the line."

"Sure. At this rate, I probably will be," he said. "The wars continue, don't they?"

"Take care of yourself," she repeated. She felt she couldn't breathe.

"Next time I see you, we will have a son."

She couldn't help it: she reached for him the way she had when he'd left for Kandahar the previous March. His great strength: she wanted it and wanted it. He lifted her off the ground in his arms, burying his face in her hair, and then bending down for a long, molten kiss.

"Wife," he said. "Wife."

"Don't."

He smiled and then he was gone again—not to the end of the world, but to a civilized place, one she could theoretically visit, at least until the pregnancy advanced or she was able, once and for all, to stay away from him.

Her appointment with India Fisher was the next day.

"I had a visitor last week," said the psychiatrist, "someone who is concerned about you."

Swan thought for a moment.

"Septimus Moore," she said.

"Of course, I told him that I could not discuss your care without your permission. He told me I could tell you about his visit," said Dr. Fisher. "He said that, if I thought he was to blame for upsetting you,

I should tell him immediately and he would do whatever I thought could rectify things."

"That sounds like him. Did he tell you he is my baby's father?"

"Yes. Of course your engagement was known in the village, as was his illness and recovery at your home, but it isn't pertinent to your care unless you wish to make it so. He said he is moving to Waverly and that, if we thought it helpful to have him involved in your office visits, he would do whatever we asked. He said he might even want to become a patient himself."

"He's suffered fifty times more than I have."

Dr. Fisher smiled again.

"That's exactly what he says about you."

CHAPTER 18

Two nights later, Swan heard from Elijah Davenport. The evening after that, Swan put on her champagne silk shirtwaist and matching pumps. The skirt was full enough and the waist generous enough for her to get away with, but it was probably the last week any of her old clothes would fit. She had a few unstructured dresses in pretty silks on order from New York. She knew the final month would be hell, silhouette-wise. She'd have to buy real maternity wear then.

Davenport was waiting for her in the entranceway of the Reynard; to make it less like a date, she'd fended off his offer to pick her up at the farm. He was in his immaculate business attire, collar pin and all. Swan had a Virgin Mary; the developer a single malt whiskey, neat. They ordered the local produce special—roasted free-range chicken, organic rice and root vegetables; a stewed fruit compote with crème fresh.

"I knew when I met you that you were a force to be reckoned with, but I didn't realize you were also the heroine of a local romantic saga," began Davenport.

"I wouldn't call the deaths of two fiancés a 'romantic saga,'" Swan corrected, but gently.

"Oh, no, of course not. I wasn't referring to those terrible tragedies," he bumbled on, trying to recover from putting his foot firmly in it.

"Perhaps you mean my most recent attempt at marriage? I'm well aware that it's caused amusement to local gossips, although it was intensely painful to me," Swan continued.

"No, no! I was attempting to characterize your dashing major and his very public courtship, but I see I should keep my mouth shut about something I know so little about." Davenport conceded defeat.

She relented.

"No, that's quite alright. Major Moore would be a larger than life figure anywhere, so it is only natural that he draws attention. I'm well aware of that," she said as their food arrived.

"Your fiancé would be a tough act for anyone to follow. He certainly has the 'movie star looks' angle covered and 'the heroic man of war' angle, as well," said Davenport. "Apparently he has everyone in Waverly so intimidated, no one dares to look sideways at you."

"He is my former fiancé. But he *is* a heroic man of war—it isn't an 'angle,'" Swan corrected again.

"Oh, of course!" Davenport backed off immediately. "I have only the 'patron of the arts' angle going for me. And some folks think I'm not so bad in the looks department, but I know when I've been outclassed there."

Swan smiled at his awkward attempt at self deprecation.

"And there are a few categories still up for grabs, although I suspect 'father of the year' may have been won before I even entered the competition," he said with the smallest of glances at her mid-section.

"Don't worry, Mr. Davenport," said Swan, "there is no competition."

"I hope your baby won't cause discord between you and your ex," Davenport continued as though she hadn't spoken at all. "You seem to have had cordial relations up to this point."

"No gunfire, if that is what you mean," Swan replied. "Major Moore is serving his country overseas, as of this week. But he does plan to make Waverly his permanent home—he bought one of Mrs. Fitzhugh's properties in Delafield to be close to his son."

"As anyone who had the good fortune to be the father of your child would want to be," Davenport agreed. His voice trailed off, and he nodded a bit obsequiously. "He'll be a formidable presence, no doubt. I, on the other hand, was only a humble Golden Gloves regional champion."

"Oh?" Swan knew nothing about boxing but she recognized the name of that national amateur competition.

"Yes, at U.V.A.," Davenport said with a smile. "But that was a long time ago."

Swan smiled back.

"You needn't worry; if Major Moore wished to fight anyone with his fists, I'm sure Marquis of Queensbury rules would apply," she observed.

"That's what they say in the Scarab." *The two creeps Sam had taken apart there must have had quite a fan club,* Swan thought. Where was any of this going?

"I suspect you think of me as a grasping, heartless tycoon, eating up historic farms and spitting out obnoxious shopping malls, but as you can see from our talk with Mrs. Osmond, I solve as many problems as I ostensibly . . . create," said Davenport.

They discussed the impact development would have on Swan's holdings and on those of several abutting property owners. Davenport was solicitously appreciative, deferential. He obviously thought he knew how to handle a pretty woman, even a pregnant one. But he was repellent to her in an indefinable way. He reminded her of the blowsy, overdressed lady friend of Philip Deveroux, she decided.

"What you landowners have to understand is that you have jobs, family responsibilities, and limited amounts of time and cash to throw at any one project to block it, while we developers can push back against you, twenty-four-seven," Davenport continued smoothly. "Eventually exhaustion sets in on your part, understandably so. If you beat back one challenger, another will immediately take his place. He has to: if you win consistently, we will be out of business, permanently. We cannot let that happen." He sounded like Attila the Hun explaining his rape and pillage policy's efficacy to the burning villagers along his way.

"You sound like the Taliban," Swan said calmly. He laughed.

"Yes, we all went to the same Josef Stalin school of world domination. Now perhaps we could have a look at the Reynard's famous pastry cart: Mrs. Lombardini, if you please."

Swan looked over her *mille fueille* and decaffeinated coffee as Davenport nursed a fine brandy.

"It is your misfortune that Taliaferro County is so close geographically to the District of Columbia, that ever-growing engine of power and jobs," he said. "Two or three counties to the south, your farms would be safe from development forever, and two or three counties south of *them* are so poor that their local governments would marry us developers to all of their most beautiful daughters to get us to put up an executive retreat or professional building anywhere in their jurisdictions."

"But destroying Waverly cannot be the solution."

"We will only 'destroy,' as you put it, *some* of Waverly, and really, *we* won't do it at all, your neighbors will do it, by selling out to us and granting the zoning we need."

"So I guess it comes down to who wins the heart and mind of Virgilia Osmond. That will determine whether my family falls into the category of collateral damage," Swan mused out loud.

"You could put it that way," Davenport agreed. "Unless someone in your family wants to marry its most beautiful daughter to one of us to keep it from happening." He smiled at Swan, showing his dental veneers in an exaggerated grin. "Check, please."

◆

Over the next week, Swan had little time to ruminate on the fate of Stone Chimneys. The Fortress delivered her fourteenth and final foal at age twenty-three, a dark bay filly. She was her usual protective, grumpy self and the source of endless comparisons to Swan's own impending motherhood. Swan felt overwhelming relief; she would never have forgiven herself if she had put the old mare through a final, fatal, pregnancy, as often happened with elderly broodmares. But The Fortress was as tough a broodmare as she had been a racehorse. When she stood up to let her last foal nurse for the first time, she gave Swan a baleful look, as though disappointed in Swan's lack of faith in her.

Two other broodmares foaled out the same cold dark week, the consequence of the great advantage Thoroughbred foals born early in the calendar year had over their May and June-foaled brethren when they got to the racetrack. Swan and Eduardo had their hands full with their three new mothers and Serve the Guns, who was close to foaling herself. Swan ate dinner off a tray in the parlor these nights and then went straight to bed. A few days after Sam's departure, she was awakened at nine P.M. by the phone ringing on the bedside table.

"Swannie?"

"You made it," she said. "It must be two A.M. there."

"A big initial parlay just broke up and I wanted to try to catch you; did I wake you?" he asked. "I can tell from your voice I did."

"The Fortress foaled . . . yesterday, so did Cosette and Silvery Pearl," Swan replied sleepily. "But everything is okay."

"Glad to hear it. Here's my phone number; I'm at a British military installation in officers' quarters, but at least it's a private room with a phone."

Swan reached for a pencil in the bedside stand and scratched down the long international string of digits.

"How are things going?" she asked, trying to wake up enough to focus on his answer.

"Oh, you know. About the same." That was code for *everything is fucked up*.

"I heard you saw Dr. Fisher," Swan said. "You shouldn't have. You aren't the problem."

"I think we should let her decide that," he said calmly. "When do you see Lige Davenport for your big pow-wow?"

"We had dinner a couple of days ago," Swan said. "He is a smooth talker, that's for sure. He has an answer for everything, but he can put his foot in his mouth as well as the next guy."

"Really? How?"

Swan laughed. "Well, I think he was trying to flirt by comparing himself to you, or at least the cardboard cut out of you." Her tone was dismissive.

"Compare himself? How? Did he whip his out?" His voice was teasing, but there was a serious intent underneath.

"Hardly. He looks like a troll, for one thing, and he basically said that, one way or the other, if he wanted Stone Chimneys, there was nothing I could do about it. Only—"

"Only what?"

"I think he was trying to come on to me—me, a pregnant, notorious man-killer. He seemed to be trying to tell me he was in the market for a human broodmare."

"How gallant," Sam said, disgusted. "When I meet this guy, I'm going to jam his tongue down his throat til it comes out his asshole and tie it in a big red bow."

"I can handle Lige Davenport. I've been handling his kind all my life. But I don't get it. He could have ten spandex specials every night of the week, and probably has. He must think I'm either naïve or desperate for male attention."

"Don't fool yourself, kid. We know a great lay when we see one."

"It's like what those two subhumans said in the Scarab; because I was able to keep a beast like you satisfied, other guys think I must be a sex goddess," Swan said wryly. "Why don't they all just bypass me and screw you, I wonder?"

He laughed.

"Get your sleep, Maw," he said warmly. "Don't let this guy paw you, remember."

"I'll remember," she said, her voice catching a little. It just sounded too much like the old days; him far away, her home, keeping each other's spirits up . . . .

The phone line went dead.

Swan felt a jolt. For a second she thought there had been an earthquake . . . no, just indigestion—but there it was again. A kick. From inside.

Sam. He had just missed it.

She thought a moment, looking at the string of numbers she had scratched out with pencil.

No. It could wait. It would have to wait. Maybe the baby had heard their voices, hers to his, and wanted to join in the conversation with Mom and Dad. Their first evening chat as a family.

Not a productive line of thought. She wiped a little self-pitying tear off her face. Then her spirits suddenly lifted: she didn't have Sam—couldn't have Sam— but she did have his little boy with her always now.

There. That was better.

She turned gently on her side. No more kicking now.

"Night, night," she said.

The thought began to form in Swan's mind that "bad luck doomed love" might actually be useful to her. Keeping a bit of company with Davenport, even in her current ridiculous state of second-semester pregnancy by another man, could work against him and his designs on Stone Chimneys. *Bad juju,* Sam had called it when arguing with Daniel, or so Daniel had said. If she was lethal to men's best interests, let her be lethal where it would do the most good.

Dr. Fisher would have a field day with this, Swan decided. At least it would make her upcoming appointments that much more entertaining. If the horse business didn't work out for her, she could always write a book. Who would believe it had all happened, though?

When Swan pulled into the Waverly Training Center the next day, Kezia Hardaway's big dually was pulled up in front of Jerusha Dutton's stalls. That was not good.

"It's Judy, not Lady," the slim, no-nonsense veterinarian reassured her client. "I think we've got a bad front tendon strain, with all the rain we've had." Jerusha's newest barn help showed up with a heavy plastic tub filled with ice. Swan went to the stall where Judy stood patiently as Jerusha eyed her front leg.

"What a shame," said Jerusha. "She was training a peach."

"Let's see how we do," Kezia announced. "We'll make her comfortable and get the heat down. Then we'll call on Dr. Green." That was the old horseman's term for turning a race horse out for rest on grass. Swan walked with Kezia back to her rig.

"Have you given any more thought to joining me as joint M.F.H. after your baby is born?" asked Kezia as she totaled up a bill for Jerusha's signature.

"Not really," Swan said. "I'm still sorting out running my two places and trying to deal with some unexpected events in the real estate market. But if I can have a bit more time—"

"Of course. We'd love to have you, and as owner of two properties critical to our country—" Kezia used "country" as in hunt "territory."

"I'll continue to join in whenever Punch and I can, once I'm back on my feet. That should be in time for cubbing," Swan said reassuringly.

"I would so appreciate it. To be master is rewarding but time consuming. I don't see how Fitch did it. You've heard that the new owners of Paintbrush Farm are not amenable to allowing Waverly access to its three hundred acres; they are concerned about liability, riders' waivers or no waivers. They want some kind of financial bond from the hunt itself." Kezia sighed. "They are attorneys, naturally. I've invited them to the kennels to see the new litter of puppies. Sometimes that helps."

"Fruit baskets at Christmas aren't enough any more, I gather," Swan said sardonically.

She was mulling over Lige Davenport as she left the training center. She popped her cell phone open: Daniel was working from High View. "May I come by?" she asked. "I'd like to talk to my banker."

"Of course. Is the rent due?" Daniel joked gently.

"No, it's this Stone Chimneys thing still," Swan said, apologetically.

"I'll put the kettle on."

Swan was at the long, winding driveway to the Delafield estate in ten minutes. The prospect of the great brick four over four, with its gracious plaster wings on each side, was breath-taking. The house was situated on a knoll above a sweeping vista of fields, streams, and rock outcroppings, there since the last hurrah of a glacier eons ago.

Swan skipped up the steps of the grand manse and entered the brick main section via its semi-circular portico. The center hallway was much larger than the entranceway at Belle Everley, with its cosy proportions, as were the rooms themselves. It had been the home of a wealthy planter/farmer in the late eighteenth century, not the modest Quaker and part-Quaker farmers who were her Bolington, Swan, Hexell, and Spaulding ancestors. Swan had insisted that Persis Fitzhugh take the prize artwork—an Edwin Landseer of sheepdogs guarding a flock at night, a James Whistler drawing, and an Albert Munnings portrait—she had brought to her marriage to Dr. Francis Fitzhugh forty years earlier. Lesser works remained to brighten the walls.

The furniture had been meticulously cared for by Fitch. It was all of a large scale, befitting the proportions of the house, and as a result had relatively little value on the open market. Who these days had houses that could hold eight-foot-tall wardrobes and highboys and linen presses, federal marble-topped pier tables, and gold ormolu clocks? A few pieces were particular treasures—an eighteenth-century mahogany muffin stand, a hunt board in a rich old-red varnish with pride of place in the dining room, and a complete set of Chinese export ware porcelain that hadn't left the corner cupboard in the dining room in two hundred and ten years. A magnificent set of ten Baltimore fancy painted chairs in chrome yellow, bright as goldfinches sitting on a fence line, was arranged against the dining room walls. Fitch had hired Italian guildsmen ten years previously to repair the plaster work throughout the house. Fitch's Hermès saddles, bridles, breastplates, and other strap goods were in the pantry for safe keeping, kept in perfect condition by Fitch's houseman, Emilio.

Emilio had a crackling fire warming the living room, which was sunny and cheerful, with Aubusson carpets, long hand-embroidered French portieres restrained by silken cord tiebacks anchored by carved walnut dogs' heads. Daniel rose from a nineteenth-century sofa to give Swan a kiss.

"Let me fill you in on Lige Davenport," she said, and she gave him the whole scoop on the dinner meeting.

"He sounds . . . slimy, Swan," Daniel said slowly. "What is your plan?"

"Well, I'm still thinking about buying Stone Chimneys, if I can, but I had another thought," Swan said. "You know the little Stubbs in the parlor at Belle Everley? Not the nicer one in the entranceway."

"Oh, no! Oh, no!" Daniel was shocked. "A mortgage on this place is better than selling that, particularly in this art market. You would never, never, never be able to replace it, not for ten times what you can sell it for. What about syndicating Oscar Mike?"

"If I do it now, it will be for one quarter of what he'll be worth at the end of his career. And I'd have armchair partners telling me what to do with my own horse while he is still racing. I've got the baby to think about. I love the little Stubbs but—"

"Swan, the Stubbs is solid gold for a lifetime, and for your baby's grandchildren's lifetimes," insisted Daniel. "What's the deal with Hetty? I know you inherited the farm when your mother died, but what about the Stubbses?"

Swan sighed.

"We share ownership of both, since they weren't of equal value. Hetty wouldn't care if I sold the lesser of the two, but I'd only get half of the proceeds. After the auction house's take, it would not be enough to pay for Stone Chimneys. But we'd still have the better one, and I'd make up the difference somehow."

"To sell the Stubbs and still have a mortgage would be a tragedy! You could get a mortgage on High View and have money in your pocket . . . unless Virgilia lets Davenport get into a bidding war with you. Do you think she'd pull that kind of stunt?"

"I don't know. She's in a strange state of mind," Swan mused. "She said to me, 'Do you know what one year in assisted living will cost in ten years? One hundred and fifty thousand dollars!' I think she is completely panicked."

"Let me get you an appraisal on this place," Daniel said, "and one on Stone Chimneys, just for comparison. Then let's see where we are." He looked at her directly, his dark, smokey eyes intense. "And Swan, that 'beautiful daughter' crack of Davenport's was tasteless. He's a slime ball. I saw him come in the bank briefly last week. I wish Septimus Moore was here for one night. Mr. Golden Gloves would be pounded into a plant spike in about thirty seconds."

That made Swan laugh.

"That sounds weird coming from you," she said. "Just a few weeks ago, you wanted me to get a restraining order against Sam. Now you want to use him as a weapon. You are an idiot."

"I was there in the Scarab, remember. Those guns really fired—for one remark. All that time in the gym—does he take steroids?"

"Daniel, a cage match between Sam and Lige is not going to solve my problems," she laughed again. "But he'd be pleased to know you'd entrust him with the physical destruction of the family's adversary. If only it wouldn't also involve him doing five to ten in Danville State Prison as a consequence."

Chapter 19

"I've got an idea," said Oliver Lentz when Swan picked up the phone the following Thursday. He was planning to take one of the Templetons' homebreds to England the following month to race at the old course at Doncaster, in south Yorkshire.

"You knew we've entered Roisterous for the William Hill Lincoln, a mile over the turf. It's a handicap, two hundred and fifty thousand added money. I think it would suit Mike very well. He likes a longer distance of ground, but I think we should bring him along," Oliver said. "As you know, if you do end up syndicating him as a stallion, his foals will appeal much more to European buyers if they've seen the sire race over there."

"Wow," said Swan. England. Sam.

"I've also gotten wind of a very nice race mare who I think could be a good prospect to replace The Fortress in your broodmare band," Oliver said. "Of course, no one could take her place, literally, but this is a beautifully conformed individual, one of the last of the Egyptian Wellses to race. She's a six-year-old with a very respectable record, over—get this—a mile and three quarters. She'd be a complete outcross to your current stock via her dam and a great cross with Mike when the time comes. You could fly into Doncaster from Heathrow, watch the race, take a look at this mare, and be home in two days."

Swan pricked up her ears. A race that long was almost unheard of in the States, and success at that distance was like crack cocaine to a distance breeder like Swan, whose stock was doing better and better over the synthetic surfaces becoming commonplace on U.S. racetracks.

"The trouble is, she is part of a distress sale," Oliver continued. "If word gets out that she is on the block, I think there will be several eager buyers in the U.K. She really is a lovely mare. Her name is Calimanco. She won at age three, four, and five against colts and mares and had been pointed at a couple of races this year that didn't fill. She is sound as a brick, the last foal out of the old Dead Bolt mare Dancing Magpie. Those Bull Lea bloodlines are impossible to come by."

"What's the ask?" Swan said. Everett Bolington had especially liked Dead Bolt as a sire, but he was out of fashion now.

"I'm not sure, but it's going to be half the price of what she'll bring if the owner decides to sell her to the highest bidder," Oliver said. "Take a look at her record and, if you're interested, I can get a DVD overnighted to you."

"Lowish six figures?" Swan dreaded asking.

"Oh, yes, I'm afraid."

"Where is the yard? There in South Yorkshire?"

"Not far from it. The Sceptre is seven miles away—that's where we will be staying; the Black Hart is right in town. I'll make a reservation and squire you around myself when you get here. Hope you don't mind a little cloak and dagger regarding where she's located. We're trying to honor the seller's wishes in this, as you might imagine."

"Let's make it the Black Hart," Swan said. "Send me the DVD, and let's plan on Mike making the trip with the Templetons."

"It looks like I'm going to England in a few weeks to see Mike race at Doncaster," she told Spaulding later in the day.

"Oh, Swan, do you think you should?"

"I'll be seven months along, but I'll be fine." Swan was determined.

"Flying internationally is such hell these days," Spaulding fretted, "even in first class."

"I'll be fine," Swan repeated.

"No need to worry," Davenport piped up, when he next saw Swan during a lunch at the Reynard. "I can always use a few days in London: I've several contacts I'd like to see in person rather than through video conferencing. If you don't mind, Miss Swan, I'll escort you over and back and leave you to your trainer and entourage while you are there."

Swan saw no reason to say no. The trip was a go.

◆

The next day, Swan got a call from the West Coast.

"Swan? It's Townsend."

"Hello, darling," said Swan, with genuine delight. "How's college?"

"Oh, okay, I guess. But I miss Virginia."

"We miss you, too, honey," said Swan comfortingly. "Maybe you could visit over the summer."

"That would be wonderful," Townsend replied, sounding more cheerful. "I hear you are going to have a baby, and I'd love to see you. Maybe I could even be of help since—" She floundered: who knew what to say about Swan and Sam breaking up, with a baby on the way?

"Yes." Swan was cheerful. "Yes, 'since.' Why don't you talk to your parents and see what they think? When do classes end?"

"May fifteenth; I could come anytime after then. Mom is going to Cannes around then and Dad is in Geneva looking for funding for his Mary Chesnut biography picture."

"What about Bernardo Holtzman, king of the KW network?" Swan asked gently.

"Oh, Swan, do you know something? Men all aren't necessarily what they seem to be."

Swan couldn't help it—she had to laugh.

"I know, darling," she commiserated. "I'm going to have one in the family soon, so I'd better not say anything more. Check with your folks. I owe you some riding lessons, remember? I promised you last summer before Fitch passed away and Sam came home so ill and . . . everything else happened."

"I will, I will! Oh, Swan, a baby boy! How fun is that!" Townsend sounded brighter than she had talking about her hunky TV star boyfriend.

◆

Over the next few weeks, Swan saw her doctors, took her anti-anxiety medication, gave Sam upbeat updates on her health, kept in touch with Virgilia, and began to let her anticipation build for her trip to England. She had been there once on an extended college trip, six weeks of pure bliss. She had spent much of it touring stately homes, attending performances at the Royal Shakespeare Company's theatre in Stratford on Avon, and relishing two weeks at the Savoy in London's West End.

As it turned out, she would have less than forty-eight hours in England. Lige could not get away for as long as he had planned, and she really simply wanted to see Mike race, inspect the mystery mare, and get home again. She did not let herself think of Septimus Moore, and she made the difficult decision to keep her whirlwind trip from him by way of her usual tortured logic. She wasn't sure she was ready for Lige and Sam to meet; she wasn't sure her vanity would allow Sam to see her broad of beam at seven months' pregnant; and she wasn't sure her willpower would hold out with Sam only an hour away from Doncaster. It would be better if she flew in, flew out, kept him in the dark. He'd never know she'd been there if, as she expected, Oscar Mike ended up a gallant also-ran to Roisterous. If Sam found out after the fact, through a photograph or some chance remark, well, she would deal with that when she came to it.

So the evening of her flight, she threw a few new additions to her wardrobe into her suitcase—rural attire, not designer wear—and put on one of her unstructured dresses, an acid green silk soft-shoulder jacket, matching peep-toed kitten-heels, and an all-weather trench coat. She was awaiting Davenport at the international gate at Dulles Airport when she was paged; he was going to be detained. He would catch up with her in England, since he could follow within a couple of hours on another airline. His profuse apologies ended the message.

Swan was relieved; she could settle in to business class with *The Girl Who Kicked the Hornet's Nest*. She'd see Davenport in the morning.

At Heathrow, she transferred to a small jet for service to Doncaster International; by one P.M. she was checking into the Black Hart, an ancient half-timbered structure in the center of the Elizabethan town, right out of a picture postcard, surrounded by a riotous garden and fronted by a much later porch. The lobby was snug and dimly lit, with a small parlor to one side, ornamented by a cozy fireplace. Swan loved it.

Her room was tiny, ancient, but charming. She changed clothes to go straight to the racetrack. She had found a narrow putty suede skirt with enough give in the waist to accommodate her belly, so she had brought her matching Vogels; a raspberry wool sweater, the Mason's frock coat, and a soft black hat with a brim. Her long thick hair always drew admiration: she decided to wear it loose for the day.

Just before she left, she checked at the desk for messages; none yet. She made her way to the track by following the crowds on the unusually busy race day. It was sunny, but very chilly for late March, and Swan was glad for her heavy clothes. Once at the track, she made her way to the rail for the third race. As the horses loaded in the starting gate, she turned her attention to the entries for the next race, since it was too late to wager on the race about to go off. She liked Forager and Hotspur Lad—she'd seen both colts run on the international feed of the horse racing channel within the previous six weeks. The country crowd was large and jolly, always a challenge for Swan, since her view was easily obstructed in groups. She stayed wedged at the rail, despite some jostling behind her: *Forager or Hotspur Lad, Forager or Hotspur Lad* . . . .

"Got a hot tip?" asked a deep voice, suddenly, above her.

She turned her head instinctively: a broad chest, the sleeve of a sports jacket stretched taut across a huge bicep. She looked up, into the sun directly overhead.

Sam. The military haircut, blue eyes, oxford cloth shirt and tie, paired with jeans and roper boots. He was knocked out with surprise. He looked down at her, scowling a little, until he saw her belly, and his face immediately softened.

"Wow. What's this?" he asked in wonderment.

"Hi," Swan replied softly, concealing her own shock. "Who's this, don't you mean? Who do you think? Am I huge?"

"No, not huge. Yes, but—no, not at all. Not like . . . not like . . . ." He struggled, then gave up. "Wow."

"I know. A lot has changed in six weeks. What are you doing here?" She suddenly looked at him suspiciously. "Did you know I was here or did you suddenly develop a yen for the races?"

"I'm a guest of an arms manufacturer looking for a little love from ISAF," he said. "They have a marquee, over there." He gestured at a tent with tables and chairs in the infield. "I saw in the newspaper this morning that Oliver was bringing the Templeton horse for the Lincoln Handicap, and there was Mike, entered in the same race. I wanted to come down and watch him run, but it never dawned on me that you'd be here. I turned around and saw all of that hair flying up in the air. It had to be you. How long have you been here? Why didn't you tell me you were coming?"

Swan chose the easier question to answer.

"Just got here. Aren't you cold?" She reached to fuss with his jacket, turning the collar up against the breeze, brushing his neck and his collarbone, then letting her hands slide down his chest, the Alpha male in all his glory. It felt wonderful to touch him.

"I'm fine," he said. "How do you feel?" He unconsciously mimicked her action, pulling her coat closed. She had added the Afghan scarf as a protection against the weather, wrapped once around her neck with the two fringed tails hanging down over her breasts. He straightened the tails with approval, chafing her hardening nipples through her shirt and bra in a way that gave her a spasm of pleasure, and pulled her loose hair over the scarf. The strong breeze lifted all of her hair again, in a huge cloud around them both. She tried to tame it with her hands.

"I'm fine; never better," Swan reported briskly, meeting his gaze. "How's the meeting going?"

Sam's smile faded. He shrugged, shorthand for *everything's a fucking mess, as usual.*

"Do you have a band for your hair? It's going to get all knotted up in this wind," he said solicitously; she obediently took off her soft hat and produced a covered elastic band from her pocket. He turned her back to him, expertly pulling all of the hair into one of his hands, and wrapped the band around it to make the long tail she was used to. Then he turned her around to face him, looking at his handiwork critically, one eyebrow cocked. That made her laugh.

"How long have you been here? Where are Oliver and Sinjon?" he asked.

"Well, I got here late last night—this morning, really. I was supposed to come with Elijah Davenport but he missed the flight." Sam's warm expression went ice-cold.

"He had business in town—London, I mean. Everyone was so concerned about me coming by myself," she forced a little, stiff laugh, "as if no pregnant woman has ever flown overseas before."

"Do you want to watch the races or get off your feet? You must be tired. Let's sit in the marquee and have something to drink," Sam proposed. He didn't want to fight. He began to pilot her toward the tent and out of the wind. Immediately, several lovely girls moved toward him, obviously from the hospitality side of the manufacturer's retinue. One, not seeing Swan on Sam's other side, slipped her arm into his from behind and snuggled close.

"Where have you been, Major? We've missed you. You promised you'd keep us all warm," she teased in a lovely, buttery, public-school accent. "Oh."

Her expression upon finding Swan equally tucked under Sam's other armpit was a mixture of surprise and alarm, but she wasn't going to cede her claim to her prime American real estate. Well, she *was* lovely, Swan observed: a cascade of blonde hair and a tall figure. She wore a snug, saucy dress and jacket too lightweight for the day's raw temperatures. High black heels and a little purse completed the outfit as she flirted, without a care in the world. *Ecce femina ipsa.*

It wasn't Saucy Girl's fault that she had crossed the path of Vlad, the Impaler of tall marines.

"Miss Susannah Bolington, Miss Emma Price-Litton," Sam announced coolly.

"Swan. Please call me Swan." She beamed, extending her hand, and let the frock coat open itself back up. Emma towered over her.

"Oh," Emma said. That seemed to be the extent of her conversation so far as Swan was concerned.

"How do you do?" Swan continued, staying put next to Sam. "Are you having any luck with the races today?"

"Oh, I don't bet," Emma Price-Litton said, still trying to sort out the lay of the land. "I've come for the . . . the s—"

"Scenery?" Swan supplied sweetly. But the English girl was not going down without a fight.

"Socializing, I was going to say. Are you here with your husband?" she countered. *Meow.* Swan had been introduced as "Miss," but Emma could be excused, given the belly in the midst of them.

Swan laughed, but Sam couldn't take any more.

"Swan has a horse in the William Lincoln," he explained. "She races them and raises them in America." He extricated himself from the tenacious English girl and steered Swan to a folding chair at a small table decorated with some exceedingly hardy flowers.

"Cup of tea?" he asked. " I know you are avoiding the hard stuff, but herbal tea is rare here."

"That would be lovely," Swan said.

Emma Price-Litton was watching their body language from a distance. Might as well put her out of her misery: Swan reached over to Sam and straightened his perfectly straight shirt collar, resting her hand on his broad collarbone before she pushed him away, just a bit, with her fingertips. He knew that gesture well; he'd felt it a hundred times in bed. It always caused his big, healthy cock to snap to attention, and this time was no different. He leaned into her, letting long tendrils of her hair that had come loose blow against his face. Then he lurched to his feet, heading off for tea and a mull.

Swan did her own mulling. She was tentatively scheduled to meet Lige for dinner. They were to return home the next day. She could steal this one evening with Sam. But what for? She still didn't envision them together long-term. She should let him have Emma. Let Emma trace the outline of the swan tattoos with her fingertips and wonder what they meant. Would she remember "Call me Swan"? Swan sighed heavily. The thought was sickening.

"I brought you a bun," Sam announced as he returned, juggling two china mugs and a plate.

"How lovely—I'm starving." Swan dug into the hot cross bun gratefully. The invisible tether that bound them had spooled itself out as he walked away and reeled itself in as he returned, strong as ever. Swan was so happy.

"Where are you staying? If I can cut myself loose at the end of the day, can I come to you?" Sam wheedled, looking intently into her eyes.

"After the race, Oliver and I are going to see a horse. I'm supposed to have dinner with . . . another party." It was as though all of her resolve had been left three thousand miles to the west. *Let him have Emma. Let him. Let him.* She sighed again. She really was hopeless.

"I'm at the Black Hart," she continued. "I go home tomorrow in late afternoon. If I like this horse, Oliver will ship her back with his string next week. When I finish my tea, I'm going to find him." She looked up at him. "You're a guest of these folks. Stay here and be nice and attentive through the last race. I'm sure it will be a full-time job keeping all these ladies warm, even for you." She couldn't resist sticking the knife in.

"Fuck them," he said, but he moved obediently, if reluctantly. Miss Emma needn't have been a lipreader to get the message from that. For the first time Swan saw for herself how Sam felt about the other women he had known. He had been a hard son of a bitch.

"You're a representative of the U.S. government, Major," she said. "Be a gentleman." Emma didn't deserve to be humiliated in front of her friends. "Just don't let her hump you here in the tent, if you please."

"I don't know why not—I'm not going to get humped any other way." He was filled with self pity. She laughed.

"Meet me at the back gate at the end of race seven then." Swan took one last swallow. "Many thanks for your hospitality, Miss Price-Litton," she called, turning in the direction of her hostess. "You might want to place a bet on number four in the five race." She smiled at Sam, rose, and left the marquee.

Swan mulled and mulled as she walked. Sam, Sam, it was always Sam, of course. Her spirits were lifted seeing the grand Mike, however, in her historic silks. She teared up thinking how proud Grandpa Bolington would have been to see the vermillion, cream, and brown at Doncaster once again. Oliver and Sinjon were overseeing Mike and the Templeton colt equally carefully as they were being saddled, instructing the jocks, folding their arms as they watched the horses walk around the saddling enclosure. The atmosphere at Doncaster, as at Lingfield, Exeter, Stratford, Ascot, Aintree, The Curragh, all the small historic country tracks throughout the United Kingdom, was more like that of the steeplechases in the United States—undulating terrain, casual patrons, bookmakers touting their odds to one and all from small stands scattered among the patrons, cars pulled up in small car parks.

Mike and Roisterous went round the walking ring one last time, and Swan met up with the Templetons. They were a gracious couple, genteel old Main Line Philadelphia, who loved their horses and loved racing and breeding them. Grace Templeton, elegant in a trim coat dress in the Templeton racing colors—cherry red and sage green—hugged Swan.

"Let's finish one-two and show these Brits a thing or two," she laughed. Thurgood Templeton was quieter, less knowledgeable about the bloodlines side of the business than Grace, but a sharp handicapper and a fierce bidder at auction when a yearling caught his eye.

Oliver stood with the three of them as Sinjon saddled both the enormous, prancing Mike and the calmer Templeton colt in the midst of a swirling field of fifteen turf specialists. Swan was torn: she wished she had asked Sam to join her in the walking ring, but it would have been awkward. Oliver and the Templetons knew she and her major were on the outs, and Sam would have had to leave his hosts. When Oliver and Sinjon gave the jocks a leg up to head to the turf course, they all clomped together to clubhouse seats where they could see the finish line. Swan looked down; she could see the marquee where Sam and Emma were no doubt bonding happily over a glass of champagne. She wondered if Emma was snugged in against Sam's ribcage, listening to his big healthy heart pumping away under her ear the way Swan did when he held her tightly, if she was—oh, why torture herself? Swan tore her eyes from the marquee and watched Mike, her wonderful Mike, about to embark on the race of his very short life.

Horses in England were not accompanied to the post by lead ponies as they were in the States, and Mike was giving his jock, a local boy, some rough moments—typical Storm Cloud behavior, it was called, after Mike's fiery sire. Swan wasn't concerned: English thoroughbreds were bigger, feistier, and less accommodating around the gate than their U.S. cousins. Hijinks were commonplace. The big field was another thing, though; seldom outside the Kentucky Derby did an American racehorse encounter fourteen competitors in one race, and at Doncaster, horses raced clockwise, the opposite of the American tradition. A small difference but one that could throw a racehorse off his game.

The fifteen loaded relatively quickly. The crowd leaned forward for the lightning fast mile on the pear-shaped grass course. A roar went up as the field sprang from the mechanical gate. Mike and Roisterous settled in behind a "rabbit," or pacesetter, but the horses' pace on the far turn seemed leisurely compared to the U.S. milers; in the United Kingdom, everyone cruised, found their positions, then dashed the last furlong like Katie, bar the door.

Mike and Roisterous dueled neck and neck, but the favorite, Herodotus V, pulled even and Mike set his large combative eye on this challenger. As they sprinted for home, a long shot came up inside Roisterous, then veered out into his path, causing the Templeton jockey to check his forward progress to avoid a collision. Mike and Herodotus, a glorious chestnut, tore ahead of the others, pounding the last strides absolutely neck and neck. It looked as though Herodotus's outstretched neck was going to beat Mike's, but Mike suddenly pushed hard; he hit the tape with the chestnut. Photo finish.

Swan was shrieking with excitement. Oliver wasn't so sure: it was hard to believe Mike had bulled his way to the lead despite his ground-eating strides at the end. It was clear, though, that Roisterous had been done in. He finished fourth behind another challenger. The Templetons were gracious in defeat while the stewards dithered a bit. Then the roar went up: dead heat for first; steward's inquiry on the horse who finished third, the one who interfered with Roisterous.

Swan and Oliver hugged. "We did it! " screamed Sinjon, the ex-pat. "A Group One!"

Swan tried to pull the Templetons along with her, but they understandably wanted to wait to learn their colt's fate. Then, they saw the inquiry had been decided in Roisterous's favor. He was placed third, ahead of the colt who had ruined his chances to battle to the finish line, little solace for the Philadelphians.

Swan, Oliver, Sinjon, Mike, Herodotus, and his connections trooped to the winner's area; each group had a winner's photo taken. The local commentators interviewed Oliver about the historic dead heat and got a word from Swan as well. Swan tried to tally the prize money: in a dead heat, first and second place money were added together and split in two. The trainer got 10 percent; the jockey got

10 percent; the Inland Revenue/IRS got . . . but who cared? Swan followed Sinjon and a groom towing the blowing, prancing Mike and Roisterous back to the stabling area for a well-earned bath and walk out to cool down.

She missed the final two races, celebrating around the horses, watching Sinjon check out the legs and feet of both stars to be sure all was to rights. She gave Mike a well-earned pat, which was, as always, followed by his ringing whinny in response. He would always be Swan's little horsey boy.

In forty-five minutes, the last race was in the record books, and Oliver had returned to the stabling area. Sinjon had another several hours of housekeeping ahead of him, while Swan and Oliver made a quick jaunt to the Yorkshire yard where the mystery mare was secreted.

"Oliver, do you mind if we add a third to the party?" Swan asked as she saw Sam striding toward them. He was hard to miss, but Oliver was unfazed.

"Not at all. Welcome, Major Moore, this is a pleasant surprise," he said amiably. They piled into the Mini Cooper rental Oliver had stowed behind the stalls. Sam gave Swan a big kiss of congratulations.

"What a horse, huh, Oliver?" Sam bragged. You would have thought he'd raised Mike himself. "Did you see that finish? I thought he was a goner, then, boom!" Sam put his arm around Swan, giving her a mammoth squeeze in his delirium.

"Oliver trained Mike, remember," Swan teased gently, but he was having none of it.

"You breed it in them, you don't train it into them—isn't that what you always say, Oliver?" crowed Sam. "Damn! I won a thousand bucks! Good old Mike!"

Oliver smiled serenely as they left Doncaster proper and putt-putted into the Yorkshire countryside in the last afternoon sun.

"That's right, Major, it's there or it isn't."

In twenty minutes they pulled into a rutted farm road, heading toward a fifteenth-century three-story stone house. Two stone barns faced each other across a cobblestone courtyard. Ten or fifteen Thoroughbreds calmly hung their heads over the stall doors, shades of grey, brown, bay, black and chestnut, blazes, stars, snips, all kinds of white markings differentiating one from another. A scruffily tweedy gentleman in his seventies was leaning against a pitchfork outside one of the barns as the Mini drove up.

"Sir Nicholas," called Oliver, getting out of the car. "May I introduce Miss Susannah Bolington of Belle Everley, Virginia, and Major Septimus Moore, United States Marine Corps. Swan, Sam, this is Sir Nicholas Renfrew of Old Chadwell." They shook hands all around. Swan recognized the name, now that she was there, of the small but ancient bloodstock breeders.

"My God, how young you are!" blurted Sir Nicholas, and Swan laughed weakly. "And a beauty! I was expecting an old battle ax, like so many American women into the horses."

Oliver blanched, but now it was Swan who was unfazed. She'd get along with the crusty old fart just fine.

"And I see you have your own string started," Sir Nicholas blundered on, looking at Swan's midsection. "Are you the responsible party?" he rasped, turning to Sam, who for once was pretty dumbfounded. "I see you are—no surprise there."

Sir Nick didn't wait for an answer. "Well, good luck to you both. I suppose you'd like to see my grand mare." He turned to one of the stalls with a grey face reaching out over the Dutch door, one with an intensely feminine expression, intelligent, fiery, a female version of Mike's own. This, then, was Calimanco. Sir Nicholas gently led the big mare out of the stall, into the deepening twilight, around the hard-surface courtyard. She was truly breath-taking, with an enormous overstep at the walk—her hind feet overreaching the print made by her front feet. A deep girth left plenty of room for heart and lungs, a beautiful hip, clean, straight, stout legs and sturdy feet made her look like a living conformation lesson in equine beauty.

"I'd only consider selling her to the breeder of The Fortress, winner of the the Dowager at a mile and a half on the turf, by God—or perhaps to the breeder of Cartouche," said the old gentleman, slyly."But since The Fortress's son just won the William Lincoln and the Zenobia colt came third, I suppose you have the inside lane."

"Why are you selling?" asked Swan quietly. "She's wonderful."

"Goddamn Inland Revenue thinks I owe them two hundred thousand pounds. Bugger 'em," the old gentleman snarled bitterly.

"I've fought them for a year, but they always win. I've got to pay up, then try to get it back. I'll be dead in the churchyard by then. Bugger 'em!"

As the mare walked around her, Swan was more and more certain: she had to have her. She had done a quick calculation: Mike had just won her one hundred thousand dollars, against all odds. It was found money.

"Does she come with a clean culture?" Even though the mare had never foaled, Swan wanted a guarantee that there was no sign of infection that might compromise the mare's breeding status.

"Do you?" sniggered the old gent. Sam bristled. Swan threw him a warning look. She was silent for a long minute.

"So," she said.

"So . . . one hundred forty thousand pounds," said Sir Nicholas. "Not a farthing less will I take."

That was almost two hundred and fifty thousand dollars.

"You've seen her race record. She won the Ascot Stakes at one and a half miles at Royal Ascot, for Christ sakes! She's never taken a bad step in her life. I could sell her to the Arabs for three times the price, but they already own everything and what they don't own they buy . . . . If she's sold, I'll want her to stay sold— with the buyer for life. No dumping her in the back field or sending her to the knacker's yard like the damn Japanese when her foaling days are over. Retired the right way, treated like a queen," said Sir Nicholas grumpily. "That's why I'm setting a beggar's price. So few real horsemen are left willing to meet my terms."

"That's the only way I'd want it, Sir Nicholas. Oliver can vouch for that. But it's a down market," said Swan mildly, "down, and staying down."

"You've got yourself the makings of a stud, miss, and I'm not referring to you, sir, Major, sir, strapping great yank that you are," Nicholas said, turning to Sam with a genial sneer. "You need one or two tiptop mares not related to himself to get a few nice foals on the ground and make his name for him. This mare will be known to every market breeder at the Keeneland or Saratoga sales, or the Tattersalls, if you please, in three years' time. Your own young squire will just be throwing his leg over his first pony by then, I reckon."

"May I discuss this with Oliver tonight?" Swan asked, never taking her eyes from Calimanco. She could already see the foal from Mike and the grey: their physical similarities would serve to strengthen their offspring, their lack of shared ancestry was all to the good in a breed as inbred as was the Thoroughbred. She had to have the mare, but she had to try to tamp down the evidence of her intense interest.

"Sure! Why not, by God? Have a leisurely pint to discuss the chance of a lifetime, why don't you? Don't mind me!" blustered the old man. He returned Calimanco to her stall with a gentle pat to the neck. It was clear he adored her, and the thought of her going so far away was painful.

"Wonderful to have met you, Sir Nicholas," said Swan. "Many thanks for the opportunity to have first crack at her." Oliver gave her a small smile.

Then Swan's cell phone rang.

"Lige, how are you?" Swan said, rolling her eyes as a warning to Sam. "Listen, I'm tied up for supper as it turns out—I'm so sorry. Horse business. I can't get to London. Yes, I'm afraid for the whole evening, such's the luck."

"Well, I was hoping we could get into the West End for a show and a late supper at the Savoy Grill," Lige said, irked.

"Yes, yes. I'm so very sorry. That would have been wonderful. I wanted to see *War Horse* very much." Swan was sincere in that. "I'll see you tomorrow, perhaps for breakfast? Or later before we head back? So sorry, but I must run—"

She snapped her phone closed.

"My God, man, she's got another one on the hook—you'd better look lively," chuckled Sir Nicholas, and Sam earned a star in his crown by not taking the old jackass apart from pure aggravation.

"We'll be in touch—tonight, I hope, sir," said Swan authoritatively.

Swan, Sam, and Oliver made their farewells and walked back to the Mini, now in almost full darkness.

"She's first-rate, Oliver, everything you said about her, and more. I have to have her," Swan said as soon as they were in the car heading back to the Black Hart. "But can he be pounded down?"

"I don't think so, Swan," sighed Oliver. "He is absolutely right about the Dubai crowd, or the Irish, if the sheiks didn't bite for some reason. He's just such a curmudgeon that he has his prejudices and, I must say, an eye for a pretty girl."

"You should have seen him inspecting your south side, Swan, while you bent over to look at the mare's front legs," said Sam grimly. "I was half expecting him to try to trade her for you."

"Poor old soul," said Oliver. "He lost Lady Renfrew to a terrible cancer three years ago, and his only son in Iraq in the first year of the war. So sad. He has no one left and is on the bottle pretty heavily. Everything is probably going to have to go for the taxes, I hear, sooner or later. Even the estate itself. It's been in the family for twelve generations."

That sobered both Sam and Swan. As they headed into Doncaster, Swan made up her mind.

"Oliver, make it happen, pending a vetting. Bring her back with you. Either Lady or Linny will have to be sold when their racing careers are over to make up for it. I don't think I could bear to sell the new filly, and Serve the Guns has done too well by me to ever leave Belle Everley."

"We don't have to worry about that now," said Oliver gently. "But I think you are making the buy of the century. Mr. Bolington would be very proud of you." Swan swallowed hard at the mention of her father. "Such a lovely name—Calimanco."

"It's a coverlet, a nineteenth-century style called a linsey woolsey," said Swan, "made with vegetable dyes on old-fashioned looms. We have one or two at the farm."

"How charming. Now, how about supper?" Oliver suggested. "I'm meeting the Templetons at the Horn and Hound, outside town."

"Sounds lovely, but I'm a little tired," Swan said, and all three of them were surprised at how genuinely tired she sounded. She was suddenly a woman seven months pregnant, with jet lag to boot. "I think I'll order from the Falstaff and eat in my room. A wonderful, wonderful day, though, Oliver. I owe it all to you and the Templetons. Please give them my sincere thanks, they are great sportsmen. They will have many wins to come with Roisterous, no doubt."

"No doubt," said Oliver, "But I suspect we will be keeping Roisterous and Mike on separate career paths from now on."

Oliver dropped Swan and Sam in front of the Elizabethan hostelry, lit from within by period lamps and two enormous fireplaces in the chilly March evening.

"Let's go in for a minute," Sam proposed. "I've hardly had a chance to see you, and you are going home tomorrow." They ducked inside, the door's low ceiling making him bend over almost double to enter.

They sat awkwardly in the little front room on two lumpy wing chairs near the smoky fire while Swan filled him in on the decision to enter Mike, making it sound like much more of a last-minute thing than it had really been. Swan told him about Dr. Fisher, Townsend Brooke coming east, and the ongoing drama of Stone Chimneys. Sam listened with a little smile on his face, as though whatever she was saying was less important than the fact that she was sitting next to him while she was saying it. She knew better than to ask what he'd seen, heard, done.

"You look good," she said, at last. "Working out, it looks like, while you're here."

"Why don't you check for yourself?" The warmth rose in his voice.

"Thanks, but no doubt Miss Emma did that pretty thoroughly. Did you succeed in keeping her toasty warm all afternoon? Wasn't it lucky she had you, since she wasn't wearing much in the clothing department?" she said, poking him with her sharp verbal stick.

"I did what you told me to do," he groused mildly. "Don't I always? Not that it ever gets me a damn thing."

She smiled. Now she'd had her fun, she was hungry and done in. She stood up to place her order for her meal. Sam stood up with her.

"I'd rather warm you up," he said.

He kissed her near the fireplace. The front door opened and closed as local pub crawlers from the track came and went. He wrapped her in his arms and pulled her close to him, even with her belly between them. She couldn't help it, she slid her hands under his jacket and wrapped her arms around his waist. She ran her hands over the slabs of muscle in his back, and that sharp spasm of pleasure like no other feeling in the world stabbed her. For a long second, it wouldn't let go of her. He flexed his arms around her and there was no way she was going to pull away from that Mars the God of War body.

"Do that again," he said. So she did, and they kissed with a real purpose, just like in the Scarab parking lot. His daunting arousal was demanding her attention: she couldn't pretend not to know where things were heading now.

"There's never been anyone like you for me," he said, and the spasm grabbed her again, stronger and longer this time. She slid her hands down around his waist, under his shirt, ruffling the fine hair of his belly, letting him feel what it would be like if they drifted lower, below his belt buckle, under his jeans.

"Don't stop," he said, very low. "Open me up."

"I can't!" she was shocked at the thought. "They'll throw us out."

But that wasn't really a no. He turned their bodies around a little so his broad back was toward the door.

"Come on," he pleaded. His voice was hoarse. "Put your hand on me. Swannie."

It was just a matter of when, not if—of what illogical little ground rules she'd set down before she succumbed, an eager beast of prey.

"No . . . no . . . ." she whimpered, panicky. "I can't . . . we can't—"

"Then take me upstairs," he countered. "Let me put my mouth on you."

"You have to agree . . . it will be like it never happened if we do," she said, choking, breathless, his packed jeans straining against her. "We can never talk about it . . . . It will be like . . . amnesia. Promise."

He would have said anything. So what if he had to agree to some ridiculous condition that she could always throw back at him . . . *I told you . . . we agreed . . .?*

They stumbled into the lift alone, so they didn't scandalize innocent tourists with her little cries, his low voice pleading with her to throw herself on the elevator mat and let him enter her right there, between floors one and two. He was giving her the coming attractions, a performance for an audience of one. Now they were getting to the feature, in widescreen. She fumbled the key card in the door, and then they were finally alone.

"This never happened," she announced again, but he didn't even bother to answer. He just kissed her the way he wanted, pressing her against the wall of the little hallway, relaxing now, sure of his future, at least for the next hour or so.

"If we do this, we need to do things . . . differently," she gasped. "I need to be on top and you can't go too . . . deep."

"Whatever you say." He kissed her throat, pulling at her clothes. His heart was pounding, pounding against her hand, and he was trembling all over. "I'll stay completely still if you want. It will be like you're fucking a dead man, I promise." He kissed her hard, just like always, his hands exploring her.

"Sounds appealing. But I'm huge . . . huge . . . bigger than a basketball. Grotesque, huh?" She was hesitant, but his hand gently spanned her belly, his fingers open, just as it had when he had spent the night at Belle Everley. He moved his hand in a circle, stopping to cradle her belly's weight from underneath.

"Wow," he said, "that is fantastic."

He felt a kick. "My God, is that him?"

"Yes, he likes that," Swan replied. "He likes to hear us . . . talk."

Sam gently pushed against her and the kicking and thumping continued.

"It doesn't hurt?"

She shook her head "Nope. The hurting part is coming down the road."

"I swear I won't—"

"No, I meant the delivery," Swan corrected, "not . . . you."

"Take your clothes off; I want to see you."

She was embarrassed by the heavy-duty underwire bra and maternity underwear that had taken the place of the frilly, frothy confections of her pre-pregnancy days.

"Holler if this grosses you out," she whispered, trying to calm her nerves.

"You are more beautiful than ever," he breathed. She wondered what hallucinogenic drug expectant fathers ingested to make them able to say such a thing with a straight face. "Look at your breasts. I've never seen anything so beautiful."

"This from someone married to a centerfold."

"Look, though," he said. They filled his big hands for the first time. "Look at how nice they are. And I like this, too," he squeezed her rounder bottom with approval. He bent his head over her breasts, sucking the nipples gently, teasing their hardness with his tongue.

"Oh, God," she whimpered. Her nerve endings were firing, firing, like a pistol on a range.

He moved down her body and she grasped the tectonic plates of muscle across his shoulders, now below her. It seemed so strange to see the top of his head. It disappeared below her belly, and his mouth found her soft, wet lips below. She was soaked for him, as always, Brazilian wax and all, and his tongue was probing, seeking, until she was suddenly made of jello. She felt as though all voluntary movements had been suspended; she was paralyzed but still able to feel every sensation he was pulling out of her. She shuddered, pressing his head gently between her thighs, as he kissed her, his lips parted as if he were eating a large, ripe peach and wanted to capture all the juice on his tongue. His body was on a mission, to make her cry his name, beg for more: *oh yes, that was fantastic*. But before she came, he lifted his head, nuzzling up her belly again, then rolled her onto her side.

"You finally have some heft to you," he panted, as he spooned her, spreading his hands across her belly, but trying to tamp down the heat. "I like heft."

"Marines," she gasped, but it didn't come out as dismissive or saucy this time. She was so close.

"Swannie, Swannie, our little baby is in there," he said in wonderment.

"Don't." She suddenly tried to twist away, but then he began to caress her with his mouth, his hands, pulling her whole body gently against him, resisting his natural impulse to fling his leg over hers or roll on top of her.

"Climb up here," he commanded, but gently, and she turned over to face him, to move into the big circle of his arms as if she had never left. She had to give him credit: he could make even a seven-month pregnant heifer like her feel like a little doll. She snugged her belly in next to him, and the sensation of him aroused against it was oddly exciting and forbidden.

"You marines," she repeated. "I can't believe this turns you on. You really will jump anything." But she had her arms around him as tightly as he had her.

Then he let her lower herself on him, panting til she found a position she liked. He soon began to guide her hipbones between his thumbs and palms, listening to her "mmnn's" to reassure him that all was well. She had been so close before, it took only a few long thrusts to make her come. But he didn't let her rest. Instead he pushed back, again, again, clenching his teeth a little as he concentrated on his control. He rolled her gently on her side facing him, and started again almost immediately, pulling deep breaths in a rhythm that kept his powerful thrusting tamped down. He ran his hand up and down her leg, following its curve, its indentation at her knee, up the outer line of her thigh to her hip bone, and back down again.

"Oh oh oh," she panted softly. She hooked her leg around his back but he gently straightened it with his hand.

"No," he said. "I'll be in too deep like that."

She pushed against his trajectory in reply, and then he thrust hard—not as hard as he could, just enough. After two nights of sex in six months, it didn't take much. He growled and his hot wet gift filled her; overflowed her.

"I've missed you . . . ten times more than you've missed me—"

"Don't—" she said, "don't say anything . . . tender." She moved just a little, and that was his signal to lift his hips so his heavy cock slipped out of her in a small, hot flood. He began to breathe normally again, swallowed.

"I can tell you how beautiful you breasts are, but I can't say how much I missed you?"

"It's too—I can't bear it." She smiled wanly. "Tell me what you tell your one-night stands. That would be okay."

"I love you and I never want to leave you."

She pulled back.

"Don't! I told you—what you tell your one-night stands. Not like me in the Scarab."

"That *is* what I tell them: for one night, you have to work fast."

She rolled her eyes: a comedian.

"You don't have to tell them anything. I know why they say yes. The blue eyes, the grin. Those arms. Fitch used to call you Major Shoulder Porn."

"Look," Sam said wearily, but he kept her tightly against him, "not everyone is like you. Not everyone takes weeks and weeks before they let you touch them. There isn't that much time spent checking each other out."

"Tell me." Her sexual experience had been limited to three short, serious relationships, all as someone's fiancée. Her sister had married the only man she'd ever known. Townsend was barely more than a child, Katie and Hannah completely inexperienced; she had no other close women friends.

"No. It feels weird talking about it with you."

"No weirder than I feel making love with this beachball sticking out of me," she retorted. He sighed. This was the price he was going to have to pay to keep her with him.

"You buy someone a drink, check them out; that's about it," he said. "You both know the drill. Sometimes the girl might be a little hesitant, so then as a gentleman you back up and say, 'Thanks for a nice evening, nice to talk to you.' Get up to leave."

"And then—"

He sighed again."Most always, she says, 'Wait.'"

"See?" Swan said. "Once she sees all of you, it's all over. Like when I saw you take your jacket off in the Scarab. I'd never seen arms like these. I wanted to crawl onto your lap and let you pull my panties off with your teeth. That's what happens to them, too."

"It's not like that. It's too damn dark in most bars, for one thing." He shrugged.

"Then when you get—where? Her place? You take off your clothes and jump right into it? Do you have a drink? Do you talk, or kiss, or grope each other, or what?"

"Don't sound so naïve; you know people who've hit and run—plenty of them," he said, slightly indignant. "I know what it sounds like. You don't have to rub my nose in it. Like I told you: I've never raw-dogged it with anyone the way I have with you. Look where it's gotten us."

"Were you tender?" She was musing out loud, but her voice caught. "How could you be, with so many of them?"

"Don't. You're only looking for a reason to kick me out on my ass." His eyes were angry and ardent at the same time.

"It all sounds . . . lonely. Pointless."

"Swannie, that's what I've been telling you for months. That's why I can't give you up. I can't." He looked at her longingly.

"Don't. Don't say any more."

He gave up.

"Your breasts are so beautiful," he said.

Now that he had her where he wanted her, Sam continued waging love through the night and into the following day, without showering or eating, dozing, then jolting himself awake against the clock, his arms around her when she slept. When it got close to the time for her to begin to pack up, he had the Falstaff send over a covered tray of Yorkshire pudding, a haddock, apricots from North Africa, fresh tomatoes, chocolate gateau, a china pot of English breakfast tea. He carried her into the bathtub and sat on the edge behind her while she soaked. Then he perched her on the side of the bed wrapped in towels. He watched as she ate everything, gathering her bare feet into his lap; so long as he held her red polished toes, she couldn't run away.

When Lige called, Sam answered the phone. When he called again, Sam answered again. The third time, Lige said, "Tell Miss Bolington I'll meet her at Doncaster International at six P.M." Then he hung up.

"Let me go with you to the airport," he said. "I might as well meet this turd."

"No."

"I don't like you going home with him."

"Can we please not argue? I have to go."

"Maybe there is something we can agree on," he ventured. "Have you thought of a name? I know it will be Bolington since you are sure it's a boy, but what about if it's a girl? Stranger mistakes have happened."

Swan hesitated. He might as well know now.

"I'm thinking about Lucinda if it is a girl, after my mother. And Lucius if it is a boy. Luke."

Sam looked as her suspiciously.

"I thought boys had the mother's surname as their first names in the old Virginia families. That's why Hetty's son is Bolington Delaney," he said.

"Bolington is his last name. Bolington Bolington is a bit ludicrous, don't you think?" Swan didn't look at him.

He looked at her, though, plenty.

"This child's last name is Moore, Swan. End of discussion. I don't care what comes before that."

She said nothing, and he knew from bitter experience that meant not only that she disagreed but also that she had no intention of discussing it any further. Talk about passive aggression.

He tried again. "Swan, we decided this."

"In theory. We made a joke about it while you were away. It wasn't a real discussion. And it was before we had broken up."

"I'm going to be the kid's father, no matter what his name. I'll have the same rights. If he goes through school with his mother's maiden name, it will remind everybody his folks weren't married. That still means something, particularly in Waverly. I want to claim this child, he's mine. It would cost you nothing to make him a Moore and it might make it easier for you to get around me, as you always want to do. That should carry some weight with you."

"Lucius . . . Bolington Moore?" She said it tentatively.

"It that so terrible?" His voice softened in spite of himself.

"No. I guess not."

"Then is it settled?"

She nodded.

"So you are doing the natural childbirth thing?" he asked as though making conversation. "You got a coach?'

"I'm thinking Hetty, if she can come to the classes in Waverly with me," Swan said.

"Will you at least e-mail me, every few days, so I know everything is going okay?" Sam began bartering. "More would be better, in case you need anything."

"Once a week," she countered. "It may be me or someone else in the family."

"Swannie—"

"Don't. For the one hundredth time: don't be . . . sweet."

"The next time we see each other, we will have a baby."

"*I* will have a baby."

"For God's sake, don't let anything happen to yourself, will you? You know what I mean."

"Having an attack of 'bad luck doomed love'?" she asked sardonically. "How do you like it? Sucks, huh?"

"I'm not going to let you push my buttons, not now," he said, satisfied but aggrieved at the same time. "I've had sex a total of three times in six months. I had more sex than that during Christmas vacation in the ninth grade. I feel great. I just hope you won't be sorry we did this."

"Depends on if we can leave it behind us, like we said," she repeated.

"Amnesia."

"Yes. Amnesia."

He sighed for the millionth time since he'd known her. But it was beginning to dawn on him: she was trying to tell him how they could be together without even realizing that she was doing it. Maybe they could live a parallel life, a shadow life, not acknowledging that they were bonded or happy or planning a future and a family together.

"You know," he said softly, "I think I rushed things last year—rushed you into bed, rushed you to get engaged—everything," he grimaced. "Maybe if we just let things go for a while. See what happens. You think I can't be patient, but I can be." He nuzzled her, knowing she was about to pull away, prolonging their time together for as long as he could. "I've never been faithful to anyone for this long, even when I was married, but I'm not complaining. I'll be home in a few months, and the baby will be here. Everything will be different."

"I've got to go. Good-bye, mountain range man," Swan said with a small smile. She smoothed her skirt, straightened the collar of her jacket, pulled her tail of hair down her back. "I'll pay the bill on my way out."

Then the bellboy arrived, and she was gone.

Chapter 20

Swan and Lige moved through Heathrow almost wordlessly. He was courteous but vexed. His ego was bruised, that was clear enough. He had said himself that her time was her own while they were in England, but he had obviously hoped for more. Those hopes had been dashed by what he assumed was Swan's one-night stand in the Black Hart. Swan debated telling him the back story and thought better of it. It fell in the category of none of his damned business. She placed quick calls to Eduardo, Hetty and Boyd, and Spaulding with some of the dead heat details; to Jerusha and Oliver, to hear how Mike had come out of the race and confirm that Calimanco would arrive at Belle Everley once she had cleared quarantine in Brookside, N.Y., in three weeks. Then she turned her attention to her slightly put-out escort, deciding to make conversation on the flight home, conversation unrelated to their real estate debate or their junket to England.

"I'm going to have a glamorous houseguest over the summer," she said as they settled into business class. "The niece of Dexter Gaylord, the television star—remember *Wall Street Meltdown*? She has been at UCLA this year but is coming to Virginia to help me with the baby. She is a beauty and has been making the L.A. scene with some actor hunk," Swan said chattily, "Bernardo—something."

"Bernardo Holtzman?" Lige showed a bit of interest. "My secretary talks about him all the time."

"Is he famous? I don't watch much broadcast TV."

"He's on *Life in the City,*" Lige replied. "She sounds glamorous. Wasn't she the little girl Hastings Fitzhugh squired around last year?"

"They split up before he passed away," Swan said. "She *is* very young." She felt like fifty, not twenty-seven, when she said it. She did feel a little maternal toward Townsend, who had a perfectly good set of parents who simply had other priorities.

"Did you end up buying your horse?" Lige was trying to keep the conversation going, a little warmer now.

Swan hid a smile. Her horse had won a huge race and a huge purse; it was the talk of the south of England and had been on the BBC news all morning at the airport, but Lige must not have connected the dots.

"Yes, I did," she said sweetly, "a very nice horse, indeed."

"Sounds like a successful trip, then," he said.

"Yes. Yes, it was, all the way around."

Lige suddenly woke up. "Oh—I saw that you won the big race yesterday and were in all of the newspapers with those fancy pants from the Kentucky Derby," he said. "I'm sorry I didn't congratulate you." He hesitated. "I did try to call your hotel room."

"Don't worry."

"Then I hope you don't mind me asking—"

Here it comes, Swan thought.

"You seemed to be sharing a room with someone."

"Yes, Major Moore is in England on . . . business," Swan said. "We had some custodial decisions to make." That was partially true.

"You seem to have had a lot of men pretty damn interested in you," Lige said in a neutral tone. Swan didn't quite know how to take that.

"Your three fiancés, your cousin, your neighbor Mr. Fitzhugh—who you foisted off on this young girl to clear the way for your major—this jockey I hear about in Waverly. Just seems to be one long parade."

"I guess I don't know what to say to that," Swan replied, a captive participant in the conversation at thirty thousand feet. Did this guy think he was being charming?

"Well, then, let me ask a straight-up question." Lige narrowed his eyes. "Where do I fit into this set-up? We've had dinner a couple of times, chit-chat on the phone, this trip . . . . What's your game? Are you moving on from the marine or am I just someone to dangle in front of him to drive him crazy?"

"I am very sorry, Mr. Davenport, if I've given you the wrong impression." Swan's voice was like ice. "I am very grateful for your solicitude on our trip. Let's please leave it at that." He was a jackass.

"Oh, now." Lige saw he had made a huge mistake. "I'm sorry if I jumped to the wrong conclusions. I'm not the smoothest guy out there at this kind of thing, I only meant—"

Swan cut him off.

"I don't want you to think you are part of any 'game,' Mr. Davenport," she said. "Having anyone in my life at this point is so alien to my current thinking, it's ludicrous. Perhaps other women in my predicament have presented themselves to you differently, but, believe me, if I never see you again, it will be all the same to me." Since she could not stand up and leave, a gesture that would have been satisfying, dramatic, and effective, Swan bent her head to her book.

Lige sat next to her, stunned into silence. He could have been on another planet as far as she was concerned. While Swan made a pretense of reading, she mulled over her behavior at the Black Hart. Runaway hormones had to bear the brunt of the blame, hormones and Sam's powerful, irresistible lovemaking. That was her story and she was sticking to it: it all was Sam's fault. The rest of the trip went that way, a long six hours. When they got to baggage claim at Dulles, Swan purposefully dragged her own bag to the short term parking lot, hauling it awkwardly, along with her belly, while the big, strapping Lige walked next to her, empty-handed except for his overnight bag. When they got to the lot, they split: she had parked at one end, he at the other.

"Good-bye and thank you," said Swan, shaking hands but not meeting his gaze. She turned on her heel and walked away. What a prick.

◆

When she got home, she hugged Flagg and Mathilde, in that order. She had brought some Melrose loose tea, Mathilde's favorite and not easily found in the States, a cunning butter soft leather change purse, some English toffees, and two souvenir racing programs signed by Oliver, Sinjon, and the Templetons, for Edgar and Eduardo. Swan gave each man an extra week's pay when a Belle Everley homebred won a Grade I stakes race, so their little keepsakes were just to show them she knew how important they were to her enterprise.

Swan turned her attention to readying High View for Historic Garden Week the second week of April. It was a melancholy exercise. She planned a display of Fitch's hunt kit and accoutrements; old family photos of Fitch and his father, Francis; and the ultimate tribute. Kezia Hardaway and the hunt staff were bringing the Waverly pack to the house on Saturday in honor of two generations of Waverly huntsmen. Swan met with Thérèse Malloy at Belle Everley the day after her return from England.

"I think everything is in order," Swan said. Unlike Belle Everley the year before, she saw no need for a big financial outlay to make High View presentable; Fitch had kept it in tiptop condition.

"It looked perfect to me," agreed Thérèse. "Those daffodil beds should still be spectacular, and our visitors will love the chance to explore the native boxwood maze by the smokehouse. We're so glad we didn't have to consider a Waterford tour." Thérèse sighed. "There are still a few among our members for whom that would be . . . unacceptable." The Quakers of Waterford had been ardent Union sympathizers during the Civil War and had organized the only Virginia military unit to fight for the North. Some old-line Waverly folks had never forgiven the village for that betrayal and still refused to set foot in it.

Thérèse sipped her tea. "I *was* wondering if you knew the current thinking of Virgilia Osmond regarding Stone Chimneys. You seem to know Mr. Davenport. What do you think is going on? I hesitate to ask Mrs. Osmond, I don't know her that well. Stone Chimneys hasn't been on the Club tour in the ten years of my presidency."

"Thérèse, I wish I knew. He wants a foothold in Waverly, and Virgilia is looking to make a move. It would be much better if a buyer could be found who wanted Stone Chimneys as a farm but was willing to pay development prices." Swan smiled at the impossibility of that.

"Lige Davenport in Waverly would be a disaster of biblical proportions," said Thérèse ominiously. "I'll be happy to tell Virgilia that to her face if you think that would help."

"Please wait. Let's not go to war with one of our own, who can't help the fact that the country's investment markets have gone into the tank. Any one of us could be in Virgilia's position." Swan meant older, alone, with financial woes and fears of the unknown. "If Fitch had left High View to me without the wherewithal to support it . . . ."

Thérèse nodded in deference.

"We'll wait . . . and hope," she said, standing up. "Of course, we are so very grateful to have High View on the garden tour, in honor of Fitch and as a reflection of your own very important position in the county."

That everyone seemed to view Swan as a key to the town's survival was intimidating. She should have had two savvy, vigorous parents in their fifties fighting these kinds of battles, people with influence, pull, political power behind the scenes—people like Fitch, a former CIA agent, for God's sake. What was she, really, other than a girl who rode horses and looked good in stretch breeches? At least, she used to look good. She was not in fighting trim to take on Lige Davenport.

Swan's eye went to the Stubbs oil on the wall of her parlor, a small intense portrait of a Newmarket Heath Thoroughbred done early in the artist's career, a little jewel that shone like the Star of India to any art historian or connoisseur whose eye fell upon it. Most Stubbses were in the great houses of England or museums around the world. Swan had this one insured for three million dollars.

Now as she looked at it, she saw not the hand of the eighteenth-century master creating great works as commissions for sporting lords. She saw Stone Chimneys, its three hundred and fifty pristine acres and beautiful house, seemingly so stout, with its foot-thick walls, but really as vulnerable as if it had been constructed of paper before a great storm. She felt like Scarlett O'Hara trying to hold on to Tara. Making a dress out of the draperies, selling a family treasure—you do what you have to do. After Thérèse left, she called Daniel.

"We need to talk to Wraggley's," she said, "the specialist in the English Romantic Period—about the little Stubbs."

CHAPTER 21

"Philippa Knight-Hughes," said Daniel, "she is Wraggley's Romantic specialist."

"Can we do it by phone? I'm just back from England and have to stay put for a while." Swan had missed two appointments with Dr. Fisher and another with Dr. Cavendish.

"Of course. The painting is listed. She'll have access to the online catalog; she will just need a condition report to determine when to send her local representative to look at the work. But, as I told you, the market is down all over. Why do you think I could pull Philippa's name off the top of my head? The bank has clients looking in the same direction to raise funds."

Swan sighed.

"What is it insured for now?" asked Daniel. She told him.

"In the name of God, I hope you go in the direction I suggested instead—mortgaging High View."

Swan fulfilled her responsibilities over the following weeks, checking with Jerusha on the status of the convalescing Judy and the flourishing Enfilade, awaiting the arrival of Calimanco from the quarantine barn, confirming Mike's safe return from overseas, seeing Dr. Fisher, and taking her meds. She felt a little better, but she didn't know whether it was because Sam was away (and safe from her negative influence), the baby was due soon (she hadn't had the Marriage in Heaven dream since she had learned she was pregnant), or she was medicated and seeing Dr. Fisher. She had told the psychiatrist her whole romantic history—the first, perfect, love with Hunt Lee, the rebound engagement to the gallant Carter Noland, Fitch, Sam—while the doctor had sat noncommittally listening, listening.

She had talked to Sam twice a week, much against her better judgment. He had an uncanny knack of knowing when and where to catch her; just when she typically sat in the entranceway to separate her bills from her personal mail; when she was having a cup of mint tea in the dining room, when she getting ready for bed. Well, it wasn't uncanny, really: he knew her schedule because he knew her, thought about her, understood her life was about routine because animals and humans depended upon her. He followed the Amnesia Rule to the letter.

So she kept the topic of conversation the progress of the pregnancy, what the obstetrician had said, when she was to make the first appointment with the pediatrician. Once he asked about the nursery, but she deflected the question; it was too painful to describe the antique furnishings or the little cradle she had placed next to the old bed they had slept in as a couple. Instead she talked about real estate and horses, two subjects of only peripheral interest to him. He seemed content just to talk to her.

Swan had begun to be concerned about her changing figure.

She stood in front of the full-length mirror in the bedroom. The baby bump of the past month or so had progressed to the "Whoa, what is in there?" stage. She had gained thirty pounds; Hetty had gained only forty when she had had her boys, but Boyd Senior was no Septimus Moore. Swan boomeranged between fears that the baby would be tiny, Spaulding and Hexell-like, or huge, Moore-like, a monster to delivery naturally. Either way, her concave belly was going to be a thing of the past as the ligaments girding her womb stretched to accommodate the son of Mars the God of War.

Hetty was due to come up for a day, leaving the boys with their Aunt Spaulding and her long-suffering houseman, Alfredo, at the Willow's Edge on her way. Swan had asked Hetty to bring her Pilates DVDs, since that was the regimen Hetty credited with her return to her pre-baby figure, not once but twice. So when Hetty arrived late one Wednesday morning with two large canvas bags, Swan wasn't surprised, not really—there must be a lot of DVDs.

"Is Mathilde here?" Hetty asked as soon as she came in the parlor.

"No, she's at Organic Natural Foods in Waverly," Swan said, suspicious. "She'll be back to make lunch. Why?"

"Because I don't want anyone to know my secret," said Hetty. "When I told you I was doing Pilates with the boys—I mean, after the boys were born—I was lying."

Swan felt a cold chill. What had Hetty done? Amphetamines? She'd lost the forty pounds overnight, it seemed, and had kept it off easily, even though she'd nursed Bud only for three months.

Hetty reached in a bag and pulled out a DVD, a sports bra, and what looked like a piece of a circus costume.

"We need to go upstairs to your bedroom; you have a DVD player in your flat screen, right? I've been belly dancing, not doing Pilates," she said.

"My God, you can't be serious, Hetty. Really?" Swan burst out laughing.

"Yes, and it has been great. I kept it from Boyd for six months, I was so embarrassed, and I've sworn him to secrecy on pain of emasculation. It is too mortifying, but it's worked, and it's a lot less stressful than ab crunches."

"What then? You've been dressing in a harem outfit?" Swan said, fingering the filmy little skirt/belt thing with a few coins attached to it.

"Laugh all you want. Do you want my help or not?" Hetty asked patiently, an older sister who knew everything and just needed the opportunity to demonstrate it. They trooped upstairs and into the bedroom.

"Pop this in the DVD player," Hetty directed, sliding her sweat pants down her hips and attaching the filmy skirt below her navel. She pulled the sports bra over her silk t-shirt.

Swan hit *play*. Five young women in sports bras, sweatpants, and filmy belt contraptions like Hetty's were standing on a beach somewhere—Santa Monica or Dubai—as Middle Eastern music—flute, drums and finger cymbals—began moaning in the background.

"Neutral pose," intoned the voice over; the women arranged their arms in natural arcs. So did Hetty, Swan noticed to her shock, and from then on, Swan watched her sister, not the video.

"Shoulders up, to the right, back, to the left," directed the voice over, and Hetty began to move her shoulders deliberately at first, then faster. "Connecting the four points into a circle. Arms above the head in the L position . . . . Now, hips forward, to the left, down, to the right. Relax the knees. Torso up, to the right, down, to the left; connect the four points into a circle, faster, now, faster, faster!"

Suddenly Hetty was twitching her hips rhythmically and moving her arms like Salome dancing with the seven veils—if Salome had also worn sweatpants. The little filmy thing's coins jingled and tinkled together, the fabric vibrating, rising and falling. Her breasts stayed serenely in place under the sports bra; everything else was pretty much in constant motion, however.

Hetty took a few steps to the left, arching her left foot, then a few steps back to the right, raising her arm gracefully above her head, dropping it behind her back, reaching out, twisting her wrist, then passing it gracefully under her jaw and extending it from the shoulder into the air, flipping the wrist at the last moment. The music ended. Swan sat down abruptly on the settee.

"Holy shit!" Swan said admiringly. "How did you learn to do that?"

"The DVDs," said Hetty with self-satisfaction. "It's all on the DVDs." She gently patted her abdomen, which was flat but feminine and, well, sexy.

"If you learn the movements now, even if you have to give up dancing for a few weeks at the end, you should be able to start up as soon as you feel up to it afterward. Those Pikeurs aren't going to hide anything, whether you have an elephant or a mouse for a kid."

"Hetty, do it again, the whole thing from the beginning," Swan commanded as she restarted the DVD player.

After lunch, Hetty showed Swan a chiffon three-panel skirt with a silk scarf girdle, a choli top, a bra covered with little coins and mirrors.

"Once you're over Sam, you'll want to be able to attract someone new," Hetty said matter-of-factly. "This is guaranteed. You don't have to be a sylph or have great cardiovascular fitness, and, well, men will go wild for it."

"Boyd? Boyd likes—this?"

"It's fun. And it helps pelvic congestion."

"I can't believe you dress up in these things; they look like Halloween costumes," Swan said, "but leave the DVDs. There is something to it, I guess. I have to hand it to you—you are surprising."

Swan tucked the DVDs and the paraphernalia deep into her summer closet, away from prying eyes. Hetty was right, it was one thing for a husband to accept changes in his wife's figure after giving birth as a small price to pay for their children. It was quite another for some man in the future to do the same. She'd begin studying the belly dancing DVDs the next day.

◆

Three days later began Historic Garden Week. This tour was light years away from the previous year's nightmare. Swan had sent Mathilde to help spell Emilio and Daniel at High View and stayed happily far from it all at Belle Everley.

That meant she was able to welcome the beautiful Calimanco that evening, when the huge Gold Chip semi van dropped her off on its way to Florida, its lights flashing like the QEII as it crawled up the driveway. The tall, elegant Thoroughbred stepped into the mare barn as though she owned it, which she did—for the night. The Belle Everley mares were in their fields with their foals. Calimanco was as stunning as Swan remembered. It was like finding a Rockette at a high school dance recital or the Crown Jewels at a swap meet. When Swan totaled her purchase price and import costs, they were upwards of two hundred and seventy-five thousand dollars. Many mares had sold for much more; but they were either proven broodmares like The Fortress in her prime, or brilliant race mares themselves. Calimanco was neither. She was just physical beauty, royal bloodlines, and—potential.

Swan called Sir Nicholas Renfrew to let him know Calimanco had arrived safely.

"Thank you; I hope the same for you, miss," the old curmudgeon said, "a safe arrival of your own."

It was almost too late in the season to breed the mare that year, although with the general financial malaise in the horse business, many stallions still had open books. Most closed down operations by Memorial Day. Swan had given some thought to breeding Calimanco to Cartouche, who was standing at stud in Kentucky, rather than lose a valuable reproductive year. He had the reputation as a fertile, gentle breeding animal, perfect for a maiden mare. She could let Calimanco settle in for a week or two then send her to Cartouche for a late-season mating. She called the Templetons' breeding manager the next day.

"Yes, of course, Miss Bolington, we will fit your mare in at the end of the month," said Bradford Taylor, the breeding manager. "The Templetons will be thrilled you've chosen Cartouche for your Calimanco. They were filled with admiration when they learned you had bought her. It isn't often we get an Egyptian Wells in the States anymore."

"Please thank the Templetons," Swan said. A seventy-five thousand dollar stud fee would put three hundred and fifty thousand dollars in Calimanco. But the resulting foal—

"Who knows?" Taylor quipped, "The way things are going, the Templetons may send Cartouche's dam, Zenobia, to Oscar Mike when the time comes. We might as well keep it all in the family."

Chapter 22

After almost four weeks of submissive silence, a huge flower arrangement arrived the week after the garden tour. At first Swan thought it was some late-arriving arrangement to commemorate Fitch's death; then she saw the card: "Let me make amends." It was signed Elijah Davenport. Swan tossed the card into the wastebasket.

"Mathilde," she called, "isn't today your day at the Catholic Ladies Relief Society? Please pull this arrangement apart and take the flowers to Waverly Hospital for the pediatrics ward. If Mr. Davenport calls, I'm not at home."

This tactic had not worked before, but Lige Davenport was no Septimus Moore.

◆

Over the next few days, Swan watched the belly dance videos when Mathilde was out and about and began to grasp the concepts of the dance itself. Each day she felt heavier, more uncomfortable. Dr. Cavendish pronounced her six weeks from delivery, but without as much certainty as Swan would have liked to hear. The baby felt as though he was making up his mind to head into the world pretty much on his own. Hetty was coming to three classes at the Waverly Recreation Center and Swan was going alone to three classes. Since Hetty had been through two natural childbirth pregnancies herself, the instructor felt comfortable giving Hetty a pass on a couple of the early sessions. Boyd Senior promised that he and Spaulding would handle the boys no matter when Swan needed her sister; Hetty was only ninety minutes away from Waverly. Swan was blasé; the mystery of mammalian birth was no mystery to someone who had helped veterinarians position malpresented foals at midnight in a freezing barn; discussed stallion libido problems with horsemen three times her age; and seen dead mares winched out of stalls before rigor mortis could set in.

She felt well, all in all, but she would tire suddenly and collapse on a sofa. Then Mathilde quietly placed a coverlet over her legs to keep her warm and Flagg flopped down next to her, snoring, within minutes himself. Swan didn't feel alone, even with Sam far away. She had baby Luke; he had pushed her bad dreams away from the moment of conception and kept her worries outside the cocoon holding the two of them. She could think of Lige Davenport and his bluster, his coarseness, even his threat to her way of life, with a cool contempt, when before she would have felt threatened, intimidated. Those few moments of panic she experienced, of fear of the unknown, were tempered by an intense eagerness to cradle her baby, to see the living embodiement of her family's future. After those first three months of misery, she was having a very good late-stage pregnancy.

But she was prudent, nonetheless. She began to minimize her activities beyond talking to her trainers; lunching at the Crossroads with Daniel; and pressing Virgilia, gently, about the price for Stone Chimneys. The appraisal on High View had come in at an astounding \$5.5 million; the one at Stone Chimneys, \$2.8 million with its current agricultural zoning.

Swan saw Dr. Fisher once a week now. She let Daniel discuss Wraggley's selling strategy on the Stubbs and carry her application for a loan against High View in the amount of \$3.5 million to the loan officer at Tidewater Financial. Although her cash flow seemed, from the outside, strong, Swan's expenses were high. Her net income was relatively low. She was land rich and cash poor.

The week after the flowers arrived, so did a repentant Elijah Davenport.

"Miss Swan, I appreciate your seeing me uninvited," he said, when Mathilde showed him into the parlor, his face a mask. "I was afraid you would refuse me if I called ahead." He was in his conservative pin striped suit and collar pin.

Swan sat down and waited.

"I understand you have a relationship with a women's charity in Waverly. I wanted to make a donation to this particular group in the hopes that concrete evidence of my sincere regret over offending you would carry more weight than would—" he hesitated, "flowers or candy." Lige must have learned the fate of his bouquet.

"You wanted to put your money where your mouth is?" Swan asked, but she did so with a small smile. She didn't look at the check; she knew it would be a whopper. "A . . . peace offering?"

"Exactly. I'd be grateful if you would accept it on the charity's behalf."

"Mathilde," Swan called across the entranceway, "could you bring us a pot of tea?" She turned back to Lige.

"Since you plan to become a resident of Waverly, it is gratifying to see that you are interested in its civic life. I'm sure I can speak on behalf of our group and offer my thanks for your generosity," she said.

"The only good thing about being a rich jackass is that you can sometimes make up for it by helping others," Lige said. He wasn't bantering anymore. "I'd hate to think that I'd made an enemy of you—for many reasons."

"Well, you needn't worry: I don't have a seat on the zoning board," Swan replied. "I have no influence on the planning committee or the health department, and, of course, the Waverly Chamber of Commerce will be over the moon with happiness when you buy Stone Chimneys."

"May I assume that you have given up your 'concern' over my pursuit of Mrs. Osmond's property?" he asked, accepting his tea in a Staffordshire cup that came from Bristol to Belle Everley as ship ballast in 1824.

"For the time being," Swan said. Why not lie? Could he have learned about her interaction with Tidewater Commercial or Wraggley's? Both companies should honor their clients' confidential transactions. Oh: Virgilia. She could have said something about Swan trying to come up with the money to buy her out.

"I have a more pressing matter occupying me for now." She glanced discreetly southward. Yes, this was the way to play it—a lady in waiting for her blessed event.

"You look marvelous," he said; she nodded a modest acknowledgment.

"I might as well admit it," he burst out. "I don't get you at all! You seem to be a girl who has spent a lot of time on her . . . personal life. You never throw your money around or flaunt your connections. You flit around town in ballet slippers like a little sprite. Now I hear not only that you are a great favorite of General Clayton and the stepdaughter of Bertrand Davis but also that your aunt is a close friend of Senator Avery, the biggest kingmaker in Virginia politics. He could make any developer's life a living hell. And you have this war hero boyfriend at your heels. I don't know . . . I just don't know. What have I gotten myself into?"

"I think you overestimate my importance in the great scheme of things," Swan said calmly, but Lige was not paying attention to her at all.

"Jesus H. Christ, is that a Stubbs?" he said, his eyes widening as he looked at the parlor wall.

"An early, minor work."

"So that one in the hall isn't a copy?" Lige said despairingly. "Some connoisseur I am." He tore his attention from the painting and looked at Swan, really looked, for perhaps the first time. "I must have seemed like the biggest jackass in the county, treating you with so little respect. You must have died laughing after I left you at Dulles. You could crush me like a bug."

"Hardly," Swan said. "You may have made a small miscalculation, but you've discovered it in time to go back to the drawing board. More tea?" Swan rose with the pot in her hand to freshen his cup.

"And I made that crack about 'beautiful daughters' . . . ." Lige mused, still staring at her. "I'm surprised I didn't get my face slapped. Or maybe you intended to get your revenge—later. My . . . comeuppance?"

Swan smiled. "Now that's a word you don't hear anymore."

Lige just stared, a hint of a smile on his face. He drained his teacup.

"Well, Miss Swan, thank you for your time. You've been very gracious." He stood up, shook her hand and turned abruptly. "I can show myself out," he said, and he was gone.

Swan mulled.

She had lost the element of surprise, although she had to give him credit: he had gone from boorish know-it-all to respectful adversary in record time. He now knew that she had resources to throw into battle if she chose to sacrifice them. She had influence if she chose to draw on it. She could retaliate. She could scheme. She could . . . well, she could do it all. Now he had to decide if *he* could do it all—if he wanted to call her bluff.

Swan called Daniel.

"He isn't the asshole we thought he was, but only because you have some pull he wasn't counting on. You aren't some Vestal Virgin to be sacrificed by the town to appease his lust for an heir," he observed. "Now you have to decide whether you want the loan or the painting sold. If you consign the painting to Wraggley's, it may be four to six months before it goes to auction. The interest rate on the High View loan would be reasonable, but you'd have to rein in some spending, unless Mike and the racing string continue to make more than they cost or unless you can increase your income from the horses. What if you found a good buyer for Serve the Guns? She could bring one hundred and fifty thousand, maybe more; you just bought that new mare . . . ."

"Gunny's February foal was not what I had hoped for, conformation-wise," said Swan softly, acknowledging this fact for the first time. "That would depress Gunny's price if she were to go on the market today."

"You could sell The Fortress to someone who wanted one more top foal. It would be a chance of a lifetime for a breeder, wouldn't it? I hesitate to even suggest it, but as your banker—"

"Never, never, never, never, never. Both Stubbses would go first."

Daniel hmmmm-ed an acknowledgment.

"What about Enfilade or Dress the Line? Couldn't they be sold as racehorses and as The Fortress's daughters? I thought you said once they were potential broodmare gold."

"They are the future of our breeding program—Luke's and mine—if they retire from racing sound," Swan said quietly.

Daniel was silent for a moment.

"What about Judy? She's laid up. Why isn't she a broodmare? She is a daughter of the Fortress, too."

"Judy was bred four times and never 'caught.' I gave up on her and put her into steeplechase training. But I could send her to a fertile local stallion, I suppose. Any foal she had would have some value, and she could then be bred next year for a top-dollar foal." Swan was thinking out loud. "Mares' fertility can change . . . just like anyone's. It will be a long shot. I'll think about it. "

"The Stubbs, then. At least we'll have the Wraggley's agent come and take a look. Do you want to be here?"

She shook her head.

"Could you do it without me?" Swan asked. "I don't think I can watch."

Daniel nodded again.

"That's how bankers get the rep as heartless SOBs."

◆

A few days later, Swan and Hetty went to the natural childbirth class in Waverly. A simple statement that "Major Moore is overseas" had been enough to satisfy anyone who didn't know the details of Swan's personal predicament. The pant-pant-pant breathing to prevent premature pushing, the supportive role of the partner, the back-rubs, seemed humorous to Swan, but Hetty quickly reminded her that it wouldn't be so funny when the time came. The younger sister shut her mouth and worked the exercises.

Swan could tell from Sam's voice, beginning around the first of May, that he was more focused on her progress; asking more questions that sounded like he had Googled third-trimester pregnancy, Braxton Hicks contractions, and all. She found this humorous as well but tried not to tease him. She had put him through enough; he was three thousand miles away as it was.

Swan found a fertile young stallion standing near Delafield and had Jerusha van a recovering Judy to his court to be bred. Jerusha still had Enfilade. Her reputation as Oscar Mike's first trainer—and Linny's, who finished a very strong second in a Grade I at Belmont at the end of April—was drawing other horse owners to her barn. Belle Everley had been good to her.

To everyone's delight, Roisterous won the Kentuckian Stakes convincingly the third Saturday in May. The following Thursday, a strange thing happened. Swan was walking up the steps after having seen Dr. Fisher when a gushing sound like no other made her look down suddenly.

Her heart twisted in her. She continued up the steps and opened the door.

"Mathilde! Call Hetty! My water just broke," Swan said in a quavering voice.

"Jesus, Mary, and Joseph," cried Mathilde from the kitchen, her hands full of flour. But she was clear-headed.

"Mrs. Delaney," Mathilde barked into the phone in the entranceway, "I'm taking Miss Swan to Waverly Hospital right now. If you call Dr. Cavendish, we'll meet you all there."

They were on their way in a few minutes. Swan called the mare barn from the car and alerted Eduardo. He'd come up to the house and take Flagg to the barn kennel until Mathilde returned.

"I'm only two weeks early, that isn't bad." Swan was thinking aloud. "I'm more worried that Hetty and I have two more classes to go to."

"I think you are going to miss those," Mathilde said sensibly. "How are you?"

"Uh . . . okay . . . okay . . . oh . . . oh . . . ." Swan was reassuring herself as a contraction hit her like a giant elastic band twisting, compressing inside her. Then it passed.

"Okay again," she reported, a little breathlessly. "But I think the speed limit is still twenty-five into Everley." Mathilde was doing fifty.

"What good is a car from the Bayerische Motoren Werke if you can't let it go when you need it?" Mathilde asked, checking the post office parking lot for Kenny Hardy's speed-trap. The coast was clear. It was no surprise that they arrived at Waverly before Dr. Cavendish, and long, long before Hetty Delaney. Swan was in Labor and Delivery waiting for them.

"Two centimeters," announced the doctor, when he had performed his exam. "We have some time left."

"I called Spaulding from the car," reported Hetty. "She's going to call Bert, and Daniel said he'd sit in the waiting room and pretend to be the nervous father if you'd like. Boyd said not to worry, two weeks is nothing and it will probably be doing you a favor . . . you'll have a seven pounder rather than a nine and halfer."

"Not 'it,' Hetty—Luke. From now on—Luke," said Swan but a contraction began to build, and Hetty held her hand. "Breathe!" said Hetty.

"Hah hah hah hah hah hah . . . ."

So for the next seven hours, Swan and Hetty walked the road traveled by female *homo sapiens* for one hundred and fifty thousand years. At nine that evening, Lucius Bolington Moore was born. When the nurse brought the baby to her, Swan was shocked. Although he had her black hair, he was the image of Septimus Moore. Blue eyes, beautiful jaw, high forehead, even the same little furrow in his brow. He looked calm and a little put out, quizzical, not sure about the whole state of the world.

Swan loved him the instant she saw him, just like the books say. Hetty sat next to her and helped her position him at her breast, letting the baby come to Swan, not her to him. It felt a little odd for a few moments as he nosed around, then caught on and began to nurse in a strong, life-force-in-action kind of way. Swan had seen it in dozens of her foals over the years so she was not surprised by the awe it inspired.

"There," Hetty announced with satisfaction, as if she had invented the whole process for mother and child. "That wasn't so hard, was it?" Even she was floored by Luke's resemblance to his warrior father.

"I guess he might have Dad's ears," she said tentatively. "But there's no need for a blood test like on those tabloid TV shows. He's his father's, all right." She sighed. "Might have been easier if he looked more like a Bolington, or if he'd been a girl."

"Don't say that. Sam's done nothing wrong. He's a wonderful guy. It just wasn't right for us." Swan looked lovingly at her new son. "Luke." She addressed him by name for the first time. "I'm *glad* he's a boy. He'll be so close in age to Junior and Bud that he'll have them to grow up with, since he'll be an only child."

"Swan—" Hetty began gently, "you are very young still. You could meet someone else someday and have a family with him, if you wanted."

"I know, Hetts, I know. You all have been wonderful about this whole thing—the baby, I mean." Swan brightened. "Anyway, I just had this guy, let me enjoy him! The thought of going through all this ever again is not appealing."

Following Hetty's expert advice, Swan had the nurses take Luke back to the hospital nursery for a couple of hours at a time so she could nap in peace. She had no anxiety about being a mother, no worries about being up to the task. Luke immediately fell into a textbook-perfect, two-hour nursing cycle.

"Hetts," Swan asked, "did you e-mail Sam?"

"Yes, honeykins, I did." Hetty looked away.

"Did you send it just as I asked?"

"Yes. *Lucius Bolington Moore born May 18, 9 P.M. EDT. Seven pounds, nine ounces. All well.* And I attached the picture from the nursery."

Within a few hours, Spaulding arrived, bearing flowers from the Lombardinis as well as Bert, who planned to see her when she went home, and Daniel. Swan's workers at Belle Everley and High View sent peonies—their fragrance filled her room. Spring flowers from Oliver Lentz, paper whites from Jerusha Dutton, anemones from the Waverly Hunt in a trophy bowl. Calla lilies from the Waverly Garden Club. Finally, a huge spray of yellow roses with a card: *Thank you, my darling girl, Love always, Sam.*

Hetty made sure Swan took care of herself with the assurance of a veteran, and the three women had a good laugh at Swan's expense at her missing her last two natural childbirth classes.

"Maybe you can get a refund," joked Hetty, "but I do appreciate that you saved me two trips to that dreary rec center. Ugh."

Swan's cell phone buzzed in her purse on the chair. Hetty looked at the caller I.D.: England.

"Sam," she said, looking at Swan. She handed her the phone.

"Swannie? Is it true? Do we have our baby?" he asked, in a tone Swan had never heard before.

"Yes, he's here and he's so . . . beautiful." She looked at Hetty and Spaulding, who gracefully moved away, toward the door, almost as one person.

"Are you okay? You must be if you can talk, right?" he said. "I saw the picture. Is he really that dark-haired?"

"Yes, it's amazing. But in every other way he looks just like you. I mean *just* like you," she said awkwardly.

"Are you sure everything is okay? The doctor said you're okay and everything? Swan, was it . . . terrible?"

"I'm fine. Don't worry," she said reassuringly. "It was . . . tough . . . but it helped that he was on the smaller side. I wouldn't have wanted a ten pounder, that's for sure. And thanks for the roses; they're beautiful."

"Why was it early? Did you know and just not tell me? Did you miscalculate, or what?"

"He looks full-term or close to it. He tested fine on the Apgar—through the roof. He's not in the NIC-U or anything. It's like the old SCUD missile attacks: not an exact science. He's just a normal little baby with a perplexed look on his face."

Sam laughed with relief.

"He's probably wondering what the hell happened. Everything was going great in there, then suddenly—eviction," he said. "I'd be perplexed, too."

Just then, the nurse arrived with the little man himself.

"Sam, Sam, hold on! He's right here," Swan said. "I'm holding the phone next to him."

"Hi, son. Hi, little Luke," said Sam from far away. When Swan took the phone back, she could hear the tears in his voice.

"You've made me the happiest guy on earth," he said to her, and they cried together on the phone.

By the time she and the baby were pulling up to the front door of Belle Everley forty-eight hours later, Swan and Luke were a team. Spaulding had done the driving honors in Swan's SUV, newly outfitted with an infant car seat, since Hetty had to head home to her own boys. Mathilde, Edgar, and Eduardo were at the steps to the old house to greet the new heir to Belle Everley. Their eyes were filled with tears.

"What's this?" Swan rebuked them gently as she held Luke up for their inspection. "Tears of joy, I hope."

"Oh, Miss Swan, he's the spitting image of—," Mathilde sobbed. "After all you have been through, I just wish—"

"I know," Swan said. "This is a happy day. Don't worry, please. Everything is going to be great."

"How do you feel, Miss Swan?" Mathilde asked anxiously.

"Well, it was a tough few hours, but nothing I couldn't handle," Swan said, minimizing those six hours of agony. They were worried enough as it was.

"I think we all could handle a nice lunch," Spaulding suggested. Edgar and Eduardo reached for the diaper bags, overnight bag, flowers, cards, bottle bags—foot soldiers in the baby army. Luke was ensconced in his little seat while the adults ate a banquet *a la* Mathilde: chicken *a la* king, a large fresh fruit salad, homemade Parker House rolls, Lady Baltimore cake, and a flan.

"No wine for me, and no coffee or real tea," Swan sighed longingly as they toasted Luke. "I'm still eating for two, only now we have separate opinions on what I can consume."

Mathilde pulled apart the floral displays, mixing the blooms with fresh ones for the tables and entranceway, and made sure the wine continued to flow. Spaulding pulled out some of the amusing outfits available for an infant that had been sent as gifts, even though Swan hadn't had a chance to have her baby shower. They all laughed at one that mocked riding attire and another in the Belle Everley racing colors.

Then Bert and Daniel Spaulding arrived. Swan was pleased to see them both. They took turns holding Luke and, like anyone with eyes, had to remark on his resemblance to Sam.

"Not a bad thing," said Bert, "since his dad looks like a movie star."

"Well, his mother isn't hard on the eyes, either," countered Daniel.

"It doesn't matter who he looks like," said Spaulding, with authority, "or what his last name is. He's a Bolington, isn't he, Swan?"

"Yes, yes, he is," Swan said quietly. "He will always be a Bolington."

◆

After lunch they all went upstairs to watch Swan put Luke in his little bed in the nursery. She had painted the room a pale Maine blue, with milk chocolate trim. He was in the old Bolington crib, also painted brown and sealed in a baby-safe sealant, with Great-grandma Swan's rocking chair next to it. Hetty had given it up prematurely in honor of the newest baby in the family.

"Welcome home, little boy," Swan murmured as she placed him, swaddled, in his bed. Luke looked at her with wide, serious eyes that slowly drooped . . . closed.

Mathilde went on phone duty while the family had one last cup of coffee in the parlor. Thérèse Malloy, Kezia Hardaway, Jerusha Dutton, Patty Lombardini—everyone knew Swan was home and wanted to leave messages of congratulations.

"Major Moore," announced Mathilde, interrupting the group. Swan went into the entranceway.

"Be sure everyone has coffee, won't you, Mathilde?" she called over her shoulder. She hadn't spoken to Sam since that first early, early morning.

"You're home," he said, with relief.

"Yes, just got here a couple of hours ago. We're having lunch," she said. "Bert, Daniel, Spaulding—"

"God, I wish I was there," he said wistfully. "How does Luke like his new digs?"

"Not saying much yet," she replied cheerfully. "He's so funny. It's like he knows he got a novice mother, and he figures he'd better help me out. Eats, sleeps, pees, poops, by the book."

"That's my boy," Sam said, with satisfaction. "He and I discussed this on the phone; he's to keep things going the marine way til I get there."

"I see from the papers the big meeting is about to get underway," Swan said.

"That's why I'm glad I caught you," Sam said. "I'm going to be tied up pretty much twenty-four-seven for the next week. Maybe longer. Some sessions may be in Kabul, so don't get worked up if you hear anything about that before I talk to you again. You could always reach me in an emergency but otherwise—"

"We'll try to keep one from happening."

"When do you see the doctor?" Sam asked.

"We go to the pediatrician early next week," Swan said. "Of course, she has seen him in the hospital already. She says he's a few weeks away from boot camp but otherwise a fine specimen."

"Great. What about you?" Sam probed, solicitous as always. "Do you get looked at again?"

"Oh yes, a number of times, and in not very dignified ways, I'm afraid. I'll spare you the gory details."

"Swan, if I was there, I wouldn't let you get away with this, you know," he said, serious now. "I'd want to know everything, go to these appointments and things with you. You laugh about it, but I want to be sure everything's really okay. I don't think you would tell me if it wasn't, and I don't trust anyone in your family to tell me a damn thing."

"Don't be silly," she said. "I'm twenty-seven and I've been involved in strenuous physical activity every day of my life for the last fifteen years. I've stacked fifty-pound hay bales, ridden broncs, and for months had your telephone pole of a—" She stopped, conscious of her guests in the next room. "Anyway, having a seven pound baby in a brand new hospital with the excellent coaching of Hetty Delaney was not a big deal."

Sam sighed.

"You'd better be telling the truth," he said. "I don't just mean physically. I'll want to know if the Marriage in Heaven dream comes back, too. But I'll let you get back to your family. Where is our little guy right now?"

"Having a nap in his room," Swan said. "I'll send a picture to your e-mail address today or tomorrow. He is looking less prune-like today and his hair isn't standing on end quite as much. It will all fall out eventually, but if he takes after me, it will grow back, big time."

"Can't wait to see it. Swan . . . " he hesitated, "you are happy you had him now, aren't you? You aren't sorry you didn't—"

"No, of course I'm not sorry," she said very softly. "He's the most wonderful person in the world, the most wonderful ever—with maybe one exception."

◆

The next day Swan looked at the belly dancing tapes on the bedroom's DVD/flat screen set up. Never too soon to think about her figure, she thought. "Let's review the Turkish figure eight and the basic Egyptian step," began the voice over. When the phone rang downstairs, she waited to see if Mathilde was going to disturb her.

"Miss Townsend from California," the housekeeper called. Swan picked Luke up and took him with her.

"Ohmygod! Ohmygod!" Townsend said. "Swan, I just heard! Ohmygod!"

"Hi, honey," Swan chuckled. "Heard what—that Roisterous won the Kentuckian?"

"Oh, please! Sure! Make fun of me! Nobody called me or said anything until I talked to Uncle Dex, who said he'd heard it from Patty Lombardini! And now you are home already! Ohmygod!"

"Sorry to tease you." Suddenly Luke gave a little yap. Flagg had booped him in the pants with his nose as Swan held the baby in her arms.

"Is that him? Ohmygod!"

"Yes, he's right here," Swan said serenely.

"You poor thing! Was it bad? Does Sam know? What does he look like? Do you need me to come right away? I can if you do," Townsend babbled.

Swan took the last question first.

"Do you still want to come? It isn't going to be glamorous, you know, honey. Not like last year, when Fitch was galavanting us around and Sam was here." Swan kept her voice matter of fact, for the younger girl's sake. "It's . . . quiet. Are you sure you want to give up Mr. Holtzman?"

Townsend heaved a sigh.

"Swan, you won't believe what went on with him. It will take six weeks just to fill you in. Do you know what a 'three-way on the freeway' is?"

Swan tried not to react one way or another.

"I do not, and I suspect I'm glad I don't," she said. "The only three-way here involves folding disposable diapers in a triangle for a better fit."

"Sounds perfect. You know, Swan, I think of you almost like a sister," she ventured plaintively. "The sister I never had, who dated the dreamy older guy and—"

"Yes, darling, I feel the same way, but understand: if you come, you are going to be a glorified babysitter, with occasional nights out at the rescue squad fund-raiser on the arm of Deputy Kenny Hardy."

"I'll make my reservations tomorrow. I can't wait to see you and the baby: Luke, is it? Which room will be mine? I think I'll rent a car for the summer so I can do some errands, and maybe I can learn to ride and to cook from Mathilde like we tried . . . last year."

"I'm so glad you want to come! It will be wonderful to have a belle back in Waverly," Swan said, and she meant it.

Chapter 23

In just a few days, Townsend was at Belle Everley, hauling three enormous suitcases and sporting a new, heavily layered hair cut. She was otherwise unchanged from the tall, blonde, elegant girl of the previous summer. She settled into one of the upstairs guest rooms, one of two that had private baths other than the master, and filled her closets with Hollywood fashion wear. She cooed over Luke, tickling him, dressing him in funny outfits, like a floppy four-tailed velvet jester's cap in red, yellow, blue, and green, then doubling over with laughter at his stoic expression.

"If Sam saw that, I'm sorry to say he'd be forced to report you," Swan warned. "That is not an approved uniform of the United States Marine Corps, even though the 'Don't ask, don't tell' policy has been rescinded."

"Oh, you can handle Sam," Townsend said blithely. "Everybody says so."

"Darling," Swan said, sounding sisterly, "I'll have to ask you not to encourage the town gossip about Sam and me. You know the things people were saying last year about Fitch. It is hurtful. So please let me handle things with Sam in my own way. He'll be back mid-July, living in Waverly." It had been confirmed: Sam was coming back to Quantico after the conference rotation ended, and living at Fitch's—now his—hunt box. "He'll be sharing custody of Luke, so he'll be in and out of here all summer. That will be hard enough without us wondering if any of our . . . personal business . . . is getting around."

"Swan, I understand. I'm sorry. It all seems so romantic from the outside but, you're right, it must be very hard to have a little baby and no one—I mean, especially since Lukie-Luke is such a little cutie pie, aren't you, Tickle Me Lukie?" Townsend gave the baby a big raspberry kiss on his neck; Luke for his part was still trying to figure out the most glamorous baby sitter ever.

Swan smiled wanly.

"Well, I have the support of a wonderful family," she said, trying to brighten up for Townsend, "and Sam and I have every intention of working out an arrangement that will allow us to co-parent effectively."

"Oh, Swan," Townsend wailed, "how can you give him up to someone else? Won't that happen if you don't take him back?"

"Honey, I've got to take one step at a time," Swan said. "Now, I'm going to nurse this little marine and put him down for his nap. I'm expecting a visitor this afternoon, someone you will be hearing a great deal about, the developer Elijah Davenport. It would be great if you could let me speak to him in peace if Luke begins to fuss while he's here."

Swan still wasn't riding, but she couldn't ignore the other drama in her life. She welcomed Lige, in his usual elegant business suit, as he got out of the Mercedes. He'd been listening to show tunes on the CD player; Swan heard "Camelot" as he shut off the engine.

"Lige," she said, extending her hand. "How nice to see you." No more "Mr. Davenport."

"Miss Swan," said Lige cordially. "I wanted to pay my respects and offer my best wishes on your blessed event." He held a small box in his hand. "You look absolutely marvelous, a vision."

Swan smiled.

"Won't you come in and have some coffee?" she asked, showing him the way.

The parlor firebox was filled with peonies. Mathilde brought in the Swan family silver coffee service. It had been in constant use all week; Swan had greeted almost all of her close friends since she'd been home, and she now was down to entertaining folks like Lige Davenport. He did at least rate a fresh pecan cake, heavily iced and garnished with Carolina berries. Mathilde prepared three plates and two coffees—Swan had to make do with herbal tea. Lige made himself at home on the sofa.

"I brought a small gift for your young man, Miss Swan," he said, "I hope you don't find that presumptuous on my part."

"Not at all, I'm sure he will be most appreciative. In fact—" Swan looked up. "You can give it to him yourself." Townsend had appeared in the doorway with Luke in her arms. "Miss Townsend Brooke and Mr. Lucius Bolington Moore, Mr. Elijah Davenport."

Lige stood up and took in the view: Townsend in a black sleeveless turtleneck, ballet flats, and khaki slacks, with her hair pulled back in a pony tail, much like a tall, blonde version of Swan herself, holding the jolly baby, already fluffed up and noticeably sturdier in his first week of life.

Swan felt an almost palpable charge in the air. In that moment, any interest Elijah Davenport might have had in her transferred itself at the speed of light to her lovely guest. Townsend slid onto the settee and settled Luke on her lap, but as soon as the baby saw Swan he fussed until he was in his mother's arms. Townsend opened the little box on her behalf.

"Oh, Swan, look, what a beautiful thing," she cried. It was an embossed sterling silver baby's rattle from the Victorian era, meant to be admired as a treasure, not used. It was engraved *LBM.*

"How very thoughtful," Swan exclaimed, genuinely surprised. "How did you find one with the correct initials?"

"Waverly Antiques has lovely Victorian keepsakes. It was not engraved until two days ago, when Mrs. Osmond apprised me of his name," Lige said with a thin smile. "So although the young man is not its first owner, he will be its last." He turned gallantly to Townsend.

"They didn't make au pairs like you when I was growing up," he murmured. "You must love children very much to devote yourself to this activity when you could be at Virginia Beach or Rehobeth for the summer."

Townsend grimaced. "I've had plenty of opportunities at the 'beach' this past year—Malibu Beach, to be specific. I'm much happier here, among friends."

"Well said," smiled Lige. "But I don't believe you spent all of your time beach combing. My secretary will shoot me if I don't inquire about a certain television star of your rumored acquaintance. She wonders if he is as 'delicious' as he seems on TV—that is her exact word," Lige said solemnly.

"Absolutely," said Townsend with a mysterious smile. "Absolutely. More coffee, Mr. Davenport?"

Swan was impressed. The insecure teenager of the previous summer was now a polished young woman who knew when to keep her own counsel.

"Perhaps Miss Swan mentioned to you that I'm often in Waverly on business," continued Lige. "I'm wondering whether you'd like to join me for lunch at the Reynard some day? I'd promise to get you back to your employer in good time."

"I'd like that." Townsend smiled.

"Townsend is as much a houseguest as she is an au pair," Swan interjected. "Her time is her own; we could work around her schedule, couldn't we, Luke?" She jiggled the baby on her lap, bending her head so she could conceal her smile at this turn of events.

"I'll look forward to that, then," said Lige, his face twenty degrees warmer than it was when he arrived. Luke began to gurgle.

"I think it is snack time, Swan," Townsend said pointedly.

"I won't keep you," Lige said, standing up. "I hope we can keep in touch, Miss Swan, once you are ready to turn your attention to matters of business. I trust I don't speak out of turn when I offer my congratulations to Major Moore, as well as yourself. Luke is a beautiful child. You are very fortunate."

"Thank you for coming and for the lovely gift. Townsend, would you show Lige out?" Swan smiled, bouncing Luke gently in her arms. She heard the door close and a few minutes later, the diesel Mercedes purr to life. She opened her shirt and Luke made little smacking noises with his mouth, his eyes bright.

"Just like your father," Swan said, "always hungry." She knew Sam would be delighted to hear about Lige's sudden U-turn in the romance department.

"Another cup of herbal tea, Swan?" asked Townsend when she came back to the parlor. "I know it's a poor substitute for coffee."

"In a minute, miss, if you please," Swan said archly. Townsend sat down. "You work fast."

"He's no older than Fitch," Townsend countered, "although kind of old-fashioned. I liked him. Don't you?"

"We've had our issues, but nothing that should concern you," Swan said. "He's hugely successful in his business and not bad looking, although he is no Bernardo Holtzman." Swan smiled.

"And no Septimus Moore," chimed in Townsend. "But really good-looking men aren't always what they are cracked up to be. Anyway, it's only a lunch. I'll still have time for Deputy Hardy if he can tear himself away from the speed trap in Everley."

Swan smiled.

"Who knew your social life would be so active so soon? And get ready for another conquest; I think I heard Cousin Daniel's car; check for me, will you?" Swan buttoned up; Luke was happy and snoozy.

The front door opened before Townsend could comply. Flagg rose in anticipation from the corner behind the fireplace.

"Anybody home?" called Daniel. "I'm on my way home myself and wanted to report on the Stubbs thing." Daniel was elegantly dressed in an Italian suit, four-in-hand knotted silk tie, and Italian shoes.

"I'm glad you're here, Daniel. Did you have a chance to spend any time with Townsend last year at Christmas?" Swan couldn't remember whether Townsend and Daniel's paths had crossed at the hunt ball or not.

Daniel's face lit up, just like every man's when Townsend was in the vicinity.

"We didn't dance, but I remember a spectacular tulip dress in white," replied Daniel gallantly. "Hi, Miss T."

"Mr. Spaulding." Townsend smiled. She was doing that alot.

"Oh, God, do I look that old?" Daniel groaned, but returned her smile. "Daniel—please."

"You just missed one of our favorite people," Swan said, "Lige Davenport. He came to see Luke but he left absolutely stunned by Townsend's charms."

"An understandable reaction," said Daniel, checking the coffee pot's warmth, "but, Miss T., Swan and Davenport are in a bit of a struggle over a potential land deal, and we will have to count on your absolute discretion. You are a great beauty, but I wouldn't put it past him to 'romance' you a bit and take advantage of your proximity to Swan to learn of our strategy."

"Oh, Daniel," Swan said, "I don't think so. You should have seen him."

"Swan, I have seen him," Daniel said. "Miss T., do you take my point?"

"Yes," Townsend nodded, becoming serious.

Daniel smiled.

"Great," he said. "Now let me see the young gentleman here." He took Luke from Swan and dandled him a bit. "Swan, he weighs a ton . . . how much has he gained?"

"More than a pound. Then I think they lose a little before they start gaining again." Swan had been reassured by the pediatrician that all was well, but Luke was on his way to being a big boy.

"And how about you?" Daniel asked, looking at her critically. "Still feeling okay?"

"Yes, fine, still a bit tired, but—"

"She's lost twenty pounds," announced Townsend with authority. "She only gained thirty-four to begin with; having the baby early kept the weight gain way down."

"You're eating, aren't you?" Daniel asked, "because you are eating for two, still, or you should be. You aren't trying to get into those damn breeches this week, are you? Be sensible."

"I'm eating three meals a day," Swan replied, in her own defense.

"But Luke eats eleven times a day," said Townsend, sensibly.

"Miss T., why don't you and Mathilde make sure she gets a bowl of hearty soup or a sandwich or something in the afternoon?" suggested Daniel. "We're the only members of the family here in town; everyone else is counting on us to keep an eye on her. And now, do you mind taking Luke upstairs to finish his nap so Swan and I can talk a minute?"

"Not at all." Townsend reached for the baby, now in a deep doze. "Let's go, Lukie-Pookie," she crooned softly as she left the parlor.

"Well, well, *well*," said Daniel, exhaling meaningfully.

"You should have seen him." Swan kept her voice low. "She came in the room holding Luke and it was like, 'Yeah, I'm buying this whole package.'"

"Well, she's never going to win a MacArthur genius award," Daniel said, "but she is a beauty and seems to have a preference for older men."

"She's been here less than a week and is on the rebound from a big-time Hollywood romance," said Swan. "She can have a little fun and take the spotlight off me at the same time. What's not to like?"

"Nothing, just—well, you heard my concern. I wouldn't put anything past him."

Swan took that in.

"Now, the Wraggley's thing," Daniel said. "They would love to take the Stubbs for sale in the fall. That gives them time to alert potential buyers via their agents and advisors, promote it through the printed catalog, et cetera."

Swan looked at the little painting on the wall where it had hung for over one hundred years. It seemed as though it was gone already. That felt horrible.

"How much of a loss do you think I'd take if I paid three million for Stone Chimneys and sold it with an historic-property designation or some other protective restriction? Do you really think it would be fifty percent?" asked Swan, dreading the answer.

"Very likely. Even if you protected Stone Chimneys, Lige might just move on to another farm, and the impact on your farms could be the same. You can't buy every farm at potential risk."

"So what's our next move?"

"The Piedmont Preservation Trust, when you are up to it. Has Virgilia given you a price as you asked?"

"Not yet, but, then, I've been occupied."

"Of course, honeykins," Daniel set his mouth grimly. "You should be sitting here with your feet up, cuddling your newborn, not fretting over this bullshit."

"With my luck, what's the chance of that?"

"At least you have a healthy baby, Sam is out of harm's way, and your loan at Tidewater is almost guaranteed to be approved. With High View as collateral, it should be a slam dunk, but there is such a glut of real estate on the market, the last thing the bank wants is any more property, I'm afraid."

"I sent Judy to a stallion, so now we'll wait and see," Swan said. "I am so grateful for your help. I know it isn't what you signed up for when you moved into High View. We thought you'd be helping Persis get an appraisal before she sold the place, not trying to protect it for our family."

"If Fitch hadn't bequeathed High View to you, Lige could be buying it from Persis and trying to buy Stone Chimneys, too, and you'd have only the Stubbs or Mike to throw at the problem. And it gives me an opportunity to help the family. I put Spaulding, my parents, even your mom, through hell a few years ago, not once but twice. They expended plenty of emotional capital on my behalf. I'm happy to do something to pay them back," he said. He studied his manicured hands in his lap.

"Then, can I ask you why you dislike Sam so intensely?" Swan was hesitant. "It can't be some form of old . . . jealousy. You are so over our puppy love."

"Am I?" he smiled. He went to the coffee service and refilled his cup. "Sam and I are two diametrically opposed individuals. He views my substance abuse as a flaw that I should be able to overcome by sucking it the fuck up. I view him as a self-righteous, judgmental SOB who turns a blind eye to his own problems, whatever their cause, but who won't cut me an inch of slack. It's okay in Sam's world for him to beat me to a pulp because he can if he wants to, but it's not okay for me to succumb to my own temptations, even if doing so hurts only myself."

Then Daniel grinned.

"And I'm pissed that he gets a pass from you on everything. Like Fitch, I think it is the eugenics principle at work. You should hear some of the fantasies about him around town—from men and women, both."

Swan shuddered.

"I'm glad I haven't. You are the subject of plenty of wishful thinking yourself: I even thought you and Miss T. might end up an item. Her Hollywood glamour would be a perfect complement to your burnished European veneer."

"I don't think a KW network's cast-off is my cup of tea, honeykins," Daniel said gently.

"Don't be unkind." Swan was defensive. "She kept Fitch interested for quite a while, and they might have gotten back together eventually. There was just too great a difference in their ages. She is lovely and sweet and wants just to be a mommy."

"Don't kid yourself, Swan. There was never anyone for Fitch but you. Fitch hoped an IED somewhere had Sam's name on it and that Fitch would be there to pick up the pieces. Fitch didn't figure on the IED that had gotten *him* getting him for good, that's all."

Swan sighed.

"This is all too sad to think about now," she said. "I'd like to get back to my little man. But you'd better make an appointment for us with the PPT—I can't count on Miss T. to handle Lige Davenport all on her own."

When the mogul showed up in the Reynard Inn the following Friday noon with Townsend Brooke on his arm, the whole town seemed to stand still. Patty Lombardini seated them at the best table in the house, probably because Townsend was in a red Cheong-sam and black silk Miu Miu stilettos. Lige did his best to entertain Miss T. and seemed to be successful, especially after Dexter Gaylord appeared out of the blue to sit with them through dessert, giving his blessing to the couple.

Swan used Townsend's date as an opportunity to send Mathilde to the fresh fish market in Delafield and get back to her shimmy DVDs in private. She put Luke in his little crib and concentrated on the first few lessons, feeling like a complete fool. She tried not to be critical of her post-baby body; she sent Sam new pictures of Luke every two or three days via e-mail but, despite his pleas, she had withheld any of herself. They were no longer engaged, and she'd be seeing him in six weeks, in any case. Sam in Delafield, virtually down the road, sharing custody of Luke—the thought was still impossible to grasp.

She hadn't made a conscious decision to sleep with Sam three of the four times she'd seen him since their break up, but she'd be a fool to think he considered them "finished." She didn't know what *she* thought. She had tried to sort it out with Dr. Fisher.

"Are you more accepting of the risk you think you pose to Major Moore because of Luke, or are you beginning to think you aren't a risk to him, after all?" Dr. Fisher had asked, but Swan hadn't been able to answer, certainly not then.

Now she wondered if she could bear the thought of Sam's loss from "bad luck doomed love" because she had Luke. The possibility seemed a betrayal of Sam. But if it allowed him back into her life, she had no doubt Sam would approve of it. Luke was already Sam's in every possible way. He would be with her when his father was redeployed, whether Sam and Swan stayed together or not. Luke was Sam's great triumph over Swan's machinations. "You've got me in your life for the next eighteen years," he'd said. What he meant was, *you've got my child in your life forever.*

It still was unresolved. Dr. Fisher suggested the anti-anxiety meds, Sam's lower-risk deployment, and the decrease in the pregnancy hormone storm might also be helping her thinking. They'd have to wait for Sam's arrival in the neighborhood for evidence one way or the other.

◆

The Monday following his lunch with Townsend, Lige Davenport asked Swan to join him at the Reynard for dinner the next evening. Swan made sure she looked her best for her engagement—hair up in a chignon, a late-spring silk frock in citron yellow with a forgiving waistline; the acid green silk jacket she'd worn on the flight he'd missed to London, citrine earrings. When she arrived, he was waiting for her. Patty showed them to the same prime table.

"You must be becoming a regular here," Swan observed as she ordered the local-produce special, duck a l'orange on a bed of organic wild rice.

"I wanted to be sure I was still in your good graces," Lige said, somewhat humbly. "I'd heard an slur regarding my attention to Miss Brooke from some local wag, and I did not want you under any misapprehension." He fussed uncharacteristically with his napkin, even after their food arrived.

"What would that be?"

"That I was entertaining her out of some ulterior motive, to ingratiate myself enough to take advantage of her."

"I think Miss T. can take care of herself," Swan said serenely, "unless you plan to use force."

"That wasn't what I meant and you know it," he snapped defensively. Then he regrouped. "I meant, to take advantage of her proximity to elicit information regarding your designs on Stone Chimneys."

"Do I have designs on Stone Chimneys?" Swan asked, sounding like Dr. Fisher. "I thought we agreed I was too busy with my newborn to pursue that strategy."

Lige smiled bitterly.

"I've learned my lesson, Miss Bolington. I no longer make such facile assumptions about you or your activities. They do an injustice to you and make me look just more the fool." He motioned for more coffee. "And I underestimated Mr. Spaulding. He has apparently arranged for an enormous line of credit to be made available to you, for what reason I do not know.

"Then I put my own foot in it by bringing up my interest in Waverly at a 'meet and greet' with Senator Avery last week in the Pump Room." This was a watering hole on Capitol Hill. "Imagine my consternation when I discovered not only that you hadn't said anything to him, but that no one else had either." He motioned to Patty for the dessert trolley and chose a piece of chess pie from the cart; Swan shook her head with a smile.

Lige took a bite of pie. "I was able to see for myself his true distress at the thought of any change coming to Waverly. You see, Miss Swan, I have no need to conceal anything. Everything is completely out in the open, above board. I hope I don't have to stoop to hoodwinking widows, teenagers, and . . . new mothers." He smiled a genuine smile. "More tea?"

Daniel was impressed when Swan reported all of this the next evening. He had stopped by Belle Everley on his way home.

"He's going with the 'let it all hang out' strategy, sure he can just bull his way through his adversaries, now that he knows who they are." He swirled a Scotch, neat, in a heavy glass tumbler as he stared at the little Stubbs in the parlor. "He's going to play David to your Goliath, believe it or not, you, with your powerful supporters and 'big' bankroll."

"What do I do?"

"Well, I'd keep seeing him whenever he calls. Miss T., too, if she is of a mind to," he said. "Just keep everything friendly-like until Virgilia is ready to quote you a price. I'm annoyed he learned of your loan application; that pisses me off. Someone probably put two and two together.

"I've set up the appointment with the PPT in Warrenton. They will explain noise abatement proffers, traffic studies, air-quality issues, roadway upgrades, groundwater quality assessment, historic byway impact—that kind of thing."

"Wow."

"Let's not get ahead of ourselves. How's Master Luke?"

"Growing like a giant weed," Swan chuckled, glad to move on to a subject she knew something about. "He's having a snooze or I'd go get him for you to inspect. Miss T. is taking in a romcom with Mathilde in Waverly—we're just one big, estrogen-heavy family around here, Luke excluded, these days." Flagg abruptly sneezed as though asking to be included in the exemption.

"He's a super kid," Daniel said warmly. "I have to hand it to Sam—he passes on great genes in the looks department. Let's hope Luke inherited your temperament, though. Is the proud father still on track to come home next month?" It was June fourth.

"So far as I know," Swan replied cautiously. "He's moving into the hunt box immediately. He only has a few things—Harry Edwards can help him pack and unload in two hours."

"Do you think he'll be able to keep his nose out of our affairs, Swan? These negotiations with Davenport are going to be sensitive. Sensitive is not a word I associate with Six-Gun Sex God Sam."

"I thought you wanted him to pound Lige Davenport 'like a plant spike.'"

"We'll use him as our last resort," Daniel smiled dryly. "Seriously, he is über-protective. Can you control him? I saw what you did in the Crossroads when he came after me, but what about his less violent behavior?"

"I don't know," Swan said cautiously. "I may have to do whatever I have to do to reassure him that Lige is not a threat emotionally or financially to me, that you and I can handle things in that regard."

Daniel hesitated for a long moment.

"You mean, start sleeping with him again? Let him move back to Belle Everley? That kind of reassurance?"

It was Swan's turn to be silent.

"I don't know, Daniel. It's still six weeks away. We may know a lot more by the time Sam is in town. But we both agree I've got to do whatever I have to do to keep Lige out of Stone Chimneys."

Something in her tone made Daniel look at her intently.

"Swan, are you already sleeping with him? Did you sleep with him before he left? Is that how you got him to let us handle Davenport without him?"

Fortunately for Swan, Luke chose that moment to begin to yip and snorkle from the upstairs nursery. She jumped up as though she was a drowning woman grasping for a life preserver, Flagg right behind her.

"You're in luck," she said. She was the one in luck. "Luke is up. I'll get him for you to say 'hi' to."

The next morning Swan was on her way to the mare barn, with Luke in his baby carrier slung over her back, when the phone rang.

"Baby?"

"You're back in the U.K.," Swan said, sitting down in the entranceway chair. "Someone here wants to say 'hi.'" She pulled Luke around to her hip and held up the phone.

"Luke?" Sam said from far away. Like clockwork, Luke gurgled cheerfully. "Hi, baby. Hi, son." His voice was soft; Swan could hear it. "Your old man says 'hi.'"

"He knows you," she said, taking the phone back. "I mean it. You should see his face."

"Well, I'm glad someone remembers me," Sam teased cheerfully. "He looks great in the pictures. When am I going to see his mom, though?"

"We were on our way to the barn," Swan reported, ducking the question. "We working types have to get to the office; we can't trot the globe to some glamorous place like England or—"

"Shit pit Herat," Sam finished for her, disgust in his voice, "or Camp Leatherneck."

"At least no one shot at you." Swan kept the larger issue at the forefront.

"Yeah, well, there is that," he acknowledged. "Everything okay?"

"Yep. Townsend is a big help; Judy may actually be in foal for the first time ever, thanks to Daniel's thinking outside the box; Calimanco, ditto; the Delaneys are all flourishing—" She took a breath. "And Luke is fantastic."

"Sounds great," he said, longingly. "I can't wait til I'm there. Home."

Swan's heart twisted in her uneasily.

"That will be in about six weeks, still, right?"

"Yep. Then it is back to the old routine at Quantico."

They were silent for a long beat. The "old routine" had been their being in love and together.

"So, how's the real estate biz?" he asked, cutting the awkward silence.

"Daniel and I are meeting with the preservation trust early in the week."

"What about Davenport? Up your skirt yet?"

"Well, he's up to something, but it isn't my skirt," she parried. "How are you? Okay, dream-wise?"

"About the same. Listen, Harry Edwards wants my stuff out of his apartment. I don't blame him—he's deploying to Japan right after I get back. I'm taking possession of the hunt box as of now; could you get the key from Tabb Fletcher and let Harry pick it up from you? He'll move my stuff into my place this week."

"Sure—no problem." So it was coming that soon: Sam's arrival in Delafield. "I'll leave it with Mathilde in case I'm not home when he arrives. I'm out and about."

"You aren't overdoing, are you? You need your rest."

"Nope. Daniel is keeping his eye on me; so are Townsend and Mathilde. Eduardo and Edgar won't let me lift a finger yet, and if I go to High View, Emilio wants to carry me into the house himself. Spaulding doesn't even call to fuss at me, she's that sure I'm being watched over."

"I'd feel better if I saw you myself. Why don't you send me a picture? You must be up to something," he said.

"I want to lose a few more pounds. I still look like a beached whale."

"When I was in Kandahar, I used to spend the nights going over every inch of you in my mind, one night starting from your toes and the next starting from your beautiful hair. The good thing was that I got to some my favorite parts of you about the same time, no matter where I started. Don't make me start doing that again," he joked.

"I'll send you a picture before you come home." She was lying. "Luke is beginning to bounce in his backpack, and Edgar and Eduardo are waiting. We just want to check one of the mares, and Private Moore has a limited time frame in which he's on board with the program."

"Gotcha." He sounded lonely and regretful, but she didn't want to hear his concern for her. It was too painful. "I should be here for the time being, mopping up."

"Was this thing a success? Worth the effort I mean?" Swan had tried to follow the progress of the peace initiative in the local papers and online, but it seemed like a lot of the same old diplomatic blah blah blah from one day to the next.

"Don't know—beginning to think I don't care," he said abruptly. "What I do care about is Luke and his beautiful mom. I was thinking about our night at the farm—"

Swan's whole body flushed, and an electrical charge boomeranged through her.

"Amnesia," she said, "remember?"

"No. There was no amnesia for farm night, only Black Hart night and Scarab night." That was true. "And I've learned enough diplomacy to know there can be no retroactive institution of such a condition without agreement among all parties. And this party ain't agreein'.

"You are becoming too savvy for your own good," Swan complained. "I liked standard issue, killing-machine Major Moore better than this diplomatic, nuance-seeking Major Moore."

"When I come home you can choose which one you want, once you've seen both of them in the sack," Sam said, with a low chuckle. "Don't say it: you gotta go—that's what you always say when I say something to make those little warning bells go off in your head."

"Ummmm," she agreed.

"I'll talk to you soon; tell Edwards thanks when you see him. I love you, Ma."

Three days later, Harry Edwards showed up in a large panel van around lunch time. He was a dark-haired version of Septimus Moore, with wide shoulders and a slim waist—only twenty-eight to Sam's almost thirty-three and closer to six feet tall than six-four.

"Sam says thanks for doing this," Swan said as she handed him the key to the hunt box.

"No problem," said Edwards. He gave her a once-over he probably thought was subtle, as if that were possible for a marine.

"Care for some coffee, Captain?" Swan asked, turning on the charm. She had decided to pump him for information, and she wanted him relaxed enough to give her an answer. He hesitated.

"Harry," he corrected. "Maybe a quick cup." Mathilde materialized with a steaming mug and a huge piece of berry cobbler on a Staffordshire plate.

"I bet you don't get much home cooking," Swan said sweetly as he began to wolf down the dessert. "I have been wondering about something," she continued. "You know a lot of our back story, Sam's and mine. I've heard something happened in Kandahar just before he got sick, after the *Washington Sun* story. Sam won't tell me what it was about."

Harry looked trapped. He revisited the cobbler.

"I'd love to show you our son, if you'd like to see him for a minute," Swan chatted along. "I'd be very grateful if you'd fill me in. I'm still worried about Sam, even though we aren't together anymore. I think something happened that contributed to . . . trouble . . . between us."

"Uh, I don't know, Swan. I think if Sam wanted you to know what happened, he'd have told you," Harry said carefully.

"But you do know," Swan pressed. "Did it have anything to do with me?"

Suddenly Townsend, in a yellow sundress, appeared with Luke in her arms, and Edwards lost all ability to follow Swan's line of questioning. He bolted to his feet, almost upending his coffee mug.

Swan gave up.

"Captain Harry Edwards, Miss Townsend Brooke and Private Lucius Moore," she said, smiling.

Edwards stood dumbstruck as Townsend extended the hand she wasn't using to balance Luke on her hip.

"How do you do, Captain Edwards?" Townsend said, sweetly. He looked as though he was grateful for the reminder as to what his name was.

"Miss—" he began, then was lost.

"Brooke," she said helpfully.

He wrenched his eyes away.

"Wow, this is Sam's Luke?" he said, awestruck. The baby, in a blue onesie and wiggly bare toes, gazed at him calmly.

"The same," Swan said quietly.

"He looks just like him," Edwards said. "Hey, Private."

Swan's heart twisted in her. Harry was meeting Luke before his own father did.

Edwards's gaze returned to Townsend, but he was speechless. Swan came to the rescue.

"Miss T. is helping me with Luke for the summer," she began. "She goes to UCLA." More silence from the marine side.

"Sam says you are deploying soon," Swan prompted.

"Yeah, but at least it isn't back to the shit pit," he said contemptuously. "Oh, I beg your pardon, Miss—"

"T." Now Townsend was the one helping him along. "My nickname in Waverly these days."

"I leave the middle of next week," Edwards returned to his trance. "But I'm afraid I've got to get the van back to Quantico." He remembered his manners: "Thanks for the cobbler, Swan. It was great seeing you again.

"And nice to meet you, Miss T."

Swan walked with him to the front door. She resumed the charm offensive.

"Harry, please," she said, touching his arm. "I just want to know everything before Sam returns from England, and I don't want to ask him directly. We've broken up, and we need to establish a new relationship as parents to Luke. If you tell me, I promise I won't ever let him know where I heard about it. I don't even want him to know I know."

Harry looked torn. Swan walked him slowly to the van in the circular driveway. She saw Sam's weight equipment, his flat-screen TV, a few boxes, through the front window. When Harry opened the driver's side door, Swan slipped into the passenger side.

"I know there was something involving another officer in Kandahar," prompted Swan. "It must have been something terrible, since no one will tell me, not even my family, who know the story."

Harry caved with a sigh.

"Those officers you had dinner with in Oceanside—Browning and Aaronson? They ended up at the airfield," he began slowly. "They are sitting in the officers' mess, just a big fucking tent, really, and they get to talking about Sam, not realizing he's behind this row of plastic trash cans stacked between the tables, okay?

"So Browning's got his back to Sam. He says to some guy sitting with them, 'Yeah we met him in Oceanside, him and that pretty farm girl of his. Great tits and ass and loaded to boot. No wonder he put her fiancé in the lead vehicle in Rashad. Once Moore saw her picture, Lee was a dead man.'" Edwards looked down to avoid meeting Swan's eyes.

Swan thought she was going to be sick.

"I thought you guys were trained to throw off personal . . . insults . . . for unit cohesion," she said, stunned lifeless.

Harry didn't move.

"So Sam stands up from behind the bins and everybody begins to move away except Aaronson and some big captain sitting next to Sam—he grabs Sam's arms, but Sam's steaming. 'Say that to my face, you fucking coward,' Sam says to Browning.

"Browning says, 'Save it for the Mujh—it's no difference to me whose girl you fuck.' Aaronson's got Browning's back, so Sam figures it's two against one, which for Sam, at his size, is a fair fight," Harry smiled thinly. "Over go the trash bins. Sam mixes it up pretty good before the captain and some other guy separate them all. That's it.

"There's an inquiry, but Sam didn't want to get into who said what, blah blah blah, horseshit. He didn't want them to repeat it, either. You're right: no verbal insult is reason for physical contact between officers. Sam figures he's heading to the brig or a court martial, but then there were mass casualties—remember? Two incidents in two days. The shit hits the fan, the fix goes in somewhere, Sam gets some kind of slap, Browning and Aaronson apologize.

"There were witnesses, but they must have taken up for Sam or stonewalled for him. Maybe the brass found out your D.C. connections and no one wanted the stink to get back home when we are supporting our noble fighting troops, blah blah horseshit. I've heard Browning has taken a medical discharge, so maybe he was losing it then anyway."

"Well, it's ridiculous. Everyone knows I killed Hunt Lee, not Sam," Swan said calmly. "But even twelve thousand miles away, I can cause trouble for him. It just proves why he's better off without me."

"Sam is a great officer," Harry said softly. "He's a fucking beast out there." She nodded imperceptibly; he continued. "He and Lee were two halves of the same brain. Which is the way you need to be. Everybody said so. They kept everybody one hundred percent safe during the worst year of the war, met every objective. They were made for it—real fucking warriors. Sam would never, never have put Lee—or anyone—intentionally in harm's way. He was always thinking three moves ahead of the Republican Guard, and the brass, too. I never heard a whiff of the bullshit those officers were slinging, ever, and I would have."

Swan was pensive as she jumped down from the van.

"Thanks for that, Harry, I really appreciate it," Swan said. "I never knew. Hunt never said."

"Well, a lot of guys were like that, particularly early on. You didn't burden your family with your shit. You'd volunteered, you were a marine, you rocked and rolled." Harry sighed. "It's different now."

"Good luck, Harry. Stay safe." Swan smiled at him. "Come out and see us when you get back." She walked around the front of the van, up the steps, to the front door. The van's engine sprang to life.

"That was a long good-bye," Townsend said. "Do you think I could have Thursday afternoon to go into town? Lige want to show me the Vermeers. Remember, we talked about going to the National Gallery of Art last year, before Fitch passed away?"

"I remember."

"Well, Lige said he could do it. I don't feel like such a dumbbell around him. In fact, I know a few things he doesn't, for a change."

"Really?" Swan was reluctant to probe what those might be.

"Yes. We may go for a swim at Lige's club, too, afterwards."

"Well, that all sounds like fun." Swan hid a smile. "What did you think of Captain Edwards? He seemed quite taken with you."

Townsend shook her head dismissively.

"Oh, I'd never go out with a marine," she said, "not after seeing what you've been through. Not in a million years." Then she rose elegantly from her chair and left Swan and Luke alone.

Chapter 24

On Friday, Daniel and Swan met with the board of the PPT. It was made up of active environmentalists, retired lobbyists and government agency types, a lawyer or two, and people with close ties to wealthy old landowners in Taliaferro County. She had last met with them about protective easements for High View. They listened somberly to Swan's account of her interactions with Lige Davenport and his interest in Stone Chimneys as an executive retreat.

"'Executive retreat,'" snorted chairman Ezekiel Harrington over his bifocals. "That's supposed to engender visions of senior managers bonding over coffee or a think-tank get-together by the pond. It always turns into an office park two years later, when the developer makes the shocking discovery that the 'executive retreat' model is an economic sink hole."

"Swan is wondering whether buying Stone Chimneys makes sense to protect her other holdings and to safeguard the quality of life in Waverly," Daniel said, his dark eyes piercing his audience. His hands were quiet but strangely powerful for a slight man. "She might want to apply for a protective easement, then sell the property to a buyer who appreciates its historic and agricultural contribution to the county."

"Well that would be wonderful, wonderful, news," said Harrington, looking at Swan in amazement. "But it would only be a stopgap measure. Mr. Davenport has prove himself a voracious consumer of agricultural land, an implacable foe of resistance in the face of his plans. He could move on to another adjacent farm and do just as much damage to Miss Bolington's property. That is, unless she has the intention of buying any property at risk of Mr. Davenport's attention."

"No, much as I'd like to be in that position, I'm not," Swan said regretfully.

"We've heard the people who bought Paintbrush Farm are already unhappy with the country culture they've encountered here," Harrington went on grimly. "It isn't so close to Belle Everley, but a commercial center anyplace within five miles of Waverly is going to have an impact. We should be prepared for any eventuality."

"It will just go on and on, then," Swan said hopelessly, "just like he said. He'll never give up."

"If we make it costly for him, it is possible he will move on to some other jurisdiction," replied Harrington with contempt. "The only other option is to convince him to move to Waverly himself. Dogs don't shit and eat in the same place, if you will pardon the crude barnyard saying."

"Move here?" Swan asked, "you mean, to live? Not to develop?"

"Look at Dayton Hartwicke," said Harrington. "He paved over half of Northern Virginia in his time but he left his own county untouched and lived in rural splendor his whole life."

The PPT spent another hour describing some of the planning terms of art Daniel had mentioned to Swan before the meeting. She took it all in, but the delaying tactics sounded convoluted and expensive and were designed to frustrate developers less committed to their goals than was Elijah Davenport. She was disheartened: she had thought that wresting Stone Chimneys from Lige—at great cost and considerable risk to herself—was her problem. It now seemed almost incidental. When she walked back into her house after the meeting, she found Townsend holding Luke in one hand and the entranceway phone in the other.

"Lige wants to take me out again tomorrow—do you mind?" Townsend asked. "He just invited me."

"Not at all. Did you two have a good time yesterday?" Swan asked, taking Luke in her arms as Townsend hung up. "You got in so late last night, I didn't have a chance to get the whole story."

"The pictures were fantastic and Lige isn't a know-it-all like—" Townsend stopped just in time, "some people can be. We went swimming at his club, had a late dinner at the Reynard, then . . ." she shrugged, "back here."

"Sounds very nice," Swan said sincerely. She took Luke into the parlor, savoring the irony: her houseguest was dating the closest thing Swan had to an adversary in Taliaferro County. But Daniel was right: they all should see as much of Lige as they could. It would only benefit them in the long run.

For the first time since Luke came home, Spaulding Hexel buzzed through Everley on her way from D.C. to the Willow's Edge. Once Townsend had moved in, Spaulding had felt free to resume her social rounds further south. She dropped by the next day, looking cool and elegant in a pale yellow Chanel sheath, matching pumps and gloves.

"You'll get wrinkled," warned Swan, as her aunt reached for Luke at the front door.

"What are a few wrinkles when someone needs a big old hug?" Spaulding crooned into the baby's warm dark head. "We don't care about wrinkles when we are holding our handsome boy, do we?"

Swan led Spaulding and the baby into the parlor and, as if by magic, Mathilde materialized with a large pitcher of iced tea and some super thin butter cookies, hot from the oven.

"Miss Swan, won't you have a nice cup of peanut soup with that tea?" Mathilde wheedled, "or some little sandwiches?"

"Bring the sandwiches, why don't you?" Spaulding suggested. "I'm watching my figure, but Swannie needs to eat for two." She shared a look with the housekeeper, who read the high sign and departed.

"I've been to a lecture at the American University with Mrs. Avery," Spaulding continued. "'The Role of Native Peoples in Modern American Culture.' The senator gave the opening remarks. Oh, here are the sandwiches—they look tempting. Cucumber? Smithfield ham? Is that smoked salmon? Lovely." Spaulding took a plate and filled it for Swan, who was now holding Luke. "How much of the weight have you lost, Swan? All but ten pounds I hear; if so, that is too much too soon—even Hetty says so." Spaulding placed the smallest of the sandwiches on her glass sandwich plate. "See? I'm going to pig out on these and I need someone to join me. Mathilde, please take Luke upstairs so Swan can eat in peace."

Swan smiled.

"I'm eating, really," she said. She did take a bite of the Smithfield ham. "Lukie is hungry pretty much all of the time, and I'm worried about this Stone Chimneys thing. Can you believe it? Townsend is out with Lige Davenport right now."

"I'm beginning to hear he's smitten. First the Reynard, then the Vermeers—the only things left are the ring and the church."

"Oh, God, I hope not." Swan was alarmed. "She's just a kid. She's only known him a few weeks. She's still getting over her lost love."

Spaulding rolled her eyes.

"Sound like someone we know?" she said gently. "I'm so happy that you and Daniel are working through this Stone Chimneys problem together. I've always thought he had a brilliant mind and that he just needed a challenge, a task, to get him over his old . . . difficulties. With Fitch gone, you can't do this on your own, barely up from childbed."

"There's a phrase you don't here anymore. These days it's more like, 'barely back at the gym.'"

"Speaking of which . . . what do you hear from Sam?" Spaulding looked at another sandwich as though it were an archeological dig.

"He's looking forward to getting back," Swan said, cautiously. "He wants to see Luke."

"Yes, I'm sure he does, so much so that he has bought into the neighborhood. Won't that be awkward?"

"It isn't what I envisioned, but he has the right to see his child," Swan said. There was a hubbub at the door—Flagg bounded up and charged into the entranceway, barking.

"*Nein!*" Swan barked back, and the big black Shepherd returned, chastened, to flop at Swan's feet.

"It's just us," announced Townsend, finding Spaulding in mid-bite. Behind her was the burly developer himself. Swan calmly made the introductions.

"Miss Hexel, please give my regards to Senator Avery when next you see him," Lige said humbly.

"I'll be happy to do that; I just saw him two hours ago in the District. Mrs. Avery and I attended a most informative presentation, introduced by the senator."

Lige smiled weakly.

"It had to do with reverence for the land, you might say," Spaulding continued, her evisceration well underway, "how native peoples understood the great strength the land could give a community when it is treated respectfully, with posterity in mind."

"Lige understands that, don't you, Lige?" Swan rescued him, strictly for the sake of hospitality.

"Ummm," Spaulding said, skeptically.

"Swan, can we bring Lukie Palookie downstairs? I want Lige to see how he's learning to smile when you tickle his belly button," asked Townsend. She tore upstairs without waiting for an answer. Lige followed her with his eyes then wrenched his attention back to his hostess.

"Sandwich?" Swan asked. "They are small but tasty." She prepared a plate of the ladies' dainties and placed it in his fist. A china tea cup soon found its way into his other hand. Lige and Spaulding exchanged glares.

"Here he is! Here's Mr. Underpants Falling Down," announced Townsend, bringing the befuddled Luke back into the parlor only minutes after he had been deposited in the nursery crib upstairs. "Look, Miss Spaulding, look how's he's grown since you were here last!" Townsend was oblivious to everyone's bemused expressions: she was acting like the proud mama herself. But Luke wasn't buying it; glamorous though Miss T. might be—he wanted Swan again. He half squalled; that got Flagg up off his feet and the whole group surged around Swan until Luke was snuggled against her.

Spaulding rolled her eyes. "He's his father's, all right," she said drily, but she smiled at the baby nonetheless.

"Lige, hasn't he grown in the last week? Watch." Miss. T. reached for Luke's tiny exposed belly button and he yapped before she had even touched him.

"I'm not sure that's a smile, T.," Lige began, but she cut him off. "Oh yes it is, isn't it, Swan? What makes men think they know anything about babies?" She gave the developer a playful swat on his arm but smiled to soften the blow.

"I'm afraid I just came in to return Miss T.," Lige said, placing his now empty plate on the hunt board with the tea service. "I'll just say good-bye here." He nodded to the ladies. "Thank you for the refreshments."

"Thursday," reminded Townsend imperiously.

Lige smiled. "Yes."

"Out you go, then." Townsend towed him into the hallway. A silence evidenced a good-bye smooch in the doorway, then the door closed and Townsend returned.

"Maybe he'll let me hold him on my lap now," Townsend observed, and it took Swan and Spaulding a second to realize she meant Luke, not Lige. But Luke was on his way to snooze land in Swan's arms: better to leave well enough alone.

"Perhaps you could tell us your plans for the fall, Townsend, dear," said Spaulding, placing another sandwich on Swan's plate. "Swan, try the smoked salmon, and the cucumber, too. They are so small you can eat them one-handed."

"Well, I suppose I have to go back to UCLA, but I wish I didn't," Townsend sighed. "William and Mary was too demanding, but UCLA was not interesting; film and TV is more complicated than I thought it would be, more . . . technical." She sounded unhappy. "I could take a year off to model—an agency was interested a couple of months ago—or take some acting classes. Uncle Dex thinks there are lots of roles on the KW network that might suit me."

Swan and Spaulding shared a look.

"Well, of course, he should know," Spaulding said sagely. "I wish there was some way you could stay here to help Swan. She is going to need it if she is going to be—" Spaulding stopped herself before she said "running three farms." Instead she went with "campaigning horses up and down the coast."

That initiated a discussion of the three racers' prospects that quickly got beyond Spaulding and Townsend's ability to follow.

"Lige and I would love to see your horses race, Swan," Townsend said, enthusiastically, nonetheless. "Of course, I saw Punch and Judy at the steeplechases, but the big tracks sound exciting. Maybe we could go to Saratoga before I go back to L.A. in August."

Swan smiled.

"That might be possible if I had you to help with Luke," she said. "In fact, it is probably the only way I could do it, but you and Lige would want it as a social outing, not a babysitting job."

"Oh no! We couldn't leave Mr. Piecake behind! Lige could carry the stroller everywhere we wanted to go and the diaper bag, too—that's what we'd have him for! It would be fun!" It was hard for Spaulding and Swan to envision the mighty entrepreneur as a stroller donkey for three hot days in August, but who knew?

"Well, Luke will be three months old by then . . . ." Swan thought of Sam and the party they'd had watching Mike the previous July. "People take babies that age everywhere. But first we have to have an entry to make the trip worthwhile." She slid the discussion back to Mike and Linny, safer territory, until it was time for Spaulding to be on her way.

Chapter 25

The next week, Swan got the call she'd been waiting for.

"Swan, it's Virgilia." Her voice was modulated but held a little frisson. "I've decided upon a price for the farm. May I come by, perhaps today?"

Swan felt her own shudder of fear: this would be it.

"Of course, darling. Would it be more convenient if Daniel and I came to you?"

"You have a newborn and a million things to do while I'm . . . ." The older woman sighed lightly. "I've got the time. About five? Could Daniel be in Waverly by then?"

"Five will be fine." The afternoon dragged on in a way it seldom did on a busy farm. The chores, the calls, the decisions, all seemed to Swan to be made against the backdrop of the sword of Damocles. Even Luke's little ways couldn't distract her. If Virgilia wanted \$3.5 million, \$3.9 million—something completely out of the question, what would she do? What could she do? If she didn't pay it, she could look forward to years of legal wrangling and delay before the inevitable defeat. If she did pay it, she'd have a crushing mortgage payment to make, month after month—selling her best foals to make the payment, cannibalizing her breeding program for Stone Chimneys.

Or the Stubbs.

She showered and put on a sundress. It was already very warm, and cooling an old house like Belle Everley on a ninety-five degree day was a challenge, even though the battalion of heat pumps hidden in the side yard behind Virginia boxwoods churned relentlessly.

Daniel arrived from town, an uncharacteristic tension in his sharp-eyed, feral face. He poured iced tea from the big pitcher Mathilde had placed on the hunt board and drank the full glass almost in one gulp. He and Swan exchanged looks. There was nothing to be said until the figure was known. Swan had asked Townsend to stay with Luke upstairs until their business downstairs was finished; then they all could sit like neighbors no matter what the outcome, admire the baby, drink iced tea. When Virgilia drove up, they looked at each other one last time.

"I'm sorry to have made you wait so long," Virgilia said as she sat in the parlor, glass in hand. Daniel stood slouching against the fireplace, hip out, the tension in his body evident. "I just felt in fairness to everyone that I wanted to be methodical, clear-headed—you know. I've come up with a price, for you alone, Swan. I haven't listed the house with Tabb or anyone else, so the farm is not officially for sale, you understand. I, too, want to be able to sleep at night, not only because I'm financially secure but also because I've loved Waverly. If I sell to you, I can stay in the neighborhood, at least for the time being, and look my friends in the eye. If I sell to Lige, I might as well pack up today and move to Myrtle Beach."

Swan was trying not to interrupt, trying to read Virgilia's decision in this speech the way the accused tries to read the jurors' decision in their body language before their verdict is announced.

"So, all that being said," Virgilia looked at Swan, "I'll sell the whole three hundred and fifty-four acres, house, and buildings, for two point nine million, to you, Swan, non-contingent, cash sale, within the next sixty days."

Swan waited a moment.

"No other offers to be entertained?" she asked.

"No other offers to be entertained."

"Done." Swan looked at Daniel. He had a faint smile on his face.

Swan stood up and went to her neighbor. She gently reached out and shook her hand, formally, then gave her a hug.

"Congratulations to both of you . . . you especially," Daniel whispered to Swan on his way to the sideboard for more tea.

There was a brief discussion—a contract offer to buy, to be executed in the next twenty-four hours, settlement attorney, closing date, livestock disbursement—then Swan called for Townsend and Luke, and it was as if nothing of importance had happened at all. There was another round of shaking hands, air-kissing, gentle chucking of Luke's chinny chin, and Virgilia was gone, a wide smile of relief on her face.

"Well, well, well. You did it, Swan—you beat the mighty land titan," Daniel said, then remembered Townsend sitting opposite him. He turned to her, his face suddenly dark again. "Miss T., let Virgilia tell Lige, won't you? It is business between him and Virgilia."

"Of course. I want what's best for Swan and Mister Wiggly. Lige Davenport is nothing to me." Townsend tossed her head. "Anyway, there are a hundred farms around here for him to fool with."

Swan sat down, suddenly spent. Three farms. A huge mortgage. No guaranteed operating income. She looked at the Stubbs. Newmarket Heath. It was so beautiful. She hoped it could stay on the wall for another hundred years.

"Once you close, Swan, you will want to start the application for the easement. Decide which one you want to apply for, get the property inspected for its agriculture, historic, cultural value—"

That made Swan laugh. "I haven't even bought it yet, and you have it sold already."

"It will get you out from under the mortgage," Daniel observed wisely, "part of it, anyway. You will have to pay off the difference in the purchase price and the sale price, of course."

"Not today." Swan relaxed in her chair.

"Miss T., again—it is very important that Swan get her contract signed before Lige hears of this from you, although Virgilia may tell him today. She's pretty naïve. Swan, you should be prepared for Lige to come back at Virgilia to try to buy it at his price. He might go as high as three and a half million; he might promise some less noxious use in exchange." Daniel was contemptuous. "He may even try to convince you to flip it. In these times, a profit of half a million dollars in a week is pretty tempting—he may think you'll gamble on selling to him and still block him through the special exemption process."

But all Swan registered was that Stone Chimneys was hers. And safe. And costly.

The family's relief was unanimous. She made sure Daniel's harshest critics, Bert and Boyd, understood how important Daniel's help had been to her, and she was pleased to see how happy he was to hear their congratulations. Swan met Virgilia the next day to sign the contract offer to buy and put down an astronomical check as earnest money. The deed was done.

Once Swan was home, she settled in to nurse Luke. Townsend had gone out for a mid-day swim in the deep pond at High View when the knocker on the big old front door banged.

"Mr. Davenport," announced Mathilde, with Lige right behind her.

"My congratulations," he smiled stiffly. "I wouldn't be much of a businessman if I didn't at least ask if you'd entertain an offer on Stone Chimneys, with whatever restrictions you'd care to apply," he said, looking Swan in the eye. "An executive retreat is what I have in mind, not a shopping mall, or landfill, or nuclear waste storage facility, or whatever else you all fear."

"Mr. Davenport," Swan began: he wasn't "Lige" now, "I'm just a farmer, not a real estate speculator. I've a contract to buy a neighbor's farm, for farming. That's all I'm really interested in, other than Luke, who, as you can see, is beginning to want my particular attention. I'm afraid I'll have to see you out. But thank you for your interest."

Lige nodded his acquiescence.

"You are a remarkable woman," he said admiringly. "I would have liked to have had you as a neighbor."

After Swan put the baby down for his nap, she looked at the clock; it was seven P.M. in England. She called Sam and left a message: *I bought the farm—literally. Stone Chimneys is now mine—and Luke's.* As usual when she announced momentous news, he called back in the middle of the night, oh-dark thirty, U.K. time.

"Congratulations," Sam said. "You are overlord of half of Virginia now, right?"

"Hardly," she croaked, her voice still scratchy from sleep, "but no matter what else Lige Davenport does, nothing will be as bad as if he'd gotten Stone Chimneys. There is the little state park, the Mellon lands—almost anyplace else would have less impact if it fell into his hands."

"How are you going to pay for it all, Swan?" Sam stopped. "Cancel that: N.O.M.D.B."

"No, I'm happy to tell you—I don't know. That's what I'll have to work out after we go to settlement in eight weeks."

"I'll be back by then. Maybe I can even help you, if you need to drop ordnance on Davenport or direct sniper fire into the mortgage company, or something."

Swan chuckled.

"I'm not sure your highly valuable skill set is going to be immediately applicable to my current situation." She muffled her laugh. "I've got to be quiet so I don't wake Luke," she whispered. "He's up at one and four A.M., but if he hears I'm awake, he's going to want a snack, just on general principle."

"Copy that. A marine knows to hit the mess hall whenever it's open. You never know when you're going to get your next meal. I've lived my whole career that way."

"Uh-oh." Swan heard Luke snuffling. "That's him. Once he's up, he'll be up for the duration."

"Copy that. All okay?" Sam was wistful. "He looks fantastic in the photo you just sent."

"All okay. He'll be a month old next week."

"I'll see him by his two-month birthday, not that I'm counting the days, or anything. Why won't you let me see you? What's wrong?"

"Nothing, I'm just too vain for my own good. That's all."

"Swan—"

"Gotta go." She didn't want to tell him that sending him her picture was too much like something a fiancée would do. He hadn't figured it out on his own yet. Why rub his nose in it by telling him?

Luke burbled.

"Coming, Mr. Peanut!" Swan said softly.

"Swan—"

"Bye. Bye, Sam."

When word got out that Swan had bought Stone Chimneys, the rejoicing was so general that Swan felt sorry for Townsend. Swan felt she had to emphasize that it wasn't personal—any developer would have been demonized in Waverly—but Townsend seemed oblivious to the animosity directed against her suitor. She let Lige escort her to the Kennedy Center for an *Oklahoma!* revival and guide her on a tour of the Manassas National Battlefield Park. Daniel took her to the occasional movie in Waverly, just to make sure she was getting out and about as much as any twenty-year-old should, particularly when Lige was tied up with business dealings.

Fortunately, Belle Everley had a clearer challenge in the third week of June. Dress the Line and the mighty Oscar Mike were going to race at Belmont Park on the same race card. Swan couldn't attend in person; the Belle Everley and High View team would have to watch the live racing feed on the giant flat screen in the parlor. Linny was contesting a fillies and mares mile on the dirt; Mike a Grade I mile-and-a-quarter turf handicap for which he would be heavily favored. He had not raced since Doncaster but continued to train like a train. Oliver Lentz was true to his word: he was keeping his two top horses, Mike and Roisterous, on separate tracks until the fall.

◆

By mid-afternoon, they were gathered in the parlor when Lige Davenport's Mercedes was heard out front. Miss T. had invited him to join them, to whet his appetite for the possible trip to Saratoga in August.

Townsend brought him in for the race before Linny's, and Swan explained the rudimentaries —how fillies and mares typically raced only against each other in the States, while colt races were open to both sexes, how horses of either sex had their "best distances" from six-furlong sprints to mile-and-a-half distance races.

Mathilde had sandwiches, soft drinks, and a tureen of French vegetable soup on the hunt board, but every eye was on the paddock for Linny's race. Belmont was Tomás's home track; he smiled confidently as he was lifted into Linny's tack. She was a compact, serious three-year-old, unlike the rambunctious Mike, but she was shiny and fit and looked a match for her five rivals.

"What a beautiful horse, Miss Swan," breathed Lige, mesmerized by the pageantry and the grand post parade.

"Thanks, but wait til you see Mike . . . six to one on Linny." Swan watched the odds scroll by on the TV crawl. She'd placed bets through Oliver but had held her big money for Mike. Then the camera caught Tomás giving Oliver, in his signature trench coat, a beaming thumbs up.

"We should have bet more," Swan groaned nervously.

"It's bad luck to change so late," said Eduardo, clutching a small figure of the Madonna in his hands.

Lige looked puzzled.

"For luck," Swan explained, "and a safe trip."

"I have St. Christopher," chimed in Mathilde, holding her medal.

"I'm a Baptist," apologized Lige, and he sounded so sincerely regretful that Swan laughed out loud.

"I hope you like the clothes you're wearing, Lige," she teased. "If Linny or Mike wins, you will have to wear them every time you go to the track, no matter what the time of year."

All kidding stopped as the assistant starters began to load the horses in the starting gate.

"Okay, okay, okay," Swan began her chant as she saw Linny load like a veteran. The other fillies were in the starting gate in forty-five seconds.

"They'rrrrrre off," cried the Belmont race caller as the fillies launched themselves smoothly up the track. Tomás let the field settle in the first quarter mile and snugged Linny in, one lane out from the rail. Swan saw Linny fight him a bit—she wanted to run too soon and didn't take kindly to Tomás's hold. Fighting the jockey like that took valuable energy out of a horse; the sooner Linny settled, the better. Tomás let her out a little more, sooner than he wanted, but it was better than strong-arming her til she sulked.

"*Vámonos, vámonos, vámonos . . .*" Edgar and Eduardo muttered together.

"Jesus, Mary, and Joseph," Mathilde prayed, her eyes fixed. "Here they come!"

Sure enough, at the top of the homestretch, Linny's competition folded like a cheap umbrella. Tomás had little trouble keeping her clear of the tiring fillies around her and brought her home two lengths ahead of the number two horse.

That started the "jump up and down" in the parlor. Mathilde brought out champagne for everyone but Swan, Townsend, and Luke. Flagg barked for a minute or two until Swan shushed him, gently though, since it was a special occasion.

"Ohmygod, Swan!" Townsend said. "Unbelievable! That was so great!"

"Another win for The Fortress," said Swan. "Dad would have been so happy."

"It's a win for you, *señorita,*" Eduardo corrected her warmly.

The horse racing channel hosts suddenly began to talk about the "historic Virginia nursery, Belle Everley" as Oliver led Linny into the winner's circle. That got everyone shrieking so that Swan couldn't hear the rest of the commentary. They had barely settled down before the cameras caught Mike being walked into the saddling area at the beautiful old track.

"Let's see if Oliver Lentz can make it two for two for Miss Susannah Bolington today at Belmont," said one of the talking heads. That set everyone shouting in glee again. "Oscar Mike is coming off a Group One win in the William Lincoln, at Doncaster on the turf in March," another intoned. "He is named for Miss Bolington's fiancé, a marine sergeant who was killed in Iraq . . . ."

Everyone in the parlor went dead silent.

"Check that—I believe her fiancé is currently serving in Afghanistan. In any case, Oscar Mike is a multiple-Grade One winner rounding into form as a four-year-old, isn't he, Jerry?"

◆

After another moment of stunned silence, everyone started to laugh uncontrollably. Swan thought she was going to pass out: she sputtered, snorted, then gagged until she downed a soda from the sideboard. Luke began to wail until Swan picked him up to comfort him.

"Shush!" Swan finally choked out as they were loading Mike in the starting gate.

"Theyrrrrrrre off," sang the race caller, and Mike was the rocket express once again.

It was a cake walk.

After several hard-fought victories, Mike just cruised around Big Sandy. Anticlimactic, really: he galloped home four lengths in front of his nearest adversary. Tomás had all he could do to wrap him up safely beyond the finish line. Lige looked at Swan with stunned admiration.

She smiled: "One hundred thousand dollars to the winner." She didn't mention her ten thousand dollars in win tickets at four to one.

Mathilde, Edgar, Emilio, Javier, and Eduardo joined hands and hopped around in a circle until Mathilde fell down breathless on the loveseat. It was general mayhem, broken only by everyone watching the enormous black Oscar Mike prance into the winner's circle, just as his little sister had an hour before. Oliver and Sinjon both had to hold him for the winners' circle photograph. Then the phone in the hall way started ringing, but they let it go to voice-mail until they had all had another good laugh over the mangled observations of the racing journalists.

"'Oh, her fiancé is dead. No, he's alive,'" paraphrased Swan, shaking her head sadly. "This is the state of journalism today. Wait til they figure out that one's dead, one's alive, but none is her fiancé and nobody's in Afghanistan."

Swan convinced Lige and Townsend to stay for dinner. They were getting around to dessert about seven thirty when she got a call on her cell phone: Oliver Lentz.

"Swan, I'm afraid we've hit a bump in the road," he said calmly. "Linny came out of the race with some heat building in the near front knee."

"Bone chips, do you think?" Swan's heart sank.

"Could be. She was a little off on it when she got back to the barn cooling out. Of course, we will stay on top of things, get the films, and see what we've got. We'll be keeping her comfortable for now."

"I know you will, Oliver, I trust you completely." Swan was calm. Better Linny than Mike.

"It's a shame, she ran a lovely race, but Tomás thinks that little fight they had at the first turn—she may have wrenched the leg, twisting it a bit," Oliver said wistfully. "The good news is that Mike looks like a million dollars—ate his dinner, looking for more, is tucked in for the night. Hardly broke a sweat. Tomás said to tell you: he's a monster."

"Thanks, Oliver," Swan was philosophical. This was the racing game. Everyone knew it.

"Swan, we will want to think about getting to the Bloodhorse Cup in the fall. He's that good. We should think about a win-and-you're-in slot." Winners of some races were automatically entered in the biggest day of racing in the year, held in October or November at different tracks around the country.

"Yes, that will be wonderful," she said, still preoccupied with Linny. "Let me know what the films show." The knee injury might be the end of her career for Dress the Line. Swan loved the filly, but if she was injured with so few races under her belt, Swan was reluctant to keep her for herself. She had learned that hard lesson from her father. Other breeders didn't feel the same way; Linny would bring a good price based on her breeding alone. That would help with the Stone Chimneys purchase.

On the other hand, it might be an injury from which Linny could recover to race again the next year. She could come home and take all the time she needed to recuperate fully. It could go either way.

And Calimanco would be home soon. She was confirmed in foal to Cartouche and would be back from Kentucky by the end of the month, along with the remarkable Judy, who was in foal to the local stallion as a ten-year-old. Swan couldn't complain. If Judy delivered a healthy foal, she would be worth sending to a top stallion the next year. As a daughter of The Fortress, she had raced successfully on the dirt and over fences for years—that was the kind of mare Swan wanted to keep for the future. A "successful career girl who started a family in her forties" type.

All this was racing through her mind as she handed around pieces of Boston cream pie to Lige and Townsend. She even took a piece. She'd keep the news about Linny to herself for the time being.

"To the Belle Everley horses," Lige said, toasting Swan with his coffee cup.

"Yes, to the horses—and its people, too." Swan was happy.

The next morning, Swan told the whole story to Sam, in abbreviated form, including the possible injury to Linny. Her philosophical tone, and Mike's one hundred thousand dollars in prize money, reassured him, and she added a rollicking account of everybody dancing, including Luke and Flagg, without mentioning the fiancé bungling of the TV crew.

"You'll be back in a few weeks," she said.

"Hope so. I'm hearing rumblings that I may be delayed a bit—weeks, not months." He was stoic. "You know how they are."

"Do we ever," she said evenly. "Well, we'll be here, whenever—Luke and I."

◆

A few days later, Swan decided to go to Furnace Mountain. Linny and Oscar Mike were back from Belmont victorious, and Swan was ready to take Luke on his first little field trip, both to show him off and to see how they did on an outing together. She was happy to have Townsend as company, so she really could not complain when the ever-present Lige added himself to the party.

"It will be good practice for Saratoga," Townsend explained, always the pragmatist. "We might as well find out if he can be useful or not."

"I'm glad you are coming," Oliver Lentz said when he heard of Swan's plans. "The Templetons will be here to see Roisterous and their string. It will give us all a chance to chat."

Swan mulled that over as she packed the SUV for the trip to the training center. She hadn't been there since early December, when she sat in the service rest area trying to decide whether to continue on to the women's health center. It was a somber thought as she buckled Luke into his baby seat and looked into his deep blue eyes. It was like looking at Sam. She couldn't get over that.

"Come on, Swan, if we're going," urged Townsend impatiently from the seat next to Luke. "The Traveling Lukester is going to be ready to eat if we don't get there on time." Swan and Lige shared an indulgent smile but obeyed.

As she pulled into the training center's long drive, Swan mulled over her options. Films had revealed bone chips in Dress the Line's front knee, fragments that could be removed surgically. Was she more valuable as a good but not spectacular racehorse or as a broodmare in the breeding shed one year sooner? Would the bloodstock market be any better if she tried to sell Linny after another year of racing, assuming she returned to her pre-injury form? These questions had kept Swan relatively quiet on the trip from Waverly, but that had only allowed Lige and Townsend to converse almost as if Swan and Luke weren't even in the car. They sounded like a married couple, Swan noted with shock, much more so that she and Sam ever had. She realized they talked about Luke, mostly, Townsend's observations on his baby ways, his development, his opinions, met with respectful attention from her older suitor. When they parked at Oliver's barn complex, Swan still had not made any decision about Linny. The Templetons' big Mercedes sedan was already in front of the barn office.

"Swan, darling," smiled Grace Templeton from the barn aisle, as she heard the SUV doors slam closed. "This must be Miss Brooke and the famous Luke." She hugged Townsend, who had Luke in her arms. "Oh, Swan, what a wonderful little gentleman you've got here!"

"Thanks, Grace," Swan said modestly. "I'd like you to meet Elijah Davenport, a friend of Townsend's and . . . mine." How else to identify him?

"How do you do?" Lige held out his hand, his typical developer's grin tamped down. He knew class when he saw it.

"We've had quite a spring, haven't we, Swan?" said Grace, as they walked arm in arm down the center barn aisle. It was as immaculate as if it had been the Templetons' living room. "And not just Luke, here."

"Yes, the William Lincoln, the Kentuckian—," Swan agreed, with a big smile herself. But her eyes went to Linny and Mike, their beautiful heads hanging over the stall doors, next to Roisterous and his brother Devotee.

"And Calimanco to our champion Cartouche, don't forget." Grace led her husband to Swan's party for introductions all around. Oliver joined them from the barn office, calm, genial, courtly as always.

"The Dream Team," Swan joshed, "the Templetons, the Bolingtons, the Lentzes—"

"And the Moores," Oliver added mischievously. "That's what I hear our newest arrival goes by." He chucked Luke under his chin. "You look absolutely marvelous, Swan. He makes up for the fact that you couldn't join us at Belmont last week for your triumph."

Mike gave his usual ringing whinny in welcome to Swan as she touched his gleaming coat. Luke looked like his fingers had been stuck in an electrical socket at the sound and was about to wail, so Townsend jiggled him desperately in her arms, jollying him out of his terror. He forgot all about it and they all laughed. The laughter stopped, though, when they looked at Linny, her front leg wrapped like the leg of an expensive table, almost to the elbow.

"Well, you know our options, Swan," Oliver said soberly. "I asked Grace and Thurgood to join us today because they have a proposal for you."

"Townsend, why don't you and I take Luke back up front?" Lige offered instantly, alert to the preamble to financial dealings. "I saw a coffee machine in the office, and perhaps I can practice changing him under your expert supervision."

Swan cast him a look of appreciation. Once they were alone, Grace Templeton spoke up.

"Swan, you know we are on the lookout for mares for Cartouche, for ourselves. We so admire your breeding program at Belle Everley, your great eye in finding Calimanco, and Mike, of course, who we've come to adore as he and Roisterous have campaigned this year."

Swan was beginning to see where Grace was going.

"You and Thurgood and I are similar horsemen—breeding, racing our own, for the improvement of the breed, and for fun, too," she smiled a winning smile.

"We'd like to make an offer for Dress the Line, just as she stands, before her surgery, to race or be sent to Cartouche, whatever Oliver feels is best for her."

Swan felt the shock roll over her.

"A young race mare daughter of The Fortress, one of the last there will ever be, would be a wonderful addition to our program, and you know we will do right by her, no matter what happens," Grace continued, taking Swan's hand.

"You have Enfilade, Serve the Guns, the new filly at home, and I heard from Oliver that Judy is in foal, to carry on for The Fortress after she's gone," Thurgood spoke up. "We may send Cartouche's dam, Zenobia, to Mike when the time comes. We may even want to buy into your stallion syndicate—and perhaps you'll want Cartouche or Roisterous for Judy or Gunny next year. It all makes sense."

"What do you think, Swan?" Oliver asked gently.

"I'd be open to the idea," Swan said carefully. "I could think of no better home for her than with you and Grace, Thurgood."

"Well, that is wonderful," Thurgood said smoothly. "We'll let you and Oliver discuss the details. He is keen on keeping Linny in his string, but he knows we'd love to get her home to Pennsylvania."

Swan stood pensively, looking at Linny pulling at her bag of alfalfa outside her stall. Cash. Cash without the worry. Cash for Stone Chimneys. Cash.

"Well, it has been a wonderful spring," Swan repeated. "Do you plan to go to Saratoga in August? Roisterous is sure to find lots to his liking there. And Imperious—is he bound for the Hopeful at the Spa?" Swan and the Templetons chatted a bit longer. Swan looked at Oscar Mike, still her great hope. If he could be syndicated; if the Templetons came in with their wonderful mares, if Calimanco produced as good as she looked, if . . . if . . . if . . . .

"Let's talk, Swan," Oliver finally said. "I know young mothers have schedules."

"Of course! So sorry to keep you, darling," said Grace. "Perhaps your au pair will let us visit with Luke for a few minutes while you and Oliver chat."

Swan and Oliver headed toward the office. Lige, Townsend, and Luke plopped down on a bench in front of the barn complex, where Grace Templeton took the baby in her arms.

"So, Swan," Oliver said, "we can schedule the surgery immediately at York Equine Medical Center. If you decide to take her home or get another opinion, you can take her to Virginia University for the surgery and she'll be an hour from Belle Everley to recuperate. I'd love to have her back, but you know that only about twenty percent of racehorses post-surgery recover their previous form. It would be three months at home, then four to six months back in training, the way I do things.

"If you took her home, you know better than I what you could do—have the surgery in Virginia and breed her for a late May foal, not ideal but doable, particularly if you keep the foal for yourself." Oliver knew Swan had thought through all of this already.

"The Templetons want to convince you not to test the open market for Linny if you decide to retire her. I know your thinking, I think. You may not necessarily want Linny for yourself, due to this injury in her three-year-old year.

"Grace and Thurgood are offering four hundred and fifty thousand dollars for her as she stands. She might bring six hundred thousand dollars on the open market, or she might not. She could go on to win in handicap and stakes company as a four-year-old. It could happen. She'd be worth eight hundred thousand then. It just depends on whether you want to take the risk or if you want the Templetons to."

Swan was silent for a long minute.

"Five hundred thousand," she said.

"Done," said Oliver. They smiled, shook hands, hugged. Then Oliver opened the office door.

"Grace, Thurgood, you have a new filly," he smiled. Then everyone hugged all around.

Swan sat with Luke on the way back to Belle Everley, letting Townsend sit with Lige in the front of the SUV. She'd taken a few minutes in the office to nurse the baby privately before the trip home, and he was settling in for a snooze in his little car seat. What a trouper, Swan thought, but the warm June sun had helped, making him drowsy.

Lige and Townsend were wild with curiosity over the turn of events at Furnace Mountain, but Swan felt it best to keep Lige in the dark about the details. She had simply announced Linny's sale to the Templetons as though it had been a routine transaction. At the top of the Thoroughbred business, it was. Broodmares still sold at auction in excess of one million dollars when the right buyers were interested, but Swan wanted to sleep at night. She was happy Linny was going to the Templetons. Forging that bond would rebound to Belle Everley's credit . . . and cash. Cash. Cash.

Chapter 26

On the Fourth of July, Sam called. Two additional weeks had been tacked onto his deployment. He would not be home now until August l. However, he'd have six full months at Quantico once he was home. You took what you could get in wartime.

◆

Fifty-five days after Luke was born, Swan swung herself back into the saddle. Edgar was there to give her a leg up and to keep an eye on Luke in his stroller outside the round pen next to the barn. Swan had chosen Punch for her maiden voyage—although he was tall, he wasn't so wide as some of her other horses, and he had a smooth way of going. Most importantly, he was 100 percent obedient to her voice, so if her physical aids were rusty, her voice would command his absolute attention. She hadn't had the heart to shoehorn herself into breeches. She'd chosen jeans and half chaps, suede mini-leggings that buckled below the knee and covered the ankle and low paddock boot to provide comfort and security in the saddle. She walked, then trotted around the little corral. She wasn't as comfortable as she had ever been, but it wasn't painful either. She was rusty all right, but there was enough of her lifetime in the saddle to give her confidence. She had gentled Punch herself in this same pen years earlier. Her father had watched from his wheelchair, due to his stroke, his eyes on his darling child as she dropped herself into the saddle. Their rider at the time had been intimidated by Punch, had refused to back him for the first time, and rather than upset Everett over it, Swan had volunteered for the job. Punch had taken to her lessons as if he'd been having them all his life.

Swan smiled. She rose into a half seat, derrière out of the saddle, and motioned for the gate to be opened. She was not on the Oscar Mike rocket express this time, but on a ground-covering land machine perfectly attuned to her wishes. It felt wonderful to be back, wonderful to be the old Swan Bolington once again.

"Enough!" Edgar was shouting. But Swan wanted more. She impulsively pointed Punch to a wooden sided coop jump in the mare field, one designed to keep livestock confined but provide safe passage for mounted riders.

"*No mas*!" shouted Edgar, back up the road, but Swan felt too wonderful.

"Easy," she said to Punch, and he compressed his stride and took off like a bird, sailing over the fence with daylight to spare. *Oww.* Well, that hurt a bit still, but she was on, through the field, swinging around the mares at a respectful distance, circling, ready to approach the same jump out of the field. That got the foals running, and that got the mares running, and Punch had to abort his take-off at the last minute to avoid a multi-horse collision and re-approach the coop at a decreased rate of speed. Then they were over and out.

"*Madre mia*!" shouted Edgar. "*No mas*!"

Punch had totally saved her butt, big time. He looked the equine equivalent of relieved as she slowed his canter, letting him relax. They approached Edgar, who was grim-faced.

"Did you see us?" Swan shouted excitedly. "Did you see how he put on the brakes just before take-off and made his adjustment? What a great guy!"

She impulsively wheeled Punch toward the service road. Off they went, not at racehorse speed but with great powerful strides heading a half mile down the Belle Everley drive, toward the hard surface road, past the mares and foals, who were still worked up after her invasion of their field. The herd got going, and Swan saw Gunny, her foal at her heels, leading the mares and foals for the first time. The Fortress was a few strides behind with the filly Swan was calling Piquet, the old French military term for sentry. The dowager had ceded her alpha mare position in the herd—not willingly, but without a fight—a harbinger.

But she was flying herself, the real Swan Bolington, set free and airborne and truly happy. She was the luckiest girl in the world at that moment. She had the decency to compose her face when she finally trotted back toward Edgar and Luke. Edgar gave her a you-just-took-ten-years-off-my-life look but offered her a steady, gentle hand out of the tack from Punch's tall back.

"Ouch," Swan grimaced as she dropped to the ground, but it had been worth it.

"I'll want to do this tomorrow, too, Edgar, same time in the morning," she said, "and every day this week, *por favor, comprende*?"

"*Si, si, señorita,*" he said. He shook his head: "*Desmasiado pronto, antes de tiempo.*" *Too much, too soon.*

"Did you see Mommy?" Swan chirped to Luke, who was brightening up at her return. "Did you see Mommy ride like the wind?"

◆

Over the next few weeks, Swan moved toward her settlement date on Stone Chimneys, lost the last of her baby weight, and made a quick trip to Richmond to see Mike just miss repeating his previous year's win in the Virginia Derby. Unlike the previous year, Swan was on her own. Townsend and Lige Davenport wanted to take a few days to head to the Greenbrier Resort in White Sulfur Springs, so Townsend agreed to babysit Luke all day Saturday in exchange.

A powerful turf specialist from the United Kingdom had flown in for the race and, at five years old, had a year on Mike. They had battled to the wire but the English colt had put his neck and shoulders half a length in front.

"Only fair," Oliver said philosophically. "We poached the Edward Lincoln, they poached the Virginia Derby. The turnaround was too fast—only four weeks since his last race. He seemed to handle that Belmont field so easily. My fault entirely." Mike still made a handsome check at the end of the day. Swan always loved to see him, her magnificent boy. Slowly the month ticked down.

She continued practicing to the belly-dancing tapes. Hetty had given her three or four colorful harem costumes, bought via the Internet, as a joke, an early birthday present. Two bras were made of golden coins, one had fringe, another was covered in beads and embroidery. The hip-hugging skirts were long and diaphanous with slits to the girdle portion, so the dancer could move freely. Swan had been afraid even to model them, but Hetty was matter of fact. "You'll put them on sooner or later," she had predicted, "you'll get tired of the sweatpants and you'll want to dress up."

"If this is what is going on at your house, Hetty, I don't know if I can ever look Boyd in the face again," Swan had said, and she was serious.

◆

The day after the Virginia Derby, Swan was playing with Luke in the parlor. She had just come in from watching Edgar walk Enfilade around the farm roads. The two-year-old filly was learning that cooperating with humans under tack was not difficult or frightening but understandable and useful. Enfilade was more like her sister Linny than her brother Oscar Mike, but she was bigger, a little broader, more substantial than Linny had been at the same age. Swan hoped that would stand her in good stead.

She was mulling over Lady's future when a Dulles Airport taxi pulled up in the driveway. A tall, big boned woman with short-cropped blonde hair turning to grey disembarked. She was in a blue summer ValUmart business suit and inexpensive blue pumps and shoulder bag.

"Mrs. Rufus Hampstead," announced Mathilde from the doorway, with the visitor behind her.

Swan stood up. She put Luke in his bouncy seat and turned to greet her unexpected guest.

"Miss Bolington?" the woman asked tentatively. "Miss Susannah Bolington?" Her accent was Kentucky hill country.

Swan nodded, smiling, extending her hand.

"I'm Julia Hampstead. I believe you know my son," said the woman, "Septimus Moore."

Swan sat back down suddenly.

"Oh," she said.

She looked at the woman, who was still standing expressionless in front of her.

"Won't you sit down?" Swan said softly.

"Is everything all right, Miss Swan?" asked Mathilde, peeking into the parlor.

"Yes, Mathilde, thank you. May we have tea, please?" Swan heard the Dulles taxi idling in the driveway, "and would you ask Mrs. Hampstead's taxi to go on its way?" She raised her eyebrows at the woman; she nodded. Swan looked at her carefully; yes, there was a strong resemblance to Sam, the jaw, the blue eyes—maybe five-foot ten. She looked to be sixty—a hard-rode sixty, but she must have been lovely in her day.

"I found you through a friend of Sam's," said Mrs. Hampstead. "I hope you don't mind me coming without calling first. There was a special on South Texas Airlines, mid-week for sixty-nine dollars each way, and I thought, 'Now or never.' So I came."

"Not at all, Mrs. Hampstead," Swan said smoothly, "but I'm afraid Sam isn't here. He is overseas." She wondered if Sam wanted his mother to know even that much.

"Oh." The woman's eyes had gone to Luke, who was peering at her with mild interest as he bounced.

"You're Sam's wife?" she asked.

"No," Swan said evenly. "I broke off our engagement. But this is his son, Lucius—Luke. Moore."

"I'd heard there was going to be a baby."

Swan went to Luke and pulled him on to her lap.

"He looks just like Sam," she said by way of information. Mrs. Hampstead looked carefully. Surely she must see Luke's resemblance to her, too.

Mathilde brought the tea set to the sideboard and poured for Swan. She handed a Staffordshire cup to Swan's guest, another to Swan, then departed silently.

"I haven't seen Sam in many years," the woman said.

"So I understand." Sam's mother: Swan was still trying to process it.

"I was widowed when Sam was almost sixteen," Mrs. Hampstead began, looking intently at Luke. "Torquil Moore was a good man when I married him in Kentucky, but the drink took its toll. By the time he died, I'd had enough. I remarried and moved to Corpus Christi with Rufus to begin again while I could. Sad to say, Rufus went down the same road Torquil had. So I had my hands full there. I didn't want to . . . rope . . . Sam into the whole thing again or to ruin his life trying to help me with mine. I'd made my choice. It was mine to live with. Rufus died last December. It was probably just as well."

She sipped her tea. She looked like she could belt back a shot and a beer herself, but underneath, there was quality there. Sam said she'd been a teacher.

"How did you find me?" Swan asked.

"A friend of Sam's met up with him last year, a school friend."

Allorene Archer?

"How old is the baby?" His grandmother was looking at him keenly now.

"A little more than two months. He was born May eighteenth," Swan said.

"And you live here all alone? What about your parents?"

"Both dead, but I have family nearby," Swan replied."You are Luke's only living grandparent, by blood."

"So you and Sam are . . . finished?"

How to describe what they were?

"Not exactly. We are trying to . . . work . . . things out." That wasn't strictly true. "But he is Luke's father. He will be in his life." Swan didn't want to reveal too much, details Sam might not want his mother to know, such as his return in a matter of weeks. "Will you excuse me?" Swan stood up and headed to the door. She skipped up the stairs to the second floor and returned with the framed photo of her and Sam they had taken of themselves in Oceanside. She handed it to Mrs. Hampstead.

"This was taken last year when we were still . . . together," Swan said.

Her guest looked at it for a long time.

"I knew he was going to be big," she said, "He was six-foot one at fifteen. Looks like he grew. And filled out. My pa was six-foot four. He was big in the arms like that." She paused, still looking at the photograph. "So I guess he likes the military."

"Well enough," said Swan. "He's a major. He's been deployed to Iraq and Afghanistan, four tours already." She thought briefly about his formal marine portrait; it was upstairs, too. "Would you like to see him in uniform?"

Julia seemed lost in thought. She didn't answer Swan directly.

Instead she said, "What did he tell you about me?"

"He said you'd had a . . . difficult . . . time with his father." That was close to true.

"We both had," Mrs. Hampstead said, without emotion. "Torquil believed in 'Spare the rod, spoil the child.' Before he died, him and Sam mixed it up pretty good a number of times. Sam had had enough."

"What was he like as a little boy?" Swan asked, hungry suddenly for the information. She thought of Sam's reaction the night Mrs. Smith and her son fled to Belle Everley.

"Quiet, but no trouble—not for me." The woman looked at Swan carefully. "My, you are so pretty." She looked back at Luke. "I've got the cancer, so they say. Maybe a year. Woman's problems."

"Oh. Oh, I'm very sorry," Swan said, and she *was* very sorry. She suddenly had an idea. "Mathilde, will you please bring the digital camera?" she called into the kitchen. She turned to Mrs. Hampstead. "Would you like me to take a picture of Luke, or of you and Luke? I'll send it to you by computer." She wanted to show it to Sam, too.

The woman nodded. She took Luke softly in her arms, and the baby for his part was happy to be there. Swan stood next to her and had Mathilde take a picture of all three of them. Then she took one of just the grandmother and grandchild. Julia smiled in that one.

"Let me have your e-mail address," Swan said, but she saw uncertainty in the older woman's eyes.

"No. I mean, I don't have one right now, but why don't you give me yours and I'll get in touch with you?"

"Fine." Swan wrote it down and handed it to her. Something made her think that was not going to happen. "But in the meantime, I'll print out a copy for you to take with you." She went back upstairs to download the two photos; then she hit print. In two minutes she returned with the color copies.

"I should be going," the woman said, looking at the photos, then at her cheap watch.

"Won't you stay for dinner? I'd like you to, please."

"I got to get back on the last flight to Corpus tonight."

"I'll drive you back to Dulles, why don't I," offered Swan spontaneously.

"No. No, thank you, but maybe you can call me another taxi."

"Of course. More tea while you wait?"

They sat there in silence. Swan desperately tried to think of something to tell Sam's mother about him, something that would cheer and comfort her.

"Sam is a wonderful man," she said softly. "He's going to be a great dad. He hasn't seen Luke yet in person, but he talks to him on the phone and is very happy to have him. It's my fault we've broken up, he did nothing wrong. He is strong and loving and . . . honorable."

Mrs. Hampstead sat in silence, looking at Luke, now back in his bouncy chair, gibbering gently to himself, pressing a soft toy soldier in his mouth.

"Well, I wish you all well," she said.

"Won't you give me your address? I'll let Sam know your . . . situation. Maybe he can help you with a doctor, or something . . . ." Swan didn't want to say *money,* but that was what she was thinking.

"No, I don't think that would be a good idea," Mrs. Hampstead said. The Waverly taxi crunched the gravel in the driveway. She stood up. "Does Sam drink?" she asked suddenly.

"No—I mean, not to excess. A beer, or a beer and a shot now and then. Marines. But, no."

"Good." The woman picked up her purse. "It was nice to meet you, Miss Bolington—you and your little boy."

"Swan," Swan said, "everyone calls me Swan—my middle name—not Susannah."

"That's right pretty. I'm Julia."

The taxi gave a courteous little beep of the horn. Julia reached out her hand.

"Good-bye." She turned and showed herself to the front door. Swan followed.

"Please take this," Swan said.

She gave Julia the picture of her and Sam at Oceanside. She could always have another printed up to replace it, and it might be of some comfort to the ill woman when she got home, Swan thought. Julia put it in her purse.

Then Swan watched the taxi drive away.

"Who was that, Miss Swan?" asked Mathilde as she came in to remove the tea set.

"The major's mother," said Swan. "He hasn't seen her in many, many years. She's . . . not well."

"Oh, that's too bad. Will she be back when the major comes home?"

"I don't think so."

Swan went to the I-Mac upstairs and attached a photo to an e-mail to Sam. She thought the less drama, the better.

> *Your mother dropped by the farm unexpectedly. She was in town just for the day. She had heard about me through Allorene Archer, I think. She saw Luke and we had a nice chat. I didn't tell her anything except that you were out of the country. I took this photo of her and Luke. If you don't want to look at them, just delete them. She is not well.*
>
> *xxxxx Swan*

She hit *send.*

◆

The next day, she received a one-word e-mail from Sam: *Thanks.*

Then the date of Sam's return was just around the corner.

"I want to meet you at Andrews so you can see Luke," Swan had said, trying to keep her voice matter of fact.

"I'm not coming in to Andrews, it's Dulles this time. Why don't I get to Quantico from there myself, pick up the truck and the Fat Boy, and come out and see you? I'll get the Mercedes later. I'll only be a couple of minutes from the hunt box once I get to the farm; that should be about three P.M."

Swan was surprised and disappointed. "If that's what you want," she said, but then she couldn't help herself: "Don't you want to see us?"

"It's not like I'm coming off a line deployment; a couple more hours won't make a big difference and it will let us meet in comfort and privacy," he argued gently. "Luke will be happier—you won't have to haul him around and wait if we are late getting processed. It's going to be ninety-five degrees. You don't want to put him through that."

Swan had seemed to acknowledge his point.

"We'll see you when you arrive, then," she had said.

She had agreed not to bring Luke to Dulles because of the heat, but she did not intend to keep her word. She woke up that morning determined to take the baby to see his father as soon as Sam was back on U.S. soil. That was the least she could do for him. She made sure Belle Everley looked its best, with flowers everywhere and Mathilde poised to prepare one of Sam's favorite dinners, a steamship round of beef, with mashed parsley potatoes, fresh tomatoes, and peach shortcake. Swan was going to give him the welcome he should have gotten the year before. She checked with the airline. All on schedule.

She put on a short amethyst silk skirt, a cream silk shell that buttoned up the front, and amethyst silk slingback kitten heels. Not a baby-friendly outfit, but she was willing to sacrifice it for Sam's homecoming. She wore her hair down and loose, despite the heat, for Sam. She put Luke in denim overalls. She left his little arms bare. At the last minute, she drew a little water soluble tattoo on his baby shoulder, a heart with *Dad* inside it—Sam should get a kick out of that. She packed a diaper bag in case the flight was late. Thank God she didn't need heavy bottles of formula.

"We should be back before noon," Swan reminded Townsend. "Perhaps you'd like the afternoon off so Sam and I can get things . . . discussed . . . before he heads over to the hunt box."

"Of course, Swan, darling. I'll take a swim and have lunch at the Crossroads, or catch up with Lige at his club in Manassas," Townsend said gently. "Tell Sam I said, 'Welcome back.'"

It was less than an hour to Dulles; Swan checked the international flight three times along the way down the highway: on time. At least they'd be back to the farm before the worst of the heat of the day closed in on them or a thunderstorm caused delays in the air.

Swan parked the SUV in the short-term lot. She decided against the stroller; she put Luke in his little ergonomic sling on her chest, with his legs spread around her waist; not glamorous, but his favorite riding position and easiest to deal with if she needed to nurse him in the ladies room. He looked up at her, pink-cheeked in the heat and serious. She kissed the top of his warm, dark little head. Her heart twisted in her: Sam's little boy. She was finally going to show her baby to his father, to let him claim her gift to him.

Swan told herself to stop thinking that way. That was how a wife thought. She was not a wife. She was a single mother, a custodial parent. She'd better start acting like it. She briefly considered turning around and hotfooting it back to Belle Everley.

She walked through the endless terminal to the international flight gates. Sam's flight had just landed, she could see it on the *Arrivals* board. He was nowhere to be seen. There was no military expressway for individual soldiers returning from non-combat areas. Sam would be just like any other American returning from Great Britain. Swan was thankful he was so tall. He'd be impossible to miss, even among the milling international passengers and their luggage, piled on big metal carts. He would not see her first—he would not be looking for a small girl in pale silk, toting a sturdy dark-haired baby in a little sling. He'd be headed for the baggage claim, ready to hoist a one-hundred-pound duffle bag onto his shoulder and add two hard-sided suitcases to his briefcase. He'd be preoccupied, heading for the cab line, alone, as he had been so many times before.

Suddenly, her internal radar pinged and she turned. There he was, in his khaki and green service uniform—although he was turned away from her, his short-cropped blond hair, powerful neck and shoulders, dwarfing 95 percent of the people surrounding him. Swan stood absolutely still, willing the invisible tether linking them to spool itself out, through the football-field-long terminal, and wrap around him, at the chemical level, alerting him to her presence.

She should have worn a brighter color, she thought suddenly. She realized she would be intensely disappointed if he didn't turn on his own, seek her out, and come directly toward her. He made another quarter turn so his broad back was now facing her. He checked his watch, looked up at the *Arrivals* board as if determining how long he'd been held up in Customs.

Luke put his hand on Swan's chest, peeping a little, looking into her face. She looked down at him and smiled. That's why she missed the exact moment Sam's chemical radar pinged within him, announcing that against all logic, she was there, just a short distance away, after all that time apart. He turned 180 degrees, as if he'd heard her call out to him, and for a second she thought she must have, because his action was so abrupt.

An overloaded luggage cart passed in front of her at that second, blocking her view, and she moved a few feet to the side to establish eye contact with him. She needn't have worried. In the three seconds it took for the porter to trundle the cart away from her, Sam had begun a huge-strided half run. In another few seconds the people in the terminal must have put two and two together; a few started to watch him, first with alarm, then with sympathy. When Swan finally saw him, he was at the double quick and accelerating toward her. Then everyone along Sam's flight path was applauding the returning major as he weaved among the passengers and luggage toward her and his son. She stood rooted to the spot, but she turned Luke gently in the sling, so his father could see his baby's face as he approached them. Her face was flushed; now everyone was looking, pausing, trying to see what the applause was for, craning their necks to see if it was some V.I.P. being whisked through the terminal.

Swan's eyes met Sam's when he was ten strides away. She smiled. *Here we are,* her smile said, *here is your child, the child I bore for you while you were trying to win a war far away from us. The child I bore out of love for you.*

When he reached them and put his arms around her, gently, careful not to crush the little sling, everyone around them cheered. Swan flushed rose red and let Sam kiss her for a long, long moment. He turned briefly to acknowledge the crowd, then he looked down into the bright little face of his child for the first time. Suddenly they were no longer the center of attention. Sam knelt on the terminal floor to peer at the baby.

"Luke," he said, "hi there, buddy." Then he stood, unstrapping the Velcro tabs and lifting the baby, pulling the sling over Swan's head so he had Luke all to himself in his arms. He kissed him, all over his little warm head. He looked into the baby's eyes and saw his own face looking back at him.

"What did I tell you? He looks just like you," Swan said, smiling quietly, reluctant to intrude on the little world of father and son. Only then could Sam yank his eyes away and look at her. He used his free arm to pull her to him, lifting her off the ground, with an open-mouthed kiss that sent her blood boiling through her. She put her arms around him and pressed herself to him so he could feel her body through the thin warm silk. He was torn: looking at Luke, then looking at Swan, then back again.

"What are you doing here? I told you I'd come to the farm," he said, but she could see he was almost speechless with delight at the sight of them both. He held Luke in one arm and Swan in the other, barely letting her feet touch the ground, as they walked through the terminal.

"Look at this—look at this baby," he murmured into Luke's ear. "What a big, big boy you've turned out to be." This made Swan laugh: never had Luke looked so small as in the huge arms of his father. He looked like a tiny elf, not a child at all. Sam nuzzled his damp hair and neck, kissed them, and caught sight of the make-believe tattoo.

"Hey, where's he been?" he said, delighted all over again, "in a bar already?" He kissed the little marking, and that made the baby squeal so Sam could hear him for the first time.

"He was born that way," Swan teased. "He inherited it from his father, I guess."

"Thank you," Sam said, his eyes filling. "Thank you for coming." They stopped briefly at the baggage carousels and Sam quickly found his suitcases and duffle bag. Swan took Luke back in her arms and let Sam carry all of his gear, effortless for him. They were at the SUV in a few minutes. Swan buckled Luke in the back seat and as she turned, Sam caught her and kissed her, lifting her off the ground yet again.

"At ease, Major," she said, when she could talk. "We're Oscar Mike. The private here has a limited time frame in which he is able to travel without requiring a MRE—the original MRE, to be precise."

Sam laughed.

"Yes, ma'am," he said, sliding into the driver's side without a second thought. Swan smiled: men.

Sam had them on the Greenway in minutes, and they settled in for the hour-long drive back to Belle Everley. It was late morning, so traffic was light, a rarity in the Washington area. Sam kept checking his rearview mirror to look at Luke, who was happily gurgling, facing backward in his little car seat, looking in the mirror attached to the seat back.

"Swan, he is beautiful," he said humbly. "You made us a beautiful little kid. He is so much more beautiful than the pictures. He has your hair and forehead, don't you think?"

"No, neither does anyone else," she teased. "My hair, yes, perhaps, but the rest of him is a clone of you. I tried to tell everyone that the milkman was to blame, but no one believed me. Your DNA must be one hundred proof."

Sam looked at her, sitting next to him, half turned in her seat to look at Luke, trying to see the baby through Sam's eyes.

"You look fantastic," he said fervently. "You don't look any different from before . . . before you were pregnant . . . at all, except for—"

She chuckled.

"Yeah, except for these," she cupped her breasts gently. "Balloon girl."

"Fantastic," he said so sincerely that she laughed outright.

"Eyes on the road, there, marine. They are here to do a job, then they'll be gone. Government issue to be rendered obsolete when no longer of service."

They teased and chatted until they hit the hard surface road to Belle Everley. They were going to have lunch there, and Sam was going to pick up the truck, with the Harley on the trailer behind it; a buddy of Harry Edwards had brought it out earlier in the week, after all. The Mercedes was still at Quantico. Sam braked as they turned into the drive to take in the view of the house, drowsing in the mid-summer heat and the shade of the box elders surrounding it.

"When I'm gone, it's hard to believe this isn't someplace I've dreamed up," he said softly. "I'm sure I'm going to wake up in stink-hole Buena Vista, or shit pit Kandahar, or armpit Fallujah. Ninety percent of the time, I'm right."

"Not today."

"No, not today." He grinned.

Mathilde was at the door to greet them, Flagg barely containing himself with joy. Sam smiled. He hugged the big dog with his free arm, as Luke bounced in his grasp.

"Hey, buddy! Thanks for keeping an eye on things here."

"Welcome back, Major Moore," Mathilde said, very formally.

"Thank you, Mathilde. It is great to be back." Sam grinned at her.

"You should have seen the terminal, Mathilde," Swan said. "Everyone applauded and cheered."

"Yeah," Sam said dryly, "they cheered someone coming from London, not Fallujah or Helmand."

"Well, when you did come back from Helmand, there was no one to cheer because you were half-dead. You got the welcome you deserved then, just one year late."

"How do you like the new master, Major?" Mathilde asked softly, looking lovingly at the baby.

"Private Moore? He's pretty fantastic." Sam blew a raspberry on Luke's neck and the baby crowed.

"Do you want lunch right away, Miss Swan?" asked Mathilde.

"No, I'd better give Lukie his lunch first, if we want him to be cheerful company for us while we eat." Swan took Luke from Sam's arms and headed into the parlor. Sam trailed after them.

Luke began to make his little smacking noises with his lips, so sweet and funny, as she sat down, turning away from Sam as she did so, out of modesty. She gently opened her shirt and Luke began to suckle immediately, as he always did. She felt Sam's eyes on her. He might as well get used to it. She let Luke grab her finger, as if he was afraid she was going to go somewhere without him, and she looked into his solemn, contented, slightly cross-eyed-looking gaze with a bemused smile. She moved him to her other breast, and he was cheerful and cooperative, as always. When he was finished, she tidied her clothes and gave him a gentle pat-pat-pat against her shoulder until he hiccuped a little.

"That should hold him," she said, matter-of-factly. "Now we can eat."

Sam looked like he was waking from a trance.

"What's for lunch?" he asked, but his voice was unsteady.

"You'll see." They'd better start as they meant to go on.

Mathilde had outdone herself—a celebratory spread in honor of Sam's return and his introduction to Luke. Afterward, she served them coffee in the parlor and left them to themselves.

"I want to know everything," Sam said gently, "how it all went, really. Not the bullshit you were slinging on the phone." He was holding Luke in his arms, now, staring, staring. He let the baby hold his little finger, like a log in his grasp.

"I told you—it was tough but I got through it," Swan said. "A big part of pain is fear of the unknown, and you don't really have fear when you are giving birth. You know you are healthy and you know your baby is, too—at least, I did—you know the bad part is coming—you can kind of prepare. You know that, when it's over, you'll feel fine again and have a wonderful baby. So that all helps. And Hetty was great. When I . . . flagged . . . she was there to keep me going instead of feeling sorry for myself. We Bolingtons are tougher than we look."

Swan looked at Luke. "I am sorry you didn't see him smile for the first time and kick and wave his arms. Townsend thinks he knows when he's about to be tickled, but I think he's still too young yet. We think he's capable of anything, no matter what the development milestone chart says. We've been going by his due date, not his birth date, but he seems to be closer in development to a three month old than a two month old."

"She's been a help, then?" Sam asked. "I thought you said she was being squired around the county by Davenport—it sounded like full time."

"No, she's been great. I don't know what I'll do when she goes. It doesn't sound like UCLA is in her future, maybe modeling or some other L.A.-based enterprise. You don't seem to have to actually do anything to earn your living there if you are tall, blonde, and beautiful."

Sam looked at her for a long, quiet moment.

"Swan, I meant what I said in Doncaster. We can take things slowly, as slowly as you want. I got carried away this morning, seeing you at Dulles. If you want us to act like parents and only parents, at least for now, I can do that," he said. "It's not the way I want things, but I don't want to be another problem for you to have to find away around all the time. I don't think that would be good for us or for Luke."

Swan looked at him cautiously. He seemed to mean it.

"That would take the pressure off. Thanks."

Sam cleared his throat.

"So, how do you want to handle things? Visitation, I mean?"

"Well, first, I'd like us not to call it visitation, I think," Swan said, by way of acknowledgment of him meeting her halfway. "Let's just call it 'your day' or 'my day.' You're on official leave, right?"

"For the next month. Then I'm back at Quantico full-time."

"Well, why don't you take him Tuesdays and Thursdays overnight this month, and one day on the weekends? I'll give you bottles to get him through his days with you; he will be fine with that, no big deal." It sounded like a good plan as she said it. "He eats a lot."

"I'm getting the nursery set up in the next day or so at the hunt box—that's my first priority." Sam was the major with a mission. "Let's introduce me to the pediatrician, just in case I need to take him if you aren't available for some reason. Why don't you walk me through his routine today, so I can be sure to get it all straight, then I'll head over to the hunt box and secure everything there."

"We could have the first hand off on Tuesday. That will let me schedule some things—going to Furnace Mountain or Tidewater Commercial for the paperwork on Stone Chimneys. I'm going to let Virgilia stay put until she finds a place in Waverly or Delafield. She's going to leave a lot of her stuff—it will make it easier to rent to a farm tenant if it's furnished." Swan was beginning to think this all might work.

"Sounds good. Now, when do I see James?" Swan stowed Luke in his stroller and, tailed by Flagg, they made their way to the barn. Sam joshed Eduardo and Edgar as he always did, *en español.* He looked at James and grinned.

"Finally—a horse that makes me look average size," he said admiringly. "I've only ridden quarter horses. I drag my feet on the ground when I'm on them."

"*No mas, no problemo,*" grinned Edgar . He said nothing about Swan being run away with.

"We'll start you on a few lessons," Swan said, "on the days you are here for Luke. You are already fit. You're really top-heavy, like a lot of men who work out, but I won't let that leaning-forward habit develop. I'll be brutal."

Now Sam grinned. "I can't wait." Edgar and Eduardo hid smiles.

"If they hadn't been there, I'd have said 'Look who's talking,' when you made that 'top-heavy' crack," Sam said, as he pushed the stroller up the hill to the house. "Are the people here the only ones happy to see me back? What about your folks? Are they happy with Luke, or at least not furious about him?"

"Oh, they love him—adore him, really. And they support me, completely."

"What about me living out here? I know Daniel is bullshit about it, and I'm hoping Luke isn't bearing the brunt of everyone's displeasure."

"They would never let that happen. I wouldn't let that happen, not to Luke."

"Okay, then." They were at the house.

"He needs his nap," Swan said as Luke began to fade. "He loves a bell sound. Peek-a-boo, that kind of thing. He can roll over one way, but not the other. I play a little light classical music if he cries, but easy listening would work, too." She smiled a little. "None of that hard rockin' stuff you like, though. He sleeps about fifteen hours a day—eats eleven times a day. Poops . . . well, let that be a surprise for you."

"It isn't going to freak you out if you are away from him overnight?"

"Not if he's with you."

"So. This is Day One," Sam said. She knew what he meant.

"Yes. Day One."

Sam stayed through dinner, talking about the mission, what he could divulge about it, anyway.

"What got things turned around in Iraq was that we finally got wise and bought ourselves clans of Sunni thugs to keep the peace with the Shias. We're going to do the same thing in Afghanistan, only we haven't yet found our clan of thugs," he said bitterly, "but we will. No one can resist power and cash, even drug lords."

Then his dark face brightened, with some effort. He talked about some of the places he'd been in Great Britain, but mostly he wanted to hear about Luke, hold Luke when he was awake, familiarize himself with the feel of his baby skin, his scent, his little sounds. At Sam's insistence he had put the baby carrier on the dining room table while they ate so he could watch the little expressions cross Luke's face.

"I missed your birthday," Sam said to Swan as he was preparing to leave. "I brought you something, a few days late. Nothing expensive, just something I found in an antiques shop."

Swan opened the box. Inside was an eighteen-carat-gold hair comb from the Edwardian era, heavy and art nouveau in style, with five long teeth.

"The dealer said only someone with a lot of hair could wear it," Sam said quietly. "Not many women these days have hair long enough and thick enough to hold the comb, I guess. I knew that would not be a problem for you."

"It's beautiful," Swan breathed. "I have nothing for you, nothing for you to open, I mean. But I did order you something." Sam's thirty-third birthday was the next day. "The blue marine boat cloak with the scarlet lining. I know you don't have one, and it can get cold here in the winter, much colder than Texas or Oceanside."

"Wow. They are rare—and all handmade." He was impressed. "Thanks."

"Do you want a party?"

"No—nothing. Just to get into a routine here. Back home."

She nodded.

"All right then."

He got up to go, reluctantly. She could feel how much he wanted to stay, to climb up the stairs with her with their baby in his arms, into the bed he still thought of as their bed. She wanted him to stay. She wanted it as much as she'd ever wanted anything. But she would let him go.

"I'll see you Tuesday."

"Yes. Sam, I'm very glad you are back. Very glad." When he bent down to kiss her, she let him see how much she wanted him. But he was going to go, to show her he could be patient. And go he did.

CHAPTER 27

Swan rode Punch the next morning and spent the rest of the day fielding endless calls about Sam's return. She told the same story to everyone: they were going to share parenting, it would be cordial, she hadn't changed her mind, he hadn't changed it for her. Townsend was the most enthusiastic about the plan. She said she thought it was "enlightened."

Swan expected the Tuesday hand-off to be uneventful. Sam arrived mid-morning in the F-250, spraying gravel from the driveway onto the lawn. When he stormed into the house, he found Swan sitting in the parlor in shorts and a soft linen short-sleeved shirt, waiting for him. He detonated.

"You pumped poor Edwards for some shit about me in Kandahar! He's a great kid, but he's no match for your devious little brain! He said you trotted out Townsend Brooke—Luke, too. What a piece of work you are."

Swan let him blow off steam—pacing around the parlor, into the dining room, back through the entranceway to the parlor and back again.

"I'd heard something last year, then you got sick and I never heard about it again," she explained calmly. "No one would tell me anything. I thought, with you coming back, here in town, us trying to establish a new relationship—"

"Don't give me your usual song and dance, please—I've had a bellyful of it!" he raged. "We aren't 'trying to establish a new relationship!' I'm trying to salvage our old relationship, and you give a pretty good impression of wanting to do the same when we're in bed, kiddo."

He finally sat down, but his whole body was tense, caged. It was an intimidating sight.

"So, are you happy now? Happy to hear the officers we had that nice dinner with accuse me of killing Hunt Lee so I could fuck you myself? Why can't you leave well enough alone—ever?"

Swan could see that under the anger he was worried sick. A fellow officer had all but called him a murderer, and he was afraid that Swan would take the calumny as another nail in the coffin of "bad luck doomed love."

"I didn't want to ask you about it," she explained, repentant. "I thought it must be terrible if Bert and everyone else didn't want to tell me. My imagination was working overtime, and knowing you were about to ship home, yes, I did ask Harry to tell me. He didn't want to, so don't be mad at him, please. I had to drag it out of him."

Sam looked at her, calculating.

"That's probably close enough to the truth—for you. Edwards felt guilty, so when I called him to pick up the Mercedes, he gave it up. He thought he owed me.

"I shouldn't blame him—you're right. You always get what you want from men. We should just send you into the Korengal as some terrorist leader's new wife and let you poison him or sell him out in your own well-meaning way. It would save a lot of heartache all the way around."

"Well, it doesn't matter now, does it?" Swan had had enough. "I thought you came for Luke. I assume you still plan to keep him overnight."

"Yes, if that is all right with you." He was beginning to come around. Swan headed up the stairs. She returned with the baby, who was cheerful and willing to go with whatever plan his parents had for him.

"He's nursing every two hours," Swan reminded Sam as she sat down to straighten Luke's booties.

He shrugged. "You can come with us."

She ignored this. "Let me feed him before you take him." She waited for Sam to get up and give her some privacy. When he didn't, she said, "I'll bring him out to you in the truck when he's finished." Still he sat. She considered getting up herself and going to the dining room. *I'm not going to be moved around in my own house, no matter how angry he is,* she thought. The baby would cool him down. She opened her shirt and Luke jiggled back and forth in anticipation.

She watched Luke as she always did, ignoring Sam. When Luke was finished, she buttoned her shirt matter-of-factly. Then she gave him another soft, effective patty-pat-pat over her shoulder until he burped.

Sam reached for the diaper bag, the bottle bag, the overnight bag, the toy bag.

"I'm sure he'd rather have this directly from the tap," he said sardonically as he stowed the bottles of milk under his arm.

"He'll be fine," she said confidently, and she believed it. "Just burp him like I did just now." Then she smiled. "And no 'giddy-up' on your knees afterward, no matter how much he chuckles, unless you're a big fan of spit up."

"Aye, aye, ma'am," Sam said and he put a cotton cap on Luke's still fuzzy dark head. "Come on, private." Swan's heart twisted at Sam's use of the little nickname: probably raging hormones. Having Sam there while she nursed the baby had been a mistake.

"You have my cell phone number. I'll bring him back tomorrow morning. We're just going to do an errand or two and hang out at my place," Sam said casually.

Swan saw Mathilde peek in from the hallway; she saw her look of pity and concern as Sam bent down to add the baby to his armful of stuff.

"Have a nice day," Swan said, not looking at either of them. She brushed her lips on Luke's head as they left the room. Her innards contracted: it felt like kissing Sam himself.

"I'm going to get on a couple of horses," she called. "When you come tomorrow, I'll give you a riding lesson."

When she came back to the house, it seemed empty. Mathilde bustled around, fixing a nice lunch. By afternoon, Swan felt the effects of missing two feedings and she pumped to add to her supply of bottled milk. She told herself it was just as if she had gone to Furnace Mountain for the day; she had missed feedings before. Both Spaulding and Hetty called, feigning casual interest in Sam's first paternal overnight with Luke. Swan could hear their concern.

"They'll be fine; he's only ten minutes from here," she said. "If he needs anything, he'll call me. It's not like he's the first man to care for a newborn."

Swan slept well, although she woke again to pump and fretted briefly at not hearing Luke's chirping and peeping from the nursery. She looked out the front window at the mare fields, mist rising in the early dawn, remembering the first tumultuous night she and Sam had spent together. What was done was done, but she had a little cry nonetheless. She was showered and dressed and heading downstairs for breakfast when she heard Sam's F-250 in the driveway.

Luke was sunny and cheerful, a good sport about everything. He pressed his little hands against Sam's mountainous shoulder with complete confidence when Sam handed him to Swan, and she suddenly wondered if Sam had actually held the baby all night while he slept. She wouldn't have put it past him. Swan took Luke in her arms and nursed him immediately in the parlor. No need to make a big deal about it, she reminded herself, but she wanted to reestablish their bond, their physical contact, immediately; she had missed her baby.

"Everything go okay?" she asked as she watched Luke with satisfaction.

"I think I need a different table or something for changing him better."

"Put rolled up blankets or towels, like bolsters, around him, on a bed or couch to keep him from rolling onto the floor."

"That's okay, just let me see what you've got. I don't want him camping out, like. I want the real thing." He went up the stairs, and Swan heard him walking around the nursery, opening drawers in the little dressing table.

"I'm turning the Mercedes and the truck in on an Escalade," he said casually as he came downstairs, "more family friendly. You'll find some marines stuff in his overnight bag." He shrugged. "I'm a sucker for dress up, I guess."

"I thought you were more a Hummer kind of guy," Swan said.

He frowned. "I've spent all the time in a humvee I'd like to, thanks."

Swan re-buttoned her shirt and pat-pat-patted Luke on her shoulder. "That's better," she said to both of them. "Do you want some coffee?"

Mathilde appeared from out of nowhere with a china mug.

"Just the way you take it, Major," she murmured with a smile. Sam took the mug gratefully, then turned to watch Swan as she straightened Luke's little onesie around his chubby neck.

"He slept good. Up at one and four. He seemed surprised I wasn't . . . you," Sam said, "but he smiled when I tickled him. I called a cadence til he fell asleep."

Swan looked alarmed. "Not *Jody, Jody six-feet four*!"

Sam looked guilty. "Well, *I* am six-feet four."

"You think *Jody, Jody six-feet four/Jody never had his ass kicked before/I'm gonna take a three-day pass/And really slap a beating on Jody's ass!* is appropriate for a baby?" Swan asked indignantly. "I've been in the Marines, before, remember!"

"He's two months old," Sam said defensively. "He won't remember."

She glowered. "'Twinkle, Twinkle, Little Star'!"

"Yes, ma'am," he said dryly. "I measured him—he's big for his age, right?"

Swan nodded. "Fifteen pounds—ninety-ninth percentile. No midget child after all."

"Wasn't your dad a six-footer? The genes are there."

"Well, genes or no, he's eating like a horse."

"You're doing a good job with him—keeping up with his appetite, I mean," Sam observed. Swan didn't know how to respond to that.

"He's pulling her down," Mathilde called in from the kitchen. "She's seven pounds lighter than before she got pregnant, in addition to the baby weight gone."

"Too much information," Swan warned from the parlor. She put Luke in his bouncy seat; he yipped contently, looking from Sam to Swan and back again.

"Aren't you eating?" Sam frowned. "Why not?"

"I am eating: three meals a day. Not that it is any of your business, either of you," but she was smiling.

"Look at her derrière," Mathilde demanded. "She's smaller than ever—the only woman that's happened to in history. Her waist is tiny."

"Enough, please!" Swan ordered more firmly. "We were talking about Luke, not Luke's mama."

"Maybe I should take you to lunch," Sam said, "just to monitor your caloric intake. You do it for the mares when they are pulled down by their foals."

"No monitoring needed, thanks," she said. Dangerous territory. She stuck in the knife. "Daniel keeps a close eye on me."

The wound registered in his face.

"Daniel. Yeah. I'm sure." Then he set his expression. "I came in my riding clothes. Am I getting a lesson or not?"

"If you're ready." Swan picked up Luke and put him in his baby sling.

Eduardo had James tacked and waiting. Sam settled in the saddle easily.

"Tighten the chin strap on your helmet, please," she ordered from the center of her riding ring. "Now make him walk on with a purpose: shoulders up and back; heels down, toes up . . . long, stretched torso; forward a little: Too much! Straighten up! Better . . . ."

After a brisk thirty minutes, Swan ended the lesson. Luke was fussing in the baby sling. Eduardo came at her call and took James from Sam, chucking Luke under his chinny chin before leaving.

"Any chance of lunch?" Sam asked calmly as they returned to the house. Swan's radar went off at a low frequency. She decided to ignore it.

"I'm sure Mathilde has a sandwich she can give you." That was an understatement.

"How does roast beef and turkey on light rye, Swiss, lettuce, tomato, potato salad, a Dos Equis, and blueberry pie sound?" the delighted Mathilde rattled off as they came into the dining room.

"Fantastic, as always," Sam said genially, "if you'll join me, Swan." She was struggling to get Luke out of his sling back pack. "Let me." He hoisted Luke out like a little peanut, then up in the air at arm's length. This caused the baby to gurgle with delight.

"I knew it!" Swan said. "You've been tossing him in the air when I wasn't around—it turns their brains to jello!" But she laughed, and the radar ping got louder.

"He's fine, he's loving it," Sam said. "He's all boy, that's all."

"All boy? Wait til you see him in one of the get-ups Townsend puts together," Swan muttered, but they ate companionably. It was more like before—before the break up. They talked about Mike, her decision to sell Linny, The Fortress's Major. They discussed Sam's plans for the hunt box. They finished lunch, and Sam stood up, but Luke began to fuss.

"Lunch time," Swan announced, "then nap time." She picked up Luke and headed toward the parlor; Sam followed Swan across the entranceway, through the first floor, to the sunny room.

"I suppose I should go," he said regretfully. He watched Swan settle herself on the sofa, turn away a bit, and open her shirt.

He turned away, too, but only slightly.

"Why do you think you're losing weight?" he asked gently. "You should just eat more. Are you taking a vitamin? Sleeping?"

"Yes, of course I am."

"You can't be worried about your figure or anything?" he asked. "Your body is perfect—always has been."

"Thanks. I appreciate the vote of confidence," she said, "but the Pikeurs are pretty unforgiving. They were not invented for new moms."

"Maybe you should feed him more formula; start weaning him . . . ." Sam sounded uncertain.

"Not yet," she replied quickly. "If Luke is going to be my only kid, I want to enjoy the experience while I can. And I think it is better for him." Her voice was confident. "I can feed him."

Sam considered that. He changed the subject. "How do you like running all these farms?"

"I'm running High View as a cattle operation, for the time being. Daniel will stay on month to month while I look for a tenant until the historic easement comes through. When I get Stone Chimneys, I'll start the easement process on *that* place and try to find a tenant in the meantime. When the market improves, I'll start looking for a buyer and try to recoup as much of the purchase price as I can. I might even find someone who actually wants to farm. Someone bought a farm as a farm recently." She was thinking of Paintbrush. "But it turns out they're already unhappy with Waverly. So I guess I'm hoping for a miracle."

Sam sat for a moment.

"I want to do something," he announced quietly. "Don't get all worked up."

He sat next to her on the sofa, gently putting his arm around her. Swan felt an overwhelming urge to lean back against him, to let her baby's father hold his whole family in his arms at once, to let herself feel completely safe, cared for, dependent on him in every way, just for a few minutes. She let him sit like that, the only sound that of the contented little baby nestled next to her, until she was ready to move Luke to her other breast. She steeled herself.

"I think you'd better go," she said quietly, and he nodded and stood up. Luke reached toward him. Swan felt her heart twist.

"I just wanted to see what that would feel like," he said, "the three of us. I'll be by Thursday morning, okay?"

"Yes, that will be fine."

He bent down and kissed the baby's head. "'Bye, little son," he said, and turned away.

But the next two times he came for Luke and dropped him off, Swan made sure she was riding two or three fields away from the house or in Waverly or at the PPT. She didn't want a repeat of that "couple" feeling, as she called it. Sam's arm around her hadn't upset her, but she hadn't liked it either. Rather, she *had* liked it, and therefore it could not be repeated. Mathilde knew Sam had overplayed his hand: Swan suspected she had told him when he came for the pick-up. Swan decided that no matter how awkward it was, she would not nurse the baby in front of him again. She knew what she could handle and what she couldn't.

The following Tuesday afternoon, she fell asleep on the loveseat in the parlor with Luke on her lap. She didn't even wake up when Sam came in the front door for the hand-off. He looked at them together for a long time, then he picked them up in his arms and carried them upstairs just as they were. He put Swan to bed and as Luke began to stir hungrily, he trundled the baby back downstairs to the kitchen before the chirping and gurgling could wake her.

"We need a bottle, " he announced. "I want to let her sleep."

"She's worn out," Mathilde said, warming a bottle of milk from the freezer in a pan on the stove. "She falls asleep over her dinner most nights. Miss Townsend is a help, but she needs her days off, just like anyone. She is just a young girl—she wants some entertainment, and Mr. Davenport is always ready to oblige. So Miss Swan does most of everything."

"Let's make her a nice full plate of food I can take up on a tray," he proposed. "I'll sit there with her until she eats it all." He pulled up a kitchen chair and expertly fed his cheerful baby, letting Mathilde bring him up to date on the local gossip about the two of them. Well, the three of them, really.

"Everybody in town thinks you are back living here," Mathilde said, looking over her glasses, "just not admitting it. Everyone thinks you have a plan."

"What do you think?" He watched Luke tuck in to his bottle.

"I don't think you do. But I hope you think of one," she said. "After all, you thought of the phone cards so I could keep you 'informed' while you were away."

Sam grinned. "But that's still our secret, isn't it?"

Mathilde sighed. "It is not easy keeping things from her. I couldn't do it if I didn't think it was what she really wanted but was afraid to admit it."

Swan was dimly aware of the gentle clatter of activity downstairs and heard her baby yipping contentedly when he'd finished the bottle. She was so very tired. She'd slept much of the afternoon away. When she finally rolled over—in her own bed, to her surprise—she saw Sam gently poking a little fire ablaze on the rare cool August day. Since he couldn't see her, she admired his back and arms for a few seconds, watching the muscles bunch and swell under his sleeveless shirt, before she remembered.

"Luke," she said anxiously.

"Playing 'Tickle me, Elmo' with Townsend, so don't worry. I'm going to bring up some real food right now, then you can feed him afterward. You need a little peace and quiet." He stood up.

"Have you been here the whole time? Didn't you take him home?"

"Swan, he *is* home; it's me who's visiting," he replied evenly, as he left the room. In a few minutes, he returned with a hot tray.

"I'd like you to eat everything on this plate. Mathilde says you've lost another couple of pounds. That's getting to be too much."

"I'm fine," she protested, but she began to eat: a hot chicken sandwich, cranberry relish, roasted new potatoes, gravy, peas. Sam sat and watched. She was as beautiful as ever to him, more so, with full ripe breasts, tiny waist, long thick hair, creamy complexion, a complete lack of consciousness of her overwhelming attractiveness, not just to him but to every heterosexual man she came across. He was plotting while she ate, trying not to push too hard but hard enough to get his way. He was wondering whether he could spend the night there, perhaps in a guest room, trying to get a foothold, establish a beachhead again in the house itself.

"You need more help," he began. "Townsend is about to leave for the summer and she is running around town with Lige."

"I'm fine, I can take care of Luke myself," she shot back. He tried a different direction.

"I miss you," he said.

"Don't."

He sat and listened contentedly to the little fire pop and sputter while she cleaned the last bite of chicken off her plate. Luke was beginning to fuss, with little burbling cries wafting up from downstairs.

"Do you want me to give him a bottle or do you want me to bring him up?" Sam asked.

"I'll feed him."

So Sam brought the baby to her.

She opened her shirt; Luke made those little smacking noises, his eyes twinkling. He bounced up and down in Sam's huge arms in anticipation of snuggling with Swan again. Sam deposited the baby on her lap then smoothly slid in behind her in the bed to watch her feed him. This time she did lean back into him. She was still warm and sleepy, and it was just too much of an effort to hold herself away from him. She tried not to turn her face into his shirt, to inhale his scent. He smelled wonderful.

"You are a great mother," he said softly, after a while. "I never thought about it before we had him, but he loves you already."

"I'm all he's got," she said, then she realized that had to have hurt him. Sam didn't let on, he had different ideas. He let the warmth of the fire and the warmth of his body relax her against him. They sat like that a long time, so long that the fire was dying out and the baby was ready to settle in for an early night. They heard Mathilde go to bed; Townsend came upstairs, then headed to her room and closed the door at the end of the corridor.

"Let me stay," he tried again, "just for the night. No sex. Just like this." He flexed his arms around her and felt that instantaneous jolt of response in her. She pulled away, but her shirt was already open. She tried to button it over her breasts as he began unbuttoning it from the bottom.

"Swan, let me, let me, let me," he murmured, and the baby looked at them both quizzically from his perch on her lap.

"No, no, no." She was struggling with a purpose. He didn't know what it was. She really meant it. *No.*

"Why? Why not?" He was whispering, his hands on her nipples now; they were wet.

"No, no, no . . . I've got no . . . no protection," she gasped. "I haven't had a . . . but that's no guarantee that—" That disclosure made up his mind.

"I'll pull out—I'll do anything—whatever you say," he promised; he was kissing her ears, her neck, making the little tent of space around Luke smaller and smaller.

"No, no, no, no," she was saying, but it wasn't *No, I don't want to,* it was *No, we shouldn't.*

"I'll just kiss you . . . below," he murmured.

"I don't think that's safe yet."

"Tell me, tell me, I'll do anything. We'll be okay—you're nursing, that's natural birth control." He kissed her neck and then down, between her breasts. They were fragrant and tender and full.

"This is a mistake," she warned, holding Luke like a little shield in front of the most embattled parts of her anatomy.

"I'll pull out, just say the word."

"This is a bad idea," Swan said to the top of his head, inhaling his scent as she rubbed his buzz cut with her cheek.

"Let's not argue," Sam replied quietly, but with finality. He gently pulled Luke from Swan's lap; the old bed was too small for the three of them. He half rolled out, his long legs hitting the floor immediately, and placed the baby in his little cradle beside the nightstand, near the fire's warmth.

"Tell me if it hurts," he murmured, rolling back next to her, but Swan was in that trance, the trance he always induced in her, that made her resistance seem foolish, unnecessary, pointless. Her body had been down this road before and was on board with the plan. She ran her hands up and down his arms, across his shoulders, down his chest, as though she was trying to decide if she could resist him.

He explored her just a little, running his hand up and down her leg, in his old way, kissing her all the time he was unbuttoning everything, sliding it all off or partially off. When she was in a mood like this, ambivalent and yet responsive, he'd learned to let things take care of themselves, not to push or pull or demand. Not to want, really—to let it happen as it was going to happen. It would work out fine that way. Eventually. Fondling, teasing her a little, letting her get into it, he finally lifted his daunting, husband-sized erection, slippery with her lubricant, and slid in, part way, just to see how it was for her.

"That's not so bad, now is it?" he moaned, then "God, you feel great . . . feel that?"

Oh, yes. It felt like a perfect fit, for the first time ever. He was on top of her starting to thrust without holding back, even a little.

"Oh. My. God." Swan was in heaven. "Oh. Sam. Ohhh."

"What, baby, what?" he murmured. She hooked one leg around his waist, the way she had wanted in the Black Hart, when he had said no. He lifted himself above her on his elbows to relieve her of his weight and began to thrust from the new trajectory. She was completely with him in every way, grabbing his waist to gain traction against his power.

"Okay?" he gasped and she answered with little "Hmmnns." The bed bucked backward against the wall, then bucked again, and again, creaking and shimmying right down to the old wooden pegged joints.

He pulled out, and his mouth found her nipples and teased out her milk until it sent a shudder through her, down to her deepest core, back up the same path way and down again. She twisted a little to short circuit the electrical charge, but he moved with her, his mouth still tasting, teasing. Her nipples felt like little grapes being squeezed for their juice. He entered her again in the next second.

"Oh. God. Oh. Sam." The bed thumped and thumped like a drum behind them. Swan ran her hand down the fine hair on his belly, to where his cock joined her flesh; both of them found that unbearable. She anchored herself against him, then pushed, pushed back, arching her back, sliding her hands over his bottom to keep him in her to the hilt, and finally went limp, like a noodle. He didn't have much to do to follow her, it had been so long. He collapsed with a long groan. Luke took that as an opportunity to chirp for attention.

"Wow," Swan breathed. "Wow." She ran her hands over the blue mountains of his shoulders. He was so strong, lean, long-bodied, like a wonderful animal she'd brought in the house from the wild.

"Sam." She looked at him as though she had never seen him before. "That was the most incredible . . . most incredible . . . most . . ." she whispered.

He looked at her, then grinned.

"Had your world rocked, did you?" he teased. But he swallowed hard and drew a deep, shaky breath from the exertion.

"What did you do?" she asked, still mired in disbelief. "Have you been . . . holding back all this time?"

"Hell, yes, I've been holding back!" He kept his voice low. "If I hadn't, you wouldn't have been able to walk for a week. Do you understand physiology at all? Anatomy? Anything in the life sciences?"

She just looked at him dreamily. She was wondering if it was endorphins that gave you the feeling that all of your joints had been gently separated from their connective tissue at some point during sex; so odd but so very pleasant.

"What have I been trying to tell you all this time?" He was half disgusted, half amused. "It used to be like docking an aircraft carrier in a tugboat slip for me." He stretched, flexed, stretched again, happy as a clam. "Now . . . it's perfect." He looked at her. "Luke made it perfect."

"Because it was uncomfortable for me, you held back . . . so it wasn't as good for you . . ." Swan began, "but now I'm still small, but not too small, and you can—"

"Let 'er rip without worrying it is going to be too big or too deep for you," he finished for her helpfully. "Which seems to have made quite a difference for you, too. I think we are making some progress here."

"Can you do that . . . all that . . . again?"

"All day, every day." Luke chirped again, with more insistence.

"He needs changing," Swan said bleakly.

The bedding under them was damp. Her clothes, unbuttoned, pulled open, wadded up, weren't much drier. Sam had shucked off all of his.

"Give me one more minute." He groaned self-pityingly, then hoisted his long legs over the bed again to tend to Luke. "I'm glad we had this little talk."

Swan laughed out loud watching a naked man change a baby's diaper in the dark. She suddenly stopped short.

"We are so screwed," she said gravely, and he knew immediately what she meant. "We are so up shit's creek."

"Nope. Not a problem."

"I'll get Plan D in the morning."

He turned as though she had slapped him.

"No, don't. Don't." It wasn't an order, but it wasn't a plea either. "We'll be fine. We'll go on the pill right away. We'll be fine; nursing cuts the chance of pregnancy by ninety percent," he said authoritatively. "Saw it on the Internet."

"I don't know what happened; it was like 'here's the boss back in town'—and my ovaries blew open," she said plaintively, shaking her head. "We are screwed."

"We'll be fine," he repeated. "Don't get Plan D, it's hormones—you're nursing. Promise me."

She sighed.

"We're not going to get pregnant. Stop freaking out," he said. "You said you haven't had a—"

"Dream on." She knew it already. He had smelled too good to her, she had been too responsive. All the physiological signs. "I could have started ovulating any time now and the flood was . . . huge." They were soaked in the evidence.

"The worst that can happen is that we have another kid. We can handle it." He didn't say, *You owe me for thinking of aborting Luke.* He didn't say, *It's not just your decision* or *You froze me out the first time.* He didn't say it because he was counting on her thinking it without him.

"We're going back on the pill," she said.

"Tomorrow."

But she didn't go back on the pill. She wanted to wait the eight days for the home test to prove her right. Within forty-eight hours she felt just as she had the first days after conceiving Luke. Flushed, aware, emotional, teary, then a burst of happiness.

First things first. If she was pregnant again, she was going to make sure she was in shape in the meantime, not for Sam, who she was now convinced was so besotted he wouldn't care what she looked like, more's the joke; not for some other man. Who could ever replace the man she had? But she still made her living riding big, powerful horses. She needed to be fit. Hetty had said it had been harder getting her figure back the second time than the first.

Sam was coming over late, so she took the opportunity before dinner, while Mathilde had run to Waverly for fresh eggs and fruit, to fire up the belly dancing DVD. She might as well get back to her routine. Swan went to her bedroom. She pulled one of the long, graceful skirts and coin-covered bras from the closet. The dress-up mood was upon her. Luke watched her from his little crib in the corner of the room. He began to smile and kick his feet when he heard the flute, the cymbals, and the drum's plaintive wail.

Swan began to dance, her arms stretched out from her sides, her hips making their four point circle, her shoulders making their four point circle; one traveling step, then another. She closed her eyes, lifting her wrists and hands in the story-telling gestures for "long, wavy hair," and "beautiful eyes, looking at you." She started the cabaret shimmy, the coins jingling provocatively.

"What the hell are you up to?"

Swan whirled around.

Sam was in the doorway. His expression was completely unreadable.

"How did you get in?" Swan stepped back, one, two, three steps. She was mortified. "What about the knock? Ever hear of it?" The music continued its provocative rhythm.

"Door was open, Flagg was downstairs. It sounded like market day in the souk, so here I am." He shrugged, but his eyes were on her. She pulled one of the filmy veil things up around her modestly.

"This is just to get back in shape after the baby. You know . . . tighten everything up a little, that's all. Like weight training is for you. You weren't supposed to see the idiotic outfit."

"Who *was*, for Christ's sake?"

"No one," Swan said miserably, "no one. It's like for Halloween. Dress up."

"Well, this certainly is a change from the Pikuers and designer things you are usually parading around in." Sam scowled. "Are you sure you aren't moonlighting at smokers in Warrenton? Entertaining the troops with a USO act?"

Swan strode to the DVD player and turned it off hard.

"Hetty did it after the boys—so you can blame it all on her," she said defensively. "I know I'm not any good at it. It's one big joke to you—you didn't have a beach ball stuck in you for eight months."

She turned away to change back into her shorts and t-shirt. "You can go on downstairs. Show's over."

"Hey, hey—wait just a damn minute," he said, the major to be obeyed. He closed the door behind him with a click.

"All right," he said quietly, heading to the DVD player, "do it again—the whole thing. From the very beginning."

An hour later, Swan was leaning over the side of her old bed, looking plaintively at the coin bra, now in three pieces, and the harem skirt, in two, spread across the wood floor.

"They will never dance again," she murmured sadly.

Sam rolled over next to her and looked down at them.

"They died for a good cause," he said. "That was without doubt the best fuck I've ever had. Ever. It beats the fuck in the Scarab that first night. It beats the three-cheerleader four-way my sophomore year at Tech and my wedding night in Vegas." He sounded as though he were in the officers' morning briefing.

Swan looked at him.

"What three-cheerleader four-way?" she asked indignantly.

But Sam just closed his eyes and moaned gently.

"It beats the weight bench fuck—"

"I'm getting the picture," Swan said patiently.

"It's a close call after last night, but I think it beats—"

"Thank you!" Swan cut him off, gently but firmly.

He turned back over, looking at her critically.

"Do that hip pop thing again."

"No. No! This was a special, one-time event, a special, freak occurrence, like Haley's Comet or—"

Sam snorted.

"You don't know much about men, do you?" he said patronizingly. "A 'one time only' event? You'll be lucky if it is a 'one time a day' event from now on."

"Don't be ridiculous. We have to get dressed. Do you see any clothes around you haven't torn in two?"

"It was that shimmy with the coins that did it . . . ." Sam sounded like he was talking to someone on the ceiling above the bed. "What other outfits do you have?" he asked moonily, "any with fringe? Or beads maybe?"

"Are you listening to me at all?" Swan asked. "Are we in the same bed? On the same planet?"

He looked at her again. "You weren't so high and mighty a few minutes ago. You were begging me to—"

"Anyone home?" called Mathilde from downstairs.

Swan abruptly turned to Sam.

"Okay, pal—here's the deal," she hissed. "If Major Gumby ever wants to visit the queen of the veils again, you will keep your mouth shut about this whole thing. It is too embarrassing."

"Luke saw it all."

"Yeah, well, he isn't due to talk in sentences for another year, is he? I'll worry about that then," Swan said, pushing his bare butt toward his side of the bed with her foot. "Get in the shower before we scandalize the help. I've got to change the linens—again."

◆

For the next eight days, Swan pushed against her worry. Conception could occur up to several days after sex, so she focused on eleven days after the world-rocking night with Sam as D-Day. In the meantime, she assessed her own physical symptoms. They were all there.

She said nothing to Sam, letting him take Luke on his days but not letting him spend the night. If they *had* dodged the bullet, they would have to use some other means of protection until the monthly pill was fully in effect.

He said nothing. Given all he had been through with her, ten days' abstinence was a piece of cake and safer than coming up with alternatives that might lead them back to the trouble they were already in. He preferred abstinence to condoms. Condoms were for hit-and-run sex, not Swan, and they could break, particularly under the weight of his heavy equipment.

But one day they talked about it. They were sitting at the old picnic table under the trees below the house after dinner, as the sun was going down. Luke was in his bouncy chair, watching Swan's hair dance and swirl in the late summer breeze, watching Sam prop his chin on his hands and take in the sunset, the mares and foals now out for the evening.

"Don't you feel better since you've had Luke? Less anxious, less worried about 'bad luck doomed love'?" he asked. "Doesn't he makes you happy—really happy?"

"Yes, of course he does. I couldn't imagine life without him now," she said, following his gaze.

"If something did happen to me—or if we really broke up for good—don't you think you could handle it better, now that you have him? You'd go on and have a happy life, don't you think? For him?" Sam turned toward her, his eyes not meeting hers.

"Yes, I think I probably would," she said carefully.

"Whatever we find out next week, we should think about having another baby," he said quietly. "I don't mean we have to get married, or that you can't send me packing for good whenever you want. You'd have even more reason to be happy, no matter what."

"Why would I need more reason to be happy? Is there something wrong with you?" She felt the old panic begin to grab hold.

"No, nothing, absolutely. I'm a beast."

She was suspicious. "Have you been having the dreams?"

"No," he said quickly, then hesitated. "Sometimes I do think about the guys. What they're doing. One hundred and fifteen degrees. Knock and talks done. Patrols over, bedding down for the night. The coms crackling in your ear . . . . It begins to eat at you. I see the little kids over there, dying, missing arms, legs . . . they are just like Luke. They are all Lukie to me now."

"I don't see how you can do it," she said softly. "Tell me, all of it, why don't you?"

He shrugged.

"What good would it do?" he said gruffly, looking back at the night horizon. "I need to grow a pair and shut the fuck up."

"What can I do to make it better, then?" Swan asked, searching his face. "I want to help."

"Nothing. Nothing . . . just . . . what I said. If you had another baby . . . . We've got a good set up between us. It would be just as easy with two as one. Look how close you and Hetty are. And I know what it's like to be an only child. No fun."

"What brought this on," she asked again, "the wait to see if this is a false alarm?"

Sam sat silently for a long time. He didn't say *We should have another child in case anything happened to Luke.* He would have eagerly thrown himself on an IED with a smile on his face for his child. But at that moment another child was just a bulwark between the love of his life and "bad luck doomed love."

"Swan, I had a shitty father and you lost yours far too soon. It would be great to make up for that with—" He almost said *a family of our own* but caught himself in time. "Some great little kids," he finished instead. "Luke is the best little kid in the world, and I'm sure another one would be, too. Money isn't a problem, it would just be your health that would be the priority."

"Septimus Anderson Moore Junior," Swan said, trying it out. "We could call him Andy. We already have one Junior in the Bolington family." She did not say *our* family.

"You're so sure it would be a boy?"

"Or Bolington Fitzhugh Moore," Swan continued, still lost in thought. "Fitch's namesake could have Fitch's inheritance, High View."

"Whatever you'd want," Sam said.

"Why do you really want to do this?" she asked again, still suspicious.

"I told you—for Luke," he lied. "In a few years, the two of them will be able to take care of you, whether we are together or not. That will give me great peace of mind when I'm deployed." He gently gathered her hair in his hand, pulling it over her shoulders, down her back.

Swan looked at him. "If we considered this, it would have to be with the understanding that things wouldn't change. I don't ever plan to get married, or cohabit, or anything else, ever again, one child or two."

"Agreed," he said promptly. "I absolutely agree that is your plan."

"Sam, you aren't having some kind of premonition, are you?" Swan was suddenly seized with fear. She put her arms around him. "Tell me if you are." She pressed her face against his arm, taking comfort in its great strength, its closeness.

"No—nothing like that," he said, holding her.

"I don't believe you! You are thinking that each time you go, it's like running across a road with your eyes closed. You may be able to get away with it once, twice, three times, but eventually you are going to get hit. You'd be crazy if it didn't eat at you—all of you— after all these tours. Your guys are all on Ambien, Valium—everybody says so."

He was silent. He looked down.

Swan looked out, out across the fields, toward the Blue Ridge, the ancient outer fortress wall of the Valley of Virginia. The Stonewall Brigade, Mosby's Raiders, the Irish Brigade had bivouacked under these trees, clattered on fine Virginia thoroughbreds or stolid farm horses across the little wooden bridges at the bottom of the far field, drawn water from the old hand-dug well at the end of the service road, stared out toward the mountains.

"But I want you to know," Swan said, suddenly calm, "if it happened to you now, I'd be okay. I'd be okay for Luke and myself, and for Hunt and Carter and Fitch, and you, too. You all want—wanted— me to have a happy life. And I will, no matter what." Part of her believed it. "I don't want you to worry about that anymore. If having another child will prove that to you, I want us to think about it. You deserve it."

◆

Nine days and counting: Swan drove to the pharmacy in Warrenton, where she was less well known, and bought three early-result pregnancy tests. Plus sign, changing colors—each considered the most sensitive on the market for early detection of human chorionic gonadotropin hormone. She went back to the farm with the intention of waiting until the following morning before she was going to use them; that's when they were the most accurate. But she had the irresistible urge to take the tests then and there. Looking at the kits made her think of when she had been in denial about her pregnancy with Luke. Now Luke was sitting happily in the crib, living repudiation of her worry that he would ruin her life.

When she emerged from the bathroom twenty minutes later, she looked at him again.

"Private Piecake, you are going to have a brother. Maybe a sister, but I'd bet the farm it is a boy. Isn't that only great?" She was smiling for the baby.

Twenty minutes after that, Swan had to hold the phone away from her ear until Sam stopped hollering.

"I gather you are happy," she said when she heard his joy begin to subside on the other end of the line.

"Aren't you? I mean I know it's too soon, too soon, and we are going to watch you every step of the way now, but please tell me you aren't sorry."

"I'm not sorry," she said. She had rehearsed this very line before she had called him so she could deliver it truthfully. "It will all be great." The poor guy deserved to hear a woman happy to be carrying his child for once. He bought it.

"You won't be sorry, I promise. You are going to be treated like a queen for the next nine months. I'll take care of everything," he said. "First, we'll get a full-time babysitter for Luke—no more movie star teenagers, but a real nanny. Then, you know, a complete physical for you, everything, and a nutritionist. Or maybe that's first before the nanny."

"So much for nothing changing," Swan murmured when he took a breath, but he was undeterred.

"You'll need to wean Luke—now. At least get him started on the formula, it won't kill him. He may even like it." Sam sounded so earnest she had to laugh.

"We have to limit your access to the Internet, Major," she said. "You are sounding much too knowledgeable about this iVillage, for-women-only stuff to be a real marine. People are going to begin to wonder about you."

"Not with two kids in twelve months, they won't," he said. "Fuck them anyway. I'm going to be a dad right from the start this time. I want to come out and celebrate—tonight. And *not* go back to the hunt box afterward." He stopped short. "You'll be due, like mid-June, right?"

"Something like that."

"I'll be deployed by then." The buoyancy drained out of his voice.

"You'll always be deployed somewhere. That doesn't change anything—like we agreed." Swan could see she was going to be repeating this a lot.

"Back up the line."

She suddenly honed in. "Do you already know?"

"Not the specifics."

"When?"

"March first."

"March first again! I hate March first!" she burst out. "Now that you proved you aren't a head case, they're going to send you back. The new surge."

"Yes."

"Fuck! Fuck! Fuck!" She was the one furious now. "How did you get on the rotation list? You aren't well! You pushed me out of bed last week: the 'if you do that again' nightmare!"

"I did?" He was surprised, but not surprised. "That's not good—particularly not now."

"Duh! When were you cleared? When were you going to tell me?"

"Just recently and when we knew about the pregnancy test."

"You could leave the Marine Corps," Swan said, for the first time meaning it, "or put in for desk duty, not for us but for you. They're going to burn you to ashes. They won't give up until they send you back in a box or a straitjacket."

"You are the one who just said I'm always going to be deployed somewhere. I thought you accepted it," he said logically. "I've got twelve years in the Corps. I'm still one of the youngest majors and they need senior officers. A lot are taking retirement."

"A lot are resigning, you mean," she said. He was silent. "They are willing to throw in the towel on their careers rather than end up like the major you replaced in the Tenth."

"No, they are retiring because they are majors at forty or forty-five, not at thirty-three, like me," Sam said. "The guys need seasoned officers more than ever. Some of them are beginning to show signs of wear and tear. PTSD, TBIs— they are a bitch to manage in the field." That was the first time Sam had ever admitted the punishing rounds of deployments were affecting the Marines as a whole, not just individuals. "The Iraqis, in particular, do not improve upon greater . . . acquaintance . . . . Everybody is willing to turn everybody else in, for a price. We've been turned into policemen over there— not what we were trained for."

He swallowed hard; then composed himself with considerable effort. "But we're not talking about me—I'm not the one going to have Septimus Moore Junior in June."

"Do you still want to celebrate with Lukie and me?" Swan said, quietly. "When can you come to us?"

"I'll be there by seven. Swannie, despite everything, I'm so very happy."

Mathilde spent the rest of the afternoon outdoing herself on a special dinner.

"Thank you Jesus, Mary, and Joseph," she had said when Swan told her, then hugged her. "The poor major," she said, "after all he's been through, he deserves it."

"Double the child support, you mean?" Swan teased, but only to keep from crying herself. Hormone storm.

By seven, a roast duckling, string potatoes, asparagus hollandaise, field greens salad and red velvet cake were ready to be served. Sam's new Escalade had barely pulled in the driveway when he was taking the front steps two at a time, grabbing Swan before she could meet him at the door and lifting her up so high she had to dodge the crystal chandelier in the hallway using both hands. When he slid her back to the floor, her hand found a package in his uniform pocket.

"What's that?" she asked suspiciously.

"For me to know and you to find out." Then he kissed her like a man truly happy. "This is the evening we should have had when we learned Luke was on the way." He dropped his eyes. He was still so hurt by that whole chain of events.

"Speaking of Mister Underpants," she said, brightly, "shall we bring him in to dinner? Miss T. is out tonight, too, so we can celebrate alone."

Mathilde brought the bouncy chair into the dining room so Luke could see his parents eat dinner as a family.

"Eat with us," Sam said to her, "this is a celebration." He gave her his big grin. "Please."

"Just a bite," she said, "then I'll leave you alone. Leave the dishes til morning, Miss Swan."

They had decided not to tell anyone else beyond the four of them, for the time being. It was still very early in the pregnancy. Swan let Mathilde and Sam try out some girls' names. With a Lucius, there was not going to be a Lucinda after all.

"Well, Susannah, of course," Mathilde said, "and Spaulding; Henrietta, since it doesn't look like Mrs. Delaney is going to have a chance to use it. What about Julia, Major?"

"I don't think so." Sam said it in a way they all recognized brought the subject to a close. He managed a tight smile.

"When can you see Dr. Cavendish, Swan?" he asked, helping himself to enormous seconds of every dish on the table.

"I should probably wait til I can look him in the eye with a straight face, since Luke and the new baby are going to be less than thirteen months apart."

Luke took that moment for a giant sneeze, and Swan brought him onto her lap as she finished her dinner. Mathilde shared a glance with Sam.

"I'll leave you two alone," she said pointedly, standing up.

"Wait," Sam said, "Swannie, don't you want to see what's in my pocket?" He pulled out the mysterious package: a jewelry box, oblong and elegant. Swan felt a jolt of excitement. It took her all of twenty seconds to open it.

"Oh," she breathed. It was a platinum necklace, with a large cabochon ruby hanging like a strawberry teardrop from its center, smooth, blood red, heavy.

"Oh," she said again.

"This completes the set," he said quietly, "the earrings, the bracelet, now the necklace."

"How did you get it so fast?" she said, but she couldn't take her eyes off it. Sam lifted her hair so she could put it on immediately. She had never felt anything like it, hanging almost between her breasts. Luke turned his head to focus on its fiery brilliance.

"They e-mailed me some time ago, saying the estate had released it after all," Sam said carefully, "then last week, when you and I thought . . . we thought . . . well, you know. I called and had it sent down on approval. Do you approve?"

"Oh," Swan said, fingering the ruby lovingly.

"I'm taking that as a yes," he said, "my beautiful girl." That was too much for Mathilde—she burst into tears, which were only made worse when Sam and Swan laughed.

"I'll leave you two alone," she fussed, wiping her eyes and rising from the table in embarrassment.

"Susannah Swan, if it is a girl," Sam said.

"Okay—but it isn't."

Chapter 28

It wasn't hard for Sam and Swan to keep up the appearance of a strictly custodial relationship. The hunt box was the perfect set up. Sam could come and go, picking up Luke, dropping him off, staying overnight, leaving the next morning, parking the Escalade at the hunt box when he took the Harley to Quantico via Belle Everley, dropping the Harley at the farm when he took Luke on little errands around Waverly. Swan changed it up by taking Luke to the hunt box herself. The only ones who knew the real state of affairs were her Belle Everley workers; not even Emilio could keep track of them. Whenever Lige Davenport asked her, Swan met him for a very public lunch at the Reynard or some Prince Arthur watering hole; it was enough to keep tongues wagging, since Lige was still keeping regular company with Townsend. Soon enough it would have to come to an end, when Swan's belly returned, but it bought Swan and Sam some privacy. They were pretty pleased with how they were managing things.

When Daniel asked Sam to meet him in the Crossroads on his way to Belle Everley for Luke, Sam agreed very reluctantly, despite what he had announced to Swan. He was back in battle dress, in solidarity with the marines still slogging away on two fronts. The camouflage utility uniform made him look taller, broader, more powerful. He was still weight training to keep up with each new crop of twenty-year-olds. Daniel was his polar opposite, slim, elegant, Continental, but strangely more confident in some ways. His months spent as Swan's closest confidant had made him so.

"You think you have this all figured out, don't you?" said Daniel when they had ordered their usual lunch at the usual banquette. "You are going to let things settle down, now that Luke is here and you've bought into the neighborhood. You think sooner or later she will change her mind, marry you, get on the way you want. But what about the first time the kid gets sick, or falls out of a tree or off a horse? What is she going to think? There's more than one kind of 'bad luck doomed love,' you know."

Sam looked at him, blindsided and furious about it.

"Listen, you little prick, if you put that idea in her head, I will kill you with my own hands," he snarled. "If David Edgeworth got probation for shooting Connie in front of the Reynard, I'll get five years, max, three suspended, being a combat veteran and all. The first crime of passion is a freebie in Taliaferro County. Or I'll just plead the PTSD. Either way, you'll be dead, won't you?"

Sam leaned forward menacingly.

"You *want* her unhappy and worked up and needy. That lets you run to the rescue and be the hero of the family for the first time in your miserable, coked-up life. Christ, even Fitch didn't sink to making her worse on purpose! Do you really think I'd give her up now?" he asked. His glare was beginning to attract notice. "Stay away from her, and stay away from my little kid."

"Well, I'm sure she's going to enjoy hearing you threatened to kill me," Daniel said companionably. "That will reassure her that you are getting well—that the old warrior spirit is under control. If you alienate her from her family and something does happen to you or, God forbid, Luke, who is she going to have to help her through it? Without us, she'll be in the psych ward. We are the ones she relies on."

"You may be in for a surprise there," Sam said quietly.

"You may be in for a surprise yourself, Major," Daniel said just as quietly. "This is all part of the plan."

That shut Sam up.

"Swan and I discussed the best way to 'distract' you from meddling in the real family business," Daniel continued serenely, "securing Stone Chimneys. You had the potential to fuck everything up with Davenport."

Sam clenched his fists under the table.

"So we agreed to let you back into her bed until Stone Chimneys was taken care of. We knew how easily you'd be . . . satisfied . . . with that." Daniel looked at Sam contemptuously. "I figured you'd never wonder why it had happened. You'd think you'd done it all yourself, given your 'prowess' in the bedroom department."

Sam stayed calm.

"Swan and I agreed to let Davenport show her around town a bit, sure—to suss out his plans for the farm. But that has all become nonoperational. He's taken a shine to Miss T., as anyone can see," he smiled grimly, "and Swan landed Stone Chimneys on her own—you said so yourself."

"We needed to keep your nose out of our strategizing, one way or the other. With your 'issues,' we couldn't take the chance that you'd ruin everything," Daniel smiled back, "although Davenport is a Golden Gloves champion, not a bar room brawler like yourself."

"You'd say anything to stir up trouble between Swan and me," Sam growled. "You've always been so fucking jealous of me you can't stand it—you and Fitch both. But Swan is mine in every way. End of discussion." He put his hands on the table.

"Well, that big dick of yours didn't buy Stone Chimneys for her, and that's what matters," Daniel battled back. "I've done that, not you. She'll have that when you're back to screwing bar girls in Tokyo. You are a temporary guest in the Belle Everley bedroom, Major, believe me."

Sam looked at Daniel in a way he'd never been looked at before. It was truly scary, not in a "thug about to beat you to death" way, but in a "small nuclear device dropping on your defenseless head" way. Nothing personal; strictly business.

"I'm afraid I'm not hungry after all," Sam said. "I'm going to thoroughly enjoy the look on your face when we announce our news." He stood up, threw down a fifty dollar bill, and stormed out, letting the door slam behind him. This caused the diners in the banquettes nearest the front windows to duck and cover defensively once again.

The Harley suited Sam perfectly in the mood he was in. He was tearing up the steps at Belle Everley in fifteen minutes. Then he was up the stairs to the second floor in fifteen seconds, his combat boots pounding the old chestnut boards, leaving Mathilde looking up the stairs after him. It sounded like the entire platoon was on its way.

"I need to talk to you," he announced to Swan, who was changing Luke in the nursery. He was roiling mad. "Tell me one thing: why did you sleep with me over the winter, here and in Doncaster? And why now, now that I'm home?"

"What?" Swan asked, alarmed. "What's wrong?"

"Tell me! Tell me! Did you plan the whole thing?" he bellowed; Luke's eyes widened in fear.

Swan took a deep breath.

"You are frightening him, Sam. Don't," she said, her voice low and even. She turned reassuringly back to Luke, tickling his pink tummy above his fresh diaper. "Don't worry, baby," she cooed. "Your silly pa has got himself all het up for some reason." She kissed Luke's forehead. "We'll get him calmed down in a minute, and then we'll come back up here for you." She plopped Luke gently in his crib, then she threw Sam a look that could kill and motioned for him to follow her downstairs.

In the parlor, she turned on him.

"He can sense your mood, you know, even though he is little," she said sharply. "This isn't your rifle company, Major. You can rage around me all you want, but don't frighten him, please." Her voice carried a clear warning beneath its veneer of cool civility.

"Then tell me the truth," he pleaded. He was pacing around the little room in tight circles, as though he could punch out all four of its walls just by extending his arms. Swan stood impassively, forcing him to detour around her each circuit.

"No, of course I didn't plan to sleep with you in Doncaster," she shot back, "not here, either. Didn't I tell you 'no' at least ten times, that we had no protection? Do you think I wanted to repeat Reproduction Roulette? What's this all about? You look like you are going to have a seizure."

"I just got bushwhacked by cousin Daniel in the Crossroads. He said you two agreed that you should take me back temporarily just to keep me from screwing up your plans for the new farm." His eyes were tormented. He stopped dead to look at her. "Swan, is that true? Having you been sleeping with me just to keep me occupied while you bought Stone Chimneys? Do you plan to dump me once the paperwork is signed?"

She looked right back.

"No," she said. "I mean—I did tell Daniel that I might have to seem to take you back. I had to cover my tracks. He was suspicious that I was going to 'backslide,' and I was worried he would find out about the Scarab, or even the Black Hart from Lige. I told him I might have to get us together again to throw him off the trail." She pulled him by the hand, gently, onto the loveseat. "I was afraid he'd catch me in a lie. He asked straight out if I was sleeping with you. I needed him. You were gone." She was getting teary. "I've got so many schemes going, I can't keep them all straight sometimes."

"God damn. I hate that guy," Sam fumed, jumping back up to pace around again, always a sign of his agitation. "He really knows how to stick the knife in. He can play me like a piano."

"It's not his fault. I'm the one who sent you away last year, not Daniel. Don't forget that." Swan set her jaw. "If you are going to be mad about it, be mad at me."

He looked at her, anguished. "Every time we are together and happy, someone fucks us up."

"It doesn't help being jerked around by the Marine Corps," she countered. But she had worked her magic on him. His pacing slowed, then stopped.

"I'll get Luke," he sighed. "We should tell everyone about the new baby now, early or not. That will shut them all up."

"What a nice reason to announce our wonderful news," she said sarcastically, as he headed upstairs. But by the time he was back with Luke, she was settled on the larger couch.

"Come here, marine," she said softly, ready to make peace in her little family. "Come and snuggle."

He put Luke in her lap and threw himself on the sofa next to her. When he had buried his head against her shoulder, she began running her free hand gently up and down his arm, feeling the anger leach out of him as she stroked the heavy muscles under his swan tattoo.

"Better now?" she murmured. She had had something on her mind for weeks. "I want to ask you about your dad."

"No."

"Yes."

"We just made up; can't we have five minutes between arguments?" he growled into her neck, but he smiled in Luke's direction to sweeten his tone.

"Did you look at the pictures I sent of your mother and Luke? The ones I took when she was here?" Swan asked.

He was silent. She took that as a yes.

"She said you and your dad had a bad relationship. I got the impression he'd been . . . stern."

Sam grimaced and burrowed deeper into her breasts.

"That's a genteel way of putting it."

"So he hit you . . . a lot."

He sat up, defeated.

"Depends on your definition of 'a lot.' If you mean every time he had a snootful, or every time he decided I'd been disrespectful, or every time I hadn't jumped when he wanted me to jump, then, yes, he hit me a lot."

"With his fist or—?"

"Belt."

"Buckle or strap?"

"Buckle. You do more damage with the buckle end."

Swan felt half-sick, but she needed to go on.

"Starting from when? How old were you?"

Sam sighed.

"Maybe twelve or thirteen. That's when the drinking got bad. He was mad all the time, home a lot, and then I began to grow. It was easier to think of me as a man when I was as tall as he was. But I was skin and bones—a skeleton—I was growing so fast. By the time I began to fill out and muscle up, he was sick, then dead. If he'd lasted another year, I could have finally given him a taste of his own medicine. I'd even have let him use the belt to make it a fair fight."

"Your mother said your stepfather drank, too, after she married him. That's why she dropped out of your life. She didn't want to pull you into a repeat of what you went through with your dad," Swan said quietly, caressing his shoulder with her fingertips.

"If you are thinking of trying to make things up between us, Swan, don't bother. It isn't going to happen," Sam said with absolute finality.

"She has cancer," Swan said softly. "She may not have long to live. I just thought you should be aware of that."

Sam shrugged.

"Well, you've sucked the story out of me, even though I told you a million times I didn't want to talk about it," he said, tired and defeated. "Why?"

"Sam, you are the father of my children. People often parent the way they were parented. I needed to know it all."

"You don't have to worry," he said quietly. "The Marine Corps became my real family; they showed me fairness—justice, really—how to be an honorable man. I might have gotten the same message at Tech if I'd been more a part of the team, but it was the Marines that did it for me. I owe them to stay in—and die, if it comes to that, too. I'd cut my own arm off before I'd ever raise it against you or Luke, and you have my permission to saw it off in my sleep if I ever even think about it. I know how to parent: do everything one hundred and eighty degrees' differently from my folks."

"Luke and I are going to make up for everything—everything—for you," Swan said. She pulled him back against her, kissing his furrowed brow. "The new baby, too. You'll see."

Swan convinced Sam to keep the news of the new baby secret, but it wasn't easy.

"We're going to be the town circus act as soon as everyone finds out. We've barely gotten off the radar screen with Luke, the showdown everyone expected with you and Daniel, the Stone Chimneys thing. Let someone else be the Waverly freak show for a few weeks," she said, persuasively. "We'll be back on the front page soon enough."

"Then tell Daniel to stay away from me," Sam fumed. "I don't want to see him or talk to him. What do you need him for now anyway? You've bought Stone Chimneys, you're going to turn him out of High View and he'll be relocating. See him when I'm not around, if you like, but I'm not going to meet with him, have a meal with him, or go on family outings with him."

Swan agreed, reluctantly. Spaulding wanted Daniel firmly ensconced in the family circle for his own good, and Swan didn't want her relatives to think Sam was responsible for pushing him out of her life. Everyone would be reconciled once the new baby was announced. It would be clear that she and Sam were, indeed, together and building a family. The evidence would be in a double stroller being pushed up and down Main Street. For anyone to draw any other conclusion would be ridiculous.

Chapter 29

Swan looked at her silhouette in the bedroom mirror. The baby bump was definitely beginning to push her waistband out, only six weeks into her pregnancy. At this rate, she and Sam would have to make their announcement before the bump revealed itself, whether they were ready or not. It was perplexing. She was back to her pre-pregnancy weight, yet her waist and belly were developing minds of their own. The belly dancing exercises had been working, she'd been riding three horses a day, toting and feeding Luke, with energy to spare for hot, steamy nights with Sam. She was disappointed, though. For some reason there were only days left for the Pikuers, and the big-shirt fashion statement would be a guaranteed giveaway.

Technically, they were still going through the motions of maintaining separate domiciles, but it was only a sliver of a technicality. Nine nights out of ten Sam could be found naked under Swan's silks, quilts, and bedcovers, swinging his long legs out of bed twice a night to scoop Luke out of the cradle next to the old bed and into Swan's sleepy arms, then back into the cradle fifteen minutes later, with her barely regaining consciousness.

◆

Early in the morning, he would pad downstairs in a big flannel robe that had "I'm Dad" written across the back in sequins, a joke gift from Harry Edwards, taking Luke with him on a subversive mission: getting him started on baby formula without Swan knowing about it. Sam had Mathilde as his coconspirator, as usual. She hid the cans of formula in the fridge in her apartment behind the kitchen. She and Sam felt it was only a matter of a few weeks before Swan would have to give up feeding Luke. They wanted him on board with the program when the time came so he wouldn't resist and upset Swan. They felt no guilt about it at all.

Four days a week Swan gave Sam riding lessons on James in the Belle Everley riding ring, their excuse for bringing him back from the hunt box to live permanently. As Sam had predicted, Waverly townsfolk became accustomed to seeing the big marine on his own, toting Luke around in the little sling strapped to his huge shoulders, not because Sam and Swan were estranged, but because he was enjoying his child while he was in Waverly fulltime. He had to be convinced that his presence at a Mommy and Me infant massage class at the Waverly Nursery School would be too disruptive to the "other" mothers, but he was allowed to sign up for a stroller fitness class, since another father was interested. The instructor drew the line at marine drills, however.

Swan bit the bullet and went to Dr. Cavendish, ostensibly for a post-postpartum check up. But the official results confirmed it. She was pregnant all right.

"Well, the world won't come to an end. You are healthy, fit, and young," Dr. Cavendish said, "but, I must say, the Marine Corps works fast. I'm glad Major Moore is out of the country six months of every year, or this would be an unsustainable rate of growth for the Bolington/Moore clan."

"Marines have to work fast," Swan said quietly, with only a hint of a smile. "Those six months abroad can be . . . eventful."

"Yes, yes, of course," said Dr. Cavendish, abashed. "We shall do our best to make these next six months *un*eventful."

"I'd like that, but . . . I seem to be getting big already," complained Swan. "Can that be possible?"

"Miss Bolington, you and I are in the same line of work," said Dr. Cavendish, "you tell me."

That left telling the Bolingtons.

"I have a surprise," Swan began, when she called Hetty the same afternoon, "one you indirectly had a hand in. I'm pregnant again."

The silence was brief but pointed.

"Really? Swan, are you sure? How can that be? My God, he's only been stateside for a few weeks! What did he do, throw you on your back in the terminal?"

"Not exactly. But you know those harem outfits? They turned out to be potently effective."

"Swan," Hetty paused, "does Sam know? Because you don't have to keep it if you don't want to. It's going to complicate things for you, big time. Don't tell him until you think it over."

Coming from Hetty, the idea was a shock. But it was no different from what Swan had thought about with Luke, was it?

"We're beyond that, Hetts. Sam knows. We're happy, so I hope you can be happy, too, or at least, not upset about it," Swan said, a little tentatively.

"Well, you know what you're doing," Hetty said, but her undertone was cool, judgmental, not happy. "You must be ready for Sam to be in your life in a big way. You've pretty much eliminated the possibility of moving on to anyone else for the foreseeable future. I gather that is what you want."

"Yes, Hetty. One way or another," Swan said, "but I've told you first, rather than Spaulding, since I wanted to keep the whole Dance of the Seven Veils thing between us. You can call her yourself and give her the news if you want."

"Will do . . . but, Swan, in the name of God, get rid of those DVDs as soon as the new baby is born!" Hetty pleaded. "In fact, I think I'll get rid of mine, too, just to be on the safe side."

It only took an hour for the Bolington phone tree to activate to its furthest branches. Daniel's was the call Swan dreaded most and Sam anticipated most.

"No wonder Sam was smirking in the Crossroads last month," Daniel said grimly.

"Hello and how are you doing, too," Swan answered, sarcasm for sarcasm.

"If biology is destiny, the two of you have the destiny thing pretty well nailed," Daniel said, "no pun intended."

"What's done is done," Swan said, conscious of Sam in the parlor with the baby. "We are happy for ourselves and for Luke, too, to have a sibling."

"I hope you'll stay happy when you see the medical bills and the mortgage payments combine into a perfect storm every month," Daniel continued calmly, "with you tied down to a one-year-old and a newborn trying to run a horse business. I'm sure Sam will be a big help from twelve thousand miles away."

"I get your drift," Swan said, coldly now. "We'll make it work."

"Daniel happy?" Sam asked cheerfully when she came into the parlor. Sam and Luke had on matching blue long-tailed stocking caps with "Kiss me, I'm a marine" knitted up their lengths. Sam was playing "Ride a Cock Horse to Banbury Cross" with Luke on his knees, now that the baby had enough strength to sit up with help.

"Concealing it pretty convincingly," Swan said, but with a smile. Then she frowned. "Stocking caps in summer?"

"Internet purchase. Good look for us?" Sam asked innocently.

"Might be if either of you had something on other than underpants. Thank God Townsend is out and it is Mathilde's day off."

◆

At eight weeks, they went to Dr. Cavendish together. Swan had the ultrasound alone, but the nurse called Sam in to see.

"Twins," Swan said, calmly, looking at him.

"Twins? Twins? Twins? You know it's twins?" Sam looked at Dr. Cavendish.

"That's what we are seeing on the ultrasound, Major Moore. Two heartbeats."

"Twin . . . boys?" Sam looked at Swan, not the doctor, for the answer.

"I'd bet the exacta on it," Swan said, "although we won't know for sure for months yet, just like with Luke."

"Holy shit. You are amazing!" he replied. "Twins! Septimus Junior *and* Bolington Fitzhugh— Andy and Fitz. Good thing we had two names. Identical?"

"There is no way of knowing yet, Major. Probably not," said Dr. Cavendish calmly.

"Three boys in one year!" Sam said delightedly, "on our way to our own combat team!"

"You're laughing now; wait til you see that first college tuition bill," observed Swan.

"Wait." Sam was serious all of a sudden. "What is the risk factor on this thing? Don't they come early? Can you deliver them . . . naturally?"

"It varies. More identicals are delivered naturally than are fraternals," replied the doctor matter-of-factly. "I'm more concerned about Swan having to go on bed rest at the end. That would be inconvenient for her, given how young Luke is, but if it has to be done, it has to be done. And yes, twins do tend to come early."

"Twins . . . ." Sam's brow was more furrowed than usual.

"They will probably be four feet tall; Luke will have gotten all of your tall genes. Better for the circus act, I suppose." Swan was still worried about the "height thing."

"No way," Sam was confident. "Six footers, all of them. I know it. We've got that thing going—what do you horse breeders call it?"

"A true nick? Hybrid vigor?"

"You know what this means, though, Swan. You can't sell Stone Chimneys. Each boy will need a farm."

Swan groaned. "God, now you are thinking like a Bolington. We've created a monster."

After they left Dr. Cavendish's, Sam was thinking logistics.

"I'm serious. I should give up the option to buy on the hunt box and move in with you. I'll pay the mortgage on Stone Chimneys, you can pay the taxes and insurance, we'll put crops in to help with income. It's an investment in all our boys' future."

"Wow," she said. "That is an . . . overwhelming . . . thought."

"Not to me—it is only great. You'll need me," Sam said with certainty. "The boys will need their father in their house, not just in their lives. You've outfoxed yourself this time, Miss I Can Raise My Child On My Own. Do you really think you can keep my three big sons in line all by your little self?"

"Why not?" Swan batted back, "I seem to manage their father pretty well."

The rest of Swan's family was speechless when they heard the news. Talk about the "deer in the headlights" look. Swan almost laughed at them herself, their expressions were so very comical. But the joke was really on her. Whatever the family had thought about prying Septimus Moore out of her life had been rendered nonoperational. Even Daniel Spaulding had trouble wrapping his mind around the three boys Swan was certain were going to make up her family in six months' time. They had no doubt that Sam had planned the whole campaign, brilliantly really, never facing them straight on, maneuvering—left oblique, straight ahead, left oblique, straight ahead—against an entrenched enemy facing him. A true military strategist, observed Bert sardonically—you had to give him credit.

If Sam and Swan had been the talk of Waverly before this development, they were now its obsession. Would Swan finally marry Sam? Would Lige Davenport move on to another farm owner victim? Would Daniel Spaulding goad Sam to the breaking point? Dr. Fisher was more subdued in her response but marveling.

"I'm glad to see my patients can still surprise me—in a good way," she said with a small smile during her first visit with Swan after the ultrasound. "How do you feel about all of this?"

"Well, pretty great, actually," Swan said truthfully. "I don't know if it is the anti-anxiety medication or the hormones or what, but fate seems to have taken me in a new direction—or is about to, anyway. It's all too much for me to try to control on my own anymore, but that prospect doesn't freak me out the way it did."

India Fisher sensed there was more.

"This is going to sound so weird—," Swan began. "It's something I haven't told anyone, not even Major Moore."

"Something you've begun to think about in relation to your baby and the children you are carrying?" asked the doctor with a small smile.

"You look like you know what I'm going to say."

"I may, if the number three is involved," Dr. Fisher agreed.

Swan nodded, impressed. "The three boys—if they do turn out to be three boys, after all."

"The three men you lost—Sergeant Lee, Captain Roland, Mr. Fitzhugh: their replacements. The ones you have given back to fate."

"Weird, isn't it?"

"Not really." Dr. Fisher met her gaze. "Karma."

"I'm giving back the three I 'took,' if you see things the way I . . . seem to," Swan said.

"Or fate is giving back the three it took from you?" ventured Dr. Fisher. "This doesn't worry you? That your so-called bad luck will 'infect' your children?"

"I was sure it would, but it doesn't. It doesn't make me worry about Major Moore, either," Swan said, "because if, God forbid, something happened to any of them, he could give me as many boys as we wanted. And if something happens to him, the boys will make sure I have a happy life without him. That's why he wants them—to take care of me."

"He has spent a lot of time trying to understand you, not just because he loves you, either. He's figured out how to get his own way, too."

"You mean getting back in the house? Getting me back?" Swan asked. "Yes, it looks like he's done that as well."

"Not just getting back into the house—back into the family, or at least back on their good side once again," said Dr. Fisher. "Do you ever ask what he dreams about?"

"Pretty grim stuff, sometimes." Eating the head of Osama bin Laden with a spoon, trying to save Hunt Lee from being blown apart in Rashad, threatening to kill someone with his bare hands if he "did that again." And, on his better days . . . .

"He'd like to be married," Swan said.

"Wouldn't you?" asked Dr. Fisher. "Now?"

"I don't know," said Swan. "It has been so painful, such a roller coaster ride."

"Think about it."

The next week, at his insistence, Sam accompanied Swan to Dr. Cavendish's office for a diet plan. The twins were booming along. If she kept it up, Swan would be almost as big at twelve weeks as she'd been with Luke at twenty-four. The doctor was reassuring.

"Your body is saying, 'Fool me once, shame on you. Fool me twice, shame on me—we're going to need the room.'"

Swan sighed. On their way out, Sam was cheerful.

"I told you, I *like* heft. Making love to a little Barbie doll is not always all it's cracked up to be. And I've always liked four-ways in bed."

"That is disgusting," Swan said, but she was cheering up.

They passed the Taliaferro county government office building, an old brick federal-style structure surrounded by a leafy little park. Sam suddenly pulled into the parking lot.

"I have an idea," he said, "let's get us a marriage license."

Swan looked at him as if he had suggested holding up the Waverly Bank and Trust.

"Why would we do that?"

"Because we are going to have two more babies in six months and the military medical benefits will come in handy; because we should have done it last year; because I'm going to be deployed; because we don't need all the fuss and flowers and dresses and guests. You planned three weddings and never got hitched. Let's not plan one and just do it." He was so earnest when he made this speech that she could think of nothing sarcastic in reply.

"Alright," she said.

The combat major took that as a go-ahead for action. He pulled her out of the truck and into the county clerk's office, paid the thirty dollars in cash, and left. It took all of fifteen minutes.

"The license is good immediately—no waiting period—for sixty days," he said.

"Why wait?" she asked.

"Don't you want me to sign a pre-nup?" He was kidding, but only partially.

"Do you want one? Afraid I'll take the Fat Boy?"

"Your family will be bullshit," Sam said.

"Let them. With what I've put you through, you deserve every penny you can wring out of me," Swan said with conviction.

"Justice of the peace or pastor?"

"Let's go home first. I want to change. And let's bring Luke," Swan sounded much calmer than she felt. "We can stop by the parsonage at Everley Methodist."

"We'll need witnesses," Sam said. In unison they said, "Mathilde, Edgar, and Eduardo."

"My family will have a coronary," Swan said.

"It couldn't happened to a nicer bunch."

◆

They drove to Belle Everley in a happy silence. Sam was certain she was going to back out, come up with some commonsense, rational reason not to do it—but she didn't. She went to the bedroom and changed into buttercream silk, matching silk pumps, her rubies. She slipped on her engagement ring for the first time in a year. She called ahead to the parsonage; the surprised Pastor Abernathy agreed to see them in half an hour. Swan dressed Luke in one of his little marines outfits. Sam came into the bedroom.

"I've got a uniform here in the closet," he said tentatively, looking at her. "You are going to be so lovely. I should change."

"Hurry up then, Major," she smiled. "I'll tell Mathilde."

"Jesus, Mary, and Joseph," cried the housekeeper when she heard the plan, "let me get my apron off. Thank goodness I've got a pork roast for dinner."

Swan called down to the barn. In fifteen minutes, they were all in the SUV and the dually, even Flagg, Swan holding a large bunch of floribunda roses from the front flower bed. Edgar and Eduardo had thrown jackets over their barn clothes. Sam looked suddenly martial in his service uniform, which was accessorized by a diaper bag. He was afraid to look at Swan at all, afraid of doing something that would cause her to change her mind. He set his jaw: the major to be obeyed. In ten minutes they were all in the little parsonage's parlor, the bride and groom, the baby, the dog, the three devoted workers, and the pastor, who had seen it all before. Except perhaps for the dog.

They said their vows—no tears, no hesitation in their voices. No one was surprised to see that Sam had a wedding ring for Swan, the perfect mate to the antique Moore engagement ring, but they were surprised to see Swan had a simple ring for Sam, one that had been tucked away safely in her jewelry box. In ten minutes, the paperwork signed, with hugs all around, they were back in the trucks headed to the old farm house. Sam looked at Swan, the shock finally registering.

"Wife," was all he said.

Mathilde charged into the kitchen to check the roast in the Aga. Then she charged out again.

"A picture," she announced. She ran for the digital camera in the closet.

"Everyone into the parlor," she ordered. She assembled them in front of the fireplace, Sam dwarfing them all, a huge smile on his face. He pulled Swan in front of him at the last minute, with Luke and her flowers in her arms, mimicking the pose of their Oceanside photo. Mathilde took the picture but insisted on a more traditional one, with Swan and Sam side by side and Edgar and Eduardo flanking them. Then Luke was over the whole thing. He began to fuss.

"One request," Swan said, "let's tell no one today. Let's just keep it for ourselves. Townsend won't be back until tomorrow, and then there will be hell to pay with the Bolingtons."

"Poor Miss Swan—I mean, Madame Moore—she hasn't been able to have a glass of champagne in months, and now she can't even celebrate her own wedding," said Mathilde as she poured five flutes. "I don't care, you can touch the wine to your lips, at least—that won't hurt."

"*A la novia*," said Edgar and Eduardo, repeating the toast they had given in exactly the same place two Christmases previously.

"Stay, both of you," Swan said impulsively. "We'll have our wedding supper, just us." The men nodded, then shook their heads unbelievingly, then became serious.

"*Gracias, Señora Moore*," said Eduardo, formally, for the first time.

They laughed away much of the afternoon. They told their versions of their history together. Everything seems funny now, now that everything had worked out. Or almost everything: they skipped over the four months in hell, when Swan had sent Sam away—and Fitch. None of that would ever be funny.

◆

After dinner—peanut soup, crown roast of pork, jalapeño corn, baby carrots, new potatoes in cream, fresh fruit trifle, *mousse au chocolate*—the men departed, still stunned. There would be no honeymoon, not right then, in any case. The next day was a work day, Swan said. Sam had to go to Quantico. More hugs all around. Mathilde cleaned up and withdrew discreetly to her rooms.

Luke had passed out from the general tumult. Swan put him in the cradle in her bedroom—their bedroom again now. They undressed, calm and happy. Swan shyly slipped on a white silk full-length nightgown, shear as gossamer, from the trousseau she had assembled but never used the year before. Sam looked at her.

"My beautiful bride," he said.

"A tubby bride," she teased, but she was pleased to see not just unquenched desire but a male's possessiveness in his eyes.

Unlike the coin bra, the nightie survived, despite being worn for less than five minutes.

"I should call Persis tomorrow," Sam said quietly when they were sated and snuggled under the silks and quilts, "and tell her I won't be buying the hunt box. I'll give sixty days' notice and move back here right away. I meant it when I said we should keep Stone Chimneys, Swan. I'll pay the mortgage, or as big a part of it as I can swing, and get you on my insurance tomorrow. Twins often need to spend time in the NIC-U, like the doctor said; those bills can be astronomical. Your own insurance will max out." Swan could tell all of this gave Sam great satisfaction. He would be the provider after all, not just a husband living in his wife's house. His family needed him.

"Okay," was all Swan said. She ran her hand gently up his arm, then back down to his big hand, with its new ring. "All mine."

"Always has been," he replied gently, "always will be."

"Well," Spaulding said the next day, "I guess none of us should be surprised, given the circumstances."

"I hope you can be happy for me," Swan said, "for us."

"Yes, my darling, of course. No one deserves happiness more."

Swan explained the whole thing—getting the license, going to Pastor Abernathy. She left out the part about keeping Stone Chimneys. That was their personal financial business, now—hers and her husband's. Spaulding had the good sense—and courtesy—not to ask. Swan heard the new formality in her tone, an acknowledgment of Swan's change in status: a married woman with new loyalties. Sam had headed off to Quantico with a sappy grin on his face, disconcerting against his battle dress.

"Talk about the happy warrior," Swan had teased as she had sent him off, with Luke in her arms. "No Taliban is going to be frightened of that."

"Laugh all you want," he batted back. "I'm prepared to be the butt of jokes all day. It's worth it, Mrs. Moore." As he had gotten into the Escalade, he turned back. "I'll stop by the hunt box and pick up my stuff. I'll be home for dinner. I don't want to be late for the old ball and chain." He had kissed her and Luke, and Swan thought she had never seen anyone so happy in her whole life. Whatever else happened, she had given him that.

"We'll be here," she had said softly.

Hetty was practical, as always.

"Sam is right about one thing: you are better off having military medical benefits. And you two have been married, for all intent and purposes, for months. To have three kids and pretend any different any more would be ridiculous, I guess. This isn't Possum Holler," she said matter-of-factly. Swan was getting used to the fact that no one's first response was happy, none of the Bolingtons', anyway.

The news traveled through Waverly with the speed of a rifle shot. Swan reconciled herself to getting nothing done but answering the phone with Luke in his bouncy chair, or his playpen, or nursing on her lap, with Flagg's anxious supervision. By mid-afternoon the Shepherd was exhausted and he and Luke were snoring in the parlor in tandem. The sound of Townsend's rental car engine broke the silence. Flagg launched himself toward the door, furious with himself for sleeping on the job. But when Townsend burst in to the parlor, he relaxed.

"Tell me—is it true? Is it some joke the two of you are pulling? Or Waverly gossip, one hundred percent wrong, as usual?" Townsend demanded, without so much as a hello. "I'm gone for two days and, boom, after two years, you do it."

"It is true," Swan said. "We decided to do it, and an hour later it was done." She recounted the sequence of events for the tenth time that day.

"Well, I'm so very happy. You two belong together. It is like a fairy tale finally come true," Townsend smiled so sincerely that for the first time Swan burst into tears.

"Don't cry, Swan, please!" Townsend said in a panic. "I'm so sorry! What did I say?"

"Nothing, darling," Swan wiped her eyes with her hand. "It's just that you are the first person other than Mathilde and the guys to be really happy for us. It caught me by surprise, that's all."

"Really?" Townsend was sobered. "Why, because you'll be a military wife? You'll have to follow him around from base to base?"

That thought was distressing to Swan as well. She wished she'd had the courage of a Nurse Edith Cavell, but she had secret hopes that General Clayton would find a way to keep Sam at Quantico, perhaps overseeing some of the specialized training marines were undertaking to prepare them for future wars, or at the Pentagon, hopes so secret she hadn't brought them up to Sam since the dinner in Oceanside.

"No, I don't think so. They are worried about his state of mind, I guess, and that he'll come between me and them because of all the history they've all built up. And he and Daniel can't stand each other."

"Well, they will get over it. They'll have to when they see all these little boys you two are going to have around here. Swan, I'm so happy and so jealous! You and Hetty will have five little boys between you, that has to be some kind of world record," Townsend said, and Swan smiled. "I know I said I'd never date a marine after seeing what you have been through, but if there was another Septimus Moore out there, believe me, I'd be married to him in a New York minute."

Swan was about to bring up Harry Edwards when the phone rang for the tenth time.

"Mrs. Osmond," said Mathilde.

"Virgilia." Swan took the phone in the hallway, expecting to field yet another round of questions and congratulations.

"Swan? Have you heard the bad news?" her neighbor asked breathlessly. Swan's heart contracted; for a second she thought, *Sam*. "It's Paintbrush Farm," continued the voice of doom, "it's been sold to Lige Davenport for two point nine million. Those lawyers wanted out."

Swan was so relieved she had to wait a moment to let her heart stop pounding.

"Oh, no," was all she could muster.

"They didn't even give anyone else a chance. And him! Such a varmint! After all he put us through—even dating Miss T.! Now we will have to fight him after all and, Swan, he will win." Virgilia was despairing.

Swan's first instinct was to say, "I'll call Daniel." Then she stopped. No, not any longer. First she would discuss it with her husband, with Sam.

"I didn't know," she said calmly. "I've been a bit preoccupied, though—perhaps you'll forgive me. Sam and I got married yesterday."

"Oh, Swan," Virgilia's tone immediately changed, "I'm so sorry to have intruded on your happiness. I didn't know." Swan could hear a very faint note of remonstration.

"No one did, darling," she said quickly. "We literally passed the clerk's office in Waverly yesterday and got a license, went to Pastor Abernathy, and that was that. I can hardly believe it myself when I tell people. But there it is, legal and everything. I'm looking at the marriage certificate right now."

"I'm very, very glad for you both. He is a wonderful man, I've always thought so," said Virgilia, "and with your family growing—well, it was time."

"Past time, according to many," Swan observed, "but thanks for the news about Paintbrush. The last of the Delafields sold it to that couple assured that they'd keep it for their lifetime. That turned out not to be the case." She couldn't keep the bitterness out of her voice. "I always loved that place—the fields of devil's paintbrush, that lovely house . . . ."

"What are we going to do? What can be done?" Virgilia was despairing and panic stricken at the same time.

"I don't know, dear. We'll think of something—talk to the PPT . . . ." Swan's mind churned. She mulled as she returned to the parlor.

"Townsend, did you know that Lige was buying a farm here in Waverly?" she asked gently.

The beauty tossed her blonde hair.

"Oh, I don't keep track of Lige Davenport's business. Who can? It's all pretty much a bore to me," she said, her interest in the subject obviously exhausted. "I'm sorry if he's still upsetting you. Do you and Sam plan to have a big party to announce your marriage? If so, I'll want to give Bernardo as much notice as I can. Season Three of his show begins shooting in a couple of weeks."

Swan hid a small smile. Certainly if there was going to be a party, Townsend couldn't bring Lige—not unless they wanted the wedding celebration to double as a hanging.

"Frankly, we haven't talked about it. But I'm sure we will do something."

"Mr. Daniel," announced Mathilde ominously from the doorway, holding the phone.

"I just heard," he said, when Swan came on the line.

"I won't ask you to be happy, but I hope you can see your way to being happy for me," Swan said, trying for reconciliation.

"Yes, of course I can," Daniel said, but with little genuine emotion.

Luke was stirring from his deep sleep and beginning to sound hungry.

"Swan, I'll try to steer clear of Sam, for your sake, but I hope you can convince him to do the same with me," Daniel said. "We're all stuck with each other now."

Swan's silence spoke volumes.

"Okay. I'm going to have to mend my ways now that he's officially part of the family—Mrs. Moore."

Luke began making grumpy, gurgling noises.

"Stuck or not, I'm afraid I've got a hungry baby in the next room," said Swan softly, "and I just heard another bit of news: Lige bought the Paintbrush Farm."

"Oh. Fuck," Daniel said. "What are you going to do?"

Swan hesitated.

"Don't know. But gotta go."

She found Townsend holding Luke on her lap. Swan opened her shirt.

"Swan, how old do you think you should be to get married?" Townsend asked as Luke snuggled into Swan's arms.

"I would have been twenty-one if I'd married Hunt when we planned," Swan said. "I certainly thought I was ready. Whether I actually would have been, I don't know. I'm glad I'm twenty-eight, not twenty-one, though, in my current predicament." She realized that sounded ominous. "I mean having the twins so soon after Luke, of course—not being married to Sam."

"But once you are married, you can't always predict what is going to happen afterward."

"Even before, you can't predict. I'm living proof."

The afternoon round of phone calls *was* predictable: Hetty and Boyd, the Lombardinis, then at the end of the afternoon, Oliver Lentz, with his update on Oscar Mike.

"Congratulations a thousand times over," he said when Swan gave him the news. "I hope you will be as happy as Decca and I have been for these twenty-five years. I'm sure I can speak for Grace and Thurgood, too. I must say, we never had our doubts that Sam was going to get his way. And you might like to know that Linny has recovered from her surgery with flying colors; their plan is to bring her back to the races next year and see what happens."

"I'm thrilled for Grace and Thurgood," Swan said sincerely. "I hope she beats the pants off every filly she meets, except for Enfilade. She will be coming to you, as usual, next month. And after that will be Trebuchet—Major. Then Piquet, the very last of the Fortresses."

"And so the years turn, Swan, dear," Oliver said.

Swan heard Sam arrive with the Escalade loaded with his belongings from the hunt box. Persis had taken his notice to vacate with good grace, Sam had said earlier in the day, and that had given Swan a thought.

She had called Daniel back from the extension upstairs.

"You might consider taking the hunt box yourself," she proposed. "You know I have to lease out High View as a working farm. Virgilia wants to stay at Stone Chimneys another few months until her new carriage house is renovated. There is very little else to rent out here, and you said town was too . . . distracting. You won't need the stalls, but the apartment isn't impossible. You could think about it."

"I appreciate that, Swan, but I'm not sure I want to stay in the same town as your strapping husband, now that he's here for good," Daniel had been philosophical. "I'm going to look further east, perhaps cut my commute into D.C."

"It was just a thought. I haven't found a tenant yet, but I'm going to have to. Sam wants us to keep Stone Chimneys." It had still sounded odd: "us."

"Really? Why, may I ask?"

"He thinks we should—" She hadn't known if Sam wanted Daniel to know all of their business. Why get into trouble the first day they were married? "Look at all of our options."

"Well, I'm glad he has become such a financial expert in one day," Daniel had said. "If I'd realized our professions were so similar I would have jumped in a humvee and gone after bin Laden myself much sooner."

Swan was too preoccupied to register his sarcasm. "Now that we are about to go to settlement, I'd like to put Sam's name on the deed with mine. Will the bank mind?"

"Can he pass a credit check?" Daniel asked, serious now. "If so, it should be no problem. It's too late to try to renegotiate your conventional loan as a VA loan and still keep to the settlement date, but otherwise, you should be good to go. You're married, in any case."

"Let's make it happen then. It's important to him," Swan said softly. "I want him to own the land with me before he goes back up the line."

"I'll ask your loan officer to get the paperwork to Sam," Daniel said.

"Thank you," Swan said. "I really mean it. I know how much you had to do with me getting the loan in the first place, despite what you said. Almost no one is getting farm loans, certainly no one with no guaranteed source of income. I couldn't have done it without you. I'll be sure Sam understands that, too. I've still got hopes for the two of you getting along eventually."

"Honey, I'm home," Sam shouted cheerfully, slamming the front door behind him. Flagg met him at full speed, as usual.

"Let's talk about the hunt box idea again before you make any final decision," Swan said anxiously into the phone.

"Swannie, you can't keep all of us clustered around you forever," Daniel said gently. "You'll tire yourself out trying to keep us in your orbit. As beautiful an orbit as it is, it's getting crowded, and will be even more so once the twins arrive. A few of us have to be thrown out into space to survive on our own."

"I don't believe that," said Swan stoutly. "I want all of you here where I can see you and take care of you."

Daniel laughed.

"Now you really do sound like the mother of the universe," he laughed. "You have a husband, a baby, and more on the way. You can't manage us all. The Moores are going to be a fulltime job, even for you. Good-bye, darling girl," and he was gone with a click.

"Hi, Miss T. Feels like I'm coming home to two wives instead of one," Sam was saying, happy as a clam, "three, counting Mathilde."

"Sam, I'm so happy for you," Townsend said, offering her cheek for a kiss, "but I'm going to be moving out next week, so you will be down one wife, at least."

"Moving out?" Swan said, coming down the stairs. But first things first: she gave Sam a long, long hug. It felt wonderful.

"Did you miss me, Ma?" he crooned into her ear. "Did you miss your old man?"

She gave him a smile, and then that little secret push away from her.

"Never gave you a thought," she teased, "too busy telling everyone our news."

"Where's Luke?" Sam was on his way upstairs to see his baby.

"Townsend, just because Sam is here for good doesn't mean you have to leave," Swan said. "It never dawned on me that you'd think so. So what if you aren't going back to school this semester? I don't want you to feel like you are being pushed out."

"I don't. I'm moving back to Uncle Dex's, at least for the time being. It's all arranged. I won't leave you high and dry. I'll keep coming during the day to take care of Lukie Palookie, until you find someone permanently. Eventually, if I stay East, I think I want to live on my own."

"When did all of this come about? Why didn't you tell me?" Swan asked, taken completely by surprise.

"I've been thinking of it for a few weeks. It just seems like the timing is right," Townsend said.

"Does this have anything to do with Lige?" Swan asked, "because, whatever my personal feeling about his activities, I would never let it interfere with our friendship. I would be sad if you thought that was even a possibility. He would always be welcome here as your friend and guest—always."

Townsend smiled at her.

"Swan, face reality. Lige's business is going to put him in conflict with people in Waverly one way or another, pretty much from now on. It would be better for everyone if I weren't living in town, I think."

"Dinner is served," announced Mathilde. A beef ragout with homemade egg noodles, field greens, local silver and gold corn, fresh fruit compote, sweet potato pie.

"In honor of Major Moore, I'm changing our menus a bit, Madame. On a day this warm we'd usually have *quenelle Lyonnaise* with gazpacho, or chilled vichyssoise and medallions of lobster. But we have a man of the house now, so I hope you approve. We cannot serve such a gentleman, protecting our country from the terrorists, little bits of seafood and lettuce for his dinner." She was solemn, as though she were announcing a change in governments.

"I do approve, Mathilde, completely," Swan said with a smile. Then she laughed.

"Just for laughing, I'm going to eat two helpings of beef," Sam said with satisfaction, "and another two ears of corn. Big guys need chow. If you ate MREs six months at a time, you'd eat a second helping, too."

Mathilde looked vindicated.

"Wait til there are four men in the family," she sniffed, "you won't be laughing, Madame, believe me. *Mon dieu,* we will have to raise cattle here ourselves, and hogs, if you are going to continue to have these—these—boys."

That got everyone laughing.

"Mathilde and I are going to be so outnumbered," Swan said sadly. "I wish you'd reconsider, Townsend, and stay."

"No, Swan, it's time," Townsend said it in a way that was final.

"I guess I'll begin to look for an au pair, then," Swan said, looking at Sam. "With the twins coming, it is going to be necessary. No way around it."

"What about that little girl who works in the Crossroads? The waitress, Kitty? She seems a peach," Sam asked. "You'll need someone who can do the heavy lifting, change a mountain of diapers, that kind of thing. Working here has to be better than slinging burgers in the Crossroads."

"I think she goes to community college," Swan said, "concentrating in early childhood development. This might work out, after all. Townsend, you can come and visit just like a regular friend and not have Luke in your arms all the time."

"Well, I will miss the little Lukotini very much," Townsend said, "but he is your son, yours and Sam's." She smiled. "I'll just have to get my own somehow."

When they went to bed that night, Swan found herself choking up when she saw Sam's weight bench, temporarily in the bedroom in its old place.

"I thought you'd get a kick out of seeing it back, one more time," he whispered. "Tomorrow I'll move it to the spare bedroom, but it deserves one last night back where we had it last year, when I was recovering."

"Sam, I just can't believe we've made this all work out. Something is going to happen—"

"Hey, don't start on that." He pulled her close to him. "Nothing is going to happen. Nothing bad, anyway. You are going to keep going to Dr. Fisher, and I'll go, too, if you want. You are going to have two more of our wonderful kids to keep us company. I'm going to get fat sitting behind a desk in some desert, jumping whenever some general says jump, then come home and take more riding lessons so I can keep up with my horsey family. We are going to win the Kentucky Derby with Major and go on horse racing TV and explain how many fiancés you've had."

"What about Lige? He has bought this farm right on our back door—on High View's back door, anyway. We are maxed out with Stone Chimneys. If he ruins Waverly, he'll ruin us, utterly." Swan had pulled herself up on her elbows, resting her chin on his chest.

"He's not going to ruin Waverly. I'm going to challenge him to a cage match—no Golden Gloves stuff—in front of the whole town. We are going to strip naked, charge admission, and sell the pay-per-view rights for so much money that he won't need to build a shopping mall on Paintbrush Farm after all. Then we'll sell *him* to the highest bidders among my one hundred ex-one night stands for a marathon sex orgy so that he can have the fifty children he wants. Problem solved." Sam stroked her long heavy hair laying like a blanket across his chest.

"Why didn't I think of that?" she smiled. "Do you think you could come up with a plan like that for the Taliban and stay home for good?"

There remained one important social obligation, a party under tents on the lawns of Belle Everley. At Spaulding and Bert's insistence, they were serving as the hosts to introduce the new master of the family's homestead and his heir, as well as to announce the impending arrival of the master and mistress's twins. Swan said that, after that, Waverly would have maxed out on Bolington/Moore drama and would leave them all in peace for at least the next two generations.

◆

It was the last week of October, almost three weeks after the sixth anniversary of Hunt Lee's death. Sam had convinced Swan to let him drive her to Arlington to lay their wreaths. He kept her stay at Hunt's grave brief, using her rare bout of morning sickness as the excuse to cut her visit short. She wanted to tell him she felt she was moving away from Hunt, that she had been doing so since she had known Sam, putting distance between Hunt's memory and her life, that it was a good sign from her perspective, but she was reluctant to say it. She thought Sam would think, *This could be me, here in Section Sixty. If she can move on from Hunt, she'll move on from me, too, if I die.* So she said nothing.

She needn't have worried. Sam had his legacy, no matter what happened to him or when it happened. Swan would never need a grave marker or a wreath or a flag to remember Sam by. She would have Luke. By the next anniversary, Sam thought, he'd be just back from Afghanistan once again, and their three babies would be reason enough to postpone her visit to Arlington, to wait until Veterans Day or Christmas time or even later. That was his plan, anyway. He wouldn't know for twelve months that it was her plan, too.

They had missed seeing Oscar Mike win the General Winder Handicap over the Labor Day weekend at Saratoga. Instead, they were going to try to make it to the Bloodhorse Cup Turf Classic the following week at Churchill Downs. Getting them all there was going to be a major logistical exercise, but Swan was determined to go. If Mike won that race against an international field, his career as a stallion would be made. He could retire to eastern Kentucky, ideally, so they could visit him easily. Grace and Thurgood Templeton were as good as their word: they were going to be part of Swan's stallion syndicate and send Cartouche's dam, Zenobia, to Mike as soon as the partnership was finalized. With the Templetons in, Swan had no worries about attracting other top breeders to Mike's studbook.

◆

The weekend of the party, Luke was christened in Everley Methodist. Just a few of them gathered in front of Pastor Abernathy: Hetty and Boyd and their boys, Spaulding and Bert, Daniel, and the Belle Everley and High View workers watched Mathilde, Luke's godmother, hold the baby as Swan and Sam stood by proudly. Then more than two hundred guests came to the old house itself. Swan sent an invitation to Julia Hampstead without telling Sam, using reverse address search, but the invitation came back as undeliverable.

Sam was in his service uniform, Swan in a Ralph Rucci grenadine silk cocktail dress, her ruby earrings, bracelet, and necklace. Her hair, now to her waist, was loose and full but braided around her face, medieval style. A social secretary, one of the few alive and kicking in the Washington, D.C., area, catalogued two hundred gifts in the living room and dining room as the endless procession of Town Cars, hummers, duallies, and BMWs was valet parked in the mare field nearest the house.

The Lombardinis catered the soirée—Maryland crab, Maine lobster, local poultry, and an entire TexMex barbeque station in honor of Sam's Texas heritage. (Sam joked they should have had a goat roast in honor of how much time he had spent in the Middle East.) Huge dessert stations, one of pastries and another of frozen sorbets and mousses, tempted the guests, accompanied by magnums of Veuve Clicquot. A local swamp band played during the buffet service. As the party wound down in the late summer twilight, Sam pulled Swan with him to the microphone at the front of the dance floor.

"I want to thank you all for coming to celebrate here with us," he said in a loud, clear voice. "Two years ago I was a broken-down marine with nothing but a motorcycle to my name, eating a burger in a little Virginia town. No family, no permanent home, no future laid out before me. Then a beautiful girl in her stocking feet came into the restaurant," he looked lovingly down at Swan. "I didn't know what Vogels were then . . . ." A chuckle spread through the crowd. "But I'll always be grateful to the Artisan for taking an hour to repair that girl's boots. Now I have, not just the belle of the South as my wife, and the beautiful son she's given me—" His voice caught, and there was dead silence while he took a second to compose himself, "not only that, but also two more little Moores on the way to take their place among you all. They will be children of Virginia, which has given me a family and a future and made me a part of its history. I hope we will be able to spend the rest of our lives here in Waverly, and I hope Swan and I can help give Waverly a great future, too." He turned and kissed Swan, lifting her off her feet, and the crowd began to clap.

For the first time ever, Sam heard from the back of the crowd the old Rebel yell, reserved for rare private occasions in the South, the "Woo-woo woo-woo woo-wooo" that was part fox hunter call, part owl hoot, and part Indian war cry, taught in a few of the old families quietly, by the last living Confederate veterans in the nineteen twenties and thirties to their sons and *their* sons and, now, their sons, too. At that, the band struck up a swamp version of "God Bless America." At the end, an "Ooh-rah!" garnered a round of applause and laughter.

Then people began to drift towards their cars.

A crème caramel Mercedes sedan wound its way into the parking area. Townsend Brooke, in saffron and cinnamon silk Indian-inspired pants and sari, was handed out of the car by Elijah Davenport in his classic suit, wingtips, and collar pin. An elegant, middle-aged couple whom Swan did not recognize was with them. A little ripple of tension spread among the guests when they realized Davenport was on the premises, so Swan pulled Sam abruptly to the foursome for an old Virginia greeting from the honorees themselves.

"Townsend, darling," Swan said, embracing the flushed girl, "and Lige, we are so very glad you were able to come." She turned to her tall husband. "Sam, I don't think you and Lige have ever actually met."

"Major Moore, my honor and pleasure," said Lige immediately, extending his hand to meet Sam's, "and my most sincere congratulations."

The men eyed each other as Alpha males typically do, observing social formality punctiliously while silently ascertaining whether they could take each other in a fight to the death. As the guest, Lige bent his head first in submission. Otherwise the two of them would have stood there glaring until daybreak. Townsend, however, was having none of it.

"Thank you for having us, Swan, Sam," she said. "I'd like you to meet my parents, Terrence and Lilith Townsend. How absolutely beautiful you look, Swannie. But where is Mister Wiggly?"

Swan gestured down the rolling lawn to a cluster of Adirondack chairs and tables, lit by candles now in the dusk. Spaulding and Bert had custody of Luke, who was watching Boyd Junior and Bud with laser-like intensity as they played in the grass at the adults' feet.

"I'll miss him so," Townsend said, looking longingly down the hill. "There will never be a baby like Tickle Me Lukie, never."

"Now, honey, don't say that," Lige remonstrated, giving her a little squeeze. "We're going to do our best to replicate him, now, aren't we?"

Swan was dumbstruck.

"Yes, that's one reason I wanted us to come today," said Townsend calmly, "I wanted our Waverly friends to hear the news first, from us, in person."

Swan felt the rumble of an oncoming train, the train of destiny, heading down the tracks toward the tall young woman in front of her.

"Lige has asked me to marry him and I've said yes, on one condition," said Townsend, "that we live in Waverly, make it our home, so that we can help keep the town beautiful and historic, just the way it is."

"She drove a hard bargain," Lige chimed in, holding his fiancée's hand in his huge paw, "so I took the bull by the horns, so to speak, and bought Paintbrush Farm as a surprise for her. We'd been there when the owners had first asked me to look at it, and I kind of got the feeling Miss T. had a yen for it, didn't I? I followed your clues pretty well."

"Yes, you did," Townsend said sweetly. "You did just fine." She looked out over the Belle Everley fields, the barns, the mares grazing in the darkening dusk. She lifted her beautiful hand, and Swan saw an enormous solitaire pink diamond in all its splendor on Townsend's ring finger.

"I asked Mother and Dad to join us, with Uncle Dex. I hope you don't mind," Townsend continued, "we don't want to steal attention from you."

"Not at all, we couldn't be happier, could we, Sam?" Swan said. "Mr. and Mrs. Townsend, I'm sure your news will be of great interest to everyone." Dexter Gaylord materialized to shepherd his sister and brother-in-law to the microphone, towing Lige and Townsend with them.

"Lilith and I are happy to announce the engagement of our daughter, Townsend, to Mr. Elijah Davenport, late of Prince Arthur County and new master of Paintbrush Farm, Waverly," said Terrence Brooke in a father-of-the-bride voice.

There was a moment of stunned silence. Swan nudged Sam and the two of them began to applaud; Spaulding, Bert, Dexter Gaylord, and the Belle Everley workers quickly followed. That broke the ice, and the whole guest list applauded with some enthusiasm. Swan went quickly to Lige and kissed his cheek, publicly bestowing on him the Bolington blessing, and Sam kissed Townsend just as publicly, although probably with more enjoyment.

"We'll be neighbors, Swan," Townsend said happily. "We want to start our family right away, so we can catch up with you and Sam."

"Yep," agreed Lige, his enormous satisfaction evident. "I had to pass Miss T.'s test with your Luke, and I guess I did."

"He'll still have to carry the diaper bags at Churchill Downs," Townsend insisted, giving her fiancé a coy look, "unless Sam wants to do it himself. Lige and I can go to the races, reopen Paintbrush to the hunt, host the Art League fund-raiser . . . . It's going to be fun."

"Darling, I am so happy for you both," Swan could say that with honest emotion. She was still trying to process it—Waverly saved, Belle Everley, High View, Stone Chimneys, all insulated from development due to the protective vigilance of its greatest threat, Lige Davenport. She pulled Townsend aside as Dexter took the Brookes and Lige through the buffet line. "Are you sure this is what you want to do? What about college and modeling and acting and . . . everything?"

"What could I do that would be more important than saving Waverly?" the beauty asked. "Lige adores me, and he wants as many children as I do. Yes, he's a little old and fuddy-duddy, but I've had fast and glamorous, too, remember. A woman has to make decisions for the long-term, not like men, who can do things in the heat of the moment." She tossed her head. "I couldn't let Belle Everley be ruined, not after all you and Sam have gone through, you especially. You are my darling sister, aren't you? And now we can be together forever." She hugged Swan and kissed her.

"Of course we can," Swan said, her eyes filling. "You know, Hetty and I once talked about men going into battle, charging into a hail of gunfire to prove their bravery to each other. But women can be resolute—and creative—in accomplishing the same mission. Even very young women."

"All's fair in love and war, Swan," said Townsend. "Napoleon said it. Or someone like that."

The next day, Daniel came by on his way into D.C. Sam had left at oh-dark thirty, but banker's hours were more civilized.

"I guess Miss T. saved the day for all of us," Daniel said. "You needn't have bought Stone Chimneys, after all."

"That's not strictly true," Swan replied, pouring coffee for him in the parlor. "It bought us some valuable time for Lige and Miss T. to warm up to each other. If some other developer had bought it for commercial use, Lige might have been reluctant to agree to settle here. Sam thinks we should keep all three of the farms for the children." Sam had had no problem with Swan telling her family his views on the subject. "They'll all deserve the opportunity to live here and raise families eventually, as he said at the party. The Bolington holdings have been shriveling up for two generations. We're expanding them again.

"And, thanks to you, I didn't sell the Stubbs in a panic. I'd be sorry now, if I had. You did that for me, and I'll always be grateful." She smiled at him. How many men had sat there on mornings just like this, watching the sun light her hair, Daniel wondered. Everett Bolington, Hunt Lee, Carter Roland, Fitch, Sam—and now him, of course.

"You and Miss T. will be settled now," he said. "You can enjoy being a newlywed, root for Oscar Mike at the Bloodhorse Cup, and wait for the twins. They will keep you occupied when Sam deploys. I, however, have decided to leave High View and perhaps Tidewater Commercial, too," he said.

"Why? Whatever for?" Swan protested.

"Oh, I think I'm ready to move on," Daniel said. "I have no desire to be your alternate husband when Sam is overseas." He smiled grimly. "That was one thing I learned from Fitch, and from my own experience, as well, I suppose."

"Where would you go? Back to Strasburg?"

"God forbid," he rolled his eyes, "perhaps the U.K. or somewhere that will allow me to make a bigger dent in my debts. But I don't have to decide today. I think I'll relax for a few days. Celebrate our victory. Then we'll see."

◆

Two nights later, Swan was aware of a car coming up the driveway, the gravel crunching as it arrived. She rolled over in bed and looked out the window—a police car with its red and blue roof light bar flashing. Flagg growled and Sam bolted upright, muscles flexed, reaching for the Walther. She put her hand on his arm.

"It's okay," she said softly, as he began actually to wake up. "I'll go down and see what it is." She gave the snoozing Luke a quick look and wrapped her kimono around her.

When she opened the front door, she came face to face with Kenny Hardy, his face a mask.

"Mrs. Moore, I'm afraid I have very bad news," he said.

"Come in, Kenny," Swan said. She felt the life draining out of her. The deputy stepped into the entranceway. Swan stepped back and searched his face.

"Mr. Daniel Spaulding was in the Scarab earlier this evening. About two hours ago, he was found deceased in his car in the parking lot, the result, we think, of a drug overdose. Of course, we don't have the toxicology report, but witnesses in the Scarab said he purchased a large amount of cocaine there tonight. He said he was celebrating."

"What's going on?" said Sam, coming down the stairs in the "I'm Dad" robe.

"Sam, you remember Deputy Hardy," Swan said mechanically. "Daniel's dead. Cocaine overdose in the Scarab parking lot earlier tonight."

"Are you sure?" Sam asked. "No foul play? Robbery? A struggle? Anything?"

"Our investigation is just beginning, Major Moore," said Kenny quietly. "Of course all of those avenues will be explored, but with eye-witness accounts of the drug buy, I think it is reasonably safe to say that is what most likely happened." He turned back to Swan. "Mrs. Moore, I am so very sorry."

"What do we do?" Swan asked. "Where is he now?"

"The coroner has finished his on-site investigation," Kenny said softly. "You should call the county morgue in the morning. There will be an autopsy, since his death would be part of a criminal investigation of the dealer who sold him the cocaine. The morgue will tell you when it can release the body to whatever funeral home or . . . arrangement . . . your family will want to make. Since Mr. Spaulding was away from home, we see no need to search High View," he continued, "but if we do, I hope we'll have your permission to do so.

"Apparently, he had made similar occasional purchases in the Scarab over the last six months or so. Were you aware of his activities in that regard, Mrs. Moore?"

"No, no. No. I thought he was doing well," Swan said. Fitch had said, "tell Daniel to stay out of the Scarab"—when? Last year? Her mind seemed frozen up: Daniel dead. After all of his hard work, celebrating the rescue of Belle Everley, her children's inheritance. Her happy life.

"I kill everyone who loves me," Swan said quietly, almost to herself. Sam put his arms around her.

"Don't," he said. He turned to Kenny. "We appreciate your coming here yourself, Deputy. Thank you. Do you need us anymore tonight? If not, I think my wife needs a little time to let this all sink in."

Sam wrapped her in his arms after he had closed the door behind Kenny.

"We should call Spaulding," he suggested, "Bert, Hetty and Boyd—who else?"

"That's all. That's all tonight, anyway," Swan said, like an automaton.

Sam punched Spaulding's number into his cell phone first; when Swan looked at him helplessly, he told Spaulding himself. Swan could hear Spaulding's heartbroken wail from where she stood. Sam gave her a few minutes to compose herself and asked what funeral home she wanted contacted: Waverly Funeral Chapel.

Then he called the Delaneys and Bert.

Mathilde materialized from her suite behind the kitchen and listened somberly, crying out a little and crossing herself. Then she pulled herself together. "Poor Mr. Daniel, he's with the Lord now," she said.

Sam looked at the girl limp in his arms.

"Swan, listen to me," he said sternly, his blue eyes like ice. "He had a problem with cocaine for ten years. *Ten years.* He tried very hard, but something was going to happen sooner or later. If it wasn't getting rid of Lige Davenport, something else would have triggered it. Tell me you understand this."

He waited. She still didn't look at him.

"This has nothing to do with us. Absolutely nothing. Nothing to do with our boys. He was a nice guy, a guy who helped us out, but he was a drug addict," he said again.

It was like talking to a ghost or maybe a log or some other inanimate object.

"I'm not going anywhere and neither is Luke," he continued. "You and I are going to see Dr. Fisher together as soon as she can see us—tomorrow, if possible. There is absolutely nothing you can do or say to drive me away. I don't care if your whole family comes after me with AK-forty sevens. I'll go AWOL from the Marines. But it isn't going to come to that, is it? Because you're upset now, but you will understand that this had nothing to do with you. You are the only thing that matters to me. You and Luke and our new babies."

She still said nothing.

"Swan," he said now, more patient, "didn't we talk about what you would do if something happened to me? You would have a happy life, wouldn't you? Happy with Luke, and now with Fitz and Andy on the way? Happy raising our boys for me? Well, I'm still here. We can still do it together. Please try to think of it this way. You can mourn Daniel. But Daniel helped us so that you and the boys would have a happy life here at the farm, didn't he? It would all be for nothing if you ruined it now. I won't let you do that."

Just then Luke cried out. Mathilde slipped upstairs to the nursery.

"Madame Moore," she called, "the baby is hungry; shall I bring him downstairs?"

"Yes!" Sam called back, "bring him down right now. Swan needs him."

Mathilde's heels clicked across the nursery floor. She stopped a moment then headed downstairs. When she brought Luke to Swan, he had the "Kiss Me" stocking cap on his little dark head.

"It's all I could find," she said apologetically. "It's the middle of the night, and I didn't want his head to be cold."

Swan looked at her baby: he looked comical in the blue cap with the long tail, so comical and yet so concerned. His little face was watching hers intently; it mirrored his father's—the same furrowed brow. She was making two generations of Moore men very worried, she realized, both at the same time. So she smiled at Luke and he smiled back. She took him in her arms and he nuzzled her hungrily.

"No, it's perfect," said Sam with relief. He put his arms around Swan and kissed her.

"How are you doing, Swannie? Okay, now?" he asked gently.

"Yes. Yes, I think I am," Swan said, with a small quaver still in her voice.

"That's my girl. My beautiful girl," Sam crooned. Then he gathered his entire family, Swan and all the boys, in his arms and carried them back upstairs to bed, safe and sound, to await the morning.

Three days later, they laid Daniel Spaulding to rest in the Waverly Methodist Cemetery, next to his parents. Daniel's death had cancelled the trip to Churchill Downs—they'd watch Mike in his big race on the flat screen once again.

Swan made it through Daniel's funeral, but only barely. Sam watched her like a hawk the whole time, but he was reassured by what he saw. She seemed to be mourning naturally, sobbing during the hymns, but holding herself together. He took her home directly afterward and sat with her for the next few days, mostly keeping to themselves in their room, playing with the baby, talking the way husbands and wives do who are helping each other through times of trouble. He was filling the role Daniel had played when he and Swan had broken up, but, of course, he couldn't know that. He mostly listened to her talk through her grief.

◆

By the end of the week, Sam was thinking of going back to Quantico at least part-days. Swan was rallying, smiling even, cheered by the baby and Sam's patient love. She expressed an interest in going to the Crossroads for lunch, just the two of them, before gathering with everyone to watch Mike's big race later that afternoon. Oliver was reasonably confident: Mike would give a good account of himself in the race of his life.

They sat in "their" booth, the one Swan was sitting in when Sam first saw her. They ordered their lunch, and Swan spontaneously propped her little ballet flats on the banquette bench, next to Sam. He pulled her feet into his lap in the playful way he always did.

"I never, never, never thought . . ." he began, looking at her. "I saw you here and I'd never seen anything, anyone as beautiful as you. Ever. That first day, I sat here and I thought, 'I could never have a chance with her . . . never . . . never . . . never . . . .'"

"And yet here you are," Swan said, wiggling her toes in his lap. "More than you bargained for, isn't that right, Major?"

"I guess, but I can handle it," he grinned. He was happy to see her happy.

"Could you handle a little more?" she asked, cocking an eyebrow. His smile faded immediately.

"What are you up to? Don't tell me it's triplets, or another farm."

"So suspicious," she murmured. "Let's eat our food first." He groaned.

"No. Argument first," he said with a sigh.

"Promise you won't just fly off the handle, but will listen with an open mind."

"Jesus H. Christ. Here we go again," Sam said, disgusted. "No. No, I won't promise not to fly off the handle or to listen with an open mind."

She kept wiggling her toes, gently pressing them deeper into his lap.

"Shit, stop that," he protested. "I promise not to—oh, fuck. Just tell me and stop wiggling."

She did. "You know how Dr. Fisher and I have been talking about the three boys taking the place of Hunt and Carter and Fitch in the cosmic scheme of things?" Swan said slowly.

He looked skeptical.

"Well, now we've lost Daniel . . . ." Here Swan swallowed hard and looked away. She took a deep breath. That was better. "We've lost Daniel, and, along that way of thinking, we are now back to a net loss of one in the 'bad-luck-doomed-love' department."

"Go on," he said, drilling her with his eyes.

"That means both Stone Chimneys and High View will be empty. We haven't found a tenant to farm either place and now we won't even have Daniel at High View. Emilio and Javier and the other staff there will be keeping an empty house or we will have to let them go," Swan continued.

"Go on."

"So I want to get in touch with your mother. I want to see if she would come back and live here, not with us but at Stone Chimneys when Virgilia leaves, and move Emilio there to keep house. It is the smaller of the two places, and High View is such a trophy house I think we will have a better shot at leasing it, at least right away. Please don't have a meltdown, please, please, please, just listen." She said this last in a hurry. His face had turned to stone.

"Just listen," she repeated. "She is Luke and the little boys' only grandparent, the only natural parent you and I have left. She is a widow, alone, and may be ill. I think I would find it comforting to have her here, particularly when you go away again. She wouldn't be living with us, she'd be at Stone Chimneys—we'd have our privacy. Please just think about it. Hetty will be busy with her boys. Spaulding lives her own life. Mathilde will be run off her feet keeping house for all of us. Even if we get Kitty," Swan lowered her voice, "to come and help me, it won't be like having a mature person. And if Miss T. has a baby, Julia will have all of us to cheer her up. It would be an act of compassion. It may give her a chance to make amends to you. And you'd be gone half the time anyway."

"Swan, there are so many reasons why that is a bad idea that I don't know where to start," Sam said very slowly. "If she is dying, how long before you are taking care of her instead of her helping you? She'll just be another loss to bear when she dies. You'll have our three in diapers, au pair or no au pair, still running the horse business, and managing the three farms. It isn't possible on your own."

"I won't be on my own, though," she said. "I'll have you."

"You can't be mother to the universe. You are still a very young girl. Harrington wants you at the PPT, Kezia for the Waverly Hunt, you'll be syndicating Mike—it's not possible."

"Sam, the way to defeat 'bad luck doomed love' is to bring more people into my life, not cut them out. When I lose one, I want to try to fill that empty place," she said. "I think she will be a comfort to me. Isn't that what you want? To know I'll be okay no matter what happens when you go away?"

His jaw was set.

"You don't know what you're asking," he said. He looked down.

"Yes, I do. And I won't do it unless you agree. She is your mother," Swan said. "It's not like it will be for years and years, but I don't want to regret not asking, at least. Can't we at least try?"

"You don't even have an address. She never contacted you, that's what you said," Sam replied, but she could see he was moving toward accepting the possibility of the idea.

"How many Mrs. Rufus Hampsteads can there be in Corpus Christi?" Swan murmured, beginning to wiggle her toes provocatively in his lap again. "Who knows? Maybe the queen of the veils can help you check with four-one-one on that."

"You are a piece of work," Sam said, looking at her, letting her fill his eyes. "What a wife I signed up for."

"An all-expenses-paid trip on the rocket express," Swan said, "riding El Diablo. The horse no woman ever tamed—no man either. But it is possible. It is possible after all."

8507555R0

Made in the USA
Charleston, SC
16 June 2011